Xenophon

Xenophon's Memorabilia of Socrates

SALZWASSER
VERLAG

Xenophon

Xenophon's Memorabilia of Socrates

Reprint of the original, first published in 1864.

1st Edition 2022 | ISBN: 978-3-75259-179-8

Verlag (Publisher): Salzwasser Verlag GmbH, Zeilweg 44, 60439 Frankfurt, Deutschland
Vertretungsberechtigt (Authorized to represent): E. Roepke, Zeilweg 44, 60439 Frankfurt, Deutschland
Druck (Print): Books on Demand GmbH, In de Tarpen 42, 22848 Norderstedt, Deutschland

ΞΕΝΟΦΩΝΤΟΣ ΑΠΟΜΝΗΜΟΝΕΥΜΑΤΑ.

XENOPHON'S

MEMORABILIA OF SOCRATES,

WITH

NOTES AND AN INTRODUCTION

NEW YORK

M.DCCC.LXIV.

INTRODUCTION.

LIFE OF SOCRATES.

PARENTAGE AND EARLY LIFE.

Socrates was of genuine Attic extraction. He spoke of himself, sportively, perhaps, as belonging to the family of the Dædalidæ of mythical renown, since his father Sophroniscus, by his devotion to the profession of a statuary, proved himself a loyal successor of the founder of the family, Dædalus.* His mother, Phænarete, was a midwife, as her son reminds us, by comparing his own relation to the mind with hers to the body.† She seems, however, to have been a woman of excellent character, and of many noble qualities.‡ The quiet, unostentatious home of these parents was in the suburbs of Athens, northwest of the Acropolis, in the borough Alopece, near Cynosarges (White-dog-town), where the school of the Cynics was held, and not very far from Mount Lycabettus, probably identical with the present hill of St.

* Plato. Euthyph. 11. B. C.: Τοῦ ἡμετέρου προγόνου, ὦ Εὐθύφρον, ἔοικεν εἶναι Δαιδάλου τὰ ὑπὸ σοῦ λεγόμενα. Cf. also Alcib. I. 121. A.

† Cf. Plato, Theaetetus, p. 149. A. and 151. A. In the latter passage he says: Πάσχουσι δὲ δὴ· οἱ ἐμοὶ ξυγγιγνόμενοι καὶ τοῦτο ταὐτὸν ταῖς τικτούσαις, κ.τ.λ.

‡ Theaetetus, p. 149. A.

George. A competence, though no superabundance of this world's goods, had been the result of their industry.

About the year 469, and early in the year, in March or April, a son was born in this retired cottage. No special prognostics, as far as we know, heralded his birth, no prodigies signalized his boyhood, and yet he was destined to be the most remarkable man, perhaps, that the world has ever seen. When of a suitable age, he was sent to the schools of his native district, where he was taught in the usual departments of learning then thought necessary, music, poetry, and gymnastic exercises. Of his attainments in the two former arts, we see no special indication in his subsequent life; and yet we hesitate not to believe, from his general character, that he fell not a whit behind his compeers, if he did not far excel them. His success in the training of his physical nature, we shall frequently have occasion to allude to in the subsequent pages. He also received instruction in the art of his father, which was probably supposed to be the profession most suited to his capacities, as well as to his birth. And he would doubtless have become world-renowned even there, if he had not been allured away to a higher sphere of exertion; for we are credibly informed, that in addition to other works carved by his hand, a draped statue of the Three Graces, which would necessarily require no small degree of skill in the use of the chisel, was thought worthy of a place in the Acropolis at Athens, near the Minerva of the master-sculptor, Phidias.*

Crito, a wealthy Athenian, in some way, perhaps, attracted to the studio of the artist by his love of the creations of the art, seems to have taken a fancy for the uncouth figure of the boy, as he bent over the half-formed mass of stone before him. "Come," said he, "leave this thoughtless, senseless mass, and these walls that imprison the free spirit, and go with me and learn something better." How long the good father was in yielding to this offer so unexpected, we know not; but sure we are, that the heart of

* This group was preserved and exhibited as the work of Socrates until the time of Pausanias. See Paus., I. 22. 8; IX. 35. 2.

the son leaped within him at the prospect of a life of culture and intellectual growth. At all events, the consent of the parents was finally obtained, for we have evidence that he made considerable progress in early life in physics, which he himself says he had a fondness for,* although afterward, when he had attained to better things, he looked upon them with some contempt, or at least without any very strong feeling in their favor ;† so true is it, that in the joy of the attainment of a desired object, the thousand little, or it may be important aids therein, are forgotten or nearly lost sight of.

Several teachers come in for their share of the honor or dishonor of his early training. According to Ion of Chios, an unimpeached contemporary witness, he accompanied the physical philosopher Archelaus from Athens to Samos, in order to avail himself of his instructions, and there is little question that he was for a time also the pupil of Anaxagoras. The Parmenides of Plato, doubtless, gives us a true picture of the zeal and enthusiasm of the young scholar in his attendance upon Parmenides and Zeno, during his earliest efforts to acquire a knowledge of the process of dialectics as pursued by them. Indeed, the natural curiosity of his mind seems to have urged him, now that the liberality of his patron had given him the means, to pursue eagerly every branch of knowledge then accessible.

The degree of satisfaction that physical science, as pursued in the age of Socrates, would give to an original and discriminating mind, was, it must be confessed, very small. The opposing dogmas, the obscurity, the confusion, the chaos in which rival sects had enveloped all nature, seem to have been too much even for his keen penetration. This we should hardly have expected.

* Plato, Phaedo. p. 96. A. where he says: *νέος ὢν θαυμαστῶς ὡς ἐπεθύμησα ταύτης τῆς σοφίας ἣν δὴ καλοῦσι περὶ φύσεως ἱστορίαν, κ.τ.λ.*—The same thing is implied in Mem. IV. 7. 3 sq.: *καίτοι οὐκ ἄπειρός γε αὐτῶν ἦν.*

† Mem. IV. 7. 5; I. 1. 11 sq., and Grote, Vol. VIII. p. 572. See also Tychsen's Dissertation Ueber. d. Prozess d. Sokrates, in Bibliothek d. Alt. Lit. u. Kunst. 1st. St. p. 43.

Some struggling rays of light, we should have supposed, would have met his eager gaze into the depths, and saved him from wholly discarding this kind of knowledge. But no; even in the maturity of his powers, he classed the working of the machinery of nature among those things which the gods had designed to be kept from the knowledge of mortals, and as a secret, the attempt to pry into which would not only prove nugatory, but would be punished as impious.* Yet, as we have before intimated, these efforts of the youth were not lost in their influence upon the character of the man.

Dissatisfied with the study of Physics, Socrates naturally turned his thoughts to more purely speculative themes, and to moral relations and duties. Even his teacher, Archelaus, might have aided in directing his attention to these subjects, by his discussions upon the foundations of justice, and upon the effect of law. But the instructions of Parmenides and Zeno are unmistakeable.†

SOCRATES AS PUBLIC TEACHER.

Precisely when Socrates deserted his father's workshop, or how long a time he devoted to study before he became a "public talker," is uncertain. He probably came into his position gradually, as his own views became more settled, and his knowledge of the errors and defects of those who professed to be teachers, and of the questionings and wants of those who frequented public places, were by degrees revealed to him. He, however, is supposed to have devoted himself to the main object of his mission when about thirty years of age. After that time, about 539 B. C., he was generally to be found in some public place in the city, with his little company of adherents, and those strangers and curious persons who had been allured into his society by the fame that had gone abroad concerning him. The external appearance

* Mem. I. 1. 7 sq.; IV. 7. 6.

† Cf. Grote, vol. viii. 568 and 473.

of the man was certainly noticeable, although not altogether attractive. Indeed, his uncomely exterior was almost proverbial. He was compared to a satyr or silenus,* and his prominent eyes, scarcely parted by the low ridge of the nose, his dilated nostrils, wide mouth, and thick lips, low and protuberant figure, and awkward movement,† were thought a sufficient ground for jests and merriment even among his friends. Neither did his soiled and worn garments, and bare feet without regard to the season, add to his personal attractions. The pale face which Aristophanes attributes to him could not certainly be indicative of infirm health, for "his physical constitution," says Grote, "was healthy, robust, and enduring to an extraordinary degree. He was not merely strong and active as an hoplite on military service, but capable of bearing fatigue or hardship, and indifferent to heat or cold to a degree which astonished all his companions."‡

The natural temper of Socrates seems not to have been without some acerbity, but his habit of self-control enabled him generally, at least, to keep it in complete subjection. Indeed, the one great principle of his life, after he had devoted himself to the instruction of others, was to reduce as much as possible all his desires and appetites. His diet and regimen was all made to conform to this, in order that his time might be the more at his disposal, for the benefit of his friends and country: thus, when Antiphon objects to his philosophy, that it does not enable him to live freely and generously, and that the legitimate result of his teachings to men would be misery, he replies: "Men rejoice when they are prosperous in their respective pursuits; but how much greater is the delight that I have in conscious advancement in virtue, and in aiding others therein." And, in conclusion: "I suppose that to want nothing is godlike (θεῖον), and to want very little is to be most nearly related to the gods; and the divine is most excellent, and that which is nearest to deity is best."§

* Plat. Symp. 215. A.

† Encyclopædia Britannica, Art. Socrates.

‡ See Grote's Greece, viii. p. 546, 547, 552.

§ Mem. I. 6. 8 sq.

We are not, however, to conclude that he had so entirely put off the character of his age and nation, as never to relax the rigidity of his life. On festal occasions, whether religious or secular, the viands and the wine were not less grateful to him than to others, yet he was careful never to cast the reins of desire wholly upon the neck of his appetites; self-command he was careful never to lose.*

The life of Socrates, with some few interruptions, which will be hereafter alluded to, seems to have passed on in an even tenor, which was the great object of his seeking. Early in the morning he was to be found in the public walks, and in the places set apart for the physical and intellectual training of the young. He went thence to the market-place, where he remained as long as the crowd set in that direction. He then passed the remainder of the day wherever he supposed he should fall in with the most of his fellow-citizens. And his biographer adds significantly: he was talking for the most part,† and that not privately, but all who wished, "sophists, military men, artisans, ambitious or studious youths," all were permitted to listen to him. "He visited all persons of interest in the city, male or female. His friendship with Aspasia is well known; and one of the most interesting chapters of Xenophon's Memorabilia recounts his visit to and dialogue with Theodote, a beautiful Hetæra or female companion."‡ He himself says in his Apology, as given us by Plato: "To all young or old who have desired to know of my words or actions, I have exhibited them; I have not spoken for money, nor kept silent for want of it; but I have freely permitted any who wished, the poor as well as the rich, to question me, and hear my answers." He also declares that he had spoken his sentiments without reserve to all. "If any one," he says, "avers that he has ever been taught any thing by me, or heard me say

* See the Symposion of Plato and Xenophon, and cf. Grote, vol. viii. 547.

† Memorab. I. 1, 10: ἔλεγε μὲν ὡς τὸ πολύ.

‡ See Mem. II. 6. 36; III. 11. 1 sq.; and Grote's Greece, viii. 555

any thing in privatė which I have not declared openly, be assured that he does not speak the truth.*

Socrates was always attended in public by "companions or listeners" more or less numerous, who were known by the citizens generally as disciples or scholars. But he and his personal friends never designated the relation between them and himself by "teacher" and "pupil" or disciples. He would thus not only have been confounded with the professed teachers of the time, who were accustomed to make pecuniary gain from their instruction, but the general and public character of his teaching would have been marred, as many would have hesitated to listen to him, or appear among his auditors, if they were, as a consequence, to be termed "disciples of Socrates."†

SOCRATES ON MILITARY DUTY.

When thirty-seven or thirty-eight years of age, near the beginning of the Peloponnesian war, Socrates, in obedience to the call of his country, enrolled himself as a foot-soldier, and marched with the army into Thrace, to aid in reclaiming the colony at Potidæa, who had revolted, and were sustained in their revolt by many of the Peloponnesians. We may suppose that Socrates did not unwillingly gird on his armor at this time, if war was necessary. It brought him into close contact with many of the young men, whom he would influence, and also gave him an opportunity to put to the test, and make a public exhibition of, some of his principles of action. The siege took place in the midst of a Thracian winter, and yet Socrates walked barefoot over snow and ice in his usual summer-clothing, and conducted himself with so much bravery, that he was thought worthy of a prize; which he, however, generously yielded to his young friend Alcibiades, whose life he had saved in battle, as an inducement for him to strive for future promotion.‡ Many anecdotes are related of his

* Apol. 33, B.

† Mem. I. 2. 6; I. 6. 13; and Grote's Hist., vol. viii. p. 555, '6.

‡ Plato Sympos. p. 219, E.

conduct during this expedition, which are at least characteristic, as great a recommendation as could be bestowed upon a large share of those told of the great men of every age.*

About six years later, in 424 B. C., Socrates was present and took part in the battle at Delium; and if all of the Athenians had exerted themselves as much and fought as bravely as Socrates, the Bœotians would doubtless have been vanquished, instead of erecting trophies over their antagonists.†

Two or three years later, when nearly fifty years old, Socrates again engaged in military service for the third and last time. Advancing age had not yet so chilled his blood as to cause him to shrink from exposure to the inclemency of a Thracian winter, or so damped his ardor as to incline him to forego personal danger when the rights of Athens were in jeopardy.

While Socrates was on his second military expedition, or at least during that year 424, the Clouds of Aristophanes was exhibited on the stage; and however misapplied, the keen wit and biting satire of this play should seem to have been too much for even the imperturbable philosopher to receive with composure, for twenty-five years afterwards, when he pleads his cause before the dikastery, he goes back to this as the fountain-head of the accusations against him, and spends most of his time in showing its injustice.

DOMESTIC LIFE OF SOCRATES.

In all probability, Socrates remained unmarried until after these military expeditions had been made, and his rigid habits of life had become fixed. It might seem that Xantippe had no great reputation for sweetness of temper before her marriage with Socrates, for when Antisthenes asks him why he did not bring the influence which he exerted so powerfully in correcting and

* It is said that he once stood for twenty-four hours on the same spot before the camp, absorbed in deep thought, with his eyes fixed on an object, as if his soul were absent from his body.—*Wiggers' Life*, Ch. 5.

† Wiggers' Life, Ch. 5.

forming others, to bear upon her, who, says he, "is the worst woman of all that exist, nay, I believe, of all that ever have existed or ever will exist;" he replies, "I see that those who wish to become best skilled in horsemanship do not select the most obedient but the most spirited horses; for they believe that after being enabled to bridle these, they will know easily how to manage others. Now, as it was my wish to converse and to live with men, I have married this woman, being firmly convinced, that in case I should be able to endure her, I should be able to endure all others."*

Yet we are inclined to think that this was an after-thought with him; and we should not much censure perturbations of temper in her, for one who professed to marry for the promotion of public interests alone, who spent his whole day in public, and brought home nothing, and, indeed, took no thought for domestic comfort, could not have contributed very much to the happiness of his family. His admonitions and advice to his son Lamprocles,† in respect to the treatment of his mother, are, however, certainly very good, and show some appreciation of what is due from a child even to a bad mother. Three children seem to have survived Socrates, for he says in his defence: "I have three sons, the eldest of whom is yet a youth, and the other two mere children."‡

HIS REGARD FOR ATHENS, AND MANNER OF EXHIBITING IT.

Socrates ever exhibited a strong attachment to his native land, and especially to Athens. He never left the city without good reasons. Even the country presented no allurements to him. In his view, man comprised all that was attractive in this vast and varied world of ours. When Phædrus§ decoyed him out into

* Xenophon's Sympos. II. 10, as quoted by Wiggers.

† Memorab. II., 2, 10 sq.

‡ Apology, p. 34, D.

§ P. 230, D.

woods and fields, and reproached him for never going beyond the walls of the city, he says, "Pardon me, my excellent friend; for I am a lover of learning; now the fields and trees will not teach me any thing, but men in the city do."

Not even the most flattering invitations from the princes of other nations had charms sufficient to withdraw him from Athens, where, he says, "Four measures of flour are sold for one obolus, the springs yield plenty of water, and I live contented with what I possess.* He occasionally, however, took a short journey, as to the Athenian games or to Delphi, and perhaps once went to Samos with his teacher Archelaus.†

Notwithstanding his regard for his native city, and the frequent inculcation of the obligation resting upon every one who was fitted for it, to aid in the administration of the affairs of the State, and the honor and happiness of a life of public service, he uniformly resisted the urgent solicitations of his friends in this particular, until, when sixty-five years of age, he once accepted the appointment of senator. This refusal of all public office was made the subject of reproach against him by Antiphon. How is it, said he, that you attempt to make others politicians, whilst you do not yourself engage in political life, if, indeed, you know any thing about it. In which way, Socrates replies, can I accomplish most for the State, by myself alone accepting office, or by exerting myself to fit as many others as possible for these duties.‡ In this we have the key to his conduct. His desire was to exert an influence, as private citizen, over the young, and those who were coming forward into political life; and it was doubtless through this persuasion that the influence of his "familiar spirit, the divine voice," was exerted; to which he attributes, in the Apology of Plato, his refusal to enter into civil life. That he could not have exerted the influence that he desired if he had not

* Diog. ii. 25; Arist. Rhet. ii. 23; Cic. Tusc, v. 12; Epictetus, Fragm 174, ed. Schweig.

† Wiggers' Life, chap. v., foot note.

‡ Mem. I. 6. 15.

remained in a private station, he expressly avers, and adduces his reasons in his apology.*

The manner in which he would have performed the duties of magistrate, and the result to his influence, is very apparent from his short experience. Soon after his appointment to the senate, an occasion offered to test his firmness in adhering to his oath of office. After the battle at the Arginusæ, the generals in command did not, as was supposed, exert themselves sufficiently to rescue the dead for burial. They were accordingly arraigned, and would have been forthwith condemned to death *in a body*, which was contrary to law, if Socrates had not stood up alone, in opposition to the people, and refused to put the vote. "I protested," he says, "against your decree, and notwithstanding all your menaces and outcries, and the orators who were standing ready to bring an accusation against me, I thought it necessary to expose myself to peril, rather than to yield to you in the perpetration of injustice."†

He also adduces one other incident which occurred while the Thirty were in office, which shows his unwavering adherence to the right amidst the greatest inducements to a contrary course. They with evil intent had ordered Socrates with four others to bring Leon from Salamis, in order to put him to death. The others obeyed the tyrants, but Socrates says: "I made known to them, both in word and deed, that (if it be not too harsh an expression), I did not care at all for death, provided I did nothing unjust or unholy, which was the great object of my solicitude;" and he adds, "The great authority of the government did not influence me to violate my sense of right. . . . But I went away home, and not improbably my life would have been taken, if that form of government had not soon been abrogated."‡

* P. 31, C.

† Apol. 32, B., and also Mem. I. 1. 18.

‡ Apolog. 32. C. D.; Memorab. iv. 4. 3.

CIRCUMSTANCES THAT LED TO THE ACCUSATION OF SOCRATES.

The life of Socrates as public discourser must have continued about thirty years. Thirty years diligently and perseveringly passed in indiscriminate conversation and dialectic subtleties! Surely something must have been accomplished during this long period of service, and something more than has reached us through the medium of his biographers. But the close of these labors,—how sad and disgraceful to the Athenians! It does not, at first, appear possible, that they who were most tolerant of dissentient opinion and speech, did actually condemn to death their greatest benefactor, and the greatest uninspired benefactor of the race of man. It should seem that there must be some mistake in the records of the affair. But no; the chain of testimony is unbroken, and can not be gainsayed. But what are the circumstances leading to the fatal result? No special occasion seems to have been given by him for reproach during the last years of his life more than during the preceding. Indeed, he appears in his apology to trace back the accusation to the early part of his career, and to indicate clearly what he supposes to be the ground of it, his attempts to convict men of their want of wisdom.

It may not be amiss to give a little more at length the causes of the hatred of the Athenians to their great benefactor. It was no one individual act of his life that had caused the public indignation to descend upon his devoted head, but, as Grote says, "The accumulated force of antipathy—the numerous and important personal enemies, each with sympathizing partizans—the long-standing and uncontradicted calumnies" which had been promulgated against him.

1. All of the Sophists, the teachers of the age, would be opposed to him, since he by precept and example discountenanced what he considered their mercenary spirit in teaching for pay. Many of them in this way amassed large fortunes, and the feeling of the times seems to be embodied in the lines of Aristophanes:*

* Clouds, 98, 99.

"These are they
Who can show pleaders how to twist a cause,
So you'll pay them for it, right or wrong."

But Xenophon says, "Socrates did not take pay of those who came to him for instruction. But by abstaining from this he believed that he was ensuring his own freedom; and he was accustomed to stigmatize those who received a compensation for services of this kind as enslavers of themselves."* In the Apology of Plato, he also says: If it has been asserted by any one that I have set myself up as a teacher of men, and received pay therefor, it is utterly false.†

He also brought their manner of teaching, as well as the objects of their instruction, into disrepute. The Sophists were accustomed to display in dress and equipage, and to make great pretensions to ability in teaching. They also communicated their thoughts in lofty words. Socrates, on the contrary, was not only himself most simple and unpretending in these particulars, but spoke with contempt of the opposite course of procedure.‡

2. He likewise offended many of those who joined themselves to him as disciples and engaged in conversation with him. His professed design was to converse with all of the most distinguished men of his time, and by cross-questioning, not only to show them their ignorance, but to oblige them to confess it; and his success in this, by means of his skill in dialectics, was unfailing. Now it is not in the nature of man to see all of his cherished thoughts turned into ridicule, and himself the object of the severest sarcasm, and the most open and unqualified derision, however beneficial it may be, without some feeling of dislike for the author; especially when there is discrimination enough to perceive that there is at least a degree of sophistry employed in accomplishing the object. Thus Xenophon, after giving an account of the manner in which Socrates corrected the false estimate which Euthydemus,

* Memorab. I. 2. 6.
† P. 19, D. E.
‡ Mem. I. 1. 11.

a mere youth, had of his own ability to enter political life without further training, says: Many of those who were thus treated by Socrates, no longer desired his society, and were considered by him as dunces; but Euthydemus supposed that one could in no other way become worthy of renown, than by associating as much as possible with Socrates.*

3. He also did not approve himself to those who discarded all advancement and progress in government, religion, and culture. The crime of innovation should seem to have been early alleged against him, and reiterated during his whole public career; and it was only from these early and continued calumnies that he felt himself in any danger. He says: "My first accusers are more to be regarded than Anytus and his accomplices, because, being numerous and well agreed among themselves, they have addressed many of you from youth up, and have falsely persuaded you that I discard the worship of the gods, and persuade others to follow in my steps."† These calumnies were first publicly disseminated when Aristophanes exhibited his comedy, the Clouds. In this comedy, Socrates, in connection with Chærephon, is held up to the most unsparing ridicule, and all the follies and misdeeds of the Sophists are embodied under this appellation. Errors which he had long before publicly discarded, and severely reproved as practised by the Sophists, he is made accountable for. It is also worthy of note, that the points in the final accusation are precisely the same that are made conspicuous by the comedian—atheism and the corruption of the youth.‡

4. His assumptions of superiority would naturally awaken the suspicion and jealousy of many, especially of the ignorant and ambitious. The response of the oracle at Delphi to Chærephon, that there was no wiser man than Socrates, and his reception of that response, and claim of a special mission from the gods, as indicated by what was supposed to be the aid of his

* Memorab. IV. 2. 1 sq. esp. 40; and cf. Grote, VIII. p. 604.

† Apol. 18. C. sq.

‡ Aristoph. Clouds.

guiding spirit, would meet with little favor from those who had seen him in his work-shop, or associated with him on terms of equality. Thus he says: "The calumnies that are heaped upon me have their foundation in a certain wisdom that I possess."*

5. His political views were offensive to many. He was not attached to the Athenian constitution in its practical bearings, although he as little approved of an oligarchy like that of the Thirty.† He even ridiculed some practices of the government; as, for example, the manner of appointing rulers. Those were not legitimate rulers who held the sceptre, nor those who were appointed by any and every body, or who had received office by lot, or obtained by force or deception, but those who knew how to rule.‡ No one would be willing to trust his life to a pilot thus chosen, or to commit any important private interest to the management of those thus designated.§ And yet no one was more rigidly observant of law.‖ Both Kritias and Alcibiades were adduced as examples of his pernicious political training.¶

It is not, then, so strange as it might at first appear, that Socrates was arraigned before the tribunal that had in charge both the morals and religion of the Athenian community. The clamors of so many classes of citizens for so many years could scarcely pass unheeded. The charges, too, were of a nature to arouse the Athenians, ever watchful over any defection from the national religion. We may, then, justly conclude that it was only the blameless life of Socrates, and the unparalleled liberality of Athens in respect to individual life and opinions, that shielded him so long from the enemies whom he had so often and severely provoked.

The most trivial circumstance may have been sufficient to cause the smothered flames of anger to burst forth, and to recall the

* Apol. 20. D.

† Grote's Greece, VIII. p. 630.

‡ Mem. III. 9. 10

§ Mem. III. 9. 11; and I. 2. 9.

‖ Mem. IV. 4. 1 sq.; and cf. Grote, VIII. 645.

¶ A sufficient defence of Socrates is found, Mem. I. 2. 9 sq.

aspersions of the comedians to recollection. And very little would probably have been enough to induce the leading individuals to set on foot the accusation, for Anytus was a personal enemy, because his son, tinctured with Socratic speculation, did not choose to tread in his father's steps, and aid in repairing a broken fortune by selling leather. The other two accusers, the one a poet and the other a rhetorician, were probably not persuaded with difficulty to avenge their respective professions, which had suffered severely from the inquisitorial proceedings of Socrates.

SOCRATES BEFORE HIS JUDGES.

But how, as it is frequently asked by Xenophon, could the judges pronounce sentence of condemnation upon a man whose life and teachings were so pure? He might have been arraigned in obedience to popular clamor; but that his judges should so mistake the character of a man of so public a life, in which no one could say that he had seen him doing, or heard him saying, any thing either impious or corrupting,* seems beyond comprehension. But it should be considered, that that very assembly by whom he was judged, was made up of those citizens, so many of whom had been annoyed, vexed, even maddened, by his cross-questioning, rebuked for superstition, or offended by his desire for political reform.

The manner, also, in which he presented himself before them and conducted his defence, was not calculated to conciliate those before alienated, but rather to repel those who were indifferent or but moderately in his favor. He was himself not anxious what the result should be, life or death. He was conscious of a life of rectitude. He declares this to his judges. He is now old, and can hope to accomplish but little more should life be prolonged. Any anxiety, any effort to influence his judges, especially after the prohibition of his guiding spirit, would be contrary

* Mem. I. 1. 20.

to the whole course of his life.* In order not to seem to discard the laws, and throw contempt upon the court; not on his own account, but "on account of the Athenians, lest they, by condemning him, should sin against the gracious blessing of the gods,"† he deigned to defend himself against the accusation of disregard to the gods of his country, and that of corrupting the youth. But no one can read his defence, as found for substance in the Apology of Plato, and take all the circumstances into account, without astonishment that no larger a majority than five or six in an assembly of more than five hundred should have voted against him.‡ And yet who would wish that he had taken a different course? Who does not feel, that in his last days he exhibited an elevation of character that "shed double and triple lustre over his whole life."§

In the final result, the affixing of the deserved penalty upon his crime, his course was not less honorable. According to the laws, he might name a penalty, between which and that of the accuser, the judges were obliged to make a selection. Now, it cannot be doubted, that if he had in sincerity chosen to name fine, exile, or imprisonment, that would have been gladly accepted. But instead of this, Socrates indignantly asks, "After all these crimes, what are my deserts? Doubtless, Athenians, if you proportion the reward to the merit, I deserve some considerable good. Now, what is it that is suitable for a poor man that is your benefactor, and wants leisure and opportunity for exciting and exhorting you? Nothing suits better with such a man than to be entertained in the Prytanæum; that is more due to him than to those of you that have brought off the trophies of victory from the horse and chariot races in the Olympic

* Plat. Apol. p. 28, E. sq.

† Plat. Apol. p. 30; Mem. IV. 4. 4; and cf. Grote, vol. VIII. p. 651.

‡ Apol. p. 36. A: θαυμάζω ἑκατέρων τῶν ψήφων τὸν γεγονότα ἀριθμόν, οὐ γὰρ ᾤμην ἔγωγε οὕτω παρ᾽ ὀλίγον ἔσεσθαι, ἀλλὰ παρὰ πολύ· νῦν δέ ὡς ἔοικεν, εἰ τρεῖς μόναι μετέπεσον τῶν ψήφων ἀποπεφεύγη ἄν. Cf. also Diog. Laert. ii. 41, quoted in Grote, vol. VIII. p. 647. Cf. also p. 654.

§ Grote, vol. VIII. p. 649.

games. For these victors purchase you a seeming happiness by their victories; but as for me, I make you really happy by mine. Besides, they stand not in need of such a supply; but I do. In justice, therefore, you ought to adjudge me a recompense worthy of myself."* But after further remarks, not calculated to conciliate, he concludes, that although he is innocent, yet, in accordance with custom, as he will not impose banishment upon himself, he will name a fine; "and perhaps," he says, "I should be able to pay you a mina of silver. But," he adds, "since Plato here, and Crito, and Critobulus, and Apollodorus, urge me to extend the sum to 30 minæ, I amerce myself in a fine of that amount, and give you them for security."†

When the final sentence of death was pronounced, Socrates, without a change of countenance, or the least indication of faltering in his course, addressed his judges, expressing his satisfaction in the result which his upright and independent conduct had brought upon him, for which he had been prepared by the silence of his monitor. He was convinced that death was no evil to him, whether it should prove a peaceful, dreamless sleep, or a passage to another state of existence, where there are no false judgments, and where he should pass his time in conversation with all the great and good who have passed away from earth, with Hesiod and Homer, Palamades, Ajax, and Ulysses. He had, however, still a few words to address to those who had decreed his death, but more in sorrow than in anger: Reproach will surely follow you for having condemned to death one who will be reputed to be wise, although not in reality so. Had you patiently delayed a little time, death in the natural order of nature would have come to me, and you would have been spared the infamy of taking the life of one who might have saved himself if he would have condescended to demean himself before you with the entreaties and supplications that you are accustomed to hear on such occasions. But our shares are fitly meted out to us; mine

* Plato, Apol. p. 36, D., Taylor's Trans.

† Plato, Apol. p. 38, B.

death, and yours infamy. You have hoped to escape the task of giving an account of your lives, as you have been compelled to do by my questions, but be assured you will find yourselves mistaken. Others, who have hitherto been restrained by my presence, will be emboldened by my death, and, young and vigorous, will be more troublesome, and harder to rid yourselves of than I have been. Far easier is it to escape censure by amending your lives, than by violently stopping the mouths of its authors.—I have not yet done. I am at that point of time which gives me a view into the future. No sooner shall I sleep in death, than the hand of the Avenger shall be laid upon you with more severity than yours is laid upon me." After giving a word of admonition in reference to the course he wishes his accusers to pursue in reference to his children, he finally says: "It is now time for us to go our respective ways, I to die and you to live; and which of us is going on a better voyage is known to God alone."*

LAST HOURS OF SOCRATES.

According to the ordinary course of procedure with the condemned at Athens, Socrates would have received the poisonous draught on the day following his condemnation. But it so chanced that the sacred ship, which was annually sent to Delos,† had set sail on the preceding day, and according to law, no person could be publicly put to death until its return, in thirty days. A month in prison and chains, we should suppose, would effectually try the spirit of the philosopher, and exhibit the dross, if it had not already been purged away. But it may truly be said of him that his last were his best days. His friends were constantly with him, and the conversations held with them, as exhibited in the Crito and Phædon of Plato, give us a picture of equanimity and cheerful resignation in the prospect of death, which few even under a Christian dispensation have ever attained

* Plat. Apol. p. 42.

† See Mem. IV. 8. 2; Plato, Crito, and cf.

unto. It would be pleasant to linger long with my readers in that prison, for the companionship of the good and great in the hour of trial is elevating, ennobling. But I must satisfy myself with two or three characteristic acts in this drama.

We find, that when left alone even, Socrates did not lose the cheerfulness which he exhibited in the presence of his friends. For he employed himself in poetic composition, in accordance with the guidance of his monitor, and produced a hymn to Apollo, whose festival was then kept at Athens, and also metrical versions of the fables of Esop, which came readily to his mind.*

He also refused to avail himself of an opportunity to escape from prison, which his friends had contrived and urged upon him, because it was contrary to law. Crito came to him with anxiety imprinted on his brow, and appearing in every motion, early in the morning of the day before it was announced that the ship would return from Delos. Socrates, however, was quietly sleeping, and his friend waited, impatiently, we may suppose, for his awaking. When Crito had expressed his astonishment at the quietness of his friend when death was so near, and Socrates had declared the assurance that had been given him that he should not die until the day after the morrow, Crito made known to him the plan that had been formed for his escape, and urged upon him, in behalf of his friends, its immediate execution. Never, perhaps, was his greatness more conspicuous than at this time. A way is opened, without his solicitation or knowledge even, for him who is unjustly condemned, to escape death. His friends are solicitous, would even, if they dared, be clamorous; but an unequivocal refusal to become a party in any infringement upon his country's laws was the only answer that could be wrung from him. He had lived obedient to law, and in the prospect of death he would not counteract the teachings of his life, or even throw a shadow over them by a moment of hesitation.

The ship at length had returned from Delos, and his disciples,

* Phædon, p. 60. E. sq.; Memorab. IV. 8.

aware that that was the last time that they should listen to him who spake as no other man had spoken to them, were early at the prison-gates. But the civil officers were before them, to announce that the execution was to take place that day. When they were admitted, they found that Socrates' chains were unloosed, and that Xantippe, with one of her children, was present. When she began to express her grief noisily, the philosopher could no longer endure it, and requested his friends to conduct her home.* When she had gone, quiet was soon restored in that prison-room, and Socrates discoursed a great part of the day with perfect cheerfulness upon topics connected with his life and the future state of existence. Many things were then said which sunk deep into the hearts of his auditors, and which, with a considerable admixture of Platonic dogmas, are to be found in the Phædon. "If," said he, "I did not hope, first of all, to find other gods who are wise and good, and then to be associated with men who have gone before me, far better than those on the earth, it would be wrong in me not to grieve at death. But, be assured, I confidently expect to join the assembly of the good. I may be mistaken in reference to this; but that I shall find divine guides of great purity and excellence, I am as confident as I can be of any thing of that nature; and on this account I meet death with composure, which otherwise I could not, and hope that something awaits the good after death, and, as has long ago been said, that it is much better with the good than with the evil."†

Toward night, after reminding his disciples that those who have distinguished themselves by a pure life, spent in beautifying the soul by the appropriate ornaments of virtue and knowledge, ought to pass quietly the time of their sojourning, as always ready for the voyage which will introduce them into those blessed mansions which he is unable to describe, but whither they will soon follow him, he says: "The grim messenger now calls

* Plat. Phæd. p. 60. A.

† Phæd. p. 63. B sq.

me, and I wish to go to the bath as preparatory to the fatal cup." He still continued to converse, as his disciples accompanied him to the bath-room, cheering them who sorrowed most of all that they should see his face and hear his voice no more. After he had returned, his children and the women of the family came to receive his last advice and benediction, which he gave at considerable length.

A little before sunset, the officer came to make the announcement that the fatal hour had arrived, but was unable formally to do so, so strongly had he become attached to his prisoner. After he had retired, and Socrates had made a passing remark concerning him, he asked Crito to bring the poison if it was in readiness, if not, to give orders to have it immediately prepared. Crito endeavored to have him postpone it for a time, but in vain. When it was brought, after asking directions what he should do after the draught, and inquiring if there was enough for a libation, took the cup with a joyful expression of face, and drank it off without the least appearance of unwillingness. As the poison began to take effect, his friends could no longer control themselves, but were compelled to give utterance to the feelings that had long struggled within them. This was too much for the dying philosopher, and reproofs were on his lips in death as well as in life. "What are ye doing, strange men? I sent away the women, most of all that these discordant notes might not be heard; for I have felt that it is fitting to die in quietness. Be composed, therefore, and silence turbulent feeling." "When we heard this," the disciple adds, "we were ashamed, and restrained our lamentations." Coldness soon began to creep over his frame, which when he perceived he said to his friends, "When it reaches here (my heart), I shall leave you;" and turning to Crito, as if with his last breath to show the injustice of the accusation of infidelity which had been made against him, he said:* "We owe a cock to Æsculapius; discharge the debt, and be sure not to for-

* Plato, Phæd. p. 118.

get it." Thus died the man who, says Xenophon, was not only the best of men, but most favored of the gods.*

SOURCES OF THE INFLUENCE OF SOCRATES.

A full discussion of the power and influence of Socrates would require a volume, rather than the very few pages which only can here be given to it. It would be necessary to give a somewhat minute account of the condition of Greece in an intellectual point of view at the time of the appearance of Socrates We should naturally speak at length of the awakening of the intellectual energies of the Greeks, which resulted in the rise of two classes of men, the dialecticians and rhetoricians, and their frequent union under the appellation of *σοφισταί*, Sophists; and point out the relation of Socrates to these men with whom he is ranked or contrasted, in connection with, or prëeminent among whom he is ridiculed or praised. But all that our present limits allow is an enumeration of some of the sources of his influence, giving prominence to those brought to view or implied in the Memorabilia.

1. His uncouth figure and appearance, peculiar habits, and pleasant voice, attracted the attention of many among a people who were ever desirous of learning some new thing,† and whose attention was gained, not merely by the graceful and the winning in the human form, but also by the strange and ludicrous.

2. The peculiarity of his method of instruction not only gained him listeners, but also retained them; especially the more cultivated of the Athenian youth. He did not teach by a continued or set discourse. He did not highly value a simple communication of knowledge to the mind in a passive state. He thought it necessary that its powers should be awakened by col-

* Mem. IV. 8. 11.

† Spintharus, a hearer of Socrates, as quoted by Grote, Hist., Vol. VIII. p. 605, says: *ὅτι οὐ πολλοῖς αὐτός γε πιθανωτέροις ἐντετυχηκὼς εἴη· τοιαύτην εἶναι τήν τε φωνὴν καὶ τὸ στόμα καὶ τὸ ἐπιφαινόμενον ἦθος, καὶ πρὸς πᾶσί τε τοῖς εἰρημένοις τὴν τοῦ εἴδους ἰδιότητα.*

lision with other minds in conversation. His illustrations, too, were not like those of the most of the teachers of his age, drawn from obscure or little known objects, but from the occupations and professions of daily life and employment. So true is this, that he was even reproached as having dwelt upon these so much as to have worn them threadbare.*

3. He turned the thoughts of his countrymen from useless speculations to the investigation of practical subjects. In this way, he not only influenced his own, but all subsequent ages. Xenophon says: "He did not, as most do, discourse upon the nature of all things, considering how that which is called by the Sophists *cosmos*, the world, exists, and by what necessary laws the heavenly bodies are governed; on the contrary, he considered those who entered into laborious investigations of that kind as fools;† and indignantly asked whether such inquirers, supposing that they already have knowledge enough of human affairs, applied themselves to the divine; or what advantage do they expect to gain by the investigation of physical phenomena? Do they think, as in the study of human affairs, to make a practical use of their knowledge, and excite and calm the winds and the rain, and produce the seasons at their pleasure, or do they seek only to gratify a prurient curiosity?" From these and numerous other passages of the Memorabilia, the difference between Socrates and his predecessors is evident. They spent their time in mere speculation upon ontological subtleties, confused and confusing; but he turned his attention to ethical, practical duties. With him the proper study of mankind was man, his duties and relations.‡ These had been assigned to man by the gods as subjects of study. These they were to understand by personal investigation, and if this was neglected, the true object of life could not be secured. It was only by diligence in learning what the gods permitted to be learned, and reverent and pious inquiry of the gods, that in

* Memorab. I. 2. 37.

† Mem. I. 1. 11.

‡ Mem. I. 1. 16.

duced them to grant information by divination upon those points which they had reserved as belonging to themselves.*

4. He accustomed those with whom he conversed to accurate definition.† This was the foundation of his success in his conversations with the young and arrogant. He would draw forth a definition or general statement from the unwary, and then, by making them acknowledge, step by step, the inadequacy or actual erroneousness of the sentiment expressed, would not only lead them to accurate statement, but to a distrust of themselves; and closely connected with this—

5. He led his auditors to careful introspection. In a conversation with Euthydemus, who supposed himself wise, and without need of instruction from others, he inquired: Have you ever been at Delphi? Yes, indeed, twice.—Did you notice the inscription, *γνῶθι σαυτόν*, found somewhere on the wall of the temple? I did.—Did you suppose that this injunction had no reference to you, or did you undertake to examine yourself carefully to see what you are?—When Euthydemus replied that he already knew himself, and had no occasion to apply this precept, and Socrates had made him acknowledge that all who have not a just appreciation of their own powers, as applied to human use, do not know themselves, he proceeded to inquire: "Is it not plain that men experience the greatest good from self-knowledge, and the greatest evil from ignorance of self? For those who know themselves know their own wants and necessities, and distinguish between what they can and cannot do, and order their lives accordingly."‡ Socrates dwelt so much upon the necessity of self-knowledge in his teachings, that it was even made the subject of ridicule.§ "To him this injunction, 'Know thyself,' was the most sacred of all precepts, and he constantly cited it,

* Mem. I. 1. 9; I. 4. 17 sq.; IV. 7.

† See Mem. IV. 6. 1 sq.; 13 sq., et al. sæp.

‡ Mem. IV. 2. 24 sq.

§ See Aristoph. Clouds, l. 842.

and strenuously enforced its obligation upon his hearers."* The influence of this teaching, with Socrates' ability† to accomplish the end aimed at, cannot be appreciated too highly. It strikes at the root of ignorance and delusion. It dispels self-conceit, and clears away the rubbish, and opens the mind to the reception of true knowledge. "To preach, to exhort, even to confute particular errors, appeared to Socrates useless, so long as the mind lay wrapped up in its habitual mist or illusion of wisdom; such mist must be dissipated before any new light could enter."‡ But it was not merely a negative process with him. He so dispelled error and ignorance from the mind, as to leave it with an unextinguishable desire for knowledge; and thus I am brought to another means of influence of Socrates.

6. His abhorrence of ignorance in every form. The worst of all ignorance was self-ignorance, and ignorance in general was folly and vice, whilst knowledge or wisdom was virtue.§ This principle formed the basis of all his instructions. The man who had knowledge and wisdom had the right of entire control over others so far as they were void of knowledge.‖ This regulated all the intercourse and relations of life. In his view, the man who sinned ignorantly was far worse than the one who erred knowingly, for the former could not conduct himself justly, however much he might desire it, whilst the latter could.¶ Knowledge, with him, was a right appreciation of one's self in all the relations of life, whether to gods or men. If, then, a parent, or child, or friend, failed to conduct rightly, it was from a want of discrimination of the right, from ignorance; and he was deserving of severe reprobation. The defectiveness of this philosophy is

* Grote, vol. VIII., p. 602.

† Mem. I. 2: *τοῖς διὰ λεγόμενοις αὐτῷ πᾶσι χρώμενον ἐν τοῖς λόγοις, ὅπως βούλοιτο.*

‡ Grote, vol. VIII., p. 603.

§ Mem. III. 9. 4 sq.

‖ See Mem. I. 2. 49, where his application of this principle to the treatment of parents is defended by Xenophon.

¶ Mem. IV. 2. 19 sq.

too palpable to require remark; and yet the influence of such teaching, especially upon the young of the age of Socrates, in rousing a spirit of inquiry and investigation, must have been very great. Neither, as a matter of fact, was this teaching so defective in a moral point of view as we should suppose from the above statement; for he was as constant in his inculcation of control over the passions and appetites, as the means of conformity to the gods, as if this, too, were a primary article of his creed. How, he reasoned for substance, can one live virtuously and temperately, who does not know what virtue or temperance is? but if he has acquired a knowledge of them by conscious effort, by diligent attention, he cannot fail to practise them. He will be inevitably lured on in the path of rectitude.

7. His honesty, simplicity, and disinterestedness of character, especially contributed to his influence. These traits shine out in almost every page of the Memorabilia. "The shortest, safest, and best way to acquire the good-will of others is to strive to possess those good qualities which you wish to seem to have."* This was not only a precept which Socrates inculcated on others, but one on which he based his own course of life. An open, frank, and generous spirit he exhibited to all. "The love of Socrates," says Potter, "was equally pure and warm, individual and catholic, firm and free, ennobling and attaching. His heartiness, frankness and pleasantry, his power of convincing his friends of their faults, and then of converting them to sounder principles and conduct; his extraordinary power of stimulating the lukewarm and encouraging the earnest; and, above all, his way of founding the most practical conduct on the highest motives, must all be studied in a variety of details before they can be adequately comprehended. Were we to attempt quotation, we should be embarrassed with all the treasures of Socrates' love—love for his friends, love for his country, love for his species—that noble love which flows in a clear pure stream in the conversations of Xenophon, but glows with equal light and warmth in those

* Mem. II. 6. 39.

admirable Socratic Dialogues of Plato, in which we seem to catch the very tone and manner, nay, the very gesture and look of Socrates, and see that Silenus face beaming not only with wit and humor, sense and feeling, but with a spirit and a grace which still make the reader of Plato hang on the lips of Socrates the live-long night."*

THE GUIDING SPIRIT (δαιμόνιον) OF SOCRATES.

Perhaps no one thing in reference to the character and teachings of Socrates, has been the subject of more diverse and contradictory opinions, than his idea of the δαιμόνιον, of which he so often speaks. Even his own friends questioned him in vain upon it, and the Delphic oracle gave no satisfactory responses to the listening ear of an eager curiosity. The commentators have been able to trace, from hints in his scattered allusions, the uncouth lineaments of the artificer of all evil, or the mild and pitying visage of one of those pure spirits, whose delight it is to walk the earth or traverse the air as the guardians and guides of erring mortals. But it is not our pleasure, were this a suitable place, to group together these several representations, but to give as well as we are able, the most probable explanation of this somewhat difficult subject.

I. The demon of Socrates was not a mere fictitious representation, devised for the sake of acquiring authority with the people. His whole character forbids the supposition. His life and his death exhibit the most unequivocal proof of the sincerity of his belief, as exhibited in his daily intercourse with his followers.

II. Socrates understood by δαιμόνιον something more than the simple voice of conscience or the internal sense. 1. The meaning of the word, and the manner in which it is employed by him, show this. Τὸ δαιμόνιον is equivalent to τὸ θεῖον, that which comes from the gods, and is so used in contrast with that which has its origin in the mind of man. So in I. 1. 9: Τοὺς δὲ

* The Greek Philosophers, Socrates and Plato, p. 119, 20.

μηδὲν τῶν τοιούτων οἰομένους εἶναι δαιμόνιον, ἀλλὰ πάντα τῆς ἀνθρωπίνης γνώμης, δαιμονᾶν ἔφη; I. 4. 2, 10, 18; IV. 3. 14; Plat. Apol. p 31. C. D. In the plural, then, τὰ δαιμόνια must correspond in general with οἱ θεοί; I. 1. 1: οὓς μὲν ἡ πόλις νομίζει θεοὺς οὐ νομίζων, ἕτερα δὲ καινὰ δαιμόνια εἰςφέρων. 2. The manner in which he invariably speaks of the guidance that he received from this source, indicates that he considered it as something supernatural. It was the voice of God: θεοῦ φωνήν, Xen. Apol. § 12, 13. It was unerring. So it was found to be, not in his own experience only, but by others who had recourse to its revelations; I. 1. 4: Καὶ πολλοῖς τῶν ξυνόντων προηγόρευε τὰ μὲν ποιεῖν, τὰ δὲ μὴ ποιεῖν, ὡς τοῦ δαιμονίου προσημαίνοντος, καὶ τοῖς μὲν πειθομένοις αὐτῷ συνέφερε, τοῖς δὲ μὴ πειθομένοις μετέμελε; Theages of Plato, p. 275–8. 3. Xenophon's testimony both to Socrates' and his own confidence in this unerring guide is beyond dispute. It was to Socrates, what the revelations of the gods through auspices, oracles, and the like, were to others, only more direct and certain. The entire reasoning of Xenophon in I. 1. 2–5 depends upon the fact, that Socrates relied upon the monitions of the δαιμόνιον as divine. How else could it be any argument that he did not discard the belief in the existence of gods?

III. Socrates' δαιμόνιον was not, on the other hand, as has often been supposed, a specific supernatural being, vouchsafed to him alone for his guidance. His exhortations to Euthydemus not to expect or desire to see the forms of the gods, but to rest satisfied with their revelation of themselves in their works, and his declaration in close connection with this, that all men might receive the same guidance as was given him, if they would only acquiesce in the requisition made upon them, to forego the desire of a physical revelation, IV. 3. 12, 13, is inconsistent with such a belief.

IV. We are now, perhaps, prepared for a more definite statement of what is meant by the Socratic demon. If what has been said is well founded, it was something beyond the dictates of mere human foresight, and yet not a specific personal deity, extrinsic from, but everywhere present with him, to give audible warnings, nor a miraculous revelation, granted as a special favor to him, but above the hopes or even the reasonable expectations of any man who will faithfully strive after its attainment. One fact in the history of the age of Socrates aids us in coming to a more precise determination in regard to this matter. The belief in guardian angels, ministering spirits sent forth on errands of mercy, was not confined to the Jews. The reliance of the ancients upon supernatural communications by various methods, and their view of the intimate connection between the deity and the human race, is too well known to need reiteration or proof. It is plain, too, that Socrates himself believed in inferior gods, who are children and ministers of the supreme God, a medium of communication between God and man, a connecting link between heaven and earth; cf. Apol. p. 27. C. D.; Memorab. IV. 3. 13, and these he called *δαιμόνια.* Two ideas, then, seem to be at the basis of this guidance of Socrates: First, his subjective fitness to receive aid from the gods, his spiritual conceptions of and obedience to them, and then, their willingness and presence to aid unerringly those who thus trust in them. The combined result of scrupulous attention to the suggestions of the inner sense and reason, and the assistance of the gods readily given to virtuous men, make up what is ascribed to the *δαιμόνιον.* It is not strange that Socrates gave it the appellation of divine. For although preparation of mind was necessary, yet it was only in matters beyond the ken of human foresight, that he was accustomed to expect supernatural aid. In his view it was equally insane and foolish to have recourse to the aid of the gods on trivial occasions, and to reject it in reference to those matters, a full knowledge of which they have reserved for themselves. Cicero's exposition of Socrates' *δαιμόνιον* is perfectly consistent with this view, although it gives rather the subjective relation of the matter, leaving the rest to be inferred; de Divinat. I. 53. 121, and 54. 122: Ut igitur, inquit, qui se tradet ita quieti, praeparato animo quum bonis cogitationibus, tum rebus ad tranquillitatem accommodatis, certa et vera cernit in somnis: sic castus sensus purusque vigilantis et ad astrorum et ad avium reliquorumque signorum et ad extorum veritatem est paratior. Hoc nimirum est illud, quod de Socrate saepe dicitur, esse divinum quiddam, quod δαιμόνιον appellat, cui semper ipse paruerit, nunquam impellenti, saepe revocanti.

In conclusion, one remark seems to be required upon an alleged contradiction between the accounts of Plato and Xenophon in regard to the office of this demon. Plato says that it only restrained him, whilst Xenophon represents it as both restraining and impelling him; cf. Plat. Apol. p. 31. C. D, and Theages, p. 128. D. with the passages above cited. The true explanation undoubtedly is, that Xenophon intends to give only a general idea of the character of this guidance; and it is not strange, that a sign which only prohibited, is spoken of also as indicating what was allowed, since the absence of a prohibition would imply permission. The object of Xenophon did not require him to draw a precise distinction between that which was positively commanded, and that which was to be inferred from silence. Besides, the fact that Socrates did consider the silence of his demon as a sign of assent, seems to be pretty well established by Plato himself. Cf. Apolog. p. 40. A. B. C; Phaedr. p. 242. B. C. On this whole subject, see Plutarch de Socratis Genio; Wiggers' Life of Socrates, Ch. III.; Ritter's Hist. Philos. II. p. 38 sq.; Tennemann's Gesch. Philos. II. 33–6, et al.; Grote's Greece, Vol. VIII. p. 557 sq.

XENOPHON AS BIOGRAPHER OF SOCRATES.

At the time of Socrates' death, 399 B. C., Xenophon was absent on the military expedition with Cyrus in Asia. And although no definite record of the fact is found, it cannot be doubted, that the Memorabilia was written soon after his return. There is a freshness of feeling and definiteness in allusion, which render it almost certain that the place of the teacher had not long been vacant, when the devoted disciple took up the pen on his behalf. The sadness which must have come over him on his return from the expedition, so unwillingly undertaken, into the land of bar-

barism, with the hope of again resuming his place with the little band of chosen friends around their companion and guide, seems yet to linger about him, and give coloring to his words. Even the absence of bitterness at the mistaken folly and injustice of the murderers, is perhaps an indication of the heartiness of his sorrow, of the subdued feeling of recent grief.

It is unnecessary at present to discuss at length the comparative merits of Plato and Xenophon, as rival biographers of Socrates.* Neither of them has given a complete and finished portrait, but both have left vivid and distinct outlines of particular parts, which need to be carefully studied and compared with discrimination, in order to supply the portions which are left in shadow, and to form a just idea of the original. But our immediate concern is with the sketch given in the present volume. We have already alluded to the facilities which Xenophon enjoyed for the execution of his work, by a long, familiar, and confidential acquaintance with his master, and with others who were so fortunate as to witness the equanimity and cheerfulness of his last hours. We might also speak of the good practical sense, the cultivated mind, and simple and graceful style of our author, but any one who is not strongly impressed with these qualities in him, before reading far in the work itself, would be little influenced by any presentation that we should be able to make. We could also express a hearty disapproval of the sentiments of those who accuse Xenophon of deficiency in warmth of feeling in defending his master. It is true he exhibits no ebullitions of passion; and how could he, and yet be the faithful and reverent disciple of one who had labored so often and so earnestly to subdue in himself and others all violent emotion? It may, we think, be asked with confidence, where we should go for an idea of Socrates as a man, a citizen, a moral teacher, if the Memorabilia were not in existence. As a philosopher, if we have skill enough to separate the Platonic from the Socratic, he is most fully exhibited in Plato. Xenophon, if he were capable of the

* See Schiermacher.

task, did not attempt to give this part of Socrates' character, except incidentally. And yet "he intimates," says Grote, "very plainly, that the conversation of Socrates was often, indeed usually of a more negative, analytical, and generalizing tendency;" . . . "destined . . . to awaken the inquisitive faculties, and lead to the rational comprehension of vice and virtue as referable to determinate general principles." Humor, in which Socrates was not deficient, we cannot find to any considerable degree in Xenophon. If he could appreciate it, which we see no reason to doubt, it was little to his purpose to give this a prominent place in his work. And besides, he could have had little heart to join in mirth over the new-made tomb of his murdered friend. He would most naturally dwell upon the serious and thoughtful developments of character at such a time.

Xenophon's principal design was, to present and illustrate the object of the life of Socrates, and thus correct wrong impressions, and rescue his memory from the calumnies which had proved so fatal. He wished to exhibit him as a good man and a useful citizen, the two points in his character which had been especially assailed by his accusers. His own practical turn of mind led him more to the consideration of the good results of his teachings, and the direct and palpable means of obtaining those results, than to mere speculations, however ingenious and subtle they might have been. It is, in fact, the basis of the character of Socrates that is given by Xenophon, the nucleus around which other qualities encircle, but without which we should often be left in darkness and doubt. We may with safety say, that no one of the pupils of Socrates had imbibed more of the genuine spirit of their teacher than Xenophon. The very absence of some of the more positive qualities of mind which are so conspicuous in Plato, enabled him to yield more implicitly to the teachings of one whose word was law to him, and fitted him to give a simple, unadorned representation of his life and character.

We do not contend that the conversations of Socrates, as recorded by Xenophon, were taken down precisely as they fell from his lips. The title indicates that they were given from recollection. They are also frequently spoken of as things remembered. We do not claim that full justice is always done to Socrates in their presentation.* This could not be expected in a brief abstract, which they undoubtedly often are. It does, however, appear to be indisputable, that Xenophon had carefully stored in his memory not only the truths themselves, but the manner in which they were presented to eager listeners. There is a minuteness and circumstantiality in many of them, and indeed a repetition,† which would have been avoided, had it not been the design of the author to give a transcript from real life. The very purpose of the author, too, in writing his book would have been frustrated, could it have been shown to be erroneous or false in respect to matters of fact. For it was without doubt written and made public while many of those with whom the conversations were held were yet living, and would have been ready to give their voice in its condemnation, had not the representation been faithful. And furthermore, his defence would have had little influence, if it could have been shown, that it was not in accordance with reality, especially as he professed to narrate that which he had heard with his own ears, or had received from the mouth of credible witnesses.

The general characteristics of this work are so well and briefly stated by an English scholar,‡ that we cannot do the reader a better service than to allow his remarks upon this point to take the place which we had reserved for our own: "The Memorabilia of Xenophon is a possession for all time; for the noble simplicity of the style is worthy of the purity and soundness of the principles. Indeed, who can mark without admiration the strong sense, the good feeling, the high principles, and the right practices of this book? It bears the same ratio to the Dialogues of Plato, that the practical teaching of the Gospels does to the doc-

* See I. 2. 53; I. 3. 1; I. 4. 2; II. 4. 1; IV. 3. 4.

† Cf. I. 4 with IV. 3; I. 5. with IV. 5, et al.

‡ Rev. J. P. Potter: Characteristics of the Greek Philosophers, Socrates and Plato pp. 7, 8.

trinal teaching of the Epistles. He who runs may read. It was a great service which Socrates rendered his countrymen. He cleared the foundations of religion and morals from whatever was obscuring and undermining them. He exhibited these foundations in all their strength, and showed that principles and conduct may be safely rested upon them. The very characteristic of Socrates' philosophy is the grand simplicity of a Doric temple. He states the great principles of religion, and morals, and politics, so clearly and convincingly, that every one must understand, and no one can deny. The sincerity of the manner is equal to the truth of the matter. And to all this must be added a genial warmth of feeling, whether it be shown in deep reverence for God, or in hearty love to man, which it is impossible to resist; for whilst Socrates states truth so convincingly as to compel assent, he urges it so kindly as to win conviction."

The text of the present edition is that of Kühner, with occa sional alterations in pointing and things of minor importance. When it appeared desirable, various readings have been given in the notes, and reasons for the one adopted, briefly stated.

In preparing the first edition, free use was made of the labors of Kühner, whenever they seemed to our purpose. We did not, however, follow him blindly, and sometimes came to results quite different from his, on the examination of a passage. We also had constantly by us, Xenophon's Memoiren; mit Einleitungen und Anmerkungen von Dr. Moritz Seyffert, Königl. Professor and Conrector am Gymn. zu Brandenberg, and sometimes received valuable aid from it, although the notes are, for the most part, made up of the translation of single words and phrases. Other editions, as those of Schneider, Weiske, Bornemann, and Greenwood, were occasionally consulted. The additions and corrections in the present edition are principally the result of experience n teaching, although the suggestions of others, either in printed notices or private correspondence, have not been unheeded or without much value. If the diligent student shall be enabled by the present volume, to gain a more thorough insight into the character of one of the greatest and best of uninspired men, and more love for, and familiarity with, the most cultivated and refined language of any age or nation, we shall feel that we have, in addition to the enjoyment which each day spent in the preparation of the volume brought with it, a full reward for our labor.

ABBREVIATIONS AND EXPLANATIONS EMPLOYED IN NOTES.

Kühn. Gr., the Translation of Kühner's Grammar by Edwards and Taylor.

L. Gr., the Larger Grammar of the same author.

El. Gr., his Elementary Grammar as prepared in English by Taylor.

B. Gr., simply *B.*, or *Buttmann*, Robinson's Buttmann, ed. 1851.

C. Gr., Crosby's Grammar.

S. or *Soph. Gr.*, Sophocles' Grammar.

Other Grammars are often referred to, but in such a way, it is believed, as not to need explanation. When references are made without naming the work, as I. 2. 5; III. 6. 3, 20; 3. 10, &c., the books, chapters, and sections of the Memorabilia are intended; and when only the name of the work, without the name of the author, is given, as *Apol. Hellen.* &c., some treatise of Xenophon is referred to.

ΞΕΝΟΦΩΝΤΟΣ

ΑΠΟΜΝΗΜΟΝΕΥΜΑΤΑ

ΞΕΝΟΦΩΝΤΟΣ

ΑΠΟΜΝΗΜΟΝΕΥΜΑΤΩΝ.

ΒΙΒΛΙΟΝ ΠΡΩΤΟΝ.

CHAPTER I.

ARGUMENT.

In the trial of Socrates, two crimes were alleged against him, as rendering him worthy of death:—1. He did not reverence the gods of the State, but introduced other new deities instead of them;—2. He corrupted the youth (§ 1). In confutation of the first accusation, the following considerations are adduced:

1. He did not omit either private or public sacrifices to the gods (§ 2).

2. He made use of divination (§ 2—9). In saying that his divinity (τὸ δαιμόνιον) made known to him future events, he did not differ from other Athenians, who do not suppose that sacrifices, the flight of birds, and other such things, of themselves make known the future, but that the gods make revelations through them. While others, then, say that they are guided by casual events, he, going back to the cause, averred that a divinity guided him; and by the confidence which he placed in the revelations made to him, he showed his confidence in the gods and his consequent belief in their existence (§ 2—5). In reference to necessary duties, he gave advice to his friends upon the manner of their performance; but in regard to things of a doubtful nature, he counselled them to ask direction from the gods; he believed it equally impious not to consult the gods in reference to those matters, the knowledge of which they had retained to themselves, and to have recourse to them in respect to things that fall within the province of human reason (§ 6—9).

3. The innocence of Socrates is also evident from the whole course of his life. He passed much of his time in public, where all could see and hear him, and yet no one could adduce an instance of impiety in word or action. He did not, like the other philosophers, employ his time in

fruitless discussions in regard to the origin of the world and other things which are beyond the bounds of human knowledge, but upon questions relating to the conduct of life both in private and public; his endeavor was to give men correct principles of action, and to make them valuable citizens (§ 10—16). Socrates confirmed his precepts by specific actions, showing how much his reverence for the gods preponderated over fear of man. It is indeed strange that the Athenians were persuaded that he was guilty of impiety, when he proved both by his actions and words, that he not only did not despise but was especially mindful of the gods (§ 17—20).

---

1 Πολλάκις ἐθαύμασα, τίσι ποτὲ λόγοις Ἀθηναίους ἔπεισαν οἱ γραψάμενοι Σωκράτην, ὡς ἄξιος εἴη θανάτου τῇ πόλει. Ἡ μὲν γὰρ γραφὴ κατ' αὐτοῦ τοιάδε τις ἦν· ἀδικεῖ Σωκράτης οὓς μὲν ἡ πόλις νομίζει θεοὺς οὐ νομίζων, ἕτερα δὲ καινὰ δαιμόνια εἰςφέρων· ἀδικεῖ δὲ καὶ τοὺς νέους διαφθείρων.

2 Πρῶτον μὲν οὖν, ὡς οὐκ ἐνόμιζεν οὓς ἡ πόλις νομίζει θεούς, ποίῳ ποτ' ἐχρήσαντο τεκμηρίῳ; θύων τε γὰρ φανερὸς ἦν πολλάκις μὲν οἴκοι, πολλάκις δὲ ἐπὶ τῶν κοινῶν τῆς πόλεως βωμῶν, καὶ μαντικῇ χρώμενος οὐκ ἀφανὴς ἦν· διετεθρύλητο γάρ, ὡς φαίη Σωκράτης τὸ δαιμόνιον ἑαυτῷ σημαίνειν· ὅθεν δὴ καὶ μάλιστά μοι δοκοῦσιν αὐτὸν αἰτιάσασθαι καινὰ δαιμόνια εἰςφέ-
3 ρειν. Ὁ δ' οὐδὲν καινότερον εἰςέφερε τῶν ἄλλων, ὅσοι μαντικὴν νομίζοντες οἰωνοῖς τε χρῶνται καὶ φήμαις καὶ συμβόλοις καὶ θυσίαις· οὗτοί τε γὰρ ὑπολαμβάνουσιν οὐ τοὺς ὄρνιθας οὐδὲ τοὺς ἀπαντῶντας εἰδέναι τὰ συμφέροντα τοῖς μαντευομένοις, ἀλλὰ τοὺς θεοὺς διὰ τού-
4 των αὐτὰ σημαίνειν, κἀκεῖνος δὲ οὕτως ἐνόμιζεν. Ἀλλ' οἱ μὲν πλεῖστοί φασιν ὑπό τε τῶν ὀρνίθων καὶ τῶν ἀπαντώντων ἀποτρέπεσθαί τε καὶ προτρέπεσθαι· Σωκράτης δὲ ὥςπερ ἐγίγνωσκεν, οὕτως ἔλεγε· τὸ δαιμόνιον γὰρ ἔφη σημαίνειν. Καὶ πολλοῖς τῶν ξυνόντων προ-

ηγόρευε τὰ μὲν ποιεῖν, τὰ δὲ μὴ ποιεῖν, ὡς τοῦ δαι-
μονίου προσημαίνοντος· καὶ τοῖς μὲν πειθομένοις αὐτῷ
συνέφερε, τοῖς δὲ μὴ πειθομένοις μετέμελε. Καίτοι τίς 5
οὐκ ἂν ὁμολογήσειεν αὐτὸν βούλεσθαι μήτ' ἠλίθιον
μήτ' ἀλαζόνα φαίνεσθαι τοῖς συνοῦσιν; ἐδόκει δ' ἂν
ἀμφότερα ταῦτα, εἰ προαγορεύων ὡς ὑπὸ θεοῦ φαι-
νόμενα κᾆτα ψευδόμενος ἐφαίνετο. Δῆλον οὖν, ὅτι
οὐκ ἂν προέλεγεν, εἰ μὴ ἐπίστευεν ἀληθεύσειν. Ταῦτα
δὲ τίς ἂν ἄλλῳ πιστεύσειεν ἢ θεῷ; πιστεύων δὲ θεοῖς
πῶς οὐκ εἶναι θεοὺς ἐνόμιζεν; Ἀλλὰ μὴν ἐποίει καὶ 6
τάδε πρὸς τοὺς ἐπιτηδείους· τὰ μὲν γὰρ ἀναγκαῖα
συνεβούλευε καὶ πράττειν, ὡς ἐνόμιζεν ἄριστ' ἂν
πραχθῆναι· περὶ δὲ τῶν ἀδήλων, ὅπως ἂν ἀποβήσοιτο,
μαντευσομένους ἔπεμπεν, εἰ ποιητέα. Καὶ τοὺς μέλ- 7
λοντας οἴκους τε καὶ πόλεις καλῶς οἰκήσειν μαντικῆς
ἔφη προςδεῖσθαι· τεκτονικὸν μὲν γὰρ ἢ χαλκευτικὸν ἢ
γεωργικὸν ἢ ἀνθρώπων ἀρχικὸν ἢ τῶν τοιούτων ἔργων
ἐξεταστικὸν ἢ λογιστικὸν ἢ οἰκονομικὸν ἢ στρατηγικὸν
γενέσθαι, πάντα τὰ τοιαῦτα μαθήματα καὶ ἀνθρώπου
γνώμῃ αἱρετέα ἐνόμιζεν εἶναι· τὰ δὲ μέγιστα τῶν ἐν
τούτοις ἔφη τοὺς θεοὺς ἑαυτοῖς καταλείπεσθαι, ὧν οὐ-
δὲν δῆλον εἶναι τοῖς ἀνθρώποις. Οὔτε γάρ τοι τῷ 8
καλῶς ἀγρὸν φυτευσαμένῳ δῆλον, ὅςτις καρπώσεται·
οὔτε τῷ καλῶς οἰκίαν οἰκοδομησαμένῳ δῆλον, ὅςτις οἰ
κήσει· οὔτε τῷ στρατηγικῷ δῆλον, εἰ συμφέρει στρα-
τηγεῖν· οὔτε τῷ πολιτικῷ δῆλον, εἰ συμφέρει τῆς πόλεως
προστατεῖν· οὔτε τῷ καλὴν γήμαντι, ἵν' εὐφραίνηται,
δῆλον, εἰ διὰ ταύτην ἀνιάσεται· οὔτε τῷ δυνατοὺς ἐν
τῇ πόλει κηδεστὰς λαβόντι δῆλον, εἰ διὰ τούτους στε-
ρήσεται τῆς πόλεως. Τοὺς δὲ μηδὲν τῶν τοιούτων 9
οἰομένους εἶναι δαιμόνιον, ἀλλὰ πάντα τῆς ἀνθρωπίνης
γνώμης, δαιμονᾶν ἔφη· δαιμονᾶν δὲ καὶ τοὺς μαντευο-
μένους, ἃ τοῖς ἀνθρώποις ἔδωκαν οἱ θεοὶ μαθοῦσι δια-
κρίνειν· οἷον εἴ τις ἐπερωτῴη, πότερον ἐπιστάμενον

ἡνιοχεῖν ἐπὶ ζεῦγος λαβεῖν κρεῖττον ἢ μὴ ἐπιστάμενον,
ἢ πότερον ἐπιστάμενον κυβερνᾶν ἐπὶ τὴν ναῦν κρεῖττον
λαβεῖν ἢ μὴ ἐπιστάμενον, ἢ ἃ ἔξεστιν ἀριθμήσαντας
ἢ μετρήσαντας ἢ στήσαντας εἰδέναι, τοὺς τὰ τοιαῦτα
παρὰ τῶν θεῶν πυνθανομένους ἀθέμιστα ποιεῖν ἡγεῖ-
το· ἔφη δὲ δεῖν ἃ μὲν μαθόντας ποιεῖν ἔδωκαν οἱ θεοὶ
μανθάνειν· ἃ δὲ μὴ δῆλα τοῖς ἀνθρώποις ἐστί, πει-
ρᾶσθαι διὰ μαντικῆς παρὰ τῶν θεῶν πυνθάνεσθαι·
τοὺς θεοὺς γὰρ οἷς ἂν ὦσιν ἵλεῳ σημαίνειν.
10 Ἀλλὰ μὴν ἐκεῖνός γε ἀεὶ μὲν ἦν ἐν τῷ φανερῷ·
πρωί τε γὰρ εἰς τοὺς περιπάτους καὶ τὰ γυμνάσια ᾔει
καὶ πληθούσης ἀγορᾶς ἐκεῖ φανερὸς ἦν, καὶ τὸ λοιπὸι
ἀεὶ τῆς ἡμέρας ἦν ὅπου πλείστοις μέλλοι συνέσεσθαι·
καὶ ἔλεγε μὲν ὡς τὸ πολύ, τοῖς δὲ βουλομένοις ἐξῆν
11 ἀκούειν. Οὐδεὶς δὲ πώποτε Σωκράτους οὐδὲν ἀσεβὲς
οὐδὲ ἀνόσιον οὔτε πράττοντος εἶδεν, οὔτε λέγοντος ἤκου-
σεν. Οὐδὲ γὰρ περὶ τῆς τῶν πάντων φύσεως ᾗπερ τῶν
ἄλλων οἱ πλεῖστοι διελέγετο, σκοπῶν, ὅπως ὁ καλού-
μενος ὑπὸ τῶν σοφιστῶν κόσμος ἔφυ, καὶ τίσιν ἀνάγκαις
ἕκαστα γίγνεται τῶν οὐρανίων, ἀλλὰ καὶ τοὺς φρον-
12 τίζοντας τὰ τοιαῦτα μωραίνοντας ἀπεδείκνυεν. Καὶ
πρῶτον μὲν αὐτῶν ἐσκόπει, πότερά ποτε νομίσαντες
ἱκανῶς ἤδη τἀνθρώπινα εἰδέναι ἔρχονται ἐπὶ τὸ περὶ
τῶν τοιούτων φροντίζειν, ἢ τὰ μὲν ἀνθρώπεια παρέντες,
τὰ δαιμόνια δὲ σκοποῦντες, ἡγοῦνται τὰ προσήκοντα
13 πράττειν. Ἐθαύμαζε δ', εἰ μὴ φανερὸν αὐτοῖς ἐστιν,
ὅτι ταῦτα οὐ δυνατόν ἐστιν ἀνθρώποις εὑρεῖν· ἐπεὶ καὶ
τοὺς μέγιστον φρονοῦντας ἐπὶ τῷ περὶ τούτων λέγειν
οὐ ταὐτὰ δοξάζειν ἀλλήλοις, ἀλλὰ τοῖς μαινομένοις
14 ὁμοίως διακεῖσθαι πρὸς ἀλλήλους. Τῶν τε γὰρ μαινο-
μένων τοὺς μὲν οὐδὲ τὰ δεινὰ δεδιέναι, τοὺς δὲ καὶ τὰ μὴ
φοβερὰ φοβεῖσθαι· καὶ τοῖς μὲν οὐδ' ἐν ὄχλῳ δοκεῖν
αἰσχρὸν εἶναι λέγειν ἢ ποιεῖν ὁτιοῦν, τοῖς δὲ οὐδ' ἐξιτη-
τέον εἰς ἀνθρώπους εἶναι δοκεῖν· καὶ τοὺς μὲν οὐθ'

ἱερὸν οὔτε βωμὸν οὔτ' ἄλλο τῶν θείων οὐδὲν τιμᾶν,
τοὺς δὲ καὶ λίθους καὶ ξύλα τὰ τυχόντα καὶ θηρία
σέβεσθαι· τῶν τε περὶ τῆς τῶν πάντων φύσεως μερι-
μνώντων τοῖς μὲν δοκεῖν ἓν μόνον τὸ ὂν εἶναι, τοῖς δ'
ἄπειρα τὸ πλῆθος· καὶ τοῖς μὲν ἀεὶ κινεῖσθαι πάντα,
τοῖς δ' οὐδὲν ἄν ποτε κινηθῆναι· καὶ τοῖς μὲν πάντα
γίγνεσθαί τε καὶ ἀπόλλυσθαι, τοῖς δὲ οὔτ' ἂν γενέσθαι
ποτὲ οὐδὲν οὔτ' ἀπολεῖσθαι. Ἐσκόπει δὲ περὶ αὐτῶν 15
καὶ τάδε· ἆρ', ὥσπερ οἱ ἀνθρώπεια μανθάνοντες ἡγοῦν-
ται τοῦθ', ὅ τι ἂν μάθωσιν, ἑαυτοῖς τε καὶ τῶν ἄλλων
ὅτῳ ἂν βούλωνται ποιήσειν, οὕτω καὶ οἱ τὰ θεῖα ζη-
τοῦντες νομίζουσιν, ἐπειδὰν γνῶσιν, αἷς ἀνάγκαις ἕκαστα
γίγνεται, ποιήσειν, ὅταν βούλωνται, καὶ ἀνέμους καὶ
ὕδατα καὶ ὥρας καὶ ὅτου δ' ἂν ἄλλου δέωνται τῶν
τοιούτων, ἢ τοιοῦτο μὲν οὐδὲν οὐδ' ἐλπίζουσιν, ἀρκεῖ
δ' αὐτοῖς γνῶναι μόνον, ᾗ τῶν τοιούτων ἕκαστα γίγνε-
ται. Περὶ μὲν οὖν τῶν ταῦτα πραγματευομένων τοι- 16
αῦτα ἔλεγεν· αὐτὸς δὲ περὶ τῶν ἀνθρωπείων ἂν ἀεὶ
διελέγετο, σκοπῶν τί εὐσεβές, τί ἀσεβές· τί καλόν, τί
αἰσχρόν· τί δίκαιον, τί ἄδικον· τί σωφροσύνη, τί μανία·
τί ἀνδρεία, τί δειλία· τί πόλις, τί πολιτικός· τί ἀρχὴ
ἀνθρώπων, τί ἀρχικὸς ἀνθρώπων· καὶ περὶ τῶν ἄλλων,
ἃ τοὺς μὲν εἰδότας ἡγεῖτο καλοὺς κἀγαθοὺς εἶναι, τοὺς
δ' ἀγνοοῦντας ἀνδραποδώδεις ἂν δικαίως κεκλῆσθαι.
Ὅσα μὲν οὖν μὴ φανερὸς ἦν ὅπως ἐγίγνωσκεν, οὐ- 17
δὲν θαυμαστὸν ὑπὲρ τούτων περὶ αὐτοῦ παραγνῶναι
τοὺς δικαστάς· ὅσα δὲ πάντες ᾔδεσαν, οὐ θαυμαστὸν,
εἰ μὴ τούτων ἐνεθυμήθησαν; Βουλεύσας γάρ ποτε 18
καὶ τὸν βουλευτικὸν ὅρκον ὀμόσας, ἐν ᾧ ἦν κατὰ τοὺς
νόμους βουλεύσειν, ἐπιστάτης ἐν τῷ δήμῳ γενόμενος,
ἐπιθυμήσαντος τοῦ δήμου παρὰ τοὺς νόμους ἐννέα στρα-
τηγοὺς μιᾷ ψήφῳ τοὺς ἀμφὶ Θράσυλλον καὶ Ἐρασι-
νίδην ἀποκτεῖναι πάντας, οὐκ ἠθέλησεν ἐπιψηφίσαι,
ὀργιζομένου μὲν αὐτῷ τοῦ δήμου, πολλῶν δὲ καὶ δυνα-

τῶν ἀπειλούντων· ἀλλὰ περὶ πλείονος ἐποιήσατο εὐορ
κεῖν ἢ χαρίσασθαι τῷ δήμῳ παρὰ τὸ δίκαιον καὶ
19 φυλάξασθαι τοὺς ἀπειλοῦντας. Καὶ γὰρ ἐπιμελεῖσθαι
θεοὺς ἐνόμιζεν ἀνθρώπων, οὐχ ὃν τρόπον οἱ πολλοὶ
νομίζουσιν· οὗτοι μὲν γὰρ οἴονται τοὺς θεοὺς τὰ μὲν
εἰδέναι, τὰ δ' οὐκ εἰδέναι· Σωκράτης δὲ πάντα μὲν
ἡγεῖτο θεοὺς εἰδέναι, τά τε λεγόμενα καὶ πραττόμενα
καὶ τὰ σιγῇ βουλευόμενα, πανταχοῦ δὲ παρεῖναι, καὶ
σημαίνειν τοῖς ἀνθρώποις περὶ τῶν ἀνθρωπείων πάν-
των.

20 Θαυμάζω οὖν, ὅπως ποτὲ ἐπείσθησαν Ἀθηναῖοι
Σωκράτην περὶ τοὺς θεοὺς μὴ σωφρονεῖν, τὸν ἀσεβὲς
μὲν οὐδέν ποτε περὶ τοὺς θεοὺς οὔτ' εἰπόντα οὔτε
πράξαντα, τοιαῦτα δὲ καὶ λέγοντα καὶ πράττοντα περὶ
θεῶν, οἷά τις ἂν καὶ λέγων καὶ πράττων εἴη τε καὶ
νομίζοιτο εὐσεβέστατος.

CHAPTER II.

ARGUMENT.

THE second accusation of the enemies of Socrates (I. 1.), that he was a corrupter of the youth, is shown to be without foundation by the following considerations:

1. He dissuaded the youth from impiety, disobedience to law, the indulgence of the sensual passions and effeminacy, and inculcated the opposite virtues, inspiring the hope, that, by the love and practice of them, they would become honorable and good. This he did, especially, by presenting himself as the most perfect example of the practice of those virtues which he inculcated (§ 1—8).

2. The accusation that Socrates made his disciples violent opposers of the established laws and usages, is confuted by the simple fact, that his teachings, showing the inconvenience and injuries resulting from the use of violence as contrasted with persuasion, must necessarily have had

the very opposite effect (§ 9—11). The disorderly conduct of Critias and Alcibiades after they had been his pupils, is no cause of reproach against him. They sought not his society from any love for his character and teachings, but as a means for the more effectual accomplishment of their ambitious purposes; and yet whilst they were with him they practised self-government; and that not from constraint but from persuasion (§ 12—18). But virtue unless constantly exercised falters and dies (§ 14—23); and Critias and Alcibiades, after leaving Socrates, were withdrawn from the continued practice of those virtues which he enjoined, by the influence of other men, and Socrates ought, in contrast with these men, to receive praise rather than blame (§ 24—29); for he faithfully admonished his pupils whenever he saw them going astray. Critias, offended by the severity of his admonitions, sought revenge after he had become a ruler of the State, by causing a law to be passed against Socrates (§ 30—38). The object of both Critias and Alcibiades in joining themselves to Socrates, is evident from their conduct; and in the case of Alcibiades, was strikingly illustrated by a conversation with his guardian Pericles (§ 24—47). In contrast with these men, all who joined themselves to Socrates with the desire of becoming wise and good, passed their whole lives in the exercise of virtue and without reproach (§ 48).

3. The accusation of inspiring in those who associated with him, a disregard of parents, relatives, and friends, rests entirely upon a misunderstanding of the nature of his teachings in this regard; for his object was to give the relation of parents and children, friends and relatives, a higher object, mutual benefit (§ 49—55).

4. The accusation made against him, of quoting from ancient poets, for the purpose of inculcating feelings of malevolence and tyranny, is absurd (§ 56—59). On the other hand, he ever exhibited the most disinterested regard for all men, both citizens and strangers (§ 60, 61).

In fine, it appears from the considerations adduced in this and the preceding chapter, that Socrates was worthy of the highest regard and honor from the city, rather than punishment (§ 62—64).

Θαυμαστὸν δὲ φαίνεταί μοι καὶ τὸ πεισθῆναί τινας, 1
ὡς Σωκράτης τοὺς νέους διέφθειρεν, ὃς πρὸς τοῖς εἰρη-
μένοις πρῶτον μὲν ἀφροδισίων καὶ γαστρὸς πάντων
ἀνθρώπων ἐγκρατέστατος ἦν, εἶτα πρὸς χειμῶνα καὶ
θέρος καὶ πάντας πόνους καρτερικώτατος, ἔτι δὲ πρὸς
τό μετρίων δεῖσθαι πεπαιδευμένος οὕτως, ὥστε πάνυ
μικρὰ κεκτημένος πάνυ ῥᾳδίως ἔχειν ἀρκοῦντα. Πῶς 2

οὖν, αὐτὸς ὢν τοιοῦτος, ἄλλους ἂν ἢ ἀσεβεῖς ἢ παρανόμους ἢ λίχνους ἢ ἀφροδισίων ἀκρατεῖς ἢ πρὸς τὸ πονεῖν μαλακοὺς ἐποίησεν; Ἀλλ' ἔπαυσε μὲν τούτων πολλοὺς ἀρετῆς ποιήσας ἐπιθυμεῖν καὶ ἐλπίδας παρασχών, ἂν ἑαυτῶν ἐπιμελῶνται, καλοὺς καὶ ἀγαθοὺς
3 ἔσεσθαι. Καίτοι γε οὐδεπώποτε ὑπέσχετο διδάσκαλος εἶναι τούτου· ἀλλὰ τῷ φανερὸς εἶναι τοιοῦτος ὢν ἐλπίζειν ἐποίει τοὺς συνδιατρίβοντας ἑαυτῷ, μιμουμένους
4 ἐκεῖνον τοιούσδε γενήσεσθαι. Ἀλλὰ μὴν καὶ τοῦ σώματος αὐτός τε οὐκ ἠμέλει τούς τ' ἀμελοῦντας οὐκ ἐπῄνει. Τὸ μὲν οὖν ὑπερεσθίοντα ὑπερπονεῖν ἀπεδοκίμαζε, τὸ δέ, ὅσα γ' ἡδέως ἡ ψυχὴ δέχεται, ταῦτα ἱκανῶς ἐκπονεῖν ἐδοκίμαζε· ταύτην γὰρ τὴν ἕξιν ὑγιεινήν τε ἱκανῶς εἶναι καὶ τὴν τῆς ψυχῆς ἐπιμέλειαν οὐκ ἐμποδίζειν ἔφη.
5 Ἀλλ' οὐ μὴν θρυπτικός γε οὐδὲ ἀλαζονικὸς ἦν οὔτ' ἀμπεχόνῃ οὔθ' ὑποδέσει οὔτε τῇ ἄλλῃ διαίτῃ· οὐ μὴν οὐδ' ἐρασιχρημάτους γε τοὺς συνόντας ἐποίει· τῶν μὲν γὰρ ἄλλων ἐπιθυμιῶν ἔπαυε, τοὺς δὲ ἑαυτοῦ ἐπιθυ-
6 μοῦντας οὐκ ἐπράττετο χρήματα. Τούτου δ' ἀπεχόμενος ἐνόμιζεν ἐλευθερίας ἐπιμελεῖσθαι· τοὺς δὲ λαμβάνοντας τῆς ὁμιλίας μισθὸν ἀνδραποδιστὰς ἑαυτῶν ἀπεκάλει, διὰ τὸ ἀναγκαῖον αὐτοῖς εἶναι διαλέγεσθαι
7 παρ' ὧν ἂν λάβοιεν τὸν μισθόν. Ἐθαύμαζε δ', εἴ τις ἀρετὴν ἐπαγγελλόμενος ἀργύριον πράττοιτο, καὶ μὴ νομίζοι τὸ μέγιστον κέρδος ἕξειν φίλον ἀγαθὸν κτησάμενος, ἀλλὰ φοβοῖτο, μὴ ὁ γενόμενος καλὸς κἀγαθὸς τῷ τὰ μέγιστα εὐεργετήσαντι μὴ τὴν μεγίστην χάριν
8 ἕξοι. Σωκράτης δὲ ἐπηγγείλατο μὲν οὐδενὶ πώποτε τοιοῦτον οὐδέν· ἐπίστευε δὲ τῶν ξυνόντων ἑαυτῷ τοὺς ἀποδεξαμένους, ἅπερ αὐτὸς ἐδοκίμαζεν, εἰς τὸν πάντα βίον ἑαυτῷ τε καὶ ἀλλήλοις φίλους ἀγαθοὺς ἔσεσθαι. πῶς ἂν οὖν ὁ τοιοῦτος ἀνὴρ διαφθείροι τοὺς νέους; εἰ μὴ ἄρα ἡ τῆς ἀρετῆς ἐπιμέλεια διαφθορά ἐστιν.

9 Ἀλλά, νὴ Δία, ὁ κατήγορος ἔφη, ὑπερορᾶν ἐποίει

τῶν καθεστώτων νόμων τοὺς συνόντας, λέγων, ὡς μω-
ρὸν εἴη τοὺς μὲν τῆς πόλεως ἄρχοντας ἀπὸ κυάμου
καθίστασθαι, κυβερνήτῃ δὲ μηδένα θέλειν κεχρῆσθαι
κυαμευτῷ, μηδὲ τέκτονι, μηδ' αὐλητῇ, μηδ' ἐπ' ἄλλα
τοιαῦτα, ἃ πολλῷ ἐλάττονας βλάβας ἁμαρτανόμενα
ποιεῖ τῶν περὶ τὴν πόλιν ἁμαρτανομένων· τοὺς δὲ
τοιούτους λόγους ἐπαίρειν ἔφη τοὺς νέους καταφρονεῖν
τῆς καθεστώσης πολιτείας, καὶ ποιεῖν βιαίους. Ἐγὼ 10
δ' οἶμαι τοὺς φρόνησιν ἀσκοῦντας καὶ νομίζοντας ἱκα-
νοὺς ἔσεσθαι τὰ συμφέροντα διδάσκειν τοὺς πολίτας
ἥκιστα γίγνεσθαι βιαίους, εἰδότας, ὅτι τῇ μὲν βίᾳ
πρόςεισιν ἔχθραι καὶ κίνδυνοι, διὰ δὲ τοῦ πείθειν ἀκιν-
δύνως τε καὶ μετὰ φιλίας ταὐτὰ γίγνεται· οἱ μὲν γὰρ
βιασθέντες ὡς ἀφαιρεθέντες μισοῦσιν, οἱ δὲ πεισθέντες
ὡς κεχαρισμένοι φιλοῦσιν. Οὐκ οὖν τῶν φρόνησιν
ἀσκούντων τὸ βιάζεσθαι, ἀλλὰ τῶν ἰσχὺν ἄνευ γνώ-
μης ἐχόντων τὰ τοιαῦτα πράττειν ἐστίν. Ἀλλὰ μὴν 11
καὶ συμμάχων ὁ μὲν βιάζεσθαι τολμῶν δέοιτ' ἂν οὐκ
ὀλίγων, ὁ δὲ πείθειν δυνάμενος, οὐδενός· καὶ γὰρ μό-
νος ἡγοῖτ' ἂν δύνασθαι πείθειν. καὶ φονεύειν δὲ τοῖς
τοιούτοις ἥκιστα συμβαίνει· τίς γὰρ ἀποκτεῖναί τινα
βούλοιτ' ἂν μᾶλλον ἢ ζῶντι πειθομένῳ χρῆσθαι;

Ἀλλ' ἔφη γε ὁ κατήγορος, Σωκράτει ὁμιλητὰ γενο- 12
μένω Κριτίας τε καὶ Ἀλκιβιάδης πλεῖστα κακὰ τὴν
πόλιν ἐποιησάτην. Κριτίας μὲν γὰρ τῶν ἐν τῇ ὀλι-
γαρχίᾳ πάντων πλεονεκτίστατός τε καὶ βιαιότατος
ἐγένετο, Ἀλκιβιάδης δὲ αὖ τῶν ἐν τῇ δημοκρατίᾳ πάν-
των ἀκρατέστατος καὶ ὑβριστότατος καὶ βιαιότατος.
Ἐγὼ δ', εἰ μέν τι κακὸν ἐκείνω τὴν πόλιν ἐποιησά- 13
την, οὐκ ἀπολογήσομαι· τὴν δὲ πρὸς Σωκράτην συνου-
σίαν αὐτοῖν, ὡς ἐγένετο, διηγήσομαι. Ἐγενέσθην μὲν 14
γὰρ δὴ τὼ ἄνδρε τούτω φύσει φιλοτιμοτάτω πάντων
Ἀθηναίων, βουλομένω τε πάντα δι' ἑαυτῶν πράττεσθαι
καὶ πάντων ὀνομαστοτάτω γενέσθαι. ᾔδεσαν δὲ Σω-

κράτην ἀπ' ἐλαχίστων μὲν χρημάτων αὐταρκέστατα
ζῶντα, τῶν ἡδονῶν δὲ πασῶν ἐγκρατέστατον ὄντα, τοῖς
δὲ διαλεγομένοις αὐτῷ πᾶσι χρώμενον ἐν τοῖς λόγοις,
15 ὅπως βούλοιτο. Ταῦτα δὲ ὁρῶντε καὶ ὄντε οἵω προεί-
ρησθον, πότερόν τις αὐτὼ φῇ τοῦ βίου τοῦ Σωκράτους
ἐπιθυμήσαντε καὶ τῆς σωφροσύνης, ἣν ἐκεῖνος εἶχεν,
ὀρέξασθαι τῆς ὁμιλίας αὐτοῦ, ἢ νομίσαντε, εἰ ὁμιλη-
σαίτην ἐκείνῳ, γενέσθαι ἂν ἱκανωτάτω λέγειν τε καὶ
16 πράττειν; Ἐγὼ μὲν γὰρ ἡγοῦμαι, θεοῦ διδόντος αὐτοῖν
ἢ ζῆν ὅλον τὸν βίον, ὥσπερ ζῶντα Σωκράτην ἑώρων,
ἢ τεθνάναι, ἑλέσθαι ἂν μᾶλλον αὐτὼ τεθνάναι. Δήλω
δ' ἐγενέσθην ἐξ ὧν ἐπραξάτην· ὡς γὰρ τάχιστα κρείτ-
τονε τῶν συγγιγνομένων ἡγησάσθην εἶναι, εὐθὺς ἀπο-
πηδήσαντε Σωκράτους ἐπραττέτην τὰ πολιτικά, ὧνπερ
ἕνεκα Σωκράτους ὠρεχθήτην.
17 Ἴσως οὖν εἴποι τις ἂν πρὸς ταῦτα, ὅτι χρῆν τὸν
Σωκράτην μὴ πρότερον τὰ πολιτικὰ διδάσκειν τοὺς
συνόντας ἢ σωφρονεῖν. Ἐγὼ δὲ πρὸς τοῦτο μὲν οὐκ
ἀντιλέγω· πάντας δὲ τοὺς διδάσκοντας ὁρῶ αὐτοὺς
δεικνύντας τε τοῖς μανθάνουσιν, ᾗπερ αὐτοὶ ποιοῦσιν
18 ἃ διδάσκουσι, καὶ τῷ λόγῳ προσβιβάζοντας. Οἶδα δὲ
καὶ Σωκράτην δεικνύντα τοῖς ξυνοῦσιν ἑαυτὸν καλὸν
κἀγαθὸν ὄντα, καὶ διαλεγόμενον κάλλιστα περὶ ἀρετῆς
καὶ τῶν ἄλλων ἀνθρωπίνων. Οἶδα δὲ κἀκείνω σωφρο-
νοῦντε, ἔστε Σωκράτει συνήστην, οὐ φοβουμένω μὴ
ζημιοῖντο ἢ παίοιντο ὑπὸ Σωκράτους, ἀλλ' οἰομένω
τότε κράτιστον εἶναι τοῦτο πράττειν.
19 Ἴσως οὖν εἴποιεν ἂν πολλοὶ τῶν φασκόντων φιλο-
σοφεῖν, ὅτι οὐκ ἄν ποτε ὁ δίκαιος ἄδικος γένοιτο, οὐδὲ
ὁ σώφρων ὑβριστής, οὐδὲ ἄλλο οὐδὲν, ὧν μάθησίς
ἐστιν, ὁ μαθὼν ἀνεπιστήμων ἄν ποτε γένοιτο. Ἐγὼ
δὲ περὶ τούτων οὐχ οὕτω γιγνώσκω· ὁρῶ γὰρ ὥσπερ
τὰ τοῦ σώματος ἔργα τοὺς μὴ τὰ σώματα ἀσκοῦντας οὐ
δυναμένους ποιεῖν, οὕτω καὶ τὰ τῆς ψυχῆς ἔργα τοὺς

μὴ τὴν ψυχὴν ἀσκοῦντας οὐ δυναμένους· οὔτε γὰρ ἃ
δεῖ πράττειν οὔτε ὧν δεῖ ἀπέχεσθαι δύνανται. Διὸ 20
καὶ τοὺς υἱεῖς οἱ πατέρες, κἂν ὦσι σώφρονες, ὅμως ἀπὸ
τῶν πονηρῶν ἀνθρώπων εἴργουσιν, ὡς τὴν μὲν τῶν
χρηστῶν ὁμιλίαν ἄσκησιν οὖσαν τῆς ἀρετῆς, τὴν δὲ
τῶν πονηρῶν κατάλυσιν. Μαρτυρεῖ δὲ καὶ τῶν ποιη-
τῶν ὅ τε λέγων·

Ἐσθλῶν μὲν γὰρ ἄπ᾽ ἐσθλὰ διδάξεαι· ἢν δὲ κακοῖσιν
Συμμίσγῃς, ἀπολεῖς καὶ τὸν ἐόντα νόον.

καὶ ὁ λέγων·

Αὐτὰρ ἀνὴρ ἀγαθὸς τοτὲ μὲν κακός, ἄλλοτε δ᾽ ἐσθλός.

Κἀγὼ δὲ μαρτυρῶ τούτοις· ὁρῶ γάρ, ὥσπερ τῶν ἐν 21
μέτρῳ πεποιημένων ἐπῶν τοὺς μὴ μελετῶντας ἐπιλαν-
θανομένους, οὕτω καὶ τῶν διδασκαλικῶν λόγων τοῖς
ἀμελοῦσι λήθην ἐγγιγνομένην. Ὅταν δὲ τῶν νουθετι-
κῶν λόγων ἐπιλάθηταί τις, ἐπιλέλησται καὶ ὧν ἡ
ψυχὴ πάσχουσα τῆς σωφροσύνης ἐπεθύμει· τούτων
δ᾽ ἐπιλαθόμενον οὐδὲν θαυμαστὸν καὶ τῆς σωφρο-
σύνης ἐπιλαθέσθαι. Ὁρῶ δὲ καὶ τοὺς εἰς φιλοποσίαν 22
προαχθέντας καὶ τοὺς εἰς ἔρωτας ἐγκυλισθέντας, ἧττον
δυναμένους τῶν τε δεόντων ἐπιμελεῖσθαι καὶ τῶν μὴ
δεόντων ἀπέχεσθαι· πολλοὶ γὰρ καὶ χρημάτων δυνά-
μενοι φείδεσθαι, πρὶν ἐρᾶν, ἐρασθέντες οὐκέτι δύνανται·
καὶ τὰ χρήματα καταναλώσαντες, ὧν πρόσθεν ἀπεί-
χοντο κερδῶν, αἰσχρὰ νομίζοντες εἶναι, τούτων οὐκ
ἀπέχονται. Πῶς οὖν οὐκ ἐνδέχεται σωφρονήσαντα 23
πρόσθεν αὖθις μὴ σωφρονεῖν, καὶ δίκαια δυνηθέντα
πράττειν αὖθις ἀδυνατεῖν; Πάντα μὲν οὖν ἔμοιγε δοκεῖ
τὰ καλὰ καὶ τἀγαθὰ ἀσκητὰ εἶναι, οὐχ ἥκιστα δὲ
σωφροσύνη· ἐν τῷ γὰρ αὐτῷ σώματι συμπεφυτευμέναι
τῇ ψυχῇ αἱ ἡδοναὶ πείθουσιν αὐτὴν μὴ σωφρονεῖν,

ἀλλὰ τὴν ταχίστην ἑαυταῖς τε καὶ τῷ σώματι χαρί-
ζεσθαι.
24 Καὶ Κριτίας δὴ καὶ Ἀλκιβιάδης, ἕως μὲν Σωκράτει
συνήστην, ἐδυνάσθην, ἐκείνῳ χρωμένω συμμάχῳ, τῶν
μὴ καλῶν ἐπιθυμιῶν κρατεῖν· ἐκείνου δ' ἀπαλλαγέντε,
Κριτίας μέν, φυγὼν εἰς Θετταλίαν, ἐκεῖ συνῆν ἀνθρώ-
ποις ἀνομίᾳ μᾶλλον ἢ δικαιοσύνῃ χρωμένοις· Ἀλκι-
βιάδης δ' αὖ διὰ μὲν κάλλος ὑπὸ πολλῶν καὶ σεμνῶν
γυναικῶν θηρώμενος, διὰ δύναμιν δὲ τὴν ἐν τῇ πόλει
καὶ τοῖς συμμάχοις ὑπὸ πολλῶν καὶ δυνατῶν κολακεύειν
ἀνθρώπων διαθρυπτόμενος, ὑπὸ δὲ τοῦ δήμου τιμώ-
μενος, καὶ ῥᾳδίως πρωτεύων, ὥσπερ οἱ τῶν γυμνικῶν
ἀγώνων ἀθληταὶ ῥᾳδίως πρωτεύοντες ἀμελοῦσι τῆς
25 ἀσκήσεως, οὕτω κἀκεῖνος ἠμέλησεν αὑτοῦ. Τοιούτων
δὲ συμβάντων αὐτοῖν, καὶ ὠγκωμένω μὲν ἐπὶ γένει,
ἐπηρμένω δ' ἐπὶ πλούτῳ, πεφυσημένω δ' ἐπὶ δυνάμει,
διατεθρυμμένω δὲ ὑπὸ πολλῶν ἀνθρώπων, ἐπὶ δὲ πᾶσι
τούτοις διεφθαρμένω καὶ πολὺν χρόνον ἀπὸ Σωκράτους
γεγονότε, τι θαυμαστόν, εἰ ὑπερηφάνω ἐγενέσθην;
26 Εἶτα, εἰ μέν τι ἐπλημμελησάτην, τούτου Σωκράτην ὁ
κατήγορος αἰτιᾶται; ὅτι δὲ νέω ὄντε αὐτώ, ἡνίκα καὶ
ἀγνωμονεστάτω καὶ ἀκρατεστάτω εἰκὸς εἶναι, Σωκράτης
παρέσχε σώφρονε, οὐδενὸς ἐπαίνου δοκεῖ τῷ κατηγόρῳ
27 ἄξιος εἶναι; Οὐ μὴν τά γε ἄλλα οὕτω κρίνεται· τίς
μὲν γὰρ αὐλητής, τίς δὲ καὶ κιθαριστής, τίς δὲ ἄλλος
διδάσκαλος ἱκανοὺς ποιήσας τοὺς μαθητάς, ἐὰν πρὸς
ἄλλους ἐλθόντες χείρους φανῶσιν, αἰτίαν ἔχει τούτου;
τίς δὲ πατήρ, ἐὰν ὁ παῖς αὐτοῦ συνδιατρίβων τῳ
σώφρων ᾖ, ὕστερον δὲ ἄλλῳ τῳ συγγενόμενος πονηρὸς
γένηται, τὸν πρόσθεν αἰτιᾶται; ἀλλ' οὐχ ὅσῳ ἂν παρὰ
τῷ ὑστέρῳ χείρων φαίνηται, τοσούτῳ μᾶλλον ἐπαινεῖ
τὸν πρότερον; ἀλλ' οἵ γε πατέρες αὐτοὶ συνόντες τοῖς
υἱέσι, τῶν παίδων πλημμελούντων, οὐκ αἰτίαν ἔχουσιν,
28 ἐὰν αὐτοὶ σωφρονῶσιν. Οὕτω δὲ καὶ Σωκράτην δίκαιον

ἦν κρίνειν· εἰ μὲν αὐτὸς ἐποίει τι φαῦλον, εἰκότως ἂν
ἐδόκει πονηρὸς εἶναι· εἰ δὲ αὐτὸς σωφρονῶν διετέλει,
πῶς ἂν δικαίως τῆς οὐκ ἐνούσης αὐτῷ κακίας αἰτίαν
ἔχοι;

Ἀλλ' εἰ καὶ μηδὲν αὐτὸς πονηρὸν ποιῶν ἐκείνους 29
φαῦλα πράττοντας ὁρῶν ἐπῄνει, δικαίως ἂν ἐπετιμᾶτο.
Κριτίαν μὲν τοίνυν αἰσθανόμενος ἐρῶντα Εὐθυδήμου
καὶ πειρῶντα χρῆσθαι, καθάπερ οἱ πρὸς τἀφροδίσια
τῶν σωμάτων ἀπολαύοντες, ἀπέτρεπε, φάσκων ἀνε-
λεύθερόν τε εἶναι καὶ οὐ πρέπον ἀνδρὶ καλῷ κἀγαθῷ,
τὸν ἐρώμενον, ᾧ βούλεται πολλοῦ ἄξιος φαίνεσθαι,
προςαιτεῖν ὥςπερ τοὺς πτωχοὺς ἱκετεύοντα καὶ δεόμε-
νον προςδοῦναι, καὶ ταῦτα μηδενὸς ἀγαθοῦ. Τοῦ δὲ 30
Κριτίου τοῖς τοιούτοις οὐχ ὑπακούοντος οὐδὲ ἀποτρε-
πομένου, λέγεται τὸν Σωκράτην, ἄλλων τε πολλῶν
παρόντων καὶ τοῦ Εὐθυδήμου, εἰπεῖν, ὅτι ὑϊκὸν αὐτῷ
δοκοίη πάσχειν ὁ Κριτίας, ἐπιθυμῶν Εὐθυδήμῳ προς-
κνῆσθαι ὥςπερ τὰ ὑΐδια τοῖς λίθοις. Ἐξ ὧν δὴ καὶ 31
ἐμίσει τὸν Σωκράτην ὁ Κριτίας, ὥςτε καί, ὅτε τῶν τριά-
κοντα ὢν νομοθέτης μετὰ Χαρικλέους ἐγένετο, ἀπεμ-
νημόνευσεν αὐτῷ, καὶ ἐν τοῖς νόμοις ἔγραψε λόγων
τέχνην μὴ διδάσκειν, ἐπηρεάζων ἐκείνῳ, καὶ οὐκ ἔχων
ὅπῃ ἐπιλάβοιτο, ἀλλὰ τὸ κοινῇ τοῖς φιλοσόφοις ὑπὸ
τῶν πολλῶν ἐπιτιμώμενον ἐπιφέρων αὐτῷ, καὶ διαβάλ-
λων πρὸς τοὺς πολλούς· οὐδὲ γὰρ ἔγωγε οὔτ' αὐτὸς
τοῦτο πώποτε Σωκράτους ἤκουσα, οὔτ' ἄλλου φάσκον-
τος ἀκηκοέναι ᾐσθόμην. Ἐδήλωσε δέ· ἐπεὶ γὰρ οἱ 32
τριάκοντα πολλοὺς μὲν τῶν πολιτῶν καὶ οὐ τοὺς χει-
ρίστους ἀπέκτεινον, πολλοὺς δὲ προετρέποντο ἀδικεῖν,
εἶπέ που ὁ Σωκράτης, ὅτι θαυμαστόν οἱ δοκοίη εἶναι,
εἴ τις γενόμενος βοῶν ἀγέλης νομεὺς καὶ τὰς βοῦς ἐλάτ-
τους τε καὶ χείρους ποιῶν μὴ ὁμολογοίη κακὸς βουκό-
λος εἶναι· ἔτι δὲ θαυμαστότερον, εἴ τις προστάτης
γενόμενος πόλεως καὶ ποιῶν τοὺς πολίτας ἐλάττους

καὶ χείρους μὴ αἰσχύνεται, μηδ' οἴεται κακὸς εἶναι
33 προστάτης τῆς πόλεως. Ἀπαγγελθέντος δὲ αὐτοῖς
τούτου, καλέσαντες ὅ τε Κριτίας καὶ ὁ Χαρικλῆς τὸν
Σωκράτην, τόν τε νόμον ἐδεικνύτην αὐτῷ καὶ τοῖς νέοις
ἀπειπέτην μὴ διαλέγεσθαι. Ὁ δὲ Σωκράτης ἐπήρετο
αὐτὼ, εἰ ἐξείη πυνθάνεσθαι, εἴ τι ἀγνοοῖτο τῶν προ-
34 αγορευμένων. Τὼ δ' ἐφάτην. Ἐγὼ τοίνυν, ἔφη, πα-
ρεσκεύασμαι μὲν πείθεσθαι τοῖς νόμοις· ὅπως δὲ μὴ
δι' ἄγνοιαν λάθω τι παρανομήσας, τοῦτο βούλομαι
σαφῶς μαθεῖν παρ' ὑμῶν· πότερον τὴν τῶν λόγων
τέχνην σὺν τοῖς ὀρθῶς λεγομένοις εἶναι νομίζοντες ἢ
σὺν τοῖς μὴ ὀρθῶς, ἀπέχεσθαι κελεύετε αὐτῆς. Εἰ
μὲν γὰρ σὺν τοῖς ὀρθῶς, δῆλον ὅτι ἀφεκτέον εἴη τοῦ
ὀρθῶς λέγειν· εἰ δὲ σὺν τοῖς μὴ ὀρθῶς, δῆλον ὅτι
35 πειρατέον ὀρθῶς λέγειν. Καὶ ὁ Χαρικλῆς ὀργισθεὶς
αὐτῷ· Ἐπειδή, ἔφη, ὦ Σώκρατες, ἀγνοεῖς, τάδε σοι
εὐμαθέστερα ὄντα προαγορεύομεν, τοῖς νέοις ὅλως μὴ
διαλέγεσθαι. Καὶ ὁ Σωκράτης· Ἵνα τοίνυν, ἔφη, μὴ
ἀμφίβολον ᾖ, ὡς ἄλλο τι ποιῶ ἢ τὰ προηγορευμένα,
ὁρίσατέ μοι, μέχρι πόσων ἐτῶν δεῖ νομίζειν νέους εἶναι
τοὺς ἀνθρώπους. Καὶ ὁ Χαρικλῆς· Ὅσου περ, εἶπε,
χρόνου βουλεύειν οὐκ ἔξεστιν, ὡς οὔπω φρονίμοις οὖσι·
36 μηδὲ σὺ διαλέγου νεωτέροις τριάκοντα ἐτῶν.—Μηδέ,
ἄν τι ὠνῶμαι, ἔφη, ἢν πωλῇ νεώτερος τριάκοντα ἐτῶν,
ἔρωμαι, ὁπόσου πωλεῖ;—Ναὶ τά γε τοιαῦτα, ἔφη ὁ
Χαρικλῆς· ἀλλά τοι σύ γε, ὦ Σώκρατες, εἴωθας, εἰδὼς
πῶς ἔχει, τὰ πλεῖστα ἐρωτᾶν· ταῦτα οὖν μὴ ἐρώτα.—
Μηδ' ἀποκρίνωμαι οὖν, ἔφη, ἄν τίς με ἐρωτᾷ νέος, ἐὰν
εἰδῶ, οἷον ποῦ οἰκεῖ Χαρικλῆς; ἢ ποῦ ἐστι Κριτίας;—
37 Ναὶ τά γε τοιαῦτα, ἔφη ὁ Χαρικλῆς. Ὁ δὲ Κριτίας·
Ἀλλὰ τῶνδέ τοί σε ἀπέχεσθαι, ἔφη, δεήσει, ὦ Σώ-
κρατες, τῶν σκυτέων καὶ τῶν τεκτόνων καὶ τῶν χαλ-
κέων· καὶ γὰρ οἶμαι αὐτοὺς ἤδη κατατετρῖφθαι διαθρυ-
λουμένους ὑπὸ σοῦ. Οὐκοῦν, ἔφη ὁ Σωκράτης, καὶ τῶν

ἑπομένων τούτοις, τοῦ τε δικαίου καὶ τοῦ ὁσίου καὶ
τῶν ἄλλων τῶν τοιούτων; Ναὶ μὰ Δί', ἔφη ὁ Χαρι-
κλῆς, καὶ τῶν βουκόλων γε· εἰ δὲ μή, φυλάττου, ὅπως
μὴ καὶ σὺ ἐλάττους τὰς βοῦς ποιήσῃς. Ἔνθα καὶ 38
δῆλον ἐγένετο, ὅτι, ἀπαγγελθέντος αὐτοῖς τοῦ περὶ τῶν
βοῶν λόγου, ὠργίζοντο τῷ Σωκράτει.

Οἷα μὲν οὖν ἡ συνουσία ἐγεγόνει Κριτίᾳ πρὸς Σω-
κράτην, καὶ ὡς εἶχον πρὸς ἀλλήλους, εἴρηται. Φαίην 39
δ' ἂν ἔγωγε μηδενὶ μηδεμίαν εἶναι παίδευσιν παρὰ
τοῦ μὴ ἀρέσκοντος. Κριτίας δὲ καὶ Ἀλκιβιάδης οὐκ
ἀρέσκοντος αὐτοῖς Σωκράτους ὡμιλησάτην, ὃν χρόνον
ὡμιλείτην αὐτῷ, ἀλλ' εὐθὺς ἐξ ἀρχῆς ὡρμηκότε προε-
στάναι τῆς πόλεως· ἔτι γὰρ Σωκράτει συνόντες οὐκ
ἄλλοις τισὶ μᾶλλον ἐπεχείρουν διαλέγεσθαι ἢ τοῖς
μάλιστα πράττουσι τὰ πολιτικά. Λέγεται γὰρ Ἀλκι- 40
βιάδην, πρὶν εἴκοσιν ἐτῶν εἶναι, Περικλεῖ ἐπιτρόπῳ
μὲν ὄντι ἑαυτοῦ, προστάτῃ δὲ τῆς πόλεως, τοιάδε
διαλεχθῆναι περὶ νόμων· Εἰπέ μοι, φάναι, ὦ Περί- 41
κλεις, ἔχοις ἄν με διδάξαι, τί ἐστι νόμος; Πάντως
δήπου, φάναι τὸν Περικλέα. Δίδαξον δὴ πρὸς τῶν
θεῶν, φάναι τὸν Ἀλκιβιάδην· ὡς ἔγωγ' ἀκούων τινῶν
ἐπαινουμένων, ὅτι νόμιμοι ἄνδρες εἰσίν, οἶμαι μὴ ἂν
δικαίως τούτου τυχεῖν τοῦ ἐπαίνου τὸν μὴ εἰδότα, τί
ἐστι νόμος. Ἀλλ' οὐδέν τι χαλεποῦ πράγματος ἐπι- 42
θυμεῖς, ὦ Ἀλκιβιάδη, φάναι τὸν Περικλέα, βουλόμενος
γνῶναι, ὅτι ἐστι νόμος· πάντες γὰρ οὗτοι νόμοι εἰσίν,
οὓς τὸ πλῆθος συνελθὸν καὶ δοκιμάσαν ἔγραψε, φρά-
ζον, ἅ τε δεῖ ποιεῖν καὶ ἃ μή.—Πότερον δὲ τἀγαθὰ
νομίσαν δεῖν ποιεῖν, ἢ τὰ κακά;—Τἀγαθά, νὴ Δία,
φάναι, ὦ μειράκιον, τὰ δὲ κακὰ οὔ.—Ἐὰν δὲ μὴ τὸ 43
πλῆθος, ἀλλ', ὥσπερ ὅπου ὀλιγαρχία ἐστίν, ὀλίγοι
συνελθόντες γράψωσιν, ὅ τι χρὴ ποιεῖν, ταῦτα τί ἐστι;
—Πάντα, φάναι, ὅσα ἂν τὸ κρατοῦν τῆς πόλεως βου-
λευσάμενον, ἃ χρὴ ποιεῖν, γράψῃ, νόμος καλεῖται.—

Καὶ ἂν τύραννος οὖν κρατῶν τῆς πόλεως γράψῃ τοῖς
πολίταις, ἃ χρὴ ποιεῖν, καὶ ταῦτα νόμος ἐστί;—Καὶ
ὅσα τύραννος ἄρχων, φάναι, γράφει, καὶ ταῦτα νόμος
44 καλεῖται.—Βία δέ, φάναι, καὶ ἀνομία τί ἐστιν, ὦ
Περίκλεις; Ἆρ' οὐχ ὅταν ὁ κρείττων τὸν ἥττω μὴ
πείσας, ἀλλὰ βιασάμενος ἀναγκάσῃ ποιεῖν, ὅ τι ἂν
αὐτῷ δοκῇ;—Ἔμοιγε δοκεῖ, φάναι τὸν Περικλέα.—
Καὶ ὅσα ἄρα τύραννος μὴ πείσας τοὺς πολίτας ἀνα-
γκάζει ποιεῖν γράφων, ἀνομία ἐστί;—Δοκεῖ μοι, φάναι
τὸν Περικλέα· ἀνατίθεμαι γὰρ τὸ ὅσα τύραννος μὴ
45 πείσας γράφει νόμον εἶναι.—Ὅσα δὲ οἱ ὀλίγοι τοὺς
πολλοὺς μὴ πείσαντες, ἀλλὰ κρατοῦντες γράφουσι,
πότερον βίαν φῶμεν, ἢ μὴ φῶμεν εἶναι;—Πάντα μοι
δοκεῖ, φάναι τὸν Περικλέα, ὅσα τις μὴ πείσας ἀναγκάζει
τινὰ ποιεῖν, εἴτε γράφων εἴτε μή, βία μᾶλλον ἢ νόμος
εἶναι.—Καὶ ὅσα ἄρα τὸ πᾶν πλῆθος κρατοῦν τῶν τὰ
χρήματα ἐχόντων γράφει μὴ πεῖσαν, βία μᾶλλον ἢ
46 νόμος ἂν εἴη;—Μάλα τοι, φάναι τὸν Περικλέα, ὦ
Ἀλκιβιάδη· καὶ ἡμεῖς, τηλικοῦτοι ὄντες, δεινοὶ τὰ τοι-
αῦτα ἦμεν· τοιαῦτα γὰρ καὶ ἐμελετῶμεν καὶ ἐσοφιζό-
μεθα, οἷά περ καὶ σὺ νῦν ἐμοὶ δοκεῖς μελετᾶν. Τὸν δὲ
Ἀλκιβιάδην φάναι· Εἴθε σοι, ὦ Περίκλεις, τότε συνε-
47 γενόμην, ὅτε δεινότατος σαυτοῦ ταῦτα ἦσθα. Ἐπεὶ
τοίνυν τάχιστα τῶν πολιτευομένων ὑπέλαβον κρείτ-
τονες εἶναι, Σωκράτει μὲν οὐκέτι προσῄεσαν· οὔτε γὰρ
αὐτοῖς ἄλλως ἤρεσκεν, εἴ τε προσέλθοιεν, ὑπὲρ ὧν
ἡμάρτανον ἐλεγχόμενοι ἤχθοντο· τὰ δὲ τῆς πόλεως
ἔπραττον, ὧνπερ ἕνεκεν καὶ Σωκράτει προσῆλθον.
48 Ἀλλὰ Κρίτων τε Σωκράτους ἦν ὁμιλητὴς καὶ Χαιρε-
φῶν, καὶ Χαιρεκράτης, καὶ Ἑρμοκράτης, καὶ Σιμμίας,
καὶ Κέβης, καὶ Φαιδώνδης, καὶ ἄλλοι, οἳ ἐκείνῳ συνῆσαν,
ουχ ἵνα δημηγορικοὶ ἢ δικανικοὶ γένοιντο, ἀλλ' ἵνα, καλοί
τε κἀγαθοὶ γενόμενοι, καὶ οἴκῳ καὶ οἰκέταις καὶ οἰκείοις
καὶ φίλοις καὶ πόλει καὶ πολίταις δύναιντο καλῶς

χρῆσθαι· καὶ τούτων οὐδεὶς, οὔτε νεώτερος οὔτε πρεσ-
βύτερος ὢν, οὔτ' ἐποίησε κακὸν οὐδὲν, οὔτ' αἰτίαν ἔσχεν.
'Αλλὰ Σωκράτης γ', ἔφη ὁ κατήγορος, τοὺς πατέρας 49
προπηλακίζειν ἐδίδασκε, πείθων μὲν τοὺς συνόντας αὐ-
τῷ σοφωτέρους ποιεῖν τῶν πατέρων, φάσκων δὲ κατὰ
νόμον ἐξεῖναι παρανοίας ἑλόντι καὶ τὸν πατέρα δῆσαι,
τεκμηρίῳ τούτῳ χρώμενος, ὡς τὸν ἀμαθέστερον ὑπὸ
τοῦ σοφωτέρου νόμιμον εἴη δεδέσθαι. Σωκράτης δὲ 50
τὸν μὲν ἀμαθίας ἕνεκα δεσμεύοντα δικαίως ἂν καὶ αὐτὸν
ᾤετο δεδέσθαι ὑπὸ τῶν ἐπισταμένων, ἃ μὴ αὐτὸς ἐπί-
σταται· καὶ τῶν τοιούτων ἕνεκα πολλάκις ἐσκόπει, τι
διαφέρει μανίας ἀμαθία· καὶ τοὺς μὲν μαινομένους
ᾤετο συμφερόντως ἂν δεδέσθαι καὶ αὐτοῖς καὶ τοῖς
φίλοις, τοὺς δὲ μὴ ἐπισταμένους τὰ δέοντα δικαίως ἂν
μανθάνειν παρὰ τῶν ἐπισταμένων. 'Αλλὰ Σωκράτης 51
γε, ἔφη ὁ κατήγορος, οὐ μόνον τοὺς πατέρας, ἀλλὰ καὶ
τοὺς ἄλλους συγγενεῖς ἐποίει ἐν ἀτιμίᾳ εἶναι παρὰ
τοῖς ἑαυτῷ συνοῦσι, λέγων, ὡς οὔτε τοὺς κάμνοντας
οὔτε τοὺς δικαζομένους οἱ συγγενεῖς ὠφελοῦσιν, ἀλλὰ
τοὺς μὲν οἱ ἰατροί, τοὺς δὲ οἱ συνδικεῖν ἐπιστάμενοι.
Ἔφη δὲ καὶ περὶ τῶν φίλων αὐτὸν λέγειν, ὡς οὐδὲν 52
ὄφελος εὔνους εἶναι, εἰ μὴ καὶ ὠφελεῖν δυνήσονται·
μόνους δὲ φάσκειν αὐτὸν ἀξίους εἶναι τιμῆς τοὺς εἰδό-
τας τὰ δέοντα καὶ ἑρμηνεῦσαι δυναμένους· ἀναπεί-
θοντα οὖν τοὺς νέους αὐτὸν, ὡς αὐτὸς εἴη σοφώτατός
τε καὶ ἄλλους ἱκανώτατος ποιῆσαι σοφούς, οὕτω δια-
τιθέναι τοὺς ἑαυτῷ συνόντας, ὥςτε μηδαμοῦ παρ'
αὐτοῖς τοὺς ἄλλους εἶναι πρὸς ἑαυτόν. 'Εγὼ δ' αὐ- 53
τὸν οἶδα μὲν καὶ περὶ πατέρων τε καὶ τῶν ἄλλων
συγγενῶν τε καὶ περὶ φίλων ταῦτα λέγοντα· καὶ
πρὸς τούτοις γε δὴ, ὅτι τῆς ψυχῆς ἐξελθούσης, ἐν ᾗ
μόνῃ γίγνεται φρόνησις, τὸ σῶμα τοῦ οἰκειοτάτου
ἀνθρώπου τὴν ταχίστην ἐξενέγκαντες ἀφανίζουσιν.
Ἔλεγε δὲ, ὅτι καὶ ζῶν ἕκαστος ἑαυτοῦ ὃ πάντων 54

μάλιστα φιλεῖ, τοῦ σώματος ὅ τι ἂν ἀχρεῖον ᾖ καὶ
ἀνωφελές, αὐτός τε ἀφαιρεῖ καὶ ἄλλῳ παρέχει· αὐτοί
τέ γε αὑτῶν ὄνυχάς τε καὶ τρίχας καὶ τύλους ἀφαι-
ροῦσι, καὶ τοῖς ἰατροῖς παρέχουσι μετὰ πόνων τε καὶ
ἀλγηδόνων καὶ ἀποτέμνειν καὶ ἀποκάειν, καὶ τούτων
χάριν οἴονται δεῖν αὐτοῖς καὶ μισθὸν τίνειν· καὶ τὸ
σίαλον ἐκ τοῦ στόματος ἀποπτύουσιν ὡς δύνανται
ποῤῥωτάτω, διότι ὠφελεῖ μὲν οὐδὲν αὐτοὺς ἐνόν, βλά-
55 πτει δὲ πολὺ μᾶλλον. Ταῦτ' οὖν ἔλεγεν οὐ τὸν μὲν
πατέρα ζῶντα κατορύττειν διδάσκων, ἑαυτὸν δὲ κατα-
τέμνειν· ἀλλ' ἐπιδεικνύων, ὅτι τὸ ἄφρον ἄτιμόν ἐστι,
παρεκάλει ἐπιμελεῖσθαι τοῦ ὡς φρονιμώτατον εἶναι
καὶ ὠφελιμώτατον, ὅπως, ἐάν τε ὑπὸ πατρός, ἐάν τε
ὑπὸ ἀδελφοῦ, ἐάν τε ὑπὸ ἄλλου τινὸς βούληται τιμᾶ-
σθαι, μὴ τῷ οἰκεῖος εἶναι πιστεύων ἀμελῇ, ἀλλὰ
πειρᾶται, ὑφ' ὧν ἂν βούληται τιμᾶσθαι, τούτοις ὠφέ-
λιμος εἶναι.

56 Ἔφη δ' αὐτὸν ὁ κατήγορος καὶ τῶν ἐνδοξοτάτων
ποιητῶν ἐκλεγόμενον τὰ πονηρότατα καὶ τούτοις μαρ-
τυρίοις χρώμενον, διδάσκειν τοὺς συνόντας κακούργους
τε εἶναι καὶ τυραννικούς· Ἡσιόδου μὲν τό·

Ἔργον δ' οὐδὲν ὄνειδος, ἀεργίη δέ τ' ὄνειδος.

Τοῦτο δὴ λέγειν αὐτὸν, ὡς ὁ ποιητὴς κελεύει μηδενὸς
ἔργου μήτε ἀδίκου μήτε αἰσχροῦ ἀπέχεσθαι, ἀλλὰ
57 καὶ ταῦτα ποιεῖν ἐπὶ τῷ κέρδει. Σωκράτης δ' ἐπειδὴ
ὁμολογήσαιτο τὸ μὲν ἐργάτην εἶναι ὠφέλιμόν τε ἀν-
θρώπῳ καὶ ἀγαθὸν εἶναι, τὸ δὲ ἀργὸν βλαβερόν τε
καὶ κακόν, καὶ τὸ μὲν ἐργάζεσθαι ἀγαθόν, τὸ δὲ ἀρ-
γεῖν κακόν, τοὺς μὲν ἀγαθόν τι ποιοῦντας ἐργάζεσθαι
τε ἔφη καὶ ἐργάτας ἀγαθοὺς εἶναι· τοὺς δὲ κυβεύον-
τας ἤ τι ἄλλο πονηρὸν καὶ ἐπιζήμιον ποιοῦντας ἀργοὺς
ἀπεκάλει. Ἐκ δὲ τούτων ὀρθῶς ἂν ἔχοι τό·

Ἔργον δ' οὐδὲν ὄνειδος, ἀεργίη δέ τ' ὄνειδος.

Τὸ δὲ Ὁμήρου ἔφη ὁ κατήγορος πολλάκις αὐτὸν λέ- 58
γειν, ὅτι Ὀδυσσεὺς

Ὅντινα μὲν βασιλῆα καὶ ἔξοχον ἄνδρα κιχείη,
Τὸν δ' ἀγανοῖς ἐπέεσσιν ἐρητύσασκε παραστάς·
Δαιμόνι', οὔ σε ἔοικε κακὸν ὣς δειδίσσεσθαι,
Ἀλλ' αὐτός τε κάθησο, καὶ ἄλλους ἵδρυε λαούς.
Ὃν δ' αὖ δήμου τ' ἄνδρα ἴδοι, βοόωντά τ' ἐφεύροι,
Τὸν σκήπτρῳ ἐλάσασκεν, ὁμοκλήσασκέ τε μύθῳ·
Δαιμόνι', ἀτρέμας ἧσο, καὶ ἄλλων μῦθον ἄκουε,
Οἳ σέο φέρτεροί εἰσι· σὺ δ' ἀπτόλεμος καὶ ἄναλκις,
Οὔτε ποτ' ἐν πολέμῳ ἐναρίθμιος, οὔτ' ἐνὶ βουλῇ.

Ταῦτα δὴ αὐτὸν ἐξηγεῖσθαι, ὡς ὁ ποιητὴς ἐπαινοίη
παίεσθαι τοὺς δημότας καὶ πένητας. Σωκράτης δ' 59
οὐ ταῦτ' ἔλεγε· καὶ γὰρ ἑαυτὸν οὕτω γ' ἂν ᾤετο δεῖν
παίεσθαι· ἀλλ' ἔφη δεῖν τοὺς μήτε λόγῳ μήτ' ἔργῳ
ὠφελίμους ὄντας, μήτε στρατεύματι μήτε πόλει μήτε
αὐτῷ τῷ δήμῳ, εἴ τι δέοι, βοηθεῖν ἱκανούς, ἄλλως τ'
ἐὰν πρὸς τούτῳ καὶ θρασεῖς ὦσι, πάντα τρόπον κω-
λύεσθαι, κἂν πάνυ πλούσιοι τυγχάνωσιν ὄντες. Ἀλλὰ 60
Σωκράτης γε τἀναντία τούτων φανερὸς ἦν καὶ δημο-
τικὸς καὶ φιλάνθρωπος ὤν· ἐκεῖνος γὰρ πολλοὺς ἐπι-
θυμητὰς καὶ ἀστοὺς καὶ ξένους λαβὼν οὐδένα πώποτε
μισθὸν τῆς συνουσίας ἐπράξατο, ἀλλὰ πᾶσιν ἀφθόνως
ἐπήρκει τῶν ἑαυτοῦ· ὧν τινες μικρὰ μέρη παρ' ἐκεί-
νου προῖκα λαβόντες πολλοῦ τοῖς ἄλλοις ἐπώλουν,
καὶ οὐκ ἦσαν, ὥσπερ ἐκεῖνος δημοτικοί· τοῖς γὰρ μὴ
ἔχουσι χρήματα διδόναι οὐκ ἤθελον διαλέγεσθαι.
Ἀλλὰ Σωκράτης γε καὶ πρὸς τοὺς ἄλλους ἀνθρώπους 61
κόσμον τῇ πόλει παρεῖχε πολλῷ μᾶλλον ἢ Λίχας τῇ
Λακεδαιμονίων, ὃς ὀνομαστὸς ἐπὶ τούτῳ γέγονε. Λίχας
μὲν γὰρ ταῖς γυμνοπαιδίαις τοὺς ἐπιδημοῦντας ἐν Λα-
κεδαίμονι ξένους ἐδείπνιζε· Σωκράτης δὲ διὰ παντὸς
τοῦ βίου τὰ ἑαυτοῦ δαπανῶν τὰ μέγιστα πάντας τοὺς

βουλομένους ὠφέλει· βελτίους γὰρ ποιῶν τοὺς συγ·
γιγνομένους ἀπέπεμπεν.
62 Ἐμοὶ μὲν δὴ Σωκράτης τοιοῦτος ὢν ἐδόκει τιμῆς
ἄξιος εἶναι τῇ πόλει μᾶλλον ἢ θανάτου. Καὶ κατὰ
τοὺς νόμους δὲ σκοπῶν ἄν τις τοῦθ' εὕροι. Κατὰ γὰρ
τοὺς νόμους, ἐάν τις φανερὸς γένηται κλέπτων ἢ λω-
ποδυτῶν ἢ βαλαντιοτομῶν ἢ τοιχωρυχῶν ἢ ἀνδραπο-
διζόμενος ἢ ἱεροσυλῶν, τούτοις θάνατός ἐστιν ἡ ζημία·
63 ὧν ἐκεῖνος πάντων ἀνθρώπων πλεῖστον ἀπεῖχεν. Ἀλ-
λὰ μὴν τῇ πόλει γε οὔτε πολέμου κακῶς συμβάντος,
οὔτε στάσεως, οὔτε προδοσίας, οὔτε ἄλλου κακοῦ οὐ-
δενὸς πώποτε αἴτιος ἐγένετο. Οὐδὲ μὴν ἰδίᾳ γε οὐδένα
πώποτε ἀνθρώπων οὔτε ἀγαθῶν ἀπεστέρησεν, οὔτε
κακοῖς περιέβαλεν· ἀλλ' οὐδ' αἰτίαν τῶν εἰρημένων
64 οὐδενὸς πώποτ' ἔσχε. Πῶς οὖν ἔνοχος ἂν εἴη τῇ
γραφῇ; ὃς ἀντὶ μὲν τοῦ μὴ νομίζειν θεούς, ὡς ἐν τῇ
γραφῇ γέγραπτο, φανερὸς ἦν θεραπεύων τοὺς θεοὺς
μάλιστα τῶν ἄλλων ἀνθρώπων· ἀντὶ δὲ τοῦ διαφθεί-
ρειν τοὺς νέους, ὃ δὴ ὁ γραψάμενος αὐτὸν ᾐτιᾶτο,
φανερὸς ἦν τῶν συνόντων τοὺς πονηρὰς ἐπιθυμίας
ἔχοντας τούτων μὲν παύων, τῆς δὲ καλλίστης καὶ μεγα-
λοπρεπεστάτης ἀρετῆς, ᾗ πόλεις τε καὶ οἴκους εὖ οἰ-
κοῦσι, προτρέπων ἐπιθυμεῖν· ταῦτα δὲ πράττων πῶς
οὐ μεγάλης ἄξιος ἦν τιμῆς τῇ πόλει;

CHAPTER III.

ARGUMENT.

The two preceding chapters contain a confutation of the accusations of the enemies of Socrates. He was neither a despiser of the gods of the State nor a corrupter of the youth. With this chapter, the more positive part of the work is commenced. The particular points of defence, which have been rapidly passed over, are again resumed in the subsequent chapters, and more fully discussed, and illustrated by the conversations of Socrates with his friends and disciples. Thus not only the injustice and malignity of his opponents, but the integrity and piety of his own life, is made more evident.

The reverence of Socrates for the gods, introduced in chap. I. § 2, is again brought into view in this chapter, and his manner of worshipping them more fully explained; and then the subject of his self-control is resumed from II. § 1 sq.

1. He both adhered to the usual manner of worshipping the gods, and enjoined it upon others to do the same (§ 1). In his prayers he merely asked for good things, believing that the gods know best what is good for man (§ 2). In sacrifices, the gods have not respect to the magnitude of the offering, but to the motives and feelings of the offerer (§ 3). The revelations made by the gods were with him paramount to all human counsels (§ 4).

2. Socrates was most abstinent in respect to food and drink, and inculcated this virtue upon others (§ 5—7); he also had command over his sensual passions (ἀφροδισίων), and ridiculed a vice prevalent in his day (§ 8—15).

Ὡς δὲ δὴ καὶ ὠφελεῖν ἐδόκει μοι τοὺς ξυνόντας τὰ 1
μὲν ἔργῳ δεικνύων ἑαυτὸν οἷος ἦν, τὰ δὲ καὶ διαλεγόμενος, τούτων δὴ γράψω, ὁπόσα ἂν διαμνημονεύσω. Τὰ μὲν τοίνυν πρὸς τοὺς θεοὺς φανερὸς ἦν καὶ ποιῶν καὶ λέγων, ᾗπερ ἡ Πυθία ὑποκρίνεται τοῖς ἐρωτῶσι, πῶς δεῖ ποιεῖν ἢ περὶ θυσίας ἢ περὶ προγόνων θεραπείας ἢ περὶ ἄλλου τινὸς τῶν τοιούτων· ἥ τε γὰρ Πυθία νόμῳ πόλεως ἀναιρεῖ ποιοῦντας εὐσεβῶς ἂν ποιεῖν, Σωκράτης τε οὕτως καὶ αὐτὸς ἐποίει καὶ τοῖς ἄλλοις παρῄνει, τοὺς δὲ ἄλλως πως ποιοῦντας περιέργους καὶ ματαίους ἐνόμιζεν εἶναι. Καὶ εὔχετο δὲ πρὸς 2
τοὺς θεοὺς ἁπλῶς τἀγαθὰ διδόναι, ὡς τοὺς θεοὺς κάλλιστα εἰδότας, ὁποῖα ἀγαθά ἐστι· τοὺς δ' εὐχομένους χρυσίον ἢ ἀργύριον ἢ τυραννίδα ἢ ἄλλο τι τῶν τοιούτων οὐδὲν διάφορον ἐνόμιζεν εὔχεσθαι, ἢ εἰ κυβείαν ἢ μάχην ἢ ἄλλο τι εὔχοιντο τῶν φανερῶς ἀδήλων ὅπως ἀποβήσοιτο. Θυσίας δὲ θύων μικρὰς ἀπὸ μικρῶν οὐδὲν ἡγεῖτο 3

μειοῦσθαι τῶν ἀπὸ πολλῶν καὶ μεγάλων πολλὰ καὶ μεγάλα θυόντων· οὔτε γὰρ τοῖς θεοῖς ἔφη καλῶς ἔχειν, εἰ ταῖς μεγάλαις θυσίαις μᾶλλον ἢ ταῖς μικραῖς ἔχαιρον· πολλάκις γὰρ ἂν αὐτοῖς τὰ παρὰ τῶν πονηρῶν μᾶλλον ἢ τὰ παρὰ τῶν χρηστῶν εἶναι κεχαρισμένα· οὔτ' ἂν τοῖς ἀνθρώποις ἄξιον εἶναι ζῆν, εἰ τὰ παρὰ τῶν πονηρῶν μᾶλλον ἦν κεχαρισμένα τοῖς θεοῖς ἢ τὰ παρὰ τῶν χρηστῶν· ἀλλ' ἐνόμιζε τοὺς θεοὺς ταῖς παρὰ τῶν εὐσεβεστάτων τιμαῖς μάλιστα χαίρειν. Ἐπαινέτης δ' ἦν καὶ τοῦ ἔπους τούτου·

Κὰδ δύναμιν δ' ἔρδειν ἱέρ' ἀθανάτοισι θεοῖσι·

καὶ πρὸς φίλους δὲ καὶ ξένους καὶ πρὸς τὴν ἄλλην δίαιταν καλὴν ἔφη παραίνεσιν εἶναι τὴν Κὰδ δύναμιν
4 ἔρδειν. Εἰ δέ τι δόξειεν αὐτῷ σημαίνεσθαι παρὰ τῶν θεῶν, ἧττον ἂν ἐπείσθη παρὰ τὰ σημαινόμενα ποιῆσαι, ἢ εἴ τις αὐτὸν ἔπειθεν ὁδοῦ λαβεῖν ἡγεμόνα τυφλὸν καὶ μὴ εἰδότα τὴν ὁδὸν ἀντὶ βλέποντος καὶ εἰδότος· καὶ τῶν ἄλλων δὲ μωρίαν κατηγόρει, οἵτινες παρὰ τὰ παρὰ τῶν θεῶν σημαινόμενα ποιοῦσί τι φυλαττόμενοι τὴν παρὰ τοῖς ἀνθρώποις ἀδοξίαν. Αὐτὸς δὲ πάντα τἀνθρώπινα ὑπερεώρα πρὸς τὴν παρὰ τῶν θεῶν ξυμβουλίαν.

5 Διαίτῃ δὲ τήν τε ψυχὴν ἐπαίδευσε καὶ τὸ σῶμα, ᾗ χρώμενος ἄν τις, εἰ μή τι δαιμόνιον εἴη, θαῤῥαλέως καὶ ἀσφαλῶς διάγοι, καὶ οὐκ ἂν ἀπορήσειε τοσαύτης δαπάνης. Οὕτω γὰρ εὐτελὴς ἦν, ὥστ' οὐκ οἶδ', εἴ τις οὕτως ἂν ὀλίγα ἐργάζοιτο, ὥστε μὴ λαμβάνειν τὰ Σωκράτει ἀρκοῦντα· σίτῳ μὲν γὰρ τοσούτῳ ἐχρῆτο, ὅσον ἡδέως ἤσθιε· καὶ ἐπὶ τούτῳ οὕτω παρεσκευασμένος ᾔει, ὥστε τὴν ἐπιθυμίαν τοῦ σίτου ὄψον αὐτῷ εἶναι· ποτὸν δὲ πᾶν ἡδὺ ἦν αὐτῷ διὰ τὸ μὴ πίνειν, εἰ μὴ
6 διψῴη. Εἰ δέ ποτε κληθεὶς ἐθελήσειεν ἐπὶ δεῖπνον

ἐλϑεῖν, ὃ τοῖς πλείστοις ἐργωδέστατόν ἐστιν, ὥςτε φυ-
λάξασϑαι τὸ ὑπὲρ τὸν καιρὸν ἐμπίπλασϑαι, τοῦτο
ῥᾳδίως πάνυ ἐφυλάττετο· τοῖς δὲ μὴ δυναμένοις τοῦτο
ποιεῖν συνεβούλευε φυλάττεσϑαι τὰ πείϑοντα μὴ πει-
νῶντας ἐσϑίειν, μηδὲ διψῶντας πίνειν· καὶ γὰρ τὰ
λυμαινόμενα γαστέρας καὶ κεφαλὰς καὶ ψυχὰς ταῦτ'
ἔφη εἶναι. Οἴεσϑαι δ' ἔφη ἐπισκώπτων καὶ τὴν Κίρ- 7
κην ὗς ποιεῖν τοιούτοις πολλοῖς δειπνίζουσαν· τὸν δὲ
Ὀδυσσέα Ἑρμοῦ τε ὑποϑημοσύνῃ καὶ αὐτὸν ἐγκρατῆ
ὄντα, καὶ ἀποσχόμενον τὸ ὑπὲρ τὸν καιρὸν τῶν τοιούτων
ἅπτεσϑαι, διὰ ταῦτα οὐδὲ γενέσϑαι ὗν.

Τοιαῦτα μὲν περὶ τούτων ἔπαιζεν ἅμα σπουδάζων· 8
ἀφροδισίων δὲ παρῄνει τῶν καλῶν ἰσχυρῶς ἀπέχεσϑαι·
οὐ γὰρ ἔφη ῥᾴδιον εἶναι τῶν τοιούτων ἁπτόμενον σω-
φρονεῖν. Ἀλλὰ καὶ Κριτόβουλόν ποτε τὸν Κρίτωνος
πυϑόμενος ὅτι ἐφίλησε τὸν Ἀλκιβιάδου υἱὸν καλὸν
ὄντα, παρόντος τοῦ Κριτοβούλου, ἤρετο Ξενοφῶντα·
Εἰπέ μοι, ἔφη, ὦ Ξενοφῶν, οὐ σὺ Κριτόβουλον ἐνόμιζες 9
εἶναι τῶν σωφρονικῶν ἀνϑρώπων μᾶλλον ἢ τῶν ϑρα-
σέων, καὶ τῶν προνοητικῶν μᾶλλον ἢ τῶν ἀνοήτων τε
καὶ ῥιψοκινδύνων;—Πάνυ μὲν οὖν, ἔφη ὁ Ξενοφῶν.—
Νῦν τοίνυν νόμιζε αὐτὸν ϑερμουργότατον εἶναι καὶ
λεωργότατον· οὗτος κἂν εἰς μαχαίρας κυβιστήσειε, κἂν
εἰς πῦρ ἅλοιτο.—Καὶ τί δή, ἔφη ὁ Ξενοφῶν, ἰδὼν 10
ποιοῦντα, τοιαῦτα κατέγνωκας αὐτοῦ;—Οὐ γὰρ οὗτος,
ἔφη, ἐτόλμησε τὸν Ἀλκιβιάδου υἱὸν φιλῆσαι, ὄντα
εὐπροςωπότατον καὶ ὡραιότατον;—Ἀλλ' εἰ μέντοι,
ἔφη ὁ Ξενοφῶν, τοιοῦτόν ἐστι τὸ ῥιψοκίνδυνον ἔργον,
κἂν ἐγὼ δοκῶ μοι τὸν κίνδυνον τοῦτον ὑπομεῖναι;—
Ὦ τλῆμον, ἔφη ὁ Σωκράτης, καὶ τί ἂν οἴει παϑεῖν 11
καλὸν φιλήσας; Ἆρ' οὐκ ἂν αὐτίκα μάλα δοῦλος μὲν
εἶναι ἀντ' ἐλευϑέρου; πολλὰ δὲ δαπανᾶν εἰς βλαβερὰς
ἡδονάς; πολλὴν δὲ ἀσχολίαν ἔχειν τοῦ ἐπιμεληϑῆναί
τινος καλοῦ κἀγαϑοῦ; σπουδάζειν δ' ἀναγκασϑῆναι,

12 ἐφ' οἷς οὐδ' ἂν μαινόμενος σπουδάσειεν;—Ὦ Ἡράκ-
λεις, ἔφη ὁ Ξενοφῶν, ὡς δεινήν τινα λέγεις δύναμιν τοῦ
φιλήματος εἶναι.—Καὶ τοῦτο, ἔφη ὁ Σωκράτης, θαυ-
μάζεις; Οὐκ οἶσθα, ἔφη, ὅτι τὰ φαλάγγια, οὐδ' ἡμιω-
βολιαῖα τὸ μέγεθος ὄντα προςαψάμενα μόνον τῷ στό-
ματι ταῖς τε ὀδύναις ἐπιτρίβει τοὺς ἀνθρώπους, καὶ
τοῦ φρονεῖν ἐξίστησιν;—Ναὶ μὰ Δί', ἔφη ὁ Ξενοφῶν·
13 ἐνίησι γάρ τι τὰ φαλάγγια κατὰ τὸ δῆγμα.—Ὦ μωρέ,
ἔφη ὁ Σωκράτης, τοὺς δὲ καλοὺς οὐκ οἴει φιλοῦντας
ἐνιέναι τι, ὅτι σὺ οὐχ ὁρᾷς; Οὐκ οἶσθ', ὅτι τοῦτο τὸ
θηρίον, ὃ καλοῦσι καλὸν καὶ ὡραῖον, τοσούτῳ δεινότερόν
ἐστι τῶν φαλαγγίων, ὅσῳ ἐκεῖνα μὲν ἁψάμενα, τοῦτο
δὲ οὐδ' ἁπτόμενον, ἐὰν δέ τις αὐτὸ θεᾶται, ἐνίησί τι
καὶ πάνυ πρόσωθεν τοιοῦτον, ὥςτε μαίνεσθαι ποιεῖν;
ἴσως δὲ καὶ οἱ Ἔρωτες τοξόται διὰ τοῦτο καλοῦνται,
ὅτι καὶ πρόσωθεν οἱ καλοὶ τιτρώσκουσιν. Ἀλλὰ συμ-
βουλεύω σοι, ὦ Ξενοφῶν, ὁπόταν ἴδῃς τινὰ καλόν,
φεύγειν προτροπάδην· σοὶ δέ, ὦ Κριτόβουλε, συμβου-
λεύω ἀπενιαυτίσαι· μόλις γὰρ ἂν ἴσως ἐν τοσούτῳ
14 χρόνῳ τὸ δῆγμα ὑγιὴς γένοιο. Οὕτω δὴ καὶ ἀφροδι-
σιάζειν τοὺς μὴ ἀσφαλῶς ἔχοντας πρὸς ἀφροδίσια ᾤετο
χρῆναι πρὸς τοιαῦτα, οἷα, μὴ πάνυ μὲν δεομένου τοῦ
σώματος, οὐκ ἂν προςδέξαιτο ἡ ψυχή, δεομένου δέ, οὐκ
ἂν πράγματα παρέχοι. Αὐτὸς δὲ πρὸς ταῦτα φανερὸς
ἦν οὕτω παρεσκευασμένος, ὥςτε ῥᾷον ἀπέχεσθαι τῶν
καλλίστων καὶ ὡραιοτάτων ἢ οἱ ἄλλοι τῶν αἰσχίστων
15 καὶ ἀωροτάτων. Περὶ μὲν δὴ βρώσεως καὶ πόσεως
καὶ ἀφροδισίων οὕτω κατεσκευασμένος ἦν· καὶ ᾤετο
οὐδὲν ἂν ἧττον ἀρκούντως ἥδεσθαι τῶν πολλὰ ἐπὶ τού-
τοις πραγματευομένων, λυπεῖσθαι δὲ πολὺ ἔλαττον.

CHAPTER IV.

ARGUMENT.

THE object of this chapter is to answer the objection, that Socrates only discoursed upon the theory of virtue and religion, without inducing others to practise them. This is done by presenting an example of the manner in which he was accustomed to correct the false notions and practices of his disciples. Aristodemus, it appears, practically disregarded the gods, and ridiculed others who served them; Socrates endeavored to restrain him by showing,

I. That there is good evidence of the intelligent agency of the gods in the works of nature. All works of art, such as paintings and statues, are the result of intelligence; much more must the creation of living beings be ascribed, not to chance, but to a designing mind (§ 3, 4). The perfection and manifest adaptedness of all parts of the human frame, and indeed of the whole organism of man, to each other and to a good end, require a belief in a living and wise creator (§ 5—7). Clear evidence of intelligence is also exhibited in the other works of nature (§ 8, 9).

Aristodemus then disowns the feeling of irreverence towards the gods, but doubts whether they condescend to take cognizance of human affairs. Socrates replies:

II. 1. The superior endowments of man, both in respect of body and still more of mind, to all other created things, show the special regard of the gods for him, and their consequent claim to reverence from him (§ 10—14).

2. The gods indicate their favor to man, by their revelations to him by means of divination (§ 15).

3. The special regard of gods to men, individually and collectively, further appears from the general belief of man in their power to reward and punish, and from the fact that both whole States and nations as well as individuals, in proportion to their age and wisdom, are reverent to the gods (§ 16).

In conclusion, the divine providence rules the world as the mind the body (§ 17); and in proportion as men sincerely worship the gods, they shall experience their readiness to assist in circumstances of doubt and darkness, and be assured, that they see and hear every thing, and are ever present to care for all. The natural effect of this conversation, the author adds, was to make those who heard him, careful of their conduct, not only in public, but when not visible to any but the all-seeing eye (§ 18, 19).

1 *Εἰ δέ τινες Σωκράτην νομίζουσιν, ὡς ἔνιοι γράφουσι
τε καὶ λέγουσι περὶ αὐτοῦ τεκμαιρόμενοι, προτρέψασθαι
μὲν ἀνθρώπους ἐπ' ἀρετὴν κράτιστον γεγονέναι, προ-
αγαγεῖν δ' ἐπ' αὐτὴν οὐχ ἱκανόν· σκεψάμενοι, μὴ μόνον
ἃ ἐκεῖνος κολαστηρίου ἕνεκα τοὺς πάντ' οἰομένους εἰδέ-
ναι ἐρωτῶν ἤλεγχεν, ἀλλὰ καὶ ἃ λέγων συνημέρευε
τοῖς συνδιατρίβουσι, δοκιμαζόντων, εἰ ἱκανὸς ἦν βελτίους
2 ποιεῖν τοὺς συνόντας. Λέξω δὲ πρῶτον, ἅ ποτε αὐτοῦ
ἤκουσα περὶ τοῦ δαιμονίου διαλεγομένου πρὸς Ἀριστό-
δημον τὸν Μικρὸν ἐπικαλούμενον. Καταμαθὼν γὰρ
αὐτὸν οὔτε θύοντα τοῖς θεοῖς, [οὔτ' εὐχόμενον,] οὔτε
μαντικῇ χρώμενον, ἀλλὰ καὶ τῶν ποιούντων ταῦτα κατα-
γελῶντα· Εἰπέ μοι, ἔφη, ὦ Ἀριστόδημε, ἔστιν οὕστινας
ἀνθρώπους τεθαύμακας ἐπὶ σοφίᾳ;—Ἔγωγε, ἔφη.—
3 Καὶ ὅς· Λέξον ἡμῖν, ἔφη, τὰ ὀνόματα αὐτῶν.—Ἐπὶ
μὲν τοίνυν ἐπῶν ποιήσει Ὅμηρον ἔγωγε μάλιστα τεθαύ-
μακα, ἐπὶ δὲ διθυράμβῳ Μελανιππίδην, ἐπὶ δὲ τραγῳ-
δίᾳ Σοφοκλέα, ἐπὶ δὲ ἀνδριαντοποιίᾳ Πολύκλειτον, ἐπὶ
4 δὲ ζωγραφίᾳ Ζεῦξιν.—Πότερά σοι δοκοῦσιν οἱ ἀπερ-
γαζόμενοι εἴδωλα ἄφρονά τε καὶ ἀκίνητα ἀξιοθαυμαστό-
τεροι εἶναι ἢ οἱ ζῷα ἔμφρονά τε καὶ ἐνεργά;—Πολύ,
νὴ Δία, οἱ ζῷα, εἴπερ γε μὴ τύχῃ τινί, ἀλλὰ ὑπὸ γνώ-
μης ταῦτα γίγνεται.—Τῶν δὲ ἀτεκμάρτως ἐχόντων, ὅτου
ἕνεκα ἔστι, καὶ τῶν φανερῶς ἐπ' ὠφελείᾳ ὄντων, πότερα
τύχης καὶ πότερα γνώμης ἔργα κρίνεις;—Πρέπει μὲν
5 τὰ ἐπ' ὠφελείᾳ γιγνόμενα γνώμης ἔργα εἶναι.—Οὐκοῦν
δοκεῖ σοι ὁ ἐξ ἀρχῆς ποιῶν ἀνθρώπους ἐπ' ὠφελείᾳ
προσθεῖναι αὐτοῖς δι' ὧν αἰσθάνονται ἕκαστα, ὀφθαλ-
μοὺς μὲν, ὥστε ὁρᾶν τὰ ὁρατά, ὦτα δὲ, ὥστε ἀκούειν
τὰ ἀκουστά; Ὀσμῶν γε μήν, εἰ μὴ ῥῖνες προσετέθησαν,
τί ἂν ἡμῖν ὄφελος ἦν; Τίς δ' ἂν αἴσθησις ἦν γλυκέων
καὶ δριμέων καὶ πάντων τῶν διὰ στόματος ἡδέων, εἰ μὴ
6 γλῶττα τούτων γνώμων ἐνειργάσθη; Πρὸς δὲ τούτοις
οὐ δοκεῖ σοι καὶ τόδε προνοίας ἔργον ἐοικέναι, τὸ, ἐπεὶ*

ἀσθενὴς μέν ἐστιν ἡ ὄψις, βλεφάροις αὐτὴν θυρῶσαι, ἅ, ὅταν μὲν αὐτῇ χρῆσθαί τι δέῃ, ἀναπετάννυται, ἐν δὲ τῷ ὕπνῳ συγκλείεται; ὡς δ᾽ ἂν μηδὲ ἄνεμοι βλάπτωσιν, ἠθμὸν βλεφαρίδας ἐμφῦσαι· ὀφρύσι τε ἀπογεισῶσαι τὰ ὑπὲρ τῶν ὀμμάτων, ὡς μηδ᾽ ὁ ἐκ τῆς κεφαλῆς ἱδρὼς κακουργῇ· τὸ δὲ τὴν ἀκοὴν δέχεσθαι μὲν πάσας φωνάς, ἐμπίπλασθαι δὲ μήποτε· καὶ τοὺς μὲν πρόσθεν ὀδόντας πᾶσι ζώοις οἵους τέμνειν εἶναι, τοὺς δὲ γομφίους οἵους παρὰ τούτων δεξαμένους λεαίνειν· καὶ στόμα μέν, δι᾽ οὗ ὧν ἐπιθυμεῖ τὰ ζῶα εἰςπέμπεται, πλησίον ὀφθαλμῶν καὶ ῥινῶν καταθεῖναι· ἐπεὶ δὲ τὰ ἀποχωροῦντα δυςχερῆ, ἀποστρέψαι τοὺς τούτων ὀχετοὺς καὶ ἀπενεγκεῖν, ᾗ δυνατὸν προσωτάτω, ἀπὸ τῶν αἰσθήσεων· ταῦτα οὕτω προνοητικῶς πεπραγμένα, ἀπορεῖς, πότερα τύχης ἢ γνώμης ἔργα ἐστίν;—Οὐ μὰ τὸν 7
Δί᾽, ἔφη, ἀλλ᾽ οὕτω γε σκοπουμένῳ πάνυ ἔοικε ταῦτα σοφοῦ τινος δημιουργοῦ καὶ φιλοζώου τεχνήματι.—Τὸ δὲ ἐμφῦσαι μὲν ἔρωτα τῆς τεκνοποιίας, ἐμφῦσαι δὲ ταῖς γειναμέναις ἔρωτα τοῦ ἐκτρέφειν, τοῖς δὲ τραφεῖσι μέγιστον μὲν πόθον τοῦ ζῆν, μέγιστον δὲ φόβον τοῦ θανάτου;—Ἀμέλει καὶ ταῦτα ἔοικε μηχανήμασί τινος ζῶα εἶναι βουλευσαμένου.—Σὺ δὲ σαυτὸν φρό- 8
νιμόν τι δοκεῖς ἔχειν;—Ἐρώτα γοῦν καὶ ἀποκρινοῦμαι.—Ἄλλοθι δὲ οὐδαμοῦ οὐδὲν οἴει φρόνιμον εἶναι; καὶ ταῦτα εἰδώς, ὅτι γῆς τε μικρὸν μέρος ἐν τῷ σώματι πολλῆς οὔσης ἔχεις, καὶ ὑγροῦ βραχὺ πολλοῦ ὄντος, καὶ τῶν ἄλλων δήπου μεγάλων ὄντων ἑκάστου μικρὸν μέρος λαβόντι τὸ σῶμα συνήρμοσταί σοι· νοῦν δὲ μόνον ἄρα οὐδαμοῦ ὄντα σὲ εὐτυχῶς πως δοκεῖς συναρπάσαι, καὶ τάδε τὰ ὑπερμεγέθη καὶ πλῆθος ἄπειρα δι᾽ ἀφροσύνην τινά, ὡς οἴει, εὐτάκτως ἔχειν;—Μὰ Δί᾽· 9
οὐ γὰρ ὁρῶ τοὺς κυρίους, ὥςπερ τῶν ἐνθάδε γιγνομένων τοὺς δημιουργούς.—Οὐδὲ γὰρ τὴν ἑαυτοῦ σύ γε ψυχὴν ὁρᾷς, ἣ τοῦ σώματος κυρία ἐστίν· ὥστε κατά γε τοῦτο

ἔξεστί σοι λέγειν, ὅτι οὐδὲν γνώμῃ, ἀλλὰ τύχῃ παντα
10 πράττεις.—Καὶ ὁ Ἀριστόδημος· Οὔτοι, ἔφη, ἐγώ, ὦ
Σώκρατες, ὑπερορῶ τὸ δαιμόνιον, ἀλλ' ἐκεῖνο μεγαλο
πρεπέστερον ἡγοῦμαι ἢ ὡς τῆς ἐμῆς θεραπείας προς-
δεῖσθαι.—Οὐκοῦν, ἔφη, ὅσῳ μεγαλοπρεπέστερον ἀξιοῖ
11 σε θεραπεύειν, τοσούτῳ μᾶλλον τιμητέον αὐτό;—Εὖ
ἴσθι, ἔφη, ὅτι, εἰ νομίζοιμι θεοὺς ἀνθρώπων τι φροντί-
ζειν, οὐκ ἂν ἀμελοίην αὐτῶν.—Ἔπειτ' οὐκ οἴει φρον-
τίζειν; οἳ πρῶτον μὲν μόνον τῶν ζώων ἄνθρωπον ὀρθὸν
ἀνέστησαν· ἡ δὲ ὀρθότης καὶ προορᾶν πλεῖον ποιεῖ
δύνασθαι, καὶ τὰ ὕπερθεν μᾶλλον θεᾶσθαι, καὶ ἧττον
κακοπαθεῖν, [οἷς] καὶ ὄψιν καὶ ἀκοὴν καὶ στόμα ἐνε-
ποίησαν· ἔπειτα τοῖς μὲν ἄλλοις ἑρπετοῖς πόδας ἔδω-
καν, οἳ τὸ πορεύεσθαι μόνον παρέχουσιν· ἀνθρώπῳ
δὲ καὶ χεῖρας προσέθεσαν, αἳ τὰ πλεῖστα οἷς εὐδαι-
12 μονέστεροι ἐκείνων ἐσμέν, ἐξεργάζονται. Καὶ μὴν
γλῶττάν γε πάντων τῶν ζώων ἐχόντων, μόνην τὴν τῶν
ἀνθρώπων ἐποίησαν οἵαν, ἄλλοτε ἀλλαχῇ ψαύουσαν
τοῦ στόματος, ἀρθροῦν τε τὴν φωνήν, καὶ σημαίνειν
πάντα ἀλλήλοις, ἃ βουλόμεθα; Τὸ δὲ καὶ τὰς τῶν
ἀφροδισίων ἡδονὰς τοῖς μὲν ἄλλοις ζώοις δοῦναι περι-
γράψαντας τοῦ ἔτους χρόνον, ἡμῖν δὲ συνεχῶς μέχρι
13 γήρως ταύτας παρέχειν; Οὐ τοίνυν μόνον ἤρκεσε τῷ
θεῷ τοῦ σώματος ἐπιμεληθῆναι, ἀλλ', ὅπερ μέγιστόν
ἐστι, καὶ τὴν ψυχὴν κρατίστην τῷ ἀνθρώπῳ ἐνέφυσε·
τίνος γὰρ ἄλλου ζώου ψυχὴ πρῶτα μὲν θεῶν τῶν τὰ
μέγιστα καὶ κάλλιστα συνταξάντων ᾔσθηται ὅτι εἰσί;
τί δὲ φῦλον ἄλλο ἢ ἄνθρωποι θεοὺς θεραπεύουσι;
ποία δὲ ψυχὴ τῆς ἀνθρωπίνης ἱκανωτέρα προφυλάτ-
τεσθαι ἢ λιμὸν ἢ δίψος ἢ ψύχη ἢ θάλπη, ἢ νόσοις
ἐπικουρῆσαι, ἢ ῥώμην ἀσκῆσαι, ἢ πρὸς μάθησιν ἐκπο-
νῆσαι, ἤ, ὅσα ἂν ἀκούσῃ ἢ ἴδῃ ἢ μάθῃ, ἱκανωτέρα
14 ἐστὶ διαμεμνῆσθαι; Οὐ γὰρ πάνυ σοι κατάδηλον, ὅτι
παρὰ τὰ ἄλλα ζῶα, ὥσπερ θεοὶ ἄνθρωποι βιοτεύουσι,

φύσει καὶ τῷ σώματι καὶ τῇ ψυχῇ κρατιστεύοντες;
Οὔτε γὰρ βοὸς ἂν ἔχων σῶμα, ἀνθρώπου δὲ γνώμην,
ἐδύνατ' ἂν πράττειν ἃ ἐβούλετο· οὔθ' ὅσα χεῖρας ἔχει,
ἄφρονα δ' ἐστί, πλέον οὐδὲν ἔχει· σὺ δὲ ἀμφοτέρων
τῶν πλείστου ἀξίων τετυχηκὼς οὐκ οἴει σοῦ θεοὺς ἐπι-
μελεῖσθαι· ἀλλ', ὅταν τί ποιήσωσι, νομιεῖς αὐτοὺς σοῦ
φροντίζειν;—Ὅταν πέμπωσιν, ὥςπερ σὺ σοὶ φὴς πέμ- 15
πειν αὐτούς, συμβούλους, ὅ τι χρὴ ποιεῖν καὶ μὴ ποιεῖν.
—Ὅταν δὲ Ἀθηναίοις, ἔφη, πυνθανομένοις τι διὰ μαν-
τικῆς φράζωσιν, οὐ καὶ σοὶ δοκεῖς φράζειν αὐτούς, οὐδ'
ὅταν τοῖς Ἕλλησι τέρατα πέμποντες προσημαίνωσιν,
οὐδ' ὅταν πᾶσιν ἀνθρώποις; ἀλλὰ μόνον σὲ ἐξαιροῦν-
τες ἐν ἀμελείᾳ κατατίθενται; Οἴει δ' ἂν τοὺς θεοὺς 16
τοῖς ἀνθρώποις δόξαν ἐμφῦσαι, ὡς ἱκανοί εἰσιν εὖ καὶ
κακῶς ποιεῖν, εἰ μὴ δυνατοὶ ἦσαν, καὶ τοὺς ἀνθρώπους
ἐξαπατωμένους τὸν πάντα χρόνον οὐδέποτ' ἂν αἰσθέ-
σθαι; Οὐχ ὁρᾷς, ὅτι τὰ πολυχρονιώτατα καὶ σοφώ-
τατα τῶν ἀνθρωπίνων, πόλεις καὶ ἔθνη, θεοσεβέστατά
ἐστι, καὶ αἱ φρονιμώταται ἡλικίαι θεῶν ἐπιμελέστα-
ται; Ὠγαθέ, ἔφη, κατάμαθε, ὅτι καὶ ὁ σὸς νοῦς ἐνὼν 17
τὸ σὸν σῶμα, ὅπως βούλεται, μεταχειρίζεται. Οἴε-
σθαι οὖν χρὴ καὶ τὴν ἐν παντὶ φρόνησιν τὰ πάντα,
ὅπως ἂν αὐτῇ ἡδὺ ᾖ, οὕτω τίθεσθαι, καὶ μὴ τὸ σὸν
μὲν ὄμμα δύνασθαι ἐπὶ πολλὰ στάδια ἐξικνεῖσθαι,
τὸν δὲ τοῦ θεοῦ ὀφθαλμὸν ἀδύνατον εἶναι ἅμα πάντα
ὁρᾶν, μηδὲ τὴν σὴν μὲν ψυχὴν καὶ περὶ τῶν ἐνθάδε
καὶ περὶ τῶν ἐν Αἰγύπτῳ καὶ ἐν Σικελίᾳ δύνασθαι
φροντίζειν, τὴν δὲ τοῦ θεοῦ φρόνησιν μὴ ἱκανὴν εἶναι
ἅμα πάντων ἐπιμελεῖσθαι. Ἢν μέντοι, ὥςπερ ἀν- 18
θρώπους θεραπεύων γιγνώσκεις τοὺς ἀντιθεραπεύειν
ἐθέλοντας, καὶ χαριζόμενος τοὺς ἀντιχαριζομένους, καὶ
συμβουλευόμενος καταμανθάνεις τοὺς φρονίμους, οὕτω
καὶ τῶν θεῶν πεῖραν λαμβάνῃς θεραπεύων, εἴ τι σοὶ
θελήσουσι περὶ τῶν ἀδήλων ἀνθρώποις συμβουλεύειν,

γνώσῃ τὸ θεῖον ὅτι τοσοῦτον καὶ τοιοῦτόν ἐστιν, ὥσθ' ἅμα πάντα ὁρᾶν, καὶ πάντα ἀκούειν, καὶ πανταχοῦ
19 παρεῖναι, καὶ ἅμα πάντων ἐπιμελεῖσθαι αὐτούς. Ἐμοὶ μὲν ταῦτα λέγων οὐ μόνον τοὺς συνόντας ἐδόκει ποιεῖν, ὁπότε ὑπὸ τῶν ἀνθρώπων ὁρῷντο, ἀπέχεσθαι τῶν ἀνοσίων τε καὶ ἀδίκων καὶ αἰσχρῶν, ἀλλὰ καὶ ὁπότε ἐν ἐρημίᾳ εἶεν, ἐπείπερ ἡγήσαιντο μηδὲν ἄν ποτε, ὧν πράττοιεν, θεοὺς διαλαθεῖν.

CHAPTER V.

ARGUMENT.

Socrates commended self-control (ἐγκράτεια), especially in regard to the indulgence of the passions, and appetite, and indolence, in the following manner:

1. He taught that any one who was destitute of this virtue, could not safely be trusted in any of the important duties or callings of life, not even as a servant (§ 1, 2). Such a man is unjust to others, and still more so to himself; for he not only squanders his estate, but destroys both body and soul; his society is especially to be avoided (§ 3, 4). Temperance or self-control is the foundation of all virtue, and the careful and hearty practice of it is the first duty (§ 4); for without it no knowledge or skill of any value can be acquired (§ 5).

2. He confirmed his precepts by the practice of the most rigid temperance, and by foregoing the acquisition of the means of self-indulgence (§ 6).

---

1 Εἰ δὲ δὴ καὶ ἐγκράτεια καλόν τε κἀγαθὸν ἀνδρὶ κτῆμά ἐστιν, ἐπισκεψώμεθα, εἴ τι προὐβίβαζε λέγων εἰς ταύτην τοιάδε· Ὦ ἄνδρες, εἰ, πολέμου ἡμῖν γενομένου, βουλοίμεθα ἑλέσθαι ἄνδρα, ὑφ' οὗ μάλιστ' ἂν αὐτοὶ μὲν σωζοίμεθα, τοὺς δὲ πολεμίους χειροίμεθα, ἆρ' ὅντιν' ἂν αἰσθανοίμεθα ἥττω γαστρὸς ἢ οἴνου ἢ

ἀφροδισίων ἢ πόνου ἢ ὕπνου, τοῦτον ἂν αἱροίμεθα; καὶ πῶς ἂν οἰηθείημεν τὸν τοιοῦτον ἢ ἡμᾶς σῶσαι, ἢ τοὺς πολεμίους κρατῆσαι; Εἰ δ' ἐπὶ τελευτῇ τοῦ βίου 2
γενόμενοι βουλοίμεθά τῳ ἐπιτρέψαι ἢ παῖδας ἄῤῥενας παιδεῦσαι, ἢ θυγατέρας παρθένους διαφυλάξαι, ἢ χρήματα διασῶσαι, ἆρ' ἀξιόπιστον εἰς ταῦτα ἡγησόμεθα τὸν ἀκρατῆ; δούλῳ δ' ἀκρατεῖ ἐπιτρέψαιμεν ἂν ἢ βοσκήματα ἢ ταμιεῖα ἢ ἔργων ἐπίστασιν; διάκονον δὲ καὶ ἀγοραστὴν τοιοῦτον ἐθελήσαιμεν ἂν προῖκα λαβεῖν; Ἀλλὰ μὴν εἴ γε μηδὲ δοῦλον ἀκρατῆ δεξαίμεθ' 3
ἄν, πῶς οὐκ ἄξιον αὐτόν γε φυλάξασθαι τοιοῦτον γενέσθαι; Καὶ γὰρ οὐχ, ὥσπερ οἱ πλεονέκται τῶν ἄλλων ἀφαιρούμενοι χρήματα ἑαυτοὺς δοκοῦσι πλουτίζειν, οὕτως ὁ ἀκρατὴς τοῖς μὲν ἄλλοις βλαβερός, ἑαυτῷ δ' ὠφέλιμος, ἀλλὰ κακοῦργος μὲν τῶν ἄλλων, ἑαυτοῦ δὲ πολὺ κακουργότερος, εἴ γε κακουργότατόν ἐστι μὴ μόνον τὸν οἶκον τὸν ἑαυτοῦ φθείρειν, ἀλλὰ καὶ τὸ σῶμα καὶ τὴν ψυχήν. Ἐν συνουσίᾳ δὲ τίς ἂν ἡσθείη τῷ 4
τοιούτῳ, ὃν εἰδείη τῷ ὄψῳ τε καὶ τῷ οἴνῳ χαίροντα μᾶλλον ἢ τοῖς φίλοις, καὶ τὰς πόρνας ἀγαπῶντα μᾶλλον ἢ τοὺς ἑταίρους; Ἆρά γε οὐ χρὴ πάντα ἄνδρα, 5
ἡγησάμενον τὴν ἐγκράτειαν ἀρετῆς εἶναι κρηπῖδα, ταύτην πρῶτον ἐν τῇ ψυχῇ κατασκευάσασθαι; Τίς γὰρ ἄνευ ταύτης ἢ μάθοι τι ἂν ἀγαθὸν ἢ μελετήσειεν ἀξιολόγως; ἢ τίς οὐκ ἂν ταῖς ἡδοναῖς δουλεύων αἰσχρῶς διατεθείη καὶ τὸ σῶμα καὶ τὴν ψυχήν; Ἐμοὶ μὲν δοκεῖ, νὴ τὴν Ἥραν, ἐλευθέρῳ μὲν ἀνδρὶ εὐκτὸν εἶναι μὴ τυχεῖν δούλου τοιούτου, δουλεύοντα δὲ ταῖς τοιαύταις ἡδοναῖς ἱκετεύειν τοὺς θεοὺς δεσποτῶν ἀγαθῶν τυχεῖν· οὕτως γὰρ ἂν μόνως ὁ τοιοῦτος σωθείη.
Τοιαῦτα δὲ λέγων ἔτι ἐγκρατέστερον τοῖς ἔργοις ἢ τοῖς 6
λόγοις ἑαυτὸν ἐπεδείκνυεν· οὐ γὰρ μόνον τῶν διὰ τοῦ σώματος ἡδονῶν ἐκράτει, ἀλλὰ καὶ τῆς διὰ τῶν χρημάτων, νομίζων τὸν παρὰ τοῦ τυχόντος χρήματα λαμ-

βάνοντα δεσπότην ἑαυτοῦ καθιστάναι, καὶ δουλεύειν δουλείαν οὐδεμιᾶς ἧττον αἰσχράν.

CHAPTER VI.

ARGUMENT.

This chapter is closely connected with the preceding, and embraces a defence of that branch of ἐγκράτεια, which was so admirably exemplified in the moderation and even abstinence of the life of Socrates, in three conversations with the sophist Antiphon.

I. Antiphon adduces the poverty, the mean and scanty diet and apparel of Socrates, as an objection to his philosophy. Philosophy, he thinks, ought to enable its votary to live freely and pleasantly, but that of Socrates had the contrary effect. By not receiving a remuneration for his instructions, to enable him to procure the pleasures of life, he by example commended to his disciples a life of misery (§ 1—3). To this reproach Socrates replied:

1. By receiving no remuneration for my instructions, I secure independence. I am compelled to converse only with those whom I choose (§ 4, 5).

2. Simple food is both more healthful and easily procured, and relishes better than that which is more expensive (§ 5). Scanty clothing and bare feet, by inuring the body to heat and cold and rough ways, obviate the necessity, and even remove the desire, of more abundant clothing (§ 6, 7).

3. Those who have higher and more permanent enjoyments can easily forego the pleasures of sense; especially, when by so doing they can command greater ability and more leisure for self-improvement, and for rendering valuable service to friends and to the State (§ 8, 9).

4. Happiness consists not in external affluence and splendor; but he who is most free from wants, is most like the gods, and consequently best (§ 10).

II. When Antiphon at another time told Socrates that he thought him δίκαιος (just), but by no means wise; since even he himself plainly indicated that he considered his instructions valueless, by receiving no remuneration for them (§ 11, 12); Socrates replied:

Both beauty and wisdom are good in themselves, and one who prostitutes either of them for money exhibits baseness and folly; but he who, by imparting knowledge, attracts others to himself and makes them his friends, is wise, and performs the part of a good citizen (§ 13); he who thus benefits his friends, reaps a richer harvest of enjoyment in his intercourse with them, than could be procured by pecuniary recompense (§ 14).

III. The third conversation seems to be appended by Xenophon to the preceding, as a sort of corollary. The wisdom of Socrates had been there called in question, on account of his refusal to receive a reward for his instructions, and to indulge in the luxury which was usual with the sophists. The leading subject of the chapter, self-control, is lost sight of in this last conversation, and a further illustration of his want of wisdom is adduced, i. e. his attempts to teach statesmanship without himself engaging in political life. The only and sufficient answer of Socrates was contained in the inquiry, whether less was accomplished for the State by fitting others for its management, than by engaging personally and alone in that employment (§ 15).

Ἄξιον δ' αὐτοῦ καὶ ἃ πρὸς Ἀντιφῶντα τὸν σοφι- 1
στὴν διελέχθη μὴ παραλιπεῖν· ὁ γὰρ Ἀντιφῶν ποτε
βουλόμενος τοὺς συνουσιαστὰς αὐτοῦ παρελέσθαι, προσ-
ελθὼν τῷ Σωκράτει, παρόντων αὐτῶν, ἔλεξε τάδε· Ὦ 2
Σώκρατες, ἐγὼ μὲν ᾤμην τοὺς φιλοσοφοῦντας εὐδαι-
μονεστέρους χρῆναι γίγνεσθαι, σὺ δέ μοι δοκεῖς τἀν-
αντία τῆς φιλοσοφίας ἀπολελαυκέναι· ζῇς γοῦν οὕτως,
ὡς οὐδ' ἂν εἷς δοῦλος ὑπὸ δεσπότῃ διαιτώμενος μεί-
νειε, σιτία τε σιτῇ καὶ ποτὰ πίνεις τὰ φαυλότατα,
καὶ ἱμάτιον ἠμφίεσαι οὐ μόνον φαῦλον, ἀλλὰ τὸ αὐτὸ
θέρους τε καὶ χειμῶνος, ἀνυπόδητός τε καὶ ἀχίτων
διατελεῖς. Καὶ μὴν χρήματά γε οὐ λαμβάνεις, ἃ καὶ 3
κτωμένους εὐφραίνει καὶ κεκτημένους ἐλευθεριώτερόν
τε καὶ ἥδιον ποιεῖ ζῆν. Εἰ οὖν, ὥσπερ καὶ τῶν ἄλλων
ἔργων οἱ διδάσκαλοι τοὺς μαθητὰς μιμητὰς ἑαυτῶν
ἀποδεικνύουσιν, οὕτω καὶ σὺ τοὺς συνόντας διαθήσεις,
νόμιζε κακοδαιμονίας διδάσκαλος εἶναι. Καὶ ὁ Σωκρά- 4
της πρὸς ταῦτα εἶπε· Δοκεῖς μοι, ἔφη, ὦ Ἀντιφῶν,
ὑπειληφέναι με οὕτως ἀνιαρῶς ζῆν, ὥστε πέπεισμαί σε

μᾶλλον ἀποθανεῖν ἂν ἑλέσθαι ἢ ζῆν ὥσπερ ἐγώ. Ἴθι
οὖν ἐπισκεψώμεθα, τί χαλεπὸν ᾔσθησαι τοὐμοῦ βίου.
5 Πότερον, ὅτι τοῖς μὲν λαμβάνουσιν ἀργύριον ἀναγκαῖόν
ἐστιν ἀπεργάζεσθαι τοῦτο, ἐφ' ᾧ ἂν μισθὸν λαμβά-
νωσιν, ἐμοὶ δὲ μὴ λαμβάνοντι οὐκ ἀνάγκη διαλέγε-
σθαι, ᾧ ἂν μὴ βούλωμαι; ἢ τὴν δίαιτάν μου φαυλί-
ζεις, ὡς ἧττον μὲν ὑγιεινὰ ἐσθίοντος ἐμοῦ ἢ σοῦ, ἧττον
δὲ ἰσχὺν παρέχοντα; ἢ ὡς χαλεπώτερα πορίσασθαι
τὰ ἐμὰ διαιτήματα τῶν σῶν διὰ τὸ σπανιώτερά τε καὶ
πολυτελέστερα εἶναι; ἢ ὡς ἡδίω σοὶ ἃ σὺ παρασκευάζῃ
ὄντα, ἢ ἐμοὶ ἃ ἐγώ; Οὐκ οἶσθ', ὅτι ὁ μὲν ἥδιστα ἐσθίων
ἥκιστα ὄψου δεῖται, ὁ δὲ ἥδιστα πίνων ἥκιστα τοῦ
6 μὴ παρόντος ἐπιθυμεῖ ποτοῦ; Τά γε μὴν ἱμάτια οἶσθ'
ὅτι οἱ μεταβαλλόμενοι ψύχους καὶ θάλπους ἕνεκα με-
ταβάλλονται, καὶ ὑποδήματα ὑποδοῦνται, ὅπως μὴ διὰ
τὰ λυποῦντα τοὺς πόδας κωλύωνται πορεύεσθαι· ἤδη
οὖν ποτε ᾔσθου ἐμὲ ἢ διὰ ψῦχος μᾶλλόν του ἔνδον
μένοντα, ἢ διὰ θάλπος μαχόμενόν τῳ περὶ σκιᾶς, ἢ
διὰ τὸ ἀλγεῖν τοὺς πόδας οὐ βαδίζοντα, ὅπου ἂν βού-
7 λωμαι; Οὐκ οἶσθ', ὅτι οἱ φύσει ἀσθενέστατοι τῷ
σώματι, μελετήσαντες τῶν ἰσχυροτάτων ἀμελησάντων
κρείττους τε γίγνονται πρὸς ἂν μελετῶσι, καὶ ῥᾷον
αὐτὰ φέρουσιν; Ἐμὲ δὲ ἄρα οὐκ οἴει τῷ σώματι ἀεὶ
τὰ συντυγχάνοντα μελετῶντα καρτερεῖν πάντα ῥᾷον
8 φέρειν σοῦ μὴ μελετῶντος; Τοῦ δὲ μὴ δουλεύειν
γαστρὶ μηδὲ ὕπνῳ καὶ λαγνείᾳ οἴει τι ἄλλο αἰτιώτε-
ρον εἶναι ἢ τὸ ἕτερα ἔχειν τούτων ἡδίω, ἃ οὐ μόνον
ἐν χρείᾳ ὄντα εὐφραίνει, ἀλλὰ καὶ ἐλπίδας παρέχοντα
ὠφελήσειν ἀεί; Καὶ μὴν τοῦτό γε οἶσθα, ὅτι οἱ μὲν
οἰόμενοι μηδὲν εὖ πράττειν οὐκ εὐφραίνονται, οἱ δὲ
ἡγούμενοι καλῶς προχωρεῖν ἑαυτοῖς ἢ γεωργίαν ἢ ναυ-
κληρίαν ἢ ἄλλ' ὅ τι ἂν τυγχάνωσιν ἐργαζόμενοι, ὡς
9 εὖ πράττοντες εὐφραίνονται. Οἴει οὖν ἀπὸ πάντων
τούτων τοσαύτην ἡδονὴν εἶναι, ὅσην ἀπὸ τοῦ ἑαυτόν

τε ἡγεῖσϑαι βελτίω γίγνεσϑαι καὶ φίλους ἀμείνους
κτᾶσϑαι; Ἐγὼ τοίνυν διατελῶ ταῦτα νομίζων. Ἐὰν
δὲ δὴ φίλους ἢ πόλιν ὠφελεῖν δέῃ, ποτέρῳ ἡ πλείων
σχολὴ τούτων ἐπιμελεῖσϑαι, τῷ, ὡς ἐγὼ νῦν, ἢ τῷ,
ὡς σὺ μακαρίζεις, διαιτωμένῳ; στρατεύοιτο δὲ πότε-
ρος ἂν ῥᾷον, ὁ μὴ δυνάμενος ἄνευ πολυτελοῦς διαίτης
ζῆν, ἢ ᾧ τὸ παρὸν ἀρκοίη; ἐκπολιορκηϑείη δὲ πότε-
ρος ἂν ϑᾶττον, ὁ τῶν χαλεπωτάτων εὑρεῖν δεόμενος,
ἢ ὁ τοῖς ῥᾴστοις ἐντυγχάνειν ἀρκούντως χρώμενος;
Ἔοικας, ὦ Ἀντιφῶν, τὴν εὐδαιμονίαν οἰομένῳ τρυφὴν 10
καὶ πολυτέλειαν εἶναι· ἐγὼ δὲ νομίζω τὸ μὲν μηδενὸς
δέεσϑαι ϑεῖον εἶναι, τὸ δ' ὡς ἐλαχίστων ἐγγυτάτω
τοῦ ϑείου· καὶ τὸ μὲν ϑεῖον κράτιστον, τὸ δὲ ἐγγυ-
τάτω τοῦ ϑείου ἐγγυτάτω τοῦ κρατίστου.

Πάλιν δέ ποτε ὁ Ἀντιφῶν διαλεγόμενος τῷ Σω- 11
κράτει εἶπεν· Ὦ Σώκρατες, ἐγώ τοι σὲ μὲν δίκαιον
νομίζω, σοφὸν δὲ οὐδ' ὁπωστιοῦν. Δοκεῖς δέ μοι καὶ
αὐτὸς τοῦτο γιγνώσκειν· οὐδένα γοῦν τῆς συνουσίας
ἀργύριον πράττῃ· καίτοι τό γε ἱμάτιον ἢ τὴν οἰκίαν
ἢ ἄλλο τι, ὧν κέκτησαι, νομίζων ἀργυρίου ἄξιον εἶναι,
οὐδενὶ ἂν μὴ ὅτι προῖκα δοίης, ἀλλ' οὐδ' ἔλαττον τῆς
ἀξίας λαβών. Δῆλον δὴ ὅτι, εἰ καὶ τὴν συνουσίαν 12
ᾤου τινὸς ἀξίαν εἶναι, καὶ ταύτης ἂν οὐκ ἔλαττον τῆς
ἀξίας ἀργύριον ἐπράττου. Δίκαιος μὲν οὖν ἂν εἴης,
ὅτι οὐκ ἐξαπατᾷς ἐπὶ πλεονεξίᾳ, σοφὸς δὲ οὐκ ἄν,
μηδενός γε ἄξια ἐπιστάμενος. Ὁ δὲ Σωκράτης πρὸς 13
ταῦτα εἶπεν· Ὦ Ἀντιφῶν, παρ' ἡμῖν νομίζεται τὴν
ὥραν καὶ τὴν σοφίαν ὁμοίως μὲν καλόν, ὁμοίως δὲ
αἰσχρὸν διατίϑεσϑαι εἶναι· τήν τε γὰρ ὥραν ἐὰν μέν
τις ἀργυρίου πωλῇ τῷ βουλομένῳ, πόρνον αὐτὸν ἀπο-
καλοῦσιν, ἐὰν δέ τις, ὃν ἂν γνῷ καλόν τε κἀγαϑὸν
ἐραστὴν ὄντα, τοῦτον φίλον ἑαυτῷ ποιῆται, σώφρονα
νομίζομεν· καὶ τὴν σοφίαν ὡσαύτως τοὺς μὲν ἀργυ-

ρίου τῷ βουλομένῳ πωλοῦντας σοφιστὰς ὥςπερ πόρνους ἀποκαλοῦσιν, ὅςτις δέ, ὃν ἂν γνῷ εὐφυᾶ ὄντα, διδάσκων ὅ τι ἂν ἔχῃ ἀγαθόν, φίλον ποιῆται, τοῦτον νομίζομεν, ἃ τῷ καλῷ κἀγαθῷ πολίτῃ προςήκει, ταῦτα
14 ποιεῖν. Ἐγὼ δ' οὖν καὶ αὐτός, ὦ Ἀντιφῶν, ὥςπερ ἄλλος τις ἢ ἵππῳ ἀγαθῷ ἢ κυνὶ ἢ ὄρνιθι ἥδεται, οὕτω καὶ ἔτι μᾶλλον ἥδομαι φίλοις ἀγαθοῖς· καί, ἐάν τι σχῶ ἀγαθόν, διδάσκω, καὶ ἄλλοις συνίστημι, παρ' ὧν ἂν ἡγῶμαι, ὠφελήσεσθαί τι αὐτοὺς εἰς ἀρετήν. Καὶ τοὺς θησαυροὺς τῶν πάλαι σοφῶν ἀνδρῶν, οὓς ἐκεῖνοι κατέλιπον ἐν βιβλίοις γράψαντες, ἀνελίττων κοινῇ σὺν τοῖς φίλοις διέρχομαι, καί, ἄν τι ὁρῶμεν ἀγαθόν, ἐκλεγόμεθα καὶ μέγα νομίζομεν κέρδος, ἐὰν ἀλλήλοις φίλοι γιγνώμεθα. Ἐμοὶ μὲν δὴ ταῦτα ἀκούοντι ἐδόκει αὐτός τε μακάριος εἶναι, καὶ τοὺς ἀκούοντας ἐπὶ καλοκἀγαθίαν ἄγειν.

15 Καὶ πάλιν ποτὲ τοῦ Ἀντιφῶντος ἐρομένου αὐτόν, πῶς ἄλλους μὲν ἡγεῖται πολιτικοὺς ποιεῖν, αὐτὸς δὲ οὐ πράττει τὰ πολιτικά, εἴπερ ἐπίσταται; Ποτέρως δ' ἄν, ἔφη, ὦ Ἀντιφῶν, μᾶλλον τὰ πολιτικὰ πράττοιμι, εἰ μόνος αὐτὰ πράττοιμι, ἢ εἰ ἐπιμελοίμην τοῦ ὡς πλείστους ἱκανοὺς εἶναι πράττειν αὐτά;

CHAPTER VII.

ARGUMENT.

This chapter is connected with the preceding by the principle of contrast. False pretension (ἀλαζονεία), based on pride and vanity, may be reckoned among the errors opposed to the ἐγκράτεια, commended in the colloquies with Antiphon which precede. Thus in chap. II. § 5, a θρυπτικὸς and ἀλιζονικὸς δίαιτα is represented as opposed to the ἐγκράτεια of Socrates' course of life, and these two chapters in connection seem to be based upon that passage. The reasoning which Socrates employed to avert his friends from false pretension, and urge them to the practice of real virtue, is briefly as follows:

The best road to honor is, in endeavoring to be what we would wish to seem to be (§ 1); for the false pretender is constantly in peril of having his knowledge put to the test, and of thus exhibiting to others his empty assumptions and base hypocrisy. He will, consequently, pass a troubled and useless life, as well as bring upon himself and others serious detriment. A course of deception is especially perilous in those who have the management of the State (§ 2—5).

Ἐπισκεψώμεθα δὲ, εἰ καὶ ἀλαζονείας ἀποτρέπων 1
τοὺς συνόντας ἀρετῆς ἐπιμελεῖσθαι προέτρεπεν· ἀεὶ
γὰρ ἔλεγεν, ὡς οὐκ εἴη καλλίων ὁδὸς ἐπ' εὐδοξίᾳ, ἢ
δι' ἧς ἄν τις ἀγαθὸς τοῦτο γένοιτο, ὃ καὶ δοκεῖν βού-
λοιτο. Ὅτι δ' ἀληθῆ ἔλεγεν, ὧδε ἐδίδασκεν· Ἐνθυ- 2
μώμεθα γάρ, ἔφη, εἴ τις μὴ ὢν ἀγαθὸς αὐλητὴς δοκεῖν βούλοιτο, τί ἂν αὐτῷ ποιητέον εἴη; ἆρ' οὐ τὰ ἔξω τῆς τέχνης μιμητέον τοὺς ἀγαθοὺς αὐλητάς; Καὶ πρῶτον μέν, ὅτι ἐκεῖνοι σκεύη τε καλὰ κέκτηνται καὶ ἀκολούθους πολλοὺς περιάγονται, καὶ τούτῳ ταῦτα ποιητέον· ἔπειτα, ὅτι ἐκείνους πολλοὶ ἐπαινοῦσι, καὶ τούτῳ πολλοὺς ἐπαινέτας παρασκευαστέον. Ἀλλὰ μὴν ἔργον γε οὐδαμοῦ ληπτέον, ἢ εὐθὺς ἐλεγχθήσεται γελοῖος ὤν, καὶ οὐ μόνον αὐλητὴς κακός, ἀλλὰ καὶ ἄνθρωπος ἀλαζών. Καίτοι πολλὰ μὲν δαπανῶν, μηδὲν δὲ ὠφελούμενος, πρὸς δὲ τούτοις κακοδοξῶν, πῶς οὐκ ἐπιπόνως τε καὶ ἀλυσιτελῶς καὶ καταγελάστως βιώσεται;
Ὡς δ' αὔτως, εἴ τις βούλοιτο στρατηγὸς ἀγαθὸς μὴ 3
ὢν φαίνεσθαι, ἢ κυβερνήτης, ἐννοῶμεν, τί ἂν αὐτῷ συμβαίνοι. Ἆρ' οὐκ ἄν, εἰ μέν, ἐπιθυμῶν τοῦ δοκεῖν ἱκανὸς εἶναι ταῦτα πράττειν, μὴ δύναιτο πείθειν, ταύτῃ λυπηρόν; εἰ δὲ πείσειεν, ἔτι ἀθλιώτερον; Δῆλον γάρ, ὅτι κυβερνᾶν τε κατασταθεὶς ὁ μὴ ἐπιστάμενος ἢ στρατηγεῖν, ἀπολέσειεν ἂν οὓς ἥκιστα βούλοιτο, καὶ

4 αὐτὸς αἰσχρῶς τε καὶ κακῶς ἀπαλλάξειεν. Ὡςαύτως
δὲ καὶ τὸ πλούσιον καὶ τὸ ἀνδρεῖον καὶ τὸ ἰσχυρὸν
μὴ ὄντα δοκεῖν ἀλυσιτελὲς ἀπέφαινε· προστάττεσθαι
γὰρ αὐτοῖς ἔφη μείζω ἢ κατὰ δύναμιν, καὶ μὴ δυνα-
μένους ταῦτα ποιεῖν, δοκοῦντας ἱκανοὺς εἶναι, συγγνώ-
5 μης οὐκ ἂν τυγχάνειν. Ἀπατεῶνα δ' ἐκάλει οὐ μικρὸν
μέν, εἴ τις ἀργύριον ἢ σκεῦος παρά του πειθοῖ λαβὼν
ἀποστεροίη, πολὺ δὲ μέγιστον, ὅςτις μηδενὸς ἄξιος ὢν
ἐξηπατήκει πείθων, ὡς ἱκανὸς εἴη τῆς πόλεως ἡγεῖ-
σθαι. Ἐμοὶ μὲν οὖν ἐδόκει καὶ τοῦ ἀλαζονεύεσθαι
ἀποτρέπειν τοὺς συνόντας τοιάδε διαλεγόμενος.

ΞΕΝΟΦΩΝΤΟΣ

ΑΠΟΜΝΗΜΟΝΕΥΜΑΤΩΝ.

ΔΕΥΤΕΡΟΝ.

CHAPTER I.

ARGUMENT.

The general subject of this chapter is the same as that of the fifth of the first Book, ἐγκράτεια. The nature and influence of the class of virtues included under that term, are here more fully explained in a conversation with Aristippus, and the necessity of their cultivation, especially to the statesman, more definitely pointed out. The course of thought may naturally enough be presented in four divisions:

1. The proper training of one who is destined to rule is presented in a series of interrogations, by which Aristippus is made to acknowledge, although entirely in opposition to his effeminate and luxurious course of life, that he must be inured to hunger, thirst, vigils, and labor, and must abstain from the indulgence of sensual passion (§ 1—7).

2. Aristippus, in answer to the question whether he ranks himself with those who wish to rule or be ruled, abjures any desire for the labor, and trouble, and servitude, to which he thinks a ruler subjects himself, and desires to live in the easiest and pleasantest manner possible (§ 8, 9). Socrates then institutes the inquiry whether the life of the ruler or ruled, masters or servants, is most pleasant (§ 10). Aristippus is willing neither to command nor obey, but desires entire freedom (§ 11). Whereupon Socrates shows that such a life as Aristippus desires, is incompatible with human society, which acknowledges but two classes; and he who withholds obedience to the more powerful will be subjected to them by force (§ 12, 13).

3. In order to avoid the dilemma in which he finds himself, Aristippus proposes not to become the citizen of any State, but to wander from place to place. In answer, Socrates, in addition to other inconveniences

and perils of a migratory life, suggests the ease with which one may be reduced to servitude, and the treatment to which an intemperate servant is naturally subjected (§ 14—16).

4. Aristippus, forced to yield every position which he has taken in opposition to the life of the statesman, brings the objection, that the voluntary submission to privation and toil which he takes upon himself, does not differ at all from that which is involuntary (§ 17). On the contrary, Socrates designates several points of difference: (1) The continuance of voluntary toil, or suffering, or privation, depends upon the will of him who assumes it. (2) The good aimed at and the hope of reward, give a satisfaction to the willing sufferer, to which the one who suffers from compulsion is a stranger (§ 17—19). (3) Whilst effeminacy and luxurious indulgence are conducive neither to soundness of body or mind, on the other hand, vigorous activity for the attainment of every thing good and noble, is conducive to the highest physical and mental excellence. Nothing of value is obtained without labor. So say the poets (§ 20); and the well-known story of Prodicus, "The Choice of Hercules," also teaches, that unless a man strive to be temperate and virtuous he cannot attain to true felicity. The chapter concludes with an admonition to Aristippus to give heed to the instructions of Ἀρετή (§ 21—34).

---

1 Ἐδόκει δέ μοι καὶ τοιαῦτα λέγων προτρέπειν τοὺς συνόντας ἀσκεῖν ἐγκράτειαν πρὸς ἐπιθυμίαν βρωτοῦ καὶ ποτοῦ καὶ λαγνείας καὶ ὕπνου, καὶ ῥίγους καὶ θάλπους καὶ πόνου. Γνοὺς δέ τινα τῶν συνόντων ἀκολαστοτέρως ἔχοντα πρὸς τὰ τοιαῦτα· Εἰπέ μοι, ἔφη, ὦ Ἀρίστιππε, εἰ δέοι σε παιδεύειν παραλαβόντα δύο τῶν νέων, τὸν μέν, ὅπως ἱκανὸς ἔσται ἄρχειν, τὸν δέ, ὅπως μηδ' ἀντιποιήσεται ἀρχῆς, πῶς ἂν ἑκάτερον παιδεύοις; Βούλει σκοπῶμεν, ἀρξάμενοι ἀπὸ τῆς τροφῆς, ὥσπερ ἀπὸ τῶν στοιχείων;—Καὶ ὁ Ἀρίστιππος ἔφη· Δοκεῖ γοῦν μοι ἡ τροφὴ ἀρχὴ εἶναι· οὐδὲ γὰρ ζῴη γ' ἄν τις,
2 εἰ μὴ τρέφοιτο.—Οὐκοῦν τὸ μὲν βούλεσθαι σίτου ἅπτεσθαι, ὅταν ὥρα ἥκῃ, ἀμφοτέροις εἰκὸς παραγίγνεσθαι;—Εἰκὸς γάρ, ἔφη.—Τὸ οὖν προαιρεῖσθαι τὸ κατεπεῖγον μᾶλλον πράττειν ἢ τῇ γαστρὶ χαρίζεσθαι πότερον ἂν αὐτῶν ἐθίζοιμεν;—Τὸν εἰς τὸ ἄρχειν, ἔφη,

νὴ Δία, παιδευόμενον, ὅπως μὴ τὰ τῆς πόλεως ἄπρακτα γίγνηται παρὰ τὴν ἐκείνου ἀρχήν.—Οὐκοῦν, ἔφη, καὶ ὅταν πιεῖν βούλωνται, τὸ δύνασθαι διψῶντα ἀνέχεσθαι τῷ αὐτῷ προςθετέον;—Πάνυ μὲν οὖν, ἔφη.—Τὸ δὲ 3
ὕπνου ἐγκρατῆ εἶναι, ὥςτε δύνασθαι καὶ ὀψὲ κοιμηθῆναι καὶ πρωῒ ἀναστῆναι καὶ ἀγρυπνῆσαι, εἴ τι δέοι, ποτέρῳ ἂν προςθείημεν;—Καὶ τοῦτο, ἔφη, τῷ αὐτῷ. —Τί δέ; ἔφη, τὸ ἀφροδισίων ἐγκρατῆ εἶναι, ὥςτε μὴ διὰ ταῦτα κωλύεσθαι πράττειν, εἴ τι δέοι;—Καὶ τοῦτο, ἔφη, τῷ αὐτῷ.—Τί δέ; τὸ μὴ φεύγειν τοὺς πόνους, ἀλλὰ ἐθελοντὴν ὑπομένειν, ποτέρῳ ἂν προςθείημεν;—Καὶ τοῦτο, ἔφη, τῷ ἄρχειν παιδευομένῳ.—Τί δέ; τὸ μαθεῖν, εἴ τι ἐπιτήδειόν ἐστι μάθημα πρὸς τὸ κρατεῖν τῶν ἀντιπάλων, ποτέρῳ ἂν προςεῖναι μᾶλλον πρέποι;—Πολὺ, νὴ Δί', ἔφη, τῷ ἄρχειν παιδευομένῳ· καὶ γὰρ τῶν ἄλλων οὐδὲν ὄφελος ἄνευ τῶν τοιούτων μαθημάτων.—Οὐκοῦν ὁ οὕτω πεπαιδευμένος 4
ἧττον ἂν δοκεῖ σοι· ὑπὸ τῶν ἀντιπάλων ἢ τὰ λοιπὰ ζῶα ἁλίσκεσθαι; Τούτων γὰρ δήπου τὰ μὲν γαστρὶ δελεαζόμενα, καὶ μάλα ἔνια δυςωπούμενα, ὅμως τῇ ἐπιθυμίᾳ τοῦ φαγεῖν ἀγόμενα πρὸς τὸ δέλεαρ ἁλίσκεται, τὰ δὲ ποτῷ ἐνεδρεύεται.—Πάνυ μὲν οὖν, ἔφη.—Οὐκοῦν καὶ ἄλλα ὑπὸ λαγνείας, οἷον οἵ τε ὄρτυγες καὶ οἱ πέρδικες, πρὸς τὴν τῆς θηλείας φωνὴν τῇ ἐπιθυμίᾳ καὶ τῇ ἐλπίδι τῶν ἀφροδισίων φερόμενοι καὶ ἐξιστάμενοι τοῦ τὰ δεινὰ ἀναλογίζεσθαι τοῖς θηράτροις ἐμπίπτουσι;—Συνέφη καὶ ταῦτα.—Οὐκοῦν δοκεῖ σοι 5
αἰσχρὸν εἶναι ἀνθρώπῳ ταὐτὰ πάσχειν τοῖς ἀφρονεστάτοις τῶν θηρίων; ὥςπερ οἱ μοιχοὶ εἰςέρχονται εἰς τὰς εἱρκτὰς εἰδότες, ὅτι κίνδυνος τῷ μοιχεύοντι ἅ τε ὁ νόμος ἀπειλεῖ παθεῖν καὶ ἐνεδρευθῆναι καὶ ληφθέντα ὑβρισθῆναι· καὶ τηλικούτων μὲν ἐπικειμένων τῷ μοιχεύοντι κακῶν τε καὶ αἰσχρῶν, ὄντων δὲ πολλῶν τῶν ἀπολυσόντων τῆς τῶν ἀφροδισίων ἐπιθυμίας, ὅμως εἰς

τὰ ἐπικίνδυνα φέρεσθαι, ἆρ' οὐκ ἤδη τοῦτο παντά-
6 πασι κακοδαιμονῶντός ἐστιν;—Ἔμοιγε δοκεῖ, ἔφη.—
Τὸ δὲ εἶναι μὲν τὰς ἀναγκαιοτάτας πλείστας πράξεις
τοῖς ἀνθρώποις ἐν ὑπαίθρῳ, οἷον τάς τε πολεμικὰς
καὶ τὰς γεωργικὰς καὶ τῶν ἄλλων οὐ τὰς ἐλαχίστας,
τοὺς δὲ πολλοὺς ἀγυμνάστως ἔχειν πρός τε ψύχη καὶ
θάλπη, οὐ δοκεῖ σοι πολλὴ ἀμέλεια εἶναι;—Συνέφη
καὶ τοῦτο.—Οὐκοῦν δοκεῖ σοι τὸν μέλλοντα ἄρχειν
ἀσκεῖν δεῖν καὶ ταῦτα εὐπετῶς φέρειν;—Πάνυ μὲν
7 οὖν, ἔφη.—Οὐκοῦν, εἰ τοὺς ἐγκρατεῖς τούτων ἁπάν-
των εἰς τοὺς ἀρχικοὺς τάττομεν, τοὺς ἀδυνάτους ταῦτα
ποιεῖν εἰς τοὺς μηδ' ἀντιποιησομένους τοῦ ἄρχειν
τάξομεν;—Συνέφη καὶ τοῦτο.—Τί οὖν; ἐπειδὴ καὶ
τούτων ἑκατέρου τοῦ φύλου τὴν τάξιν οἶσθα, ἤδη ποτ'
ἐπεσκέψω, εἰς ποτέραν τῶν τάξεων τούτων σαυτὸν
8 δικαίως ἂν τάττοις;—Ἔγωγ', ἔφη ὁ Ἀρίστιππος·
καὶ οὐδαμῶς γε τάττω ἐμαυτὸν εἰς τὴν τῶν ἄρχειν
βουλομένων τάξιν. Καὶ γὰρ πάνυ μοι δοκεῖ ἄφρονος
ἀνθρώπου εἶναι τὸ, μεγάλου [ἔργου] ὄντος τοῦ ἑαυτῷ
τὰ δέοντα παρασκευάζειν, μὴ ἀρκεῖν τοῦτο, ἀλλὰ προς-
αναθέσθαι τὸ και τοῖς ἄλλοις πολίταις, ὧν δέονται,
πορίζειν· καὶ ἑαυτῷ μὲν πολλὰ ὧν βούλεται ἐλλεί-
πειν, τῆς δὲ πόλεως προεστῶτα, ἐὰν μὴ πάντα, ὅσα
ἡ πόλις βούλεται, καταπράττῃ, τούτου δίκην ὑπέχειν,
9 τοῦτο πῶς οὐ πολλὴ ἀφροσύνη ἐστί; Καὶ γὰρ ἀξιοῦ-
σιν αἱ πόλεις τοῖς ἄρχουσιν, ὥςπερ ἐγὼ τοῖς οἰκέταις,
χρῆσθαι· ἐγώ τε γὰρ ἀξιῶ τοὺς θεράποντας ἐμοὶ μὲν
ἄφθονα τὰ ἐπιτήδεια παρασκευάζειν, αὐτοὺς δὲ μηδε-
νὸς τούτων ἅπτεσθαι· αἵ τε πόλεις οἴονται χρῆναι
τοὺς ἄρχοντας ἑαυταῖς μὲν ὡς πλεῖστα ἀγαθὰ πορί-
ζειν, αὐτοὺς δὲ πάντων τούτων ἀπέχεσθαι. Ἐγὼ οὖν
τοὺς μὲν βουλομένους πολλὰ πράγματα ἔχειν αὐτοῖς
τε καὶ ἄλλοις παρέχειν οὕτως ἂν παιδεύσας εἰς τοὺς
ἀρχικοὺς καταστήσαιμι· ἐμαυτὸν τοίνυν τάττω εἰς

τοὺς βουλομένους ᾖ ῥᾷστά τε καὶ ἥδιστα βιοτεύειν.
Καὶ ὁ Σωκράτης ἔφη· Βούλει οὖν καὶ τοῦτο σκεψώ- 10
μεθα, πότεροι ἥδιον ζῶσιν, οἱ ἄρχοντες, ἢ οἱ ἀρχό-
μενοι;—Πάνυ μὲν οὖν, ἔφη.—Πρῶτον μὲν τοίνυν
τῶν ἐθνῶν, ὧν ἡμεῖς ἴσμεν, ἐν μὲν τῇ Ἀσίᾳ Πέρσαι
μὲν ἄρχουσιν, ἄρχονται δὲ Σύροι καὶ Φρύγες καὶ Λυ-
δοί· ἐν δὲ τῇ Εὐρώπῃ Σκύθαι μὲν ἄρχουσι, Μαιῶ-
ται δὲ ἄρχονται· ἐν δὲ τῇ Λιβύῃ Καρχηδόνιοι μὲν
ἄρχουσι, Λίβυες δὲ ἄρχονται. Τούτων οὖν ποτέρους
ἥδιον οἴει ζῆν; ἢ τῶν Ἑλλήνων, ἐν οἷς καὶ αὐτὸς εἶ,
πότεροί σοι δοκοῦσιν ἥδιον, οἱ κρατοῦντες, ἢ οἱ κρατ-
ούμενοι ζῆν;—Ἀλλ᾽ ἐγώ τοι, ἔφη ὁ Ἀρίστιππος, 11
οὐδὲ εἰς τὴν δουλείαν αὖ ἐμαυτὸν τάττω· ἀλλ᾽ εἶναί
τίς μοι δοκεῖ μέση τούτων ὁδός, ἣν πειρῶμαι βαδί-
ζειν, οὔτε δι᾽ ἀρχῆς, οὔτε διὰ δουλείας, ἀλλὰ δι᾽ ἐλευ-
θερίας, ἥπερ μάλιστα πρὸς εὐδαιμονίαν ἄγει.—Ἀλλ᾽ 12
εἰ μέντοι, ἔφη ὁ Σωκράτης, ὥσπερ οὔτε δι᾽ ἀρχῆς
οὔτε διὰ δουλείας ἡ ὁδὸς αὕτη φέρει, οὕτως μηδὲ δι᾽
ἀνθρώπων, ἴσως ἄν τι λέγοις· εἰ μέντοι ἐν ἀνθρώποις
ὢν μήτε ἄρχειν ἀξιώσεις μήτε ἄρχεσθαι, μήτε τοὺς
ἄρχοντας ἑκὼν θεραπεύσεις, οἶμαί σε ὁρᾶν, ὡς ἐπί-
στανται οἱ κρείττονες τοὺς ἥττονας καὶ κοινῇ καὶ ἰδίᾳ
κλαίοντας καθιστάντες δούλοις χρῆσθαι· ἢ λανθά- 13
νουσί σε οἱ ἄλλων σπειράντων καὶ φυτευσάντων τόν
τε σῖτον τέμνοντες καὶ δενδροκοποῦντες, καὶ πάντα
τρόπον πολιορκοῦντες τοὺς ἥττονας καὶ μὴ θέλοντας
θεραπεύειν, ἕως ἂν πείσωσιν ἑλέσθαι δουλεύειν ἀντὶ
τοῦ πολεμεῖν τοῖς κρείττοσι; καὶ ἰδίᾳ αὖ οἱ ἀνδρεῖοι
καὶ δυνατοὶ τοὺς ἀνάνδρους καὶ ἀδυνάτους οὐκ οἶσθα
ὅτι καταδουλωσάμενοι καρποῦνται;—Ἀλλ᾽ ἐγώ τοι,
ἔφη, ἵνα μὴ πάσχω ταῦτα, οὐδ᾽ εἰς πολιτείαν ἐμαυ-
τὸν κατακλείω, ἀλλὰ ξένος πανταχοῦ εἰμι. Καὶ ὁ 14
Σωκράτης ἔφη· Τοῦτο μέντοι ἤδη λέγεις δεινὸν πά-
λαισμα· τοὺς γὰρ ξένους, ἐξ οὗ ὅ τε Σίννις καὶ ὁ

Σκείρων καὶ ὁ Προκρούστης ἀπέθανον, οὐδεὶς ἔτι ἀδι-
κεῖ· ἀλλὰ νῦν οἱ μὲν πολιτευόμενοι ἐν ταῖς πατρίσι
καὶ νόμους τίθενται, ἵνα μὴ ἀδικῶνται, καὶ φίλους
πρὸς τοῖς ἀναγκαίοις καλουμένοις ἄλλους κτῶνται
βοηθούς, καὶ ταῖς πόλεσιν ἐρύματα περιβάλλονται,
καὶ ὅπλα κτῶνται, οἷς ἀμύνονται τοὺς ἀδικοῦντας, καὶ
πρὸς τούτοις ἄλλους ἔξωθεν συμμάχους κατασκευ-
15 άζονται· καὶ οἱ μὲν πάντα ταῦτα κεκτημένοι ὅμως
ἀδικοῦνται· σὺ δὲ οὐδὲν μὲν τούτων ἔχων, ἐν δὲ ταῖς
ὁδοῖς, ἔνθα πλεῖστοι ἀδικοῦνται, πολὺν χρόνον διατρί-
βων, εἰς ὁποίαν δ' ἂν πόλιν ἀφίκῃ, τῶν πολιτῶν πάν-
των ἥττων ὤν, καὶ τοιοῦτος, οἵοις μάλιστα ἐπιτίθεν-
ται οἱ βουλόμενοι ἀδικεῖν, ὅμως διὰ τὸ ξένος εἶναι οὐκ
ἂν οἴει ἀδικηθῆναι; ἦ, διότι αἱ πόλεις σοι κηρύττου-
σιν ἀσφάλειαν καὶ προσιόντι καὶ ἀπιόντι, θαῤῥεῖς;
ἢ διότι καὶ δοῦλος ἂν οἴει τοιοῦτος εἶναι, οἷος μηδενὶ
δεσπότῃ λυσιτελεῖν; τίς γὰρ ἂν ἐθέλοι ἄνθρωπον ἐν
οἰκίᾳ ἔχειν πονεῖν μὲν μηδὲν ἐθέλοντα, τῇ δὲ πολυ-
16 τελεστάτῃ διαίτῃ χαίροντα; Σκεψώμεθα δὲ καὶ τοῦτο,
πῶς οἱ δεσπόται τοῖς τοιούτοις οἰκέταις χρῶνται· ἆρα
οὐ τὴν μὲν λαγνείαν αὐτῶν τῷ λιμῷ σωφρονίζουσι;
κλέπτειν δὲ κωλύουσιν ἀποκλείοντες ὅθεν ἄν τι λα-
βεῖν ᾖ; τοῦ δὲ δραπετεύειν δεσμοῖς ἀπείργουσι; τὴν
ἀργίαν δὲ πληγαῖς ἐξαναγκάζουσιν; ἢ σὺ πῶς ποιεῖς,
ὅταν τῶν οἰκετῶν τινα τοιοῦτον ὄντα καταμανθάνῃς;
17 —Κολάζω, ἔφη, πᾶσι κακοῖς, ἕως ἂν δουλεύειν ἀνα-
γκάσω. Ἀλλὰ γάρ, ὦ Σώκρατες, οἱ εἰς τὴν βασιλι-
κὴν τέχνην παιδευόμενοι, ἣν δοκεῖς μοι σὺ νομίζειν
εὐδαιμονίαν εἶναι, τί διαφέρουσι τῶν ἐξ ἀνάγκης κακο-
παθούντων, εἴ γε πεινήσουσι καὶ διψήσουσι καὶ ῥιγώ-
σουσι καὶ ἀγρυπνήσουσι καὶ τἆλλα πάντα μοχθή-
σουσιν ἑκόντες; ἐγὼ μὲν γὰρ οὐκ οἶδ', ὅ τι διαφέρει
τὸ αὐτὸ δέρμα ἑκόντα ἢ ἄκοντα μαστιγοῦσθαι, ἢ ὅλως
τὸ αὐτὸ σῶμα πᾶσι τοῖς τοιούτοις ἑκόντα ἢ ἄκοντα

πολιορκεῖσθαι, ἄλλο γε ἢ ἀφροσύνη πρόσεστι τῷ θέλοντι τὰ λυπηρὰ ὑπομένειν.—Τί δέ, ὦ Ἀρίστιππε, 18
ὁ Σωκράτης ἔφη, οὐ δοκεῖ σοι τῶν τοιούτων διαφέρειν τὰ ἑκούσια τῶν ἀκουσίων, ᾗ ὁ μὲν ἑκὼν πεινῶν φάγοι ἄν, ὁπότε βούλοιτο; καὶ ὁ ἑκὼν διψῶν πίοι, καὶ τἆλλα ὡςαύτως· τῷ δ᾽ ἐξ ἀνάγκης ταῦτα πάσχοντι οὐκ ἔξεστιν, ὁπόταν βούληται, παύεσθαι; ἔπειτα ὁ μὲν ἑκουσίως ταλαιπωρῶν ἐπ᾽ ἀγαθῇ ἐλπίδι πονῶν εὐφραίνεται, οἷον οἱ τὰ θηρία θηρῶντες ἐλπίδι τοῦ λήψεσθαι ἡδέως μοχθοῦσι. Καὶ τὰ μὲν τοιαῦτα 19
ἆθλα τῶν πόνων μικροῦ τινος ἄξιά ἐστι· τοὺς δὲ πονοῦντας, ἵνα φίλους ἀγαθοὺς κτήσωνται, ἢ ὅπως ἐχθροὺς χειρώσωνται, ἢ ἵνα δυνατοὶ γενόμενοι καὶ τοῖς σώμασι καὶ ταῖς ψυχαῖς καὶ τὸν ἑαυτῶν οἶκον καλῶς οἰκῶσι, καὶ τοὺς φίλους εὖ ποιῶσι, καὶ τὴν πατρίδα εὐεργετῶσι, πῶς οὐκ οἴεσθαι χρὴ τούτους καὶ πονεῖν ἡδέως εἰς τὰ τοιαῦτα, καὶ ζῆν εὐφραινομένους, ἀγαμένους μὲν ἑαυτούς, ἐπαινουμένους δὲ καὶ ζηλουμένους ὑπὸ τῶν ἄλλων; Ἔτι δὲ αἱ μὲν ῥᾳδιουρ- 20
γίαι καὶ ἐκ τοῦ παραχρῆμα ἡδοναὶ οὔτε σώματι εὐεξίαν ἱκαναί εἰσιν ἐνεργάζεσθαι, ὥς φασιν οἱ γυμνασταί, οὔτε ψυχῇ ἐπιστήμην ἀξιόλογον οὐδεμίαν ἐμποιοῦσιν· αἱ δὲ διὰ καρτερίας ἐπιμέλειαι τῶν καλῶν τε κἀγαθῶν ἔργων ἐξικνεῖσθαι ποιοῦσιν, ὥς φασιν οἱ ἀγαθοὶ ἄνδρες· λέγει δέ που καὶ Ἡσίοδος·

Τὴν μὲν γὰρ κακότητα καὶ ἰλαδὸν ἔστιν ἑλέσθαι
Ῥηϊδίως· λείη μὲν ὁδός, μάλα δ᾽ ἐγγύθι ναίει.
Τῆς δ᾽ ἀρετῆς ἱδρῶτα θεοὶ προπάροιθεν ἔθηκαν
Ἀθάνατοι· μακρὸς δὲ καὶ ὄρθιος οἶμος ἐς αὐτὴν
Καὶ τρηχὺς τὸ πρῶτον· ἐπὴν δ᾽ εἰς ἄκρον ἵκηται,
Ῥηϊδίη δὴ ἔπειτα πέλει, χαλεπή περ ἐοῦσα.

Μαρτυρεῖ δὲ καὶ Ἐπίχαρμος ἐν τῷδε·

Τῶν πόνων πωλοῦσιν ἡμῖν πάντα τἀγάθ᾽ οἱ θεοί.

Καὶ ἐν ἄλλῳ δὲ τόπῳ φησίν·

Ὦ πονηρέ, μὴ τὰ μαλακὰ μώεο, μὴ τὰ σκλήρ' ἔχῃς.

21 Καὶ Πρόδικος δὲ ὁ σοφὸς ἐν τῷ συγγράμματι τῷ περὶ τοῦ Ἡρακλέους, ὅπερ δὴ καὶ πλείστοις ἐπιδείκνυται, ὡσαύτως περὶ τῆς ἀρετῆς ἀποφαίνεται ὧδέ πως λέγων, ὅσα ἐγὼ μέμνημαι· φησὶ γὰρ Ἡρακλέα, ἐπεὶ ἐκ παίδων εἰς ἥβην ὡρμᾶτο, ἐν ᾗ οἱ νέοι ἤδη αὐτοκράτορες γιγνόμενοι δηλοῦσιν, εἴτε τὴν δι' ἀρετῆς ὁδὸν τρέψονται ἐπὶ τὸν βίον, εἴτε τὴν διὰ κακίας, ἐξελθόντα εἰς ἡσυχίαν καθῆσθαι, ἀποροῦντα, ὁποτέ-
22 ραν τῶν ὁδῶν τράπηται· καὶ φανῆναι αὐτῷ δύο γυναῖκας προϊέναι μεγάλας, τὴν μὲν ἑτέραν εὐπρεπῆ τε ἰδεῖν καὶ ἐλευθέριον, φύσει κεκοσμημένην τὸ μὲν σῶμα καθαρότητι, τὰ δὲ ὄμματα αἰδοῖ, τὸ δὲ σχῆμα σωφροσύνῃ, ἐσθῆτι δὲ λευκῇ· τὴν δ' ἑτέραν τεθραμμένην μὲν εἰς πολυσαρκίαν τε καὶ ἁπαλότητα, κεκαλλωπισμένην δὲ τὸ μὲν χρῶμα, ὥστε λευκοτέραν τε καὶ ἐρυθροτέραν τοῦ ὄντος δοκεῖν φαίνεσθαι, τὸ δὲ σχῆμα, ὥστε δοκεῖν ὀρθοτέραν τῆς φύσεως εἶναι, τὰ δὲ ὄμματα ἔχειν ἀναπεπταμένα, ἐσθῆτα δέ, ἐξ ἧς ἂν μάλιστα ὥρα διαλάμποι, κατασκοπεῖσθαι δὲ θαμὰ ἑαυτήν, ἐπισκοπεῖν δὲ καί, εἴ τις ἄλλος αὐτὴν θεᾶται, πολλάκις δὲ καὶ εἰς τὴν ἑαυτῆς σκιὰν ἀποβλέ-
23 πειν. Ὡς δ' ἐγένοντο πλησιαίτερον τοῦ Ἡρακλέους, τὴν μὲν πρόσθεν ῥηθεῖσαν ἰέναι τὸν αὐτὸν τρόπον, τὴν δ' ἑτέραν φθάσαι βουλομένην προσδραμεῖν τῷ Ἡρακλεῖ καὶ εἰπεῖν· Ὁρῶ σε, ὦ Ἡράκλεις, ἀποροῦντα, ποίαν ὁδὸν ἐπὶ τὸν βίον τράπῃ· ἐὰν οὖν ἐμὲ φίλην ποιησάμενος, ἐπὶ τὴν ἡδίστην τε καὶ ῥᾴστην ὁδὸν ἄξω σε, καὶ τῶν μὲν τερπνῶν οὐδενὸς ἄγευστος
24 ἔσῃ, τῶν δὲ χαλεπῶν ἄπειρος διαβιώσῃ. Πρῶτον μὲν γὰρ οὐ πολέμων οὐδὲ πραγμάτων φροντιεῖς, ἀλλὰ σκοπούμενος διέσῃ, τί ἂν κεχαρισμένον ἢ σιτίον ἢ

ποτὸν εὕροις, ἢ τί ἂν ἰδὼν ἢ τί ἀκούσας τερφθείης,
ἢ τίνων ὀσφραινόμενος ἢ ἁπτόμενος ἡσθείης, τίσι δὲ
παιδικοῖς ὁμιλῶν μάλιστ' ἂν εὐφρανθείης, καὶ πῶς ἂν
μαλακώτατα καθεύδοις, καὶ πῶς ἂν ἀπονώτατα τού-
των πάντων τυγχάνοις. Ἐὰν δὲ ποτε γένηταί τις 25
ὑποψία σπάνεως ἀφ' ὧν ἔσται ταῦτα, οὐ φόβος, μή
σε ἀγάγω ἐπὶ τὸ πονοῦντα καὶ ταλαιπωροῦντα τῷ
σώματι καὶ τῇ ψυχῇ ταῦτα πορίζεσθαι· ἀλλ' οἷς ἂν
οἱ ἄλλοι ἐργάζωνται, τούτοις σὺ χρήσῃ, οὐδενὸς ἀπε-
χόμενος, ὅθεν ἂν δυνατὸν ᾖ τι κερδᾶναι· πανταχόθεν
γὰρ ὠφελεῖσθαι τοῖς ἐμοὶ ξυνοῦσιν ἐξουσίαν ἔγωγε
παρέχω. Καὶ ὁ Ἡρακλῆς ἀκούσας ταῦτα· Ὦ γύναι, 26
ἔφη, ὄνομα δέ σοι τί ἐστιν; Ἡ δέ· Οἱ μὲν ἐμοὶ
φίλοι, ἔφη, καλοῦσί με Εὐδαιμονίαν, οἱ δὲ μισοῦντές
με ὑποκοριζόμενοι ὀνομάζουσί με Κακίαν. Καὶ ἐν 27
τούτῳ ἡ ἑτέρα γυνὴ προσελθοῦσα εἶπε· Καὶ ἐγὼ ἥκω
πρὸς σέ, ὦ Ἡράκλεις, εἰδυῖα τοὺς γεννήσαντάς σε,
καὶ τὴν φύσιν τὴν σὴν ἐν τῇ παιδείᾳ καταμαθοῦσα·
ἐξ ὧν ἐλπίζω, εἰ τὴν πρὸς ἐμὲ ὁδὸν τράποιο, σφόδρ'
ἄν σε τῶν καλῶν καὶ σεμνῶν ἐργάτην ἀγαθὸν γενέ-
σθαι, καὶ ἐμὲ ἔτι πολὺ ἐντιμοτέραν καὶ ἐπ' ἀγαθοῖς
διαπρεπεστέραν φανῆναι· οὐκ ἐξαπατήσω δέ σε προ-
οιμίοις ἡδονῆς, ἀλλ', ᾗπερ οἱ θεοὶ διέθεσαν, τὰ ὄντα
διηγήσομαι μετ' ἀληθείας. Τῶν γὰρ ὄντων ἀγαθῶν 28
καὶ καλῶν οὐδὲν ἄνευ πόνου καὶ ἐπιμελείας θεοὶ δι-
δόασιν ἀνθρώποις· ἀλλ' εἴτε τοὺς θεοὺς ἵλεως εἶναί
σοι βούλει, θεραπευτέον τοὺς θεούς· εἴτε ὑπὸ φίλων
ἐθέλεις ἀγαπᾶσθαι, τοὺς φίλους εὐεργετητέον· εἴτε
ὑπό τινος πόλεως ἐπιθυμεῖς τιμᾶσθαι, τὴν πόλιν
ὠφελητέον· εἴτε ὑπὸ τῆς Ἑλλάδος πάσης ἀξιοῖς ἐπ'
ἀρετῇ θαυμάζεσθαι, τὴν Ἑλλάδα πειρατέον εὖ ποιεῖν·
εἴτε γῆν βούλει σοι καρποὺς ἀφθόνους φέρειν, τὴν
γῆν θεραπευτέον· εἴτε ἀπὸ βοσκημάτων οἴει δεῖν
πλουτίζεσθαι, τῶν βοσκημάτων ἐπιμελητέον· εἴτε διὰ

πολέμου ὁρμᾷς αὔξεσθαι, καὶ βούλει δύνασθαι τους τε φίλους ἐλευθεροῦν καὶ τοὺς ἐχθροὺς χειροῦσθαι, τὰς πολεμικὰς τέχνας αὐτάς τε παρὰ τῶν ἐπισταμένων μαθητέον, καὶ ὅπως αὐταῖς δεῖ χρῆσθαι ἀσκητέον· εἰ δὲ καὶ τῷ σώματι βούλει δυνατὸς εἶναι, τῇ γνώμῃ ὑπηρετεῖν ἐθιστέον τὸ σῶμα καὶ γυμναστέον
29 σὺν πόνοις καὶ ἱδρῶτι. Καὶ ἡ Κακία ὑπολαβοῦσα εἶπεν, ὥς φησι Πρόδικος· Ἐννοεῖς, ὦ Ἡράκλεις, ὡς χαλεπὴν καὶ μακρὰν ὁδὸν ἐπὶ τὰς εὐφροσύνας ἡ γυνή σοι αὕτη διηγεῖται; ἐγὼ δὲ ῥᾳδίαν καὶ βραχεῖαν ὁδὸν
30 ἐπὶ τὴν εὐδαιμονίαν ἄξω σε. Καὶ ἡ Ἀρετὴ εἶπεν· Ὦ τλῆμον, τί δὲ σὺ ἀγαθὸν ἔχεις; ἢ τί ἡδὺ οἶσθα, μηδὲν τούτων ἕνεκα πράττειν ἐθέλουσα; ἥτις οὐδὲ τὴν τῶν ἡδέων ἐπιθυμίαν ἀναμένεις, ἀλλά, πρὶν ἐπιθυμῆσαι, πάντων ἐμπίπλασαι, πρὶν μὲν πεινῆν ἐσθίουσα, πρὶν δὲ διψῆν πίνουσα, [καὶ] ἵνα μὲν ἡδέως φάγῃς, ὀψοποιοὺς μηχανωμένη, ἵνα δὲ ἡδέως πίνῃς, οἴνους τε πολυτελεῖς παρασκευάζῃ, καὶ τοῦ θέρους χιόνα περιθέουσα ζητεῖς· ἵνα δὲ καθυπνώσῃς ἡδέως, οὐ μόνον τὰς στρωμνὰς μαλακάς, ἀλλὰ καὶ τὰς κλίνας καὶ τὰ ὑπόβαθρα ταῖς κλίναις παρασκευάζῃ· οὐ γὰρ διὰ τὸ πονεῖν, ἀλλὰ διὰ τὸ μηδὲν ἔχειν, ὅ τι ποιῇς, ὕπνου ἐπιθυμεῖς· τὰ δὲ ἀφροδίσια πρὸ τοῦ δέεσθαι ἀναγκάζεις, πάντα μηχανωμένη, καὶ γυναιξὶ καὶ ἀνδράσι χρωμένη· οὕτω γὰρ παιδεύεις τοὺς ἑαυτῆς φίλους, τῆς μὲν νυκτὸς ὑβρίζουσα, τῆς δ' ἡμέρας
31 τὸ χρησιμώτατον κατακοιμίζουσα. Ἀθάνατος δὲ οὖσα ἐκ θεῶν μὲν ἀπέρριψαι, ὑπὸ δὲ ἀνθρώπων ἀγαθῶν ἀτιμάζῃ· τοῦ δὲ πάντων ἡδίστου ἀκούσματος, ἐπαίνου ἑαυτῆς, ἀνήκοος εἶ, καὶ τοῦ πάντων ἡδίστου θεάματος ἀθέατος· οὐδὲν γὰρ πώποτε σεαυτῆς ἔργον καλὸν τεθέασαι. Τίς δ' ἄν σοι λεγούσῃ τι πιστεύσειε; τίς δ' ἂν δεομένῃ τινὸς ἐπαρκέσειεν; ἢ τίς ἂν εὖ φρονῶν τοῦ σοῦ θιάσου τολμήσειεν εἶναι; οἳ νέοι μὲν ὄντες

τοῖς σώμασιν ἀδύνατοί εἰσι, πρεσβύτεροι δὲ γενόμενοι
ταῖς ψυχαῖς ἀνόητοι, ἀπόνως μὲν λιπαροὶ διὰ νεότη-
τος τρεφόμενοι, ἐπιπόνως δὲ αὐχμηροὶ διὰ γήρως περ-
ῶντες, τοῖς μὲν πεπραγμένοις αἰσχυνόμενοι, τοῖς δὲ
πραττομένοις βαρυνόμενοι, τὰ μὲν ἡδέα ἐν τῇ νεότητι
διαδραμόντες, τὰ δὲ χαλεπὰ εἰς τὸ γῆρας ἀποθέμενοι.
Ἐγὼ δὲ σύνειμι μὲν θεοῖς, σύνειμι δὲ ἀνθρώποις τοῖς 32
ἀγαθοῖς· ἔργον δὲ καλὸν οὔτε θεῖον οὔτε ἀνθρώπινον
χωρὶς ἐμοῦ γίγνεται· τιμῶμαι δὲ μάλιστα πάντων
καὶ παρὰ θεοῖς καὶ παρὰ ἀνθρώποις, οἷς προςήκει,
ἀγαπητὴ μὲν συνεργὸς τεχνίταις, πιστὴ δὲ φύλαξ
οἴκων δεσπόταις, εὐμενὴς δὲ παραστάτις οἰκέταις,
ἀγαθὴ δὲ συλλήπτρια τῶν ἐν εἰρήνῃ πόνων, βεβαία
δὲ τῶν ἐν πολέμῳ σύμμαχος ἔργων, ἀρίστη δὲ φιλίας
κοινωνός. Ἔστι δὲ τοῖς μὲν ἐμοῖς φίλοις ἡδεῖα μὲν 33
καὶ ἀπράγμων σίτων καὶ ποτῶν ἀπόλαυσις· ἀνέχον-
ται γὰρ, ἕως ἂν ἐπιθυμήσωσιν αὐτῶν. Ὕπνος δ'
αὐτοῖς πάρεστιν ἡδίων ἢ τοῖς ἀμόχθοις, καὶ οὔτε ἀπο-
λείποντες αὐτὸν ἄχθονται, οὔτε διὰ τοῦτον μεθιᾶσι
τὰ δέοντα πράττειν. Καὶ οἱ μὲν νέοι τοῖς τῶν πρεσ-
βυτέρων ἐπαίνοις χαίρουσιν, οἱ δὲ γεραίτεροι ταῖς
τῶν νέων τιμαῖς ἀγάλλονται· καὶ ἡδέως μὲν τῶν πα-
λαιῶν πράξεων μέμνηνται, εὖ δὲ τὰς παρούσας ἥδον-
ται πράττοντες, δι' ἐμὲ φίλοι μὲν θεοῖς ὄντες, ἀγα-
πητοὶ δὲ φίλοις, τίμιοι δὲ πατρίσιν· ὅταν δ' ἔλθῃ
τὸ πεπρωμένον τέλος, οὐ μετὰ λήθης ἄτιμοι κεῖνται,
ἀλλὰ μετὰ μνήμης τὸν ἀεὶ χρόνον ὑμνούμενοι θάλ-
λουσι. Τοιαῦτά σοι, ὦ παῖ τοκέων ἀγαθῶν Ἡρά-
κλεις, ἔξεστι διαπονησαμένῳ τὴν μακαριστοτάτην εὐ-
δαιμονίαν κεκτῆσθαι. Οὕτω πως διώκει Πρόδικος 34
τὴν ὑπ' Ἀρετῆς Ἡρακλέους παίδευσιν, ἐκόσμησε μέν-
τοι τὰς γνώμας ἔτι μεγαλειοτέροις ῥήμασιν ἢ ἐγὼ
νῦν. Σοὶ δ' οὖν ἄξιον, ὦ Ἀρίστιππε, τούτων ἐνθυ-

μουμένῳ πειρᾶσθαί τι καὶ τῶν εἰς τὸν μέλλοντα χρονον τοῦ βίου φροντίζειν.

CHAPTER II.

ARGUMENT.

The remaining chapters of Book II., which treat of filial piety (Chap. II.), the relation of brothers (Chap. III.), and of friendship (Chap. IV.—IX.), are founded on Book I. Chap. II. § 49—55, and contain a more complete defence of Socrates against the three points of accusation but slightly examined there.

The present chapter contains a conversation with his son Lamprocles, who had become much embittered towards his mother Xantippe, on account of her severity. The strong regard for the parental relation, which Socrates felt and inculcated, is here made evident. The course of thought is somewhat as follows:

1. Those, first, are justly accused of ingratitude, who, having received favors, do not, when they are able, make a return. Secondly, ingratitude is injustice (§ 1, 2). Thirdly, ingratitude is criminal in proportion to the magnitude of favors received. But the greatest favors are bestowed by parents upon children, especially by the mother (§ 3—6). Acerbity of temper or severity of treatment on the part of the mother, does not excuse a want of filial regard and respect; for the recollection of the sufferings, toil, and anxiety of the mother for the child, especially during the early period of his existence, and the certainty that her severity does not arise from ill-will, but from the highest regard to his well-being, should secure from him a willing obedience, and prompt and hearty service (§ 7—12).

2. To these strongest and subjective arguments for filial piety, an objective one is added: The State recognizes the sacredness of the obligation of children to parents, by punishing its violation; and all men despise the disobedient and ungrateful child (§ 13, 14).

---

1 *Αἰσθόμενος δέ ποτε Λαμπροκλέα, τὸν πρεσβύτατον υἱὸν ἑαυτοῦ, πρὸς τὴν μητέρα χαλεπαίνοντα· Εἰπέ μοι, ἔφη, ὦ παῖ, οἶσθά τινας ἀνθρώπους ἀχαρίστους*

καλουμένους;—Καὶ μάλα, ἔφη ὁ νεανίσκος.—Καταμεμάθηκας οὖν τοὺς τί ποιοῦντας τὸ ὄνομα τοῦτο ἀποκαλοῦσιν;—Ἔγωγε, ἔφη· τοὺς γὰρ εὖ παθόντας, ὅταν δυνάμενοι χάριν ἀποδοῦναι μὴ ἀποδῶσιν, ἀχαρίστους καλοῦσιν.—Οὐκοῦν δοκοῦσί σοι ἐν τοῖς ἀδίκοις καταλογίζεσθαι τοὺς ἀχαρίστους;—Ἔμοιγε, ἔφη.—
Ἤδη δέ ποτ' ἐσκέψω, εἰ ἄρα, ὥσπερ τὸ ἀνδραποδί- 2
ζεσθαι τοὺς μὲν φίλους ἄδικον εἶναι δοκεῖ, τοὺς δὲ πολεμίους δίκαιον, καὶ τὸ ἀχαριστεῖν πρὸς μὲν τοὺς φίλους ἄδικόν ἐστι, πρὸς δὲ τοὺς πολεμίους δίκαιον;—Καὶ μάλα, ἔφη· καὶ δοκεῖ μοι, ὑφ' οὗ ἄν τις εὖ παθὼν, εἴτε φίλου εἴτε πολεμίου, μὴ πειρᾶται χάριν ἀπο-
διδόναι, ἄδικος εἶναι.—Οὐκοῦν, εἴ γε οὕτως ἔχει τοῦτο, 3
εἰλικρινής τις ἂν εἴη ἀδικία ἡ ἀχαριστία;—Συνωμολόγει.—Οὐκοῦν, ὅσῳ ἄν τις μείζω ἀγαθὰ παθὼν μὴ ἀποδιδῷ χάριν, τοσούτῳ ἀδικώτερος ἂν εἴη;—Συνέφη καὶ τοῦτο.—Τίνας οὖν, ἔφη, ὑπὸ τίνων εὕροιμεν ἂν μείζονα εὐεργετημένους ἢ παῖδας ὑπὸ γονέων; οὓς οἱ γονεῖς ἐκ μὲν οὐκ ὄντων ἐποίησαν εἶναι, τοσαῦτα δὲ καλὰ ἰδεῖν καὶ τοσούτων ἀγαθῶν μετασχεῖν, ὅσα οἱ θεοὶ παρέχουσι τοῖς ἀνθρώποις· ἃ δὴ καὶ οὕτως ἡμῖν δοκεῖ παντὸς ἄξια εἶναι, ὥστε πάντες τὸ καταλιπεῖν αὐτὰ πάντων μάλιστα φεύγομεν· καὶ αἱ πόλεις ἐπὶ τοῖς μεγίστοις ἀδικήμασι ζημίαν θάνατον πεποιήκασιν, ὡς οὐκ ἂν μείζονος κακοῦ φόβῳ τὴν ἀδικίαν παύσον-
τες. Καὶ μὴν οὐ τῶν γε ἀφροδισίων ἕνεκα παιδο- 4
ποιεῖσθαι τοὺς ἀνθρώπους ὑπολαμβάνεις, ἐπεὶ τούτου γε τῶν ἀπολυσόντων μεσταὶ μὲν αἱ ὁδοί, μεστὰ δὲ τὰ οἰκήματα· φανεροὶ δ' ἐσμὲν καὶ σκοπούμενοι, ἐξ ὁποίων ἂν γυναικῶν βέλτιστα ἡμῖν τέκνα γένοιτο, αἷς συνελ-
θόντες τεκνοποιούμεθα. Καὶ ὁ μέν γε ἀνὴρ τήν τε 5
συντεκνοποιήσουσαν ἑαυτῷ τρέφει, καὶ τοῖς μέλλουσιν ἔσεσθαι παισὶ προπαρασκευάζει πάντα, ὅσα ἂν οἴηται συνοίσειν αὐτοῖς πρὸς τὸν βίον, καὶ ταῦτα ὡς ἂν

δύνηται πλεῖστα· ἡ δὲ γυνὴ ὑποδεξαμένη τε φέρει τὸ
φορτίον τοῦτο, βαρυνομένη τε καὶ κινδυνεύουσα περὶ
τοῦ βίου, καὶ μεταδιδοῦσα τῆς τροφῆς ἧς καὶ αὐτὴ
τρέφεται, καὶ σὺν πολλῷ πόνῳ διενέγκασα καὶ τεκοῦσα,
τρέφει τε καὶ ἐπιμελεῖται, οὔτε προπεπονθυῖα οὐδὲν
ἀγαθὸν, οὔτε γιγνῶσκον τὸ βρέφος ὑφ' ὅτου εὖ πά-
σχει, οὐδὲ σημαίνειν δυνάμενον, ὅτου δεῖται, ἀλλ' αὐτὴ
στοχαζομένη τά τε συμφέροντα καὶ κεχαρισμένα πει-
ρᾶται ἐκπληροῦν, καὶ τρέφει πολὺν χρόνον καὶ ἡμέρας
καὶ νυκτὸς ὑπομένουσα πονεῖν, οὐκ εἰδυῖα, τίνα τούτων
6 χάριν ἀπολήψεται. Καὶ οὐκ ἀρκεῖ θρέψαι μόνον, ἀλ-
λὰ καί, ἐπειδὰν δόξωσιν ἱκανοὶ εἶναι οἱ παῖδες μαν-
θάνειν τι, ἃ μὲν ἂν αὐτοὶ ἔχωσιν οἱ γονεῖς ἀγαθὰ
πρὸς τὸν βίον, διδάσκουσιν· ἃ δ' ἂν οἴωνται ἄλλον
ἱκανώτερον εἶναι διδάξαι, πέμπουσι πρὸς τοῦτον δα-
πανῶντες, καὶ ἐπιμελοῦνται πάντα ποιοῦντες, ὅπως οἱ
7 παῖδες αὐτοῖς γένωνται ὡς δυνατὸν βέλτιστοι.—Πρὸς
ταῦτα ὁ νεανίσκος ἔφη· Ἀλλά τοι, εἰ καὶ πάντα ταῦτα
πεποίηκε καὶ ἄλλα τούτων πολλαπλάσια, οὐδεὶς ἂν
δύναιτο αὐτῆς ἀνασχέσθαι τὴν χαλεπότητα.—Καὶ ὁ
Σωκράτης· Πότερα δὲ οἴει, ἔφη, θηρίου ἀγριότητα δυς-
φορωτέραν εἶναι, ἢ μητρός;—Ἐγὼ μὲν οἶμαι, ἔφη,
τῆς μητρός, τῆς γε τοιαύτης.—Ἤδη πώποτε, οὖν ἡ
δακοῦσα κακόν τί σοι ἔδωκεν ἢ λακτίσασα, οἷα ὑπὸ
8 θηρίων ἤδη πολλοὶ ἔπαθον;—Ἀλλά, νὴ Δία, ἔφη,
λέγει, ἃ οὐκ ἄν τις ἐπὶ τῷ βίῳ παντὶ βούλοιτο ἀκοῦ-
σαι.—Σὺ δὲ πόσα, ἔφη ὁ Σωκράτης, οἴει ταύτῃ δυς-
άνεκτα καὶ τῇ φωνῇ καὶ τοῖς ἔργοις ἐκ παιδίου δυς-
κολαίνων καὶ ἡμέρας καὶ νυκτὸς πράγματα παρασχεῖν,
πόσα δὲ λυπῆσαι κάμνων;—Ἀλλ' οὐδεπώποτε αὐτήν,
ἔφη, οὔτ' εἶπα οὔτ' ἐποίησα οὐδέν, ἐφ' ᾧ ᾐσχύνθη.—
9 Τί δ'; οἴει, ἔφη, χαλεπώτερον εἶναί σοι ἀκούειν ὧν
αὐτὴ λέγει, ἢ τοῖς ὑποκριταῖς, ὅταν ἐν ταῖς τραγῳδίαις
ἀλλήλους τὰ ἔσχατα λέγωσιν;—Ἀλλ', οἶμαι, ἐπειδὴ

οὐκ οἴονται τῶν λεγόντων οὔτε τὸν ἐλέγχοντα ἐλέγ-
χειν, ἵνα ζημιώσῃ, οὔτε τὸν ἀπειλοῦντα ἀπειλεῖν, ἵνα
κακόν τι ποιήσῃ, ῥᾳδίως φέρουσι.—Σὺ δ' εὖ εἰδὼς,
ὡς, ὅ τι λέγει σοι ἡ μήτηρ, οὐ μόνον οὐδὲν κακὸν
νοοῦσα λέγει, ἀλλὰ καὶ βουλομένη σοι ἀγαθὰ εἶναι,
ὅσα οὐδενὶ ἄλλῳ, χαλεπαίνεις; ἢ νομίζεις κακόνουν
τὴν μητέρα σοι εἶναι;—Οὐ δῆτα, ἔφη, τοῦτό γε οὐκ
οἴομαι.—Καὶ ὁ Σωκράτης· Οὐκοῦν, ἔφη, σὺ ταύτην, 10
εὔνουν τέ σοι οὖσαν καὶ ἐπιμελομένην, ὡς μάλιστα
δύναται, κάμνοντος, ὅπως ὑγιαίνῃς τε καὶ ὅπως τῶν
ἐπιτηδείων μηδενὸς ἐνδεὴς ἔσῃ, καὶ πρὸς τούτοις πολλὰ
τοῖς θεοῖς εὐχομένην ἀγαθὰ ὑπὲρ σοῦ, καὶ εὐχὰς ἀπο-
διδοῦσαν, χαλεπὴν εἶναι φῄς; ἐγὼ μὲν οἶμαι, εἰ τοι-
αύτην μὴ δύνασαι φέρειν μητέρα, τἀγαθά σε οὐ
δύνασθαι φέρειν. Εἰπὲ δέ μοι, ἔφη, πότερον ἄλλον 11
τινὰ οἴει δεῖν θεραπεύειν, ἢ παρεσκεύασαι μηδενὶ ἀν-
θρώπων πειρᾶσθαι ἀρέσκειν, μηδ' ἕπεσθαι, μηδὲ
πείθεσθαι μήτε στρατηγῷ μήτε ἄλλῳ ἄρχοντι;—
Ναὶ μὰ Δί' ἔγωγε, ἔφη.—Οὐκοῦν, ἔφη ὁ Σωκράτης, 12
καὶ τῷ γείτονι βούλει σὺ ἀρέσκειν, ἵνα σοι καὶ πῦρ
ἐναύῃ, ὅταν τούτου δέῃ, καὶ ἀγαθοῦ τέ σοι γίγνηται
συλλήπτωρ, καί, ἄν τι σφαλλόμενος τύχῃς, εὐνοϊκῶς
ἐγγύθεν βοηθῇ σοι;—Ἔγωγε, ἔφη.—Τί δέ; συνο-
δοιπόρον ἢ σύμπλουν, ἢ εἴ τῳ ἄλλῳ ἐντυγχάνοις, οὐ-
δὲν ἄν σοι διαφέροι φίλον ἢ ἐχθρὸν γενέσθαι, ἢ καὶ
τῆς παρὰ τούτων εὐνοίας οἴει δεῖν ἐπιμελεῖσθαι;—
Ἔγωγε, ἔφη.—Εἶτα τούτων μὲν ἐπιμελεῖσθαι παρε- 13
σκεύασαι, τὴν δὲ μητέρα τὴν πάντων μάλιστά σε
φιλοῦσαν οὐκ οἴει δεῖν θεραπεύειν; οὐκ οἶσθ', ὅτι
καὶ ἡ πόλις ἄλλης μὲν ἀχαριστίας οὐδεμιᾶς ἐπιμε-
λεῖται, οὐδὲ δικάζει, ἀλλὰ περιορᾷ τοὺς εὖ πεπονθότας
χάριν οὐκ ἀποδιδόντας, ἐὰν δέ τις γονέας μὴ θερα-
πεύῃ, τούτῳ δίκην τε ἐπιτίθησι, καὶ ἀποδοκιμάζουσα
οὐκ ἐᾷ ἄρχειν τοῦτον, ὡς οὔτε ἂν τὰ ἱερὰ εὐσεβῶς

θυόμενα ὑπὲρ τῆς πόλεως, τούτου θύοντος, οὔτε ἄλλο καλῶς καὶ δικαίως οὐδὲν ἂν τούτου πράξαντος; Καὶ νὴ Δία ἐάν τις τῶν γονέων τελευτησάντων τοὺς τάφους μὴ κοσμῇ, καὶ τοῦτο ἐξετάζει ἡ πόλις ἐν ταῖς τῶν
14 ἀρχόντων δοκιμασίαις. Σὺ οὖν, ὦ παῖ, ἂν σωφρονῇς, τοὺς μὲν θεοὺς παραιτήσῃ συγγνώμονάς σοι εἶναι, εἴ τι παρημέληκας τῆς μητρός, μή σε καὶ οὗτοι νομίσαντες ἀχάριστον εἶναι οὐκ ἐθέλωσιν εὖ ποιεῖν· τοὺς δὲ ἀνθρώπους αὖ φυλάξῃ, μή σε αἰσθόμενοι τῶν γονέων ἀμελοῦντα πάντες ἀτιμάσωσιν, εἶτα ἐν ἐρημίᾳ φίλων ἀναφανῇς· εἰ γάρ σε ὑπολάβοιεν πρὸς τοὺς γονεῖς ἀχάριστον εἶναι, οὐδεὶς ἂν νομίσειεν εὖ σε ποιήσας χάριν ἀπολήψεσθαι.

CHAPTER III.

ARGUMENT.

Socrates perceiving that two brothers, the elder Chaerephon and the younger Chaerecrates, were at variance with each other, admonished the latter to seek a reconciliation. He suggests the following motives and inducements to fraternal concord:

1. A brother ought to be valued above all wealth (§ 1); since possessions are insecure and their enjoyment uncertain, without companions and friends; and the best friend is a brother, who is so by a natural relation, and on account of whom one receives honor from men, and is less exposed to their hostile assaults (§ 2—4).

2. It follows, then, since a brother is to be so highly valued, that even though his alienation and hostility be great, it should not cause hatred, but rather induce one, laying aside all angry feeling, to seek to appease him (§ 5—9). The means of reconciliation are easy; by first exhibiting fraternal affection and kindness, a reciprocation of it will be secured (§ 10—13). The advances, Socrates teaches Chaerecrates, should be on his part (§ 14—16). You can rely, he adds, upon the honorable and noble feeling of your brother for success (§ 16—18).

3. Brothers ought not to be at variance with one another; for as the members of the body, which are by nature in pairs, are for mutual aid, so are brothers, who, if friendly, although far separated, are still able from a natural affinity to be of special service to each other (§ 18, 19).

Χαιρεφῶντα δέ ποτε καὶ Χαιρεκράτην, ἀδελφὼ μὲν 1
ὄντε ἀλλήλοιν, ἑαυτῷ δὲ γνωρίμω, αἰσθόμενος διαφε-
ρομένω, ἰδὼν τὸν Χαιρεκράτην. Εἰπέ μοι, ἔφη, ὦ Χαι-
ρέκρατες, οὐ δήπου καὶ σὺ εἶ τῶν τοιούτων ἀνθρώπων,
οἳ χρησιμώτερον νομίζουσι χρήματα ἢ ἀδελφούς; καὶ
ταῦτα τῶν μὲν ἀφρόνων ὄντων, τοῦ δὲ φρονίμου, καὶ
τῶν μὲν βοηθείας δεομένων, τοῦ δὲ βοηθεῖν δυναμένου,
καὶ πρὸς τούτοις τῶν μὲν πλειόνων ὑπαρχόντων, τοῦ δὲ
ἑνός. Θαυμαστὸν δὲ καὶ τοῦτο, εἴ τις τοὺς μὲν ἀδελ- 2
φοὺς ζημίαν ἡγεῖται, ὅτι οὐ καὶ τὰ τῶν ἀδελφῶν
κέκτηται, τοὺς δὲ πολίτας οὐχ ἡγεῖται ζημίαν, ὅτι οὐ
καὶ τὰ τῶν πολιτῶν ἔχει, ἀλλ' ἐνταῦθα μὲν δύναται
λογίζεσθαι, ὅτι κρεῖττον σὺν πολλοῖς οἰκοῦντα ἀσφα-
λῶς ἀρκοῦντα ἔχειν, ἢ μόνον διαιτώμενον τὰ τῶν
πολιτῶν ἐπικινδύνως πάντα κεκτῆσθαι, ἐπὶ δὲ τῶν
ἀδελφῶν τὸ αὐτὸ τοῦτο ἀγνοοῦσι. Καὶ οἰκέτας μὲν οἱ 3
δυνάμενοι ὠνοῦνται, ἵνα συνεργοὺς ἔχωσι, καὶ φίλους
κτῶνται, ὡς βοηθῶν δεόμενοι, τῶν δ' ἀδελφῶν ἀμελοῦ-
σιν ὥσπερ ἐκ πολιτῶν μὲν γιγνομένους φίλους, ἐξ
ἀδελφῶν δὲ οὐ γιγνομένους. Καὶ μὴν πρὸς φιλίαν 4
μέγα μὲν ὑπάρχει τὸ ἐκ τῶν αὐτῶν φῦναι, μέγα δὲ
τὸ ὁμοῦ τραφῆναι, ἐπεὶ καὶ τοῖς θηρίοις πόθος τις
ἐγγίγνεται τῶν συντρόφων· πρὸς δὲ τούτοις καὶ οἱ
ἄλλοι ἄνθρωποι τιμῶσί τε μᾶλλον τοὺς συναδέλφους
ὄντας τῶν ἀναδέλφων, καὶ ἧττον τούτοις ἐπιτίθενται.
Καὶ ὁ Χαιρεκράτης εἶπεν· Ἀλλ' εἰ μέν, ὦ Σώκρατες, 5
μὴ μέγα εἴη τὸ διάφορον, ἴσως ἂν δέοι φέρειν τὸν
ἀδελφὸν καὶ μὴ μικρῶν ἕνεκα φεύγειν· ἀγαθὸν γάρ,
ὥσπερ καὶ σὺ λέγεις, ἀδελφός, ὢν οἷον δεῖ· ὁπότε μέντοι

παντὸς ἐνδέοι, καὶ πᾶν το ἐναντιώτατον εἴη, τί ἂν τις
6 ἐπιχειροίη τοῖς ἀδυνάτοις; Καὶ ὁ Σωκράτης ἔφη·
Πότερα δέ, ὦ Χαιρέκρατες, οὐδενὶ ἀρέσαι δύναται Χαι
ρεφῶν, ὥςπερ οὐδὲ σοί, ἢ ἔστιν οἷς καὶ πάνυ ἀρέσκει;
Διὰ τοῦτο γάρ τοι, ἔφη, ὦ Σώκρατες, ἄξιόν ἐστιν
ἐμοὶ μισεῖν αὐτόν, ὅτι ἄλλοις μὲν ἀρέσκειν δύναται,
ἐμοὶ δέ, ὅπου ἂν παρῇ, πανταχοῦ καὶ ἔργῳ καὶ λόγῳ
7 ζημία μᾶλλον ἢ ὠφέλειά ἐστιν. Ἆρ᾽ οὖν, ἔφη ὁ Σω-
κράτης, ὥςπερ ἵππος τῷ ἀνεπιστήμονι μέν, ἐγχειροῦντι
δὲ χρῆσθαι ζημία ἐστίν, οὕτω καὶ ἀδελφός, ὅταν τις
αὐτῷ μὴ ἐπιστάμενος ἐγχειρῇ χρῆσθαι, ζημία ἐστίν;
8 Πῶς δ᾽ ἂν ἐγώ, ἔφη ὁ Χαιρεκράτης, ἀνεπιστήμων εἴην
ἀδελφῷ χρῆσθαι, ἐπιστάμενός γε καὶ εὖ λέγειν τὸν
εὖ λέγοντα, καὶ εὖ ποιεῖν τὸν εὖ ποιοῦντα; τὸν μέν-
τοι καὶ λόγῳ καὶ ἔργῳ πειρώμενον ἐμὲ ἀνιᾶν οὐκ ἂν
δυναίμην οὔτ᾽ εὖ λέγειν, οὔτ᾽ εὖ ποιεῖν, ἀλλ᾽ οὐδὲ
9 πειράσομαι. Καὶ ὁ Σωκράτης ἔφη· Θαυμαστά γε
λέγεις, ὦ Χαιρέκρατες, εἰ κύνα μέν, εἴ σοι ἦν ἐπὶ
προβάτοις ἐπιτήδειος ὤν, καὶ τοὺς μὲν ποιμένας ἠσπά-
ζετο, σοὶ δὲ προςιόντι ἐχαλέπαινεν, ἀμελήσας ἂν τοῦ
ὀργίζεσθαι ἐπειρῶ εὖ ποιήσας πραΰνειν αὐτόν, τὸν δὲ
ἀδελφὸν φῂς μέν μέγα ἂν ἀγαθὸν εἶναι, ὄντα πρὸς
σὲ οἷον δεῖ, ἐπίστασθαι δὲ ὁμολογῶν καὶ εὖ ποιεῖν
καὶ εὖ λέγειν, οὐκ ἐπιχειρεῖς μηχανᾶσθαι, ὅπως σοι
10 ὡς βέλτιστος ἔσται; Καὶ ὁ Χαιρεκράτης· Δέδοικα,
ἔφη, ὦ Σώκρατες, μὴ οὐκ ἔχω ἐγὼ τοσαύτην σοφίαν,
ὥςτε Χαιρεφῶντα ποιῆσαι πρὸς ἐμὲ οἷον δεῖ. Καὶ
μὴν οὐδέν γε ποικίλον, ἔφη ὁ Σωκράτης, οὐδὲ καινὸν
δεῖ ἐπ᾽ αὐτόν, ὡς ἐμοὶ δοκεῖ, μηχανᾶσθαι, οἷς δὲ καὶ
σὺ ἐπίστασαι αὐτὸς οἴομαι ἂν αὐτὸν ἁλόντα περὶ
11 πολλοῦ ποιεῖσθαί σε.—Οὐκ ἂν φθάνοις, ἔφη, λέγων,
εἴ τι ᾔσθησαί με φίλτρον ἐπιστάμενον, ὃ ἐγὼ εἰδὼς
λέληθα ἐμαυτόν.—Λέγε δή μοι, ἔφη, εἴ τινα τῶν
γνωρίμων βούλοιο κατεργάσασθαι, ὁπότε θύοι, καλεῖν

σε ἐπὶ δεῖπνον, τί ἂν ποιοίης;—Δῆλον, ὅτι κατάρχοιμι ἂν τοῦ αὐτός, ὅτε θύοιμι, καλεῖν ἐκεῖνον.—
Εἰ δὲ βούλοιο τῶν φίλων τινὰ προτρέψασθαι, ὁπότε 12
ἀποδημοίης, ἐπιμελεῖσθαι τῶν σῶν, τί ἂν ποιοίης;—Δῆλον, ὅτι πρότερος ἂν ἐγχειροίην ἐπιμελεῖσθαι τῶν
ἐκείνου, ὁπότε ἀποδημοίη.—Εἰ δὲ βούλοιο ξένον ποιῆ- 13
σαι ὑποδέχεσθαι σεαυτόν, ὁπότε ἔλθοις εἰς τὴν ἐκείνου, τί ἂν ποιοίης;—Δῆλον, ὅτι καὶ τοῦτον πρότερος ὑποδεχοίμην ἄν, ὁπότε ἔλθοι Ἀθήναζε· καὶ εἴ γε βουλοίμην αὐτὸν προθυμεῖσθαι διαπράττειν μοι ἐφ' ἃ ἥκοιμι, δῆλον, ὅτι καὶ τοῦτο δέοι ἂν πρότερον αὐτὸν
ἐκείνῳ ποιεῖν.—Πάντ' ἄρα σύ γε τὰ ἐν ἀνθρώποις 14
φίλτρα ἐπιστάμενος πάλαι ἀπεκρύπτου· ἢ ὀκνεῖς, ἔφη, ἄρξαι, μὴ αἰσχρὸς φανῇς, ἐὰν πρότερος τὸν ἀδελφὸν εὖ ποιῇς; καὶ μὴν πλείστου γε δοκεῖ ἀνὴρ ἐπαίνου ἄξιος εἶναι, ὃς ἂν φθάνῃ τοὺς μὲν πολεμίους κακῶς ποιῶν, τοὺς δὲ φίλους εὐεργετῶν· εἰ μὲν οὖν ἐδόκει μοι Χαιρεφῶν ἡγεμονικώτερος εἶναι σοῦ πρὸς τὴν φύσιν ταύτην, ἐκεῖνον ἂν ἐπειρώμην πείθειν πρότερον ἐγχειρεῖν τῷ σε φίλον ποιεῖσθαι· νῦν δέ μοι σὺ δοκεῖς ἡγούμενος
μᾶλλον ἂν ἐξεργάζεσθαι τοῦτο. Καὶ ὁ Χαιρεκράτης 15
εἶπεν· Ἄτοπα λέγεις, ὦ Σώκρατες, καὶ οὐδαμῶς πρὸς σοῦ, ὅς γε κελεύεις ἐμὲ νεώτερον ὄντα καθηγεῖσθαι· καίτοι τούτου γε παρὰ πᾶσιν ἀνθρώποις τἀναντία νομίζεται, τὸν πρεσβύτερον ἡγεῖσθαι παντὸς καὶ ἔργου
καὶ λόγου. Πῶς; ἔφη ὁ Σωκράτης· οὐ γὰρ καὶ ὁδοῦ 16
παραχωρῆσαι τὸν νεώτερον πρεσβυτέρῳ συντυγχάνοντι πανταχοῦ νομίζεται, καὶ καθήμενον ὑπαναστῆναι, καὶ κοίτῃ μαλακῇ τιμῆσαι, καὶ λόγων ὑπεῖξαι; ὠγαθέ, μὴ ὄκνει, ἔφη, ἀλλ' ἐγχείρει τὸν ἄνδρα καταπραΰνειν, καὶ πάνυ ταχύ σοι ὑπακούσεται· οὐχ ὁρᾷς, ὡς φιλότιμός ἐστι καὶ ἐλευθέριος; τὰ μὲν γὰρ πονηρὰ ἀνθρώπια οὐκ ἂν ἄλλως μᾶλλον ἕλοις, ἢ εἰ διδοίης τι, τοὺς δὲ καλοὺς κἀγαθοὺς ἀνθρώπους προσφιλῶς

17 χρώμενος μάλιστ' ἂν κατεργάσαιο. Καὶ ὁ Χαιρεκράτης εἶπεν· Ἐὰν οὖν, ἐμοῦ ταῦτα ποιοῦντος, ἐκεῖνος μηδὲν βελτίων γίγνηται; Τί γὰρ ἄλλο, ἔφη ὁ Σωκράτης, ἢ κινδυνεύσεις ἐπιδεῖξαι, σὺ μὲν χρηστός τε καὶ φιλάδελφος εἶναι, ἐκεῖνος δὲ φαῦλός τε καὶ οὐκ ἄξιος εὐεργεσίας; Ἀλλ' οὐδὲν οἶμαι τούτων ἔσεσθαι· νομίζω γὰρ αὐτόν, ἐπειδὰν αἴσθηταί σε προκαλούμενον ἑαυτὸν εἰς τὸν ἀγῶνα τοῦτον, πάνυ φιλονεικήσειν, ὅπως περιγένηταί σου καὶ λόγῳ καὶ ἔργῳ εὖ
18 ποιῶν. Νῦν μὲν γὰρ οὕτως, ἔφη, διάκεισθον, ὥσπερ εἰ τὼ χεῖρε, ἃς ὁ θεὸς ἐπὶ τὸ συλλαμβάνειν ἀλλήλαιν ἐποίησεν, ἀφεμένω τούτου τράποιντο πρὸς τὸ διακωλύειν ἀλλήλω, ἢ εἰ τὼ πόδε θείᾳ μοίρᾳ πεποιημένω πρὸς τὸ συνεργεῖν ἀλλήλοιν ἀμελήσαντε τούτου
19 ἐμποδίζοιεν ἀλλήλω. Οὐκ ἂν πολλὴ ἀμαθία εἴη καὶ κακοδαιμονία τοῖς ἐπ' ὠφελείᾳ πεποιημένοις ἐπὶ βλάβῃ χρῆσθαι; Καὶ μὴν ἀδελφώ γε, ὡς ἐμοὶ δοκεῖ, ὁ θεὸς ἐποίησεν ἐπὶ μείζονι ὠφελείᾳ ἀλλήλοιν, ἢ χεῖρέ τε καὶ πόδε καὶ ὀφθαλμὼ τἆλλά τε, ὅσα ἀδελφὰ ἔφυσεν ἀνθρώποις. Χεῖρες μὲν γάρ, εἰ δέοι αὐτὰς τὰ πλέον ὀργυιᾶς διέχοντα ἅμα ποιῆσαι, οὐκ ἂν δύναιντο, πόδες δὲ οὐδ' ἂν ἐπὶ τὰ ὀργυιὰν διέχοντα ἔλθοιεν ἅμα, ὀφθαλμοὶ δέ, οἱ καὶ δοκοῦντες ἐπὶ πλεῖστον ἐξικνεῖσθαι, οὐδ' ἂν τῶν ἔτι ἐγγυτέρω ὄντων τὰ ἔμπροσθεν ἅμα καὶ τὰ ὄπισθεν ἰδεῖν δύναιντο, ἀδελφὼ δέ, φίλω ὄντε, καὶ πολὺ διεστῶτε πράττετον ἅμα καὶ ἐπ' ὠφελείᾳ ἀλλήλοιν.

CHAPTER IV.

ARGUMENT.

This first chapter upon *friendship* (see Argument to Book II. Chap. II.), gives a general view of *its value.* Many who acknowledge in general terms the worth of friends, appear least of all anxious to acquire or retain them (§ 1—4). But yet no possession is more desirable or permanent than that of a good friend; for he cares for another's property and business, shares his fortune whether prosperous or adverse, and is sometimes even more solicitous for the health and prosperity of his friend than for his own (§ 5—7).

Ἤκουσα δέ ποτε αὐτοῦ καὶ περὶ φίλων διαλεγο- 1
μένου, ἐξ ὧν ἔμοιγε ἐδόκει μάλιστ' ἄν τις ὠφελεῖσθαι πρὸς φίλων κτῆσίν τε καὶ χρείαν· τοῦτο μὲν γὰρ δὴ πολλῶν ἔφη ἀκούειν, ὡς πάντων κτημάτων κράτιστον ἂν εἴη φίλος σαφὴς καὶ ἀγαθός, ἐπιμελουμένους δὲ παντὸς μᾶλλον ὁρᾶν ἔφη τοὺς πολλοὺς ἢ φίλων κτή-
σεως. Καὶ γὰρ οἰκίας καὶ ἀγροὺς καὶ ἀνδράποδα καὶ 2
βοσκήματα καὶ σκεύη κτωμένους τε ἐπιμελῶς ὁρᾶν ἔφη, καὶ τὰ ὄντα σώζειν πειρωμένους, φίλον δέ, ὃ μέγιστον ἀγαθὸν εἶναί φασιν, ὁρᾶν ἔφη τοὺς πολλοὺς οὔτε ὅπως κτήσονται φροντίζοντας, οὔτε ὅπως οἱ ὄντες
ἑαυτοῖς σώζωνται. Ἀλλὰ καὶ καμνόντων φίλων τε 3
καὶ οἰκετῶν ὁρᾶν τινας ἔφη τοῖς μὲν οἰκέταις καὶ ἰατροὺς εισαγοντας, καὶ τἆλλα πρὸς ὑγιείαν ἐπιμελῶς παρασκευάζοντας, τῶν δὲ φίλων ὀλιγωροῦντας, ἀποθανόντων τε ἀμφοτέρων ἐπὶ μὲν τοῖς οἰκέταις ἀχθομένους καὶ ζημίαν ἡγουμένους, ἐπὶ δὲ τοῖς φίλοις οὐδὲν οἰομένους ἐλαττοῦσθαι, καὶ τῶν μὲν ἄλλων κτημάτων οὐδὲν ἐῶντας ἀθεράπευτον οὐδ' ἀνεπίσκεπτον, τῶν δὲ
φίλων ἐπιμελείας δεομένων ἀμελοῦντας. Ἔτι δὲ πρὸς 4

τουτοις ὁρᾶν ἔφη τοὺς πολλοὺς τῶν μὲν ἄλλων κτημάτων, καὶ πάνυ πολλῶν αὐτοῖς ὄντων, τὸ πλῆθος εἰδότας, τῶν δὲ φίλων, ὀλίγων ὄντων, οὐ μόνον τὸ πλῆθος ἀγνοοῦντας, ἀλλὰ καὶ τοῖς πυνθανομένοις τοῦτο καταλέγειν ἐγχειρήσαντας, οὓς ἐν τοῖς φίλοις ἔθεσαν, πάλιν τούτους ἀνατίθεσθαι· τοσοῦτον αὐτοὺς τῶν φίλων φροντίζειν. Καίτοι πρὸς ποῖον κτῆμα τῶν ἄλλων παραβαλλόμενος φίλος ἀγαθὸς οὐκ ἂν πολλῷ κρείττων φανείη; ποῖος γὰρ ἵππος ἢ ποῖον ζεῦγος οὕτω χρήσιμον, ὥσπερ ὁ χρηστὸς φίλος, ποῖον δὲ ἀνδράποδον οὕτως εὔνουν καὶ παραμόνιμον, ἢ ποῖον ἄλλο
6 κτῆμα οὕτω πάγχρηστον; Ὁ γὰρ ἀγαθὸς φίλος ἑαυτὸν τάττει πρὸς πᾶν τὸ ἐλλεῖπον τῷ φίλῳ καὶ τῆς τῶν ἰδίων κατασκευῆς καὶ τῶν κοινῶν πράξεων, καί, ἄν τέ τινα εὖ ποιῆσαι δέῃ, συνεπισχύει, ἄν τέ τις φόβος ταράττῃ, συμβοηθεῖ τὰ μὲν συναναλίσκων, τὰ δὲ συμπράττων, καὶ τὰ μὲν συμπείθων, τὰ δὲ βιαζόμενος, καὶ εὖ μὲν πράττοντας πλεῖστα εὐφραίνων, σφαλ-
7 λομένους δὲ πλεῖστα ἐπανορθῶν. Ἃ δὲ αἵ τε χεῖρες ἑκάστῳ ὑπηρετοῦσι, καὶ οἱ ὀφθαλμοὶ προορῶσι, καὶ τὰ ὦτα προακούουσι, καὶ οἱ πόδες διανύτουσι, τούτων φίλος εὐεργετῶν οὐδενὸς λείπεται· πολλάκις δέ, ἃ πρὸ αὑτοῦ τις οὐκ ἐξειργάσατο ἢ οὐκ εἶδεν ἢ οὐκ ἤκουσεν ἢ οὐ διήνυσε, ταῦτα ὁ φίλος πρὸ τοῦ φίλου ἐξήρκεσεν. Ἀλλ' ὅμως ἔνιοι δένδρα μὲν πειρῶνται θεραπεύειν τοῦ καρποῦ ἕνεκεν, τοῦ δὲ παμφορωτάτου κτήματος, ὃ καλεῖται φίλος, ἀργῶς καὶ ἀνειμένως οἱ πλεῖστοι ἐπιμέλονται.

CHAPTER V.

ARGUMENT.

The following short conversation appears to have been called forth by the neglect of a very poor friend by one of the disciples of Socrates, and was held in the presence of the offender as an admonition to him (§ 1). It seems, at first view, to be aimed at the neglected rather than the neglecting friend. But the application which it was designed that the offender should make to himself, seems to be this: since you do not show yourself useful to your friend, when he is in distress, you must expect that you in turn will be deserted by others as a worthless friend.

The value of friends is as various as that of slaves (§ 2, 3). Whoever then would not be discarded by his friends, as a slave of little value is disposed of by its owner, must seek to become as useful to them as possible (§ 4, 5).

Ἤκουσα δέ ποτε καὶ ἄλλον αὐτοῦ λόγον, ὅς ἐδόκει 1
μοι προτρέπειν τὸν ἀκούοντα ἐξετάζειν ἑαυτὸν, ὁπόσου τοῖς φίλοις ἄξιος εἴη. Ἰδὼν γάρ τινα τῶν ξυνόντων ἀμελοῦντα φίλου πενίᾳ πιεζομένου, ἤρετο Ἀντισθένη ἐναντίον τοῦ ἀμελοῦντος αὐτοῦ καὶ ἄλλων πολλῶν·
Ἆρ', ἔφη, ὦ Ἀντίσθενες, εἰσί τινες ἀξίαι φίλων, ὥς- 2
περ οἰκετῶν; Τῶν γὰρ οἰκετῶν ὁ μέν που δύο μναῖν ἄξιός ἐστιν, ὁ δὲ οὐδ' ἡμιμναίου, ὁ δὲ πέντε μνῶν, ὁ δὲ καὶ δέκα· Νικίας δὲ ὁ Νικηράτου λέγεται ἐπιστάτην εἰς τἀργύρια πρίασθαι ταλάντου· σκοποῦμαι δὴ τοῦτο, ἔφη, εἰ ἄρα, ὥσπερ τῶν οἰκετῶν, οὕτω καὶ τῶν
φίλων εἰσὶν ἀξίαι. Ναὶ μὰ Δί', ἔφη ὁ Ἀντισθένης· 3
ἐγὼ γοῦν βουλοίμην ἂν τὸν μέν τινα φίλον μοι εἶναι μᾶλλον ἢ δύο μνᾶς, τὸν δ' οὐδ' ἂν ἡμιμναίου προτιμησαίμην, τὸν δὲ καὶ πρὸ δέκα μνῶν ἑλοίμην ἄν, τὸν δὲ πρὸ πάντων χρημάτων καὶ πόνων πριαίμην ἂν φίλον
μοι εἶναι. Οὐκοῦν, ἔφη ὁ Σωκράτης, εἴ γε ταῦτα 4

τοιαῦτά ἐστι, καλῶς ἂν ἔχοι ἐξετάζειν τινὰ ἑαυτὸν,
πόσου ἄρα τυγχάνει τοῖς φίλοις ἄξιος ὤν, καὶ πειρᾶ-
σθαι ὡς πλείστου ἄξιος εἶναι, ἵνα ἧττον αὐτὸν οἱ φί-
λοι προδιδῶσιν· ἐγὼ γάρ τοι, ἔφη, πολλάκις ἀκούω
τοῦ μὲν, ὅτι προὔδωκεν αὐτὸν φίλος ἀνήρ, τοῦ δὲ, ὅτι
μνᾶν ἀνθ' ἑαυτοῦ μᾶλλον εἵλετο ἀνὴρ, ὃν ᾤετο φίλον
5 εἶναι. Τὰ τοιαῦτα πάντα σκοπῶ, μὴ, ὥσπερ ὅταν τις
οἰκέτην πονηρὸν πωλῇ καὶ ἀποδίδωται τοῦ εὑρόντος,
οὕτω καὶ τὸν πονηρὸν φίλον, ὅταν ἐξῇ τὸ πλεῖον τῆς
ἀξίας λαβεῖν, ἐπαγωγὸν ᾖ προδίδοσθαι· τοὺς δὲ χρη-
στοὺς οὔτε οἰκέτας πάνυ τι πωλουμένους ὁρῶ, οὔτε
φίλους προδιδομένους.

CHAPTER VI.

ARGUMENT.

This chapter treats of the selection, proving, and acquisition of friends, and of the real foundation of friendship:

1. Those only should be chosen as friends, who are temperate (ἐγκρατεῖς), faithful, obliging and prompt in the performance of the offices of kindness, and are not contentious, avaricious, and ungrateful (§ 1—5).

2. In order to determine whether a person is worthy to be a friend, it is necessary to consider his treatment of other friends (§ 6, 9).

3. When any one appears to be worthy of friendship, he may be sought as a friend in the following manner: First, it should be inquired, whether the gods approve the alliance (§ 8). Then, we should make known our regard to the individual whom we would wish to be our friend both in word and deed (§ 9—13). Friendship, however, can exist only between those who are good and honorable (§ 14—16). The dissensions and animosities which indeed exist among the good, and cannot but exist among the bad, are the result of a mixed nature, partly inclined to friendship and partly to hostility, and should not discourage in the attempt to acquire valuable friends; for a prevailing friendliness is predominant over the baser passions in good men, and

unites them together, by means of the virtue which restrains and subjects to reason the desires which lead to dissension (§ 17—28).

4. Friendship is founded not on external beauty, but on noble qualities of mind (§ 30—32). It originates in admiration, which is followed by regard or good will (§ 33, 34), and necessarily demands the possession of the virtues which give value to a friend (§ 35). But as truth is the foundation of all real friendship (§ 36—38), the shortest, surest, and best way to the attainment of friends, is to be what you wish them to believe you to be, i. e., good, ἀγαθός (§ 39).

Ἐδόκει δέ μοι καὶ εἰς τὸ δοκιμάζειν φίλους ὁποί- 1
ους ἄξιον κτᾶσθαι φρενοῦν τοιάδε λέγων· Εἰπέ μοι,
ἔφη, ὦ Κριτόβουλε, εἰ δεοίμεθα φίλου ἀγαθοῦ, πῶς
ἂν ἐπιχειροίημεν σκοπεῖν; ἆρα πρῶτον μὲν ζητητέον,
ὅςτις ἄρχει γαστρός τε καὶ φιλοποσίας καὶ λαγνείας
καὶ ὕπνου καὶ ἀργίας; ὁ γὰρ ὑπὸ τούτων κρατού-
μενος οὔτ' αὐτὸς ἑαυτῷ δύναιτ' ἂν οὔτε φίλῳ τὰ δέοντα
πράττειν;—Μὰ Δί', οὐ δῆτα, ἔφη.—Οὐκοῦν τοῦ μὲν
ὑπὸ τούτων ἀρχομένου ἀφεκτέον δοκεῖ σοι εἶναι;—
Πάνυ μὲν οὖν, ἔφη.—Τί γάρ; ἔφη, ὅςτις δαπανηρὸς 2
ὢν μὴ αὐτάρκης ἐστίν, ἀλλ' ἀεὶ τῶν πλησίον δεῖται,
καὶ λαμβάνων μὲν μὴ δύναται ἀποδιδόναι, μὴ λαμβά-
νων δὲ τὸν μὴ διδόντα μισεῖ, οὐ δοκεῖ σοι καὶ οὗτος
χαλεπὸς φίλος εἶναι;—Πάνυ, ἔφη.—Οὐκοῦν ἀφεκτέον
καὶ τούτου;—Ἀφεκτέον μέντοι, ἔφη.—Τί γάρ; ὅςτις 3
χρηματίζεσθαι μὲν δύναται, πολλῶν δὲ χρημάτων ἐπι-
θυμεῖ, καὶ διὰ τοῦτο δυςξύμβολός ἐστι, καὶ λαμβάνων
μὲν ἥδεται, ἀποδιδόναι δὲ οὐ βούλεται;—Ἐμοὶ μὲν
δοκεῖ, ἔφη, οὗτος ἔτι πονηρότερος ἐκείνου εἶναι.—Τί 4
δέ; ὅςτις διὰ τὸν ἔρωτα τοῦ χρηματίζεσθαι μηδὲ πρὸς
ἓν ἄλλο σχολὴν ποιεῖται, ἢ ὁπόθεν αὐτὸς κερδανεῖ;—
Ἀφεκτέον καὶ τούτου, ὡς ἐμοὶ δοκεῖ· ἀνωφελὴς γὰρ
ἂν εἴη τῷ χρωμένῳ.—Τί δέ; ὅςτις στασιώδης τέ ἐστι
καὶ θέλων πολλοὺς τοῖς φίλοις ἐχθροὺς παρέχειν;—
Φευκτέον, νὴ Δία, καὶ τοῦτον.—Εἰ δέ τις τούτων μὲν

τῶν κακῶν μηδὲν ἔχοι, εὖ δὲ πάσχων ἀνέχεται, μηδὲν
φροντίζων τοῦ ἀντευεργετεῖν;—Ἀνωφελὴς ἂν εἴη καὶ
οὗτος· ἀλλὰ ποῖον, ὦ Σώκρατες, ἐπιχειρήσομεν φίλον
5 ποιεῖσθαι;—Οἶμαι μέν, ὃς τἀναντία τούτων ἐγκρατὴς
μέν ἐστι τῶν διὰ τοῦ σώματος ἡδονῶν, εὔορκος δὲ καὶ
εὐξύμβολος ὢν τυγχάνει, καὶ φιλόνεικος πρὸς τὸ μὴ
ἐλλείπεσθαι εὖ ποιῶν τοὺς εὐεργετοῦντας αὐτὸν, ὥςτε
6 λυσιτελεῖν τοῖς χρωμένοις.—Πῶς οὖν ἂν ταῦτα δοκι-
μάσαιμεν, ὦ Σώκρατες, πρὸ τοῦ χρῆσθαι;—Τοὺς μὲν
ἀνδριαντοποιούς, ἔφη, δοκιμάζομεν, οὐ τοῖς λόγοις αὐ-
τῶν τεκμαιρόμενοι, ἀλλ' ὃν ἂν ὁρῶμεν τοὺς πρόσθεν
ἀνδριάντας καλῶς εἰργασμένον, τούτῳ πιστεύομεν καὶ
7 τοὺς λοιποὺς εὖ ποιήσειν.—Καὶ ἄνδρα δὴ λέγεις, ἔφη,
ὃς ἂν τοὺς φίλους τοὺς πρόσθεν εὖ ποιῶν φαίνηται,
δῆλον εἶναι καὶ τοὺς ὑστέρους εὐεργετήσοντα;—Καὶ
γὰρ ἵπποις, ἔφη, ὃν ἂν τοῖς πρόσθεν ὁρῶ καλῶς χρώ-
μενον, τοῦτον καὶ ἄλλοις οἶμαι καλῶς χρῆσθαι.—
8 Εἶεν, ἔφη· ὃς δ' ἂν ἡμῖν ἄξιος φιλίας δοκῇ εἶναι, πῶς
χρὴ φίλον τοῦτον ποιεῖσθαι;—Πρῶτον μέν, ἔφη, τὰ
παρὰ τῶν θεῶν ἐπισκεπτέον, εἰ συμβουλεύουσιν αὐτὸν
φίλον ποιεῖσθαι.—Τί οὖν; ἔφη, ὃν ἂν ἡμῖν τε δοκῇ
καὶ οἱ θεοὶ μὴ ἐναντιῶνται, ἔχεις εἰπεῖν, ὅπως οὗτος
9 θηρατέος;—Μὰ Δί', ἔφη, οὐ κατὰ πόδας, ὥσπερ ὁ
λαγώς, οὐδ' ἀπάτῃ, ὥσπερ αἱ ὄρνιθες, οὐδὲ βίᾳ, ὥς-
περ οἱ ἐχθροί· ἄκοντα γὰρ φίλον ἑλεῖν ἐργῶδες·
χαλεπὸν δὲ καὶ δήσαντα κατέχειν, ὥσπερ δοῦλον·
ἐχθροὶ γὰρ μᾶλλον ἢ φίλοι γίγνονται ταῦτα πάσχον-
10 τες.—Φίλοι δὲ πῶς; ἔφη.—Εἶναι μέν τινάς φασιν
ἐπῳδάς, ἃς οἱ ἐπιστάμενοι ἐπᾴδοντες οἷς ἂν βούλων-
ται φίλους ἑαυτοῖς ποιοῦνται, εἶναι δὲ καὶ φίλτρα, οἷς
οἱ ἐπιστάμενοι πρὸς οὓς ἂν βούλωνται χρώμενοι φι-
λοῦνται ὑπ' αὐτῶν.—Πόθεν οὖν, ἔφη, ταῦτα μάθοι-
11 μεν ἄν;—Ἃ μὲν αἱ Σειρῆνες ἐπῇδον τῷ Ὀδυσσεῖ,
ἤκουσας Ὁμήρου, ὧν ἐστιν ἀρχὴ τοιάδε τις·

Δεῦρ' ἄγε δὴ πολύαιν' Ὀδυσεῦ, μέγα κῦδος Ἀχαιῶν.

—Ταύτην οὖν, ἔφη, τὴν ἐπῳδήν, ὦ Σώκρατες, καὶ τοῖς ἄλλοις ἀνθρώποις αἱ Σειρῆνες ἐπᾴδουσαι κατεῖχον, ὥστε μὴ ἀπιέναι ἀπ' αὐτῶν τοὺς ἐπᾳσθέντας;—Οὔκ· ἀλλὰ τοῖς ἐπ' ἀρετῇ φιλοτιμουμένοις οὕτως
ἐπῇδον.—Σχεδόν τι λέγεις τοιαῦτα χρῆναι ἑκάστῳ 12
ἐπᾴδειν, οἷα μὴ νομιεῖ ἀκούων τὸν ἐπαινοῦντα καταγελῶντα λέγειν· οὕτω μὲν γὰρ ἐχθίων τ' ἂν εἴη, καὶ ἀπελαύνοι τοὺς ἀνθρώπους ἀφ' ἑαυτοῦ, εἰ τὸν εἰδότα, ὅτι μικρός τε καὶ αἰσχρὸς καὶ ἀσθενής ἐστιν, ἐπαινοίη λέγων, ὅτι καλός τε καὶ μέγας καὶ ἰσχυρός
ἐστιν. Ἄλλας δέ τινας οἶσθα ἐπῳδάς;—Οὔκ· ἀλλ' 13
ἤκουσα μέν, ὅτι Περικλῆς πολλὰς ἐπίσταιτο, ἃς ἐπᾴδων τῇ πόλει ἐποίει αὐτὴν φιλεῖν αὐτόν.—Θεμιστοκλῆς δὲ πῶς ἐποίησε τὴν πόλιν φιλεῖν αὐτόν;—Μὰ Δί' οὐκ ἐπᾴδων, ἀλλὰ περιάψας τι ἀγαθὸν αὐτῇ.—
Δοκεῖς μοι λέγειν, ὦ Σώκρατες, ὡς, εἰ μέλλοιμεν ἀγα- 14
θόν τινα κτήσασθαι φίλον, αὐτοὺς ἡμᾶς ἀγαθοὺς δεῖ γενέσθαι λέγειν τε καὶ πράττειν.—Σὺ δ' ᾤου, ἔφη ὁ Σωκράτης, οἷόν τ' εἶναι πονηρὸν ὄντα χρηστοὺς φί-
λους κτήσασθαι;—Ἑώρων γάρ, ἔφη ὁ Κριτόβουλος, 15
ῥήτοράς τε φαύλους ἀγαθοῖς δημηγόροις φίλους ὄντας, καὶ στρατηγεῖν οὐχ ἱκανοὺς πάνυ στρατηγικοῖς ἀν-
δράσιν ἑταίρους.—Ἆρ' οὖν, ἔφη, καί, περὶ οὗ διαλε- 16
γόμεθα, οἶσθά τινας, οἳ ἀνωφελεῖς ὄντες ὠφελίμους δύνανται φίλους ποιεῖσθαι;—Μὰ Δί' οὐ δῆτ', ἔφη· ἀλλ' εἰ ἀδύνατόν ἐστι πονηρὸν ὄντα καλοὺς κἀγαθοὺς φίλους κτήσασθαι, ἐκεῖνο ἤδη μέλει μοι, εἰ ἔστιν αὐτὸν καλὸν κἀγαθὸν γενόμενον ἐξ ἑτοίμου τοῖς καλοῖς
κἀγαθοῖς φίλον εἶναι.—Ὃ ταράττει σε, ὦ Κριτό- 17
βουλε, ὅτι πολλάκις ἄνδρας καὶ καλὰ πράττοντας καὶ τῶν αἰσχρῶν ἀπεχομένους ὁρᾷς ἀντὶ τοῦ φίλους εἶναι στασιάζοντας ἀλλήλοις καὶ χαλεπώτερον χρωμένους

18 τῶν μηδενὸς ἀξίων ἀνθρώπων.—Καὶ οὐ μόνον γ',
ἔφη ὁ Κριτόβουλος, οἱ ἰδιῶται τοῦτο ποιοῦσιν, ἀλλὰ
καὶ πόλεις αἱ τῶν τε καλῶν μάλιστα ἐπιμελόμεναι,
καὶ τὰ αἰσχρὰ ἥκιστα προσιέμεναι, πολλάκις πολε-
19 μικῶς ἔχουσι πρὸς ἀλλήλας. Ἃ λογιζόμενος πάνυ
ἀθύμως ἔχω πρὸς τὴν τῶν φίλων κτῆσιν· οὔτε γὰρ
τοὺς πονηροὺς ὁρῶ φίλους ἀλλήλοις δυναμένους εἶναι·
πῶς γὰρ ἂν ἢ ἀχάριστοι ἢ ἀμελεῖς ἢ πλεονέκται ἢ
ἄπιστοι ἢ ἀκρατεῖς ἄνθρωποι δύναιντο φίλοι γενέ-
σθαι; Οἱ μὲν οὖν πονηροὶ πάντως ἔμοιγε δοκοῦσιν
20 ἀλλήλοις ἐχθροὶ μᾶλλον ἢ φίλοι πεφυκέναι. Ἀλλὰ
μήν, ὥσπερ σὺ λέγεις, οὐδ' ἂν τοῖς χρηστοῖς οἱ πονη-
ροί ποτε συναρμόσειαν εἰς φιλίαν· πῶς γὰρ οἱ τὰ
πονηρὰ ποιοῦντες τοῖς τὰ τοιαῦτα μισοῦσι φίλοι γέ-
νοιντ' ἄν; Εἰ δὲ δὴ καὶ οἱ ἀρετὴν ἀσκοῦντες στασιά-
ζουσί τε περὶ τοῦ πρωτεύειν ἐν ταῖς πόλεσι, καὶ
φθονοῦντες ἑαυτοῖς μισοῦσιν ἀλλήλους, τίνες ἔτι φίλοι
ἔσονται, καὶ ἐν τίσιν ἀνθρώποις εὔνοια καὶ πίστις
21 ἔσται; Ἀλλ' ἔχει μέν, ἔφη ὁ Σωκράτης, ποικίλως
πως ταῦτα, ὦ Κριτόβουλε· φύσει γὰρ ἔχουσιν οἱ
ἄνθρωποι τὰ μὲν φιλικά· δέονταί τε γὰρ ἀλλήλων,
καὶ ἐλεοῦσι, καὶ συνεργοῦντες ὠφελοῦσι καὶ τοῦτο
συνιέντες χάριν ἔχουσιν ἀλλήλοις· τὰ δὲ πολεμικά·
τά τε γὰρ αὐτὰ καλὰ καὶ ἡδέα νομίζοντες ὑπὲρ τού-
των μάχονται, καὶ διχογνωμονοῦντες ἐναντιοῦνται·
πολεμικὸν δὲ καὶ ἔρις καὶ ὀργή, καὶ δυσμενὲς μὲν ὁ
22 τοῦ πλεονεκτεῖν ἔρως, μισητὸν δὲ ὁ φθόνος. Ἀλλ'
ὅμως διὰ τούτων πάντων ἡ φιλία διαδυομένη συνά-
πτει τοὺς καλούς τε κἀγαθούς· διὰ γὰρ τὴν ἀρετὴν
αἱροῦνται μὲν ἄνευ πόνου τὰ μέτρια κεκτῆσθαι μᾶλ-
λον, ἢ διὰ πολέμου πάντων κυριεύειν, καὶ δύνανται
πεινῶντες καὶ διψῶντες ἀλύπως σίτου καὶ ποτοῦ κοι-
νωνεῖν, καὶ τοῖς τῶν ὡραίων ἀφροδισίοις ἡδόμενοι
23 ἐγκαρτερεῖν, ὥστε μὴ λυπεῖν οὓς μὴ προσήκει· δύνανται

δὲ καὶ χρημάτων οὐ μόνον τοῦ πλεονεκτεῖν ἀπεχόμενοι νομίμως κοινωνεῖν, ἀλλὰ καὶ ἐπαρκεῖν ἀλλήλοις· δύνανται δὲ καὶ τὴν ἔριν οὐ μόνον ἀλύπως, ἀλλὰ καὶ συμφερόντως ἀλλήλοις διατίθεσθαι, καὶ τὴν ὀργὴν κωλύειν εἰς τὸ μεταμελησόμενον προϊέναι· τὸν δὲ φθόνον παντάπασιν ἀφαιροῦσι τὰ μὲν ἑαυτῶν ἀγαθὰ τοῖς φίλοις οἰκεῖα παρέχοντες, τὰ δὲ τῶν φίλων ἑαυτῶν νομίζοντες. Πῶς οὖν οὐκ εἰκὸς τοὺς καλούς τε κἀγα- 24
θοὺς καὶ τῶν πολιτικῶν τιμῶν μὴ μόνον ἀβλαβεῖς, ἀλλὰ καὶ ὠφελίμους ἀλλήλοις κοινωνοὺς εἶναι; οἱ μὲν γὰρ ἐπιθυμοῦντες ἐν ταῖς πόλεσι τιμᾶσθαί τε καὶ ἄρχειν, ἵνα ἐξουσίαν ἔχωσι χρήματά τε κλέπτειν καὶ ἀνθρώπους βιάζεσθαι καὶ ἡδυπαθεῖν, ἄδικοί τε καὶ πονηροὶ ἂν εἶεν καὶ ἀδύνατοι ἄλλῳ συναρμόσαι.
Εἰ δέ τις ἐν πόλει τιμᾶσθαι βουλόμενος, ὅπως αὐτός 25
τε μὴ ἀδικῆται, καὶ τοῖς φίλοις τὰ δίκαια βοηθεῖν δύνηται, καὶ ἄρξας ἀγαθόν τι ποιεῖν τὴν πατρίδα πειρᾶται, διὰ τί ὁ τοιοῦτος ἄλλῳ τοιούτῳ οὐκ ἂν δύναιτο συναρμόσαι; πότερον τοὺς φίλους ὠφελεῖν μετὰ τῶν καλῶν κἀγαθῶν ἧττον δυνήσεται, ἢ τὴν πόλιν εὐεργετεῖν ἀδυνατώτερος ἔσται καλούς τε κἀγαθοὺς ἔχων συνεργούς; Ἀλλὰ καὶ ἐν τοῖς γυμνικοῖς 26
ἀγῶσι δῆλόν ἐστιν, ὅτι, εἰ ἐξῆν τοῖς κρατίστοις συνθεμένους ἐπὶ τοὺς χείρους ἰέναι, πάντας ἂν τοὺς ἀγῶνας οὗτοι ἐνίκων, καὶ πάντα τὰ ἆθλα οὗτοι ἐλάμβανον. Ἐπεὶ οὖν ἐκεῖ μὲν οὐκ ἐῶσι τοῦτο ποιεῖν, ἐν δὲ τοῖς πολιτικοῖς, ἐν οἷς οἱ καλοὶ κἀγαθοὶ κρατιστεύουσιν, οὐδεὶς κωλύει, μεθ' οὗ ἄν τις βούληται, τὴν πόλιν εὐεργετεῖν, πῶς οὖν οὐ λυσιτελεῖ τοὺς βελτίστους φίλους κτησάμενον πολιτεύεσθαι, τούτοις κοινωνοῖς καὶ συνεργοῖς τῶν πράξεων μᾶλλον ἢ ἀνταγωνισταῖς χρώμενον; Ἀλλὰ μὴν κἀκεῖνο δῆλον, ὅτι, κἂν πολεμῇ 27
τίς τινι, συμμάχων δεήσεται, καὶ τούτων πλειόνων, ἐὰν καλοῖς κἀγαθοῖς ἀντιτάττηται. Καὶ μὴν οἱ συμμαχεῖν

ἐθέλοντες εὖ ποιητέοι, ἵνα θέλωσι προθυμεῖσθαι· πολὺ δὲ κρεῖττον τοὺς βελτίστους ἐλάττονας εὖ ποιεῖν ἢ τοὺς χείρονας πλείονας ὄντας· οἱ γὰρ πονηροὶ πολὺ πλειόνων εὐεργεσιῶν ἢ οἱ χρηστοὶ δέονται.
28 Ἀλλὰ θαῤῥῶν, ἔφη, ὦ Κριτόβουλε, πειρῶ ἀγαθὸς γίγνεσθαι, καὶ τοιοῦτος γιγνόμενος θηρᾶν ἐπιχείρει τοὺς καλούς τε κἀγαθούς. Ἴσως δ' ἄν τί σοι κἀγὼ συλλαβεῖν εἰς τὴν τῶν καλῶν τε κἀγαθῶν θήραν ἔχοιμι διὰ τὸ ἐρωτικὸς εἶναι· δεινῶς γάρ, ὧν ἂν ἐπιθυμήσω ἀνθρώπων, ὅλος ὥρμημαι ἐπὶ τὸ φιλῶν τε αὐτοὺς ἀντιφιλεῖσθαι ὑπ' αὐτῶν, καὶ ποθῶν ἀντιποθεῖσθαι, καὶ ἐπιθυμῶν ξυνεῖναι καὶ ἀντεπιθυμεῖ-
29 σθαι τῆς ξυνουσίας. Ὁρῶ δὲ καὶ σοὶ τούτων δεῆσον, ὅταν ἐπιθυμήσῃς φιλίαν πρός τινας ποιεῖσθαι. Μὴ σὺ οὖν ἀποκρύπτου με, οἷς ἂν βούλοιο φίλος γενέσθαι· διὰ γὰρ τὸ ἐπιμελεῖσθαι τοῦ ἀρέσαι τῷ ἀρέσκοντί μοι οὐκ ἀπείρως οἶμαι ἔχειν πρὸς θήραν
30 ἀνθρώπων. Καὶ ὁ Κριτόβουλος ἔφη· Καὶ μήν, ὦ Σώκρατες, τούτων ἐγὼ τῶν μαθημάτων πάλαι ἐπιθυμῶ, ἄλλως τε καὶ εἰ ἐξαρκέσει μοι ἡ αὐτὴ ἐπιστήμη ἐπὶ τοὺς ἀγαθοὺς τὰς ψυχὰς καὶ ἐπὶ τοὺς καλοὺς
31 τὰ σώματα. Καὶ ὁ Σωκράτης ἔφη· Ἀλλ', ὦ Κριτόβουλε, οὐκ ἔνεστιν ἐν τῇ ἐμῇ ἐπιστήμῃ τὸ τὰς χεῖρας προσφέροντα ὑπομένειν ποιεῖν τοὺς καλούς· πέπεισμαι δὲ καὶ ἀπὸ τῆς Σκύλλης διὰ τοῦτο φεύγειν τοὺς ἀνθρώπους, ὅτι τὰς χεῖρας αὐτοῖς προσέφερε· τὰς δέ γε Σειρῆνας, ὅτι τὰς χεῖρας οὐδενὶ προσέφερον, ἀλλὰ πᾶσι πόῤῥωθεν ἐπῇδον, πάντας φασὶν ὑπομένειν, καὶ ἀκού-
32 οντας αὐτῶν κηλεῖσθαι. Καὶ ὁ Κριτόβουλος ἔφη· Ὡς οὐ προσοίσοντος τὰς χεῖρας, εἴ τι ἔχεις ἀγαθὸν εἰς φίλων κτῆσιν, δίδασκε. Οὐδὲ τὸ στόμα οὖν, ἔφη ὁ Σωκράτης, πρὸς τὸ στόμα προσοίσεις; Θάῤῥει, ἔφη ὁ Κριτόβουλος· οὐδὲ γὰρ τὸ στόμα πρὸς τὸ στόμα προσοίσω οὐδενί, ἐὰν μὴ καλὸς ᾖ. Εὐθύς, ἔφη, σύ γε,

ὦ Κριτόβουλε, τοὐναντίον τοῦ συμφέροντος εἴρηκας· οἱ μὲν γὰρ καλοὶ τὰ τοιαῦτα οὐχ ὑπομένουσιν, οἱ δὲ αἰσχροὶ καὶ ἡδέως προςίενται, νομίζοντες διὰ τὴν ψυχὴν καλοὶ καλεῖσθαι. Καὶ ὁ Κριτόβουλος ἔφη· Ὡς 33
τοὺς μὲν καλοὺς φιλήσοντός μου, τοὺς δ' ἀγαθοὺς καταφιλήσοντος, θαῤῥῶν δίδασκε τῶν φίλων τὰ θηρατικά. Καὶ ὁ Σωκράτης ἔφη· Ὅταν οὖν, ὦ Κριτόβουλε, φίλος τινὶ βούλῃ γενέσθαι, ἐάσεις με κατειπεῖν σου πρὸς αὐτὸν, ὅτι ἄγασαί τε αὐτοῦ, καὶ ἐπιθυμεῖς φίλος αὐτοῦ εἶναι;—Κατηγόρει, ἔφη ὁ Κριτόβουλος· οὐδένα γὰρ οἶδα μισοῦντα τοὺς ἐπαινοῦντας.—Ἐὰν 34
δέ σου προσκατηγορήσω, ἔφη, ὅτι διὰ τὸ ἄγασθαι αὐτοῦ καὶ εὐνοϊκῶς ἔχεις πρὸς αὐτόν, ἆρα μὴ διαβάλλεσθαι δόξεις ὑπ' ἐμοῦ;—Ἀλλὰ καὶ αὐτῷ μοι, ἔφη, ἐγγίγνεται εὔνοια πρὸς οὓς ἂν ὑπολάβω εὐνοϊκῶς ἔχειν πρὸς ἐμέ.—Ταῦτα μὲν δή, ἔφη ὁ Σωκράτης, ἐξέσται 35
μοι λέγειν περὶ σοῦ πρὸς οὓς ἂν βούλῃ φίλους ποιήσασθαι· ἐὰν δέ μοι ἔτι ἐξουσίαν δῷς λέγειν περὶ σοῦ, ὅτι ἐπιμελής τε τῶν φίλων εἶ, καὶ οὐδενὶ οὕτω χαίρεις ὡς φίλοις ἀγαθοῖς, καὶ ἐπί τε τοῖς καλοῖς ἔργοις τῶν φίλων ἀγάλλῃ οὐχ ἧττον ἢ ἐπὶ τοῖς ἑαυτοῦ, καὶ ἐπὶ τοῖς ἀγαθοῖς τῶν φίλων χαίρεις οὐδὲν ἧττον ἢ ἐπὶ τοῖς ἑαυτοῦ, ὅπως τε ταῦτα γίγνηται τοῖς φίλοις, οὐκ ἀποκάμνεις μηχανώμενος, καὶ ὅτι ἔγνωκας ἀνδρὸς ἀρετὴν εἶναι νικᾶν τοὺς μὲν φίλους εὖ ποιοῦντα, τοὺς δ' ἐχθροὺς κακῶς, πάνυ ἂν οἶμαί σοι ἐπιτήδειον εἶναι με σύνθηρον τῶν ἀγαθῶν φίλων.—Τί οὖν, ἔφη ὁ 36
Κριτόβουλος, ἐμοὶ τοῦτο λέγεις, ὥσπερ οὐκ ἐπὶ σοὶ ὄν, ὅ τι ἂν βούλῃ, περὶ ἐμοῦ λέγειν;—Μὰ Δί' οὐχ, ὥς ποτε ἐγὼ Ἀσπασίας ἤκουσα· ἔφη γὰρ τὰς ἀγαθὰς προμνηστρίδας μετὰ μὲν ἀληθείας τἀγαθὰ διαγγελλούσας δεινὰς εἶναι συνάγειν ἀνθρώπους εἰς κηδείαν, ψευδομένας δ' οὐκ ὠφελεῖν ἐπαινούσας· τοὺς γὰρ ἐξαπατηθέντας ἅμα μισεῖν ἀλλήλους τε καὶ τὴν

προμνησαμένην· ἃ δὴ καὶ ἐγὼ πεισθεὶς ὀρθῶς ἔχειν, ἡγοῦμαι οὐκ ἐξεῖναί μοι περὶ σοῦ λέγειν ἐπαινοῦντι
37 οὐδὲν, ὅ τι ἂν μὴ ἀληθεύω. — Σὺ μὲν ἄρα, ἔφη ὁ Κριτόβουλος, τοιοῦτός μοι φίλος εἶ, ὦ Σώκρατες, οἷος, ἂν μέν τι αὐτὸς ἔχω ἐπιτήδειον εἰς τὸ φίλους κτήσασθαι, συλλαμβάνειν μοι· εἰ δὲ μή, οὐκ ἂν ἐθέλοις πλάσας τι εἰπεῖν ἐπὶ τῇ ἐμῇ ὠφελείᾳ. — Πότερα δ' ἄν, ἔφη ὁ Σωκράτης, ὦ Κριτόβουλε, δοκῶ σοι μᾶλλον ὠφελεῖν σε τὰ ψευδῆ ἐπαινῶν, ἢ πείθων πειρᾶσθαί σε
38 ἀγαθὸν ἄνδρα γενέσθαι; Εἰ δὲ μὴ φανερὸν οὕτω σοι, ἐκ τῶνδε σκέψαι· εἰ γάρ σε βουλόμενος φίλον ποιῆσαι ναυκλήρῳ ψευδόμενος ἐπαινοίην, φάσκων ἀγαθὸν εἶναι κυβερνήτην, ὁ δέ μοι πεισθεὶς ἐπιτρέψειέ σοι τὴν ναῦν μὴ ἐπισταμένῳ κυβερνᾶν, ἔχεις τινὰ ἐλπίδα μὴ ἂν σαυτόν τε καὶ τὴν ναῦν ἀπολέσαι; ἢ εἴ σοι πείσαιμι κοινῇ τὴν πόλιν ψευδόμενος, ὡς ἂν στρατηγικῷ τε καὶ δικαστικῷ καὶ πολιτικῷ, ἑαυτὴν ἐπιτρέψαι, τί ἂν οἴει σεαυτὸν καὶ τὴν πόλιν ὑπὸ σοῦ παθεῖν; ἢ εἴ τινας ἰδίᾳ τῶν πολιτῶν πείσαιμι ψευδόμενος, ὡς ὄντι οἰκονομικῷ τε καὶ ἐπιμελεῖ, τὰ ἑαυτῶν ἐπιτρέψαι, ἆρ' οὐκ ἂν πεῖραν διδοὺς ἅμα τε
39 βλαβερὸς εἴης, καὶ καταγέλαστος φαίνοιο; Ἀλλὰ συντομωτάτη τε καὶ ἀσφαλεστάτη καὶ καλλίστη ὁδός, ὦ Κριτόβουλε, ὅ τι ἂν βούλῃ δοκεῖν ἀγαθὸς εἶναι, τοῦτο καὶ γενέσθαι ἀγαθὸν πειρᾶσθαι. Ὅσαι δ' ἐν ἀνθρώποις ἀρεταὶ λέγονται, σκοπούμενος εὑρήσεις πάσας μαθήσει τε καὶ μελέτῃ αὐξανομένας. Ἐγὼ μὲν οὖν, ὦ Κριτόβουλε, οἶμαι δεῖν ἡμᾶς ταύτῃ θηρᾶσθαι· εἰ δὲ σύ πως ἄλλως γιγνώσκεις, δίδασκε. — Καὶ ὁ Κριτόβουλος· Ἀλλ' αἰσχυνοίμην ἄν, ἔφη, ὦ Σώκρατες, ἀντιλέγων τούτοις· οὔτε γὰρ καλὰ οὔτε ἀληθῆ λέγοιμ' ἄν.

CHAPTER VII.

ARGUMENT.

In the three preceding chapters, the theoretical instructions of Socrates in regard to the relation of friends is explained, and in those which follow, to the end of the book, Xenophon exhibits the manner in which he applied these precepts in the instruction and admonition of his disciples and friends.

At the time of the insurrection of Thrasybulus and his followers against the government of the thirty tyrants, there was a great dearth of provisions in Athens. Socrates having learned from Aristarchus that he was much troubled to know how to provide for a large number of relatives, who had assembled at his house (§ 1—3), shows him the folly of supposing that any degradation is attached to engaging in the pursuits requisite for procuring the necessaries of life (§ 4—8). He then points out the mutual bad effect upon himself and friends of living in their present state, and the contrasted effect of inducing them to engage in the employments best suited to their capacities and characters (§ 9, 10). Aristarchus approves the recommendation of Socrates (§ 11).

After procuring the materials of industry for the women, by borrowing money, Aristarchus finds the experiment to be successful, and, returning, relates his experience to Socrates; he however states one obstacle which yet remained to the entire success of his plan; i. e. his own inactivity, which was a source of uneasiness to the women. Socrates counsels him to relate to them the fable of the watch-dog (§ 12—14).

Καὶ μὴν τὰς ἀπορίας γε τῶν φίλων τὰς μὲν δι' 1
ἄγνοιαν ἐπειρᾶτο γνώμῃ ἀκεῖσθαι, τὰς δὲ δι' ἔνδειαν
διδάσκων κατὰ δύναμιν ἀλλήλοις ἐπαρκεῖν. Ἐρῶ δὲ
καὶ ἐν τούτοις ἃ σύνοιδα αὐτῷ. Ἀρίσταρχον γάρ
ποτε ὁρῶν σκυθρωπῶς ἔχοντα· Ἔοικας, ἔφη, ὦ Ἀρί-
σταρχε, βαρέως φέρειν τι· χρὴ δὲ τοῦ βάρους μετα-
διδόναι τοῖς φίλοις· ἴσως γὰρ ἄν τί σε καὶ ἡμεῖς
κουφίσαιμεν. Καὶ ὁ Ἀρίσταρχος· Ἀλλὰ μήν, ἔφη, 2
ὦ Σώκρατες, ἐν πολλῇ γέ εἰμι ἀπορίᾳ· ἐπεὶ γὰρ

ἐστασίασεν ἡ πόλις, πολλῶν φυγόντων εἰς τὸν Πειραιᾶ, συνεληλύθασιν ὡς ἐμὲ καταλελειμμέναι ἀδελφαί τε καὶ ἀδελφιδαῖ καὶ ἀνεψιαὶ τοσαῦται, ὥςτ' εἶναι ἐν τῇ οἰκίᾳ τεσσαρεςκαίδεκα τοὺς ἐλευθέρους· λαμβάνομεν δὲ οὔτε ἐκ τῆς γῆς οὐδέν· οἱ γὰρ ἐναντίοι κρατοῦσιν αὐτῆς· οὔτε ἀπὸ τῶν οἰκιῶν· ὀλιγανθρωπία γὰρ ἐν τῷ ἄστει γέγονε· τὰ ἔπιπλα δὲ οὐδεὶς ὠνεῖται, οὐδὲ δανείσασθαι οὐδαμόθεν ἔστιν ἀργύριον, ἀλλὰ πρότερον ἄν τίς μοι δοκεῖ ἐν τῇ ὁδῷ ζητῶν εὑρεῖν ἢ δανειζόμενος λαβεῖν. Χαλεπὸν μὲν οὖν ἐστιν, ὦ Σώκρατες, τοὺς οἰκείους περιορᾶν ἀπολλυμένους, ἀδύνατον
3 δὲ τοσούτους τρέφειν ἐν τοιούτοις πράγμασιν. Ἀκούσας οὖν ταῦτα ὁ Σωκράτης· Τί ποτέ ἐστιν, ἔφη, ὅτι ὁ Κεράμων μὲν πολλοὺς τρέφων οὐ μόνον ἑαυτῷ τε καὶ τούτοις τὰ ἐπιτήδεια δύναται παρέχειν, ἀλλὰ καὶ περιποιεῖται τοσαῦτα, ὥςτε καὶ πλουτεῖν, σὺ δὲ πολλοὺς τρέφων δέδοικας, μὴ δι' ἔνδειαν τῶν ἐπιτηδειων ἅπαντες ἀπόλησθε;—Ὅτι νὴ Δί', ἔφη, ὁ μὲν δούλους
4 τρέφει, ἐγὼ δὲ ἐλευθέρους.—Καὶ πότερον, ἔφη, τοὺς παρὰ σοὶ ἐλευθέρους οἴει βελτίους εἶναι, ἢ τοὺς παρὰ Κεράμωνι δούλους;—Ἐγὼ μὲν οἶμαι, ἔφη, τοὺς παρὰ ἐμοὶ ἐλευθέρους.—Οὐκοῦν, ἔφη, αἰσχρὸν τὸν μὲν ἀπὸ τῶν πονηροτέρων εὐπορεῖν, σὲ δὲ πολλῷ βελτίους ἔχοντα ἐν ἀπορίαις εἶναι;—Νὴ Δί', ἔφη· ὁ μὲν γὰρ τεχνίτας τρέφει, ἐγὼ δὲ ἐλευθερίως πεπαιδευμένους.—
5 Ἆρ' οὖν, ἔφη, τεχνῖταί εἰσιν οἱ χρήσιμόν τι ποιεῖν ἐπιστάμενοι;—Μάλιστά γε, ἔφη.—Οὐκοῦν χρήσιμά γ' ἄλφιτα;—Σφόδρα γε.—Τί δὲ ἄρτοι;—Οὐδὲν ἧττον.—Τί γάρ; ἔφη, ἱμάτιά τε ἀνδρεῖα καὶ γυναικεῖα, καὶ χιτωνίσκοι καὶ χλαμύδες καὶ ἐξωμίδες;—Σφόδρα γε, ἔφη, καὶ πάντα ταῦτα χρήσιμα.—Ἔπειτα, ἔφη, οἱ παρὰ σοὶ τούτων οὐδὲν ἐπίστανται ποιεῖν;—Πάντα
6 μὲν οὖν, ὡς ἐγῷμαι.—Εἶτ' οὐκ οἶσθα, ὅτι ἀφ' ἑνὸς μὲν τούτων, ἀλφιτοποιίας, Ναυσικύδης οὐ μόνον ἑαυτόν

γε καὶ τοὺς οἰκέτας τρέφει, ἀλλὰ πρὸς τούτοις καὶ ὗς πολλὰς καὶ βοῦς, καὶ περιποιεῖται τοσαῦτα, ὥστε καὶ τῇ πόλει πολλάκις λειτουργεῖν, ἀπὸ δὲ ἀρτοποιίας Κύρηβος τήν τε οἰκίαν πᾶσαν διατρέφει καὶ ζῇ δαψιλῶς, Δημέας δὲ ὁ Κολλυτεὺς ἀπὸ χλαμυδουργίας, Μένων δ' ἀπὸ χλανιδοποιίας, Μεγαρέων δ' οἱ πλεῖστοι, ἔφη, ἀπὸ ἐξωμιδοποιίας διατρέφονται ;—Νὴ Δί', ἔφη· οὗτοι μὲν γὰρ ὠνούμενοι βαρβάρους ἀνθρώπους ἔχουσιν, ὥστ' ἀναγκάζειν ἐργάζεσθαι ἃ καλῶς ἔχει, ἐγὼ δ' ἐλευθέρους τε καὶ συγγενεῖς.—Ἔπειτ', ἔφη, 7
ὅτι ἐλεύθεροί τ' εἰσὶ καὶ συγγενεῖς σοι, οἴει χρῆναι μηδὲν αὐτοὺς ποιεῖν ἄλλο ἢ ἐσθίειν καὶ καθεύδειν ; Πότερον καὶ τῶν ἄλλων ἐλευθέρων τοὺς οὕτω ζῶντας ἄμεινον διάγοντας ὁρᾷς καὶ μᾶλλον εὐδαιμονίζεις, ἢ τούς, ἃ ἐπίστανται χρήσιμα πρὸς τὸν βίον, τούτων ἐπιμελομένους ; ἢ τὴν μὲν ἀργίαν καὶ τὴν ἀμέλειαν αἰσθάνῃ τοῖς ἀνθρώποις πρός τε τὸ μαθεῖν ἃ προσήκει ἐπίστασθαι, καὶ πρὸς τὸ μνημονεύειν ἃ ἂν μάθωσι, καὶ πρὸς τὸ ὑγιαίνειν τε καὶ ἰσχύειν τοῖς σώμασι, καὶ πρὸς τὸ κτήσασθαί τε καὶ σώζειν τὰ χρήσιμα πρὸς τὸν βίον ὠφέλιμα ὄντα, τὴν δὲ ἐργασίαν καὶ τὴν ἐπιμέλειαν οὐδὲν χρήσιμα ; Ἔμαθον δέ, ἃ φῂς αὐτὰς ἐπί- 8
στασθαι, πότερον ὡς οὔτε χρήσιμα ὄντα πρὸς τὸν βίον, οὔτε ποιήσουσαι αὐτῶν οὐδέν, ἢ τοὐναντίον, ὡς καὶ ἐπιμελησόμεναι τούτων, καὶ ὠφελησόμεναι ἀπ' αὐτῶν ; ποτέρως γὰρ ἂν μᾶλλων ἄνθρωποι σωφρονοῖεν, ἀργοῦντες, ἢ τῶν χρησίμων ἐπιμελούμενοι ; ποτέρως δ' ἂν δικαιότεροι εἶεν, εἰ ἐργάζοιντο, ἢ εἰ ἀργοῦντες βουλεύοιντο περὶ τῶν ἐπιτηδείων ; Ἀλλὰ καὶ νῦν μέν, 9
ὡς ἐγᾦμαι, οὔτε σὺ ἐκείνας φιλεῖς, οὔτε ἐκεῖναι σέ· σὺ μὲν ἡγούμενος αὐτὰς ἐπιζημίους εἶναι σεαυτῷ, ἐκεῖναι δὲ σὲ ὁρῶσαι ἀχθόμενον ἐφ' ἑαυταῖς. Ἐκ δὲ τούτων κίνδυνος μείζω τε ἀπέχθειαν γίγνεσθαι, καὶ τὴν προγεγονυῖαν χάριν μειοῦσθαι. Ἐὰν δὲ προστα-

τήσῃς, ὅπως ἐνεργοὶ ὦσι, σὺ μὲν ἐκείνας φιλήσεις,
ὁρῶν ὠφελίμους σεαυτῷ οὔσας, ἐκεῖναι δὲ σὲ ἀγαπή-
σουσιν, αἰσθόμεναι χαίροντά σε αὐταῖς, τῶν δὲ προ-
γεγονυιῶν εὐεργεσιῶν ἥδιον μεμνημένοι τὴν ἀπ' ἐκεί-
νων χάριν αὐξήσετε, καὶ ἐκ τούτων φιλικώτερόν τε καὶ
10 οἰκειότερον ἀλλήλοις ἕξετε. Εἰ μὲν τοίνυν αἰσχρόν
τι ἔμελλον ἐργάσασθαι, θάνατον ἀντ' αὐτοῦ προαι-
ρετέον ἦν· νῦν δὲ, ἃ μὲν δοκεῖ κάλλιστα καὶ πρεπω-
δέστερα γυναικὶ εἶναι, ἐπίστανται, ὡς ἔοικε· πάντες
δὲ, ἃ ἐπίστανται, ῥᾷστά τε καὶ τάχιστα καὶ κάλλιστα
καὶ ἥδιστα ἐργάζονται. Μὴ οὖν ὄκνει, ἔφη, ταῦτα
εἰςηγεῖσθαι αὐταῖς, ἃ σοί τε λυσιτελήσει κἀκείναις,
11 καί, ὡς εἰκός, ἡδέως ὑπακούσονται.—'Αλλά, νὴ τοὺς
θεούς, ἔφη ὁ 'Αρίσταρχος, οὕτως μοι δοκεῖς καλῶς λέ-
γειν, ὦ Σώκρατες, ὥςτε πρόσθεν μὲν οὐ προςιέμην
δανείσασθαι, εἰδὼς, ὅτι ἀναλώσας, ὅ τι ἂν λάβω, οὐχ
ἕξω ἀποδοῦναι, νῦν δέ μοι δοκῶ εἰς ἔργων ἀφορμὴν
ὑπομένειν αὐτὸ ποιῆσαι.

12 'Εκ τούτων δὲ ἐπορίσθη μὲν ἀφορμή, ἐωνήθη δὲ
ἔρια· καὶ ἐργαζόμεναι μὲν ἠρίστων, ἐργασάμεναι δὲ
ἐδείπνουν, ἱλαραὶ δὲ ἀντὶ σκυθρωπῶν ἦσαν· καὶ ἀντὶ
ὑφορωμένων ἑαυτὰς ἡδέως ἀλλήλας ἑώρων· καὶ αἱ μὲν
ὡς κηδεμόνα ἐφίλουν, ὁ δὲ ὡς ὠφελίμους ἠγάπα.
Τέλος δὲ ἐλθὼν πρὸς τὸν Σωκράτην χαίρων διηγεῖτο
ταῦτά τε, καὶ ὅτι αἰτιῶνται αὐτὸν μόνον τῶν ἐν τῇ
13 οἰκίᾳ ἀργὸν ἐσθίειν. Καὶ ὁ Σωκράτης ἔφη· Εἶτα
οὐ λέγεις αὐταῖς τὸν τοῦ κυνὸς λόγον; φασὶ γάρ,
ὅτε φωνήεντα ἦν τὰ ζῷα, τὴν ὄϊν πρὸς τὸν δεσπότην
εἰπεῖν· Θαυμαστὸν ποιεῖς, ὃς ἡμῖν μὲν ταῖς καὶ ἔριά
σοι καὶ ἄρνας καὶ τυρὸν παρεχούσαις οὐδὲν δίδως,
ὅ τι ἂν μὴ ἐκ τῆς γῆς λάβωμεν, τῷ δὲ κυνί, ὃς οὐδὲν
τοιοῦτόν σοι παρέχει, μεταδίδως οὗπερ αὐτὸς ἔχεις
14 σίτου. Τὸν κύνα οὖν ἀκούσαντα εἰπεῖν· Ναὶ μὰ Δία·
ἐγὼ γάρ εἰμι ὁ καὶ ὑμᾶς αὐτὰς σώζων, ὥςτε μητε

ὑπ' ἀνθρώπων κλέπτεσθαι, μήτε ὑπὸ λύκων ἁρπάζεσθαι, ἐπεὶ ὑμεῖς γε, εἰ μὴ ἐγὼ προφυλάττοιμι ὑμᾶς, οὐδ' ἂν νέμεσθαι δύναισθε, φοβούμεναι, μὴ ἀπόλησθε. Οὕτω δὴ λέγεται καὶ τὰ πρόβατα συγχωρῆσαι τὸν κύνα προτιμᾶσθαι. Καὶ σὺ οὖν ἐκείναις λέγε, ὅτι ἀντὶ κυνὸς εἶ φύλαξ καὶ ἐπιμελητής, καὶ διὰ σὲ οὐδ' ὑφ' ἑνὸς ἀδικούμεναι ἀσφαλῶς τε καὶ ἡδέως ἐργαζόμεναι ζῶσιν.

CHAPTER VIII.

ARGUMENT.

Eutherus, an old friend of Socrates, had lost his paternal estate by the peace of Theramenes between the Athenians and Spartans, and was compelled to engage in manual labor to procure his daily bread (§ 1). Socrates urges him to engage in some pursuit better suited to his age, and recommends that of a *villicus*, an overseer or steward to some person of wealth (§ 2, 3). The objection of Eutherus, that there is something slavish in obliging one's self to be accountable to another, Socrates obviates by the comparison of those who engage in public life, who are rather considered more free on account of their employment, and by the suggestion, that it is impossible to engage in any pursuit which is wholly devoid of this accountability. Each one should apply himself with zeal and alacrity to that which is best suited to his station and ability (§ 4—6).

---

1 Ἄλλον δέ ποτε ἀρχαῖον ἑταῖρον διὰ χρόνου ἰδών, Πόθεν, ἔφη, Εὔθηρε, φαίνῃ; — Ὑπὸ μὲν τὴν κατάλυσιν τοῦ πολέμου, ἔφη, ὦ Σώκρατες, ἐκ τῆς ἀποδημίας, νυνὶ μέντοι αὐτόθεν· ἐπειδὴ γὰρ ἀφῃρέθημεν τὰ ἐν τῇ ὑπερορίᾳ κτήματα, ἐν δὲ τῇ Ἀττικῇ ὁ πατήρ μοι οὐδὲν κατέλιπεν, ἀναγκάζομαι νῦν ἐπιδημήσας τῷ σώματι ἐργαζόμενος τὰ ἐπιτήδεια πορίζεσθαι· δοκεῖ

δέ μοι τοῦτο κρεῖττον εἶναι ἢ δέεσθαί τινος ἀνθρώπων, ἄλλως τε καὶ μηδὲν ἔχοντα, ἐφ' ὅτῳ ἂν δανει-
2 ζοίμην.—Καὶ πόσον χρόνον οἴει σοι, ἔφη, τὸ σῶμα ἱκανὸν εἶναι μισθοῦ τὰ ἐπιτήδεια ἐργάζεσθαι;—Μὰ τὸν Δί', ἔφη, οὐ πολὺν χρόνον.—Καὶ μήν, ἔφη, ὅταν γε πρεσβύτερος γένῃ, δῆλον, ὅτι δαπάνης μὲν δεήσῃ, μισθὸν δὲ οὐδείς σοι θελήσει τῶν τοῦ σώματος ἔργων
3 διδόναι.—Ἀληθῆ λέγεις, ἔφη.—Οὐκοῦν, ἔφη, κρεῖττόν ἐστιν αὐτόθεν τοῖς τοιούτοις τῶν ἔργων ἐπιτίθεσθαι, ἃ καὶ πρεσβυτέρῳ γενομένῳ ἐπαρκέσει, καὶ προσελθόντα τῳ τῶν πλείονα χρήματα κεκτημένων, τῷ δεομένῳ τοῦ συνεπιμελησομένου, ἔργων τε ἐπιστατοῦντα καὶ συγκομίζοντα καρποὺς καὶ συμφυλάττοντα
4 τὴν οὐσίαν ὠφελοῦντα ἀντωφελεῖσθαι.—Χαλεπῶς ἄν, ἔφη, ἐγώ, ὦ Σώκρατες, δουλείαν ὑπομείναιμι.—Καὶ μὴν οἵ γε ἐν ταῖς πόλεσι προστατεύοντες καὶ τῶν δημοσίων ἐπιμελόμενοι οὐ δουλοπρεπέστεροι ἕνεκα τού-
5 του, ἀλλ' ἐλευθεριώτεροι νομίζονται.—Ὅλως μήν, ἔφη, ὦ Σώκρατες, τὸ ὑπαίτιον εἶναί τινι οὐ πάνυ προσίεμαι.—Καὶ μήν, ἔφη, Εὔθηρε, οὐ πάνυ γε ῥᾴδιόν ἐστιν εὑρεῖν ἔργον, ἐφ' ᾧ οὐκ ἄν τις αἰτίαν ἔχοι· χαλεπὸν γὰρ οὕτω τι ποιῆσαι, ὥστε μηδὲν ἁμαρτεῖν, χαλεπὸν δὲ καὶ ἀναμαρτήτως τι ποιήσαντα μὴ ἀγνώμονι κριτῇ περιτυχεῖν, ἐπεὶ καὶ οἷς νῦν ἐργάζεσθαι φῄς, θαυμάζω εἰ ῥᾴδιόν ἐστιν ἀνέγκλητον διαγίνεσθαι.
6 Χρὴ οὖν πειρᾶσθαι τούς τε φιλαιτίους φεύγειν, καὶ τοὺς εὐγνώμονας διώκειν, καὶ τῶν πραγμάτων, ὅσα μὲν δύνασαι ποιεῖν, ὑπομένειν, ὅσα δὲ μὴ δύνασαι, φυλάττεσθαι, ὅ τι δ' ἂν πράττῃς, τούτων ὡς κάλλιστα καὶ προθυμότατα ἐπιμελεῖσθαι· οὕτω γὰρ ἥκιστα μέν σε οἶμαι ἐν αἰτίᾳ εἶναι, μάλιστα δὲ τῇ ἀπορίᾳ βοήθειαν εὑρεῖν, ῥᾷστα δὲ καὶ ἀκινδυνότατα ζῆν καὶ εἰς τὸ γῆρας διαρκέστατα.

CHAPTER IX.

ARGUMENT.

Crito, a rich and worthy man, complained to Socrates of the herd of sycophants by whom he was annoyed (§ 1). Socrates recommended to him Archedemus, a poor but honest man, who was well qualified, both by his ability to speak and act, to protect him from all their injustice (§ 2—4). Archedemus was employed, and not only won the esteem and friendship of Crito, but his aid was much sought by the friends of Crito in the management of their business. He thus not only obtained pecuniary advantage, but authority and distinction (§ 5—8).

Οἶδα δέ ποτε αὐτὸν καὶ Κρίτωνος ἀκούσαντα, ὡς 1
χαλεπὸν ὁ βίος Ἀθήνησιν εἴη ἀνδρὶ βουλομένῳ τὰ ἑαυτοῦ πράττειν. Νῦν γάρ, ἔφη, ἐμέ τινες εἰς δίκας ἄγουσιν, οὐχ ὅτι ἀδικοῦνται ὑπ' ἐμοῦ, ἀλλ' ὅτι νομίζουσιν ἥδιον ἄν με ἀργύριον τελέσαι ἢ πράγματα ἔχειν.
Καὶ ὁ Σωκράτης· Εἰπέ μοι, ἔφη, ὦ Κρίτων, κύνας δὲ 2
τρέφεις, ἵνα σοι τοὺς λύκους ἀπὸ τῶν προβάτων ἀπερύκωσι;—Καὶ μάλα, ἔφη· μᾶλλον γάρ μοι λυσιτελεῖ τρέφειν ἢ μή.—Οὐκ ἂν οὖν θρέψαις καὶ ἄνδρα, ὅστις ἐθέλοι τε καὶ δύναιτό σου ἀπερύκειν τοὺς ἐπιχειροῦντας ἀδικεῖν σε;—Ἡδέως γ' ἄν, ἔφη, εἰ μὴ φοβοίμην,
ὅπως μὴ ἐπ' αὐτόν με τράποιτο.—Τί δ'; ἔφη, οὐχ 3
ὁρᾷς, ὅτι πολλῷ ἥδιόν ἐστι χαριζόμενον οἵῳ σοὶ ἀνδρὶ ἢ ἀπεχθόμενον ὠφελεῖσθαι; εὖ ἴσθι, ὅτι εἰσὶν ἐνθάδε τῶν τοιούτων ἀνδρῶν οἳ πάνυ ἂν φιλοτιμηθεῖεν φίλῳ σοι χρῆσθαι.

Καὶ ἐκ τούτων ἀνευρίσκουσιν Ἀρχέδημον, πάνυ 4
μὲν ἱκανὸν εἰπεῖν τε καὶ πρᾶξαι, πένητα δέ· οὐ γὰρ ἦν οἷος ἀπὸ παντὸς κερδαίνειν, ἀλλά, φιλόχρηστός τε καὶ εὐφυέστερος ὤν, ἀπὸ τῶν συκοφαντῶν λαμβάνειν.

Τούτῳ οὖν ὁ Κρίτων, ὁπότε συγκομίζοι ἢ σῖτον ἢ ἔλαιον
ἢ οἶνον ἢ ἔρια ἢ ἄλλο τι τῶν ἐν ἀγρῷ γιγνομένων χρη-
σίμων πρὸς τὸν βίον, ἀφελὼν [ἂν] ἔδωκε· καὶ ὁπότε
5 θύοι, ἐκάλει, καὶ τὰ τοιαῦτα πάντα ἐπεμελεῖτο. Νο-
μίσας δὲ ὁ Ἀρχέδημος ἀποστροφήν οἱ τὸν Κρίτωνος
οἶκον μάλα περιεῖπεν αὐτόν· καὶ εὐθὺς τῶν συκοφαν-
τούντων τὸν Κρίτωνα ἀνευρήκει πολλὰ μὲν ἀδικήματα,
πολλοὺς δὲ ἐχθρούς, καὶ αὐτῶν τινα προσεκαλέσατο
εἰς δίκην δημοσίαν, ἐν ᾗ αὐτὸν ἔδει κριθῆναι, ὅ τι δεῖ
6 παθεῖν ἢ ἀποτῖσαι. Ὁ δὲ, συνειδὼς αὑτῷ πολλὰ καὶ
πονηρὰ, πάντ' ἐποίει, ὥστε ἀπαλλαγῆναι τοῦ Ἀρχεδή-
μου. Ὁ δὲ Ἀρχέδημος οὐκ ἀπηλλάττετο, ἕως τόν τε
7 Κρίτωνα ἀφῆκε, καὶ αὐτῷ χρήματα ἔδωκεν. Ἐπεὶ δὲ
τοῦτό τε καὶ ἄλλα τοιαῦτα ὁ Ἀρχέδημος διεπράξατο,
ἤδη τότε, ὥσπερ, ὅταν νομεὺς ἀγαθὸν κύνα ἔχῃ, καὶ οἱ
ἄλλοι νομεῖς βούλονται πλησίον αὐτοῦ τὰς ἀγέλας ἱστά-
ναι, ἵνα τοῦ κυνὸς ἀπολαύωσιν, οὕτω καὶ Κρίτωνος πολ-
λοὶ τῶν φίλων ἐδέοντο καὶ σφίσι παρέχειν φύλακα
8 τὸν Ἀρχέδημον. Ὁ δὲ Ἀρχέδημος τῷ Κρίτωνι ἡδέως
ἐχαρίζετο, καὶ οὐχ ὅτι μόνος ὁ Κρίτων ἐν ἡσυχίᾳ ἦν,
ἀλλὰ καὶ οἱ φίλοι αὐτοῦ· εἰ δέ τις αὐτῷ τούτων, οἷς
ἀπήχθετο, ὀνειδίζοι, ὡς ὑπὸ Κρίτωνος ὠφελούμενος
κολακεύοι αὐτόν· Πότερον οὖν, ἔφη ὁ Ἀρχέδημος,
αἰσχρόν ἐστιν εὐεργετούμενον ὑπὸ χρηστῶν ἀνθρώπων
καὶ ἀντευεργετοῦντα τοὺς μὲν τοιούτους φίλους ποιεῖ-
σθαι, τοῖς δὲ πονηροῖς διαφέρεσθαι, ἢ τοὺς μὲν καλοὺς
κἀγαθοὺς ἀδικεῖν πειρώμενον ἐχθροὺς ποιεῖσθαι, τοῖς
δὲ πονηροῖς συνεργοῦντα πειρᾶσθαι φίλους ποιεῖσθαι,
καὶ χρῆσθαι τούτοις ἀντ' ἐκείνων; Ἐκ δὲ τούτου εἷς
τε τῶν Κρίτωνος φίλων Ἀρχέδημος ἦν, καὶ ὑπὸ τῶν
ἄλλων Κρίτωνος φίλων ἐτιμᾶτο.

CHAPTER X.

ARGUMENT.

Socrates admonished his friend Diodorus, who was possessed of wealth, to secure to himself the friendship of Hermogenes, a poor but worthy man, by giving him pecuniary aid.

If we offer rewards, he reasoned, for a slave who has run away, or care for one that is sick, should we not much rather see to it that a friend, who is of far more value than a slave, is not crushed under the burden of poverty (§ 1, 2). Hermogenes is able to be of more value than many slaves, and may now be firmly secured as a friend at a very small price (§ 3, 4). Socrates refused to send Hermogenes to Diodorus, but urged Diodorus to go to him (§ 5), which he did, and the result verified the prediction of Socrates (§ 6).

Οἶδα δὲ καὶ Διοδώρῳ αὐτὸν ἑταίρῳ ὄντι τοιάδε δια- 1
λεχθέντα· Εἰπέ μοι, ἔφη, ὦ Διόδωρε, ἄν τίς σοι τῶν
οἰκετῶν ἀποδρᾷ, ἐπιμελῇ, ὅπως ἀνακομίσῃ; — Καὶ 2
ἄλλους γε νὴ Δί', ἔφη, παρακαλῶ, σῶστρα τούτου
ἀνακηρύσσων.—Τί γάρ; ἔφη, ἐάν τίς σοι κάμνῃ τῶν
οἰκετῶν, τούτου ἐπιμελῇ, καὶ παρακαλεῖς ἰατρούς, ὅπως
μὴ ἀποθάνῃ;—Σφόδρα γ', ἔφη.—Εἰ δέ τίς σοι τῶν
γνωρίμων, ἔφη, πολὺ τῶν οἰκετῶν χρησιμώτερος ὤν,
κινδυνεύει δι' ἔνδειαν ἀπολέσθαι, οὐκ οἴει σοι ἄξιον
εἶναι ἐπιμεληθῆναι, ὅπως διασωθῇ; Καὶ μὴν οἶσθά 3
γε, ὅτι οὐκ ἀγνώμων ἐστὶν Ἑρμογένης, αἰσχύνοιτο δ'
ἄν, εἰ ὠφελούμενος ὑπὸ σοῦ μὴ ἀντωφελοίη σε· καί-
τοι τὸ ὑπηρέτην ἑκόντα τε καὶ εὔνουν καὶ παράμονον
καὶ τὸ κελευόμενον ἱκανὸν ποιεῖν ἔχειν, καὶ μὴ μόνον
τὸ κελευόμενον ἱκανὸν ὄντα ποιεῖν, ἀλλὰ δυνάμενον
καὶ ἀφ' ἑαυτοῦ χρήσιμον εἶναι, καὶ προνοεῖν καὶ προ-
βουλεύεσθαι, πολλῶν οἰκετῶν οἶμαι ἀντάξιοι εἶναι.

4 Οἱ μέντοι ἀγαθοὶ οἰκονόμοι, ὅταν τὸ πολλοῦ ἄξιον
μικροῦ ἐξῇ πρίασθαι, τότε φασὶ δεῖν ὠνεῖσθαι· νῦν
δὲ διὰ τὰ πράγματα εὐωνοτάτους ἔστι φίλους ἀγαθοὺς
5 κτήσασθαι. Καὶ ὁ Διόδωρος· Ἀλλὰ καλῶς γε, ἔφη,
λέγεις, ὦ Σώκρατες, καὶ κέλευσον ἐλθεῖν ὡς ἐμὲ τὸν
Ἑρμογένην.—Μὰ Δί', ἔφη, οὐκ ἔγωγε· νομίζω γὰρ
οὔτε σοὶ κάλλιον εἶναι τὸ καλέσαι ἐκεῖνον τοῦ αὐτὸν
ἐλθεῖν πρὸς ἐκεῖνον, οὔτε ἐκείνῳ μεῖζον ἀγαθὸν τὸ
6 πραχθῆναι ταῦτα ἢ σοί. Οὕτω δὴ ὁ Διόδωρος ᾤχετο
πρὸς τὸν Ἑρμογένην, καὶ οὐ πολὺ τελέσας ἐκτήσατο
φίλον, ὃς ἔργον εἶχε σκοπεῖν, ὅ τι ἂν ἢ λέγων ἢ πράττων ὠφελοίη τε καὶ εὐφραίνοι Διόδωοον.

ΞΕΝΟΦΩΝΤΟΣ

ΑΠΟΜΝΗΜΟΝΕΥΜΑΤΩΝ.

ΤΡΙΤΟΝ.

CHAPTER I.

ARGUMENT.

The first seven chapters of Book III. relate to the duties of those who engage in the management of civil and military affairs, and comprise a more complete refutation of that branch of the second accusation of Socrates, stated and briefly controverted in I. 2. 9 sq.

The subject of this chapter is, the duties and qualifications of a military commander.

Socrates urged a young Athenian, who desired to become a general, to put himself under the instruction of a professed teacher of the art of managing an army. Knowledge is the more necessary for the general, since the whole State in time of danger is intrusted to him, and the most important consequences are dependent upon his skill in the duties of his calling (§ 1—3). When the pupil returned, thinking himself, without doubt, qualified for any office in the army, Socrates sportively inquired of him, what and how he had been taught, and was told that he learned only tactics (§ 4, 5). Socrates explained to him that although the ability to arrange an army is important, still it is but one among many prerequisites for a good general (§ 6—8). He further shows him that arbitrary rules for arranging an army, without discrimination in regard to the character of the troops, and without reference to time, place, and other contingencies, are of little value, and sends him back to his teacher to question him on these points (§ 9—11).

Ὅτι δὲ τοὺς ὀρεγομένους τῶν καλῶν ἐπιμελεῖς ὢν 1
ὀρέγοιντο ποιῶν ὠφέλει, νῦν τοῦτο διηγήσομαι· ἀκούσας

γάρ ποτε Διονυσόδωρον εἰς τὴν πόλιν ἥκειν ἐπαγγελλόμενον στρατηγεῖν διδάξειν, ἔλεξε πρός τινα τῶν ξυνόντων, ὃν ᾐσθάνετο βουλόμενον τῆς τιμῆς ταύτης ἐν
2 τῇ πόλει τυγχάνειν· Αἰσχρὸν μέντοι, ὦ νεανία, τὸν βουλόμενον ἐν τῇ πόλει στρατηγεῖν, ἐξὸν τοῦτο μαθεῖν, ἀμελῆσαι αὐτοῦ, καὶ δικαίως ἂν οὗτος ὑπὸ τῆς πόλεως ζημιοῖτο πολὺ μᾶλλον, ἢ εἴ τις ἀνδριάντας ἐργολα-
3 βοίη, μὴ μεμαθηκὼς ἀνδριαντοποιεῖν. Ὅλης γὰρ τῆς πόλεως ἐν τοῖς πολεμικοῖς κινδύνοις ἐπιτρεπομένης τῷ στρατηγῷ, μεγάλα τά τε ἀγαθὰ κατορθοῦντος αὐτοῦ καὶ τὰ κακὰ διαμαρτάνοντος εἰκὸς γίγνεσθαι· πῶς οὖν οὐκ ἂν δικαίως ὁ τοῦ μὲν μανθάνειν τοῦτο ἀμελῶν, τοῦ δὲ αἱρεθῆναι ἐπιμελόμενος ζημιοῖτο; Τοιαῦτα μὲν
4 δὴ λέγων ἔπεισεν αὐτὸν ἐλθόντα μανθάνειν. Ἐπεὶ δὲ μεμαθηκὼς ἧκε, προσέπαιζεν αὐτῷ λέγων· Οὐ δοκεῖ ὑμῖν, ὦ ἄνδρες, ὥσπερ Ὅμηρος τὸν Ἀγαμέμνονα γεραρὸν ἔφη εἶναι, καὶ [οὕτως] ὅδε στρατηγεῖν μαθὼν γεραρώτερος φαίνεσθαι; καὶ γὰρ ὥσπερ ὁ κιθαρίζειν μαθὼν, καὶ ἐὰν μὴ κιθαρίζῃ, κιθαριστής ἐστι, καὶ ὁ μαθὼν ἰᾶσθαι, κἂν μὴ ἰατρεύῃ, ὅμως ἰατρός ἐστιν, οὕτω καὶ ὅδε ἀπὸ τοῦδε τοῦ χρόνου διατελεῖ στρατηγὸς ὤν, κἂν μηδεὶς αὐτὸν ἕληται· ὁ δὲ μὴ ἐπιστάμενος οὔτε στρατηγὸς οὔτε ἰατρός ἐστιν, οὐδὲ ἐὰν ὑπὸ
5 πάντων ἀνθρώπων αἱρεθῇ. Ἀτάρ, ἔφη, ἵνα καὶ, ἐὰν ἡμῶν τις ταξιαρχῇ ἢ λοχαγῇ σοι, ἐπιστημονέστεροι τῶν πολεμικῶν ὦμεν, λέξον ἡμῖν, πόθεν ἤρξατό σε διδάσκειν τὴν στρατηγίαν. Καὶ ὅς· Ἐκ τοῦ αὐτοῦ, ἔφη, εἰς ὅπερ καὶ ἐτελεύτα· τὰ γὰρ τακτικὰ ἐμέ γε
6 καὶ ἄλλο οὐδὲν ἐδίδαξεν. Ἀλλὰ μήν, ἔφη ὁ Σωκράτης, τοῦτό γε πολλοστὸν μέρος ἐστὶ στρατηγίας· καὶ γὰρ παρασκευαστικὸν τῶν εἰς τὸν πόλεμον τὸν στρατηγὸν εἶναι χρή, καὶ ποριστικὸν τῶν ἐπιτηδείων τοῖς στρατιώταις, καὶ μηχανικόν, καὶ ἐργαστικόν, καὶ ἐπιμελῆ, καὶ καρτερικόν, καὶ ἀγχίνουν, καὶ φιλόφρονά τε

καὶ ὠμόν, καὶ ἁπλοῦν τε καὶ ἐπίβουλον, καὶ φυλακτικόν τε καὶ κλέπτην, καὶ προετικὸν καὶ ἅρπαγα, καὶ φιλόδωρον καὶ πλεονέκτην, καὶ ἀσφαλῆ καὶ ἐπιθετικόν, καὶ ἄλλα πολλὰ καὶ φύσει καὶ ἐπιστήμῃ δεῖ τὸν εὖ στρατηγήσοντα ἔχειν. Καλὸν δὲ καὶ τὸ τακτι- 7
κὸν εἶναι· πολὺ γὰρ διαφέρει στράτευμα τεταγμένον ἀτάκτου· ὥςπερ λίθοι τε καὶ πλίνθοι καὶ ξύλα καὶ κέραμος ἀτάκτως μὲν ἐῤῥιμμένα οὐδὲν χρήσιμά ἐστιν, ἐπειδὰν δὲ ταχθῇ κάτω μὲν καὶ ἐπιπολῆς τὰ μήτε σηπόμενα μήτε τηκόμενα, οἵ τε λίθοι καὶ ὁ κέραμος, ἐν μέσῳ δὲ αἵ τε πλίνθοι καὶ τὰ ξύλα, ὥςπερ ἐν οἰκοδομίᾳ, συντίθεται, τότε γίγνεται πολλοῦ ἄξιον
κτῆμα οἰκία. Ἀλλὰ πάνυ, ἔφη ὁ νεανίσκος, ὅμοιον, 8
ὦ Σώκρατες, εἴρηκας· καὶ γὰρ ἐν τῷ πολέμῳ τούς τε πρώτους ἀρίστους δεῖ τάττειν καὶ τοὺς τελευταίους, ἐν δὲ μέσῳ τοὺς χειρίστους, ἵνα ὑπὸ μὲν τῶν ἄγωνται,
ὑπὸ δὲ αὖ τῶν ὠθῶνται.—Εἰ μὲν τοίνυν, ἔφη, καὶ 9
διαγιγνώσκειν σε τοὺς ἀγαθοὺς καὶ τοὺς κακοὺς ἐδίδαξεν· εἰ δὲ μή, τί σοι ὄφελος ὧν ἔμαθες; οὐδὲ γὰρ εἴ σε ἀργύριον ἐκέλευσε πρῶτον μὲν καὶ τελευταῖον τὸ κάλλιστον τάττειν, ἐν μέσῳ δὲ τὸ χείριστον, μὴ διδάξας διαγιγνώσκειν τό τε καλὸν καὶ τὸ κίβδηλον, οὐδὲν ἄν σοι ὄφελος ἦν.—Ἀλλὰ μὰ Δί', ἔφη, οὐκ ἐδίδαξεν, ὥστε αὐτοὺς ἂν ἡμᾶς δέοι τούς τε ἀγαθοὺς
καὶ τοὺς κακοὺς κρίνειν.—Τί οὖν οὐ σκοποῦμεν, ἔφη, 10
πῶς ἂν αὐτῶν μὴ διαμαρτάνοιμεν;—Βούλομαι, ἔφη ὁ νεανίσκος.—Οὔκουν, ἔφη, εἰ μὲν ἀργύριον δέοι ἁρπάζειν, τοὺς φιλαργυρωτάτους πρώτους καθιστάντες ὀρθῶς ἂν τάττοιμεν;—Ἔμοιγε δοκεῖ.—Τί δὲ τοὺς κινδυνεύειν μέλλοντας; ἆρα τοὺς φιλοτιμοτάτους προτακτέον;—Οὗτοι γοῦν εἰσιν, ἔφη, οἱ ἕνεκα ἐπαίνου κινδυνεύειν ἐθέλοντες· οὐ τοίνυν οὗτοί γε ἄδηλοι, ἀλλ'
ἐπιφανεῖς πανταχοῦ ὄντες εὐαίρετοι ἂν εἶεν.—Ἀτάρ, 11
ἔφη, πότερά σε τάττειν μόνον ἐδίδαξεν, ἢ καὶ ὅποι

καὶ ὅπως χρηστέον ἑκάστῳ τῶν ταγμάτων; — Οὐ πάνυ, ἔφη.—Καὶ μὴν πολλά γ' ἐστί, πρὸς ἃ οὔτε τάττειν οὔτε ἄγειν ὡςαύτως προςήκει.—Ἀλλὰ μὰ Δί', ἔφη, οὐ διεσαφήνιζε ταῦτα.—Νὴ Δί', ἔφη, πάλιν τοίνυν ἐλθὼν ἐπανερώτα· ἢν γὰρ ἐπίστηται, καὶ μὴ ἀναιδὴς ᾖ, αἰσχυνεῖται ἀργύριον εἰληφὼς ἐνδεᾶ σε ἀποπέμψασθαι.

CHAPTER II.

ARGUMENT.

Socrates, in conversation with an Athenian who had been appointed to a command in the army, on the authority of Homer, compares a general to a shepherd. His duty is to provide for the safety and comfort of his soldiers, and to lead them on to the successful subjugation of their enemies (§ 1). He must not merely fight bravely himself, but inspire his followers with military ardor. Like a good prince he should not care for his own happiness alone, but wisely conduct others to good fortune (§ 2—4).

---

1 Ἐντυχὼν δέ ποτε στρατηγεῖν ᾑρημένῳ τῳ· Τοῦ ἕνεκεν, ἔφη, Ὅμηρον οἴει τὸν Ἀγαμέμνονα προςαγορεῦσαι ποιμένα λαῶν; ἆρά γε ὅτι, ὥςπερ τὸν ποιμένα ἐπιμελεῖσθαι δεῖ, ὅπως σῶαί τε ἔσονται αἱ ὄϊες, καὶ τὰ ἐπιτήδεια ἕξουσι, [καὶ οὗ ἕνεκα τρέφονται, τοῦτο ἔσται,] οὕτω καὶ τὸν στρατηγὸν ἐπιμελεῖσθαι δεῖ, ὅπως σῶοί τε οἱ στρατιῶται ἔσονται, καὶ τὰ ἐπιτήδεια ἕξουσι, καὶ, οὗ ἕνεκα στρατεύονται, τοῦτο ἔσται; στρατεύονται δὲ, ἵνα κρατοῦντες τῶν πολεμίων εὐδαιμονέ-
2 στεροι ὦσιν· ἢ τί δήποτε οὕτως ἐπήνεσε τὸν Ἀγαμέμνονα εἰπών,

Ἀμφότερον, βασιλεύς τ' ἀγαθός, κρατερός τ' αἰχμητής;

ἆρά γε ὅτι αἰχμητής τε κρατερὸς ἂν εἴη, οὐκ
εἰ μόνος αὐτὸς εὖ ἀγωνίζοιτο πρὸς τοὺς πολεμίους,
ἀλλ' εἰ καὶ παντὶ τῷ στρατοπέδῳ τούτου αἴτιος εἴη;
καὶ βασιλεὺς ἀγαθός, οὐκ εἰ μόνον τοῦ ἑαυτοῦ
βίου καλῶς προεστήκοι, ἀλλ' εἰ καί, ὧν βασιλεύοι,
τούτοις εὐδαιμονίας αἴτιος εἴη; Καὶ γὰρ βασιλεὺς αἱ- 3
ρεῖται, οὐχ ἵνα ἑαυτοῦ καλῶς ἐπιμελῆται, ἀλλ' ἵνα καὶ
οἱ ἑλόμενοι δι' αὐτὸν εὖ πράττωσι· καὶ στρατεύονται
δὲ πάντες, ἵνα ὁ βίος αὐτοῖς ὡς βέλτιστος ᾖ· καὶ
στρατηγοὺς αἱροῦνται τούτου ἕνεκα, ἵνα πρὸς τοῦτο
αὐτοῖς ἡγεμόνες ὦσι. Δεῖ οὖν τὸν στρατηγοῦντα τοῦτο 4
παρασκευάζειν τοῖς ἑλομένοις αὐτὸν στρατηγόν· καὶ
γὰρ οὔτε κάλλιον τούτου ἄλλο ῥᾴδιον εὑρεῖν, οὔτε
αἴσχιον τοῦ ἐναντίου. Καὶ οὕτως ἐπισκοπῶν, τίς εἴη
ἀγαθοῦ ἡγεμόνος ἀρετή, τὰ μὲν ἄλλα περιῄρει, κατέ-
λειπε δὲ τὸ εὐδαίμονας ποιεῖν, ὧν ἂν ἡγῆται.

CHAPTER III.

ARGUMENT.

After representing, in general, that the object of the 'prefect of the horse' is not the gratification of personal vanity, but the improvement of the forces under him, Socrates more specifically designates his duty as twofold: the care of the horse and of the rider (§ 1, 2).

1. He must give his personal attention to the care and training of the horses, and not leave them to the management of their riders alone (§ 3, 4).

2. Care for the rider, requires attention to his mounting, sitting firmly in the saddle, and the managing of his weapons (§ 5, 6); to his courage and alacrity in opposing the enemy, and to his prompt obedience to orders (§ 7, 8). And as an inducement to the prompt obedience and service of the soldier, the commander must perform his own duties well (§ 9)· and inculcate the honor and utility that result from obe-

dience (§ 10). In fine, the ability to speak in public should be cultivated, not only as a means of procuring obedience and discipline, but also for the excitement of military ambition and love of glory, that thus the desired object of warfare may be the more readily attained (§ 11—15).

---

1 Καὶ ἱππαρχεῖν δέ τινι ᾑρημένῳ οἶδά ποτε αὐτὸν τοιάδε διαλεχθέντα· Ἔχοις ἄν, ἔφη, ὦ νεανία, εἰπεῖν ἡμῖν, ὅτου ἕνεκα ἐπεθύμησας ἱππαρχεῖν; οὐ γὰρ δὴ τοῦ πρῶτος τῶν ἱππέων ἐλαύνειν· καὶ γὰρ οἱ ἱπποτοξόται τούτου γε ἀξιοῦνται, προελαύνουσι γοῦν καὶ τῶν ἱππάρχων.—Ἀληθῆ λέγεις, ἔφη.—Ἀλλὰ μὴν οὐδὲ τοῦ γνωσθῆναί γε, ἐπεὶ καὶ οἱ μαινόμενοί γε ὑπὸ πάντων γιγνώσκονται.—Ἀληθές, ἔφη, καὶ τοῦτο λέ-
2 γεις.—Ἀλλ' ἆρα ὅτι τὸ ἱππικὸν οἴει τῇ πόλει βέλτιον ἂν ποιήσας παραδοῦναι, καί, εἴ τις χρεία γίγνοιτο ἱππέων, τούτων ἡγούμενος ἀγαθοῦ τινος αἴτιος γενέσθαι τῇ πόλει;—Καὶ μάλα, ἔφη.—Καὶ ἔστι γε, νὴ Δί', ἔφη, ὁ Σωκράτης, καλόν, ἐὰν δύνῃ ταῦτα ποιῆσαι. Ἡ δὲ ἀρχή που, ἐφ' ἧς ᾕρησαι, ἵππων τε καὶ ἀμβα-
3 τῶν ἐστιν;—Ἔστι γὰρ οὖν, ἔφη.—Ἴθι δὴ λέξον ἡμῖν πρῶτον τοῦτο, ὅπως διανοῇ τοὺς ἵππους βελτίους ποιῆσαι;—Καὶ ὅς. Ἀλλὰ τοῦτο μέν, ἔφη, οὐκ ἐμὸν οἶμαι τὸ ἔργον εἶναι, ἀλλὰ ἰδίᾳ ἕκαστον δεῖν τοῦ ἑαυτοῦ ἵππου
4 ἐπιμελεῖσθαι.—Ἐὰν οὖν, ἔφη ὁ Σωκράτης, παρέχωνταί σοι τοὺς ἵππους οἱ μὲν οὕτως κακόποδας ἢ κακοσκελεῖς ἢ ἀσθενεῖς, οἱ δὲ οὕτως ἀτρόφους, ὥστε μὴ δύνασθαι ἀκολουθεῖν, οἱ δὲ οὕτως ἀναγώγους, ὥστε μὴ μένειν, ὅπου ἂν σὺ τάξῃς, οἱ δὲ οὕτως λακτιστάς, ὥστε μηδὲ τάξαι δυνατὸν εἶναι, τί σοι τοῦ ἱππικοῦ ὄφελος ἔσται; ἢ πῶς δυνήσῃ τοιούτων ἡγούμενος ἀγαθόν τι ποιῆσαι τὴν πόλιν;—Καὶ ὅς· Ἀλλὰ καλῶς τε λέγεις, ἔφη καὶ πειράσομαι τῶν ἵππων εἰς τὸ δυνατὸν
5 ἐπιμελεῖσθαι.—Τί δέ; τοὺς ἱππέας οὐκ ἐπιχειρήσεις, ἔφη, βελτίονας ποιῆσαι;—Ἔγωγ', ἔφη.—Οὐκοῦν πρῶ-

τον μὲν ἀναβατικωτέρους ἐπὶ τοὺς ἵππους ποιήσεις αὐτούς;—Δεῖ γοῦν, ἔφη· καὶ γάρ, εἴ τις αὐτῶν καταπέσοι, μᾶλλον ἂν οὕτω σώζοιτο.—Τί γάρ; ἐάν που 6
κινδυνεύειν δέῃ, πότερον ἐπαγαγεῖν τοὺς πολεμίους ἐπὶ τὴν ἄμμον κελεύσεις, ἔνθαπερ εἰώθατε ἱππεύειν, ἢ πειράσῃ τὰς μελέτας ἐν τοιούτοις ποιεῖσθαι χωρίοις, ἐν οἵοισπερ οἱ πολέμιοι γίγνονται;—Βέλτιον γοῦν, ἔφη.—Τί γάρ; τοῦ βάλλειν ὡς πλείστους ἀπὸ τῶν 7
ἵππων ἐπιμέλειάν τινα ποιήσῃ;—Βέλτιον γοῦν, ἔφη, καὶ τοῦτο.—Θήγειν δὲ τὰς ψυχὰς τῶν ἱππέων καὶ ἐξοργίζειν πρὸς τοὺς πολεμίους, εἴπερ ἀλκιμωτέρους ποιεῖν, διανενόησαι;—Εἰ δὲ μή, ἀλλὰ νῦν γε πειράσομαι, ἔφη.—Ὅπως δέ σοι πείθωνται οἱ ἱππεῖς, 8
πεφρόντικάς τι; ἄνευ γὰρ δὴ τούτου οὔτε ἵππων οὔτε ἱππέων ἀγαθῶν καὶ ἀλκίμων οὐδὲν ὄφελος.—Ἀληθῆ λέγεις, ἔφη· ἀλλὰ πῶς ἄν τις μάλιστα, ὦ Σώκρατες, ἐπὶ τοῦτο αὐτοὺς προτρέψαιτο;—Ἐκεῖνο μὲν δήπου 9
οἶσθα, ὅτι ἐν παντὶ πράγματι οἱ ἄνθρωποι τούτοις μάλιστα ἐθέλουσι πείθεσθαι, οὓς ἂν ἡγῶνται βελτίστους εἶναι· καὶ γὰρ ἐν νόσῳ, ὃν ἂν ἡγῶνται ἰατρικώτατον εἶναι, τούτῳ μάλιστα πείθονται, καὶ ἐν πλοίῳ οἱ πλέοντες, ὃν ἂν κυβερνητικώτατον, καὶ ἐν γεωργίᾳ, ὃν ἂν γεωργικώτατον.—Καὶ μάλα, ἔφη.—Οὐκοῦν εἰκός, ἔφη, καὶ ἐν ἱππικῇ, ὃς ἂν μάλιστα εἰδὼς φαίνηται ἃ δεῖ ποιεῖν, τούτῳ μάλιστα ἐθέλειν τοὺς ἄλλους πείθεσθαι.—Ἐὰν οὖν, ἔφη, ἐγώ, ὦ Σώκρατες, 10
βέλτιστος ὢν αὐτῶν δῆλος ὦ, ἀρκέσει μοι τοῦτο εἰς τὸ πείθεσθαι αὐτοὺς ἐμοί;—Ἐάν γε πρὸς τούτῳ, ἔφη, διδάξῃς αὐτούς, ὡς τὸ πείθεσθαί σοι κάλλιόν τε καὶ σωτηριώτερον αὐτοῖς ἔσται.—Πῶς οὖν, ἔφη, τοῦτο διδάξω;—Πολὺ νὴ Δί', ἔφη, ῥᾷον, ἢ εἴ σοι δέοι διδάσκειν, ὡς τὰ κακὰ τῶν ἀγαθῶν ἀμείνω καὶ λυσιτελέστερά ἐστι.—Λέγεις, ἔφη, σὺ τὸν ἵππαρχον 11
πρὸς τοῖς ἄλλοις ἐπιμελεῖσθαι δεῖν· καὶ τοῦ λέγειν

δύνασθαι;—Σὺ δ' ᾤου, ἔφη, χρῆναι σιωπῇ ἱππαρ-
χεῖν; ἢ οὐκ ἐντεθύμησαι, ὅτι, ὅσα τε νόμῳ μεμαθή-
καμεν κάλλιστα ὄντα, δι' ὧν γε ζῆν ἐπιστάμεθα,
ταῦτα πάντα διὰ λόγου ἐμάθομεν, καὶ εἴ τι ἄλλο
καλὸν μανθάνει τις μάθημα, διὰ λόγου μανθάνει;
καὶ οἱ ἄριστα διδάσκοντες μάλιστα λόγῳ χρῶνται,
καὶ οἱ τὰ σπουδαιότατα μάλιστα ἐπιστάμενοι κάλ-
12 λιστα διαλέγονται; Ἢ τόδε οὐκ ἐντηθύμησαι, ὡς,
ὅταν γε χορὸς εἷς ἐκ τῆςδε τῆς πόλεως γίγνηται,
ὥςπερ ὁ εἰς Δῆλον πεμπόμενος, οὐδεὶς ἄλλοθεν οὐ-
δαμόθεν τούτῳ ἐφάμιλλος γίγνεται, οὐδὲ εὐανδρία ἐν
ἄλλῃ πόλει ὁμοία τῇ ἐνθάδε συνάγεται;—Ἀληθῆ
13 λέγεις, ἔφη.—Ἀλλὰ μὴν οὔτε εὐφωνίᾳ τοσοῦτον δια-
φέρουσιν Ἀθηναῖοι τῶν ἄλλων, οὔτε σωμάτων μεγέθει
καὶ ῥώμῃ, ὅσον φιλοτιμίᾳ, ἥπερ μάλιστα παροξύνει
πρὸς τὰ καλὰ καὶ ἔντιμα.—Ἀληθές, ἔφη, καὶ τοῦτο.
14 —Οὐκοῦν οἴει, ἔφη, καὶ τοῦ ἱππικοῦ τοῦ ἐνθάδε εἴ
τις ἐπιμεληθείη, ὡς πολὺ ἂν καὶ τούτῳ διενέγκοιεν
τῶν ἄλλων, ὅπλων τε καὶ ἵππων παρασκευῇ καὶ
εὐταξίᾳ, καὶ τῷ ἑτοίμως κινδυνεύειν πρὸς τοὺς πολε-
μίους, εἰ νομίσειαν ταῦτα ποιοῦντες ἐπαίνου καὶ τιμῆς
15 τεύξεσθαι.—Εἰκός γε, ἔφη.—Μὴ τοίνυν ὄκνει, ἔφη,
ἀλλὰ πειρῶ τοὺς ἄνδρας ἐπὶ ταῦτα προτρέπειν, ἀφ
ὧν αὐτός τε ὠφεληθήσῃ, καὶ οἱ ἄλλοι πολῖται διὰ
σέ.—Ἀλλὰ νὴ Δία πειράσομαι, ἔφη.

CHAPTER IV.

ARGUMENT.

Nicomachides complained to Socrates that Antisthenes, who neither had experience in military affairs, or knowledge of any thing but to amass wealth, had been chosen as leader of the army, instead of himself, who had devoted his life to such pursuits, and bore the marks of previous warfare (§ 1, 2). Socrates replied: Since Antisthenes has shown skill in the management of his own affairs, and as a leader of the chorus, and is ambitious of a good name, he may be safely trusted with the army (§ 3—5). A man who has knowledge and skill will be successful as a leader any where; for the same qualities are demanded in presiding over the chorus and in conducting private affairs, as in commanding the State or army (§ 6—12).

Ἰδὼν δέ ποτε Νικομαχίδην ἐξ ἀρχαιρεσιῶν ἀπι- 1
όντα ἤρετο. Τίνες, ὦ Νικομαχίδη, στρατηγοὶ ᾕρηνται;
Καὶ ὅς· Οὐ γάρ, ἔφη, ὦ Σώκρατες, τοιοῦτοί εἰσιν
Ἀϑηναῖοι, ὥςτε ἐμὲ μὲν οὐχ εἵλοντο, ὃς ἐκ καταλόγου
στρατευόμενος κατατέτριμμαι καὶ λοχαγῶν καὶ ταξιαρ-
χῶν καὶ τραύματα ὑπὸ τῶν πολεμίων τοσαῦτα ἔχων·
ἅμα δὲ τὰς οὐλὰς τῶν τραυμάτων ἀπογυμνούμενος ἐπε-
δείκνυεν· Ἀντισϑένην δέ, ἔφη, εἵλοντο τὸν οὔτε ὁπλί-
την πώποτε στρατευσάμενον, ἔν τε τοῖς ἱππεῦσιν οὐδὲν
περίβλεπτον ποιήσαντα, ἐπιστάμενόν τε ἄλλο οὐδὲν ἢ
χρήματα συλλέγειν; Οὐκοῦν, ἔφη ὁ Σωκράτης, τοῦτο 2
μὲν ἀγαϑόν, εἴγε τοῖς στρατιώταις ἱκανὸς ἔσται τὰ
ἐπιτήδεια πορίζειν; Καὶ γὰρ οἱ ἔμποροι, ἔφη, ὁ Νικο-
μαχίδης, χρήματα συλλέγειν ἱκανοί εἰσιν· ἀλλ' οὐχ
ἕνεκα τούτου καὶ στρατηγεῖν δύναιντ' ἄν. Καὶ ὁ Σω- 3
κράτης ἔφη· Ἀλλὰ καὶ φιλόνεικος Ἀντισϑένης ἐστίν,
ὃ στρατηγῷ προςεῖναι ἐπιτήδειόν ἐστιν· οὐχ ὁρᾷς, ὅτι
καί, ὁσάκις κεχορήγηκε, πᾶσι τοῖς χοροῖς νενίκηκε;
Μὰ Δί', ἔφη ὁ Νικομαχίδης, ἀλλ' οὐδὲν ὅμοιόν ἐστι
χοροῦ τε καὶ στρατεύματος προεστάναι. Καὶ μήν, 4
ἔφη ὁ Σωκράτης, οὐδὲ ᾠδῆς γε ὁ Ἀντισϑένης, οὐδὲ
χορῶν διδασκαλίας ἔμπειρος ὢν ὅμως ἐγένετο ἱκανὸς
εὑρεῖν τοὺς κρατίστους ταῦτα. Καὶ ἐν τῇ στρατιᾷ
οὖν, ἔφη ὁ Νικομαχίδης, ἄλλους μὲν εὑρήσει τοὺς
τάξοντας ἀνϑ' ἑαυτοῦ, ἄλλους δὲ τοὺς μαχουμένους.
Οὐκοῦν, ἔφη ὁ Σωκράτης, ἐάν γε καὶ ἐν τοῖς πολε- 5

μικοῖς τοὺς κρατίστους, ὥσπερ ἐν τοῖς χορικοῖς, ἐξευρίσκῃ τε καὶ προαιρῆται, εἰκότως ἂν καὶ τούτου νικηφόρος εἴη· καὶ δαπανᾶν δ' αὐτὸν εἰκὸς μᾶλλον ἂν ἐθέλειν εἰς τὴν ξὺν ὅλῃ τῇ πόλει τῶν πολεμικῶν
6 νίκην ἢ εἰς τὴν ξὺν τῇ φυλῇ τῶν χορικῶν. Λέγεις σύ, ἔφη, ὦ Σώκρατες, ὡς τοῦ αὐτοῦ ἀνδρός ἐστι χορηγεῖν τε καλῶς καὶ στρατηγεῖν;—Λέγω ἔγωγ', ἔφη, ὡς, ὅτου ἄν τις προστατεύῃ, ἐὰν γιγνώσκῃ τε ὧν δεῖ, καὶ ταῦτα πορίζεσθαι δύνηται, ἀγαθὸς ἂν εἴη προστάτης, εἴτε χοροῦ, εἴτε οἴκου, εἴτε πόλεως, εἴτε στρα-
7 τεύματος προστατεύοι.—Καὶ ὁ Νικομαχίδης· Μὰ Δί', ἔφη, ὦ Σώκρατες, οὐκ ἄν ποτε ᾤμην ἐγὼ σοῦ ἀκοῦσαι, ὡς ἀγαθοὶ οἰκονόμοι ἀγαθοὶ στρατηγοὶ ἂν εἶεν. —Ἴθι δή, ἔφη, ἐξετάσωμεν τὰ ἔργα ἑκατέρου αὐτῶν, ἵνα εἰδῶμεν, πότερον τὰ αὐτά ἐστιν, ἢ διαφέρει τι.—
8 Πάνυ γε, ἔφη.—Οὐκοῦν, ἔφη, τὸ μὲν τοὺς ἀρχομένους κατηκόους τε καὶ εὐπειθεῖς ἑαυτοῖς παρασκευάζειν ἀμφοτέρων ἐστὶν ἔργον;—Καὶ μάλα, ἔφη.—Τί δέ; τὸ προστάττειν ἕκαστα τοῖς ἐπιτηδείοις πράττειν;—Καὶ τοῦτ' ἔφη.—Καὶ μὴν καὶ τὸ τοὺς κακοὺς κολάζειν, καὶ τοὺς ἀγαθοὺς τιμᾶν, ἀμφοτέροις οἶμαι προσήκειν.
9 —Πάνυ μὲν οὖν, ἔφη.—Τὸ δὲ τοὺς ὑπηκόους εὐμενεῖς ποιεῖσθαι πῶς οὐ καλὸν ἀμφοτέροις;—Καὶ τοῦτ', ἔφη.—Συμμάχους δὲ καὶ βοηθοὺς προσάγεσθαι δοκεῖ σοι συμφέρειν ἀμφοτέροις, ἢ οὔ;—Πάνυ μὲν οὖν, ἔφη.—Ἀλλὰ φυλακτικοὺς τῶν ὄντων οὐκ ἀμφοτέρους εἶναι προσήκει;—Σφόδρα γ', ἔφη.—Οὐκοῦν καὶ ἐπιμελεῖς καὶ φιλοπόνους ἀμφοτέρους εἶναι προσήκει περὶ
10 τὰ αὑτῶν ἔργα;—Ταῦτα μέν, ἔφη, πάντα ὁμοίως ἀμφοτέρων ἐστίν· ἀλλὰ τὸ μάχεσθαι οὐκέτι ἀμφοτέρων.—Ἀλλ' ἐχθροί γέ τοι ἀμφοτέροις γίγνονται; —Καὶ μάλα, ἔφη, τοῦτό γε.—Οὐκοῦν τὸ περιγενέ-
11 σθαι τούτων ἀμφοτέροις συμφέρει;—Πάνυ γε, ἔφη· ἀλλ' ἐκεῖνο παριείς, ἂν δέῃ μάχεσθαι, τί ὠφελήσει ἡ

οἰκονομική;—Ἐνταῦθα δήπου καὶ πλεῖστον, ἔφη· ὁ γὰρ ἀγαθὸς οἰκονόμος, εἰδὼς, ὅτι οὐδὲν οὕτω λυσιτελές τε καὶ κερδαλέον ἐστίν, ὡς τὸ μαχόμενον τοὺς πολεμίους νικᾶν, οὐδὲ οὕτως ἀλυσιτελές τε καὶ ζημιῶδες, ὡς τὸ ἡττᾶσθαι, προθύμως μὲν τὰ πρὸς τὸ νικᾶν συμφέροντα ζητήσει καὶ παρασκευάσεται, ἐπιμελῶς δὲ τὰ πρὸς τὸ ἡττᾶσθαι φέροντα σκέψεται καὶ φυλάξεται, ἐνεργῶς δ', ἂν τὴν παρασκευὴν ὁρᾷ νικητικὴν οὖσαν, μαχεῖται, οὐχ ἥκιστα δὲ τούτων, ἐὰν ἀπαράσκευος ᾖ, φυλάξεται συνάπτειν μάχην. Μὴ 12
καταφρόνει, ἔφη, ὦ Νικομαχίδη, τῶν οἰκονομικῶν ἀνδρῶν· ἡ γὰρ τῶν ἰδίων ἐπιμέλεια πλήθει μόνον διαφέρει τῆς τῶν κοινῶν, τὰ δὲ ἄλλα παραπλήσια ἔχει, τὸ δὲ μέγιστον, ὅτι οὔτε ἄνευ ἀνθρώπων οὐδετέρα γίγνεται, οὔτε δι' ἄλλων μὲν ἀνθρώπων τὰ ἴδια πράττεται, δι' ἄλλων δὲ τὰ κοινά· οὐ γὰρ ἄλλοις τισὶν ἀνθρώποις οἱ τῶν κοινῶν ἐπιμελόμενοι χρῶνται ἢ οἷσπερ οἱ τὰ ἴδια οἰκονομοῦντες· οἷς οἱ ἐπιστάμενοι χρῆσθαι καὶ τὰ ἴδια καὶ τὰ κοινὰ καλῶς πράττουσιν, οἱ δὲ μὴ ἐπιστάμενοι ἀμφοτέρωθι πλημμελοῦσιν.

CHAPTER V.

ARGUMENT.

This chapter consists of a colloquy of Socrates with Pericles the younger, upon the means of restoring the Athenians to their former valor and glory in war. It should seem, from some allusions in § 4, to have taken place soon after the battle at Delos, B. C. 424.

The Athenians, Socrates argues, are in possession of all the advantages and qualities necessary for the conquest of their enemies (§ 1—3). The very fact that they, on account of several disastrous engagements, fear the enemies which they formerly despised, will cause them to be more obedient to a good leader, and will banish sloth, arrogance, and all insubordination or irregularity (§ 4—6). If then they be obedient, the next step is, to incite their courage and stimulate their ambition, by recounting to them the virtues and valor of their ancestors, which are committed to them as a sacred inheritance (§ 7—12). Their present degeneracy is occasioned by their prosperity which induced carelessness (§ 13). The only way of restoring them to their pristine splendor, is in bringing them back to former manners and habits, or in leading them to imitate the virtues of the Lacedemonians (§ 13—15). There is no occasion to be disheartened on account of present factions and dissensions; they have among them the elements of union, and only need well-informed and skilful leaders, to make them obedient and efficient in war as well as in other occupations (§ 17—21). Hence the importance of knowledge and thorough training for those who are to guide the army (§ 22—24). Finally, Socrates alludes to the advantages of Attica for self-defence, and enjoins upon Pericles active exertion as a military commander (§ 25—28).

---

1 Περικλεῖ δέ ποτε, τῷ τοῦ πάνυ Περικλέους υἱῷ,
διαλεγόμενος· Ἐγώ τοι, ἔφη, ὦ Περίκλεις, ἐλπίδα ἔχω
σοῦ στρατηγήσαντος ἀμείνω τε καὶ ἐνδοξοτέραν τὴν
πόλιν εἰς τὰ πολεμικὰ ἔσεσθαι, καὶ τῶν πολεμίων
κρατήσειν. Καὶ ὁ Περικλῆς· Βουλοίμην ἄν, ἔφη, ὦ
Σώκρατες, ἃ λέγεις· ὅπως δὲ ταῦτα γένοιτ' ἄν, οὐ
δύναμαι γνῶναι. Βούλει οὖν, ἔφη ὁ Σωκράτης, διαλο-
γιζόμενοι περὶ αὐτῶν ἐπισκοπῶμεν, ὅπου ἤδη τὸ δυνα-
2 τόν ἐστιν;—Βούλομαι, ἔφη.—Οὔκουν οἶσθα, ἔφη, ὅτι
πλήθει μὲν οὐδὲν μείους εἰσὶν Ἀθηναῖοι Βοιωτῶν;—
Οἶδα γάρ, ἔφη.—Σώματα δὲ ἀγαθὰ καὶ καλὰ πότε-
ρον ἐκ Βοιωτῶν οἴει πλείω ἂν ἐκλεχθῆναι, ἢ ἐξ Ἀθη-
νῶν;—Οὐδὲ ταύτῃ μοι δοκοῦσι λείπεσθαι.—Εὐμενε-
στέρους δὲ ποτέρους ἑαυτοῖς εἶναι νομίζεις;—Ἀθηναίους
ἔγωγε· Βοιωτῶν μὲν γὰρ πολλοί, πλεονεκτούμενοι ὑπὸ
Θηβαίων, δυσμενῶς αὐτοῖς ἔχουσιν· Ἀθήνησι δέ οὐδὲν
3 ὁρῶ τοιοῦτον.—Ἀλλὰ μὴν φιλοτιμότατοί γε καὶ φιλο-
φρονέστατοι πάντων εἰσίν, ἅπερ οὐχ ἥκιστα παροξύνει
κινδυνεύειν ὑπὲρ εὐδοξίας τε καὶ πατρίδος.—Οὐδὲ ἐν

τούτοις Ἀθηναῖοι μεμπτοί.—Καὶ μὴν προγόνων γε
καλὰ ἔργα οὐκ ἔστιν οἷς μείζω καὶ πλείω ὑπάρχει ἢ
Ἀθηναίοις· ᾧ πολλοὶ ἐπαιρόμενοι προτρέπονταί τε
ἀρετῆς ἐπιμελεῖσθαι καὶ ἄλκιμοι γίγνεσθαι.—Ταῦτα 4
μὲν ἀληθῆ λέγεις πάντα, ὦ Σώκρατες· ἀλλ' ὁρᾷς, ὅτι,
ἀφ' οὗ ἥ τε σὺν Τολμίδῃ τῶν χιλίων ἐν Λεβαδείᾳ
συμφορὰ ἐγένετο καὶ ἡ μεθ' Ἱπποκράτους ἐπὶ Δηλίῳ,
ἐκ τούτων τεταπείνωται μὲν ἡ τῶν Ἀθηναίων δόξα
πρὸς τοὺς Βοιωτούς, ἐπῆρται δὲ τὸ τῶν Θηβαίων
φρόνημα πρὸς τοὺς Ἀθηναίους, ὥστε Βοιωτοὶ μέν, οἱ
πρόσθεν οὐδ' ἐν τῇ ἑαυτῶν τολμῶντες Ἀθηναίοις ἄνευ
Λακεδαιμονίων τε καὶ τῶν ἄλλων Πελοποννησίων ἀντι-
τάττεσθαι, νῦν ἀπειλοῦσιν αὐτοὶ καθ' ἑαυτοὺς ἐμβα-
λεῖν εἰς τὴν Ἀττικήν, Ἀθηναῖοι δέ, οἱ πρότερον, ὅτε
Βοιωτοὶ μόνοι ἐγένοντο, πορθοῦντες τὴν Βοιωτίαν, φο-
βοῦνται, μὴ Βοιωτοὶ δῃώσωσι τὴν Ἀττικήν. Καὶ ὁ 5
Σωκράτης· Ἀλλ' αἰσθάνομαι μέν, ἔφη, ταῦτα οὕτως
ἔχοντα· δοκεῖ δέ μοι ἀνδρὶ ἀγαθῷ ἄρχοντι νῦν εὐαρε-
στοτέρως διακεῖσθαι ἡ πόλις· τὸ μὲν γὰρ θάρσος
ἀμέλειάν τε καὶ ῥᾳθυμίαν καὶ ἀπείθειαν ἐμβάλλει, ὁ
δὲ φόβος προσεκτικωτέρους τε καὶ εὐπειθεστέρους καὶ
εὐτακτοτέρους ποιεῖ. Τεκμήραιο δ' ἂν τοῦτο καὶ ἀπὸ 6
τῶν ἐν ταῖς ναυσίν· ὅταν μὲν γὰρ δήπου μηδὲν φο-
βῶνται, μεστοί εἰσιν ἀταξίας, ἔστ' ἂν δὲ ἢ χειμῶνα ἢ
πολεμίους δείσωσιν, οὐ μόνον τὰ κελευόμενα πάντα
ποιοῦσιν, ἀλλὰ καὶ σιγῶσι καραδοκοῦντες τὰ προσ-
ταχθησόμενα, ὥσπερ χορευταί.—Ἀλλὰ μήν, ἔφη ὁ 7
Περικλῆς, εἴγε νῦν μάλιστα πείθοιντο, ὥρα ἂν εἴη
λέγειν, πῶς ἂν αὐτοὺς προτρεψαίμεθα πάλιν ἀνερεθι-
σθῆναι τῆς ἀρχαίας ἀρετῆς τε καὶ εὐκλείας καὶ εὐδαι-
μονίας.—Οὐκοῦν, ἔφη ὁ Σωκράτης, εἰ μὲν ἐβουλόμεθα 8
χρημάτων αὐτούς, ὧν οἱ ἄλλοι εἶχον, ἀντιποιεῖσθαι,
ἀποδεικνύντες αὐτοῖς ταῦτα πατρῷά τε ὄντα καὶ προσ-
ήκοντα, μάλιστ' ἂν οὕτως αὐτοὺς ἐξορμῷμεν ἀντέχεσθαι

τούτων· ἐπεὶ δὲ τοῦ μετ' ἀρετῆς πρωτεύειν αὐτοὺς
ἐπιμελεῖσθαι βουλόμεθα, τοῦτ' αὖ δεικτέον ἐκ πα-
λαιοῦ μάλιστα προσῆκον αὐτοῖς, καὶ ὡς τούτου ἐπι-
9 μελούμενοι πάντων ἂν εἶεν κράτιστοι.—Πῶς οὖν ἂν
τοῦτο διδάσκοιμεν;—Οἶμαι μέν, εἰ τούς γε παλαιο-
τάτους, ὧν ἀκούομεν, προγόνους αὐτῶν ἀναμιμνήσκοι-
10 μεν αὐτοὺς ἀκηκοότας ἀρίστους γεγονέναι.—Ἆρα
λέγεις τὴν τῶν θεῶν κρίσιν, ἣν οἱ περὶ Κέκροπα δι'
ἀρετὴν ἔκριναν;—Λέγω γάρ, καὶ τὴν Ἐρεχθέως γε
τροφὴν καὶ γένεσιν, καὶ τὸν πόλεμον τὸν ἐπ' ἐκείνου
γενόμενον πρὸς τοὺς ἐκ τῆς ἐχομένης ἠπείρου πάσης,
καὶ τὸν ἐφ' Ἡρακλειδῶν πρὸς τοὺς ἐν Πελοποννήσῳ,
καὶ πάντας τοὺς ἐπὶ Θησέως πολεμηθέντας, ἐν οἷς
πᾶσιν ἐκεῖνοι δῆλοι γεγόνασι τῶν καθ' ἑαυτοὺς ἀν-
11 θρώπων ἀριστεύσαντες. Εἰ δὲ βούλει, ἃ ὕστερον οἱ
ἐκείνων μὲν ἀπόγονοι, οὐ πολὺ δὲ πρὸ ἡμῶν γεγονό-
τες, ἔπραξαν, τὰ μὲν αὐτοὶ καθ' ἑαυτοὺς ἀγωνιζόμενοι
πρὸς τοὺς κυριεύοντας τῆς τε Ἀσίας πάσης καὶ τῆς
Εὐρώπης μέχρι Μακεδονίας, καὶ πλείστην τῶν προγε-
γονότων δύναμιν καὶ ἀφορμὴν κεκτημένους, καὶ μέ-
γιστα ἔργα κατειργασμένους, τὰ δὲ καὶ μετὰ Πελο-
ποννησίων ἀριστεύοντες καὶ κατὰ γῆν καὶ κατὰ
θάλατταν· οἳ δὴ καὶ λέγονται πολὺ διενεγκεῖν τῶν
καθ' ἑαυτοὺς ἀνθρώπων.—Λέγονται γάρ, ἔφη.—
12 Τοιγαροῦν πολλῶν μὲν μεταναστάσεων ἐν τῇ Ἑλλάδι
γεγονυιῶν διέμειναν ἐν τῇ ἑαυτῶν, πολλοὶ δὲ ὑπὲρ
δικαίων ἀντιλέγοντες ἐπέτρεπον ἐκείνοις, πολλοὶ δὲ
ὑπὸ κρειττόνων ὑβριζόμενοι κατέφευγον πρὸς ἐκείνους.
13 —Καὶ ὁ Περικλῆς· Καὶ θαυμάζω γε, ἔφη, ὦ Σώ-
κρατες, ἡ πόλις ὅπως ποτ' ἐπὶ τὸ χεῖρον ἔκλινεν.—
Ἐγὼ μέν, ἔφη, οἶμαι, ὁ Σωκράτης, ὥσπερ καὶ ἄλλοι
τινὲς διὰ τὸ πολὺ ὑπερενεγκεῖν καὶ κρατιστεῦσαι
καταῤῥᾳθυμήσαντες ὑστερίζουσι τῶν ἀντιπάλων, οὕτω
καὶ Ἀθηναίους πολὺ διενεγκόντας ἀμελῆσαι ἑαυτῶν.

καὶ διὰ τοῦτο χείρους γεγονέναι.—Νῦν οὖν, ἔφη, τί 14
ἂν ποιοῦντες ἀναλάβοιεν τὴν ἀρχαίαν ἀρετήν;—Καὶ
ὁ Σωκράτης· Οὐδὲν ἀπόκρυφον δοκεῖ μοι εἶναι, ἀλλ'
εἰ μὲν ἐξευρόντες τὰ τῶν προγόνων ἐπιτηδεύματα μη-
δὲν χεῖρον ἐκείνων ἐπιτηδεύοιεν, οὐδὲν ἂν χείρους ἐκεί-
νων γενέσθαι· εἰ δὲ μή, τούς γε νῦν πρωτεύοντας
μιμούμενοι, καὶ τούτοις τὰ αὐτὰ ἐπιτηδεύοντες, ὁμοίως
μὲν τοῖς αὐτοῖς χρώμενοι, οὐδὲν ἂν χείρους ἐκείνων εἶεν·
εἰ δ' ἐπιμελέστερον, καὶ βελτίους.—Λέγεις, ἔφη, πόῤῥω 15
που εἶναι τῇ πόλει τὴν καλοκἀγαθίαν· πότε γὰρ οὕ-
τως Ἀθηναῖοι, ὥσπερ Λακεδαιμόνιοι, ἢ πρεσβυτέρους
αἰδέσονται; οἳ ἀπὸ τῶν πατέρων ἄρχονται καταφρο-
νεῖν τῶν γεραιτέρων· ἢ σωμασκήσουσιν οὕτως; οἳ οὐ
μόνον αὐτοὶ εὐεξίας ἀμελοῦσιν, ἀλλὰ καὶ τῶν ἐπιμε-
λουμένων καταγελῶσι. Πότε δὲ οὕτω πείσονται τοῖς 16
ἄρχουσιν; οἳ καὶ ἀγάλλονται ἐπὶ τῷ καταφρονεῖν τῶν
ἀρχόντων· ἢ πότε οὕτως ὁμονοήσουσιν; οἵ γε ἀντὶ
μὲν τοῦ συνεργεῖν ἑαυτοῖς τὰ συμφέροντα ἐπηρεάζου-
σιν ἀλλήλοις, καὶ φθονοῦσιν ἑαυτοῖς μᾶλλον ἢ τοῖς
ἄλλοις ἀνθρώποις· μάλιστα δὲ πάντων ἔν τε ταῖς
ἰδίαις συνόδοις καὶ ταῖς κοιναῖς διαφέρονται, καὶ πλεί-
στας δίκας ἀλλήλοις δικάζονται, καὶ προαιροῦνται
μᾶλλον οὕτω κερδαίνειν ἀπ' ἀλλήλων ἢ συνωφελοῦν-
τες αὐτούς· τοῖς δὲ κοινοῖς ὥσπερ ἀλλοτρίοις χρώ-
μενοι, περὶ τούτων αὖ μάχονται, καὶ ταῖς εἰς τὰ
τοιαῦτα δυνάμεσι μάλιστα χαίρουσιν. Ἐξ ὧν πολλὴ 17
μὲν ἀπειρία καὶ κακία τῇ πόλει ἐμφύεται, πολλὴ δὲ
ἔχθρα καὶ μῖσος ἀλλήλων τοῖς πολίταις ἐγγίγνεται,
δι' ἃ ἔγωγε μάλα φοβοῦμαι ἀεί, μή τι μεῖζον ἢ ὥστε
φέρειν δύνασθαι κακὸν τῇ πόλει συμβῇ.—Μηδαμῶς, 18
ἔφη ὁ Σωκράτης, ὦ Περίκλεις, οὕτως ἡγοῦ ἀνηκέστῳ
πονηρίᾳ νοσεῖν Ἀθηναίους· οὐχ ὁρᾷς, ὡς εὔτακτοι
μέν εἰσιν ἐν τοῖς ναυτικοῖς, εὐτάκτως δ' ἐν τοῖς γυμ-
νικοῖς ἀγῶσι πείθονται τοῖς ἐπιστάταις, οὐδένων δὲ

καταδεέστερον ἐν τοῖς χοροῖς ὑπηρετοῦσι τοῖς διδασκά-
19 λοις ;—Τοῦτο γάρ τοι, ἔφη, καὶ θαυμαστόν ἐστι, τὸ
τοὺς μὲν τοιούτους πειθαρχεῖν τοῖς ἐφεστῶσι, τοὺς δὲ
ὁπλίτας καὶ τοὺς ἱππεῖς, οἳ δοκοῦσι καλοκἀγαθίᾳ
προκεκρίσθαι τῶν πολιτῶν, ἀπειθεστάτους εἶναι πάν-
20 των.—Καὶ ὁ Σωκράτης ἔφη· Ἡ δὲ ἐν Ἀρείῳ πάγῳ
βουλή, ὦ Περίκλεις, οὐκ ἐκ τῶν δεδοκιμασμένων καθί-
σταται ;—Καὶ μάλα, ἔφη.—Οἶσθα οὖν τινας, ἔφη,
κάλλιον ἢ νομιμώτερον ἢ σεμνότερον ἢ δικαιότερον
τάς τε δίκας δικάζοντας καὶ τἆλλα πάντα πράττον-
τας ;—Οὐ μέμφομαι, ἔφη, τούτοις.—Οὐ τοίνυν, ἔφη,
δεῖ ἀθυμεῖν, ὡς οὐκ εὐτάκτων ὄντων Ἀθηναίων.—
21 Καὶ μὴν ἔν γε τοῖς στρατιωτικοῖς, ἔφη, ἔνθα μάλιστα
δεῖ σωφρονεῖν τε καὶ εὐτακτεῖν καὶ πειθαρχεῖν, οὐδενὶ
τούτων προσέχουσιν.—Ἴσως γάρ, ἔφη ὁ Σωκράτης,
ἐν τούτοις οἱ ἥκιστα ἐπιστάμενοι ἄρχουσιν αὐτῶν·
οὐχ ὁρᾷς, ὅτι κιθαριστῶν μὲν καὶ χορευτῶν καὶ ὀρχη-
στῶν οὐδὲ εἷς ἐπιχειρεῖ ἄρχειν μὴ ἐπιστάμενος, οὐδὲ
παλαιστῶν οὐδὲ παγκρατιαστῶν ; ἀλλὰ πάντες, ὅσοι
τούτων ἄρχουσιν, ἔχουσι δεῖξαι, ὁπόθεν ἔμαθον ταῦτα,
ἐφ' οἷς ἐφεστᾶσι, τῶν δὲ στρατηγῶν οἱ πλεῖστοι αὐ-
22 τοσχεδιάζουσιν. Οὐ μέντοι σέ γε τοιοῦτον ἐγὼ νομίζω
εἶναι, ἀλλ' οἶμαί σε οὐδὲν ἧττον ἔχειν εἰπεῖν, ὁπότε
στρατηγεῖν ἢ ὁπότε παλαίειν ἤρξω μανθάνειν· καὶ
πολλὰ μὲν οἶμαί σε τῶν πατρῴων στρατηγημάτων πα-
ρειληφότα διασώζειν, πολλὰ δὲ πανταχόθεν συνενηνο-
χέναι, ὁπόθεν οἷόν τε ἦν μαθεῖν τι ὠφέλιμον εἰς στρα-
23 τηγίαν. Οἶμαι δὲ σε πολλὰ μεριμνᾶν, ὅπως μὴ λάθῃς
σεαυτὸν ἀγνοῶν τι τῶν εἰς στρατηγίαν ὠφελίμων, καὶ
ἐάν τι τοιοῦτον αἴσθῃ σεαυτὸν μὴ εἰδότα, ζητεῖν τοὺς
ἐπισταμένους ταῦτα, οὔτε δώρων οὔτε χαρίτων φειδό-
μενον, ὅπως μάθῃς παρ' αὐτῶν ἃ μὴ ἐπίστασαι, καὶ
24 συνεργοὺς ἀγαθοὺς ἔχῃς. Καὶ ὁ Περικλῆς· Οὐ λανθά-
νεις με, ὦ Σώκρατες, ἔφη, ὅτι οὐδ' οἰόμενός με τούτων

ἐπιμελεῖσϑαι ταῦτα λέγεις, ἀλλ' ἐγχειρῶν με διδά-
σκειν, ὅτι τὸν μέλλοντα στρατηγεῖν τούτων ἁπάντων
ἐπιμελεῖσϑαι δεῖ· ὁμολογῶ μέντοι κἀγώ σοι ταῦτα.—
Τοῦτο δ', ἔφη, ὦ Περίκλεις, κατανενόηκας, ὅτι πρό- 25
κειται τῆς χώρας ἡμῶν ὄρη μεγάλα, καϑήκοντα ἐπὶ
τὴν Βοιωτίαν, δι' ὧν εἰς τὴν χώραν εἴσοδοι στεναί τε
καὶ προσάντεις εἰσί, καὶ ὅτι μέση διέζωσται ὄρεσιν
ἐρυμνοῖς;—Καὶ μάλα, ἔφη.—Τί δέ; σὺ ἐκεῖνο ἀκή- 26
κοας, ὅτι Μυσοὶ καὶ Πισίδαι ἐν τῇ βασιλέως χώρᾳ
κατέχοντες ἐρυμνὰ πάνυ χωρία, καὶ κούφως ὡπλισμέ-
νοι, δύνανται, πολλὰ μὲν τὴν βασιλέως χώραν κατα-
ϑέοντες κακοποιεῖν, αὐτοὶ δὲ ζῆν ἐλεύϑεροι;—Καὶ
τοῦτό γ', ἔφη, ἀκούω.—Ἀϑηναίους δ' οὐκ ἂν οἴει, 27
ἔφη, μέχρι τῆς ἐλαφρᾶς ἡλικίας ὡπλισμένους κουφο-
τέροις ὅπλοις, καὶ τὰ προκείμενα τῆς χώρας ὄρη
κατέχοντας, βλαβεροὺς μὲν τοῖς πολεμίοις εἶναι, με-
γάλην δὲ προβολὴν τοῖς πολίταις τῆς χώρας κατε-
σκευάσϑαι; Καὶ ὁ Περικλῆς· Πάντ' οἶμαι, ἔφη, ὦ
Σώκρατες, καὶ ταῦτα χρήσιμα εἶναι. Εἰ τοίνυν, ἔφη 28
ὁ Σωκράτης, ἀρέσκει σοι ταῦτα, ἐπιχείρει αὐτοῖς, ὦ
ἄριστε· ὅ τι μὲν γὰρ ἂν τούτων καταπράξῃς, καὶ σοὶ
καλὸν ἔσται καὶ τῇ πόλει ἀγαϑόν, ἐὰν δέ τι ἀδυνα-
τῇς, οὔτε τὴν πόλιν βλάψεις, οὔτε σεαυτὸν καται-
σχυνεῖς.

CHAPTER VI.

ARGUMENT.

Glauco, a brother of the philosopher Plato, ridiculously persisting in haranguing the people in the assembly (δημηγορεῖν), in opposition to the wishes of his friends, with the hope of obtaining honor and influence in the State, was averted from his course by a conversation with Socrates (§ 1).

Socrates first gained the favorable attention of Glauco, by a representation of the importance of the office that he desired, and of the honor that was attached to it (§ 2). He then by a series of questions exhibited to Glauco his entire want of qualifications for performing adequately the duties pertaining to it (§ 3—13). By this means Glauco was prepared for the advice, that he should begin a preparation for so important a trust, by undertaking the management of his uncle's affairs (§ 14). The objection that his uncle might not be willing to intrust his estate to him gave Socrates occasion to inculcate the sentiment, that one who is not thoroughly acquainted with public business, will not be able, as a ruler to advance the prosperity or provide for the safety of the State, nor to gain for himself any renown (§ 14—18).

---

1 *Γλαύκωνα δὲ τὸν Ἀρίστωνος, ὅτ' ἐπεχείρει δημη-*
γορεῖν ἐπιθυμῶν προστατεύειν τῆς πόλεως, οὐδέπω
εἴκοσιν ἔτη γεγονώς, ὄντων ἄλλων οἰκείων τε καὶ φί-
λων οὐδεὶς ἐδύνατο παῦσαι ἑλκόμενόν τε ἀπὸ τοῦ
βήματος καὶ καταγέλαστον ὄντα, Σωκράτης δὲ εὔνους
ὢν αὐτῷ διά τε Χαρμίδην τὸν Γλαύκωνος καὶ διὰ
2 *Πλάτωνα μόνος ἔπαυσεν· ἐντυχὼν γὰρ αὐτῷ πρῶτον*
μὲν εἰς τὸ ἐθελῆσαι ἀκούειν τοιάδε λέξας κατέσχεν·
Ὦ Γλαύκων, ἔφη, προστατεύειν ἡμῖν διανενόησαι τῆς
πόλεως;—Ἔγωγ', ἔφη, ὦ Σώκρατες.—Νὴ Δί', ἔφη,
καλὸν γάρ, εἴπερ τι καὶ ἄλλο τῶν ἐν ἀνθρώποις·
δῆλον γάρ, ὅτι, ἐὰν τοῦτο διαπράξῃ, δυνατὸς μὲν ἔσῃ
αὐτὸς τυγχάνειν ὅτου ἂν ἐπιθυμῇς, ἱκανὸς δὲ τοὺς φί-
λους ὠφελεῖν, ἐπαρεῖς δὲ τὸν πατρῷον οἶκον, αὐξήσεις
δὲ τὴν πατρίδα, ὀνομαστὸς δ' ἔσῃ πρῶτον μὲν ἐν τῇ
πόλει, ἔπειτα ἐν τῇ Ἑλλάδι, ἴσως δὲ ὥσπερ Θεμιστο-
κλῆς καὶ ἐν τοῖς βαρβάροις, ὅπου δ' ἂν ᾖς, πανταχοῦ
3 *περίβλεπτος ἔσῃ. Ταῦτ' οὖν ἀκούων ὁ Γλαύκων ἐμε-*
γαλύνετο καὶ ἡδέως παρέμενε. Μετὰ δὲ ταῦτα ὁ Σω-
κράτης· Οὐκοῦν, ἔφη, τοῦτο μέν, ὦ Γλαύκων, δῆλον,
ὅτι, εἴπερ τιμᾶσθαι βούλει, ὠφελητέα σοι ἡ πόλις
ἐστίν;—Πάνυ μὲν οὖν, ἔφη.—Πρὸς θεῶν, ἔφη, μὴ
τοίνυν ἀποκρύψῃ, ἀλλ' εἰπὸν ἡμῖν, ἐκ τίνος ἄρξῃ τὴν

πόλιν εὐεργετεῖν; Ἐπεὶ δὲ ὁ Γλαύκων διεσιώπησεν, 4
ὡς ἂν τότε σκοπῶν, ὁπόθεν ἄρχοιτο· Ἆρ', ἔφη ὁ Σωκράτης, ὥςπερ, φίλου οἶκον εἰ αὐξῆσαι βούλοιο, πλουσιώτερον αὐτὸν ἐπιχειροίης ἂν ποιεῖν, οὕτω καὶ τὴν πόλιν πειράσῃ πλουσιωτέραν ποιῆσαι; — Πάνυ μὲν
οὖν, ἔφη.—Οὐκοῦν πλουσιωτέρα γ' ἂν εἴη, προςόδων 5
αὐτῇ πλειόνων γενομένων;—Εἰκὸς γοῦν, ἔφη.—Λέξον δή, ἔφη, ἐκ τίνων νῦν αἱ πρόςοδοι τῇ πόλει καὶ πόσαι τινές εἰσι; δῆλον γάρ, ὅτι ἔσκεψαι, ἵνα, εἰ μέν τινες αὐτῶν ἐνδεῶς ἔχουσιν, ἐκπληρώσῃς, εἰ δὲ παραλείπονται, προςπορίσῃς.—Ἀλλὰ μὰ Δί', ἔφη ὁ Γλαύκων,
ταῦτά γε οὐκ ἐπέσκεμμαι.—Ἀλλ', εἰ τοῦτο, ἔφη, παρέ- 6
λιπες, τάς γε δαπάνας τῆς πόλεως ἡμῖν εἰπέ· δῆλον γάρ, ὅτι καὶ τούτων τὰς περιττὰς ἀφαιρεῖν διανοῇ.—Ἀλλὰ μὰ τὸν Δί', ἔφη, οὐδὲ πρὸς ταῦτά πω ἐσχόλασα.—Οὐκοῦν, ἔφη, τὸ μὲν πλουσιωτέραν τὴν πόλιν ποιεῖν ἀναβαλούμεθα· πῶς γὰρ οἷόν τε μὴ εἰδότα γε τὰ ἀναλώματα καὶ τὰς προςόδους ἐπιμεληθῆναι τούτων;—
Ἀλλ', ὦ Σώκρατες, ἔφη ὁ Γλαύκων, δυνατόν ἐστι καὶ 7
ἀπὸ πολεμίων τὴν πόλιν πλουτίζειν.—Νὴ Δία, σφόδρα γ', ἔφη ὁ Σωκράτης, ἐάν τις αὐτῶν κρείττων ᾖ· ἥττων δὲ ὢν καὶ τὰ ὄντα προςαποβάλοι ἄν.—Ἀληθῆ
λέγεις, ἔφη.—Οὐκοῦν, ἔφη, τόν γε βουλευσόμενον πρὸς 8
οὕςτινας δεῖ πολεμεῖν τήν τε τῆς πόλεως δύναμιν καὶ τὴν τῶν ἐναντίων εἰδέναι δεῖ, ἵνα, ἐὰν μὲν ἡ τῆς πόλεως κρείττων ᾖ, συμβουλεύῃ ἐπιχειρεῖν τῷ πολέμῳ, ἐαν δὲ ἥττων τῶν ἐναντίων, εὐλαβεῖσθαι πείθῃ.—
Ὀρθῶς λέγεις, ἔφη.—Πρῶτον μὲν τοίνυν, ἔφη, λέξον 9
ἡμῖν τῆς πόλεως τήν τε πεζικὴν καὶ τὴν ναυτικὴν δύναμιν, εἶτα τὴν τῶν ἐναντίων.—Ἀλλὰ μὰ τὸν Δί', ἔφη, οὐκ ἂν ἔχοιμί σοι οὕτως γε ἀπὸ στόματος εἰπεῖν. —Ἀλλ', εἰ γέγραπταί σοι, ἔνεγκε, ἔφη· πάνυ γὰρ ἡδέως ἂν τοῦτο ἀκούσαιμι.—Ἀλλὰ μὰ τὸν Δί', ἔφη,
οὐδὲ γέγραπταί μοί πω.—Οὐκοῦν, ἔφη, καὶ περὶ πολέ- 10

μου συμβουλεύειν τήν γε πρώτην ἐπισχήσομεν· ἴσως γὰρ καὶ διὰ τὸ μέγεθος αὐτῶν ἄρτι ἀρχόμενος τῆς προστατείας οὔπω ἐξήτακας. Ἀλλά τοι περί γε φυλακῆς τῆς χώρας οἶδ' ὅτι σοι μεμέληκε, καὶ οἶσθα, ὁπόσαι τε φυλακαὶ ἐπίκαιροί εἰσι καὶ ὁπόσαι μή, καὶ ὁπόσοι τε φρουροὶ ἱκανοί εἰσι καὶ ὁπόσοι μή εἰσι, καὶ τὰς μὲν ἐπικαίρους φυλακὰς συμβουλεύσειν μείζονας
11 ποιεῖν, τὰς δὲ περιττὰς ἀφαιρεῖν.—Νὴ Δί', ἔφη ὁ Γλαύκων, ἁπάσας μὲν οὖν ἔγωγε, ἕνεκά γε τοῦ οὕτως αὐτὰς φυλάττεσθαι, ὥστε κλέπτεσθαι τὰ ἐκ τῆς χώρας. —Ἐὰν δέ τις ἀφέλῃ γ', ἔφη, τὰς φυλακάς, οὐκ οἴει καὶ ἁρπάζειν ἐξουσίαν ἔσεσθαι τῷ βουλομένῳ; ἀτάρ, ἔφη, πότερον ἐλθὼν αὐτὸς ἐξήτακας τοῦτο, ἢ πῶς οἶσθα, ὅτι κακῶς φυλάττονται; — Εἰκάζω, ἔφη. — Οὐκοῦν, ἔφη, καὶ περὶ τούτων, ὅταν μηκέτι εἰκάζωμεν, ἀλλ' ἤδη εἰδῶμεν, τότε συμβουλεύσομεν;—Ἴσως, ἔφη ὁ Γλαύ-
12 κων, βέλτιον.—Εἴς γε μήν, ἔφη, τἀργύρια οἶδ' ὅτι οὐκ ἀφῖξαι, ὥστ' ἔχειν εἰπεῖν, διότι νῦν ἐλάττω ἢ πρόσθεν προσέρχεται αὐτόθεν.—Οὐ γὰρ οὖν ἐλήλυθα, ἔφη. Καὶ γὰρ νὴ Δί', ἔφη ὁ Σωκράτης, λέγεται βαρὺ τὸ χωρίον εἶναι, ὥστε, ὅταν περὶ τούτου δέῃ συμβουλεύειν, αὕτη σοι ἡ πρόφασις ἀρκέσει. Σκώπτομαι,
13 ἔφη ὁ Γλαύκων.—Ἀλλ' ἐκείνου γέ τοι, ἔφη, οἶδ' ὅτι οὐκ ἠμέληκας, ἀλλ' ἔσκεψαι, καὶ πόσον χρόνον ἱκανός ἐστιν ὁ ἐκ τῆς χώρας γιγνόμενος σῖτος διατρέφειν τὴν πόλιν, καὶ πόσου εἰς τὸν ἐνιαυτὸν προσδέεται, ἵνα μὴ τοῦτό γε λάθῃ σέ ποτε ἡ πόλις ἐνδεὴς γενομένη, ἀλλ' εἰδὼς ἔχῃς ὑπὲρ τῶν ἀναγκαίων συμβουλεύων τῇ πόλει βοηθεῖν τε καὶ σώζειν αὐτήν. Λέγεις, ἔφη ὁ Γλαύκων, παμμέγεθες πρᾶγμα, εἴγε καὶ τῶν τοιούτων
14 ἐπιμελεῖσθαι δεήσει. Ἀλλὰ μέντοι, ἔφη ὁ Σωκράτης, οὐδ' ἂν τὸν ἑαυτοῦ ποτε οἶκον καλῶς τις οἰκήσειεν, εἰ μὴ πάντα μὲν εἴσεται, ὧν προσδέεται, πάντων δὲ ἐπιμελόμενος ἐκπληρώσει· ἀλλ' ἐπεὶ ἡ μὲν πόλις ἐκ

πλειόνων ἢ μυρίων οἰκιῶν συνέστηκε, χαλεπὸν δέ ἐστιν
ἅμα τοσούτων οἴκων ἐπιμελεῖσθαι, πῶς οὐχ ἕνα, τὸν
τοῦ θείου, πρῶτον ἐπειράθης αὐξῆσαι; δέεται δέ· κἂν
μὲν τοῦτον δύνῃ, καὶ πλείοσιν ἐπιχειρήσεις· ἕνα δὲ μὴ
δυνάμενος ὠφελῆσαι, πῶς ἂν πολλούς γε δυνηθείης;
ὥσπερ εἴ τις ἓν τάλαντον μὴ δύναιτο φέρειν, πῶς οὐ
φανερὸν, ὅτι πλείω γε φέρειν οὐδ' ἐπιχειρητέον αὐτῷ;
Ἀλλ' ἔγωγ', ἔφη ὁ Γλαύκων, ὠφελοίην ἂν τὸν τοῦ 15
θείου οἶκον, εἴ μοι ἐθέλοι πείθεσθαι. Εἶτα, ἔφη ὁ
Σωκράτης, τὸν θεῖον οὐ δυνάμενος πείθειν, Ἀθηναίους
πάντας μετὰ τοῦ θείου νομίζεις δυνήσεσθαι ποιῆσαι
πείθεσθαί σοι; Φυλάττου, ἔφη, ὦ Γλαύκων, ὅπως μὴ 16
τοῦ εὐδοξεῖν ἐπιθυμῶν εἰς τοὐναντίον ἔλθῃς· ἢ οὐχ
ὁρᾷς, ὡς σφαλερόν ἐστι τὸ, ἃ μὴ οἶδέ τις, ταῦτα
λέγειν ἢ πράττειν; ἐνθυμοῦ δὲ τῶν ἄλλων ὅσους
οἶσθα τοιούτους, οἷοι φαίνονται καὶ λέγοντες ἃ μὴ
ἴσασι καὶ πράττοντες, πότερά σοι δοκοῦσιν ἐπὶ τοῖς
τοιούτοις ἐπαίνου μᾶλλον ἢ ψόγου τυγχάνειν; καὶ
πότερον θαυμάζεσθαι μᾶλλον ἢ καταφρονεῖσθαι;
Ἐνθυμοῦ δὲ καὶ τῶν εἰδότων ὅ τι τε λέγουσι καὶ 17
ὅ τι ποιοῦσι, καί, ὡς ἐγὼ νομίζω, εὑρήσεις ἐν πᾶσιν
ἔργοις τοὺς μὲν εὐδοκιμοῦντάς τε καὶ θαυμαζομένους
ἐκ τῶν μάλιστα ἐπισταμένων ὄντας, τοὺς δὲ κακο-
δοξοῦντάς τε καὶ καταφρονουμένους ἐκ τῶν ἀμαθε-
στάτων. Εἰ οὖν ἐπιθυμεῖς εὐδοκιμεῖν τε καὶ θαυμά- 18
ζεσθαι ἐν τῇ πόλει, πειρῶ κατεργάσασθαι ὡς μάλιστα
τὸ εἰδέναι ἃ βούλει πράττειν· ἐὰν γὰρ τούτῳ διενέ-
γκας τῶν ἄλλων ἐπιχειρῇς τὰ τῆς πόλεως πράττειν,
οὐκ ἂν θαυμάσαιμι, εἰ πάνυ ῥᾳδίως τύχοις ὧν ἐπι-
θυμεῖς.

CHAPTER VII.

ARGUMENT.

This chapter is the counterpart of the preceding. Socrates encourages Charmides, a man of great worth and ability, to engage in public life, although averse to it.

One who is able to advance the interests of the State, and thereby to obtain glory and honor, is under a twofold obligation to exercise his talents (§ 1, 2). Socrates says, that he has learned that Charmides possesses this ability, by noticing his conversation with other statesmen (§ 3). He who can express his thoughts or give his opinion among them, can certainly speak in the assembly of the people (§ 4—7); for if those who are most wise and powerful are not, those who have less knowledge and power need not be, feared (§ 8). Seek, Socrates adds, a right understanding of yourself, which will impart confidence; and neglect not to give your exertions for the advantage of the State, that you may thus benefit not the citizens alone, but yourself and friends (§ 9).

---

1 Χαρμίδην δὲ τὸν Γλαύκωνος ὁρῶν ἀξιόλογον μὲν ἄνδρα ὄντα, καὶ πολλῷ δυνατώτερον τῶν τὰ πολιτικὰ τότε πραττόντων, ὀκνοῦντα δὲ προσιέναι τῷ δήμῳ καὶ τῶν τῆς πόλεως πραγμάτων ἐπιμελεῖσθαι· Εἰπέ μοι, ἔφη, ὦ Χαρμίδη, εἴ τις ἱκανὸς ὢν τοὺς στεφανίτας ἀγῶνας νικᾶν καὶ διὰ τοῦτο αὐτός τε τιμᾶσθαι καὶ τὴν πατρίδα ἐν τῇ Ἑλλάδι εὐδοκιμωτέραν ποιεῖν μὴ θέλοι ἀγωνίζεσθαι, ποῖόν τινα τοῦτον νομίζοις ἂν τὸν ἄνδρα εἶναι; — Δῆλον, ὅτι, ἔφη, μαλακόν τε καὶ δειλόν.—

2 Εἰ δέ τις, ἔφη, δυνατὸς ὢν τῶν τῆς πόλεως πραγμάτων ἐπιμελόμενος τήν τε πόλιν αὔξειν καὶ αὐτὸς διὰ τοῦτο τιμᾶσθαι ὀκνοίη δὴ τοῦτο πράττειν, οὐκ ἂν εἰκότως δειλὸς νομίζοιτο; — Ἴσως, ἔφη· ἀτὰρ πρὸς τί με ταῦτ' ἐρωτᾷς; — Ὅτι, ἔφη, οἶμαί σε δυνατὸν ὄντα ὀκνεῖν ἐπιμελεῖσθαι, καὶ ταῦτα ὧν ἀνάγκη σοι μετέ-

χειν πολίτῃ γε ὄντι.—Τὴν δὲ ἐμὴν δύναμιν, ἔφη ὁ 3
Χαρμίδης, ἐν ποίῳ ἔργῳ καταμαθὼν ταῦτά μου κατα-
γιγνώσκεις;—Ἐν ταῖς συνουσίαις, ἔφη, αἷς σύνει τοῖς
τὰ τῆς πόλεως πράττουσι· καὶ γάρ, ὅταν τι ἀνακοι-
νῶνταί σοι, ὁρῶ σε καλῶς συμβουλεύοντα, καὶ ὅταν τι
ἁμαρτάνωσιν, ὀρθῶς ἐπιτιμῶντα.—Οὐ ταὐτόν ἐστιν, 4
ἔφη, ὦ Σώκρατες, ἰδίᾳ τε διαλέγεσθαι καὶ ἐν τῷ πλή-
θει ἀγωνίζεσθαι.—Καὶ μήν, ἔφη, ὅ γε ἀριθμεῖν δυνά-
μενος οὐδὲν ἧττον ἐν τῷ πλήθει ἢ μόνος ἀριθμεῖ, καὶ
οἱ κατὰ μόνας ἄριστα κιθαρίζοντες, οὗτοι καὶ ἐν τῷ
πλήθει κρατιστεύουσιν.—Αἰδῶ δὲ καὶ φόβον, ἔφη, οὐχ 5
ὁρᾷς ἔμφυτά τε ἀνθρώποις ὄντα καὶ πολλῷ μᾶλλον ἐν
τοῖς ὄχλοις ἢ ἐν ταῖς ἰδίαις ὁμιλίαις παριστάμενα;—
Καὶ σέ γε διδάξων, ἔφη, ὥρμημαι, ὅτι οὔτε τοὺς φρο-
νιμωτάτους αἰδούμενος οὔτε τοὺς ἰσχυροτάτους φοβού-
μενος ἐν τοῖς ἀφρονεστάτοις τε καὶ ἀσθενεστάτοις
αἰσχύνῃ λέγειν· πότερον γὰρ τοὺς γναφεῖς αὐτῶν, ἢ 6
τοὺς σκυτεῖς, ἢ τοὺς τέκτονας, ἢ τοὺς χαλκεῖς, ἢ τοὺς
γεωργούς ἢ τοὺς ἐμπόρους, ἢ τούς, ἐν τῇ ἀγορᾷ μετα-
βαλλομένους καὶ φροντίζοντας, ὅ τι ἐλάττονος πριά-
μενοι πλείονος ἀποδῶνται, αἰσχύνῃ; ἐκ γὰρ τούτων
ἁπάντων ἡ ἐκκλησία συνίσταται. Τί δὲ οἴει διαφέρειν 7
ὃ σὺ ποιεῖς ἢ τῶν ἀσκητῶν ὄντα κρείττω τοὺς ἰδιώτας
φοβεῖσθαι; οὐ γὰρ τοῖς πρωτεύουσιν ἐν τῇ πόλει, ὧν
ἔνιοι καταφρονοῦσί σου, ῥᾳδίως διαλεγόμενος, καὶ τῶν
ἐπιμελομένων τοῦ τῇ πόλει διαλέγεσθαι πολὺ περιών,
ἐν τοῖς μηδὲ πώποτε φροντίσασι τῶν πολιτικῶν, μηδὲ
σοῦ καταπεφρονηκόσιν ὀκνεῖς λέγειν, δεδιώς, μὴ κατα-
γελασθῇς;—Τί δ'; ἔφη, οὐ δοκοῦσί σοι πολλάκις οἱ 8
ἐν τῇ ἐκκλησίᾳ τῶν ὀρθῶς λεγόντων καταγελᾶν;—
Καὶ γὰρ οἱ ἕτεροι, ἔφη· διὸ καὶ θαυμάζω σου, εἰ
ἐκείνους, ὅταν τοῦτο ποιῶσι, ῥᾳδίως χειρούμενος, τού-
τοις δὲ μηδένα τρόπον οἴει δυνήσεσθαι προσενεχθῆναι.
Ὠγαθέ, μὴ ἀγνόει σεαυτόν, μηδὲ ἁμάρτανε ἃ οἱ πλεῖ- 9

στοι ἁμαρτάνουσιν· οἱ γὰρ πολλοὶ ὡρμηκότες ἐπὶ τὸ σκοπεῖν τὰ τῶν ἄλλων πράγματα οὐ τρέπονται ἐπὶ τὸ ἑαυτοὺς ἐξετάζειν· μὴ οὖν ἀποῤῥᾳθύμει τούτου, ἀλλὰ διατείνου μᾶλλον πρὸς τὸ σεαυτῷ προσέχειν· καὶ μὴ ἀμέλει τῶν τῆς πόλεως, εἴ τι δυνατόν ἐστι διὰ σὲ βέλτιον ἔχειν· τούτων γὰρ καλῶς ἐχόντων, οὐ μόνον οἱ ἄλλοι πολῖται, ἀλλὰ καὶ οἱ σοὶ φίλοι καὶ αὐτὸς σὺ οὐκ ἐλάχιστα ὠφελήσῃ.

CHAPTER VIII.

ARGUMENT.

The remaining chapters of the third Book are of a miscellaneous nature, not directly connected with the preceding chapters and not connected with each other. They contain practical explanations of ethical principles, conversations with artists and workmen in regard to their occupations, apothegms and precepts in reference to exercise, regimen, etc. Their object seems to be to show the extent and value of Socrates' instructions, and thus they indirectly have a bearing upon the second accusation against him.

The present chapter shows in what manner he answered the somewhat captious questions of Aristippus, in reference to the good and beautiful, by showing their practical utility in life. Nothing, he says, is absolutely good or evil, but only in reference to its object (§ 1—3). The same is true of the beautiful, which does not differ from the good, and they both are comprehended in the useful (§ 4—10).

1 Ἀριστίππου δ' ἐπιχειροῦντος ἐλέγχειν τὸν Σωκράτην, ὥςπερ αὐτὸς ὑπ' ἐκείνου τὸ πρότερον ἠλέγχετο, βουλόμενος τοὺς συνόντας ὠφελεῖν ὁ Σωκράτης ἀπεκρίνατο, οὐχ ὥςπερ οἱ φυλαττόμενοι, μή πῃ ὁ λόγος ἐπαλλαχθῇ, ἀλλ' ὡς ἂν πεπεισμένοι μάλιστα πράτ-
2 τειν τὰ δέοντα. Ὁ μὲν γὰρ αὐτὸν ἤρετο, εἴ τι εἰδείη

ἀγαθόν, ἵνα, εἴ τι εἴποι τῶν τοιούτων, οἷον ἢ σιτίον,
ἢ ποτὸν ἢ χρήματα, ἢ ὑγίειαν, ἢ ῥώμην, ἢ τόλμαν
δεικνύοι δὴ τοῦτο κακὸν ἐνίοτε ὄν· ὁ δὲ εἰδώς, ὅτι, ἐάν
τι ἐνοχλῇ ἡμᾶς, δεόμεθα τοῦ παύσοντος, ἀπεκρίνατο,
ᾗπερ καὶ ποιεῖν κράτιστον· Ἀρά γε, ἔφη, ἐρωτᾷς με 3
εἴ τι οἶδα πυρετοῦ ἀγαθόν.—Οὐκ ἔγωγ', ἔφη.—Ἀλλ
ὀφθαλμίας ;— Οὐδὲ τοῦτο.—Ἀλλὰ λιμοῦ ;— Οὐδε
λιμοῦ.—Ἀλλὰ μήν, ἔφη, εἴγ' ἐρωτᾷς με, εἴ τι ἀγαθὸν
οἶδα, ὃ μηδενὸς ἀγαθόν ἐστιν, οὔτ' οἶδα, ἔφη, οὔτε
δέομαι.

Πάλιν δὲ τοῦ Ἀριστίππου ἐρωτῶντος αὐτόν, εἴ τι 4
εἰδείη καλόν ;— Καὶ πολλά, ἔφη.—Ἀρ' οὖν, ἔφη,
πάντα ὅμοια ἀλλήλοις ;—Ὡς οἷόν τε μὲν οὖν, ἔφη,
ἀνομοιότατα ἔνια.—Πῶς οὖν, ἔφη, τὸ τῷ καλῷ ἀνό-
μοιον καλὸν ἂν εἴη ;—Ὅτι, νὴ Δί', ἔφη, ἔστι μὲν τῷ
καλῷ πρὸς δρόμον ἀνθρώπῳ ἄλλος ἀνόμοιος, καλὸς
πρὸς πάλην, ἔστι δὲ ἀσπίς, καλὴ πρὸς τὸ προβα-
λέσθαι, ὡς ἔνι ἀνομοιοτάτη τῷ ἀκοντίῳ, καλῷ πρὸς
τὸ σφόδρα τε καὶ ταχὺ φέρεσθαι.— Οὐδὲν διαφερόν- 5
τως, ἔφη, ἀποκρίνῃ μοι ἢ ὅτε σε ἠρώτησα, εἴ τι
ἀγαθὸν εἰδείης.—Σὺ δ' οἴει, ἔφη, ἄλλο μὲν ἀγαθόν,
ἄλλο δὲ καλὸν εἶναι ; οὐκ οἶσθ', ὅτι πρὸς ταὐτὰ πάν-
τα καλά τε κἀγαθά ἐστιν ; Πρῶτον μὲν γὰρ ἡ ἀρετὴ
οὐ πρὸς ἄλλα μὲν ἀγαθόν, πρὸς ἄλλα δὲ καλόν ἐστιν,
ἔπειτα οἱ ἄνθρωποι τὸ αὐτό τε καὶ πρὸς τὰ αὐτὰ
καλοὶ κἀγαθοὶ λέγονται, πρὸς τὰ αὐτὰ δὲ καὶ τὰ
σώματα τῶν ἀνθρώπων καλά τε κἀγαθὰ φαίνεται,
πρὸς ταὐτὰ δὲ καὶ τἆλλα πάντα, οἷς ἄνθρωποι χρῶν-
ται, καλά τε κἀγαθὰ νομίζεται, πρὸς ἅπερ ἂν εὔχρη-
στα ᾖ.—Ἀρ' οὖν, ἔφη, καὶ κόφινος κοπροφόρος καλόν 6
ἐστιν ;—Νὴ Δί', ἔφη, καὶ χρυσῆ γε ἀσπὶς αἰσχρόν,
ἐὰν πρὸς τὰ ἑαυτῶν ἔργα ὁ μὲν καλῶς πεποιημένος ᾖ,
ἡ δὲ κακῶς.—Λέγεις σύ, ἔφη, καλά τε καὶ αἰσχρὰ τὰ
αὐτὰ εἶναι ;—Καὶ νὴ Δί' ἔγωγ', ἔφη, ἀγαθά τε καὶ 7

κακά· πολλάκις γὰρ τό τε λιμοῦ ἀγαθὸν πυρετοῦ κα-
κόν ἐστι, καὶ τὸ πυρετοῦ ἀγαθὸν λιμοῦ κακόν ἐστι,
πολλάκις δὲ τὸ μὲν πρὸς δρόμον καλὸν πρὸς πάλην
αἰσχρόν, τὸ δὲ πρὸς πάλην καλὸν πρὸς δρόμον αἰσχρόν·
πάντα γὰρ ἀγαθὰ μὲν καὶ καλά ἐστι, πρὸς ἃ ἂν εὖ
ἔχῃ, κακὰ δὲ καὶ αἰσχρά, πρὸς ἃ ἂν κακῶς.
8 Καὶ οἰκίας δὲ λέγων τὰς αὐτὰς καλάς τε εἶναι καὶ
χρησίμους παιδεύειν ἔμοιγ' ἐδόκει, οἵας χρὴ οἰκοδο-
μεῖσθαι. Ἐπεσκόπει δὲ ὧδε· Ἆρά γε τὸν μέλλοντα
οἰκίαν, οἵαν χρή, ἔχειν τοῦτο δεῖ μηχανᾶσθαι, ὅπως
9 ἡδίστη τε ἐνδιαιτᾶσθαι καὶ χρησιμωτάτη ἔσται; Τού-
του δὲ ὁμολογουμένου· Οὔκουν ἡδὺ μὲν θέρους ψυχει-
νὴν ἔχειν, ἡδὺ δὲ χειμῶνος ἀλεεινήν;—Ἐπειδὴ δὲ καὶ
τοῦτο συμφαῖεν· Οὔκουν ἐν ταῖς πρὸς μεσημβρίαν
βλεπούσαις οἰκίαις τοῦ μὲν χειμῶνος ὁ ἥλιος εἰς τὰς
παστάδας ὑπολάμπει, τοῦ δὲ θέρους ὑπὲρ ἡμῶν αὐτῶν
καὶ τῶν στεγῶν πορευόμενος σκιὰν παρέχει; Οὔκουν
εἴ γε καλῶς ἔχει ταῦτα οὕτω γίγνεσθαι, οἰκοδομεῖν δεῖ
ὑψηλότερα μὲν τὰ πρὸς μεσημβρίαν, ἵνα ὁ χειμερινὸς
ἥλιος μὴ ἀποκλείηται, χθαμαλώτερα δὲ τὰ πρὸς ἄρ-
10 κτον, ἵνα οἱ ψυχροὶ μὴ ἐμπίπτωσιν ἄνεμοι; Ὡς δὲ
συνελόντι εἰπεῖν, ὅποι πάσας ὥρας αὐτός τε ἂν ἥδιστα
καταφεύγοι καὶ τὰ ὄντα ἀσφαλέστατα τιθοῖτο, αὕτη
ἂν εἰκότως ἡδίστη τε καὶ καλλίστη οἴκησις εἴη· γρα-
φαὶ δὲ καὶ ποικιλίαι πλείονας εὐφροσύνας ἀποστεροῦ-
σιν ἢ παρέχουσι. Ναοῖς γε μὴν καὶ βωμοῖς χώραν
ἔφη εἶναι πρεπωδεστάτην, ἥτις ἐμφανεστάτη οὖσα ἀστι-
βεστάτη εἴη· ἡδὺ μὲν γὰρ ἰδόντας προσεύξασθαι, ἡδὺ
δὲ ἁγνῶς ἔχοντας προσιέναι.

CHAPTER IX.

ARGUMENT.

This chapter consists of definitions and explanations of several terms expressive of moral qualities.

1. Although some men have by nature more *courage* than others, yet this quality may be strengthened by precept and practice (§ 1—3).

2. *Wisdom and discretion* (σωφροσύνη) cannot be separated; since every one who knows the right, and acts accordingly, is both wise and discreet. But as every one does what seems best to him, he who *does* not the right, is not only not discreet, but not wise (§ 4).

3. *Justice*, and every other virtue is wisdom (σοφία) (§ 5).

4. The opposite of wisdom is *insanity* (μανία); but ignorance is not insanity, yet self-ignorance is next akin to it. Great aberration of understanding is commonly called insanity, but Socrates understood by it the mistaking of the good, which has its foundation in want of self-knowledge (§ 6, 7).

5. *Envy* is the pain or sorrow felt at the prosperity of friends. It is the companion of fools and not of wise men (§ 8).

6. *Idleness* is not entire inactivity, for all do something, but a vacuity of all useful employment (§ 9).

7. Those who bear the sceptre are not necessarily *kings* and princes, but only those who have the skill and ability to govern (§ 10—13).

8. The best employment of life is εὐπραξία, good conduct, which is to be distinguished from εὐτυχία, good fortune; as πρᾶξις from τύχη (§ 14, 15).

Πάλιν δὲ ἐρωτώμενος, ἡ ἀνδρία πότερον εἴη δι- 1
δακτὸν, ἢ φυσικόν; Οἶμαι μέν, ἔφη, ὥσπερ σῶμα
σώματος ἰσχυρότερον πρὸς τοὺς πόνους φύεται, οὕτω
καὶ ψυχὴν ψυχῆς ἐῤῥωμενεστέραν πρὸς τὰ δεινὰ φύ-
σει γίγνεσθαι· ὁρῶ γὰρ ἐν τοῖς αὐτοῖς νόμοις τε καὶ
ἔθεσι τρεφομένους πολὺ διαφέροντας ἀλλήλων τόλμῃ.
Νομίζω μέντοι πᾶσαν φύσιν μαθήσει καὶ μελέτῃ πρὸς 2
ἀνδρίαν αὔξεσθαι· δῆλον μὲν γάρ, ὅτι Σκύθαι καὶ

Θρᾷκες οὐκ ἂν τολμήσειαν ἀσπίδας καὶ δόρατα λα-
βόντες Λακεδαιμονίοις διαμάχεσθαι, φανερὸν δὲ, ὅτι
καὶ Λακεδαιμόνιοι οὔτ' ἂν Θρᾳξὶν ἐν πέλταις καὶ ἀκον-
τίοις, οὔτε Σκύθαις ἐν τόξοις ἐθέλοιεν ἂν διαγωνίζε-
3 σθαι. Ὁρῶ δ' ἔγωγε καὶ ἐπὶ τῶν ἄλλων πάντων
ὁμοίως καὶ φύσει διαφέροντας ἀλλήλων τοὺς ἀνθρώ-
πους, καὶ ἐπιμελείᾳ πολὺ ἐπιδιδόντας· ἐκ δὲ τούτων
δῆλόν ἐστιν, ὅτι πάντας χρὴ καὶ τοὺς εὐφυεστέρους
καὶ τοὺς ἀμβλυτέρους τὴν φύσιν, ἐν οἷς ἂν ἀξιόλογοι
βούλωνται γενέσθαι, ταῦτα καὶ μανθάνειν καὶ μελετᾶν.
4 Σοφίαν δὲ καὶ σωφροσύνην οὐ διώριζεν, ἀλλὰ
τὸν τὰ μὲν καλά τε καὶ ἀγαθὰ γιγνώσκοντα χρῆσθαι
αὐτοῖς, καὶ τὸν τὰ αἰσχρὰ εἰδότα εὐλαβεῖσθαι, σοφόν
τε καὶ σώφρονα ἔκρινεν. Προσερωτώμενος δὲ, εἰ τοὺς
ἐπισταμένους μὲν ἃ δεῖ πράττειν, ποιοῦντας δὲ τἀναν-
τία, σοφούς τε καὶ ἐγκρατεῖς εἶναι νομίζοι· Οὐδέν γε
μᾶλλον, ἔφη, ἢ ἀσόφους τε καὶ ἀκρατεῖς· πάντας γὰρ
οἶμαι, προαιρουμένους ἐκ τῶν ἐνδεχομένων ἃ οἴονται
συμφορώτατα αὐτοῖς εἶναι, ταῦτα πράττειν. Νομίζω
οὖν τοὺς μὴ ὀρθῶς πράττοντας οὔτε σοφοὺς οὔτε σώ-
5 φρονας εἶναι. Ἔφη δὲ καὶ τὴν δικαιοσύνην καὶ
τὴν ἄλλην πᾶσαν ἀρετὴν σοφίαν εἶναι· τά τε γὰρ
δίκαια καὶ πάντα, ὅσα ἀρετῇ πράττεται, καλά τε καὶ
ἀγαθὰ εἶναι· καὶ οὔτ' ἂν τοὺς ταῦτα εἰδότας ἄλλο ἀντὶ
τούτων οὐδὲν προελέσθαι, οὔτε τοὺς μὴ ἐπισταμένους
δύνασθαι πράττειν, ἀλλὰ καὶ ἐὰν ἐγχειρῶσιν, ἁμαρ-
τάνειν· οὕτω καὶ τὰ καλά τε καὶ ἀγαθὰ τοὺς μὲν σο-
φοὺς πράττειν, τοὺς δὲ μὴ σοφοὺς οὐ δύνασθαι, ἀλλὰ
καὶ ἐὰν ἐγχειρῶσιν, ἁμαρτάνειν· ἐπεὶ οὖν τά τε δίκαια
καὶ τὰ ἄλλα καλά τε καὶ ἀγαθὰ πάντα ἀρετῇ πράτ-
τεται, δῆλον εἶναι, ὅτι καὶ δικαιοσύνη καὶ ἡ ἄλλη πᾶσα
6 ἀρετὴ σοφία ἐστί. Μανίαν γε μὴν ἐναντίον μὲν ἔφη
εἶναι σοφίᾳ, οὐ μέντοι γε τὴν ἀνεπιστημοσύνην μανίαν
ἐνόμιζε, τὸ δὲ ἀγνοεῖν ἑαυτὸν, καὶ μὴ ἃ οἶδε δοξάζειν

τε καὶ οἴεσθαι γιγνώσκειν, ἐγγυτάτω μανιας ἐλογίζετο εἶναι· τοὺς μέντοι πολλοὺς ἔφη, ἃ μὲν οἱ πλεῖστοι ἀγνοοῦσι, τοὺς διημαρτηκότας τούτων οὐ φάσκειν μαίνεσθαι τοὺς δὲ διημαρτηκότας, ὧν οἱ πολλοὶ γιγνώσκουσι, μαινομένους καλεῖν· ἐάν τε γάρ τις μέγας 7
οὕτως οἴηται εἶναι, ὥστε κύπτειν τὰς πύλας τοῦ τείχους διεξιών, ἐάν τε οὕτως ἰσχυρός, ὥστ' ἐπιχειρεῖν οἰκίας αἴρεσθαι, ἢ ἄλλῳ τῳ ἐπιτίθεσθαι τῶν πᾶσι δήλων ὅτι ἀδύνατά ἐστι, τοῦτον μαίνεσθαι φάσκειν, τοὺς δὲ μικρὸν διαμαρτάνοντας οὐ δοκεῖν τοῖς πολλοῖς μαίνεσθαι, ἀλλ', ὥσπερ τὴν ἰσχυρὰν ἐπιθυμίαν ἔρωτα καλοῦσιν, οὕτω καὶ τὴν μεγάλην παράνοιαν μανίαν αὐτους καλεῖν.

Φθόνον δὲ σκοπῶν, ὅ τι εἴη, λύπην μέν τινα 8
ἐξεύρισκεν αὐτὸν ὄντα, οὔτε μέντοι τὴν ἐπὶ φίλων ἀτυχίαις, οὔτε τὴν ἐπ' ἐχθρῶν εὐτυχίαις γιγνομένην, ἀλλὰ μόνους ἔφη φθονεῖν τοὺς ἐπὶ ταῖς τῶν φίλων εὐπραξίαις ἀνιωμένους. Θαυμαζόντων δέ τινων, εἴ τις φιλῶν τινα ἐπὶ τῇ εὐπραξίᾳ αὐτοῦ λυποῖτο, ὑπεμίμνησκεν, ὅτι πολλοὶ οὕτως πρός τινας ἔχουσιν, ὥστε κακῶς μὲν πράττοντας μὴ δύνασθαι περιορᾶν, ἀλλὰ βοηθεῖν ἀτυχοῦσιν, εὐτυχούντων δὲ λυπεῖσθαι· τοῦτο δὲ φρονίμῳ μὲν ἀνδρὶ οὐκ ἂν συμβῆναι, τοὺς ἠλιθίους δὲ ἀεὶ πάσχειν αὐτό.

Σχολὴν δὲ σκοπῶν, τί εἴη, ποιοῦντας μέν τι 9
[ὅλως ἅπαντας, σχολάζοντας μέντοι] τοὺς πλείστους ἔφη εὑρίσκειν· καὶ γὰρ τοὺς πεττεύοντας καὶ τοὺς γελωτοποιοῦντας ποιεῖν τι· πάντας δὲ τούτους ἔφη σχολάζειν· ἐξεῖναι γὰρ αὐτοῖς ἰέναι πράξοντας τὰ βελτίω τούτων· ἀπὸ μέντοι τῶν βελτιόνων ἐπὶ τὰ χείρω ἰέναι οὐδένα σχολάζειν, εἰ δέ τις ἴοι, τοῦτον ἀσχολίας αὐτῷ οὔσης κακῶς ἔφη τοῦτο πράττειν.

Βασιλεῖς δὲ καὶ ἄρχοντας οὐ τοὺς τὰ σκῆπτρα 10
ἔχοντας ἔφη εἶναι, οὐδὲ τοὺς ὑπὸ τῶν τυχόντων αἱρε-

θέντας, οὐδὲ τοὺς κλήρῳ λαχόντας, οὐδὲ τοὺς βιασαμένους, οὐδὲ τοὺς ἐξαπατήσαντας, ἀλλὰ τοὺς ἐπιστα-
11 μένους ἄρχειν. Ὁπότε γάρ τις ὁμολογήσειε τοῦ μὲν ἄρχοντος εἶναι τὸ προστάττειν ὅ τι χρὴ ποιεῖν, τοῦ δὲ ἀρχομένου τὸ πείθεσθαι, ἐπεδείκνυεν ἔν τε νηῒ τὸν μὲν ἐπιστάμενον ἄρχοντα, τὸν δὲ ναύκληρον καὶ τοὺς ἄλλους τοὺς ἐν τῇ νηῒ πάντας πειθομένους τῷ ἐπισταμένῳ, καὶ ἐν γεωργίᾳ τοὺς κεκτημένους ἀγρούς, καὶ ἐν νόσῳ τοὺς νοσοῦντας, καὶ ἐν σωμασκίᾳ τοὺς σωμασκοῦντας, καὶ τοὺς ἄλλους πάντας, οἷς ὑπάρχει τι ἐπιμελείας δεόμενον, ἂν μὲν αὐτοὶ ἡγῶνται ἐπίστασθαι ἐπιμελεῖσθαι,—εἰ δὲ μή, τοῖς ἐπισταμένοις οὐ μόνον παροῦσι πειθομένους, ἀλλὰ καὶ ἀπόντας μεταπεμπομένους, ὅπως ἐκείνοις πειθόμενοι τὰ δέοντα πράττωσιν· ἐν δὲ ταλασίᾳ καὶ τὰς γυναῖκας ἐπεδείκνυεν ἀρχούσας τῶν ἀνδρῶν, διὰ τὸ τὰς μὲν εἰδέναι,
12 ὅπως χρὴ ταλασιουργεῖν, τοὺς δὲ μὴ εἰδέναι. Εἰ δέ τις πρὸς ταῦτα λέγοι, ὅτι τῷ τυράννῳ ἔξεστι μὴ πείθεσθαι τοῖς ὀρθῶς λέγουσι· Καὶ πῶς ἄν, ἔφη, ἐξείη μὴ πείθεσθαι, ἐπικειμένης γε ζημίας, ἐάν τις τῷ εὖ λέγοντι μὴ πείθηται; ἐν ᾧ γὰρ ἄν τις πράγματι μὴ πείθηται τῷ εὖ λέγοντι, ἁμαρτήσεται δήπου, ἁμαρ-
13 τάνων δὲ ζημιωθήσεται. Εἰ δὲ φαίη τις τῷ τυράννῳ ἐξεῖναι καὶ ἀποκτεῖναι τὸν εὖ φρονοῦντα· Τὸν δὲ ἀποκτείνοντα, ἔφη, τοὺς κρατίστους τῶν συμμάχων οἴει ἀζήμιον γίγνεσθαι, ἢ ὡς ἔτυχε ζημιοῦσθαι; πότερον γὰρ ἂν μᾶλλον οἴει σώζεσθαι τὸν ταῦτα ποιοῦντα, ἢ οὕτω καὶ τάχιστ' ἂν ἀπολέσθαι;

4 Ἐρομένου δέ τινος αὐτόν, τί δοκοίη αὐτῷ κράτιστον ἀνδρὶ ἐπιτήδευμα εἶναι, ἀπεκρίνατο, Εὐπραξίαν. Ἐρομένου δὲ πάλιν, εἰ καὶ τὴν εὐτυχίαν ἐπιτήδευμα νομίζοι εἶναι· Πᾶν μὲν οὖν τοὐναντίον ἔγωγ', ἔφη, τύχην καὶ πρᾶξιν ἡγοῦμαι· τὸ μὲν γὰρ μὴ ζητοῦντα ἐπιτυχεῖν τινι τῶν δεόντων εὐτυχίαν οἶμαι

εἶναι, τὸ δὲ μαθόντα τε καὶ μελετήσαντά τι εὖ ποιεῖν εὐπραξίαν νομίζω, καὶ οἱ τοῦτο ἐπιτηδεύοντες δοκοῦσί μοι εὖ πράττειν. Καὶ ἀρίστους δὲ καὶ θεοφιλεστάτους ἔφη εἶναι ἐν μὲν γεωργίᾳ τοὺς τὰ γεωργικὰ εὖ πράττοντας, ἐν δ' ἰατρείᾳ τοὺς τὰ ἰατρικά, ἐν δὲ πολιτείᾳ τοὺς τὰ πολιτικά, τὸν δὲ μηδὲν εὖ πράττοντα οὔτε χρήσιμον οὐδὲν ἔφη εἶναι, οὔτε θεοφιλῆ.

CHAPTER X.

ARGUMENT.

Socrates also sought to be useful to artists and mechanics, by conversing with them in regard to their employments:

1. Painting consists not merely in copying exactly all the objects that come within the circle of vision; even the highest beauty of the human figure is not found in any one individual, but must be consummated by the union of all the separate beauties of different persons, with the emotions expressed in the eyes, countenance, and the whole mien (§ 1—5).

2. In statuary, not only must the motions of the body be imitated, but thoughts and feelings designated in such a manner, that the statue shall seem to be endowed with life (§ 6—8).

3. With Pistias, he conversed upon the manner of constructing the breast-plate, so that it would best protect the body, with the least impediment to its free and easy motion (§ 9—15).

Ἀλλὰ μὴν καὶ εἴ ποτε τῶν τὰς τέχνας ἐχόντων 1
καὶ ἐργασίας ἕνεκα χρωμένων αὐταῖς διαλέγοιτό τινι, καὶ τούτοις ὠφέλιμος ἦν· εἰςελθὼν μὲν γάρ ποτε πρὸς Παῤῥάσιον τὸν ζωγράφον καὶ διαλεγόμενος αὐτῷ· Ἆρα, ἔφη, ὦ Παῤῥάσιε γραφική ἐστιν ἡ εἰκασία τῶν ὁρωμένων; τὰ γοῦν κοῖλα καὶ τὰ ὑψηλά, καὶ τὰ σκοτεινὰ καὶ τὰ φωτεινά, καὶ τὰ σκληρὰ καὶ τὰ μαλακά, καὶ τὰ τραχέα καὶ τὰ λεῖα, καὶ τὰ νέα καὶ τὰ παλαιὰ

σώματα διὰ τῶν χρωμάτων ἀπεικάζοντες ἐκμιμεῖσθε.—
2 Ἀληθῆ λέγεις, ἔφη.—Καὶ μὴν τά γε καλὰ εἴδη ἀφομοιοῦντες, ἐπειδὴ οὐ ῥᾴδιον ἑνὶ ἀνθρώπῳ περιτυχεῖν ἄμεμπτα πάντα ἔχοντι, ἐκ πολλῶν συνάγοντες τὰ ἐξ ἑκάστου κάλλιστα, οὕτως ὅλα τὰ σώματα καλὰ ποιεῖτε
3 φαίνεσθαι; — Ποιοῦμεν γάρ, ἔφη, οὕτως. — Τί γάρ; ἔφη, τὸ πιθανώτατόν τε καὶ ἥδιστον καὶ φιλικώτατον καὶ ποθεινότατον καὶ ἐρασμιώτατον ἀπομιμεῖσθε τῆς ψυχῆς ἦθος; ἢ οὐδὲ μιμητόν ἐστι τοῦτο;—Πῶς γὰρ ἄν, ἔφη, μιμητὸν εἴη, ὦ Σώκρατες, ὃ μήτε συμμετρίαν, μήτε χρῶμα, μήτε ὧν σὺ εἶπας ἄρτι μηδὲν ἔχει, μηδὲ
4 ὅλως ὁρατόν ἐστιν;—Ἆρ᾽ οὖν, ἔφη, γίγνεται ἐν ἀνθρώπῳ τό τε φιλοφρόνως καὶ τὸ ἐχθρῶς βλέπειν πρός τινας;—Ἔμοιγε δοκεῖ, ἔφη.—Οὔκουν τοῦτό γε μιμητὸν ἐν τοῖς ὄμμασιν;—Καὶ μάλα, ἔφη.—Ἐπὶ δὲ τοῖς τῶν φίλων ἀγαθοῖς καὶ τοῖς κακοῖς ὁμοίως σοι δοκοῦσιν ἔχειν τὰ πρόσωπα οἵ τε φροντίζοντες καὶ οἱ μή;—Μὰ Δί᾽ οὐ δῆτα, ἔφη· ἐπὶ μὲν γὰρ τοῖς ἀγαθοῖς φαιδροί, ἐπὶ δὲ τοῖς κακοῖς σκυθρωποὶ γίγνονται.—Οὔκουν, ἔφη, καὶ ταῦτα δυνατὸν ἀπεικάζειν;—Καὶ μάλα,
5 ἔφη.—Ἀλλὰ μὴν καὶ τὸ μεγαλοπρεπές τε καὶ ἐλευθέριον καὶ τὸ ταπεινόν τε καὶ ἀνελεύθερον, καὶ τὸ σωφρονητικόν τε καὶ φρόνιμον καὶ τὸ ὑβριστικόν τε καὶ ἀπειρόκαλον καὶ διὰ τοῦ προσώπου καὶ διὰ τῶν σχημάτων καὶ ἑστώτων καὶ κινουμένων ἀνθρώπων διαφαίνει. — Ἀληθῆ λέγεις, ἔφη. — Οὔκουν καὶ ταῦτα μιμητά;—Καὶ μάλα, ἔφη.—Πότερον οὖν, ἔφη, νομίζεις ἥδιον ὁρᾶν τοὺς ἀνθρώπους, δι᾽ ὧν τὰ καλά τε κἀγαθὰ καὶ ἀγαπητὰ ἤθη φαίνεται, ἢ δι᾽ ὧν τὰ αἰσχρά τε καὶ πονηρὰ καὶ μισητά;—Πολὺ νὴ Δί᾽, ἔφη διαφέρει, ὦ Σώκρατες.

6 Πρὸς δὲ Κλείτωνα τὸν ἀνδριαντοποιὸν εἰσελθών ποτε καὶ διαλεγόμενος αὐτῷ· Ὅτι μέν, ἔφη, ὦ Κλείτων, ἀλλοίους ποιεῖς δρομεῖς τε καὶ παλαιστὰς

καὶ πύκτας καὶ παγκρατιαστάς, ὁρῶ τε καὶ οἶδα· ὃ δὲ μάλιστα ψυχαγωγεῖ διὰ τῆς ὄψεως τοὺς ἀνθρώπους, τὸ ζωτικὸν φαίνεσθαι, πῶς τοῦτο ἐνεργάζῃ τοῖς ἀνδριᾶσιν; Ἐπεὶ δὲ ἀπορῶν ὁ Κλείτων οὐ ταχὺ ἀπεκρί- 7
νατο· Ἆρ', ἔφη, τοῖς τῶν ζώντων εἴδεσιν ἀπεικάζων τὸ ἔργον ζωτικωτέρους ποιεῖς φαίνεσθαι τοὺς ἀνδριάντας;—Καὶ μάλα, ἔφη.—Οὔκουν τά τε ὑπὸ τῶν σχημάτων κατασπώμενα καὶ τὰ ἀνασπώμενα ἐν τοῖς σώμασι, καὶ τὰ συμπιεζόμενα καὶ τὰ διελκόμενα, καὶ τὰ ἐντεινόμενα καὶ τὰ ἀνιέμενα ἀπεικάζων ὁμοιότερά τε τοῖς ἀληθινοῖς καὶ πιθανώτερα ποιεῖς φαίνεσθαι;—Πάνυ μὲν οὖν, ἔφη.—Τὸ δὲ καὶ τὰ πάθη τῶν ποιούν- 8
των τι σωμάτων ἀπομιμεῖσθαι οὐ ποιεῖ τινα τέρψιν τοῖς θεωμένοις;—Εἰκὸς γοῦν, ἔφη.—Οὔκουν καὶ τῶν μὲν μαχομένων ἀπειλητικὰ τὰ ὄμματα ἀπεικαστέον, τῶν δὲ νενικηκότων εὐφραινομένων ἡ ὄψις μιμητέα;—Σφόδρα γ', ἔφη.—Δεῖ ἄρα, ἔφη, τὸν ἀνδριαντοποιὸν τὰ τῆς ψυχῆς ἔργα τῷ εἴδει προςεικάζειν.

Πρὸς δὲ Πιστίαν τὸν θωρακοποιὸν εἰςελθών, 9
ἐπιδείξαντος αὐτοῦ τῷ Σωκράτει θώρακας εὖ εἰργασμένους· Νὴ τὴν Ἥραν, ἔφη, καλόν γε, ὦ Πιστία, τὸ εὕρημα τῷ τὰ μὲν δεόμενα σκέπης τοῦ ἀνθρώπου σκεπάζειν τὸν θώρακα, ταῖς δὲ χερσὶ μὴ κωλύειν χρῆσθαι. Ἀτάρ, ἔφη, λέξον μοι, ὦ Πιστία, διὰ τί οὔτε ἰσχυροτέ- 10
ρους οὔτε πολυτελεστέρους τῶν ἄλλων ποιῶν τοὺς θώρακας πλείονος πωλεῖς;—Ὅτι, ἔφη, ὦ Σώκρατες, εὐρυθμοτέρους ποιῶ.—Τὸν δὲ ῥυθμόν, ἔφη, πότερα μέτρῳ ἢ σταθμῷ ἐπιδεικνύων πλείονος τιμᾷ; οὐ γὰρ δὴ ἴσους γε πάντας οὐδὲ ὁμοίους οἶμαί σε ποιεῖν, εἴγε ἁρμόττοντας ποιεῖς.—Ἀλλὰ νὴ Δί', ἔφη, ποιῶ· οὐδὲν γὰρ ὄφελός ἐστι θώρακος ἄνευ τούτου.—Οὔκουν, ἔφη, σώματά γε 11
ἀνθρώπων τὰ μὲν εὔρυθμά ἐστι, τὰ δὲ ἄρρυθμα;—Πάνυ μὲν οὖν, ἔφη.—Πῶς οὖν, ἔφη, τῷ ἀρρύθμῳ σώματι ἁρμόττοντα τὸν θώρακα εὔρυθμον ποιεῖς;—

12 Ὥςπερ καὶ ἁρμόττοντα, ἔφη· ὁ ἁρμόττων γάρ ἐστιν
εὔρυθμος.—Δοκεῖς μοι, ἔφη ὁ Σωκράτης, τὸ εὔρυθμον
οὐ καθ' ἑαυτὸ λέγειν, ἀλλὰ πρὸς τὸν χρώμενον, ὥς-
περ ἂν εἰ φαίης ἀσπίδα, ᾧ ἂν ἁρμόττῃ, τούτῳ εὔρυ-
θμον εἶναι, καὶ χλαμύδα, καὶ τἆλλα ὡςαύτως ἔοικεν
13 ἔχειν τῷ σῷ λόγῳ. Ἴσως δὲ καὶ ἄλλο τι οὐ μικρὸν
ἀγαθὸν τῷ ἁρμόττειν πρόςεστι.—Δίδαξον, ἔφη, ὦ
Σώκρατες, εἴ τι ἔχεις.—Ἧττον, ἔφη, τῷ βάρει πιέ-
ζουσιν οἱ ἁρμόττοντες τῶν ἀναρμόστων, τὸν αὐτὸν
σταθμὸν ἔχοντες· οἱ μὲν γὰρ ἀνάρμοστοι ἢ ὅλοι ἐκ
τῶν ὤμων κρεμάμενοι, ἢ καὶ ἄλλο τι τοῦ σώματος
σφόδρα πιέζοντες δύςφοροι καὶ χαλεποὶ γίγνονται, οἱ
δὲ ἁρμόττοντες, διειλημμένοι τὸ βάρος τὸ μὲν ὑπὸ τῶν
κλειδῶν καὶ ἐπωμίδων, τὸ δὲ ὑπὸ τῶν ὤμων, τὸ δὲ
ὑπὸ τοῦ στήθους, τὸ δὲ ὑπὸ τοῦ νώτου, τὸ δὲ ὑπὸ
τῆς γαστρός, ὀλίγου δεῖν οὐ φορήματι, ἀλλὰ προς-
14 θήματι ἐοίκασιν.—Εἴρηκας, ἔφη, αὐτό, δι' ὅπερ ἔγωγε
τὰ ἐμὰ ἔργα πλείστου ἄξια νομίζω εἶναι· ἔνιοι μέντοι
τοὺς ποικίλους καὶ τοὺς ἐπιχρύσους θώρακας μᾶλλον
ὠνοῦνται.—Ἀλλὰ μήν, ἔφη, εἴγε διὰ ταῦτα μὴ ἁρ-
μόττοντας ὠνοῦνται, κακὸν ἔμοιγε δοκοῦσι ποικίλον τε
15 καὶ ἐπίχρυσον ὠνεῖσθαι. Ἀτάρ, ἔφη, τοῦ σώματος
μὴ μένοντος, ἀλλὰ τοτὲ μὲν κυρτουμένου, τοτὲ δὲ ὀρ-
θουμένου, πῶς ἂν ἀκριβεῖς θώρακες ἁρμόττοιεν;—
Οὐδαμῶς, ἔφη.—Λέγεις, ἔφη, ἁρμόττειν οὐ τοὺς ἀκρι-
βεῖς, ἀλλὰ τοὺς μὴ λυποῦντας ἐν τῇ χρείᾳ.—Αὐτός,
ἔφη, τοῦτο λέγεις, ὦ Σώκρατες, καὶ πάνυ ὀρθῶς ἀπο-
δέχῃ

CHAPTER XI.

ARGUMENT.

SOCRATES having heard of the beauty of a famous courtezan Theodota, visits her with some of his disciples (§ 1), and finds her engaged with a painter. After instituting the inquiry whether they conferred or received greater favor by looking at so great beauty (§ 2, 3), Socrates converses jestingly with Theodota upon the value of friends and the best means of obtaining them (§ 4—9). Lasting friendship, he says, is not secured by beauty of person and the arts of love alone, but by kindness (§ 10—12). In the gratification of sensual desire the greatest moderation should be preserved, lest satiety and disgust ensue (§ 13, 14). The interview is concluded by a playful dialogue between Theodota and Socrates (§ 15—18).

Γυναικὸς δέ ποτε οὔσης ἐν τῇ πόλει καλῆς, ᾗ ὄνομα 1
ἦν Θεοδότη, καὶ οἵας συνεῖναι τῷ πείθοντι, μνησθέν-
τος αὐτῆς τῶν παρόντων τινὸς καὶ εἰπόντος, ὅτι κρεῖτ-
τον εἴη λόγου τὸ κάλλος τῆς γυναικός, καὶ ζωγράφους
φήσαντος εἰσιέναι πρὸς αὐτὴν ἀπεικασομένους, οἷς ἐκεί-
νην ἐπιδεικνύειν ἑαυτῆς ὅσα καλῶς ἔχοι· Ἰτέον ἂν εἴη
θεασομένους, ἔφη ὁ Σωκράτης· οὐ γὰρ δὴ ἀκούσασί γε
τὸ λόγου κρεῖττον ἔστι καταμαθεῖν. Καὶ ὁ διηγησά-
μενος· Οὐκ ἂν φθάνοιτ', ἔφη, ἀκολουθοῦντες. Οὕτω 2
μὲν δὴ πορευθέντες πρὸς τὴν Θεοδότην, καὶ καταλα-
βόντες ζωγράφῳ τινὶ παρεστηκυῖαν ἐθεάσαντο· παυ-
σαμένου δὲ τοῦ ζωγράφου· Ὦ ἄνδρες, ἔφη ὁ Σωκρά-
της, πότερον ἡμᾶς δεῖ μᾶλλον Θεοδότῃ χάριν ἔχειν,
ὅτι ἡμῖν τὸ κάλλος ἑαυτῆς ἐπέδειξεν, ἢ ταύτην ἡμῖν,
ὅτι ἐθεασάμεθα; ἆρ' εἰ μὲν ταύτῃ ὠφελιμωτέρα ἐστὶν
ἡ ἐπίδειξις, ταύτην ἡμῖν χάριν ἑκτέον, εἰ δὲ ἡμῖν ἡ θέα,
ἡμᾶς ταύτῃ; Εἰπόντος δέ τινος, ὅτι δίκαια λέγοι·

3 *Οὐκοῦν, ἔφη, αὕτη μὲν ἤδη τε τὸν παρ' ἡμῶν ἔπαινον
κερδαίνει, καὶ ἐπειδὰν εἰς πλείους διαγγείλωμεν, πλείω
ὠφελήσεται, ἡμεῖς δὲ ἤδη τε, ὧν ἐϑεασάμεϑα, ἐπιϑυ-
μοῦμεν ἅψασϑαι, καὶ ἄπιμεν ὑποκνιζόμενοι, καὶ ἀπελ-
ϑόντες ποϑήσομεν· ἐκ δὲ τούτων εἰκὸς ἡμᾶς μὲν ϑερα-
πεύειν, ταύτην δὲ ϑεραπεύεσϑαι. Καὶ ἡ Θεοδότη· Νὴ
Δί', ἔφη, εἰ τοίνυν ταῦϑ' οὕτως ἔχει, ἐμὲ ἂν δέοι ὑμῖν
4 τῆς ϑέας χάριν ἔχειν. Ἐκ δὲ τούτου ὁ Σωκράτης ὁρῶν
αὐτήν τε πολυτελῶς κεκοσμημένην, καὶ μητέρα παροῦ-
σαν αὐτῇ ἐν ἐσϑῆτι καὶ ϑεραπείᾳ οὐ τῇ τυχούσῃ, καὶ
ϑεραπαίνας πολλὰς καὶ εὐειδεῖς, καὶ οὐδὲ ταύτας ἠμε-
λημένως ἐχούσας, καὶ τοῖς ἄλλοις τὴν οἰκίαν ἀφϑόνως
κατεσκευασμένην· Εἰπέ μοι, ἔφη, ὦ Θεοδότη, ἔστι σοι
ἀγρός; Οὐκ ἔμοιγ', ἔφη.—Ἀλλ' ἄρα οἰκία προσόδους
ἔχουσα;—Οὐδὲ οἰκία, ἔφη.—Ἀλλὰ μὴ χειροτέχναι
τινές;—Οὐδὲ χειροτέχναι, ἔφη.—Πόϑεν οὖν, ἔφη,
τἀπιτήδεια ἔχεις;—Ἐάν τις, ἔφη, φίλος μοι γενό-
5 μενος εὖ ποιεῖν ἐϑέλῃ, οὗτός μοι βίος ἐστί.—Νὴ τὴν
Ἥραν, ἔφη, ὦ Θεοδότη, καλόν γε τὸ κτῆμα· καὶ
πολλῷ κρεῖττον οἰῶν τε καὶ βοῶν καὶ αἰγῶν φίλων
ἀγέλην κεκτῆσϑαι. Ἀτάρ, ἔφη, πότερον τῇ τύχῃ ἐπι-
τρέπεις, ἐάν τίς σοι φίλος, ὥσπερ μυῖα, προσπτῆται,
6 ἢ καὶ αὐτή τι μηχανᾷ;—Πῶς δ' ἄν, ἔφη, ἐγὼ τούτου
μηχανὴν εὕροιμι;—Πολὺ νὴ Δί', ἔφη, προσηκόντως
μᾶλλον ἢ αἱ φάλαγγες· οἶσϑα γάρ, ὡς ἐκεῖναι ϑηρῶσι
τὰ πρὸς τὸν βίον· ἀράχνια γὰρ δήπου λεπτὰ ὑφηνά-
μεναι, ὅ τι ἂν ἐνταῦϑα ἐμπέσῃ, τούτῳ τροφῇ χρῶν-
7 ται.—Καὶ ἐμοὶ οὖν, ἔφη, συμβουλεύεις ὑφήνασϑαί τι
ϑήρατρον;—Οὐ γὰρ δὴ οὕτως γε ἀτεχνῶς οἴεσϑαι
χρὴ τὸ πλείστου ἄξιον ἄγρευμα, φίλους, ϑηράσειν·
οὐχ ὁρᾷς, ὅτι καὶ τὸ μικροῦ ἄξιον, τοὺς λαγώς, ϑη-
8 ρῶντες πολλὰ τεχνάζουσιν; Ὅτι μὲν γὰρ τῆς νυκτὸς
νέμονται, κύνας νυκτερευτικὰς πορισάμενοι, ταύταις αὐ-
τοὺς ϑηρῶσιν, ὅτι δὲ μεϑ' ἡμέραν ἀποδιδράσκουσιν*

ἄλλας κτῶνται κύνας, αἵτινες, ᾗ ἂν ἐκ τῆς νομῆς εἰς τὴν εὐνὴν ἀπέλθωσι, τῇ ὀσμῇ αἰσθανόμεναι εὑρίσκουσιν αὐτούς, ὅτι δὲ ποδώκεις εἰσίν, ὥςτε καὶ ἐκ τοῦ φανεροῦ τρέχοντες ἀποφεύγειν, ἄλλας αὖ κύνας ταχείας παρασκευάζονται, ἵνα κατὰ πόδας ἁλίσκωνται, ὅτι δὲ καὶ ταύτας αὐτῶν τινες ἀποφεύγουσι, δίκτυα ἱστᾶσιν εἰς τὰς ἀτραπούς, ᾗ φεύγουσιν, ἵν' εἰς ταῦτα
ἐμπίπτοντες συμποδίζωνται. — Τίνι οὖν, ἔφη, τοιούτῳ 9
φίλους ἂν ἐγὼ θηρῴην; — Ἐὰν νὴ Δί', ἔφη, ἀντὶ κυνὸς κτήσῃ, ὅςτις σοι ἰχνεύων μὲν τοὺς φιλοκάλους καὶ πλουσίους εὑρήσει, εὑρὼν δὲ μηχανήσεται, ὅπως
ἐμβάλῃ αὐτοὺς εἰς τὰ σὰ δίκτυα. — Καὶ ποῖα, ἔφη, 10
ἐγὼ δίκτυα ἔχω; — Ἓν μὲν δήπου, ἔφη, καὶ μάλα εὖ περιπλεκόμενον, τὸ σῶμα, ἐν δὲ τούτῳ ψυχήν, ᾗ καταμανθάνεις, καὶ ὡς ἂν ἐμβλέπουσα χαρίζοιο, καὶ ὅ τι ἂν λέγουσα εὐφραίνοις, καὶ ὅτι δεῖ τὸν μὲν ἐπιμελόμενον ἀσμένως ὑποδέχεσθαι, τὸν δὲ τρυφῶντα ἀποκλείειν, καὶ ἀῤῥωστήσαντός γε φίλου φροντιστικῶς ἐπισκέψασθαι, καὶ καλόν τι πράξαντος σφόδρα συνησθῆναι, καὶ τῷ σφόδρα σοῦ φροντίζοντι ὅλῃ τῇ ψυχῇ κεχαρίσθαι· φιλεῖν γε μὴν εὖ οἶδ' ὅτι ἐπίστασαι οὐ μόνον μαλακῶς, ἀλλὰ καὶ εὐνοϊκῶς· καὶ ὅτι ἀρεστοί σοί εἰσιν οἱ φίλοι, οἶδ' ὅτι οὐ λόγῳ, ἀλλ' ἔργῳ ἀναπείθεις. — Μὰ τὸν Δί', ἔφη ἡ Θεοδότη, ἐγὼ τούτων
οὐδὲν μηχανῶμαι. — Καὶ μήν, ἔφη, πολὺ διαφέρει τὸ 11
κατὰ φύσιν τε καὶ ὀρθῶς ἀνθρώπῳ προςφέρεσθαι· καὶ γὰρ δὴ βίᾳ μὲν οὔτ' ἂν ἕλοις οὔτε κατάσχοις φίλον, εὐεργεσίᾳ δὲ καὶ ἡδονῇ τὸ θηρίον τοῦτο ἁλώσιμόν τε καὶ παραμόνιμόν ἐστιν. — Ἀληθῆ λέγεις,
ἔφη. — Δεῖ τοίνυν, ἔφη, πρῶτον μὲν τοὺς φροντίζοντάς 12
σου τοιαῦτα ἀξιοῦν, οἷα ποιοῦσιν αὐτοῖς σμικρότατα μελήσει, ἔπειτα δὲ αὐτὴν ἀμείβεσθαι χαριζομένην τὸν αὐτὸν τρόπον· οὕτω γὰρ ἂν μάλιστα φίλοι γίγνοιντο, καὶ πλεῖστον χρόνον φιλοῖεν, καὶ μέγιστα εὐεργετοῖεν.

13 Χαρίζοιο δ' ἂν μάλιστα, εἰ δεομένοις δωροῖο τὰ παρὰ σεαυτῆς· ὁρᾷς γάρ, ὅτι καὶ τῶν βρωμάτων τὰ ἥδιστα, ἐὰν μέν τις προσφέρῃ, πρὶν ἐπιθυμεῖν, ἀηδῆ φαίνεται, κεκορεσμένοις δὲ καὶ βδελυγμίαν παρέχει, ἐὰν δέ τις προσφέρῃ λιμὸν ἐμποιήσας, κἂν φαυλότερα ᾖ, πάνυ
14 ἡδέα φαίνεται.—Πῶς οὖν ἄν, ἔφη, ἐγὼ λιμὸν ἐμποιεῖν τῳ τῶν παρ' ἐμοὶ δυναίμην;—Εἰ νὴ Δί', ἔφη, πρῶτον μὲν τοῖς κεκορεσμένοις μήτε προσφέροις μήτε ὑπομιμνήσκοις, ἕως ἂν τῆς πλησμονῆς παυσάμενοι πάλιν δέωνται, ἔπειτα τοὺς δεομένους ὑπομιμνήσκοις ὡς κοσμιωτάτῃ τε ὁμιλίᾳ καὶ τῷ φαίνεσθαι βουλομένη χαρίζεσθαι, καὶ διαφεύγουσα, ἕως ἂν ὡς μάλιστα δεηθῶσι· τηνικαῦτα γὰρ πολὺ διαφέρει τὰ αὐτὰ δῶρα, ἢ πρὶν
15 ἐπιθυμῆσαι, διδόναι.—Καὶ ἡ Θεοδότη· Τί οὖν οὐ σύ μοι, ἔφη, ὦ Σώκρατες, ἐγένου συνθηρατὴς τῶν φίλων; —Ἐάν γε νὴ Δί', ἔφη, πείθῃς με σύ.—Πῶς οὖν ἄν, ἔφη, πείσαιμί σε;—Ζητήσεις, ἔφη, τοῦτο αὐτὴ καὶ
16 μηχανήσῃ, ἐάν τί μου δέῃ.—Εἴσιθι τοίνυν, ἔφη, θαμινά. Καὶ ὁ Σωκράτης ἐπισκώπτων τὴν αὑτοῦ ἀπραγμοσύνην· Ἀλλ', ὦ Θεοδότη, ἔφη, οὐ πάνυ μοι ῥᾴδιόν ἐστι σχολάσαι· καὶ γὰρ ἴδια πράγματα πολλὰ καὶ δημόσια παρέχει μοι ἀσχολίαν, εἰσὶ δὲ καὶ φίλαι μοι, αἳ οὔτε ἡμέρας οὔτε νυκτὸς ἀφ' αὑτῶν ἐάσουσί με ἀπιέναι, φίλτρα τε μανθάνουσαι παρ' ἐμοῦ καὶ ἐπῳ-
17 δάς.—Ἐπίστασαι γάρ, ἔφη, καὶ ταῦτα, ὦ Σώκρατες; —Ἀλλὰ διὰ τί οἴει, ἔφη, Ἀπολλόδωρόν τε τόνδε καὶ Ἀντισθένην οὐδέποτέ μου ἀπολείπεσθαι; διὰ τί δὲ καὶ Κέβητα καὶ Σιμμίαν Θήβηθεν παραγίγνεσθαι; εὖ ἴσθι, ὅτι ταῦτα οὐκ ἄνευ πολλῶν φίλτρων τε καὶ
18 ἐπῳδῶν καὶ ἰύγγων ἐστί.—Χρῆσον τοίνυν μοι, ἔφη, τὴν ἴυγγα, ἵνα ἐπὶ σοὶ πρῶτον ἕλκω αὐτήν.—Ἀλλὰ μὰ Δί', ἔφη, οὐκ αὐτὸς ἕλκεσθαι πρὸς σὲ βούλομαι, ἀλλὰ σὲ πρὸς ἐμὲ πορεύεσθαι.—Ἀλλὰ πορεύσομαι, ἔφη· μόνον ὑποδέχου.—Ἀλλ' ὑποδέξομαί σε, ἔφη, ἐὰν μή τις φιλωτέρα σου ἔνδον ᾖ.

CHAPTER XII.

ARGUMENT.

Socrates enjoined upon Epigenes, one of his disciples, who, although a youth, was suffering from physical debility, the duty of engaging in gymnastic exercises. As a citizen of Athens, and hence bound to fight against her enemies, he, as much as those who contended in the Olympic Games, needed to cultivate his physical powers. The dangers and inconveniences are many to those who neglect physical exercise, whilst those who are robust and firm in health, can easily extricate themselves from peril and danger, and by succoring their friends and country, obtain honor and glory, and thus provide happily for the future life of themselves and families (§ 1—4). But health is not a boon to be desired for warlike purposes only; it contributes to soundness and vigor of mind, and cannot be neglected with impunity (§ 5—8).

Ἐπιγένην δὲ τῶν ξυνόντων τινά, νέον τε ὄντα καὶ 1
τὸ σῶμα κακῶς ἔχοντα, ἰδών· Ὡς ἰδιωτικῶς, ἔφη, τὸ σῶμα ἔχεις, ὦ Ἐπίγενες. Καὶ ὅς· Ἰδιώτης μέν, ἔφη, εἰμί, ὦ Σώκρατες.—Οὐδέν γε μᾶλλον, ἔφη, τῶν ἐν Ὀλυμπίᾳ μελλόντων ἀγωνίζεσθαι· ἢ δοκεῖ σοι μικρὸς εἶναι ὁ περὶ τῆς ψυχῆς πρὸς τοὺς πολεμίους ἀγών, ὃν Ἀθηναῖοι θήσουσιν, ὅταν τύχωσιν; Καὶ μὴν οὐκ 2
ὀλίγοι μὲν διὰ τὴν τῶν σωμάτων καχεξίαν ἀποθνήσκουσί τε ἐν τοῖς πολεμικοῖς κινδύνοις, καὶ αἰσχρῶς σώζονται, πολλοὶ δὲ δι' αὐτὸ τοῦτο ζῶντες ἁλίσκονται, καὶ ἁλόντες ἤτοι δουλεύουσι τὸν λοιπὸν βίον, ἐὰν οὕτω τύχωσι, τὴν χαλεπωτάτην δουλείαν, ἢ εἰς τὰς ἀνάγκας τὰς ἀλγεινοτάτας ἐμπεσόντες, καὶ ἐκτίσαντες ἐνίοτε πλείω τῶν ὑπαρχόντων αὐτοῖς, τὸν λοιπὸν βίον ἐνδεεῖς τῶν ἀναγκαίων ὄντες καὶ κοκοπαθοῦντες διαζῶσι, πολλοὶ δὲ δόξαν αἰσχρὰν κτῶνται, διὰ τὴν τοῦ
σώματος ἀδυναμίαν δοκοῦντες ἀποδειλιᾶν· ἢ καταφρο- 3

νεῖς τῶν ἐπιτιμίων τῆς καχεξίας τούτων, καὶ ῥᾳδίως ἂν οἴει φέρειν τὰ τοιαῦτα; καὶ μὴν οἶμαί γε πολλῷ ῥᾴω καὶ ἡδίω τούτων εἶναι ἃ δεῖ ὑπομένειν τὸν ἐπιμελόμενον τῆς τοῦ σώματος εὐεξίας· ἢ ὑγιεινότερόν τε καὶ εἰς τἆλλα χρησιμώτερον νομίζεις εἶναι τὴν καχεξίαν τῆς εὐεξίας; ἢ τῶν διὰ τὴν εὐεξίαν γιγνο-
4 μένων καταφρονεῖς; Καὶ μὴν πάντα γε τἀναντία συμβαίνει τοῖς εὖ τὰ σώματα ἔχουσιν ἢ τοῖς κακῶς· καὶ γὰρ ὑγιαίνουσιν οἱ τὰ σώματα εὖ ἔχοντες καὶ ἰσχύουσι, καὶ πολλοὶ μὲν διὰ τοῦτο ἐκ τῶν πολεμικῶν ἀγώνων σώζονταί τε εὐσχημόνως, καὶ τὰ δεινὰ πάντα διαφεύγουσι, πολλοὶ δὲ φίλοις τε βοηθοῦσι καὶ τὴν πατρίδα εὐεργετοῦσι, καὶ διὰ ταῦτα χάριτός τε ἀξιοῦνται, καὶ δόξαν μεγάλην κτῶνται, καὶ τιμῶν καλλίστων τυγχάνουσι, καὶ διὰ ταῦτα τόν τε λοιπὸν βίον ἥδιον καὶ κάλλιον διαζῶσι, καὶ τοῖς ἑαυτῶν παισὶ καλ-
5 λίους ἀφορμὰς εἰς τὸν βίον καταλείπουσιν. Οὔτοι χρή, ὅτι ἡ πόλις οὐκ ἀσκεῖ δημοσίᾳ τὰ πρὸς τὸν πόλεμον, διὰ τοῦτο καὶ ἰδίᾳ ἀμελεῖν, ἀλλὰ μηδὲν ἧττον ἐπιμελεῖσθαι· εὖ γὰρ ἴσθι, ὅτι οὐδὲ ἐν ἄλλῳ οὐδενὶ ἀγῶνι, οὐδὲ ἐν πράξει οὐδεμιᾷ μεῖον ἕξεις διὰ τὸ βέλτιον τὸ σῶμα παρεσκευάσθαι· πρὸς πάντα γάρ, ὅσα πράττουσιν ἄνθρωποι, χρήσιμον τὸ σῶμά ἐστιν· ἐν πάσαις δὲ ταῖς τοῦ σώματος χρείαις πολὺ διαφέρει
6 ὡς βέλτιστα τὸ σῶμα ἔχειν· ἐπεὶ καὶ ἐν ᾧ δοκεῖς ἐλαχίστην σώματος χρείαν εἶναι, ἐν τῷ διανοεῖσθαι, τίς οὐκ οἶδεν, ὅτι καὶ ἐν τούτῳ πολλοὶ μεγάλα σφάλλονται, διὰ τὸ μὴ ὑγιαίνειν τὸ σῶμα; καὶ λήθη δὲ καὶ ἀθυμία καὶ δυσκολία καὶ μανία πολλάκις πολλοῖς διὰ τὴν τοῦ σώματος καχεξίαν εἰς τὴν διάνοιαν ἐμπίπτουσιν οὕτως, ὥστε καὶ τὰς ἐπιστήμας ἐκβάλλειν.
7 Τοῖς δὲ τὰ σώματα εὖ ἔχουσι πολλὴ ἀσφάλεια καὶ οὐδεὶς κίνδυνος διά γε τὴν τοῦ σώματος καχεξίαν τοιοῦτόν τι παθεῖν, εἰκὸς δὲ μᾶλλον πρὸς τὰ ἐναντία τῶν

διὰ τὴν καχεξίαν γιγνομένων καὶ τὴν εὐεξίαν χρήσιμον εἶναι· καίτοι τῶν γε τοῖς εἰρημένοις ἐναντίων ἕνεκα τί οὐκ ἄν τις νοῦν ἔχων ὑπομείνειεν;—Αἰσχρὸν δὲ 8
καὶ τὸ διὰ τὴν ἀμέλειαν γηρᾶσαι πρὶν ἰδεῖν ἑαυτὸν, ποῖος ἂν κάλλιστος καὶ κράτιστος τῷ σώματι γένοιτο· ταῦτα δὲ οὐκ ἔστιν ἰδεῖν ἀμελοῦντα· οὐ γὰρ ἐθέλει αὐτόματα γίγνεσθαι.

CHAPTER XIII.

ARGUMENT.

Several short sayings or apothegms of Socrates upon the conduct of life, are preserved in this chapter. They are briefly the following:

1. Rusticity of conduct as well as physical deformity should be overlooked (§ 1).
2. The best remedy for loss of appetite is fasting (§ 2).
3. The necessity of guarding against being too much troubled by the little ills of life, such as the impalatableness of food and drink (§ 3).
4. If you would correct a servant's faults, see to it that you are not yourself equally culpable (§ 4).
5. One who is accustomed to walk every day, need not fear a long journey, which may be considered merely as an extended walk; still it is better to hasten in starting, than while on a journey (§ 5).
6. A man of liberal training cannot honorably allow himself to be excelled, in encountering difficulties, by a slave (§ 6).

Ὀργιζομένου δέ ποτέ τινος, ὅτι προςειπών τινα 1
χαίρειν οὐκ ἀντιπροςερρήθη· Γελοῖον, ἔφη, τὸ, εἰ μὲν τὸ σῶμα κάκιον ἔχοντι ἀπήντησάς τῳ, μὴ ἂν ὀργίζεσθαι, ὅτι δὲ τὴν ψυχὴν ἀγροικοτέρως διακειμένῳ περιέτυχες, τοῦτό σε λυπεῖ.

Ἄλλου δὲ λέγοντος, ὅτι ἀηδῶς ἐσθίοι· Ἀκουμενός, 2
ἔφη, τούτου φάρμακον ἀγαθὸν διδάσκει. Ἐρομένου δέ·

Ποῖον; Παύσασθαι ἐσθίοντα, ἔφη· καὶ ἥδιόν τε καὶ εὐτελέστερον καὶ ὑγιεινότερον [φησὶ] διάξειν παυσάμενον.

3 *Ἄλλου δ' αὖ λέγοντος, ὅτι θερμὸν εἴη παρ' ἑαυτῷ τὸ ὕδωρ, ὃ πίνοι· Ὅταν ἄρ', ἔφη, βούλῃ θερμῷ λούσασθαι, ἕτοιμον ἔσται σοι.—Ἀλλὰ ψυχρόν, ἔφη, ὥστε λούσασθαι, ἐστίν.—Ἆρ' οὖν, ἔφη, καὶ οἱ οἰκέται σου ἄχθονται πίνοντές τε αὐτὸ καὶ λουόμενοι αὐτῷ; —Μὰ τὸν Δί', ἔφη· ἀλλὰ καὶ πολλάκις τεθαύμακα, ὡς ἡδέως αὐτῷ πρὸς ἀμφότερα ταῦτα χρῶνται.—Πότερον δέ, ἔφη, τὸ παρὰ σοὶ ὕδωρ θερμότερον πιεῖν ἐστιν, ἢ τὸ ἐν Ἀσκληπιοῦ;—Τὸ ἐν Ἀσκληπιοῦ, ἔφη. —Πότερον δὲ λούσασθαι ψυχρότερον, τὸ παρὰ σοί, ἢ τὸ ἐν Ἀμφιαράου;—Τὸ ἐν Ἀμφιαράου, ἔφη.—Ἐνθυμοῦ οὖν, ἔφη, ὅτι κινδυνεύεις δυσαρεστότερος εἶναι τῶν τε οἰκετῶν καὶ τῶν ἀῤῥωστούντων.*

4 *Κολάσαντος δέ τινος ἰσχυρῶς ἀκόλουθον ἤρετο, τί χαλεπαίνοι τῷ θεράποντι.—Ὅτι, ἔφη, ὀψοφαγίστατός τε ὢν βλακίστατός ἐστι, καὶ φιλαργυρώτατος ὢν ἀργότατος.—Ἤδη ποτὲ οὖν ἐπεσκέψω, πότερος πλειόνων πληγῶν δεῖται, σὺ ἢ ὁ θεράπων;*

5 *Φοβουμένου δέ τινος τὴν εἰς Ὀλυμπίαν ὁδόν· Τί, ἔφη, φοβῇ σὺ τὴν πορείαν; οὐ καὶ οἴκοι σχεδὸν ὅλην τὴν ἡμέραν περιπατεῖς; καὶ ἐκεῖσε πορευόμενος, περιπατήσας ἀριστήσεις, περιπατήσας δειπνήσεις καὶ ἀναπαύσῃ· οὐκ οἶσθα, ὅτι, εἰ ἐκτείναις τοὺς περιπάτους, οὓς ἐν πέντε ἢ ἓξ ἡμέραις περιπατεῖς, ῥᾳδίως ἂν Ἀθήνηθεν εἰς Ὀλυμπίαν ἀφίκοιο; Χαριέστερον δὲ καὶ προεξορμᾶν ἡμέρᾳ μιᾷ μᾶλλον ἢ ὑστερίζειν· τὸ μὲν γὰρ ἀναγκάζεσθαι περαιτέρω τοῦ μετρίου μηκύνειν τὰς ὁδοὺς χαλεπόν, τὸ δὲ μιᾷ ἡμέρᾳ πλείονας πορευθῆναι πολλὴν ῥᾳστώνην παρέχει· κρεῖττον οὖν ἐν τῇ ὁρμῇ σπεύδειν ἢ ἐν τῇ ὁδῷ.*

6 *Ἄλλου δὲ λέγοντος, ὡς παρετάθη μακρὰν ὁδὸν*

πορευθείς, ἤρετο αὐτὸν, εἰ καὶ φορτίον ἔφερε.—Μὰ Δί' οὐκ ἔγωγ', ἔφη, ἀλλὰ τὸ ἱμάτιον.—Μόνος δ' ἐπορεύου, ἔφη, ἢ καὶ ἀκόλουθός σοι ἠκολούθει;—Ἠκολούθει, ἔφη.—Πότερον κενός, ἔφη, ἢ φέρων τι;—Φέρων νὴ Δί', ἔφη, τά τε στρώματα καὶ τἆλλα σκεύη.—Καὶ πῶς δή, ἔφη, ἀπήλλαχεν ἐκ τῆς ὁδοῦ;—Ἐμοὶ μὲν δοκεῖ, ἔφη, βέλτιον ἐμοῦ.—Τί οὖν; ἔφη, εἰ τὸ ἐκείνου φορτίον ἔδει σὲ φέρειν, πῶς ἂν οἴει διατεθῆναι;—Κακῶς νὴ Δί', ἔφη· μᾶλλον δὲ οὐδ' ἂν ἠδυνήθην κομίσαι.—Τὸ οὖν τοσούτῳ ἧττον τοῦ παιδὸς δύνασθαι πονεῖν πῶς ἠσκημένου δοκεῖ σοι ἀνδρὸς εἶναι;

CHAPTER XIV.

ARGUMENT.

XENOPHON gives in this chapter a specimen of the conversation by which Socrates sought to benefit his friends on festive occasions.

1. The manner in which he effected an equal distribution in the furnishing of the food at a feast, is explained (§ 1).

2. One who ate little or no bread with his other food, Socrates called a gourmand, ὀψοφάγος (§ 2—4).

3. A caution is given against too luxurious living, as an offence against the art of cookery, and as injurious to the offender (§ 5, 6).

4. He is said to live well, who eats food that is not injurious to body or mind, and is easily obtained (§ 7).

Ὁπότε δὲ τῶν ξυνιόντων ἐπὶ τὸ δεῖπνον οἱ μὲν 1 μικρὸν ὄψον, οἱ δὲ πολὺ φέροιεν, ἐκέλευεν ὁ Σωκράτης τὸν παῖδα τὸ μικρὸν ἢ εἰς τὸ κοινὸν τιθέναι, ἢ διανέμειν ἑκάστῳ τὸ μέρος. Οἱ οὖν τὸ πολὺ φέροντες ᾐσχύνοντο τό τε μὴ κοινωνεῖν τοῦ εἰς τὸ κοινὸν τιθεμένου, καὶ τὸ μὴ ἀντιτιθέναι τὸ ἑαυτῶν· ἐτίθεσαν οὖν καὶ τὸ ἑαυτῶν εἰς τὸ κοινόν· καὶ ἐπεὶ οὐδὲν πλέον εἶχον τῶν μικρὸν φερομένων, ἐπαύοντο πολλοῦ ὀψωνοῦντες.

2 Καταμαθὼν δέ τινα τῶν ξυνδειπνούντων τοῦ μὲν σίτου πεπαυμένον, τὸ δὲ ὄψον αὐτὸ καθ' αὑτὸ ἐσθίοντα, λόγου ὄντος περὶ ὀνομάτων, ἐφ' οἵῳ ἔργῳ ἕκαστον εἴη· Ἔχοιμεν ἄν, ἔφη, ὦ ἄνδρες, εἰπεῖν, ἐπὶ ποίῳ ποτὲ ἔργῳ ἄνθρωπος ὀψοφάγος καλεῖται; ἐσθίουσι μὲν γὰρ δὴ πάντες ἐπὶ τῷ σίτῳ ὄψον, ὅταν παρῇ· ἀλλ' οὐκ οἶμαί πω ἐπί γε τούτῳ ὀψοφάγοι καλοῦνται.
3 — Οὐ γὰρ οὖν, ἔφη τις τῶν παρόντων. — Τί γάρ; ἔφη, ἐάν τις ἄνευ τοῦ σίτου τὸ ὄψον αὐτὸ ἐσθίῃ, μὴ ἀσκήσεως, ἀλλ' ἡδονῆς ἕνεκα, πότερον ὀψοφάγος εἶναι δοκεῖ, ἢ οὔ; — Σχολῇ γ' ἄν, ἔφη, ἄλλος τις ὀψοφάγος εἴη. — Καί τις ἄλλος τῶν παρόντων. Ὁ δὲ μικρῷ σίτῳ, ἔφη, πολὺ ὄψον ἐπεσθίων; — Ἐμοὶ μέν, ἔφη ὁ Σωκράτης, καὶ οὗτος δοκεῖ δικαίως ἂν ὀψοφάγος καλεῖσθαι· καὶ ὅταν γε οἱ ἄλλοι ἄνθρωποι τοῖς θεοῖς εὔχωνται πολυκαρπίαν, εἰκότως ἂν οὗτος πολυοψίαν
4 εὔχοιτο. Ταῦτα δὲ τοῦ Σωκράτους εἰπόντος, νομίσας ὁ νεανίσκος εἰς αὑτὸν εἰρῆσθαι τὰ λεχθέντα, τὸ μὲν ὄψον οὐκ ἐπαύσατο ἐσθίων, ἄρτον δὲ προσέλαβεν. Καὶ ὁ Σωκράτης καταμαθών· Παρατηρεῖτ', ἔφη, τοῦτον οἱ πλησίον, ὁπότερα τῷ σίτῳ ὄψῳ, ἢ τῷ ὄψῳ σίτῳ χρήσεται.

5 Ἄλλον δέ ποτε τῶν συνδείπνων ἰδὼν ἐπὶ τῷ ἑνὶ ψωμῷ πλειόνων ὄψων γευόμενον· Ἆρα γένοιτ' ἄν, ἔφη, πολυτελεστέρα ὀψοποιία ἢ μᾶλλον τὰ ὄψα λυμαινομένη, ἢ ἣν ὀψοποιεῖται ὁ ἅμα πολλὰ ἐσθίων καὶ ἅμα παντοδαπὰ ἡδύσματα εἰς τὸ στόμα λαμβάνων; πλείω μέν γε τῶν ὀψοποιῶν συμμιγνύων πολυτελέστερα ποιεῖ, ἃ δὲ ἐκεῖνοι μὴ συμμιγνύουσιν, ὡς οὐχ ἁρμόττοντα, ὁ συμμιγνύων, εἴπερ ἐκεῖνοι ὀρθῶς ποιοῦσιν, ἁμαρτάνει τε καὶ καταλύει τὴν τέχνην αὐτῶν.

Καίτοι πῶς οὐ γελοῖόν ἐστι παρασκευάζεσϑαι μὲν 6
ὀψοποιοὺς τοὺς ἄριστα ἐπισταμένους, αὐτὸν δὲ μηδ᾽
ἀντιποιούμενον τῆς τέχνης ταύτης τὰ ὑπ᾽ ἐκείνων
ποιούμενα μετατιϑέναι; καὶ ἄλλο δέ τι προςγίγνεται
τῷ ἅμα πολλὰ ἐπεσϑίειν ἐϑισϑέντι· μὴ παρόντων γὰρ
πολλῶν μειονεκτεῖν ἄν τι δοκοίη, ποϑῶν τὸ σύνηϑες·
ὁ δὲ συνεϑισϑεὶς τὸν ἕνα ψωμὸν ἑνὶ ὄψῳ προπέμ-
πειν, ὅτε μὴ παρείη πολλά, δύναιτ᾽ ἂν ἀλύπως τῷ ἑνὶ
χρῆσϑαι.

Ἔλεγε δὲ καὶ, ὡς τὸ εὐωχεῖσϑαι ἐν τῇ Ἀϑηναίων 7
γλώττῃ ἐσϑίειν καλοῖτο· τὸ δὲ εὖ προςκεῖσϑαι ἔφη
ἐπὶ τῷ ταῦτα ἐσϑίειν, ἅτινα μήτε τὴν ψυχὴν μήτε τὸ
σῶμα λυποίη, μήτε δυςεύρετα εἴη· ὥςτε καὶ τὸ εὐωχεῖ-
σϑαι τοῖς κοσμίως διαιτωμένοις ἀνετίϑει.

ΞΕΝΟΦΩΝΤΟΣ

ΑΠΟΜΝΗΜΟΝΕΥΜΑΤΩΝ.

ΤΕΤΑΡΤΟΝ.

CHAPTER I.

ARGUMENT.

In the preceding Books, Xenophon illustrates the manner in which Socrates benefitted his fellow-citizens in general; in this Book he exhibits him more particularly in his relation to his disciples, his selection of and manner of instructing them, and such like things. The first two chapters are closely connected, and show, first, the kind of persons whom he preferred as pupils; and secondly, the different manner in which he treated different individuals, and attempted to win them over to an attendance upon his instructions.

1. Socrates' love for the youth was not founded on beauty of person, but upon mental and moral excellence; by which he understood facility in learning, a good memory, and a desire of acquiring and using every species of useful knowledge. Those who were possessed of these qualities he supposed would themselves be made better and happier by instruction, and would in turn communicate good to others (§ 1, 2).

2. He adapted his instructions to the character of his pupils First, he showed those who trusted to their natural endowments or genius, and despised instruction, that they were in especial danger of running into error and folly (§ 3, 4). Secondly, those who trusted to their wealth as a means of procuring every good thing, he recalled to sanity, by showing the folly of supposing that any one who was uninstructed could understand what is good or evil, or adapt his exertions to the attainment of the good; and, in fine, the impossibility of maintaining the

appearance of goodness, and the consequent esteem of others, by means of wealth (§ 5).

---

1 Οὕτω δὲ ὁ Σωκράτης ἦν ἐν παντὶ πράγματι καὶ πάντα τρόπον ὠφέλιμος, ὥςτε τῷ σκοπουμένῳ τοῦτο, καὶ εἰ μετρίως αἰσθανομένῳ, φανερὸν εἶναι, ὅτι οὐδὲν ὠφελιμώτερον ἦν τοῦ Σωκράτει συνεῖναι, καὶ μετ' ἐκείνου διατρίβειν ὁπουοῦν καὶ ἐν ὁτῳοῦν πράγματι· ἐπεὶ καὶ τὸ ἐκείνου μεμνῆσθαι μὴ παρόντος οὐ μικρὰ ὠφέλει τοὺς εἰωθότας τε αὐτῷ συνεῖναι καὶ ἀποδεχομένους ἐκεῖνον· καὶ γὰρ παίζων οὐδὲν ἧττον ἢ σπουδάζων
2 ἐλυσιτέλει τοῖς συνδιατρίβουσι. Πολλάκις γὰρ ἔφη μὲν ἄν τινος ἐρᾶν, φανερὸς δ' ἦν οὐ τῶν τὰ σώματα πρὸς ὥραν, ἀλλὰ τῶν τὰς ψυχὰς πρὸς ἀρετὴν εὖ πεφυκότων ἐφιέμενος· ἐτεκμαίρετο δὲ τὰς ἀγαθὰς φύσεις ἐκ τοῦ ταχύ τε μανθάνειν οἷς προσέχοιεν καὶ μνημονεύειν ἃ ἂν μάθοιεν, καὶ ἐπιθυμεῖν τῶν μαθημάτων πάντων, δι' ὧν ἔστιν οἰκίαν τε καλῶς οἰκεῖν καὶ πόλιν, καὶ τὸ ὅλον ἀνθρώποις τε καὶ ἀνθρωπίνοις πράγμασιν εὖ χρῆσθαι· τοὺς γὰρ τοιούτους ἡγεῖτο παιδευθέντας οὐκ ἂν μόνον αὐτούς τε εὐδαίμονας εἶναι καὶ τοὺς ἑαυτῶν οἴκους καλῶς οἰκεῖν, ἀλλὰ καὶ ἄλλους ἀνθρώπους
3 καὶ πόλεις δύνασθαι εὐδαίμονας ποιεῖν. Οὐ τὸν αὐτὸν δὲ τρόπον ἐπὶ πάντας ᾔει, ἀλλὰ τοὺς μὲν οἰομένους φύσει ἀγαθοὺς εἶναι, μαθήσεως δὲ καταφρονοῦντας, ἐδίδασκεν, ὅτι αἱ ἄρισται δοκοῦσαι εἶναι φύσεις μάλιστα παιδείας δέονται, ἐπιδεικνύων τῶν τε ἵππων τοὺς εὐφυεστάτους, θυμοειδεῖς τε καὶ σφοδροὺς ὄντας, εἰ μὲν ἐκ νέων δαμασθεῖεν, εὐχρηστοτάτους καὶ ἀρίστους γιγνομένους, εἰ δὲ ἀδάμαστοι γένοιντο, δυςκαθεκτοτάτους καὶ φαυλοτάτους· καὶ τῶν κυνῶν τῶν εὐφυεστάτων, φιλοπόνων τε οὐσῶν καὶ ἐπιθετικῶν τοῖς θηρίοις, τὰς μὲν καλῶς ἀχθείσας ἀρίστας γίγνεσθαι πρὸς τὰς θήρας καὶ χρησιμωτάτας, ἀναγώγους δὲ γιγνομένας

ματαίους τε καὶ μανιώδεις καὶ δυςπειθεστάτας. Ὁμοίως 4
δὲ καὶ τῶν ἀνθρώπων τοὺς εὐφυεστάτους, ἐῤῥωμενε-
στάτους τε ταῖς ψυχαῖς ὄντας καὶ ἐξεργαστικωτάτους
ὧν ἂν ἐγχειρῶσι, παιδευθέντας μὲν καὶ μαθόντας ἃ
δεῖ πράττειν ἀρίστους τε καὶ ὠφελιμωτάτους γίγνε-
σθαι (πλεῖστα γὰρ καὶ μέγιστα ἀγαθὰ ἐργάζεσθαι),
ἀπαιδεύτους δὲ καὶ ἀμαθεῖς γενομένους κακίστους τε
καὶ βλαβερωτάτους γίγνεσθαι· κρίνειν γὰρ οὐκ ἐπι-
σταμένους ἃ δεῖ πράττειν πολλάκις πονηροῖς ἐπιχει-
ρεῖν πράγμασι, μεγαλείους δὲ καὶ σφοδροὺς ὄντας δυς-
καθέκτους τε καὶ δυςαποτρέπτους εἶναι· διὸ πλεῖστα
καὶ μέγιστα κακὰ ἐργάζονται. Τοὺς δ' ἐπὶ πλούτῳ 5
μέγα φρονοῦντας καὶ νομίζοντας οὐδὲν προςδεῖσθαι
παιδείας, ἐξαρκέσειν δέ σφισι τὸν πλοῦτον οἰομένους
πρὸς τὸ διαπράττεσθαί τε ὅ τι ἂν βούλωνται καὶ
τιμᾶσθαι ὑπὸ τῶν ἀνθρώπων, ἐφρένου λέγων, ὅτι μω-
ρὸς μὲν εἴη, εἴ τις οἴεται μὴ μαθὼν τά τε ὠφέλιμα
καὶ τὰ βλαβερὰ τῶν πραγμάτων διαγνώσεσθαι, μωρὸς
δ', εἴ τις μὴ διαγιγνώσκων μὲν ταῦτα, διὰ δὲ τὸν πλοῦ-
τον ὅ τι ἂν βούληται ποριζόμενος οἴεται δυνήσεσθαι
καὶ τὰ συμφέροντα πράττειν, ἠλίθιος δ', εἴ τις μὴ δυνά-
μενος τὰ συμφέροντα πράττειν εὖ τε πράττειν οἴεται
καὶ τὰ πρὸς τὸν βίον αὐτῷ ἢ καλῶς ἢ ἱκανῶς παρε-
σκευάσθαι, ἠλίθιος δὲ καὶ, εἴ τις οἴεται διὰ τὸν πλοῦ-
τον μηδὲν ἐπιστάμενος δόξειν τὶ ἀγαθὸς εἶναι, ἢ μηδὲν
ἀγαθὸς εἶναι δοκῶν εὐδοκιμήσειν.

CHAPTER II.

ARGUMENT.

The method of instruction which Socrates pursued with different individuals is further developed in this chapter, by an example. Having heard that one Euthydemus, a mere youth, had conceived the notion that he was possessed of great wisdom, and that he should soon distinguish himself as a statesman, without any aid from teachers, he sought to convince him that many who thought themselves wise were fools, and that thorough instruction and discipline could by no means be superseded by any natural endowments.

He first repaired with some of his disciples to the shop near the forum, where Euthydemus, who was not of a suitable age to appear in the public assembly, was accustomed to harangue his fellow-citizens. He then in his presence, in answer to the question whether Themistocles' influence in the State was the result of natural endowments or of thorough discipline, showed the folly of supposing that the successful pursuit of the inferior arts and employments, required the instruction of teachers, whilst the more important one of governing the State could be assumed at will (§ 1, 2). At another time, he, in the presence of Euthydemus, showed with much dexterity the folly of a public speaker, who pretended to have never learned any thing from teachers (§ 3—5); and after he had gained the attention of Euthydemus, although he yet took no part in the discussion, Socrates again recurred to the necessity of previous training to one who would rule (§ 6, 7).

After Socrates had thus excited the interest of Euthydemus, he repaired to the shop of the young man, unattended by his disciples, and after praising his taste in collecting a library, inquired what use he intended to make of his books, and what pursuit in life he intended to follow. He finally obtained, by means of his interrogations, the unwilling confession, that his aspirations were for political honor (§ 8—11). Socrates praises the art which he calls royal, and by a series of questions upon the qualities and knowledge requisite for a statesman, and upon the abstract notion of *good* and *evil*, obliges Euthydemus to confess his ignorance of that with which he had before supposed himself perfectly acquainted, and that he could not accordingly abjure the name of uncultivated, ἀνδραποδώδης (§ 8—22).

Socrates then recommended to Euthydemus, who finds himself in a state of entire uncertainty what course to pursue, to learn to know himself, as the foundation of all true knowledge, and the source of all real prosperity and happiness in life (§ 23—29). He also replied indirectly to the question of Euthydemus in regard to the manner of entering upon self-knowledge, by interrogatories in reference to good and evil, the useful and injurious, as pertaining to happiness, and also in regard to the nature of government, which gave Euthydemus a still deeper sense of his ignorance (§ 30—39).

The result of these exertions of Socrates was not to drive Euthydemus from him, as was frequently the case with others, but to make him a fast adherent. Hence Socrates ceased to confound him with questions, and imparted to him, with all simplicity and clearness, the knowledge of which he saw that he had need (§ 40).

---

*Τοῖς δὲ νομίζουσι παιδείας τε τῆς ἀρίστης τετυχη- 1
κέναι καὶ μέγα φρονοῦσιν ἐπὶ σοφίᾳ ὡς προςεφέρετο, νῦν διηγήσομαι. Καταμαθὼν γὰρ Εὐθύδημον τὸν καλὸν γράμματα πολλὰ συνειλεγμένον ποιητῶν τε καὶ σοφιστῶν τῶν εὐδοκιμωτάτων, καὶ ἐκ τούτων ἤδη τε νομίζοντα διαφέρειν τῶν ἡλικιωτῶν ἐπὶ σοφίᾳ, καὶ μεγάλας ἐλπίδας ἔχοντα πάντων διοίσειν τῷ δύνασθαι λέγειν τε καὶ πράττειν, πρῶτον μὲν αἰσθανόμενος αὐτὸν διὰ νεότητα οὔπω εἰς τὴν ἀγορὰν εἰςιόντα, εἰ δέ τι βούλοιτο διαπράξασθαι, καθίζοντα εἰς ἡνιοποιεῖόν τι τῶν ἐγγὺς τῆς ἀγορᾶς, εἰς τοῦτο καὶ αὐτὸς ᾔει τῶν μεθ' ἑαυτοῦ τινας ἔχων. Καὶ πρῶτον μὲν πυνθανο- 2
μένου τινὸς, πότερον Θεμιστοκλῆς διὰ συνουσίαν τινὸς τῶν σοφῶν ἢ φύσει τοσοῦτον διήνεγκε τῶν πολιτῶν, ὥςτε πρὸς ἐκεῖνον ἀποβλέπειν τὴν πόλιν, ὁπότε σπουδαίου ἀνδρὸς δεηθείη, ὁ Σωκράτης βουλόμενος κινεῖν τὸν Εὐθύδημον εὔηθες ἔφη εἶναι τὸ οἴεσθαι τὰς μὲν ὀλίγου ἀξίας τέχνας μὴ γίγνεσθαι σπουδαίους ἄνευ διδασκάλων ἱκανῶν, τὸ δὲ προεστάναι πόλεως, πάντων ἔργων μέγιστον ὄν, ἀπὸ ταὐτομάτου παραγίγνεσθαι τοῖς ἀνθρώποις. Πάλιν δέ ποτε παρόντος τοῦ Εὐθυ- 3
δήμου, ὁρῶν αὐτὸν ἀποχωροῦντα τῆς συνεδρίας καὶ*

φυλαττόμενον, μὴ δόξῃ τὸν Σωκράτην θαυμάζειν ἐπὶ
σοφίᾳ· "Ὅτι μέν, ἔφη, ὦ ἄνδρες, Εὐθύδημος οὑτοσὶ ἐν
ἡλικίᾳ γενόμενος, τῆς πόλεως λόγον περί τινος προτι-
θείσης, οὐκ ἀφέξεται τοῦ συμβουλεύειν, εὔδηλόν ἐστιν
ἐξ ὧν ἐπιτηδεύει· δοκεῖ δέ μοι καλὸν προοίμιον τῶν
δημηγοριῶν παρασκευάσασθαι φυλαττόμενος μὴ δόξῃ
μανθάνειν τι παρά του· δῆλον γάρ, ὅτι λέγειν ἀρχό-
4 μενος ὧδε προοιμιάσεται· "Παρ' οὐδενὸς μὲν πώποτε,
ὦ ἄνδρες Ἀθηναῖοι, οὐδὲν ἔμαθον, οὐδ' ἀκούων τινὰς
εἶναι λέγειν τε καὶ πράττειν ἱκανοὺς ἐζήτησα τούτοις
ἐντυχεῖν, οὐδ' ἐπεμελήθην τοῦ διδάσκαλόν μοί τινα
γενέσθαι τῶν ἐπισταμένων, ἀλλὰ καὶ τἀναντία· διατε-
τέλεκα γὰρ φεύγων οὐ μόνον τὸ μανθάνειν τι παρά
τινος, ἀλλὰ καὶ τὸ δόξαι· ὅμως δὲ ὅ τι ἂν ἀπὸ ταὐτο-
5 μάτου ἐπίῃ μοι συμβουλεύσω ὑμῖν." Ἁρμόσειε δ' ἂν
οὕτω προοιμιάζεσθαι καὶ τοῖς βουλομένοις παρὰ τῆς
πόλεως ἰατρικὸν ἔργον λαβεῖν· ἐπιτήδειόν γ' ἂν αὐτοῖς
εἴη τοῦ λόγου ἄρχεσθαι ἐντεῦθεν· "Παρ' οὐδενὸς μὲν
πώποτε, ὦ ἄνδρες Ἀθηναῖοι, τὴν ἰατρικὴν τέχνην ἔμα-
θον, οὐδ' ἐζήτησα διδάσκαλον ἐμαυτῷ γενέσθαι τῶν
ἰατρῶν οὐδένα· διατετέλεκα γὰρ φυλαττόμενος οὐ μό-
νον τὸ μαθεῖν τι παρὰ τῶν ἰατρῶν, ἀλλὰ καὶ τὸ δόξαι
μεμαθηκέναι τὴν τέχνην ταύτην· ὅμως δέ μοι τὸ ἰατρι-
κὸν ἔργον δότε· πειράσομαι γὰρ ἐν ὑμῖν ἀποκινδυνεύων
μανθάνειν." Πάντες οὖν οἱ παρόντες ἐγέλασαν ἐπὶ
6 τῷ προοιμίῳ. Ἐπεὶ δὲ φανερὸς ἦν ὁ Εὐθύδημος ἤδη
μὲν οἷς ὁ Σωκράτης λέγοι προσέχων, ἔτι δὲ φυλαττό-
μενος αὐτός τι φθέγγεσθαι, καὶ νομίζων τῇ σιωπῇ
σωφροσύνης δόξαν περιβάλλεσθαι, τότε ὁ Σωκράτης,
βουλόμενος αὐτὸν παῦσαι τούτου· Θαυμαστὸν γάρ,
ἔφη, τί ποτε οἱ βουλόμενοι κιθαρίζειν ἢ αὐλεῖν ἢ ἱπ-
πεύειν ἢ ἄλλο τι τῶν τοιούτων ἱκανοὶ γενέσθαι πειρῶν-
ται ὡς συνεχέστατα ποιεῖν ὅ τι ἂν βούλωνται δυνατοὶ
γενέσθαι, καὶ οὐ καθ' ἑαυτούς, ἀλλὰ παρὰ τοῖς ἀρί-

στοις δοκοῦσιν εἶναι, πάντα ποιοῦντες καὶ ὑπομένοντες ἕνεκα τοῦ μηδὲν ἄνευ τῆς ἐκείνων γνώμης ποιεῖν, ὡς οὐκ ἂν ἄλλως ἀξιόλογοι γενόμενοι· τῶν δε βουλομένων δυνατῶν γενέσθαι λέγειν τε καὶ πράττειν τὰ πολιτικὰ νομίζουσί τινες ἄνευ παρασκευῆς καὶ ἐπιμελείας αὐτόματοι ἐξαίφνης δυνατοὶ ταῦτα ποιεῖν ἔσεσθαι.
Καίτοι γε τοσούτῳ ταῦτα ἐκείνων δυςκατεργαστότερα 7
φαίνεται, ὅσῳ περ πλειόνων περὶ ταῦτα πραγματευομένων ἐλάττους οἱ κατεργαζόμενοι γίγνονται· δῆλον οὖν, ὅτι καὶ ἐπιμελείας δέονται πλείονος καὶ ἰσχυροτέρας οἱ τούτων ἐφιέμενοι ἢ οἱ ἐκείνων. Κατ' ἀρχὰς 8
μὲν οὖν, ἀκούοντος Εὐθυδήμου, τοιούτους λόγους ἔλεγε Σωκράτης· ὡς δ' ᾔσθετο αὐτὸν ἑτοιμότερον ὑπομένοντα, ὅτε διαλέγοιτο, καὶ προθυμότερον ἀκούοντα, μόνος ἦλθεν εἰς τὸ ἡνιοποιεῖον·. παρακαθεζομένου δ' αὐτῷ τοῦ Εὐθυδήμου· Εἰπέ μοι, ἔφη, ὦ Εὐθύδημε, τῷ ὄντι, ὥσπερ ἐγὼ ἀκούω, πολλὰ γράμματα συνῆχας τῶν λεγομένων σοφῶν ἀνδρῶν γεγονέναι; Νὴ τὸν Δί', ἔφη, ὦ Σώκρατες· καὶ ἔτι γε συνάγω, ἕως ἂν κτήσωμαι ὡς ἂν δύνωμαι πλεῖστα. Νὴ τὴν Ἥραν, ἔφη ὁ 9
Σωκράτης, ἄγαμαί γέ σου, διότι οὐκ ἀργυρίου καὶ χρυσίου προείλου θησαυροὺς κεκτῆσθαι μᾶλλον ἢ σοφίας· δῆλον γὰρ, ὅτι νομίζεις ἀργύριον καὶ χρυσίον οὐδὲν βελτίους ποιεῖν τοὺς ἀνθρώπους, τὰς δὲ τῶν σοφῶν ἀνδρῶν γνώμας ἀρετῇ πλουτίζειν τοὺς κεκτημένους. Καὶ ὁ Εὐθύδημος ἔχαιρεν ἀκούων ταῦτα, νομίζων δοκεῖν τῷ Σωκράτει ὀρθῶς μετιέναι τὴν σοφίαν. Ὁ δὲ καταμαθὼν αὐτὸν ἡσθέντα τῷ ἐπαίνῳ 10
τούτῳ· Τί δὲ δὴ βουλόμενος ἀγαθὸς γενέσθαι, ἔφη, ὦ Εὐθύδημε, συλλέγεις τὰ γράμματα; Ἐπεὶ δὲ διεσιώπησεν ὁ Εὐθύδημος σκοπῶν ὅ τι ἀποκρίναιτο, πάλιν ὁ Σωκράτης· Ἆρα μὴ ἰατρός; ἔφη· πολλὰ γὰρ καὶ ἰατρῶν ἐστι συγγράμματα. Καὶ ὁ Εὐθύδημος· Μὰ Δί', ἔφη, οὐκ ἔγωγε.—Ἀλλὰ μὴ ἀρχι-

τέκτων βούλει γενέσθαι; γνωμονικοῦ γὰρ ἀνδρὸς καὶ τοῦτο δεῖ.—Οὔκουν ἔγωγ', ἔφη.—Ἀλλὰ μὴ γεωμέτρης ἐπιθυμεῖς, ἔφη, γενέσθαι ἀγαθός, ὥσπερ ὁ Θεόδωρος;—Οὐδὲ γεωμέτρης, ἔφη.—Ἀλλὰ μὴ ἀστρολόγος, ἔφη, βούλει γενέσθαι; Ὡς δὲ καὶ τοῦτο ἠρνεῖτο· Ἀλλὰ μὴ ῥαψῳδός; ἔφη· καὶ γὰρ τὰ Ὁμήρου σέ φασιν ἔπη πάντα κεκτῆσθαι.—Μὰ Δί' οὐκ ἔγωγ', ἔφη· τοὺς γάρ τοι ῥαψῳδοὺς οἶδα τὰ μὲν ἔπη
11 ἀκριβοῦντας, αὐτοὺς δὲ πάνυ ἠλιθίους ὄντας. Καὶ ὁ Σωκράτης ἔφη· Οὐ δήπου, ὦ Εὐθύδημε, ταύτης τῆς ἀρετῆς ἐφίεσαι, δι' ἣν ἄνθρωποι πολιτικοὶ γίγνονται, καὶ οἰκονομικοί, καὶ ἄρχειν ἱκανοί, καὶ ὠφέλιμοι τοῖς τε ἄλλοις ἀνθρώποις καὶ ἑαυτοῖς; Καὶ ὁ Εὐθύδημος· Σφόδρα γ', ἔφη, ὦ Σώκρατες, ταύτης τῆς ἀρετῆς δέομαι. Νὴ Δί', ἔφη ὁ Σωκράτης, τῆς καλλίστης ἀρετῆς καὶ μεγίστης ἐφίεσαι τέχνης· ἔστι γὰρ τῶν βασιλέων αὕτη, καὶ καλεῖται βασιλική· ἀτάρ, ἔφη, κατανενόηκας, εἰ οἷόν τ' ἐστὶ μὴ ὄντα δίκαιον ἀγαθὸν ταῦτα γενέσθαι;—Καὶ μάλα, ἔφη, καὶ οὐχ οἷόν τέ γε ἄνευ
12 δικαιοσύνης ἀγαθὸν πολίτην γενέσθαι.—Τί οὖν; ἔφη, σὺ δὴ τοῦτο κατείργασαι;—Οἶμαί γε, ἔφη, ὦ Σώκρατες, οὐδενὸς ἂν ἧττον φανῆναι δίκαιος.—Ἆρ' οὖν, [ἔφη,] τῶν δικαίων ἐστὶν ἔργα, ὥσπερ τῶν τεκτόνων;—Ἔστι μέντοι, ἔφη.—Ἆρ' οὖν, ἔφη, ὥσπερ οἱ τέκτονες ἔχουσι τὰ ἑαυτῶν ἔργα ἐπιδεῖξαι, οὕτως οἱ δίκαιοι τὰ ἑαυτῶν ἔχοιεν ἂν διεξηγήσασθαι; Μὴ οὖν, ἔφη ὁ Εὐθύδημος, οὐ δύναμαι ἐγὼ τὰ τῆς δικαιοσύνης ἔργα ἐξηγήσασθαι; καὶ νὴ Δί' ἔγωγε τὰ τῆς ἀδικίας· ἐπεὶ οὐκ ὀλίγα ἐστὶ καθ' ἑκάστην ἡμέραν τοιαῦτα
13 ὁρᾶν τε καὶ ἀκούειν. Βούλει οὖν, ἔφη ὁ Σωκράτης, γράψωμεν ἐνταυθοῖ μὲν δέλτα, ἐνταυθοῖ δὲ ἄλφα; εἶτα ὅ τι μὲν ἂν δοκῇ ἡμῖν τῆς δικαιοσύνης ἔργον εἶναι πρὸς τὸ δέλτα τιθῶμεν, ὅ τι δ' ἂν τῆς ἀδικίας, πρὸς τὸ ἄλφα;—Εἴ τί σοι δοκεῖ, ἔφη, προσδεῖν

τοῦτων, ποίει ταῦτα. Καὶ ὁ Σωκράτης γράψας ὥς- 14
περ εἶπεν· Οὐκοῦν, ἔφη, ἔστιν ἐν ἀνθρώποις [τὸ] ψεύδεσθαι;—Ἔστι μέντοι, ἔφη.—Ποτέρωσε οὖν, ἔφη, θῶμεν τοῦτο;—Δῆλον, ἔφη, ὅτι πρὸς τὴν ἀδικίαν.—Οὐκοῦν, ἔφη, καὶ τὸ ἐξαπατᾶν ἔστι;—Καὶ μάλα, ἔφη.—Τοῦτο οὖν ποτέρωσε θῶμεν; Καὶ τοῦτο δῆλον ὅτι, ἔφη, πρὸς τὴν ἀδικίαν.—Τί δέ; τὸ κακουργεῖν;—Καὶ τοῦτο, ἔφη.—Τὸ δὲ ἀνδραποδίζεσθαι; Καὶ τοῦτο.—Πρὸς δὲ τῇ δικαιοσύνῃ οὐδὲν ἡμῖν τούτων κείσεται, ὦ Εὐθύδημε;—Δεινὸν γὰρ ἂν εἴη, ἔφη.
—Τί δ᾽; ἐάν τις στρατηγὸς αἱρεθεὶς ἄδικόν τε καὶ 15
ἐχθρὰν πόλιν ἐξανδραποδίσηται, φήσομεν τοῦτον ἀδικεῖν;—Οὐ δῆτα, ἔφη.—Δίκαια δὲ ποιεῖν οὐ φήσομεν;—Καὶ μάλα.—Τί δ᾽; ἐὰν ἐξαπατᾷ πολεμῶν αὐτοῖς;—Δίκαιον, ἔφη, καὶ τοῦτο.—Ἐὰν δὲ κλέπτῃ τε καὶ ἁρπάζῃ τὰ τούτων, οὐ δίκαια ποιήσει;—Καὶ μάλα, ἔφη· ἀλλ᾽ ἐγώ σε τὸ πρῶτον ὑπελάμβανον πρὸς τοὺς φίλους μόνον ταῦτα ἐρωτᾶν.—Οὔκουν, ἔφη, ὅσα πρὸς τῇ ἀδικίᾳ ἐθήκαμεν, πάντα καὶ πρὸς τῇ
δικαιοσύνῃ θετέον ἂν εἴη;—Ἔοικεν, ἔφη.—Βούλει, 16
οὖν, ἔφη, ταῦτα οὕτω θέντες διορισώμεθα πάλιν, πρὸς μὲν τοὺς πολεμίους δίκαιον εἶναι τὰ τοιαῦτα ποιεῖν, πρὸς δὲ τοὺς φίλους ἄδικον, ἀλλὰ δεῖν πρός γε τούτους ὡς ἁπλούστατον εἶναι; Πάνυ μὲν οὖν, ἔφη ὁ
Εὐθύδημος. Τί οὖν; ἔφη ὁ Σωκράτης, ἐάν τις στρα- 17
τηγὸς ὁρῶν ἀθύμως ἔχον τὸ στράτευμα ψευσάμενος φήσῃ συμμάχους προσιέναι, καὶ τῷ ψεύδει τούτῳ παύσῃ τὰς ἀθυμίας τοῦ στρατεύματος, ποτέρωθι τὴν ἀπάτην ταύτην θήσομεν;—Δοκεῖ μοι, ἔφη, πρὸς τὴν δικαιοσύνην.—Ἐὰν δέ τις υἱὸν ἑαυτοῦ δεόμενον φαρμακείας καὶ μὴ προσιέμενον φάρμακον ἐξαπατήσας ὡς σιτίον τὸ φάρμακον δῷ, καὶ τῷ ψεύδει χρησάμενος οὕτως ὑγιᾶ ποιήσῃ, ταύτην αὖ τὴν ἀπάτην ποῖ θετέον;—Δοκεῖ μοι, ἔφη, καὶ ταύτην εἰς τὸ αὐτό.—

*Τί δ᾽; ἐάν τις, ἐν ἀθυμίᾳ ὄντος φίλου, δείσας μὴ
διαχρήσηται ἑαυτόν, κλέψῃ ἢ ἁρπάσῃ ἢ ξίφος ἢ ἄλλο
τι τοιοῦτον, τοῦτο αὖ ποτέρωσε θετέον;—Καὶ τοῦτο
18 νὴ Δί᾽, ἔφη, πρὸς τὴν δικαιοσύνην.—Λέγεις, ἔφη, σὺ
οὐδὲ πρὸς τοὺς φίλους ἅπαντα δεῖν ἁπλοΐζεσθαι;—
Μὰ Δί᾽ οὐ δῆτα, ἔφη· ἀλλὰ μετατίθεμαι τὰ εἰρημένα,
εἴπερ ἔξεστι.—Δεῖ γέ τοι, ἔφη ὁ Σωκράτης, ἐξεῖναι
19 πολὺ μᾶλλον ἢ μὴ ὀρθῶς τιθέναι. Τῶν δὲ δὴ τοὺς
φίλους ἐξαπατώντων ἐπὶ βλάβῃ, ἵνα μηδὲ τοῦτο πα-
ραλίπωμεν ἄσκεπτον, πότερος ἀδικώτερός ἐστιν, ὁ ἑκών,
ἢ ὁ ἄκων;—᾽Αλλ᾽, ὦ Σώκρατες, οὐκέτι μὲν ἔγωγε
πιστεύω οἷς ἀποκρίνομαι· καὶ γὰρ τὰ πρόσθεν πάντα
νῦν ἄλλως ἔχειν δοκεῖ μοι ἢ ὡς ἐγὼ τότε ᾤόμην·
ὅμως δὲ εἰρήσθω μοι ἀδικώτερον εἶναι τὸν ἑκόντα
20 ψευδόμενον τοῦ ἄκοντος.—Δοκεῖ δέ σοι μάθησις καὶ
ἐπιστήμη τοῦ δικαίου εἶναι, ὥσπερ τῶν γραμμάτων;
῎Εμοιγε.—Πότερον δὲ γραμματικώτερον κρίνεις, ὃς ἂν
ἑκὼν μὴ ὀρθῶς γράφῃ καὶ ἀναγιγνώσκῃ, ἢ ὃς ἂν
ἄκων;—῞Ος ἂν ἑκών, ἔγωγε· δύναιτο γὰρ ἄν, ὁπότε
βούλοιτο, καὶ ὀρθῶς αὐτὰ ποιεῖν.—Οὐκοῦν ὁ μὲν ἑκὼν
μὴ ὀρθῶς γράφων γραμματικὸς ἂν εἴη, ὁ δὲ ἄκων
ἀγράμματος;—Πῶς γὰρ οὔ;—Τὰ δίκαια δὲ πότε-
ρον ὁ ἑκὼν ψευδόμενος καὶ ἐξαπατῶν οἶδεν, ἢ ὁ ἄκων;
—Δῆλον, ὅτι ὁ ἑκών.—Οὐκοῦν γραμματικώτερον μὲν
τὸν ἐπιστάμενον γράμματα τοῦ μὴ ἐπισταμένου φῂς
εἶναι;—Ναί.—Δικαιότερον δὲ τὸν ἐπιστάμενον τὰ
δίκαια τοῦ μὴ ἐπισταμένου;—Φαίνομαι· δοκῶ δέ μοι
21 καὶ ταῦτα, οὐκ οἶδ᾽ ὅπως, λέγειν.—Τί δὲ δή, ὃς ἂν
βουλόμενος τἀληθῆ λέγειν μηδέποτε τὰ αὐτὰ περὶ
τῶν αὐτῶν λέγῃ, ἀλλ᾽ ὁδόν τε φράζων τὴν αὐτὴν τοτὲ
μὲν πρὸς ἕω, τοτὲ δὲ πρὸς ἑσπέραν φράζῃ, καὶ λογι-
σμὸν ἀποφαινόμενος τὸν αὐτὸν τοτὲ μὲν πλείω, τοτὲ δ᾽
ἐλάττω ἀποφαίνηται, τί σοι δοκεῖ ὁ τοιοῦτος;—Δῆλος
22 νὴ Δί᾽ εἶναι, ὅτι ἃ ᾤετο εἰδέναι οὐκ οἶδεν.—Οἶσθα*

δέ τινας ἀνδραποδώδεις καλουμένους;—Ἔγωγε.—Πότερον διὰ σοφίαν, ἢ δι' ἀμαθίαν;—Δῆλον, ὅτι δι' ἀμαθίαν.—Ἆρ' οὖν διὰ τὴν τοῦ χαλκεύειν ἀμαθίαν τοῦ ὀνόματος τούτου τυγχάνουσιν;—Οὐ δῆτα.—Ἀλλ' ἄρα διὰ τὴν τοῦ τεκταίνεσθαι;—Οὐδὲ διὰ ταύτην.—Ἀλλὰ διὰ τὴν τοῦ σκυτεύειν;—Οὐδὲ δι' ἓν τούτων, ἔφη, ἀλλὰ καὶ τοὐναντίον· οἱ γὰρ πλεῖστοι τῶν γε τὰ τοιαῦτα ἐπισταμένων ἀνδραποδώδεις εἰσιν.—Ἆρ' οὖν τῶν τὰ καλὰ καὶ ἀγαθὰ καὶ δίκαια μὴ εἰδότων
τὸ ὄνομα τοῦτ' ἐστίν;—Ἔμοιγε δοκεῖ, ἔφη.—Οὐκοῦν 23
δεῖ παντὶ τρόπῳ διατειναμένους φεύγειν, ὅπως μὴ ἀνδράποδα ὦμεν.—Ἀλλά, νὴ τοὺς θεούς, ἔφη, ὦ Σώκρατες, πάνυ ᾤμην φιλοσοφεῖν φιλοσοφίαν, δι' ἧς ἂν μάλιστα ἐνόμιζον παιδευθῆναι τὰ προςήκοντα ἀνδρὶ καλοκἀγαθίας ὀρεγομένῳ· νῦν δὲ πῶς οἴει με ἀθύμως ἔχειν, ὁρῶντα ἐμαυτὸν διὰ μὲν τὰ προπεπονημένα οὐδὲ τὸ ἐρωτώμενον ἀποκρίνεσθαι δυνάμενον ὑπὲρ ὧν μάλιστα χρὴ εἰδέναι, ἄλλην δὲ ὁδὸν οὐδεμίαν ἔχοντα,
ἣν ἂν πορευόμενος βελτίων γενοίμην;—Καὶ ὁ Σω- 24
κράτης· Εἰπέ μοι, ἔφη, ὦ Εὐθύδημε, εἰς Δελφοὺς δὲ ἤδη πώποτε ἀφίκου;—Καὶ δίς γε νὴ Δία, ἔφη.—Κατέμαθες οὖν πρὸς τῷ ναῷ που γεγραμμένον τὸ Γνῶθι σαυτόν;—Ἔγωγε.—Πότερον οὖν οὐδέν σοι τοῦ γράμματος ἐμέλησεν, ἢ προςέσχες τε καὶ ἐπεχείρησας σαυτὸν ἐπισκοπεῖν, ὅςτις εἴης;—Μὰ Δί' οὐ δῆτα, ἔφη· καὶ γὰρ δὴ πάνυ τοῦτό γε ᾤμην εἰδέναι· σχολῇ γὰρ ἂν ἄλλο τι ᾔδειν, εἴγε μηδ' ἐμαυτὸν ἐγί-
γνωσκον.—Πότερα δέ σοι δοκεῖ γιγνώσκειν ἑαυτὸν 25
ὅςτις τοὔνομα τὸ ἑαυτοῦ μόνον οἶδεν, ἢ ὅςτις, ὥςπερ οἱ τοὺς ἵππους ὠνούμενοι οὐ πρότερον οἴονται γιγνώσκειν, ὃν ἂν βούλωνται γνῶναι, πρὶν ἂν ἐπισκέψωνται, πότερον εὐπειθής ἐστιν, ἢ δυςπειθής, καὶ πότερον ἰσχυρός ἐστιν ἢ ἀσθενής, καὶ πότερον ταχὺς ἢ βραδύς, καὶ τἆλλα τὰ πρὸς τὴν τοῦ ἵππου χρείαν ἐπι-

τήδειά τε καὶ ἀνεπιτήδεια ὅπως ἔχει, οὕτως ὁ ἑαυτὸν ἐπισκεψάμενος, ὁποῖός ἐστι πρὸς τὴν ἀνθρωπίνην χρείαν, ἔγνωκε τὴν αὑτοῦ δύναμιν;—Οὕτως ἔμοιγε δοκεῖ, ἔφη, ὁ μὴ εἰδὼς τὴν ἑαυτοῦ δύναμιν ἀγνοεῖν
26 ἑαυτόν.—Ἐκεῖνο δὲ οὐ φανερόν, ἔφη, ὅτι διὰ μὲν τὸ εἰδέναι ἑαυτοὺς πλεῖστα ἀγαθὰ πάσχουσιν οἱ ἄνθρωποι, διὰ δὲ τὸ ἐψεῦσθαι ἑαυτῶν πλεῖστα κακά; οἱ μὲν γὰρ ἑαυτοὺς εἰδότες τά τε ἐπιτήδεια ἑαυτοῖς ἴσασι, καὶ διαγιγνώσκουσιν ἅ τε δύνανται καὶ ἃ μή· καὶ ἃ μὲν ἐπίστανται πράττοντες πορίζονταί τε ὧν δέονται καὶ εὖ πράττουσιν, ὧν δὲ μὴ ἐπίστανται ἀπεχόμενοι ἀναμάρτητοι γίγνονται καὶ διαφεύγουσι τὸ κακῶς πράττειν· διὰ τοῦτο δὲ καὶ τοὺς ἄλλους ἀνθρώπους δυνάμενοι δοκιμάζειν καὶ διὰ τῆς τῶν ἄλλων χρείας τά τε
27 ἀγαθὰ πορίζονται καὶ τὰ κακὰ φυλάττονται. Οἱ δὲ μὴ εἰδότες, ἀλλὰ διεψευσμένοι τῆς ἑαυτῶν δυνάμεως πρός τε τοὺς ἄλλους ἀνθρώπους καὶ τἆλλα ἀνθρώπινα πράγματα ὁμοίως διάκεινται· καὶ οὔτε ὧν δέονται ἴσασιν, οὔτε ὅ τι πράττουσιν, οὔτε οἷς χρῶνται, ἀλλὰ πάντων τούτων διαμαρτάνοντες τῶν τε ἀγαθῶν
28 ἀποτυγχάνουσι καὶ τοῖς κακοῖς περιπίπτουσι. Καὶ οἱ μὲν εἰδότες ὅ τι ποιοῦσιν, ἐπιτυγχάνοντες ὧν πράττουσιν, εὔδοξοί τε καὶ τίμιοι γίγνονται· καὶ οἵ τε ὅμοιοι τούτοις ἡδέως χρῶνται, οἵ τε ἀποτυγχάνοντες τῶν πραγμάτων ἐπιθυμοῦσι τούτους ὑπὲρ αὑτῶν βουλεύεσθαι, καὶ προΐστασθαί τε ἑαυτῶν τούτους, καὶ τὰς ἐλπίδας τῶν ἀγαθῶν ἐν τούτοις ἔχουσι, καὶ διὰ πάντα ταῦτα πάντων μάλιστα τούτους ἀγαπῶσιν.
29 Οἱ δὲ μὴ εἰδότες ὅ τι ποιοῦσι, κακῶς δὲ αἱρούμενοι, καὶ οἷς ἂν ἐπιχειρήσωσιν ἀποτυγχάνοντες, οὐ μόνον ἐν αὐτοῖς τούτοις ζημιοῦνταί τε καὶ κολάζονται, ἀλλὰ καὶ ἀδοξοῦσι διὰ ταῦτα καὶ καταγέλαστοι γίγνονται, καὶ καταφρονούμενοι καὶ ἀτιμαζόμενοι ζῶσιν· ὁρᾷς δὲ καὶ τῶν πόλεων ὅτι ὅσαι ἂν ἀγνοήσασαι τὴν ἑαυτῶν

δύναμιν κρείττοσι πολεμήσωσιν, αἱ μὲν ἀνάστατοι
γίγνονται, αἱ δ' ἐξ ἐλευθέρων δοῦλαι. Καὶ ὁ Εὐθύ-
δημος· Ὡς πάνυ μοι δοκοῦν, ἔφη, ὦ Σώκρατες, περὶ 30
πολλοῦ ποιητέον εἶναι τὸ ἑαυτὸν γιγνώσκειν, οὕτως
ἴσθι· ὁπόθεν δὲ χρὴ ἄρξασθαι ἐπισκοπεῖν ἑαυτόν,
τοῦτο πρὸς σὲ ἀποβλέπω εἴ μοι ἐθελήσαις ἂν ἐξηγή-
σασθαι. Οὐκουν, ἔφη ὁ Σωκράτης, τὰ μὲν ἀγαθὰ 31
καὶ τὰ κακὰ ὁποῖά ἐστι, πάντως που γιγνώσκεις;—
Νὴ Δί', ἔφη· εἰ γὰρ μηδὲ ταῦτα οἶδα, καὶ τῶν ἀνδρα-
πόδων φαυλότερος ἂν εἴην.—Ἴθι δή, ἔφη, καὶ ἐμοὶ
ἐξήγησαι αὐτά.—Ἀλλ' οὐ χαλεπόν, ἔφη· πρῶτον
μὲν γὰρ αὐτὸ τὸ ὑγιαίνειν ἀγαθὸν εἶναι νομίζω, τὸ δὲ
νοσεῖν κακόν, ἔπειτα τὰ αἴτια ἑκατέρου αὐτῶν, καὶ
ποτὰ καὶ βρωτὰ καὶ ἐπιτηδεύματα, τὰ μὲν πρὸς τὸ
ὑγιαίνειν φέροντα ἀγαθά, τὰ δὲ πρὸς τὸ νοσεῖν κακά.
—Οὐκοῦν, ἔφη, καὶ τὸ ὑγιαίνειν καὶ τὸ νοσεῖν, ὅταν 32
μὲν ἀγαθοῦ τινος αἴτια γίγνηται, ἀγαθὰ ἂν εἴη, ὅταν
δὲ κακοῦ, κακά.—Πότε δ' ἄν, ἔφη, τὸ μὲν ὑγιαίνειν
κακοῦ αἴτιον γένοιτο, τὸ δὲ νοσεῖν ἀγαθοῦ;—Ὅταν
νὴ Δί', ἔφη, στρατείας τε αἰσχρᾶς καὶ ναυτιλίας βλα-
βερᾶς καὶ ἄλλων πολλῶν τοιούτων οἱ μὲν διὰ ῥώμην
μετασχόντες ἀπόλωνται, οἱ δὲ δι' ἀσθένειαν ἀπολει-
φθέντες σωθῶσιν.—Ἀληθῆ λέγεις· ἀλλ' ὁρᾷς, ἔφη,
ὅτι καὶ τῶν ὠφελίμων οἱ μὲν διὰ ῥώμην μετέχουσιν,
οἱ δὲ δι' ἀσθένειαν ἀπολείπονται.—Ταῦτα οὖν, ἔφη,
ποτὲ μὲν ὠφελοῦντα, ποτὲ δὲ βλάπτοντα μᾶλλον
ἀγαθὰ ἢ κακά ἐστιν;—Οὐδὲν μὰ Δία φαίνεται κατά
γε τοῦτον τὸν λόγον. Ἀλλ' ἥ γέ τοι σοφία, ὦ Σώ- 33
κρατες, ἀναμφισβητήτως ἀγαθόν ἐστιν· ποῖον γὰρ ἂν
τις πρᾶγμα οὐ βέλτιον πράττοι σοφὸς ὢν ἢ ἀμαθής;
—Τί δαί; τὸν Δαίδαλον, ἔφη, οὐκ ἀκήκοας, ὅτι
ληφθεὶς ὑπὸ Μίνω διὰ τὴν σοφίαν ἠναγκάζετο ἐκείνῳ
δουλεύειν, καὶ τῆς τε πατρίδος ἅμα καὶ τῆς ἐλευθε-
ρίας ἐστερήθη, καὶ ἐπιχειρῶν ἀποδιδράσκειν μετὰ τοῦ

υἱοῦ τόν τε παῖδα ἀπώλεσε καὶ αὐτὸς οὐκ ἠδυνήθη σωθῆναι, ἀλλ' ἀπενεχθεὶς εἰς τοὺς βαρβάρους πάλιν ἐκεῖ ἐδούλευεν;—Λέγεται νὴ Δί', ἔφη, ταῦτα.—Τὰ δὲ Παλαμήδους οὐκ ἀκήκοας πάθη; τοῦτον γὰρ δὴ πάντες ὑμνοῦσιν, ὡς διὰ σοφίαν φθονηθεὶς ὑπὸ τοῦ Ὀδυσσέως ἀπόλλυται.—Λέγεται καὶ ταῦτα, ἔφη.—Ἄλλους δὲ πόσους οἴει διὰ σοφίαν ἀναρπάστους πρὸς
34 βασιλέα γεγονέναι, καὶ ἐκεῖ δουλεύειν;—Κινδυνεύει, ἔφη, ὦ Σώκρατες, ἀναμφιλογώτατον ἀγαθὸν εἶναι τὸ εὐδαιμονεῖν.—Εἴγε μή τις αὐτό, ἔφη, ὦ Εὐθύδημε, ἐξ ἀμφιλόγων ἀγαθῶν συντιθείη.—Τί δ' ἄν, ἔφη, τῶν εὐδαιμονικῶν ἀμφίλογον εἴη;—Οὐδέν, ἔφη, εἴγε μὴ προσθήσομεν αὐτῷ κάλλος, ἢ ἰσχύν, ἢ πλοῦτον, ἢ δόξαν, ἢ καί τι ἄλλο τῶν τοιούτων.—Ἀλλὰ νὴ Δία προσθήσομεν, ἔφη· πῶς γὰρ ἄν τις ἄνευ τούτων
35 εὐδαιμονοίη;—Νὴ Δί', ἔφη, προσθήσομεν ἄρα ἐξ ὧν πολλὰ καὶ χαλεπὰ συμβαίνει τοῖς ἀνθρώποις· πολλοὶ μὲν γὰρ διὰ τὸ κάλλος ὑπὸ τῶν ἐπὶ τοῖς ὡραίοις παρακεκινηκότων διαφθείρονται, πολλοὶ δὲ διὰ τὴν ἰσχὺν μείζοσιν ἔργοις ἐπιχειροῦντες οὐ μικροῖς κακοῖς περιπίπτουσι, πολλοὶ δὲ διὰ τὸν πλοῦτον διαθρυπτόμενοί τε καὶ ἐπιβουλευόμενοι ἀπόλλυνται, πολλοὶ δὲ διὰ δόξαν καὶ πολιτικὴν δύναμιν μεγάλα κακὰ πε-
36 πόνθασιν.—Ἀλλὰ μήν, ἔφη, εἴγε μηδὲ τὸ εὐδαιμονεῖν ἐπαινῶν ὀρθῶς λέγω, ὁμολογῶ μηδὲ ὅ τι πρὸς τοὺς θεοὺς εὔχεσθαι χρὴ εἰδέναι. Ἀλλὰ ταῦτα μέν, ἔφη ὁ Σωκράτης, ἴσως διὰ τὸ σφόδρα πιστεύειν εἰδέναι οὐδ' ἔσκεψαι· ἐπεὶ δὲ πόλεως δημοκρατουμένης παρασκευάζῃ προεστάναι, δῆλον, ὅτι δημοκρατίαν γε οἶσθα
37 τί ἐστι.—Πάντως δήπου, ἔφη.—Δοκεῖ οὖν σοι δυνατὸν εἶναι δημοκρατίαν εἰδέναι μὴ εἰδότα δῆμον;—Μὰ Δί' οὐκ ἔμοιγε.—Καὶ τί νομίζεις δῆμον εἶναι;—Τοὺς πένητας τῶν πολιτῶν ἔγωγε.—Καὶ τοὺς πένητας ἄρα οἶσθα;—Πῶς γὰρ οὔ;—Ἆρ' οὖν καὶ τοὺς

πλουσίους οἶσθα;—Οὐδέν γε ἧττον ἢ καὶ τοὺς πένη-
τας.—Ποίους δὲ πένητας καὶ ποίους πλουσίους κα-
λεῖς;—Τοὺς μέν, οἶμαι, μὴ ἱκανὰ ἔχοντας εἰς ἃ δεῖ
τελεῖν πένητας, τοὺς δὲ πλείω τῶν ἱκανῶν πλουσίους;
—Καταμεμάθηκας οὖν, ὅτι ἐνίοις μὲν πάνυ ὀλίγα 38
ἔχουσιν οὐ μόνον ἀρκεῖ ταῦτα, ἀλλὰ καὶ περιποιοῦν-
ται ἀπ' αὐτῶν, ἐνίοις δὲ πάνυ πολλὰ οὐχ ἱκανά ἐστι;
Καὶ νὴ Δί', ἔφη ὁ Εὐθύδημος, ὀρθῶς γάρ με ἀνα-
μιμνήσκεις, οἶδα γὰρ καὶ τυράννους τινάς, οἳ δι' ἔν-
δειαν, ὥσπερ οἱ ἀπορώτατοι, ἀναγκάζονται ἀδικεῖν.
Οὔκουν, ἔφη ὁ Σωκράτης, εἴγε ταῦτα οὕτως ἔχει, τοὺς 39
μὲν τυράννους εἰς τὸν δῆμον θήσομεν, τοὺς δὲ ὀλίγα
κεκτημένους, ἐὰν οἰκονομικοὶ ὦσιν, εἰς τοὺς πλουσίους;
Καὶ ὁ Εὐθύδημος ἔφη· Ἀναγκάζει με καὶ ταῦτα
ὁμολογεῖν, δηλονότι ἡ ἐμὴ φαυλότης· καὶ φροντίζω,
μὴ κράτιστον ᾖ μοι σιγᾶν· κινδυνεύω γὰρ ἁπλῶς
οὐδὲν εἰδέναι.

Καὶ πάνυ ἀθύμως ἔχων ἀπῆλθε καὶ καταφρο-
νήσας ἑαυτοῦ καὶ νομίσας τῷ ὄντι ἀνδράποδον εἶναι.
Πολλοὶ μὲν οὖν τῶν οὕτω διατεθέντων ὑπὸ Σωκρά- 40
τους οὐκέτι αὐτῷ προσῄεσαν, οὓς καὶ βλακωτέρους
ἐνόμιζεν, ὁ δὲ Εὐθύδημος ὑπέλαβεν οὐκ ἂν ἄλλως
ἀνὴρ ἀξιόλογος γενέσθαι, εἰ μὴ ὅ τι μάλιστα Σω-
κράτει συνείη· καὶ οὐκ ἀπελείπετο ἔτι αὐτοῦ, εἰ μή
τι ἀναγκαῖον εἴη· ἔνια δὲ καὶ ἐμιμεῖτο ὧν ἐκεῖνος
ἐπετήδευεν· ὁ δὲ ὡς ἔγνω αὐτὸν οὕτως ἔχοντα, ἥκιστα
μὲν διετάραττεν, ἁπλούστατα δὲ καὶ σαφέστατα ἐξη-
γεῖτο ἅ τε ἐνόμιζεν εἰδέναι δεῖν καὶ ἐπιτηδεύειν κρα-
τιστα εἶναι.

CHAPTER III.

ARGUMENT.

In the two preceding chapters, we have a brief exemplification of Socrates' method of acquainting himself with the character of different individuals, and gaining them as listeners to his instructions. Xenophon next presents more particularly the manner of his treatment of his disciples, and the subjects on which he was most accustomed to dwell in his teachings.

It was his earnest desire, first of all, to make them reasonable beings, and to inspire them with sentiments of reverence and gratitude to the gods, without which all knowledge would only give them ability to do evil (§ 1, 2). In a conversation with Euthydemus he first explained the care of the gods for men in providing for all their necessities and ministering to their happiness (§ 3—9). They have even made and sustained other animals for the use of man (§ 10). Besides the pleasures of sense they have given him reason, the ability to express his thoughts and feelings in language, and the knowledge of the future, by means of divination (§ 11, 12). In answer to the intimation of Euthydemus that Socrates is himself especially favored by the gods, alluding to his guiding deity (δαιμόνιον), he answers, for substance, that all would be guided as well as himself, if they did not look for visible deities, but gave heed to their revelations of themselves in their works (§ 12—14). It is also the duty of all to honor and reverence the gods according to their ability (§ 15—18).

The general similarity of the contents of this chapter with Book I. chap. IV, will not escape notice. There Socrates attempts to convince the skeptical Aristodemus that the gods have a direct regard for individual men. In this chapter, the real existence and agency of the gods is made prominent.

---

1 Τὸ μὲν οὖν λεκτικοὺς καὶ πρακτικοὺς καὶ μηχανικοὺς γίγνεσθαι τοὺς συνόντας οὐκ ἔσπευδεν, ἀλλὰ πρότερον τούτων ᾤετο χρῆναι σωφροσύνην αὐτοῖς ἐγγενέσθαι· τοὺς γὰρ ἄνευ τοῦ σωφρονεῖν ταῦτα δυναμένους ἀδικωτέρους τε καὶ δυνατωτέρους κακουργεῖν

ἐνόμιζεν εἶναι. Πρῶτον μὲν δὴ περὶ θεοὺς ἐπειρᾶτο 2
σώφρονας ποιεῖν τοὺς συνόντας. Ἄλλοι μὲν οὖν αὐτῷ
πρὸς ἄλλους οὕτως ὁμιλοῦντι παραγενόμενοι διηγοῦντο,
ἐγὼ δέ, ὅτε πρὸς Εὐθύδημον τοιάδε διελέγετο, παρε-
γενόμην. Εἰπέ μοι, ἔφη, ὦ Εὐθύδημε, ἤδη ποτέ σοι 3
ἐπῆλθεν ἐνθυμηθῆναι, ὡς ἐπιμελῶς οἱ θεοὶ ὧν οἱ ἄν-
θρωποι δέονται κατεσκευάκασι; Καὶ ὅς· Μὰ τὸν Δί', ἔφη, οὐκ ἔμοιγε.—Ἀλλ' οἶσθά γ', ἔφη, ὅτι πρῶτον μὲν φωτὸς δεόμεθα, ὃ ἡμῖν οἱ θεοὶ παρέχουσιν;—Νὴ Δί', ἔφη, ὅ γ' εἰ μὴ εἴχομεν, ὅμοιοι τοῖς τυφλοῖς ἂν ἦμεν ἕνεκά γε τῶν ἡμετέρων ὀφθαλμῶν.—Ἀλλὰ μὴν καὶ ἀναπαύσεώς γε δεομένοις ἡμῖν νύκτα παρέ-
χουσι κάλλιστον ἀναπαυτήριον.—Πάνυ γ', ἔφη, καὶ 4
τοῦτο χάριτος ἄξιον.—Οὔκουν καί, ἐπειδὴ ὁ μὲν ἥλιος φωτεινὸς ὢν τάς τε ὥρας τῆς ἡμέρας ἡμῖν καὶ τἆλλα πάντα σαφηνίζει, ἡ δὲ νὺξ διὰ τὸ σκοτεινὴ εἶναι ἀσαφεστέρα ἐστίν, ἄστρα ἐν τῇ νυκτὶ ἀνέφηναν, ἃ ἡμῖν τὰς ὥρας τῆς νυκτὸς ἐμφανίζει, καὶ διὰ τοῦτο πολλὰ ὧν δεόμεθα πράττομεν;—Ἔστι ταῦτα, ἔφη.—Ἀλλὰ μὴν ἥ γε σελήνη οὐ μόνον τῆς νυκτός, ἀλλὰ καὶ τοῦ μηνὸς τὰ μέρη φανερὰ ἡμῖν ποιεῖ.—Πάνυ μὲν οὖν,
ἔφη.—Τὸ δ', ἐπεὶ τροφῆς δεόμεθα, ταύτην ἡμῖν ἐκ 5
τῆς γῆς ἀναδιδόναι, καὶ ὥρας ἁρμοττούσας πρὸς τοῦτο παρέχειν, αἳ ἡμῖν οὐ μόνον ὧν δεόμεθα πολλὰ καὶ παντοῖα παρασκευάζουσιν, ἀλλὰ καὶ οἷς εὐφραινόμεθα;
—Πάνυ, ἔφη, καὶ ταῦτα φιλάνθρωπα.—Τὸ δὲ καὶ 6
ὕδωρ ἡμῖν παρέχειν οὕτω πολλοῦ ἄξιον, ὥστε καὶ φυτεύειν τε καὶ συναύξειν τῇ γῇ καὶ ταῖς ὥραις πάντα τὰ χρήσιμα ἡμῖν, συντρέφειν δὲ καὶ αὐτοὺς ἡμᾶς, καὶ μιγνύμενον πᾶσι τοῖς τρέφουσιν ἡμᾶς εὐκατεργαστότερά τε καὶ ὠφελιμώτερα καὶ ἡδίω ποιεῖν αὐτά, καί, ἐπειδὴ πλείστου δεόμεθα τούτου, ἀφθονέστατον αὐτὸ
παρέχειν ἡμῖν;—Καὶ τοῦτο, ἔφη, προνοητικόν.—Τὸ 7
δὲ καὶ τὸ πῦρ πορίσαι ἡμῖν, ἐπίκουρον μὲν ψύχους, ἐπι-

κουρον δὲ σκότους, συνεργὸν δὲ πρὸς πᾶσαν τέχνην καὶ πάντα, ὅσα ὠφελείας ἕνεκα ἄνθρωποι κατασκευάζονται; ὡς γὰρ συνελόντι εἰπεῖν, οὐδὲν ἀξιόλογον ἄνευ πυρὸς ἄνθρωποι τῶν πρὸς τὸν βίον χρησίμων κατασκευάζονται. — Ὑπερβάλλει, ἔφη, καὶ τοῦτο φιλαν-
8 θρωπίᾳ. — [Τὸ δὲ καὶ ἀέρα ἡμῖν ἀφθόνως οὕτω πανταχοῦ διαχῦσαι, οὐ μόνον πρόμαχον καὶ σύντροφον ζωῆς, ἀλλὰ καὶ πελάγη περᾶν δι' αὐτοῦ καὶ τὰ ἐπιτήδεια ἄλλους ἀλλαχόθι καὶ ἐν ἀλλοδαπῇ στελλομένους πορίζεσθαι, πῶς οὐχ ὑπὲρ λόγον; — Ἀνέκφραστον. —] Τὸ δὲ τὸν ἥλιον, ἐπειδὰν ἐν χειμῶνι τράπηται, προσιέναι τὰ μὲν ἁδρύνοντα, τὰ δὲ ξηραίνοντα, ὧν καιρὸς διελήλυθεν, καὶ ταῦτα διαπραξάμενον μηκέτι ἐγγυτέρω προσιέναι, ἀλλ' ἀποτρέπεσθαι φυλαττόμενον, μή τι ἡμᾶς μᾶλλον τοῦ δέοντος θερμαίνων βλάψῃ, καὶ ὅταν αὖ πάλιν ἀπιὼν γένηται, ἔνθα καὶ ἡμῖν δῆλόν ἐστιν, ὅτι, εἰ προσωτέρω ἄπεισιν, ἀποπαγησόμεθα ὑπὸ τοῦ ψύχους, πάλιν αὖ τρέπεσθαι καὶ προσχωρεῖν, καὶ ἐνταῦθα τοῦ οὐρανοῦ ἀναστρέφεσθαι, ἔνθα ὢν μάλιστα ἡμᾶς ὠφελοίη; — Νὴ τὸν Δί', ἔφη, καὶ ταῦτα
9 παντάπασιν ἔοικεν ἀνθρώπων ἕνεκα γιγνόμενα. — Τὸ δ' αὖ, ἐπειδὴ καὶ τοῦτο φανερὸν, ὅτι οὐκ ἂν ὑπενέγκαιμεν οὔτε τὸ καῦμα οὔτε τὸ ψῦχος, εἰ ἐξαπίνης γίγνοιτο, οὕτω μὲν κατὰ μικρὸν προσιέναι τὸν ἥλιον, οὕτω δὲ κατὰ μικρὸν ἀπιέναι, ὥστε λανθάνειν ἡμᾶς εἰς ἑκάτερα τὰ ἰσχυρότατα καθισταμένους; Ἐγὼ μέν, ἔφη ὁ Εὐθύδημος, ἤδη τοῦτο σκοπῶ, εἰ ἄρα τί ἐστι τοῖς θεοῖς ἔργον ἢ ἀνθρώπους θεραπεύειν, ἐκεῖνο δὲ μόνον ἐμποδίζει με, ὅτι καὶ τἆλλα ζῷα τούτων μετέχει.
10 Οὐ γὰρ καὶ τοῦτ', ἔφη ὁ Σωκράτης φανερὸν, ὅτι καὶ ταῦτα ἀνθρώπων ἕνεκα γίγνεταί τε καὶ ἀνατρέφεται; τί γὰρ ἄλλο ζῷον αἰγῶν τε καὶ οἴων καὶ ἵππων καὶ βοῶν καὶ ὄνων καὶ τῶν ἄλλων ζώων τοσαῦτα ἀγαθὰ ἀπολαύει, ὅσα ἄνθρωποι; ἐμοὶ μὲν γὰρ δοκεῖ πλείω

τῶν φονῶν· τρέφονται γοῦν καὶ χρηματίζονται οὐδὲν ἧττον ἀπὸ τούτων ἢ ἀπ' ἐκείνων· πολὺ δὲ γένος ἀνθρώπων τοῖς μὲν ἐκ τῆς γῆς φυομένοις εἰς τροφὴν οὐ χρῶνται, ἀπὸ δὲ βοσκημάτων γάλακτι καὶ τυρῷ καὶ κρέασι τρεφόμενοι ζῶσι· πάντες δὲ τιθασσεύοντες καὶ δαμάζοντες τὰ χρήσιμα τῶν ζώων εἴς τε πόλεμον καὶ εἰς ἄλλα πολλὰ συνεργοῖς χρῶνται.—Ὁμογνωμονῶ σοι καὶ τοῦτ', ἔφη· ὁρῶ γὰρ αὐτῶν καὶ τὰ πολὺ ἰσχυρότερα ἡμῶν οὕτως ὑποχείρια γιγνόμενα τοῖς ἀνθρώποις, ὥστε χρῆσθαι αὐτοῖς ὅ τι ἂν βούλωνται.—Τὸ δ', 11
ἐπειδὴ πολλὰ μὲν καλὰ καὶ ὠφέλιμα, διαφέροντα δὲ ἀλλήλων ἐστί, προςθεῖναι τοῖς ἀνθρώποις αἰσθήσεις ἁρμοττούσας πρὸς ἕκαστα, δι' ὧν ἀπολαύομεν πάντων τῶν ἀγαθῶν· τὸ δὲ καὶ λογισμὸν ἡμῖν ἐμφῦσαι, ᾧ περὶ ὧν αἰσθανόμεθα λογιζόμενοί τε καὶ μνημονεύοντες καταμανθάνομεν, ὅπῃ ἕκαστα συμφέρει, καὶ πολλὰ μηχανώμεθα, δι' ὧν τῶν τε ἀγαθῶν ἀπολαύομεν καὶ τὰ κακὰ ἀλεξόμεθα· τὸ δὲ καὶ ἑρμηνείαν δοῦναι, δι' 12
ἧς πάντων τῶν ἀγαθῶν μεταδίδομέν τε ἀλλήλοις διδάσκοντες καὶ κοινωνοῦμεν, καὶ νόμους τιθέμεθα, καὶ πολιτευόμεθα;—Παντάπασιν ἐοίκασιν, ὦ Σώκρατες, οἱ θεοὶ πολλὴν τῶν ἀνθρώπων ἐπιμέλειαν ποιεῖσθαι. —Τὸ δὲ καί, εἰ ἀδυνατοῦμεν τὰ συμφέροντα προνοεῖσθαι ὑπὲρ τῶν μελλόντων, ταύτῃ αὐτοὺς ἡμῖν συνεργεῖν, διὰ μαντικῆς τοῖς πυνθανομένοις φράζοντας τὰ ἀποβησόμενα, καὶ διδάσκοντας, ᾗ ἂν ἄριστα γίγνοιντο; —Σοὶ δ', ἔφη, ὦ Σώκρατες, ἐοίκασιν ἔτι φιλικώτερον ἢ τοῖς ἄλλοις χρῆσθαι, εἴ γε μηδὲ ἐπερωτώμενοι ὑπό σου προσημαίνουσί σοι ἅ τε χρὴ ποιεῖν καὶ ἃ μή.— Ὅτι δέ γε ἀληθῆ λέγω, καὶ σὺ γνώσῃ, ἂν μὴ ἀνα- 13
μένῃς, ἕως ἂν τὰς μορφὰς τῶν θεῶν ἴδῃς, ἀλλ' ἐξαρκῇ σοι τὰ ἔργα αὐτῶν ὁρῶντι σέβεσθαι καὶ τιμᾶν τοὺς θεούς. Ἐννόει δέ, ὅτι καὶ αὐτοὶ οἱ θεοὶ οὕτως ὑποδεικνύουσιν· οἵ τε γὰρ ἄλλοι ἡμῖν τἀγαθὰ διδόντες

οὐδὲν τούτων εἰς τοὐμφανὲς ἰόντες διδόασι, καὶ ὁ τον ὅλον κόσμον συντάττων τε καὶ συνέχων, ἐν ᾧ πάντα καλὰ καὶ ἀγαθά ἐστι, καὶ ἀεὶ μὲν χρωμένοις ἀτριβῆ τε καὶ ὑγιᾶ καὶ ἀγήρατα παρέχων, θᾶττον δὲ νοήματος ἀναμαρτήτως ὑπηρετοῦντα, οὗτος τὰ μέγιστα μὲν πράττων ὁρᾶται, τάδε δὲ οἰκονομῶν ἀόρατος ἡμῖν ἐστιν.
14 Ἐννόει δ', ὅτι καὶ ὁ πᾶσι φανερὸς δοκῶν εἶναι ἥλιος οὐκ ἐπιτρέπει τοῖς ἀνθρώποις ἑαυτὸν ἀκριβῶς ὁρᾶν, ἀλλ', ἐάν τις αὐτὸν ἀναιδῶς ἐγχειρῇ θεᾶσθαι, τὴν ὄψιν ἀφαιρεῖται. Καὶ τοὺς ὑπηρέτας δὲ τῶν θεῶν εὑρήσεις ἀφανεῖς ὄντας· κεραυνός τε γὰρ ὅτι μὲν ἄνωθεν ἀφίεται, δῆλον, καὶ ὅτι οἷς ἂν ἐντύχῃ πάντων κρατεῖ, ὁρᾶται δ' οὔτ' ἐπιών, οὔτε κατασκήψας, οὔτε ἀπιών· καὶ ἄνεμοι αὐτοὶ μὲν οὐχ ὁρῶνται, ἃ δὲ ποιοῦσι φανερὰ ἡμῖν ἐστι, καὶ προσιόντων αὐτῶν αἰσθανόμεθα. Ἀλλὰ μὴν καὶ ἀνθρώπου γε ψυχή, ἥ, εἴπερ τι καὶ ἄλλο τῶν ἀνθρωπίνων, τοῦ θείου μετέχει, ὅτι μὲν βασιλεύει ἐν ἡμῖν, φανερόν, ὁρᾶται δὲ οὐδ' αὐτή. Ἃ χρὴ κατανοοῦντα μὴ καταφρονεῖν τῶν ἀοράτων, ἀλλ' ἐκ τῶν γιγνομένων τὴν δύναμιν αὐτῶν καταμαν-
15 θάνοντα τιμᾶν τὸ δαιμόνιον. Ἐγὼ μέν, ὦ Σώκρατες, ἔφη ὁ Εὐθύδημος, ὅτι μὲν οὐδὲ μικρὸν ἀμελήσω τοῦ δαιμονίου, σαφῶς οἶδα, ἐκεῖνο δὲ ἀθυμῶ, ὅτι μοι δοκεῖ τὰς τῶν θεῶν εὐεργεσίας οὐδ' ἂν εἷς ποτε ἀνθρώ-
16 πων ἀξίαις χάρισιν ἀμείβεσθαι. Ἀλλὰ μὴ τοῦτο ἀθύμει, ἔφη, ὦ Εὐθύδημε· ὁρᾷς γάρ, ὅτι ὁ ἐν Δελφοῖς θεός, ὅταν τις αὐτὸν ἐπερωτᾷ, πῶς ἂν τοῖς θεοῖς χαρίζοιτο, ἀποκρίνεται· Νόμῳ πόλεως· νόμος δὲ δήπου πανταχοῦ ἐστι κατὰ δύναμιν ἱεροῖς θεοὺς ἀρέσκεσθαι· πῶς οὖν ἄν τις κάλλιον καὶ εὐσεβέστερον τιμῴη θεούς, ἢ ὡς αὐτοὶ κελεύουσιν, οὕτω ποιῶν;
17 Ἀλλὰ χρὴ τῆς μὲν δυνάμεως μηδὲν ὑφίεσθαι· ὅταν γάρ τις τοῦτο ποιῇ, φανερὸς δήπου ἐστὶ τότε οὐ τιμῶν θεούς· χρὴ οὖν μηδὲν ἐλλείποντα κατὰ δύναμιν τιμᾶν

τοὺς ϑεοὺς ϑαῤῥεῖν τε καὶ ἐλπίζειν τὰ μέγιστα ἀγα-
ϑά· οὐ γὰρ παρ' ἄλλων γ' ἄν τις μείζω ἐλπίζων
σωφρονοίη ἢ παρὰ τῶν τὰ μέγιστα ὠφελεῖν δυνα-
μένων, οὐδ' ἂν ἄλλως μᾶλλον, ἢ εἰ τούτοις ἀρέσκοι,
ἀρέσκοι δὲ πῶς ἂν μᾶλλον, ἢ εἰ ὡς μάλιστα πείϑοιτο
αὐτοῖς; Τοιαῦτα μὲν δὴ λέγων τε καὶ αὐτὸς ποιῶν 18
εὐσεβεστέρους τε καὶ σωφρονεστέρους τοὺς συνόντας
παρεσκεύαζεν.

CHAPTER IV.

ARGUMENT.

Justice, δικαιοσύνη or τὸ δίκαιον, is the subject of this chapter, as piety, σωφροσύνη περὶ ϑεούς, was of the preceding. Socrates inculcated this upon his disciples:

1. By his example; especially by his regard for law and his undeviating obedience to it, both in private and public life (§ 1—5).

2. By precept; an example of which is given in a conversation with Hippia, a sophist: After a considerable colloquy, the purport of which is that justice consists rather in right action than in ingenious and novel theories, Socrates defines it as obedience to law: τὸ νόμιμον δίκαιον εἶναι (§ 6—12); and he who is obedient to the laws, which are the prescriptions of the citizens in reference to what they shall do or abstain from doing, is just, and the reverse (§ 13). The fact that the laws are changed is no objection to them (§ 14). Those are indeed the best rulers who, like Lycurgus, make the citizens most obedient to the laws, and that State will best acquit itself in peace and war, whose laws are obeyed (§ 15). Even peace and concord in the State and families, and honor and confidence among individual citizens, are dependent upon obedience to law (§ 16—18).

But all laws are not written, Socrates adds; some are given by the gods to the whole human race, and are to be observed at all times. The violation of these laws brings certain punishment with it, and thus a higher than human authority is evinced for them (§ 19—24). The gods, then, prescribe only just laws, and thus show that every thing that is *νόμιμον* is *δίκαιον* (§ 25).

---

1 Ἀλλὰ μὴν καὶ περὶ τοῦ δικαίου γε οὐκ ἀπεκρύ-
πτετο ἣν εἶχε γνώμην, ἀλλὰ καὶ ἔργῳ ἀπεδείκνυτο,
ἰδίᾳ τε πᾶσι νομίμως τε καὶ ὠφελίμως χρώμενος,
καὶ κοινῇ ἄρχουσί τε ἃ οἱ νόμοι προστάττοιεν πειθό-
μενος καὶ κατὰ πόλιν καὶ ἐν ταῖς στρατείαις οὕτως,
2 ὥστε διάδηλος εἶναι παρὰ τοὺς ἄλλους εὐτακτῶν, καὶ
ὅτε ἐν ταῖς ἐκκλησίαις ἐπιστάτης γενόμενος οὐκ ἐπέ-
τρεψε τῷ δήμῳ παρὰ τοὺς νόμους ψηφίσασθαι, ἀλλὰ
σὺν τοῖς νόμοις ἠναντιώθη τοιαύτῃ ὁρμῇ τοῦ δήμου,
ἣν οὐκ ἂν οἶμαι ἄλλον οὐδένα ἄνθρωπον ὑπομεῖναι·
3 καὶ ὅτε οἱ τριάκοντα προσέταττον αὐτῷ παρὰ τοὺς νό-
μους τι, οὐκ ἐπείθετο· τοῖς τε γὰρ νέοις ἀπαγορευόν-
των αὐτῶν μὴ διαλέγεσθαι, καὶ προσταξάντων ἐκείνῳ
τε καὶ ἄλλοις τισὶ τῶν πολιτῶν ἀγαγεῖν τινα ἐπὶ
θανάτῳ, μόνος οὐκ ἐπείσθη διὰ τὸ παρὰ τοὺς νόμους
4 αὐτῷ προστάττεσθαι· καὶ ὅτε τὴν ὑπὸ Μελήτου γρα-
φὴν ἔφευγε, τῶν ἄλλων εἰωθότων ἐν τοῖς δικαστηρίοις
πρὸς χάριν τε τοῖς δικασταῖς διαλέγεσθαι καὶ κολα-
κεύειν καὶ δεῖσθαι παρὰ τοὺς νόμους, καὶ διὰ τὰ τοι-
αῦτα πολλῶν πολλάκις ὑπὸ τῶν δικαστῶν ἀφιεμένων,
ἐκεῖνος οὐδὲν ἠθέλησε τῶν εἰωθότων ἐν τῷ δικαστηρίῳ
παρὰ τοὺς νόμους ποιῆσαι, ἀλλὰ ῥᾳδίως ἂν ἀφεθεὶς
ὑπὸ τῶν δικαστῶν, εἰ καὶ μετρίως τι τούτων ἐποίησε,
προείλετο μᾶλλον τοῖς νόμοις ἐμμένων ἀποθανεῖν ἢ
5 παρανομῶν ζῆν. Καὶ ἔλεγε δὲ οὕτως καὶ πρὸς ἄλλους
μὲν πολλάκις, οἶδα δέ ποτε αὐτὸν καὶ πρὸς Ἱππίαν
τὸν Ἠλεῖον περὶ τοῦ δικαίου τοιάδε διαλεχθέντα· διὰ
χρόνου γὰρ ἀφικόμενος ὁ Ἱππίας Ἀθήναζε παρεγένετο
τῷ Σωκράτει λέγοντι πρός τινας, ὡς θαυμαστὸν εἴη τὸ,
εἰ μέν τις βούλοιτο σκυτέα διδάξασθαί τινὰ ἢ τέκτονα
ἢ χαλκέα ἢ ἱππέα, μὴ ἀπορεῖν, ὅποι ἂν πέμψας τούτοι

τύχοι· φασὶ δέ τινες καὶ ἵππον καὶ βοῦν τῷ βουλομένῳ δικαίους ποιήσασθαι πάντα μεστὰ εἶναι τῶν διδαξόντων· ἐὰν δέ τις βούληται ἢ αὐτὸς μαθεῖν τὸ δίκαιον, ἢ υἱὸν ἢ οἰκέτην διδάξασθαι, μὴ εἰδέναι, ὅποι ἂν ἐλθὼν τύχοι
τούτου. Καὶ ὁ μὲν Ἱππίας ἀκούσας ταῦτα, ὥςπερ 6
ἐπισκώπτων αὐτόν· Ἔτι γὰρ σύ, ἔφη, ὦ Σώκρατες, ἐκεῖνα τὰ αὐτὰ λέγεις, ἃ ἐγὼ πάλαι ποτέ σου ἤκουσα; Καὶ ὁ Σωκράτης· Ὃ δέ γε τούτου δεινότερον, ἔφη, ὦ Ἱππία, οὐ μόνον ἀεὶ τὰ αὐτὰ λέγω, ἀλλὰ καὶ περὶ τῶν αὐτῶν· σὺ δ' ἴσως διὰ τὸ πολυμαθὴς εἶναι περὶ τῶν αὐτῶν οὐδέποτε τὰ αὐτὰ λέγεις.—Ἀμέλει, ἔφη,
πειρῶμαι καινόν τι λέγειν ἀεί.—Πότερον, ἔφη, καὶ 7
περὶ ὧν ἐπίστασαι, οἷον περὶ γραμμάτων, ἐάν τις ἔρηταί σε, πόσα καὶ ποῖα Σωκράτους ἐστίν, ἄλλα μὲν πρότερον, ἄλλα δὲ νῦν πειρᾷ λέγειν; ἢ περὶ ἀριθμῶν τοῖς ἐρωτῶσιν, εἰ τὰ δὶς πέντε δέκα ἐστίν, οὐ τὰ αὐτὰ νῦν, ἃ καὶ πρότερον, ἀποκρίνῃ;—Περὶ μὲν τούτων, ἔφη, ὦ Σώκρατες, ὥςπερ σύ, καὶ ἐγὼ ἀεὶ τὰ αὐτὰ λέγω, περὶ μέντοι τοῦ δικαίου πάνυ οἶμαι νῦν ἔχειν εἰπεῖν, πρὸς ἃ οὔτε σύ, οὔτ' ἂν ἄλλος οὐδεὶς δύναιτ'
ἀντειπεῖν.—Νὴ τὴν Ἥραν, ἔφη, μέγα λέγεις ἀγαθὸν 8
εὑρηκέναι, εἰ παύσονται μὲν οἱ δικασταὶ δίχα ψηφιζόμενοι, παύσονται δὲ οἱ πολῖται περὶ τῶν δικαίων ἀντιλέγοντές τε καὶ ἀντιδικοῦντες καὶ στασιάζοντες, παύσονται δὲ αἱ πόλεις διαφερόμεναι περὶ τῶν δικαίων καὶ πολεμοῦσαι· καὶ ἐγὼ μὲν οὐκ οἶδ', ὅπως ἂν ἀπολειφθείην σου πρὸ τοῦ ἀκοῦσαι τηλικοῦτον ἀγαθὸν
εὑρηκότος.—Ἀλλὰ μὰ Δί', ἔφη, οὐκ ἀκούσῃ, πρίν γ' 9
ἂν αὐτὸς ἀποφήνῃ, ὅ τι νομίζεις τὸ δίκαιον εἶναι· ἀρκεῖ γάρ, ὅτι τῶν ἄλλων καταγελᾷς ἐρωτῶν μὲν καὶ ἐλέγχων πάντας, αὐτὸς δ' οὐδενὶ θέλων ὑπέχειν λόγον, οὐδὲ
γνώμην ἀποφαίνεσθαι περὶ οὐδενός.—Τί δέ; ὦ Ἱπ- 10
πία, ἔφη, οὐκ ᾔσθησαι, ὅτι ἐγὼ ἃ δοκεῖ μοι δίκαια εἶναι οὐδὲν παύομαι ἀποδεικνύμενος;—Καὶ ποῖος δή

σοι, ἔφη, οὗτος ὁ λόγος ἐστίν;—Εἰ δὲ μὴ λόγῳ, ἔφη ἀλλ' ἔργῳ ἀποδείκνυμαι· ἢ οὐ δοκεῖ σοι ἀξιοτεκμαρτότερον τοῦ λόγου τὸ ἔργον εἶναι;—Πολύ γε νὴ Δί', ἔφη· δίκαια μὲν γὰρ λέγοντες πολλοὶ ἄδικα ποιοῦσι,
11 δίκαια δὲ πράττων οὐδ' ἂν εἷς ἄδικος εἴη.—Ἤισθησαι οὖν πώποτέ μου ἢ ψευδομαρτυροῦντος, ἢ συκοφαντοῦντος, ἢ φίλους ἢ πόλιν εἰς στάσιν ἐμβάλλοντος, ἢ ἄλλο τι ἄδικον πράττοντος;—Οὐκ ἔγωγε, ἔφη.—Τὸ δὲ τῶν ἀδίκων ἀπέχεσθαι οὐ δίκαιον ἡγῇ;—Δῆλος, εἶ, ἔφη, ὦ Σώκρατες, καὶ νῦν διαφεύγειν ἐγχειρῶν τὸ ἀποδείκνυσθαι γνώμην, ὅ τι νομίζεις τὸ δίκαιον· οὐ γὰρ ἃ πράττουσιν οἱ δίκαιοι, ἀλλ', ἃ μὴ πράττουσι,
12 ταῦτα λέγεις.—Ἀλλ' ᾤμην ἔγωγε, ἔφη ὁ Σωκράτης, τὸ μὴ θέλειν ἀδικεῖν ἱκανὸν δικαιοσύνης ἐπίδειγμα εἶναι· εἰ δέ σοι μὴ δοκεῖ, σκέψαι, ἐὰν τόδε σοι μᾶλλον ἀρέσκῃ· φημὶ γὰρ ἐγὼ τὸ νόμιμον δίκαιον εἶναι.—Ἆρα τὸ αὐτὸ λέγεις, ὦ Σώκρατες, νόμιμόν τε καὶ δί-
13 καιον εἶναι;—Ἔγωγε, ἔφη.—Οὐ γὰρ αἰσθάνομαι σου, ὁποῖον νόμιμον, ἢ ποῖον δίκαιον λέγεις.—Νόμους δὲ πόλεως, ἔφη, γιγνώσκεις;—Ἔγωγε, ἔφη.—Καὶ τίνας τούτους νομίζεις;—Ἃ οἱ πολῖται, ἔφη, συνθέμενοι ἅ τε δεῖ ποιεῖν καὶ ὧν ἀπέχεσθαι ἐγράψαντο.—Οὔκουν, ἔφη, νόμιμος μὲν ἂν εἴη ὁ κατὰ ταῦτα πολιτευόμενος, ἄνομος δὲ ὁ ταῦτα παραβαίνων;—Πάνυ μὲν οὖν, ἔφη.—Οὔκουν καὶ δίκαια μὲν ἂν πράττοι ὁ τούτοις πειθόμενος, ἄδικα δ' ὁ τούτοις ἀπειθῶν;—Πάνυ μὲν οὖν.—Οὔκουν ὁ μὲν τὰ δίκαια πράττων δίκαιος, ὁ δὲ τὰ ἄδικα ἄδικος;—Πῶς γὰρ οὔ;—Ὁ μὲν ἄρα νόμιμος δίκαιός ἐστιν, ὁ δὲ ἄνομος ἄδικος.
14 Καὶ ὁ Ἱππίας· Νόμους δ', ἔφη, ὦ Σώκρατες, πῶς ἄν τις ἡγήσαιτο σπουδαῖον πρᾶγμα εἶναι ἢ τὸ πείθεσθαι αὐτοῖς, οὕς γε πολλάκις αὐτοὶ οἱ θέμενοι ἀποδοκιμάσαντες μετατίθενται;—Καὶ γὰρ πόλεμον, ἔφη ὁ Σωκράτης πολλάκις ἀράμεναι αἱ πόλεις πάλιν εἰρήνην

ποιοῦνται. — Καὶ μάλα, ἔφη. — Διάφορον οὖν τι οἴει
ποιεῖν, ἔφη, τοὺς τοῖς νόμοις πειθομένους φαυλίζων,
ὅτι καταλυθεῖεν ἂν οἱ νόμοι, ἢ εἰ τοὺς ἐν τοῖς πολέ-
μοις εὐτακτοῦντας ψέγοις, ὅτι γένοιτ' ἂν εἰρήνη; ἢ
καὶ τοὺς ἐν τοῖς πολέμοις ταῖς πατρίσι προθύμως
βοηθοῦντας μέμφῃ; — Μὰ Δί' οὐκ ἔγωγ', ἔφη. Λυ- 15
κοῦργον δὲ τὸν Λακεδαιμόνιον, ἔφη ὁ Σωκράτης, κατα-
μεμάθηκας, ὅτι οὐδὲν ἂν διάφορον τῶν ἄλλων πόλεων
τὴν Σπάρτην ἐποίησεν, εἰ μὴ τὸ πείθεσθαι τοῖς νό-
μοις μάλιστα ἐνειργάσατο αὐτῇ; τῶν δὲ ἀρχόντων ἐν
ταῖς πόλεσιν οὐκ οἶσθα, ὅτι, οἵτινες ἂν τοῖς πολίταις
αἰτιώτατοι ὦσι τοῦ τοῖς νόμοις πείθεσθαι, οὗτοι ἄρι-
στοί εἰσι; καὶ πόλις, ἐν ᾗ μάλιστα οἱ πολῖται τοῖς
νόμοις πείθονται, ἐν εἰρήνῃ τε ἄριστα διάγει καὶ ἐν
πολέμῳ ἀνυπόστατός ἐστιν; Ἀλλὰ μὴν καὶ ὁμόνοιά 16
γε μέγιστόν τε ἀγαθὸν δοκεῖ ταῖς πόλεσιν εἶναι, καὶ
πλειστάκις ἐν αὐταῖς αἵ τε γερουσίαι καὶ οἱ ἄριστοι
ἄνδρες παρακελεύονται τοῖς πολίταις ὁμονοεῖν, καὶ
πανταχοῦ ἐν τῇ Ἑλλάδι νόμος κεῖται τοὺς πολίτας
ὀμνύναι ὁμονοήσειν, καὶ πανταχοῦ ὀμνύουσι τὸν ὅρκον
τοῦτον· οἶμαι δ' ἐγὼ ταῦτα γίγνεσθαι, οὐχ ὅπως τοὺς
αὐτοὺς χοροὺς κρίνωσιν οἱ πολῖται, οὐδ' ὅπως τοὺς
αὐτοὺς αὐλητὰς ἐπαινῶσιν, οὐδ' ὅπως τοὺς αὐτοὺς
ποιητὰς αἱρῶνται, οὐδ' ἵνα τοῖς αὐτοῖς ἥδωνται, ἀλλ'
ἵνα τοῖς νόμοις πείθωνται· τούτοις γὰρ τῶν πολιτῶν
ἐμμενόντων, αἱ πόλεις ἰσχυρόταταί τε καὶ εὐδαιμονέ-
σταται γίγνονται· ἄνευ δὲ ὁμονοίας οὔτ' ἂν πόλις εὖ
πολιτευθείη, οὔτ' οἶκος καλῶς οἰκηθείη. Ἰδίᾳ δὲ πῶς 17
μὲν ἄν τις ἧττον ὑπὸ πόλεως ζημιοῖτο, πῶς δ' ἂν μᾶλ-
λον τιμῷτο, ἢ εἰ τοῖς νόμοις πείθοιτο; πῶς δ' ἂν
ἧττον ἐν τοῖς δικαστηρίοις ἡττῷτο, ἢ πῶς ἂν μᾶλλον
νικῴη; τίνι δ' ἄν τις μᾶλλον πιστεύσειε παρακατα-
θέσθαι ἢ χρήματα, ἢ υἱούς, ἢ θυγατέρας, τίνα δ' ἂν
ἡ πόλις ὅλη ἀξιοπιστότερον ἡγήσαιτο τοῦ νομίμου;

παρὰ τίνος δ' ἂν μᾶλλον τῶν δικαίων τύχοιεν ἢ γονεῖς, ἢ οἰκεῖοι, ἢ οἰκέται, ἢ φίλοι, ἢ πολῖται, ἢ ξένοι; τίνι δ' ἂν μᾶλλον πολέμιοι πιστεύσειαν ἢ ἀνοχάς, ἢ σπονδάς, ἢ συνθήκας περὶ εἰρήνης; τίνι δ' ἂν μᾶλλον ἢ τῷ νομίμῳ σύμμαχοι ἐθέλοιεν γίγνεσθαι, τῷ δ' ἂν μᾶλλον οἱ σύμμαχοι πιστεύσειαν ἢ ἡγεμονίαν, ἢ φρουραρχίαν, ἢ πόλεις; τίνα δ' ἄν τις εὐεργετήσας ὑπολάβοι χάριν κομιεῖσθαι μᾶλλον ἢ τὸν νόμιμον; ἢ τίνα μᾶλλον ἄν τις εὐεργετήσειεν ἢ παρ' οὗ χάριν ἀπολήψεσθαι νομίζει; τῷ δ' ἄν τις βούλοιτο μᾶλλον φίλος εἶναι ἢ τῷ τοιούτῳ, ἢ τῷ ἧττον ἐχθρός; τῷ δ' ἄν τις ἧττον πολεμήσειεν ἢ ᾧ ἂν μάλιστα μὲν φίλος εἶναι βούλοιτο, ἥκιστα δ' ἐχθρός, καὶ ᾧ πλεῖστοι μὲν φίλοι καὶ σύμμαχοι βούλοιντο εἶναι, ἐλάχιστοι δ'
18 ἐχθροὶ καὶ πολέμιοι; Ἐγὼ μὲν οὖν, ὦ Ἱππία, τὸ αὐτὸ ἐπιδείκνυμι νόμιμόν τε καὶ δίκαιον εἶναι, σὺ δ' εἰ τἀναντία γιγνώσκεις, δίδασκε. Καὶ ὁ Ἱππίας· Ἀλλά, μὰ τὸν Δία, ἔφη, ὦ Σώκρατες, οὔ μοι δοκῶ τἀναντία γιγνώσκειν οἷς εἴρηκας περὶ τοῦ δικαίου.—
19 Ἀγράφους δέ τινας οἶσθα, ἔφη, ὦ Ἱππία, νόμους;—Τούς γ' ἐν πάσῃ, ἔφη, χώρᾳ κατὰ ταὐτὰ νομιζομένους.—Ἔχοις ἂν οὖν εἰπεῖν, ἔφη, ὅτι οἱ ἄνθρωποι αὐτοὺς ἔθεντο;—Καὶ πῶς ἄν, ἔφη, οἵ γε οὔτε συνελθεῖν ἅπαντες ἂν δυνηθεῖεν, οὔτε ὁμόφωνοί εἰσι;—Τίνας οὖν, ἔφη, νομίζεις τεθεικέναι τοὺς νόμους τούτους; Ἐγὼ μέν, ἔφη, θεοὺς οἶμαι τοὺς νόμους τούτους τοῖς ἀνθρώποις θεῖναι· καὶ γὰρ παρὰ πᾶσιν ἀνθρώ-
20 ποις πρῶτον νομίζεται τοὺς θεοὺς σέβειν.—Οὔκουν καὶ γονέας τιμᾶν πανταχοῦ νομίζεται;—Καὶ τοῦτο, ἔφη.—Οὔκουν καὶ μήτε γονέας παισὶ μίγνυσθαι, μήτε παῖδας γονεῦσιν;—Οὐκέτι μοι δοκεῖ, ἔφη, ὦ Σώκρατες, οὗτος θεοῦ νόμος εἶναι.—Τί δή; ἔφη.—Ὅτι
21 αἰσθάνομαι τινας, ἔφη, παραβαίνοντας αὐτόν.—Καὶ γὰρ ἄλλα πολλά, ἔφη, παρανομοῦσιν· ἀλλ' οὖν δίκην

γέ τοι διδόασιν οἱ παραβαίνοντες τοὺς ὑπὸ τῶν θεῶν κειμένους νόμους, ἣν οὐδενὶ τρόπῳ δυνατὸν ἀνθρώπῳ διαφυγεῖν, ὥσπερ τοὺς ὑπ' ἀνθρώπων κειμένους νόμους ἔνιοι παραβαίνοντες διαφεύγουσι τὸ δίκην διδόναι, οἱ μὲν λανθάνοντες, οἱ δὲ βιαζόμενοι.—Καὶ ποίαν, ἔφη, 22
δίκην, ὦ Σώκρατες, οὐ δύνανται διαφεύγειν γονεῖς τε παισὶ καὶ παῖδες γονεῦσι μιγνύμενοι;—Τὴν μεγίστην νὴ Δί', ἔφη· τί γὰρ ἂν μεῖζον πάθοιεν ἄνθρωποι τεκνοποιούμενοι τοῦ κακῶς τεκνοποιεῖσθαι;—Πῶς οὖν 23
ἔφη, κακῶς οὗτοι τεκνοποιοῦνται, οὕς γε οὐδὲν κωλύει ἀγαθοὺς αὐτοὺς ὄντας ἐξ ἀγαθῶν παιδοποιεῖσθαι;—Ὅτι νὴ Δί', ἔφη, οὐ μόνον ἀγαθοὺς δεῖ τοὺς ἐξ ἀλλήλων παιδοποιουμένους εἶναι, ἀλλὰ καὶ ἀκμάζοντας τοῖς σώμασιν· ἢ δοκεῖ σοι ὅμοια τὰ σπέρματα εἶναι τὰ τῶν ἀκμαζόντων τοῖς τῶν μήπω ἀκμαζόντων ἢ τῶν παρηκμακότων;—Ἀλλὰ μὰ Δί', ἔφη, οὐκ εἰκὸς ὅμοια εἶναι.—Πότερα οὖν, ἔφη, βελτίω;—Δῆλον ὅτι, ἔφη, τὰ τῶν ἀκμαζόντων.—Τὰ τῶν μὴ ἀκμαζόντων ἄρα οὐ σπουδαῖα;—Οὐκ εἰκὸς μὰ Δί', ἔφη.—Οὔκουν οὕτω γε οὐ δεῖ παιδοποιεῖσθαι;—Οὐ γὰρ οὖν, ἔφη.—Οὔκουν οἵ γε οὕτω παιδοποιούμενοι ὡς οὐ δεῖ παιδοποιοῦνται;—Ἔμοιγε δοκεῖ, ἔφη.—Τίνες οὖν ἄλλοι, ἔφη, κακῶς ἂν παιδοποιοῖντο, εἴγε μὴ οὗτοι;—Ὁμογνωμονῶ σοι, ἔφη, καὶ τοῦτο.—Τί δέ; τοὺς εὖ ποιοῦντας 24
ἀντευεργετεῖν οὐ πανταχοῦ νόμιμόν ἐστι;—Νόμιμον, ἔφη· παραβαίνεται δὲ καὶ τοῦτο.—Οὔκουν καὶ οἱ τοῦτο παραβαίνοντες δίκην διδόασι, φίλων μὲν ἀγαθῶν ἔρημοι γιγνόμενοι, τοὺς δὲ μισοῦντας ἑαυτοὺς ἀναγκαζόμενοι διώκειν· ἢ οὐχ οἱ μὲν εὖ ποιοῦντες τοὺς χρωμένους ἑαυτοῖς ἀγαθοὶ φίλοι εἰσίν, οἱ δὲ μὴ ἀντευεργετοῦντες τοὺς τοιούτους διὰ μὲν τὴν ἀχαριστίαν μισοῦνται ὑπ' αὐτῶν, διὰ δὲ τὸ μάλιστα λυσιτελεῖν τοῖς τοιούτοις χρῆσθαι τούτους μάλιστα διώκουσι;—Νὴ τὸν Δί', ὦ Σώκρατες, ἔφη, θεοῖς ταῦτα πάντα

ἔοικε· τὸ γὰρ τοὺς νόμους αὐτοὺς τοῖς παραβαίνουσι τὰς τιμωρίας ἔχειν βελτίονος ἢ κατ᾽ ἄνϑρωπον νομοϑέτου δοκεῖ μοι εἶναι.—Πότερον οὖν, ὦ Ἱππία, τοὺς ϑεοὺς ἡγῇ τὰ δίκαια νομοϑετεῖν, ἢ ἄλλα τῶν δικαίων;—Οὐκ ἄλλα μὰ Δί᾽, ἔφη· σχολῇ γὰρ ἂν ἄλλος γέ τις τὰ δίκαια νομοϑετήσειεν, εἰ μὴ ϑεός.—Καὶ τοῖς ϑεοῖς ἄρα, ὦ Ἱππία, τὸ αὐτὸ δίκαιόν τε καὶ νόμιμον εἶναι ἀρέσκει.

Τοιαῦτα λέγων τε καὶ πράττων δικαιοτέρους ἐποίει τοὺς πλησιάζοντας.

CHAPTER V.

ARGUMENT.

Having in the two preceding chapters showed the manner in which Socrates laid the foundation for a good character in his pupils, by inculcating the practice of religion and morality, Xenophon proceeds to his instructions which have a more direct bearing on practical life. In this chapter he presents the manner in which Socrates endeavored to qualify his disciples for action. He went back to the source from which energy in action springs, i. e., temperance or self-control, ἐγκράτεια. This virtue he recommended by his example and by his instructions (§ 1, 2). A conversation which he held with Euthydemus was substantially as follows:

The servitude of the passions is most abject; for they not only prevent from doing the greatest good, in which the highest freedom consists, but, confounding good and evil, urge to the commission of great evil (§ 2—7). As intemperance is the greatest of evils, so on the contrary the greatest virtues arise from temperance (§ 8—10). The man who is under the dominion of his passions is fitted for no virtuous action, and does not materially differ from a beast. But the man of temperate habits, is attended by the best gifts of fortune, and is most worthy and happy (§ 11, 12).

With this conversation Book I. chap. V, and VI. § 5; also Book II. chap. I. § 21—34, may be compared.

Ὡς δὲ καὶ πρακτικωτέρους ἐποίει τοὺς συνόντας 1
ἑαυτῷ, νῦν αὖ τοῦτο λέξω· νομίζων γὰρ ἐγκράτειαν ὑπάρχειν ἀγαθὸν εἶναι τῷ μέλλοντι καλόν τι πράξειν, πρῶτον μὲν αὐτὸς φανερὸς ἦν τοῖς συνοῦσιν ἠσκηκὼς ἑαυτὸν μάλιστα πάντων ἀνθρώπων, ἔπειτα διαλεγόμενος προετρέπετο πάντων μάλιστα τοὺς συνόντας πρὸς
ἐγκράτειαν. Ἀεὶ μὲν οὖν περὶ τῶν πρὸς ἀρετὴν χρη- 2
σίμων αὐτός τε διετέλει μεμνημένος καὶ τοὺς συνόντας πάντας ὑπομιμνήσκων· οἶδα δέ ποτε αὐτὸν καὶ πρὸς Εὐθύδημον περὶ ἐγκρατείας τοιάδε διαλεχθέντα· Εἰπέ μοι, ἔφη, ὦ Εὐθύδημε, ἆρα καλὸν καὶ μεγαλεῖον νομίζεις εἶναι καὶ ἀνδρὶ καὶ πόλει κτῆμα ἐλευθερίαν;—
Ὡς οἷόν τέ γε μάλιστα, ἔφη.—Ὅστις οὖν ἄρχεται 3
ὑπὸ τῶν διὰ τοῦ σώματος ἡδονῶν, καὶ διὰ ταύτας μὴ δύναται πράττειν τὰ βέλτιστα, νομίζεις τοῦτον ἐλεύθερον εἶναι;—Ἥκιστα, ἔφη.—Ἴσως γὰρ ἐλεύθερον φαίνεταί σοι τὸ πράττειν τὰ βέλτιστα, εἶτα τὸ ἔχειν τοὺς κωλύσοντας τὰ τοιαῦτα ποιεῖν ἀνελεύθερον νομί-
ζεις;—Παντάπασί γε, ἔφη.—Παντάπασιν ἄρα σοι 4
δοκοῦσιν οἱ ἀκρατεῖς ἀνελεύθεροι εἶναι;—Νὴ τὸν Δί', ἔφη, εἰκότως.—Πότερον δέ σοι δοκοῦσιν οἱ ἀκρατεῖς κωλύεσθαι μόνον τὰ κάλλιστα πράττειν, ἢ καὶ ἀναγκάζεσθαι τὰ αἴσχιστα ποιεῖν;—Οὐδὲν ἧττον ἔμοιγ', ἔφη, δοκοῦσι ταῦτα ἀναγκάζεσθαι ἢ ἐκεῖνα κωλύεσθαι.
—Ποίους δέ τινας δεσπότας ἡγῇ τοὺς τὰ μὲν ἄριστα 5
κωλύοντας, τὰ δὲ κάκιστα ἀναγκάζοντας;—Ὡς δυνατὸν νὴ Δί', ἔφη, κακίστους.—Δουλείαν δὲ ποίαν κακίστην νομίζεις εἶναι;—Ἐγὼ μέν, ἔφη, τὴν παρὰ τοῖς κακίστοις δεσπόταις.—Τὴν κακίστην ἄρα δουλείαν οἱ
ἀκρατεῖς δουλεύουσιν;—Ἔμοιγε δοκεῖ, ἔφη.—Σοφίαν 6
δὲ τὸ μέγιστον ἀγαθὸν οὐ δοκεῖ σοι ἀπείργουσα τῶν ἀνθρώπων ἡ ἀκρασία εἰς τοὐναντίον αὐτοὺς ἐμβάλλειν; ἢ οὐ δοκεῖ σοι προσέχειν τε τοῖς ὠφελοῦσι καὶ καταμανθάνειν αὐτὰ κωλύειν ἀφέλκουσα ἐπὶ τὰ ἡδέα,

καὶ πολλάκις αἰσθανομένους τῶν ἀγαθῶν τε καὶ τῶν κακῶν ἐκπλήξασα ποιεῖν τὸ χεῖρον ἀντὶ τοῦ βελτίονος
7 αἱρεῖσθαι;—Γίγνεται τοῦτ', ἔφη.—Σωφροσύνης δέ, ὦ Εὐθύδημε, τίνι ἂν φαίημεν ἧττον ἢ τῷ ἀκρατεῖ προσήκειν; αὐτὰ γὰρ δήπου τὰ ἐναντία σωφροσύνης καὶ ἀκρασίας ἔργα ἐστίν.—Ὁμολογῶ καὶ τοῦτο, ἔφη. —Τοῦ δ' ἐπιμελεῖσθαι ὧν προσήκει οἴει τι κωλυτικώτερον ἀκρασίας εἶναι;—Οὔκουν ἔγωγε, ἔφη.—Τοῦ δὲ ἀντὶ τῶν ὠφελούντων τὰ βλάπτοντα προαιρεῖσθαι ποιοῦντος, καὶ τούτων μὲν ἐπιμελεῖσθαι, ἐκείνων δὲ ἀμελεῖν πείθοντος, καὶ τοῖς σωφρονοῦσι τὰ ἐναντία ποιεῖν ἀναγκάζοντος οἴει τι ἀνθρώπῳ κάκιον εἶναι;—
8 Οὐδέν, ἔφη.—Οὔκουν τὴν ἐγκράτειαν τῶν ἐναντίων ἢ τὴν ἀκρασίαν εἰκὸς τοῖς ἀνθρώποις αἰτίαν εἶναι;—Πάνυ μὲν οὖν, ἔφη.—Οὔκουν καὶ τῶν ἐναντίων τὸ αἴτιον εἰκὸς ἄριστον εἶναι;—Εἰκὸς γάρ, ἔφη.—Ἔοικεν ἄρα, ἔφη, ὦ Εὐθύδημε, ἄριστον ἀνθρώπῳ ἡ ἐγκρά-
9 τεια εἶναι;—Εἰκότως γάρ, ἔφη, ὦ Σώκρατες.—Ἐκεῖνο δέ, ὦ Εὐθύδημε, ἤδη πώποτε ἐνεθυμήθης;—Ποῖον; ἔφη.—Ὅτι καὶ ἐπὶ τὰ ἡδέα, ἐφ' ἅπερ μόνα δοκεῖ ἡ ἀκρασία τοὺς ἀνθρώπους ἄγειν, αὐτὴ μὲν οὐ δύναται ἄγειν, ἡ δ' ἐγκράτεια πάντων μάλιστα ἥδεσθαι ποιεῖ. —Πῶς; ἔφη.—Ὥσπερ ἡ μὲν ἀκρασία, οὐκ ἐῶσα καρτερεῖν οὔτε λιμόν, οὔτε δίψαν, οὔτε ἀφροδισίων ἐπιθυμίαν, οὔτε ἀγρυπνίαν, δι' ὧν μόνων ἔστιν ἡδέως μὲν φαγεῖν τε καὶ πιεῖν καὶ ἀφροδισιάσαι, ἡδέως δ' ἀναπαύσασθαί τε καὶ κοιμηθῆναι, καὶ περιμείναντας καὶ ἀνασχομένους, ἕως ἂν ταῦτα ὡς ἔνι ἥδιστα γένηται, κωλύει τοῖς ἀναγκαιοτάτοις τε καὶ συνεχεστάτοις ἀξιολόγως ἥδεσθαι· ἡ δ' ἐγκράτεια μόνη ποιοῦσα καρτερεῖν τὰ εἰρημένα μόνη καὶ ἥδεσθαι ποιεῖ ἀξίως μνήμης ἐπὶ τοῖς εἰρημένοις.—Παντάπασιν, ἔφη, ἀληθῆ λέγεις.
10 —Ἀλλὰ μὴν τοῦ μαθεῖν τι καλὸν καὶ ἀγαθόν, καὶ τοῦ ἐπιμεληθῆναι τῶν τοιούτων τινός, δι' ὧν ἄν τις

καὶ τὸ ἑαυτοῦ σῶμα καλῶς διοικήσειε, καὶ τὸν ἑαυτοῦ οἶκον καλῶς οἰκονομήσειε, καὶ φίλοις καὶ πόλει ὠφέλιμος γένοιτο, καὶ ἐχθροὺς κρατήσειεν, ἀφ' ὧν οὐ μόνον ὠφέλειαι, ἀλλὰ καὶ ἡδοναὶ μέγισται γίγνονται, οἱ μὲν ἐγκρατεῖς ἀπολαύουσι πράττοντες αὐτὰ, οἱ δ' ἀκρατεῖς οὐδενὸς μετέχουσι· τῷ γὰρ ἂν ἧττον φήσαιμεν τῶν τοιούτων προσήκειν ἢ ᾧ ἥκιστα ἔξεστι ταῦτα πράττειν, κατεχομένῳ ἐπὶ τῷ σπουδάζειν περὶ τὰς ἐγγυτάτω ἡδονάς;—Καὶ ὁ Εὐθύδημος· Δοκεῖς μοι, ἔφη, 11
ὦ Σώκρατες, λέγειν, ὡς ἀνδρὶ ἥττονι τῶν διὰ τοῦ σώματος ἡδονῶν πάμπαν οὐδεμιᾶς ἀρετῆς προσήκει.—Τί γὰρ διαφέρει, ἔφη, ὦ Εὐθύδημε, ἄνθρωπος ἀκρατὴς θηρίου τοῦ ἀμαθεστάτου; ὅστις γὰρ τὰ μὲν κράτιστα μὴ σκοπεῖ, τὰ ἥδιστα δ' ἐκ παντὸς τρόπου ζητεῖ ποιεῖν, τί ἂν διαφέροι τῶν ἀφρονεστάτων βοσκημάτων; ἀλλὰ τοῖς ἐγκρατέσι μόνοις ἔξεστι σκοπεῖν τὰ κράτιστα τῶν πραγμάτων, καὶ ἔργῳ καὶ λόγῳ διαλέγοντας κατὰ γένη τὰ μὲν ἀγαθὰ προαιρεῖσθαι, τῶν δὲ κακῶν ἀπέχεσθαι. Καὶ οὕτως ἔφη ἀρίστους τε καὶ 12
εὐδαιμονεστάτους ἄνδρας γίγνεσθαι, καὶ διαλέγεσθαι δυνατωτάτους· ἔφη δὲ καὶ τὸ διαλέγεσθαι ὀνομασθῆναι ἐκ τοῦ συνιόντας κοινῇ βουλεύεσθαι διαλέγοντας κατὰ γένη τὰ πράγματα· δεῖν οὖν πειρᾶσθαι ὅ τι μάλιστα πρὸς τοῦτο ἑαυτὸν ἕτοιμον παρασκευάζειν, καὶ τούτου μάλιστα ἐπιμελεῖσθαι· ἐκ τούτου γὰρ γίγνεσθαι ἄνδρας ἀρίστους τε καὶ ἡγεμονικωτάτους καὶ διαλεκτικωτάτους.

CHAPTER VI.

ARGUMENT.

SOCRATES also endeavored to make his disciples more expert in reasoning, *διαλεκτικωτέρους*. He supposed that those who had clear notions themselves could communicate them to others, but those who were ignorant were themselves liable to be deceived and to deceive others. He accordingly constantly labored to communicate definite ideas or definitions of things (§ 1). Some of his definitions are as follows:

1. Piety, *εὐσέβεια*, is the knowledge of that which is established by the laws in regard to the worship of the gods (§ 1—4). [Compare with this, Book III. chap. VIII., where every virtue is represented as consisting in wisdom, *σοφία*.]

2. Justice is the knowledge of the laws of the State, in regard to intercourse with men (§ 5, 6).

3. Wisdom, *σοφία*, is the knowledge of that in which one is versed (§ 7).

4. The good and beautiful, which are equivalent to each other, are discerned by their utility. Yet that which is useful is not so in itself, but in its relation to other things (§ 8, 9).

5. Manliness, *ἀνδρία*, consists in knowing how to conduct ourselves in circumstances of difficulty and danger (§ 10, 11).

6. Definitions of several terms which relate to civil affairs, such as of kingdom, tyranny, aristocracy, etc. (§ 12).

In fine, Xenophon adds several particulars concerning Socrates' manner of disputation (§ 13—15).

---

1 Ὡς δὲ καὶ διαλεκτικωτέρους ἐποίει τοὺς συνόντας, πειράσομαι καὶ τοῦτο λέγειν· Σωκράτης γὰρ τοὺς μὲν εἰδότας, τί ἕκαστον εἴη τῶν ὄντων, ἐνόμιζε καὶ τοῖς ἄλλοις ἂν ἐξηγεῖσθαι δύνασθαι, τοὺς δὲ μὴ εἰδότας οὐδὲν ἔφη θαυμαστὸν εἶναι αὐτούς τε σφάλλεσθαι καὶ ἄλλους σφάλλειν· ὧν ἕνεκα σκοπῶν σὺν τοῖς συνοῦσι, τί ἕκαστον εἴη τῶν ὄντων, οὐδέποτ' ἔληγε. Πάντα μὲν οὖν, ᾗ διωρίζετο, πολὺ ἔργον ἂν εἴη διεξελθεῖν

ἐν ὅσοις δὲ καὶ τὸν τρόπον τῆς ἐπισκέψεως δηλώσειν οἶμαι, τοσαῦτα λέξω. Πρῶτον δὲ περὶ εὐσεβείας ὧδέ 2
πως ἐσκόπει· Εἰπέ μοι, ἔφη, ὦ Εὐθύδημε, ποῖόν τι νομίζεις εὐσέβειαν εἶναι; Καὶ ὅς· Κάλλιστον νὴ Δί', ἔφη.—Ἔχεις οὖν εἰπεῖν, ὁποῖός τις ὁ εὐσεβής ἐστιν; —Ἐμοὶ μὲν δοκεῖ, ἔφη, ὁ τοὺς θεοὺς τιμῶν.—Ἔξεστι δὲ ὃν ἄν τις βούληται τρόπον τοὺς θεοὺς τιμᾶν;—Οὔκ· ἀλλὰ νόμοι εἰσί καθ' οὓς δεῖ τοῦτο ποιεῖν.—
Οὔκουν ὁ τοὺς νόμους τούτους εἰδὼς εἰδείη ἄν, ὡς δεῖ 3
τοὺς θεοὺς τιμᾶν;—Οἶμαι ἔγωγ', ἔφη.—Ἆρ' οὖν ὁ εἰδὼς τοὺς θεοὺς τιμᾶν οὐκ ἄλλως οἴεται δεῖν τοῦτο ποιεῖν ἢ ὡς οἶδεν;—Οὐ γὰρ οὖν, ἔφη.—Ἄλλως δέ τις θεοὺς τιμᾷ ἢ ὡς οἴεται δεῖν;—Οὐκ οἶμαι, ἔφη.—
Ὁ ἄρα τὰ περὶ τοὺς θεοὺς νόμιμα εἰδὼς νομίμως ἂν 4
τοὺς θεοὺς τιμῴη;—Πάνυ μὲν οὖν.—Οὔκουν ὅ γε νομίμως τιμῶν ὡς δεῖ τιμᾷ;—Πῶς γὰρ οὔ;—Ὁ δέ γε ὡς δεῖ τιμῶν εὐσεβής ἐστι;—Πάνυ μὲν οὖν, ἔφη. —Ὁ ἄρα τὰ περὶ τοὺς θεοὺς νόμιμα εἰδὼς ὀρθῶς ἂν ἡμῖν εὐσεβὴς ὡρισμένος εἴη;—Ἐμοὶ γοῦν, ἔφη, δοκεῖ.

Ἀνθρώποις δὲ ἆρα ἔξεστιν ὃν ἄν τις τρόπον βού- 5
ληται χρῆσθαι;—Οὔκ· ἀλλὰ καὶ περὶ τούτους ὁ εἰδὼς ἅ ἐστι νόμιμα, καθ' ἃ δεῖ πως ἀλλήλοις χρῆσθαι, νόμιμος ἂν εἴη.—Οὔκουν οἱ κατὰ ταῦτα χρώμενοι ἀλλήλοις ὡς δεῖ χρῶνται;—Πῶς γὰρ οὔ;—Οὔκουν οἵ γε ὡς δεῖ χρώμενοι καλῶς χρῶνται;—Πάνυ μὲν οὖν, ἔφη.—Οὔκουν οἵ γε τοῖς ἀνθρώποις καλῶς χρώμενοι καλῶς πράττουσι τἀνθρώπεια πράγματα;—Εἰκός γ', ἔφη.—Οὔκουν οἱ τοῖς νόμοις πειθόμενοι δίκαια οὗτοι ποιοῦσι;—Πάνυ μὲν οὖν, ἔφη.
—Δίκαια δὲ οἶσθα, ἔφη, ὁποῖα καλεῖται;—Ἃ οἱ 6
νόμοι κελεύουσιν, [ἔφη].—Οἱ ἄρα ποιοῦντες ἃ οἱ νόμοι κελεύουσι δίκαιά τε ποιοῦσι καὶ ἃ δεῖ;—Πῶς γὰρ οὔ;—Οὔκουν οἵ γε τὰ δίκαια ποιοῦντες δίκαιοί εἰσιν;

—Οἶμαι ἔγωγ', ἔφη.—Οἴει οὖν τινας πείθεσθαι τοῖς νόμοις μὴ εἰδότας ἃ οἱ νόμοι κελεύουσιν;—Οὐκ ἔγωγ', ἔφη.—Εἰδότας δὲ ἃ δεῖ ποιεῖν οἴει τινὰς οἴεσθαι δεῖν μὴ ποῖειν ταῦτα;—Οὐκ οἶμαι, ἔφη.—Οἶδας δέ τινας ἄλλα ποιοῦντας ἢ ἃ οἴονται δεῖν;—Οὐκ ἔγωγ', ἔφη.—Οἱ ἄρα τὰ περὶ ἀνθρώπους νόμιμα εἰδότες τὰ δίκαια οὗτοι ποιοῦσιν;—Πάνυ μὲν οὖν, ἔφη.—Οὔκουν οἵ γε τὰ δίκαια ποιοῦντες δίκαιοί εἰσι;—Τίνες γὰρ ἄλλοι; ἔφη.—Ὀρθῶς ἄν ποτε ἄρα ὁριζοίμεθα ὁριζόμενοι δικαίους εἶναι τοὺς εἰδότας τὰ περὶ ἀνθρώπους νόμιμα;—Ἔμοιγε δοκεῖ, ἔφη.

7 Σοφίαν δὲ τί ἂν φήσαιμεν εἶναι; εἰπέ μοι, πότερά σοι δοκοῦσιν οἱ σοφοὶ, ἃ ἐπίστανται, ταῦτα σοφοὶ εἶναι, ἢ εἰσί τινες ἃ μὴ ἐπίστανται σοφοί;—Ἃ ἐπίστανται δῆλον ὅτι, ἔφη· πῶς γὰρ ἄν τις, ἅ γε μὴ ἐπίσταιτο, ταῦτα σοφὸς εἴη;—Ἆρ' οὖν οἱ σοφοὶ ἐπιστήμῃ σοφοί εἰσι;—Τίνι γάρ, ἔφη, ἄλλῳ τις ἂν εἴη σοφός, εἴ γε μὴ ἐπιστήμῃ;—Ἄλλο δέ τι σοφίαν οἴει εἶναι ἢ ᾧ σοφοί εἰσιν;—Οὐκ ἔγωγε.—Ἐπιστήμη ἄρα σοφία ἐστίν;—Ἔμοιγε δοκεῖ.—Ἆρ' οὖν δοκεῖ σοι ἀνθρώπῳ δυνατὸν εἶναι τὰ ὄντα πάντα ἐπίστασθαι;—Οὐδὲ μὰ Δί' ἔμοιγε πολλοστὸν μέρος αὐτῶν.—Πάντα μὲν ἄρα σοφὸν οὐχ οἷόν τε ἄνθρωπον εἶναι;—Μὰ Δί', οὐ δῆτα, ἔφη.—Ὃ ἄρα ἐπίσταται ἕκαστος, τοῦτο καὶ σοφός ἐστιν;—Ἔμοιγε δοκεῖ.

8 Ἆρ' οὖν, ὦ Εὐθύδημε, καὶ τἀγαθὸν οὕτω ζητητέον ἐστί;—Πῶς; ἔφη.—Δοκεῖ σοι τὸ αὐτὸ πᾶσιν ὠφέλιμον εἶναι;—Οὐκ ἔμοιγε.—Τί δέ; τὸ ἄλλῳ ὠφέλιμον οὐ δοκεῖ σοι ἐνίοτε ἄλλῳ βλαβερὸν εἶναι;—Καὶ μάλα, ἔφη.—Ἄλλο δ' ἄν τι φαίης ἀγαθὸν εἶναι ἢ τὸ ὠφέλιμον;—Οὐκ ἔγωγ', ἔφη.—Τὸ ἄρα ὠφέλιμον ἀγαθόν ἐστιν, ὅτῳ ἂν ὠφέλιμον ᾖ;—Δοκεῖ μοι, ἔφη.

9 Τὸ δὲ καλὸν ἔχοιμεν ἄν πως ἄλλως εἰπεῖν, ἤ, ει ἔστιν, ὀνομάζεις καλὸν ἢ σῶμα ἢ σκεῦος ἢ ἄλλ' ὁτιοῦν,

ὃ οἶσθα πρὸς πάντα καλὸν ὄν;—Μὰ Δί' οὐκ ἔγωγ', ἔφη.—Ἆρ' οὖν, πρὸς ὃ ἂν ἕκαστον χρήσιμον ᾖ, πρὸς τοῦτο ἑκάστῳ καλῶς ἔχει χρῆσθαι;—Πάνυ μὲν οὖν, ἔφη.—Καλὸν δὲ πρὸς ἄλλο τί ἐστιν ἕκαστον, ἢ πρὸς ὃ ἑκάστῳ καλῶς ἔχει χρῆσθαι;—Οὐδὲ πρὸς ἓν ἄλλο, ἔφη.—Τὸ χρήσιμον ἄρα καλόν ἐστι, πρὸς ὃ ἂν ᾖ Χρήσιμον;—Ἔμοιγε δοκεῖ, ἔφη.

Ἀνδρίαν δέ, ὦ Εὐθύδημε, ἆρα τῶν καλῶν νομίζεις 10
εἶναι;—Κάλλιστον μὲν οὖν ἔγωγ', ἔφη.—Χρήσιμον ἄρα οὐ πρὸς τὰ ἐλάχιστα νομίζεις τὴν ἀνδρίαν;—Μὰ Δί', ἔφη, πρὸς τὰ μέγιστα μὲν οὖν.—Ἆρ' οὖν δοκεῖ σοι πρὸς τὰ δεινά τε καὶ ἐπικίνδυνα χρήσιμον εἶναι τὸ ἀγνοεῖν αὐτά;—Ἥκιστά γ', ἔφη.—Οἱ ἄρα μὴ φοβούμενοι τὰ τοιαῦτα διὰ τὸ μὴ εἰδέναι τί ἐστιν οὐκ ἀνδρεῖοί εἰσιν;—Νὴ Δί', ἔφη, πολλοὶ γὰρ ἂν οὕτω γε τῶν τε μαινομένων καὶ τῶν δειλῶν ἀνδρεῖοι εἶεν.—Τί δὲ οἱ καὶ τὰ μὴ δεινὰ δεδοικότες;—Ἔτι γε, νὴ Δία, ἧττον, ἔφη.—Ἆρ' οὖν τοὺς μὲν ἀγαθοὺς πρὸς τὰ δεινὰ καὶ ἐπικίνδυνα ὄντας ἀνδρείους ἡγῇ εἶναι, τοὺς δὲ κακοὺς δειλούς;—Πάνυ μὲν οὖν, ἔφη.
—Ἀγαθοὺς δὲ πρὸς τὰ τοιαῦτα νομίζεις ἄλλους τινὰς 11
ἢ τοὺς δυναμένους αὐτοῖς καλῶς χρῆσθαι;—Οὔκ, ἀλλὰ τούτους, ἔφη.—Κακοὺς δὲ ἄρα τοὺς οἵους τούτοις κακῶς χρῆσθαι;—Τίνας γὰρ ἄλλους; ἔφη.—Ἆρ' οὖν ἕκαστοι χρῶνται, ὡς οἴονται δεῖν;—Πῶς γὰρ ἄλλως; ἔφη.—Ἆρα οὖν οἱ μὴ δυνάμενοι καλῶς χρῆσθαι ἴσασιν, ὡς δεῖ χρῆσθαι;—Οὐ δήπου γε, ἔφη.—Οἱ ἄρα εἰδότες, ὡς δεῖ χρῆσθαι, οὗτοι καὶ δύνανται;—Μόνοι γ', ἔφη.—Τί δέ; οἱ μὴ διημαρτηκότες ἆρα κακῶς χρῶνται τοῖς τοιούτοις;—Οὐκ οἴομαι, ἔφη.—Οἱ ἄρα κακῶς χρώμενοι διημαρτήκασιν;—Εἰκός γ', ἔφη.—Οἱ μὲν ἄρα ἐπιστάμενοι τοῖς δεινοῖς τε καὶ ἐπικινδύνοις καλῶς χρῆσθαι ἀνδρεῖοί εἰσιν, οἱ δὲ διαμαρτάνοντες τούτου δειλοί;—Ἔμοιγε δοκοῦσιν, ἔφη.

12 Βασιλείαν δὲ καὶ τυραννίδα ἀρχὰς μὲν ἀμφοτέρας
ἡγεῖτο εἶναι, διαφέρειν δὲ ἀλλήλων ἐνόμιζε· τὴν μὲν
γὰρ ἑκόντων τε τῶν ἀνθρώπων καὶ κατὰ νόμους τῶν
πόλεων ἀρχὴν βασιλείαν ἡγεῖτο, τὴν δὲ ἀκόντων τε
καὶ μὴ κατὰ νόμους, ἀλλ' ὅπως ὁ ἄρχων βούλοιτο,
τυραννίδα· καὶ ὅπου μὲν ἐκ τῶν τὰ νόμιμα ἐπιτε-
λούντων αἱ ἀρχαὶ καθίστανται, ταύτην τὴν πολιτείαν
ἀριστοκρατίαν ἐνόμιζεν εἶναι, ὅπου δ' ἐκ τιμημάτων,
πλουτοκρατίαν, ὅπου δ' ἐκ πάντων δημοκρατίαν.
13 Εἰ δέ τις αὐτῷ περί του ἀντιλέγοι μηδὲν ἔχων
σαφὲς λέγειν, ἀλλ' ἄνευ ἀποδείξεως ἤτοι σοφώτερον
φάσκων εἶναι ὃν αὐτὸς λέγοι ἢ πολιτικώτερον ἢ ἀν-
δρειότερον ἢ ἄλλο τι τῶν τοιούτων, ἐπὶ τὴν ὑπόθεσιν
14 ἐπανῆγεν ἂν πάντα τὸν λόγον ὧδέ πως· Φῂς σὺ
ἀμείνω πολίτην εἶναι ὃν σὺ ἐπαινεῖς ἢ ὃν ἐγώ;—
Φημὶ γὰρ οὖν.—Τί οὖν οὐκ ἐκεῖνο πρῶτον ἐπεσκεψά-
μεθα, τί ἐστιν ἔργον ἀγαθοῦ πολίτου; — Ποιῶμεν
τοῦτο.—Οὔκουν ἐν μὲν χρημάτων διοικήσει κρατοίη
ἂν ὁ χρήμασιν εὐπορωτέραν ποιῶν τὴν πόλιν;—Πάνυ
μὲν οὖν, ἔφη.—'Εν δέ γε πολέμῳ ὁ καθυπερτέραν
τῶν ἀντιπάλων;—Πῶς γὰρ οὔ;—'Εν δὲ πρεσβείᾳ
ἆρα ὃς ἂν φίλους ἀντὶ πολεμίων παρασκευάζῃ;—
Εἰκότως γε.—Οὔκουν καὶ ἐν δημηγορίᾳ ὁ στάσεις τε
παύων καὶ ὁμόνοιαν ἐμποιῶν;—"Εμοιγε δοκεῖ. Οὕτω
δὲ τῶν λόγων ἐπαναγομένων καὶ τοῖς ἀντιλέγουσιν
15 αὐτοῖς φανερὸν ἐγίγνετο τἀληθές. 'Οπότε δὲ αὐτός
τι τῷ λόγῳ διεξίοι, διὰ τῶν μάλιστα ὁμολογουμένων
ἐπορεύετο, νόμιζων ταύτην τὴν ἀσφάλειαν εἶναι λόγου·
τοιγαροῦν πολὺ μάλιστα ὧν ἐγὼ οἶδα, ὅτε λέγοι, τοὺς
ἀκούοντας ὁμολογοῦντας παρεῖχεν· ἔφη δὲ καὶ Ὅμη-
ρον τῷ 'Οδυσσεῖ ἀναθεῖναι τὸ ἀσφαλῆ ῥήτορα εἶναι,
ὡς ἱκανὸν αὐτὸν ὄντα διὰ τῶν δοκούντων τοῖς ἀνθρώ-
ποις ἄγειν τοὺς λόγους.

CHAPTER VII.

ARGUMENT.

In the preceding chapters Xenophon has exhibited the manner in which Socrates made his disciples, πρακτικούς and διαλεκτικούς; he now proceeds to his influence in making them skilful in the application of every art and science to the uses of life, i. e., μηχανικούς, and thus independent of aid from others. He taught what and how much was useful for them to know of the separate arts and sciences, as of Geometry, Astronomy, and Arithmetic (§ 1—8). He also inculcated special care of health (§ 9); and that those who desired knowledge that was beyond the limits of human investigation should consult the gods by means of divination (§ 10).

It should be taken into the account, in forming a judgment of the contents of this chapter, that Socrates, in his more general instructions to his pupils, has in mind the subtleties and useless speculations of many of the sophists, and wishes in opposition to them to give prominence to the practical in life. This too is the part of his teaching that is especially important, for the accomplishment of Xenophon's design in writing his book, to bring to view. It must not be supposed that Socrates would limit all investigation, to the narrow bounds which he seems to prescribe here, or that he did not with his more gifted pupils, such as Plato and even Xenophon, enter upon far more subtle and elevated themes of discourse.

---

1 Ὅτι μὲν οὖν ἁπλῶς τὴν ἑαυτοῦ γνώμην ἀπεφαίνετο Σωκράτης πρὸς τοὺς ὁμιλοῦντας αὐτῷ, δοκεῖ μοι δῆλον ἐκ τῶν εἰρημένων εἶναι, ὅτι δὲ καὶ αὐτάρκεις ἐν ταῖς προσηκούσαις πράξεσιν αὐτοὺς εἶναι ἐπεμελεῖτο, νῦν τοῦτο λέξω· πάντων μὲν γὰρ ὧν ἐγὼ οἶδα μάλιστα ἔμελεν αὐτῷ εἰδέναι, ὅτου τις ἐπιστήμων εἴη τῶν συνόντων αὐτῷ, ὧν δὲ προσήκει ἀνδρὶ καλῷ κἀγαθῷ εἰδέναι, ὅ τι μὲν αὐτὸς εἰδείη, πάντων προθυμότατα ἐδίδασκεν, ὅτου δὲ αὐτὸς ἀπειρότερος εἴη, πρὸς τοὺς ἐπισταμένους ἦγεν αὐτούς. Ἐδίδασκε δὲ καὶ μέχρι 2

ὅτου δέοι ἔμπειρον εἶναι ἑκάστου πράγματος τὸν ὀρθῶς πεπαιδευμένον· αὐτίκα γεωμετρίαν μέχρι μὲν τούτου ἔφη δεῖν μανθάνειν, ἕως ἱκανός τις γένοιτο, εἴ ποτε δεήσειε, γῆν μέτρῳ ὀρθῶς ἢ παραλαβεῖν ἢ παραδοῦναι ἢ διανεῖμαι, ἢ ἔργον ἀποδείξασθαι· οὕτω δὲ τοῦτο ῥᾴδιον εἶναι μαθεῖν, ὥστε τὸν προσέχοντα τὸν νοῦν τῇ μετρήσει ἅμα τήν τε γῆν ὁπόση ἐστὶν εἰδέναι, καὶ ὡς
3 μετρεῖται ἐπιστάμενον ἀπιέναι. Τὸ δὲ μέχρι τῶν δυσξυνέτων διαγραμμάτων γεωμετρίαν μανθάνειν ἀπεδοκίμαζεν· ὅ τι μὲν γὰρ ὠφελοίη ταῦτα, οὐκ ἔφη ὁρᾶν· καίτοι οὐκ ἄπειρός γε αὐτῶν ἦν· ἔφη δὲ ταῦτα ἱκανὰ εἶναι ἀνθρώπου βίον κατατρίβειν, καὶ ἄλλων πολλῶν
4 τε καὶ ὠφελίμων μαθημάτων ἀποκωλύειν. Ἐκέλευε δὲ καὶ ἀστρολογίας ἐμπείρους γίγνεσθαι, καὶ ταύτης μέντοι μέχρι τοῦ νυκτός τε ὥραν καὶ μηνὸς καὶ ἐνιαυτοῦ δύνασθαι γιγνώσκειν ἕνεκα πορείας τε καὶ πλοῦ κα φυλακῆς, καὶ ὅσα ἄλλα ἢ νυκτός, ἢ μηνός, ἢ ἐνιαυτοῦ πράττεται, πρὸς ταῦτ᾽ ἔχειν τεκμηρίοις χρῆσθαι, τὰς ὥρας τῶν εἰρημένων διαγιγνώσκοντας· καὶ ταῦτα δὲ ῥᾴδια εἶναι μαθεῖν παρά τε [τῶν] νυκτοθηρῶν καὶ κυβερνητῶν καὶ ἄλλων πολλῶν, οἷς ἐπιμελὲς ταῦτα
5 εἰδέναι. Τὸ δὲ μέχρι τούτου ἀστρονομίαν μανθάνειν, μέχρι τοῦ καὶ τὰ μὴ ἐν τῇ αὐτῇ περιφορᾷ ὄντα καὶ τοὺς πλάνητάς τε καὶ ἀσταθμήτους ἀστέρας γνῶναι, καὶ τὰς ἀποστάσεις αὐτῶν ἀπὸ τῆς γῆς καὶ τὰς περιόδους καὶ τὰς αἰτίας αὐτῶν ζητοῦντας κατατρίβεσθαι, ἰσχυρῶς ἀπέτρεπεν· ὠφέλειαν μὲν γὰρ οὐδεμίαν οὐδ᾽ ἐν τούτοις ἔφη ὁρᾶν· καίτοι οὐδὲ τούτων γε ἀνήκοος ἦν· ἔφη δὲ καὶ ταῦτα ἱκανὰ εἶναι κατατρίβειν ἀνθρώπου βίον, καὶ πολλῶν καὶ ὠφελίμων ἀποκωλύειν.
6 Ὅλως δὲ τῶν οὐρανίων, ᾗ ἕκαστα ὁ θεὸς μηχανᾶται, φροντιστὴν γίγνεσθαι ἀπέτρεπεν· οὔτε γὰρ εὑρετὰ ἀνθρώποις αὐτὰ ἐνόμιζεν εἶναι, οὔτε χαρίζεσθαι θεοῖς ἂν ἡγεῖτο τὸν ζητοῦντα ἃ ἐκεῖνοι σαφηνίσαι οὐκ ἐβου-

λήθησαν· κινδυνεῦσαι δ᾽ ἂν ἔφη καὶ παραφρονῆσαι τὸν ταῦτα μεριμνῶντα, οὐδὲν ἧττον ἢ Ἀναξαγόρας παρεφρόνησεν, ὁ μέγιστον φρονήσας ἐπὶ τῷ τὰς τῶν θεῶν μηχανὰς ἐξηγεῖσθαι. Ἐκεῖνος γὰρ λέγων μὲν 7
τὸ αὐτὸ εἶναι πῦρ τε καὶ ἥλιον ἠγνόει, ὡς τὸ μὲν πῦρ οἱ ἄνθρωποι ῥᾳδίως καθορῶσιν, εἰς δὲ τὸν ἥλιον οὐ δύνανται ἀντιβλέπειν· καὶ ὑπὸ μὲν τοῦ ἡλίου καταλαμπόμενοι τὰ χρώματα μελάντερα ἔχουσιν, ὑπὸ δὲ τοῦ πυρὸς οὔ· ἠγνόει δὲ, ὅτι καὶ τῶν ἐκ τῆς γῆς φυομένων ἄνευ μὲν ἡλίου αὐγῆς οὐδὲν δύναται καλῶς αὔξεσθαι, ὑπὸ δὲ τοῦ πυρὸς θερμαινόμενα πάντα ἀπόλλυται· φάσκων δὲ τὸν ἥλιον λίθον διάπυρον εἶναι καὶ τοῦτο ἠγνόει, ὅτι λίθος μὲν ἐν πυρὶ ὢν οὔτε λάμπει, οὔτε πολὺν χρόνον ἀντέχει, ὁ δὲ ἥλιος τὸν πάντα χρόνον πάντων λαμπρότατος ὢν διαμένει.
Ἐκέλευε δὲ καὶ λογισμοὺς μανθάνειν, καὶ τούτων δὲ 8
ὁμοίως τοῖς ἄλλοις ἐκέλευε φυλάττεσθαι τὴν μάταιον πραγματείαν, μέχρι δὲ τοῦ ὠφελίμου πάντα καὶ αὐτὸς συνεπεσκόπει καὶ συνδιεξῄει τοῖς συνοῦσι. Προέτρεπε 9
δὲ σφόδρα καὶ ὑγιείας ἐπιμελεῖσθαι τοὺς συνόντας, παρά τε τῶν εἰδότων μανθάνοντας ὅσα ἐνδέχοιτο, καὶ ἑαυτῷ ἕκαστον προσέχοντα διὰ παντὸς τοῦ βίου, τί βρῶμα ἢ τί πόμα ἢ ποῖος πόνος συμφέροι αὐτῷ, καὶ πῶς τούτοις χρώμενος ὑγιεινότατ᾽ ἂν διάγοι· τοῦ γὰρ οὕτω προσέχοντος ἑαυτῷ ἔργον ἔφη εἶναι εὑρεῖν ἰατρὸν τὰ πρὸς ὑγίειαν συμφέροντα αὐτῷ μᾶλλον διαγιγνώσκοντα ἑαυτοῦ. Εἰ δέ τις μᾶλλον ἢ κατὰ τὴν ἀνθρω- 10
πίνην σοφίαν ὠφελεῖσθαι βούλοιτο, συνεβούλευε μαντικῆς ἐπιμελεῖσθαι· τὸν γὰρ εἰδότα, δι᾽ ὧν οἱ θεοὶ τοῖς ἀνθρώποις περὶ τῶν πραγμάτων σημαίνουσιν, οὐδέποτ᾽ ἔρημον ἔφη γίγνεσθαι συμβουλῆς θεῶν.

CHAPTER VIII.

ARGUMENT.

The last section of the preceding chapter furnishes a transition to the subject of the last and closing chapter of these Reminiscences of the Life and Death of Socrates. This chapter is fitly occupied with the closing scenes of his mortal life. It might be objected that the *δαιμόνιον*, in which the philosopher so confidently trusted during his life, forsook him in his last hours, since he suffered a violent death. But not so thought the philosopher or his pupil. His death rather showed the especial regard of the gods for him; since, first, he thus escaped the evils of old age which were fast coming upon him; and, secondly, in his trial and during the thirty days that intervened between it and his death, he exhibited a magnanimity and cheerfulness, which obtained for him immortal honor (§ 3). In proof of this Xenophon adduces a conversation which he held with Hermogenes after his condemnation. The leading thoughts in it are as follows:

Socrates replies to Hermogenes' entreaty that he will take into consideration the defence that he is to make, that his whole life, passed in the exercise of virtue, is his best defence. The fear of the injustice of the judges does not influence him, since his guiding genius dissuades him from making a defence; for if he should continue to live, he might be deprived of his powers of improvement and usefulness by age, and die with less honor than now (§ 5—8). The disgrace of an unjust condemnation would fall upon his judges, not upon himself; he should rather be held in grateful remembrance, since he had not only not done evil to men, but had always exerted himself for their improvement (§ 9, 10).

Xenophon concludes the chapter and his work, by an allusion to the regard felt for Socrates by all virtuous persons who knew him, and by a brief recapitulation of the qualities on which his own admiration, reverence, and esteem were based, and on account of, and by means of which, he had endeavored to commend him to others (§ 11).

---

1 Εἰ δέ τις, ὅτι φάσκοντος αὐτοῦ τὸ δαιμόνιον ἑαυτῷ προσημαίνειν, ἅ τε δέοι καὶ ἃ μὴ δέοι ποιεῖν, ὑπὸ τῶν δικαστῶν κατεγνώσθη θάνατος, οἴεται αὐτὸν ἐλέγχε

σθαι περὶ τοῦ δαιμονίου ψευδόμενον, ἐννοησάτω πρῶτον μὲν, ὅτι οὕτως ἤδε τότε πόῤῥω τῆς ἡλικίας ἦν, ὥςτ', εἰ καὶ μὴ τότε, οὐκ ἂν πολλῷ ὕστερον τελευτῆσαι τὸν βίον, εἶτα ὅτι τὸ μὲν ἀχθεινότατον τοῦ βίου καὶ ἐν ᾧ πάντες τὴν διάνοιαν μειοῦνται ἀπέλειπεν, ἀντὶ δὲ τούτου τῆς ψυχῆς τὴν ῥώμην ἐπιδειξάμενος εὔκλειαν προςεκτήσατο, τήν τε δίκην πάντων ἀνθρώπων ἀληθέστατα καὶ ἐλευθεριώτατα καὶ δικαιότατα εἰπὼν, καὶ τὴν κατάγνωσιν τοῦ θανάτου πρᾳότατα καὶ
ἀνδρωδέστατα ἐνεγκών. Ὁμολογεῖται γὰρ οὐδένα πω 2
τῶν μνημονευομένων ἀνθρώπων κάλλιον θάνατον ἐνεγκεῖν· ἀνάγκη μὲν γὰρ ἐγένετο αὐτῷ μετὰ τὴν κρίσιν τριάκοντα ἡμέρας βιῶναι διὰ τὸ Δήλια μὲν ἐκείνου τοῦ μηνὸς εἶναι, τὸν δὲ νόμον μηδένα ἐᾶν δημοσίᾳ ἀποθνήσκειν, ἕως ἂν ἡ θεωρία ἐκ Δήλου ἐπανέλθῃ· καὶ τὸν χρόνον τοῦτον ἅπασι τοῖς συνήθεσι φανερὸς ἐγένετο οὐδὲν ἀλλοιότερον διαβιοὺς ἢ τὸν ἔμπροσθεν χρόνον· καίτοι τὸν ἔμπροσθέν γε πάντων ἀνθρώπων μάλιστα
ἐθαυμάζετο ἐπὶ τῷ εὐθύμως τε καὶ εὐκόλως ζῆν. Καὶ 3
πῶς ἄν τις κάλλιον ἢ οὕτως ἀποθάνοι; ἢ ποῖος ἂν εἴη θάνατος καλλίων ἢ ὃν ἂν κάλλιστά τις ἀποθάνοι; ποῖος δ' ἂν γένοιτο θάνατος εὐδαιμονέστερος τοῦ καλλίστου; ἢ ποῖος θεοφιλέστερος τοῦ εὐδαιμονεστάτου;
Λέξω δὲ καὶ ἃ Ἑρμογένους τοῦ Ἱππονίκου ἤκουσα 4
περὶ αὐτοῦ· ἔφη γάρ, ἤδη Μελήτου γεγραμμένου αὐτὸν τὴν γραφήν, αὐτὸς ἀκούων αὐτοῦ πάντα μᾶλλον ἢ περὶ τῆς δίκης διαλεγομένου λέγειν αὐτῷ, ὡς χρὴ σκοπεῖν ὅ τι ἀπολογήσεται, τὸν δὲ τὸ μὲν πρῶτον εἰπεῖν· Οὐ γὰρ δοκῶ σοι τοῦτο μελετῶν διαβεβιωκέναι; ἐπεὶ δὲ αὐτὸν ἤρετο, ὅπως; εἰπεῖν αὐτὸν, ὅτι οὐδὲν ἄλλο ποιῶν διαγεγένηται ἢ διασκοπῶν μὲν τά τε δίκαια καὶ τὰ ἄδικα, πράττων δὲ τὰ δίκαια καὶ τῶν ἀδίκων ἀπεχόμενος, ἥνπερ νομίζοι καλλίστην μελέτην ἀπολογίας
εἶναι. Αὐτὸς δὲ πάλιν εἰπεῖν· Οὐχ ὁρᾷς, ὦ Σώκρατες, 5

ὅτι οἱ Ἀθήνησι δικασταὶ πολλοὺς μὲν ἤδη μηδὲν ἀδικοῦντας λόγῳ παραχθέντες, ἀπέκτειναν, πολλοὺς δὲ ἀδικοῦντας ἀπέλυσαν; Ἀλλὰ νὴ τὸν Δία, φάναι αὐτόν, ὦ Ἑρμόγενες, ἤδη μου ἐπιχειροῦντος φροντίσαι τῆς πρὸς τοὺς δικαστὰς ἀπολογίας, ἠναντιώθη τὸ δαι-
6 μόνιον. Καὶ αὐτὸς εἰπεῖν· Θαυμαστὰ λέγεις· τὸν δέ· Θαυμάζεις, φάναι, εἰ τῷ θεῷ δοκεῖ βέλτιον εἶναι ἐμὲ τελευτᾶν τὸν βίον ἤδη; οὐκ οἶσθ', ὅτι μέχρι μὲν τοῦδε τοῦ χρόνου ἐγὼ οὐδενὶ ἀνθρώπων ὑφείμην ἂν οὔτε βέλτιον οὔθ' ἥδιον ἐμοῦ βεβιωκέναι; ἄριστα μὲν γὰρ οἶμαι ζῆν τοὺς ἄριστα ἐπιμελομένους τοῦ ὡς βελτίστους γίγνεσθαι, ἥδιστα δὲ τοὺς μάλιστα αἰσθανο-
7 μένους, ὅτι βελτίους γίγνονται. Ἃ ἐγὼ μέχρι τοῦδε τοῦ χρόνου ᾐσθανόμην ἐμαυτῷ συμβαίνοντα, καὶ τοῖς ἄλλοις ἀνθρώποις ἐντυγχάνων καὶ πρὸς τοὺς ἄλλους παραθεωρῶν ἐμαυτὸν οὕτω διατετέλεκα περὶ ἐμαυτοῦ γιγνώσκων· καὶ οὐ μόνον ἐγώ, ἀλλὰ καὶ οἱ ἐμοὶ φίλοι οὕτως ἔχοντες περὶ ἐμοῦ διατελοῦσιν, οὐ διὰ τὸ φιλεῖν ἐμέ, καὶ γὰρ οἱ τοὺς ἄλλους φιλοῦντες οὕτως ἂν εἶχον πρὸς τοὺς ἑαυτῶν φίλους, ἀλλὰ διόπερ καὶ αὐτοὶ ἂν
8 οἴονται ἐμοὶ συνόντες βέλτιστοι γίγνεσθαι. Εἰ δὲ βιώσομαι πλείω χρόνον, ἴσως ἀναγκαῖον ἔσται τὰ τοῦ γήρως ἐπιτελεῖσθαι, καὶ ὁρᾶν τε καὶ ἀκούειν ἧττον, καὶ διανοεῖσθαι χεῖρον, καὶ δυσμαθέστερον καὶ ἐπιλησμονέστερον ἀποβαίνειν, καὶ ὧν πρότερον βελτίων ἦν, τούτων χείρω γίγνεσθαι· ἀλλὰ μὴν ταῦτά γε μὴ αἰσθανομένῳ μὲν ἀβίωτος ἂν εἴη ὁ βίος, αἰσθανόμενον δὲ πῶς οὐκ ἀνάγκη χεῖρόν τε καὶ ἀηδέστερον ζῆν;
9 Ἀλλὰ μὴν εἴ γε ἀδίκως ἀποθανοῦμαι, τοῖς μὲν ἀδίκως ἐμὲ ἀποκτείνασιν αἰσχρὸν ἂν εἴη τοῦτο· εἰ γὰρ τὸ ἀδικεῖν αἰσχρόν ἐστι, πῶς οὐκ αἰσχρὸν καὶ τὸ ἀδίκως ὁτιοῦν ποιεῖν; ἐμοὶ δὲ τί αἰσχρὸν τὸ ἑτέρους μὴ δύνασθαι περὶ ἐμοῦ τὰ δίκαια μήτε γνῶναι μήτε ποιῆσαι;
10 Ὁρῶ δ' ἔγωγε καὶ τὴν δόξαν τῶν προγεγονότων ἀνθρώ-

πων ἐν τοῖς ἐπιγιγνομένοις οὐχ ὁμοίαν καταλειπομένην τῶν τε ἀδικησάντων καὶ τῶν ἀδικηθέντων· οἶδα δὲ, ὅτι καὶ ἐγὼ ἐπιμελείας τεύξομαι ὑπ' ἀνθρώπων, καὶ ἐὰν νῦν ἀποθάνω, οὐχ ὁμοίως τοῖς ἐμὲ ἀποκτείνασιν· οἶδα γὰρ ἀεὶ μαρτυρήσεσθαί μοι, ὅτι ἐγὼ ἠδίκησα μὲν οὐδένα πώποτε ἀνθρώπων, οὐδὲ χείρω ἐποίησα, βελτίους δὲ ποιεῖν ἐπειρώμην ἀεὶ τοὺς ἐμοὶ συνόντας. Τοιαῦτα μὲν πρὸς Ἑρμογένην τε διελέχθη καὶ πρὸς τοὺς ἄλ-
λους. Τῶν δὲ Σωκράτην γιγνωσκόντων, οἷος ἦν, οἱ 11
ἀρετῆς ἐφιέμενοι πάντες ἔτι καὶ νῦν διατελοῦσι πάντων μάλιστα ποθοῦντες ἐκεῖνον, ὡς ὠφελιμώτατον ὄντα πρὸς ἀρετῆς ἐπιμέλειαν. Ἐμοὶ μὲν δὴ τοιοῦτος ὢν, οἷον ἐγὼ διήγημαι, εὐσεβὴς μὲν οὕτως, ὥστε μηδὲν ἄνευ τῆς τῶν θεῶν γνώμης ποιεῖν, δίκαιος δὲ, ὥςτε βλάπτειν μὲν μηδὲ μικρὸν μηδένα, ὠφελεῖν δὲ τὰ μέγιστα τοὺς χρωμένους αὐτῷ, ἐγκρατὴς δὲ, ὥςτε μηδέποτε προαιρεῖσθαι τὸ ἥδιον ἀντὶ τοῦ βελτίονος, φρόνιμος δὲ, ὥςτε μὴ διαμαρτάνειν κρίνων τὰ βελτίω καὶ τὰ χείρω, μηδὲ ἄλλου προςδέεσθαι, ἀλλ' αὐτάρκης εἶναι πρὸς τὴν τούτων γνῶσιν, ἱκανὸς δὲ καὶ λόγῳ εἰπεῖν τε καὶ διορίσασθαι τὰ τοιαῦτα, ἱκανὸς δὲ καὶ ἄλλους δοκιμάσαι τε καὶ ἁμαρτάνοντας ἐξελέγξαι καὶ προτρέψασθαι ἐπ' ἀρετὴν καὶ καλοκἀγαθίαν, ἐδόκει τοιοῦτος εἶναι, οἷος ἂν εἴη ἄριστός τε ἀνὴρ καὶ εὐδαιμονέστατος· εἰ δέ τῳ μὴ ἀρέσκει ταῦτα, παραβάλλων τὸ ἄλλων ἦθος πρὸς ταῦτα οὕτω κρινέτω.

NOTES.

NOTES.

ΞΕΝΟΦΩΝΤΟΣ ΑΠΟΜΝΗΜΟΝΕΥΜΑΤΩΝ: *ἀπομνημονεύματα*, from *ἀπομνημονεύειν*, things related from memory. It is not, however, restricted to that which fell under the author's own observation, but includes also particulars which he received from other witnesses. The Latin term Memorabilia, things memorable or worthy to be remembered, although it does not correspond precisely to the Greek word, is a very good designation of the contents of these Books, and as such is very commonly used in English. We not unfrequently affix the termination *ana* to proper names to designate much the same thing; as Johnsoniana, the memorable sayings of Johnson. Aulus Gellius (N. H. XIV. 3.) called these books: Libros quos dictorum atque factorum Socratis commentarios composuit Xenophon. And some modern editors, as Kühner, retain Commentarii as the most fitting title of the work. Cicero de Nat. Deor. I. 12, refers to Xenophon in iis, quae a Socrate dicta retulit.

Instead of *ἀπομνημονευμάτων*, two Mss. Victorii have *ὑπομνήματα*; and one, Parisiensis F. has *ἐκ τῶν τοῦ Ξενοφῶντος ὑπομνημονευμάτων*, i. e., memoranda, things written down in order that they may be remembered. This name does not seem to apply so well to the contents of a work which consists not merely of hasty sketches, but in many parts exhibits signs of elaboration; still the two words *ἀπομνημονεύματα* and *ὑπομνήματα* may have been used, even in ancient times, as nearly synonymous. Thus *ὑπομνήματα* seems to be used like *ἀπομνημονεύματα* in Polybius 1. 1. 1., 6. 32. 4 et al.

BOOK I.

CHAPTER I.

1.—Πολλάκις ἐθαύμασα, τίσι . . . λόγοις; the interrogative *τίσι* instead of *οἷστισι*. Thus in Laced. Rep. I. 1, we find the compound *ὅστις*: *ἐθαύμασα, ὅτῳ ποτὲ τρόπῳ τοῦτ' ἐγένετο*; Apol. 11, and § 20 below;

but in IV. 2. 6: θαυμαστὸν ... τί ποτε ... πειρῶνται, the simple pronoun τί. In indirect questions the simple interrogatives τίς, ποῖος, πότερος, πῶς, etc., are somewhat often (Buttmann, 139. m. 63, says rather strongly, "just as often") employed instead of the compounds ὅστις, ὁποῖος, ὁπότερος, ὅπως, giving the phrase in a degree the force of a direct question. See Kühn. Gr. § 344, 3. R. 1; El. Gr. § 187. (9) R. 2. Sometimes both classes of words are used in the same sentence. See Plat. Gorg. p. 448. E. For the use of the modes in indirect interrogations, see Kühn. Gr. § 344. 6; B. 139. H. —— ποτέ is often added to interrogative pronouns to indicate the desire for an answer, or astonishment or wonder; see Kühn. Gr. § 344. R. 2. Comp. § 2 and note upon it in § 20; III. 14. 2; IV. 2. 6. For the similar use of tandem in Latin to denote impatience for an answer to a question, see Zumpt's Lat. Gr. § 287. —— λόγοις, *arguments.* —— οἱ γραψάμενοι Σωκράτην. The Mid. Voice here indicates causation: Those who caused his name to be written down, i. e., *the accusers of Socrates.* Kühn. Gr. 250. R. 2. Crosby, 559. d. So in Plat. Apol. Socr. p. 41. D.: διὰ τοῦτο ... ἔγωγε καταψηφισαμένοις μου ... οὐ πάνυ χαλεπαίνω, the participle is used, followed however by the genitive. Cicero, in Tusc. Disp. 1. 41. 99, also employs a similar phrase: Ii, a quibus accusatus sum. But accusator is sometimes used in Latin.—Socrates in his Apology speaks of two classes of accusers: those who had long been his enemies, many of whom, "setting a comedian [Aristophanes] at the head of the charge," themselves remained in concealment. The principal points of this first accusation, he says, may be found in the Comedy (the Clouds) of Aristophanes. See v. 248 sq. Those most active in the last trial (Apol. Socr. p. 23. B.), were Melitus, a man of rank and wealth, and author of poor tragedies (Aristoph. Ranae. v. 1302 sq. and also Stallb. Plato, Apol. Socr. 23. B.), Anytus, a tanner (Xenophon, Apol. § 29), and Lycon an orator (Aristoph. Vesp. 1301). Thus it is said: "Melitus stands by the poets, Anytus represents the politicians and tradesmen, and Lycon appears for the orators." The part that each took is more definitely stated by Max. Tyr., Diss. 9. 2: Σωκράτην Μέλιτος μὲν ἐγράψατο, Ἄνυτος δὲ εἰσήγαγε, Λύκων δὲ ἐδίωκε, κ.τ.λ., cf. Brandis' Gesch. Gr. u. Rom. Philosophy, Vol. II. p. 28 sq. The trial took place in the large court, called Ἡλιαία; concerning which see Potter's Gr. Antiquities I. p. 123; Fiske's Man. of Class. Lit. p. 185. —— ὡς ἄξιος εἴη θανάτου τῇ πόλει, *that Socrates was worthy of death in respect to the State.* For ὡς, see note 2 below. In some phrases, and especially after ὡς, the Dative denotes the person *in whose judgment*, or in whose view a thing is; here more definitely, *from the State*, as it respects the State. See B. 133. 7. Kühn. Gr. § 284. (10) b.; L. Gr. II. 581. *e.*, and Rost 105, p. 501. Cf.

I. 2. 62, 63; II. 5. 1. The Optat. mode, εἴη, with ὡς after the Aor. Tense, ἔπεισα, in the final clause here is used instead of the Subj., to indicate that this was merely a persuasion of others, not believed by the writer; see Kühn. Gr. § 330. 2, and R. 2. (a).

Ἡ μέν. The particle μέν is usually followed by δέ or an equivalent word, and calls the attention to a distinction that is to be made between the clause in which it stands and the succeeding one. But the following adversative particle, and even the whole antithetic clause, may be omitted, as here, and be merely supplied by the mind; μέν is then called solitarium. See Kühn. Gr. § 322. R. 4; L. Gr. § 734. 2. Rost. § 134. Plato, Phaed. 58. A., and Stallbaum's note in h. l. Homer often omits the adversative clause after μὲν γάρ; e. g. Il. V. 901. Cf. also note, I. 2. 62: ἐμοὶ μὲν, κ.τ.λ.; I. 5. 5; II. 6. 1, 3, 5; III. 12. 1, and Hackett's Plut. De Sera, etc. p. 120. —— γραφή; an Attic law-term for an indictment for a public offence, and hence opposed to δική a private action. It is, however, as well as γράφεσθαι, sometimes used in reference to private accusations. For the occasions on which the γραφή was used, see Meier and Schömann, Att. Process S. 198 sq. and Fiske's Man. p. 186, and also the word γραφή in the Index of Meier and Schömann. —— τοιάδε τις ἦν, *was for substance this*, Lat. haec fere; so τίς is frequently used with pronouns and numerals to give indefiniteness to the assertion. Kühn. Gr. 303. 4; L. Gr. II. § 638. 5. Crosby 517. Cf. II. 6. 11. Bornemann, Cyrop. II. 1. 2. and ὧδέ πως II. 1. 21 below.

Ἀδικεῖ Σωκράτης οὓς μὲν . . . ἕτερα δὲ καινὰ δαιμόνια εἰσφέρων. Μέν is here, as commonly, followed by δέ, introducing the counterpart of the declaration with μέν. It has been stated that the latter particle is sometimes omitted. Μέν too is frequently omitted in poetry and sometimes in prose; cf. II. 2. 8. and 6. 22. Cyropaed. IV, 3, 21: πολλὰ γάρ φασι καὶ ἵππον ἀνθρώποις τοῖς ὀφθαλμοῖς προορῶντα δηλοῦν, πολλὰ δὲ τοῖς ὠσὶ προακούοντα σημαίνειν. So especially where the corresponding clauses are far separated, as in I. 2. 21. In III. 13. 5. both particles are omitted. The position here, after the words contrasted, is the most common, though the particles frequently qualify the predicate or the whole clause, and then take a different position; Kühner Gr. 322, R. 2. For unusual positions of these particles, see also note, § 12. —— It should be noticed that in order to make good English the μὲν . . . δὲ must be rendered variously. Frequently the force of μέν is given merely by the tone of voice or emphasis, and sometimes the δέ is best translated by *while*, and both particles, by *both . . . and*, *whilst . . . yet*, etc. Either distinction and distribution may be indicated by these particles, or simple connection, relation; see B. 149. 11–13. —— νομίζει οὓς . . . οὐ νομίζων, κ.τ.λ., in not reverencing those, etc. The participle here introduces a clause indicative of way or manner; so εἰσφέρων and διαφθείρων; see Kühn. Gr. § 312. (e). The Latin would take a more specific form injuste agit Socrates, quod deos non ducit, etc. The participle may be said to have been a favorite part of speech with the Greeks, and the beautiful conciseness which its use often gave to a sentence, and the varied shades of idea which it so briefly designates, may well be considered a sufficient justification of this partiality. Νομίζειν θεούς, means, to believe in the gods, to honor as gods, colere deos, although even without the article it may sometimes signify, to believe in the existence of gods, deos esse credere, for which ἡγεῖσθαι θεούς is the more usual phrase. Hence οἱ νενομισμένοι θεοί, the gods which are publicly received and worshipped, and in § 3 μαντικὴν νομίζειν, to put confidence in, to practise divination. It is used in a somewhat similar manner in the phrase: βίον or τέχνην νομίζειν, as in Aesch., Choeph. 994 (1003): ἀργυροστερῆ βίον νομίζων, leading a robber's life. For the meaning of δαιμόνια, deities, Lat. dii, see the Introduction. —— ἀδικεῖ δὲ καί, the repetition of ἀδικεῖ here instead of a mere connection by particles *both . . . and*, cum . . . tum, is perhaps an imitation of the fulness and definiteness of the style in judicial proceedings. Anaphora, however, is oftener employed in Greek than in Latin where some rhetorical effect seems generally to be indicated by it. See πολλάκις μεν . . . πολλάκις δέ in § 2.

2.—Πρῶτον μὲν, introduces the first part of the accusation, namely, that of impiety, and δέ in chap. II. 1, without any word answering to πρῶτον, introducing the second accusation, may be considered as corresponding with it. —— οὖν is perhaps derived from the neut. part. ἐόν, ὄν of the verb εἶναι, and hence refers to the present (being) state of things, hence = *thus, so*, and in general marks a sequence or dependence of the thought on what has gone before; and then, a necessary consequence or deduction, Latin ergo or igitur. It is related to ἄρα in meaning, but has a wider range, and frequently denotes a *strong* conclusive force, which is not indicated by that particle. It here denotes the transition from the statement of the subject of discourse, to the examination of it, Lat. igitur, *then;* see Kühn. Gr. § 324. 3 (b). Hartung, Gr. Partik. II. 18 sq. Arn. 2 Gr. Pr. Com. Ch. 44. —— ὡς is frequently used especially after *verba sentiendi et declarandi* with much the same significance as ὅτι, but perhaps the manner, the *how*, may be generally hinted at when ὡς is used, but the mere fact when ὅτι is employed; cf. just below: ὡς φαίη and see Lewis, Plat. Contr. Ath. p. 3. —— ποίῳ ποτ'; the force of ποτέ may be given here by *possible, what possible*, etc., see note upon τίσι ποτέ § 1, above, and § 20 below —— θύων τε; to this τέ the καί with μαντικῇ corresponds. The connection by τέ ... καί, *both .. and, not only ... but also,* or simply, *and,* with the last clause, is employed where two ideas are to be brought together as one whole, the second being *generally,* not always, the more important, and hence receiving the stronger particle, καί. The connection by καί ... καί, on the other hand, is used where two distinct particulars are brought together. See Kühn. Gr. § 321. I. 1. (a). —— πολλάκις μὲν ... πολλάκις δὲ; the correlative particles μὲν ... δέ as above § 1; and πολλάκις is perhaps repeated for the sake of emphasis; cf. note upon ἀδίκει, § 1. —— οἴκοι; i. e., ἐν τῇ αὐλῇ. The αὐλή was the open space, or court, around which the house was built, in which was placed the altar for private and domestic sacrifices. See Becker's Charikles, p. 202; Wachsmuth, Hellen. Alterthumskunde II. S. 415 sq.; Plato, De Repub. 328. C. So among the Romans it was in the compluvium. —— μαντικῇ, *divination,* divinatio or vaticinia, and μαντικῇ χρώμενος, supplying one's own need with, *using divination,* whilst χράω in the Act. Voice means, to give the needful answer. —— διετεθρύλητο γὰρ, it was very commonly reported, pervulgatum erat. Γάρ introduces a proof that he made use of divination. On the subject of divination among the Greeks, see Fiske's Manual and Wachsmuth, Hellen. Alterthumskunde, II. § 136. —— ἑαυτῷ σημαίνειν. In 4 below προσημαίνειν is used, as there is in that place direct reference to making known *future* events, while here only the fact of a revelation or disclosure is brought into view. —— φαίη; optative in oratio obliqua; see Kühn. § 345. 4. and 330. 2. In general, not always, in dependent clauses, the Opt. is used after the Histor., and the Subj. after the Primary tenses. —— τὸ δαιμόνιον; see Introduction. —— ὅθεν δὴ καὶ μάλιστά; from which very thing (ὅθεν δή) they seem most especially (καὶ μάλ.) to have accused him, etc. Δή here qualifies the particle ὅθεν and gives it definiteness and force; see Kühn. Gr. § 315. 2. Καὶ strengthens the superlative adj. μάλιστα; see Kühn. Gr. § 239. 1. R. 1. —— αὐτὸν αἰτιάσασθαι ... εἰσφέρειν. Αἰτιάσασθαι. The verb αἰτιάομαι is generally, like other verbs of kindred signification, followed by the Accus. of the person and Gen. (sometimes the Accus.) of the thing, but here by the Accus. with the Inf. So also in II. 7. 12.

3.—Οὐδὲν καινότερον εἰσέφερε τῶν ἄλλων; for this compendious comparison so common in Greek, by which the attribute of one object is compared with the other object itself, see Kühn. Gr. § 323. R. 6, and Felton's Note, Hom. Il. I. 163. —— μαντικὴν νομίζοντες, see note, § 1. —— φήμαις καὶ συμβόλοις καὶ θυσίαις. Φῆμαι are omens taken from the words of men. Cicero de Divin. I. 45. 102: seque solum deorum voces Pythagorei observitaverunt, sed etiam hominum quae vocant omina; Eustath., Il. κ. p. 799: φήμη οὐ τὴν ἁπλῶς ἀνθρωπίνην δηλοῖ λαλιάν, ἀλλά τινα θειοτέραν, δηλωτικὴν τοῦ μέλλοντος Xen. Apol. 12. Σύμβολα are various occurrences from which things concealed and future were supposed to be known; as thunder, lightning, the casual meeting of men (οἱ ἀπαντῶντες), and other things of the like kind. Θυσίαι, extispiscia, the examination of the entrails, the *exta*, of victims, which was performed by the ἱεροσκόπος, the Haruspex. Cf. the Prometheus 484—500, where Prom. enumerates the different kinds of divination which he had taught man.—— οὗτοί τε ... κἀκεῖνος δέ. Τε here stands related to καί in κἀκεῖνος, and contrasts οὗτοί with -κεῖνος. Καί ... δὲ like the Latin, et ... et vero, or et vero etiam, or atque etiam. The δὲ here connects, *and*, and καί means *also*. See B. 149. 10. Its position after καί with one or more words between is common in Attic Greek; see Xen. Anab. 2. 6. 8; 2. 6. below, etc. This position in Tragedy has been denied. But see Aesch. Prom. 975 and Wellauer's note upon it; and Kühn. Gr. 321. I. 1. (c). The use of the particles καὶ ... δέ in this way is quite frequent in Xenophon; cf. I. 2. 11, 62; 3. 2; II. 1. 20, 21 et al.; more rare in Thucyd. or Plato. In like manner relative enunciations are connected by καὶ ... δέ to what precedes, as in I. 1. 15: καὶ ἀνέμους καὶ ὕδατα καὶ ὥρας καὶ ὅτου δ' ἂν ἄλλου δέωνται, Sympos. II. 9. Cf. Kühn. Gr. § 322. R. 7; L. Gr. 737. 2; Rost, § 134; Hartung Gr. Partik. I. p. 181 sq., and for the difference between the significance of καὶ δέ and δὲ καί, Hoogeveen, p. 118. XXII. —— τοὺς ἀπαντῶντας, with ἀνθρώπους implied, the ἐνοδίους συμβόλους of Aeschylus Prom. 488.

4.—Ἀλλ' οἱ μὲν πλεῖστοί. Σωκράτης δέ. Ἀλλά (from the pron. ἄλλος, other, another) denotes naturally difference, separation, restriction, change, etc. It is very frequent in transitions from one subject to another, especially in colloquies, in quick answers or objections. Upon its origin and different significations, see Hartung Gr. Partik. II. 30 sq. Kühn. Gr. § 322. 6 and L. Gr. II. § 741, and Anm. 1, 2, 3. It here merely limits or restricts the meaning of the preceding affirmation, ὁ δ' οὐδὲν καινότερον εἰσέφερε, κ.τ.λ.: *yet* or *however* the multitude, etc. See Kühn. Gr. § 322. 6.—For the position and force of μὲν (whilst) ... δὲ, see note § 1. —— οἱ πλεῖστοι, the many, the multitude, Lat. plerique or vulgus. —— ἀποτρέπεσθαι ... προτρέπεσθαι, deterreri or revocari ... impelli, to dissuade from, or hinder, ... to persuade, urge forward. —— πολλοῖς τῶν ξυνόντων, many of his pupils, disciples, literally, those who were with him, associates; Latin: cum quibus erat, or quorum consuetudine utebatur. The Greeks were much more fond of this partitive construction after numerals, etc. than the Latins The pupils of Socrates are never called μαθηταί, since he disclaimed the appellation of teacher, διδάσκαλος. See Wiggers' Life of Socrates, ch. IV. and cf. note, I. 2. 3. —— προηγόρευε, was accustomed to foretell or forewarn, like προεῖπον; the imperf., as frequently, denoting repeated or customary action. See Kühn. El. Gr. § 152. 9. R. 4. —— τὰ μὲν ποιεῖν; τὰ δὲ μὴ ποιεῖν; acc. to Plato the *genius* of Socrates only dissuaded him from doing and did not incite him to action. See Theag. p. 128 D. et al., and cf. Introd. —— ὡς τοῦ δαιμονίου προσημαίνοντος. This phrase is equivalent to the participle of the verb to think or say, and the Accus. with the Infin.: λέγων τὸ δαιμόνιον προσημαίνειν. Ὡς with the genitive of the participle frequently indicates the subjective ground of the foregoing action; as here the real cause in the mind of Socrates which enabled him to forewarn, etc. See Kühn. Gr. § 312. 6. (b); L. Gr. II. § 671. The Latins would use quod, with the subjunctive mode. Cf. 2. 20; 3. 2; 6, 5; II. 3. 3, et al. —— μὴ πειθομένοις. Μή is used with participles and adjectives when they may be resolved by a conditional clause. Latin: si qui autem non parebant. See Kühn. Gr. § 318. 5; El. Gr. § 177. 5; L. Gr. II. § 715. 2. —— μετέμελε, had cause of repentance.

5.—Καίτοι signifies, *but, and yet, however*, Lat. *verum, sed tamen;* and *although*, quanquam; here *and yet.* See Hartung Gr. Partik. II. p. 365. 6. —— τίς οὐκ ἂν ὁμολογήσειεν; This form of the 1st Aor. Opt. in -ειας, -ειε(ν) commonly termed Aeolic, is used more frequently by Attic writers than the regular form; see Kühn. Gr. § 116. 9. According to Eustathius this form denoted the desire for an immediate result: ὁ δὲ εἰπὼν τύψειας, ἢ λέξειας, ἢ γράψειας, εὔχεται τάχιον ἀνυσθῆναι, ὃ εὔχεται; but this distinction between it and the regular form does not seem to have been always observed. For the use of the optative with ἄν by Attic writers to describe certain opinions, and sometimes even actual facts, see Kühn. Gr. § 260 (4) (a) and (c); and for the use of οὐκ and not μή in such cases, see also (a). —— ἐδόκει δ' ἂν [sc. εἶναι] ... ἐφαίνετο. The Subjunctive Imperf. is used in Latin in hypothetical clauses, like the Imperf. with ἄν here, for the pluperfect, when the writer wishes to convey the idea that the thing continued a long time, or was often repeated. Often also when the continued action has reference not to past only, but extends even to the present or future time. See Zumpt's Lat. Gr. § 525. Cf. Kühn. note upon Cic. Tusc. Disp. I. 12. 27. The reason of the use of the Imperf. instead of the Pluperf. seems to be, that the writer in mind places himself back in the past. Here, for example, Socrates would have seemed a fool if he had appeared to those of his own age to speak falsely. So οὐκ ἂν προέλεγεν, εἰ μὴ ἐπίστευεν, indicates the custom of Socrates when he was yet alive. Cf. note 1. 1. 16, 28, 29, 59. After δοκεῖν, the Inf. εἶναι is often to be supplied, as in I. 7. 1, 4; Anab. VII. 1. 6: ὡς ἂν αὐτῷ δοκῇ ἀσφαλές.

Κᾆτα. κᾆτα (καὶ εἶτα) and κἄπειτα (καὶ ἔπειτα) are often used after participles, where we might expect εἶτα and ἔπειτα. These participles originally denote sequence in time, but the transition is easy to the idea in this and similar passages, where the *strangeness* or *inconsistency* of doing the second thing after the first has been done, is indicated, *then, after that, after all.* See Stallb. Plat. Gorg. p. 457. B. and Phaedr. p. 40, and Kühn. Gr. § 312. R. 8, and L. Gr. II. § 667. c.—— Δῆλον οὖν, ὅτι, ἂν προέλεγεν, εἰ, κ.τ.λ. It is clear that Socrates would not have made predictions if he had not, etc.: patet igitur non eam praedicere nisi crederet. When the reality both of the condition (εἰ προαγ, κ.τ.λ.) and that which is consequent upon the condition is denied, we have εἰ with the indicative of the hist. tenses in the Protasis and the same mode with ἄν in the Apodosis; see Kühn. Gr. § 339. I. b; L. Gr. II. § 820.—— ἀληθεύσειν; Verbs in -ευω from nouns or adjectives indicate the being in a condition, or the exercise of that indicated by the primitive. See Kühn. Gr. § 232. (b). The idea of *real* truth is prominent in this word and not the mere *utterance* of truth: that it was truth which he uttered. See Lewis' Contr. Atheos p. 97 sq.—ταῦτα (i. e., ἀληθεύσειν). The Latin method of using the sing. *hoc*, is more logically definite, but the Greeks seemed to prefer to extend the thought by the use of the plural; see Kühn. Gr. § 241. 3. The idea here is: The knowledge of future events belongs only to the gods. No one then could feel confident in predicting the future, unless he referred his knowledge to them.—— Πιστεύων δὲ θεοῖς πῶς οὐκ, κ.τ.λ., since he put confidence in the gods, how is it possible that he did not, etc. See note, § 1. For this use of the Greek participle where we use a particle with a verb, see Kühn. Gr. § 312. (b). It will be noticed, that in the statement of the accusations made against Socrates, § 1 above, it is not said that he denied the existence of all gods, although in the more particular statement of the accusations in Plato, Apol. Socr. 26. C. this is affirmed by Melitus.

6.—Ἀλλὰ μήν; Lat. at or sed vero. These particles introduce another and stronger proof that Socrates believed in the existence of the gods; so, in reasoning, these particles denote a transition to a new and stronger argument. Ἀλλά denotes change, transition, and μήν, = Lat. vero, confirmation, *but further* or *besides.* See note, § 4 above, and cf. I. 2. 4; II. 6, 27.—— καὶ τάδε, κ.τ.λ., also these things (which follow) he did for his friends. As if he had said, (οὐ μόνον ταῦτα, ἃ ἔλεξα, ἀλλὰ) *καὶ τάδε.* Cf. note, § 7: *καὶ ἀνδ. κ.τ.λ.* For the use of *καί* referring to a suppressed clause, see Arn. 2. Gr. Pr. Comp. 348. —— *τὰ μὲν γὰρ ἀναγκαῖα.* Γάρ, compounded of *γε* (indicating confirmation) and *ἄρα* (result or consequence), may express a reason, an explanation, or assurance, as the meaning of the one or the other particle predominates. It is often used as explicative after demonstratives, etc., and sometimes it need scarcely be rendered into English at all; here after *τάδε* it = *namely, to wit.* See B. Gr. 149. 17; Kühn. Gr. § 324. 2; L. Gr. II. § 754. 1. β.; Matt. II. § 615. 2.; Hartung Gr. Partik. I. § 467 sq. Cf. II. 6. 38: *ἐκ τῶνδε σκέψαι· εἰ γάρ κ.τ.λ.* IV. 4. 5. —— *τὰ . . . ἀναγκαῖα, things necessary* (to be done), i. e., here, things about the result of which there is no question. —— *συνεβούλευε*; this and following verbs in the Imperf. denote customary action; see note, § 4: *προηγόρευε.* —— *καὶ πράττειν, ὡς ἐνόμιζεν,* i. e., *οὕτω καὶ πρ.*, contrasting the doing (*πράττειν*) with the thinking (*ἐνόμιζεν*). The correlative is not unfrequently omitted, as in Herod. I. 79: *ὡς δέ οἱ ταῦτα ἔδοξε, καὶ ἐποίεε κατὰ τάχος.* But in comparisons where it is in both members of the sentence we find *καί* repeated, as in I. 6. 3. *ὥσπερ καὶ . . . οὕτω καί*; III. 5. 13. Anab. II. 1. 22. and Stallb. Plato Apol. p. 22. D. For the cases where one *καί* is omitted, see Kühn. L. Gr. II. § 729. —— *ἂν πραχθῆναι*; for the use of the infinitive with *ἄν* after Verba sentiendi, see Kühn. Gr. § 260. 5. (a).

Περὶ δὲ ἀδήλων, ὅπως ἂν ἀποβήσοιτο, but in regard to those things whose result would be doubtful (if performed). The idea would be more extended in Latin: de iis autem rebus, in quibus obscurum erat quomodo eventurae essent, or quarum incertus esset eventus. Ἄν is omitted here in some editions, as in Ernesti, but apparently without good reason. The fact of its omission in 3. 2: *ἢ εἰ ἄλλο τι εὔχοιντο τῶν φανερῶς ἀδήλων ὅπως ἀποβήσοιτο,* proves nothing. The idea there is simply: if they may pray for those things, the result of which is *plainly* uncertain; but here the expression is intended to indicate the uncertainty with less definiteness. See Kühn. Gr. § 260. (4). and R. 7. —— *μαντευσομένους,* oraculum consulere, to consult an oracle. This use of the Fut. Participle after verbs of sending, etc., denoting purpose, where we may use *that,* in order that, or *in order to,* with the infinitive or the simple infinitive with *to,* is frequent in Greek; see Kühn. Gr. § 312. 4. (c); B. 144. The Present Participle is also used in a similar manner, as in the phrase *ἔπεμψεν αὐτὸν ἀγγέλλοντα.* —— *εἰ ποιητέα.* The conjunction *εἰ* is used to denote a wavering between two possibilities, and hence is often found after verbs of deliberating, inquiring, etc., *whether, whether or not.* The context alone can decide whether the phrase which it introduces is to be understood affirmatively or negatively. Cf. Anab. I. 3. 5: *εἰ μὲν δὴ δίκαια ποιήσω, οὐκ οἶδα,* I am ignorant, whether or not I shall do, etc. See also Anab. III. 2. 22. Even in the phrase, *οὐκ οἶδ' εἰ*, this particle has an affirmative force, and also a negative as in I. 3. 5. See Kühn. Gr. § 344. 5. (i). Cf. the use of si in Latin, Zumpt's Lat. Gr. § 354. *fin.*, and of an after dubito, etc., which however has an affirmative force, Kühn. Tusc. Disp. IV. 22. 50. For the construction of the verbal Adj., see Kühn. Gr. § 284. 3. (12); B. 134. 10.

7.—Καὶ τοὺς. Καί, *and so, accordingly*, is here an expletive particle, introducing examples in illustration and confirmation of the preceding sentiment. Comp. Anab. § I. 9. 6. and V. 2. 29. For a similar use of et in Latin, Livy II. 13 is sometimes quoted: Ita honorata virtute feminae quoque ad publica decora excitatae. Et Claelia virgo ... dux agminis virginum inter tela hostium Tiberim tranavit. See also Kühn. Tusc. Disp. I. 34. 82.——τοὺς μέλλοντας οἴκους τε καὶ πόλεις καλῶς οἰκήσειν, those who would manage either domestic or public affairs well. Τε καί, see n. 2 above. Οἰκήσειν is here nearly synonymous with διοικεῖν. Cf. § 8; note, I. 2. 64; II. 1. 19; III. 6. 14; IV. 1. 2.——προσδεῖσθαι, *have need, besides* (in addition to other things, πρός).——τεκτονικὸν μὲν γὰρ ἢ χαλκευτικὸν ... πάντα τὰ τοιαῦτα μαθήματα, κ.τ.λ. The idea is: that all such arts as those of the architect, brasier, etc., are to be undertaken, in accordance with human judgment and insight alone, without consulting oracles. The καί with ἀνθρώπου γνώμῃ, as in § 6: καὶ τάδε (where see note), strictly refers to a suppressed clause; as if the author had said: καὶ ἀνθ. γνώμῃ, καὶ οὐ μόνον θεῶν γνώμῃ, cf. 2. 4. καὶ τοῦ σώματος ... οὐκ ἠμέλει (οὐ μόνον τῆς ψυχῆς, ἀλλὰ καὶ τοῦ σώματος). 18: οἶδα καὶ Σωκράτην (ὥσπερ ἄλλους διδασκάλους, οὕτω καὶ Σ.) 21. See Kühn. Gr. § 321. R. 5; L. Gr. II. § 728, and Hartung Gr. Partik. 1. p. 133 sq.——τῶν τοιούτων ἔργων; i. e., such works as are ἐν τῇ τεκτονικῇ, χαλκευτικῇ, etc. The adjj. τεκτονικόν, etc., are in the Accus. predicate after γενέσθαι, and ἄνθρωπον is to be supplied with that verb. For the idea of *ability, fitness, aptness*, implied in the termination -ικός, see Kühn. Gr. § 234. 1. (b).——ἐξεταστικός, an investigator, one who points out the excellences and defects of a thing, or is employed in θεωρίᾳ not in πράξει. For the Genitive with verbals in -ικος, see B. 132. 13; S. 187. 2. Kühn. L. Gr. II. § 530. hh.——γνώμῃ, Dat of means. Instead of the simple Dat. sometimes ἐν with the Dat. is pleonastically used (B. 147. 2. (a), for the means or instrument. Διὰ with the Gen. is used if a person is indicated, and sometimes of things; even after Pass. verbs, when the person is the means and not the efficient cause, i. e., where *per* would be used in Latin. B. 147. 2. (a). See also the constr of ἀπό with the Gen. of means in I. 2. 14.

8.—Τὰ δὲ μέγιστα, but the most important things in these arts, i. e., which would result from the practice of these arts, the gods have reserved for themselves, δὲ here answering to μέν in § 7: τεκτον. μὲν γάρ. See § 1 above; the sense will be most distinctly brought out by rendering: *for although ... yet.* For the use of the infinitive εἶναι in the subordinate clause, see Kühn. Gr. § 345. 6. and cf. with Zumpt's Lat. Gr. § 603, and III. 11. 1. Also Apolog. § 3, 4, 5, and Anab. II. 2. 1. and Bornemann's note in h. l.—γάρ τοι. Γάρ introduces the proof or illustration of the fact, that the gods reserve for themselves, etc., which has just been affirmed, and τοι adds confirmation, *indeed.* φυτευσαμένῳ. There is great force in the use of the Mid. Voice here and in the corresponding clause: οἰκοδομησαμένῳ, indicating the object in planting, &c., the individual's own interest. δῆλον ὅστις, κ.τ.λ. Δῆλον need not be repeated in translation. Xenophon in comparisons and parallel phrases loves to retain the full expression which would be avoided in Latin as well as in our own language. For the use of εἰ see note, § 6, and for the use of the indicative mode, Kühn. Gr. § 344. 6; Buttm. § 139. 22, 3. In the first two cases, with συμφέρει, εἰ may be rendered *whether*, and in the last two *whether ... not*, Lat. an.—τῷ πολιτικῷ, one who takes part in the government.—ἀνιάσεται ... στερήσεται; for this use of Fut. middle for passives, see Buttm. Gr. § 113. 6. Compare below II. 7. 8; III. 3. 15, and IV. 8. 10. Plato often uses Fut. Mid. in the same way. See examples collected by Schneid. upon Civit. V. 470. A.

9.—Δαιμόνιον, *pertains to,* or *comes into the province of, the deity,* as contrasted with τῆς ἀνθρωπίνης γνώμης.—Ἀλλὰ πάντα τῆς ἀνθρωπίνης γνώμης, but that all things fall within the province of human reason or intelligence. The Latins in such disjunctive phrases generally express each member fully.—δαιμονᾶν, *to be insane,* according to Hesychius: ὑπὸ δαίμονος κατέχεσθαι. The beauty and force of the oxymoron here with μηδὲν δαιμόνιον οἰομένους εἶναι will not escape the notice of the student.—δὲ καί, *and also.*—τοὺς μαντευομένους ... ἀνθρώποις ... μαθοῦσι διακρίνειν; in those things which the gods give to men to understand by learning, (by knowledge of the things themselves). Μαντευομένους and μαθοῦσι are placed in contrast here. Μαθοῦσι denotes the means, and is put in the dative by attraction to ἀνθρώποις, see Buttm. § 142. 2. (b). As the subject of the Inf. is omitted, the Part. takes the case in which that subject is found with the preceding verb; so sometimes in Latin, as the phrase: licet illis esse beatis.—οἷον, ut, velut, *for instance,* a frequent use in Attic Greek.—ἐπὶ ζεῦγος λαβεῖν ... ἐπὶ τὴν ναῦν ... λαβεῖν. We should naturally expect the insertion of the Article before ζεῦγος, or its omission before ναῦν.

But the construction seems to have been designed by the author. According to Kühn. ἐπὶ ζεῦγος without the article has the force of the Latin ad vehendum; with λαβεῖν, ad vehend. adhibere; as the phrase, ἰέναι ἐπὶ δεῖπνον, may be translated by ad coenandum, I. 3. 6. Anab VII. 3. 15; Herod. I. 37: ἐπὶ θήραν ἰέναι, venatum ire. See Kühn L. Gr. II. § 484. Anm.—— With ναῦν the article has the force of a possessive pronoun. Sauppius explains the phrase ἐπὶ τὴν ναῦν, by, in navem, quam quis habet. See Kühn. Gr. § 244. 4. Cf. III. 9. 11: ἔν τε νηΐ, in navigando, in nave regenda,—indicating the action of navigating, as just after, ἐν γεωργίᾳ does that of cultivating the fields, and ἐν σωμασκίᾳ, that of exercising the body, and ἐν νόσῳ, the condition of sickness. On the other hand, with the article, in II. 6. 38: τὴν ναῦν, his ship, and 7. 2. ἐν τῇ οἰκίᾳ, in my house, et al. The use of the article in Greek where we use the possessive pron. is frequent, particularly with the names of things that stand in some special relation, as *son, friend, master*, etc. See B. 127. 8.—— ἀριθμήσαντας ἢ μετρήσαντες . . . εἰδέναι; i. e., things that may be determined by the processes familiarly known among men. These participles denote the means (Kühn. Gr. 312. 4. (e), and are equivalent to the Abl. of the Gerund in Latin. For the accusative with the Infin. without attraction after ἔξεστι, where the Dat. is not expressed, see Kühn. Gr. § 307. Rem.; L. Gr. II. § 645 and 647; and cf. III. 12. 8: ταῦτα δὲ οὐκ ἔστιν ἰδεῖν ἀμελοῦντα. The dative of the noun is also sometimes used, whilst the accusative of the Part. with the Infin. is retained, as in I. 2. 49; II. 6. 26: εἰ ἐξῆν τοῖς κρατίστοις συνθεμένους ἐπὶ τοὺς χείρους ἰέναι; III. 9. 9; IV. 5. 11. In like manner the construction varies after δοῦναι; II. 8. 1; Cyr. I. 6. 5. See Krüger in Disquisit. Gram. III. § 359—372; Stallb. Plat. de Rep. IX. p. 586. E.; Rost's Gr. § 121.—— τοὺς τὰ τοιαῦτα, κ.τ.λ. This enunciation is asyndic, because it contains a brief summary or recapitulation of what precedes; so often with τὰ τοιαῦτα. See Kühn. Gr. § 325. (e).; L. Gr. II. § 760. b., and cf. II. 1. 33; 3. 19; 5. 5; IV. 3. 13. et al.—— ποιεῖν ἀθέμιστα, nefarie agere. Some editions read ἀθέμιτα, but ἀθέμιστα is best authorized. The phrase is a more extended expression for δαιμονᾶν above.—— ἔφη δὲ, *since, he said.* Δέ here introduces the ground, or reason of the preceding assertion, like the Latin cum. See Hartung Gr. Partik. S. 167. ἃ μὲν . . . ἃ δὲ, et haec, quae...et illa, quae.—— μαθόντας, *having learned*, or, by gaining a knowledge of; the Part. indicates the manner or means, Kühn. Gr. § 312. 4. (e).—— ἔδωκαν, have given or permitted, with the Infin. μανθάνειν. For the use of this form of the Aorist, see Kühn. § 173. 2. and cf. IV. 2. 15.—— ἵλεῳ Attic Nom. plural.

The idea of Socrates which lies at the basis of the preceding represen tation, § 6—9, in respect to divination, seems to be, that all phenomena are divided into two classes; in one, the connection of antecedent and consequent is invariable, and can be traced by study; and hence the connected future results are within the sphere of human attainment. In the other, there is no invariable or ascertainable sequence, and the knowledge and results are reserved by the gods for themselves, and only made known to mortals by means of omens, prophecy, or some other inspired communication from themselves. These two classes of events he supposed to be radically distinct, and not to be confounded, without impiety;' see Grote's Hist. of Greece, Vol. I. ch. 16, p. 498.

10.—Ἀλλὰ μὴν, *moreover*, see § 6 above.——γε qualifies ἐκεῖνος after which it is placed, and gives it emphasis; but its force cannot well be expressed in English without a circumlocution; *he was one who*, etc. ——ἀεὶ μὲν ἦν ἐν τῷ φανερῷ, he was always in view of the citizens, in public. Δὲ in § 11, (Οὐδεὶς δὲ) answers to this μὲν, and a μὲν... δὲ in similar construction intervenes: ἔλεγε μὲν... τοῖς δέ.——τε... καὶ, both... and; see Kühn. Gr. § 321. I. (a).——περιπάτους; the portico constructed for those who walked for exercise. Literally, *walkings*, just as in Latin ambulatio is used for ambulacrum. See Kühn. Cic. Tusc. Disp. IV. 4. 7. Thus Aristotle and his followers received the name Peripatetics, because they gave instruction in the place for walking, περιπάτος.——τὰ γυμνάσια. The Grecian Gymnasia were employed as a place of exercise, amusement, and instruction. The sophists and rhetoricians often assembled their pupils there for instruction. For a detailed account of them and their influence on Grecian life, see Becker, Char. p. 228 sq.——πληθούσης ἀγορᾶς, at the time of full market; i. e., the last half of the forenoon, perhaps from nine to about twelve o'clock, called also περὶ πλήθουσαν ἀγοράν. In general, the genitive is used of time when it is indefinite and continued, the dative when it is definite; and the accusative denotes duration of time, (B. 132. 14. a; 133. 4. e. and 131. 9. See Becker, Charicles, p. 219. According to Dio Chrysostom the day was divided into five parts: 1. πρωΐ, morning; 2. περὶ ἀγοράν, full market; 3. μεσημβρία, noon; 4. δείλη, afternoon; 5. ἑσπέρα, evening. Another division into twelve parts is given in Herodotus, 2. 109, as introduced into Greece from Babylonia.——ἐκεῖ φανερὸς ἦν, *was to be seen there*. φανερός from φαίνω, hence open to sight, *to be seen*.——μέλλοι, optative (subjunct. in Latin). The *oratio obliqua* is used in subordinate clauses in connection with the *oratio recta* as indicating the intention, wish, or feeling of the person spoken of. See Kühn. Gr. § 345. 4; L. Gr. II. 845. Anm., and cf. Cic. Tusc. Disp. V. 21. 62.——καὶ ἔλεγε, *he was conversing*, engaged in conversation.——ὡς τὸ πολύ, plerumque, *usually*.

11.—Σωκρατους οὐδὲν ἀσεβὲς . . . οὔτε πράττοντος εἶδεν, οὔτε λέγοντος ἤκουσεν. Ἰδεῖν is here construed with the genitive of the participle, so as to preserve a unity of construction with the parallel phrase, λέγοντος ἤκουσεν. See Kühn. L. Gr. § 528. Anm. 3. Some commentators govern the genitive by οὐδέν, but the method of construction above given seems preferable. Cf. § 20. Bornemann renders this passage: Nemo unquam vidit vel audivit, quum Socr. impium aliquid... faceret aut diceret. —— οὐδὲ γὰρ περὶ τῆς τῶν πάντων φύσεως, ᾗπερ, κ.τ.λ., for he did not reason (was not accustomed to discourse, διελέγετο, Imperf.) concerning the nature of all things in the same manner as, etc. Ἧιπερ, the fem. relative ᾗ with the strengthening particle περ (from πέρι), used adverbially, with ὁδῷ implied. Οἱ πλεῖστοι, most of the other philosophers, the sophists. Xenophon does not intend to be understood, as saying that Socrates never discoursed upon physics, as the contrary appears from IV. 8. 10; Sympos. VI. 6 sq.; Plato's Apol.; Phaedo, p. 96 and 97, and Diog. Laert. II. 45; but that he did not spend his time like the sophists, in useless questions concerning the origin of the world and the motions of celestial bodies, etc., but upon the human and divine nature and their relations, and upon the divine government, and such like things of a practical nature. Cf. note upon τοὺς φροντίζοντας, κ.τ.λ., below, and upon § 16. His objections were rather against the manner in which investigations in physics were pursued, which led to the confusion of the intellect and to atheism, than against the pursuits themselves. —— σκοπῶν, ὅπως . . . καὶ τίσιν. It is not often that in indirect questions, the first member has the form of the *oratio obliqua* while the last has the pronoun of the direct interrogation, as here. Yet such cases do occur, as in Plato, Repub. III. 414. D., and they seem designed to throw stress upon the last member. Much oftener ὅστις follows τίς, and ὁποῖος, ποῖος. See Kühn. Gr. § 344. R. 1; L. Gr. II. § 837, n. 2; Rost, Gr. § 123, b.

Ὁ καλούμενος, κ.τ.λ., the κόσμος, *so called* by the sophists, see B. 144. 7. N. 10. —— σοφιστῶν; the noun σοφιστής was orig. used in an honorable sense, and is so used by Xenophon in IV. 2. 1. = σοφός, for one skilled in any art, wise, learned. Aeschylus, however, uses it once, Prom. 146, with the implication of artfulness; and after those who professed to teach wisdom prostituted their talents for unworthy purposes, it was commonly employed as a term of reproach: sophists. At a later period the primitive meaning was again restored to it. This name designated a class of men rather than a school in philosophy. The sophists were the teachers, the wandering professors of their age. Many of them acquired great wealth by their profession. Protagoras, the first who assumed this title, (about the eighty-fourth Olympiad,) is said to have demanded of single pupils: centenas minas; see Plat. Protag. p. 328 and 349, and Diog. Laert. IX. 58. Gorgias and others also received large sums of their pupils for instruction. The arrogant assumptions of the sophists are well known. The boast of their most accomplished leader, that he could by his eloquence "make the worse appear the better reason," has been considered as the guiding principle of their conduct and the foundation of their instructions. Socrates and his followers were the direct antagonists of the Sophists, and much of Socrates' teaching was directed against them. Our limits do not allow a more extended exhibition of their peculiarities at present. We shall have occasion to notice frequent allusions to them in the sequel. For original sources of information aside from Xenophon, see Plato, especially in Protagoras and Euthydemus, Aristotle Rhet. II. 24, et al.; Isocrates contra Sophistas, Aristophanes, especially in the Clouds, (with which consult Mitchell's Preliminary Discussion,) all of which must be taken with many grains of allowance. For connected accounts, see especially Grote's Greece, Vol. VIII. Chaps. LXVII. and LXVIII., Ritter's History of Ancient Philosophy, Vol. I. p. 525 sq. Eng. Tr., and other Histories of Ancient Philosophy. In Lewes' Biographical History of Philosophy a defence of them is attempted, which may be consulted, although Grote's Discussion leaves little to be desired on that side of the question. Also see Bibl. Repository, Vol. XII. p. 50, and Quart. Review, No. 42. p. 289. —— κόσμος, *order*, and hence the world, as exhibiting order and arrangement. Comp. Lat. mundus. It appears to be used here as parallel with φύσις ἡ τῶν πάντων. This signification of the term seems to have originated with Pythagoras, see Bentley Opusc. Philol. p. 347, 445; Photius Bibl. Cod. 659. Plato in his Gorgias 507 E. and 508 A. explains the meaning: φασὶ δ' οἱ σοφοὶ... καὶ οὐρανὸν καὶ γῆν καὶ θεοὺς καὶ ἀνθρώπους τὴν κοινωνίαν συνέχειν, κ.τ.λ.... καὶ τὸ ὅλον τοῦτο... κόσμον καλοῦσιν. The phraseology here indicates that this use of the word κόσμος belonged to educated rather than common life. —— ἔφυ, in some Mss. and Editt. ἔχει. —— ἀνάγκαις, necessary laws = the laws of nature. Abstract nouns assume in the Plur. a concrete signification, and denote parts or specific instances under a general class. Thus ἀνάγκη denotes the necessity of fate, and ανάγκαι parts of this necessity, laws. Cf. the use of the word in III. 12. 2., and Anab. IV. 5. 15, and see Kühn. Gr. § 243. 3. (3); L. Gr. II. § 408, and for a similar usage in Latin. Tusc. Disc. IV. 2. 3. p. 295. —— Ἀλλὰ καί. We might expect μόνον with the preceding negative, but these words are sometimes used without it, meaning *but even* or *nay even;* see Arn. 2 Gr. Com. 16. a. —— τοὺς φροντίζοντας τὰ τοιαῦτα, those investigating such things φροντίζω, with the accusative, corresponds in meaning with the Latin scrutari, or investigare; but with the genitive, with which it is most frequently construed, or with the preposition περί and the Gen., it is in transitive, and the noun in the Gen. denotes that which causes thought or anxiety. Cf. III. 7. 7, and § 12 below. See Kühn. Gr. § 274. 1. and R. 1; L. Gr. II. 533. 1. μεριμνάω is used much in the same way, cf. note, § 14; III. 5, 23. Thus in Aristophanes' Clouds, φροντιστήριον, μεριμνοφροντισταί (v. 101) are given as appellations of those who engage in minute and harassing investigations in physics. See further upon Socrates' opinion of such pursuits, note § 16.

12.—Μὲν here has for its correlative δὲ in the beginning of § 15: ἐσκόπει δὲ, κ.τ.λ. —— αὐτῶν ἐσκόπει, κ.τ.λ. Αὐτῶν is in the genitive after ἐσκόπει, referring back to φροντίζοντας τὰ τοιαῦτα. See Note upon I. 6. 4: τὶ χαλεπὸν, κ.τ.λ.; and for the constr. of the genitive, Kühn. Gr. § 273. 5. f., and L. Gr. II. § 528 and Anm. 3. —— τἀνθρώπινα. Some editions and Mss. have τἀνθρώπεια. The two words are used almost promiscuously, see Kühn. in h. l. —— τὰ μὲν ἀνθρώπεια . . . τὰ δαιμόνια δὲ; a similar collocation of the particles μὲν . . . δὲ is found in 2, 24: διὰ μὲν κάλλος, κ.τ.λ.; II. 1. 16; III. 9. 8; IV. 5. 11. Τὰ ἀνθρώπεια, res humanae, and τὰ δαιμόνια, res divinae, when contrasted, designate things which relate to man as such, his duties, etc., in contrast with things of a speculative nature, questions in physics, metaphysics, etc., called also οὐράνια in IV. 7. 6. Cf. Cic. Acad. I. 15.

13.—Ἐθαύμαζε δ', εἰ μή. Εἰ is here used somewhat like ὅτι; so not unfrequently in Attic discourse after verbs indicating emotion, and followed by the Indic. where the doubt is merely rhetorical, for ὅτι or ὡς, in order to avoid harshness of expression. Athenian urbanity did not allow the direct imputation of such actions, etc., as excited the emotion indicated by the verb used; they accordingly threw a coloring of doubt over them by the use of the interrogative form of discourse. See Kühn. L. Gr. II. 339. R. 7; Buttm. § 149. m. 60, and Rost § 121. Anm. 5. p. 601. Cf. § 17; I. 2. 7; III. 7. 8; 9. 8, and observe a similar usage of the Latin si after miror in Cic. Amicit. XV. 53. —— φανερὸν αὐτοῖς ἐστιν ὅτι ..οὐ δυνατόν ἐστιν. For the use of the indicative mode in oratio obliqua, see Kühn. Gr. § 345. 5., and cf. § 12 above, ἐσκόπει πότερα . . . ἔρχονται, I. 2. 29, 50; II. 7. 12, et al. —— ἐπεὶ καὶ τοὺς μέγιστον φρονοῦντας, κ.τ.λ., since even those who are most confident in disputing upon these matters, etc. —— Instead of μέγιστον φρον. we might expect μέγα φρονεῖν. In the poets this superlative neuter sing. is used as an adverb, as in Eurip. Heracl. 792, but its use is rare in good prose writers. Cf. Plato, Phaed. 257. E. ——δοξάζειν; for the use of the infinitive, see note and references, § 8 above: δῆλον εἶναι. The same idea is further developed in IV. 7. 6.

14.—Τῶν τε γὰρ μαινομένων . . . τῶν τε. . μεριμνώντων. Γάρ introduces the proof of the previous assertion, which is contained in the parallel clauses introduced by τε—τε, *both—and*, or better, *like as—so*. Xenophon rarely joined phrases in this way by τε—τε. Yet they are found, as in I. 2. 4, and 3, 1; IV. 2. 28, and a few other passages. This form of connection is much oftener used by the older Epic writers. See Rost's Gr. § 134. 4. a., and Kühn. L. Gr. § 722, 3.——τοὺς μὲν . . . τοὺς δὲ, τοῖς μὲν . . . τοῖς δὲ. The Latins use greater variety in such expressions, as partim . . . partim, pars . . . pars, alii . . . alii, hi . . . illi, etc.——δεδιέναι . . . φοβεῖσθαι, *to fear* . . . to be *frightened*, Latin, metuere or verere . . . timere, in accordance with the distinction between δέος and φόβος. The former is fear of something foreseen or meditated upon, the latter, sudden fright.——οὐδ' ἐν ὄχλῳ, not even in a crowd, Latin, turba.——εἰς ἀνθρώπους εἶναι, to be out of doors, or among men.——ἱερὸν, a temple.——καὶ λίθους καὶ ξύλα τὰ τυχόντα. Some, as Schneider, suppose that by λίθους and ξύλα, Socrates understood idols made of these materials, but τὰ τυχόντα (of whatever kind, however worthless,) belongs to both words and seems to preclude that meaning. He speaks of what are sometimes termed *Feteiches*.——τιμᾶν . . . σέβεσθαι, to honor . . . revere.——μεριμνώντων, a more poetic and grave word than φροντίζω in § 12 above, designating those who anxiously and carefully inquire into things obscure. Lat. perscrutari anxie or solicite.——ἓν μόνον τὸ ὂν εἶναι, Lat.: unum esse ea, quae sint. Many philosophers, as Thales, Pythagoras, Xenophanes, and others, laid down the general proposition: ἕνα τὸν κόσμον. See Stobaeus Ecl. Phys. I. 23. p. 496, and cf. Plato, Sophist. 242. D. and Parmenides, where he alludes to and explains the sentiment of Xenophanes, the founder of the Eleatic school of philosophy: ἓν εἶναι τὰ πάντα καλούμενα. Acad. II. 37. 118: unum esse omnia. Particular accounts of these speculations and their authors may be found in Ritter's, Lewes', and Brandis' Histories.——ἄπειρα τὸ πλῆθος. Τὰ ὄντα εἶναι is to be supplied from the preceding τὸ ὄν; ἄπειρα is in the neut. plur. Allusion is probably made here to Leucippus, who lived about 500 B. C. and was the author of the Atomic theory, and his pupil Democritus who went even beyond his teacher in his speculations.——ἀεὶ κινεῖσθαι πάντα. See Stobaeus Ecl. Phys. I. 20. p. 396, as quoted by Kühn. in h. l. Heraclitus of Ephesus surnamed σκοτεινός, "the obscure," affirmed that every thing was subject to constant change, which he called τὴν τῶν πάντων ῥοήν, and this is what constitutes life. See Plutarch.

Decret. I. 23 Plato Theaetetus, p. 180. D. et al., and Cratylus, 402. A. λέγει που Ἡράκλειτος, ὅτι πάντα χωρεῖ καὶ οὐδὲν μένει. —— οὐδὲν ἄν ποτε κινηθῆναι; the theory of Zeno Eleates. See Aristotle, Phys. VI. 9. For an account of these two opposing systems of philosophy, the germ of the modern sensuous and supersensuous schools, see Lewis' Contr. Ath. p. 152 sq. Seiffert says that ἄν here may be translated, *facile.* But according to Kühner, the infinitive with ἄν both here and just below (ἂν γενέσθαι) has the same meaning as the optative with ἄν in an independent clause. It softens the assertion. Cf. § 16: ἡγεῖτο .. ἀνδραποδώδεις ἄν, κ.τ.λ.

15.—Καὶ τάδε, *this also,* this in addition to what has been stated. Τάδε is plural, where in Latin and English the singular would be used. See note, § 5 above: ταῦτα. —— ἆρ'; this interrogative particle from the illative ἄρα does not of itself decide whether an affirmative or negative answer is expected, ἆρ' οὐ being used in the former case and ἆρα μή in the latter; and yet ἆρα is used in several cases like ἆρ' οὐ, as in Alcestis 229, 771, see Kühn. Gr. § 344. 5. (b). —— ὥρας, *the seasons of the year.* —— καὶ ὅτου δ' ἄν. Καὶ . . . δὲ, denique, *and in fine,* or *and also.* See note, § 3: κἀκεῖνος δέ ἀρκεῖ δὲ. Instead of the adversative conjunctive particle in such cases as this, the Latin employs more commonly the copulative que or atque.

16.—Μὲν οὖν. Οὖν, especially in repetitions and recapitulations, loses much of its deductive force and confirms the truth of what is said, *surely, indeed.* Especially in such combinations as γοῦν, γὰρ οὖν, οὔκουν, μῶν and μὲν οὖν, "οὖν denotes the feeling of *certainty* raised to indifference." Ar. 2 Gr. Comp. 454. Kühn. Gr. § 324. (b). —— πραγματευομένων τοιαῦτα, those giving their time and labor to such things. —— αὐτὸς δὲ is contrasted with τῶν ταῦτα πραγματ. κ.τ.λ. —— περὶ τῶν ἀνθρωπείων ἂν ἀεὶ διελέγετο. Ἄν is omitted in some editions, but without good authority. It is often used with the Indic. of the Histor. tenses, indicating that the action was *repeated* or *customary,* though dependent on conditions only suggested by the particle. So here with the indicative imperfect it indicates that the thing was not done once, but as often as the occasion required. Hermann ad Vig. explains it: quotiescunque occasio ferret. Cf. IV. 6. 13, and Anab. I. 5. 2 and Krüger's and Owen's notes upon it; also see B. Gr. 139. 12; Kühn. Gr. § 260. R. 6 and Examples; Rost's Gr. § 120. c. γ. It is placed here after τῶν ἀνθρωπείων, since that is emphatic. See Kühn. Gr. § 261. 2; L. Gr. II. § 457. The practical bearing of the teaching of Socrates is here brought distinctly to view. So also in IV. 7. et al. See Ritter's Hist.

Phil. II. p. 45 sq.; Brandis, II. 35, and Wiggers' Life of Socr. Ch. IV. The often quoted eulogium of Cicero, Tusc. Quaest. V. 16, seems to be well merited: Socrates autem primus philosophorum devocavit e coelo et in urbibus collocavit et in domos etiam introduxit, etc. Cf. also Cic. de Finib. II. 1: S. qui parens phil. jure dici potest, and Tusc. Quaest. V. 3. —— σκοπῶν, *considering.* —— τί σωφροσύνη, τί μανία, soundness of mind, sana mens... insania (Cic. Tusc. Disp. III. 4), amentia (Catal. II. 11). —— τί ἀνδρεία, τί δειλία. Some editions read ἀνδρία here, but without good reason. See Kühn. upon the passage. Ἀνδρεία is from the adj. ἀνδρεῖος, and corresponds to the Latin *virtus* in one of its signiff., *manliness, courage,* and hence is the proper contrast of δειλία. —— τί πολιτικός, rerum civilium peritus, *a statesman.* For the force of the termination -ικός in πολιτικός and ἀρχικός, see note upon 7 above. —— καὶ περὶ τῶν ἄλλων, to sum up the whole in one general proposition. —— ἃ τοὺς μὲν εἰδότ. κ.τ.λ. This position of the relative with the antecedent or subordinate part of the sentence is common both in Latin and Greek. See Zumpt, § 812. The omission of the antecedent when it is a general word, such as χρῆμα, πρᾶγμα, or can be easily supplied, is common. See Sophocles' Gr. § 150. 5. —— καλοὺς κἀγαθοὺς ... ἀνδραποδώδεις. Those are properly called καλοὺς κἀγαθούς, who are distinguished for physical, intellectual, and moral excellence combined, and the words are appropriately placed in contrast with ἀνδραποδώδεις, the servile, low. Cf. I. 2. 29; IV. 2. 39; Plat. Theag. 130, B. In Socrates' idea, expressed by these words, moral excellence seems to be predominant, as this was the highest excellence with him; another might use them with more direct reference to honorable birth or intellectual preëminence. For the derivation of ἀγαθός from ἄγαμαι, to wonder at, admire, etc., see Plato, Cratylus, p. 412, and Lewis' Plato contr. Atheos. p. 1, n. 2; and cf. Cicero's explanation of the meaning of the word *bonus,* Offic. I. 7. 20. and De Orat. I. 47. 204. —— ἂν δικ. κεκλῆσθαι for ἄν with the Infin., see Kühn. Gr. § 260. 5. a. It may be rendered here in English by *seem:* should seem to be justly called, or, *might* justly be called.

17.—Ὅσα μὲν οὖν μὴ φανερὸς ἦν ὅπως ἐγίγνωσκεν, κ.τ.λ. For the position of the adjective clause here and the use of the demonstrative τούτων, see Kühn. Gr. § 332. 8. —— οὖν denotes conclusion or inference from what precedes; see note, § 2 above, and cf. also § 20. The negative μή, not οὐ, is used on account of the condition implied in the relative construction: εἰ μή τινα φαν. ἦν ὅ ἐγίγν. —— ὅπως ἐγίγνωσκεν, how he thought, what his opinion was. —— ὑπὲρ τούτων, instead of the usual περί τούτ. on account of the following περί. Seiffert renders the whole clause: In qua ergo non appareret quid ille sentiret, in hoc inique de eo sententiam tulisse judices nihil mirum est. For the signification of εἰ after οὐ θαυμαστόν, see § 13 and grammatical references there. —— παραγνῶναι, from the trop. meaning of παρά, aside from, *beyond*, comes in composition that of *missing, failing;* hence, here, παραγνῶναι signifies to misjudge, *to judge wrongly.* —— τούτων ἐνεθυμήθησαν. The verb ἐνθυμεῖσθαι in construction with the genitive of the thing with or without the prep. περί, signifies, to meditate with one's self, to think upon, but with the accusative it means to ponder, to lay to heart. But it is not common in either of these constructions. For examples, see II. 1. 34; IV. 5. 9. A different construction is also found; i. e., with the genitive of the person who is the object of consideration and the accusative of the thing, or some secondary enunciation which takes its place, as in III. 6. 16: ἐνθυμοῦ δὲ τῶν ἄλλων, κ.τ.λ.

18.—Βουλεύσας, Aor. Part., *having been made senator*, senator factus, indicating *individual* and *completed* action; in the present, βουλεύειν, *to be senator*, I. 2. 35, action as in progress and incomplete. A similar distinction in the meaning of the Aor. and Pres. is frequent. Thus ἄρξας, having been made magistrate, III. 5. 1, but ἄρχειν, to be archon, II. 2. 13; σοῦ στρατηγήσαντος, you having been made leader; βασιλεύσας, having been made king; ταμιεύσας, quaestor factus. In like manner ἰσχύων, potens, and ἰσχύσας, potens factus; ἀσθενῶν, one sick, ἀσθενήσας, one who has been attacked by disease, Cyrop. 1. 4. 2; δυνάμενος, potens, and δυνηθείς, potentium nactus. The place of senator was the only civil office ever held by Socrates. See Plat. Apol. p. 32, B. —— βουλευτικὸν ὅρκον ὀμόσας ἐν ᾧ ἦν ... ἐπιστάτης ... γενόμενος, having taken the senator's oath (*lit.* in which it was that) etc., being ἐπιστάτης, he would not put the vote. The joining together of participles without connectives, as here, was common both among poets and prose writers. They were thus enabled to introduce several particulars into a sentence with energy and brevity. See Kühn. L. Gr. II § 676. 2, and cf. I. 2. 22; II. 2. 5; III. 13, 5, and Bornemann's Anab III. 1, 13. Stallb.; Plat. Euthyphr. p. 127; Phaedr. p. 9; Phileb. p. 53 So genitives absolute as just below: ἐπιθυμήσαντος τοῦ δήμου .. ὀργιζομένου τοῦ δήμου, which may be translated: when the people desired, ... although the people were enraged. But, where the design of successive participles is the same, they are joined by the particles καί, τὲ ... καί, δὲ, etc., as βουλεύσας καὶ ὀμόσας. Even genitives absolute are joined in this way with nominatives, see I. 2. 25: τοιούτων δὲ συμβάντων αὐτοῖν καὶ ὠγκωμένω ... ἐπὶ γένει, when such things had happened to them, and (when) etc. Cf. Thucyd. I. 65. and Anab. I. 10. 6. with Krüger's note; also see examples collected by Poppo, Thuc. III. 84, 2. (Part. III. Vol. 2, p. 334 sq.)

Ἐπιστάτης. The βουλὴ τῶν πεντακοσίων, or Athenian Senate, was composed of 500 members, chosen from the ten tribes (φυλαί). These 500 were divided according to the ten φυλαί, into ten πρυτάνεις, each of which presided over the state thirty-five or thirty-six days. From these *prytanes* ten were chosen each week, called πρόεδροι, who had the whole management of affairs for the time. The leader of these was called chief president, ἐπιστάτης, which was the office held by Socrates at the time alluded to in the text. See G. F. Schömann, de Comit. Athen. Ch. VII. p. 83 sq., and K. F. Hermann, Lehrb. d. Gr. Staatsalterth. § 127. —— παρὰ τοὺς νόμους. The unlawfulness of the act consisted in voting for their condemnation all together (μιᾷ ψήφῳ) instead of separately: κρίνειν δίχα ἕκαστον. See the law in Thirlwall's Hist. of Greece, App. XIII. The position of the words, μιᾷ ψήφῳ, directly after ἐννέα στρατηγούς, is chosen, to indicate the contrast between ἐννέα and μιᾷ, thus bringing into view, merely by the position, the principal point, in which the unlawfulness consisted. See Kühn. Gr. § 348. 10; L. Gr. II. § 716. 4. —— ἐννέα στρατηγοὺς ... τοὺς ἀμφὶ Θράσυλλον καὶ Ἐρασινίδην, κ.τ.λ., Thrasyllus and Erasinides with the other admirals, nine in all. For the elliptical construction, see Kühn. Gr. § 263. d.; L. Gr. II. 474. d. The occurrence here alluded to was briefly as follows: After the victory of the Athenians over the Peloponnesians off the Arginusae, three little islands between Lesbos and Aeolis (B. C. 404), it was decided by the admirals that they should pursue the enemy with their fleet, leaving behind some inferior officers, ταξιάρχαι, with men for the purpose of burying the dead. But a storm that immediately arose, prevented the performance of this most necessary office for the repose of the souls of the departed, and the leaders of the army were publicly arraigned for failure in duty in this matter. It was at their trial when all the other *prytanes* yielded to the clamor of the people for their condemnation, that Socrates remained unshaken, and refused to put the vote: οὐκ ἠθέλησεν ἐπιψηφίσαι. By refusing to do it, he put a stop to their proceeding at the time, as it could be done by no other than an ἐπιστάτης. Thus the condemnation was at least postponed until the next day, when a new *prytanis* came into office. For a more particular account, see Thirlwall's Hist. of Greece, Ch. XXX. Vol. I. p. 475 sq.; Mitford's Hist. Ch. 20. 2 and 3. Thrasyllus and Erasinides alone are named, because the latter proposed and urged that they all should pursue the enemy: ἐπὶ τοὺς ἐς Μιτυλήνην πολεμίους τὴν τακίστην πλεῖν ἅπαντας; and the former advised the leaving behind of ships and men for burying the dead: τὰς μὲν ναῦς καταλιπεῖν ταῖς δὲ ἐπὶ τοὺς πολεμίους πλεῖν Xen. Hellen. I. 7. 31 sq. Also cf. Xen. Hellen. I. 6. 28, 7 sq.; Diod. Sicul. XIII. 620 sq.; Plat. Apol. p. 32, and IV. 4. 2 below. —— περὶ πλείονος ἐποιήσατο, he thought it better, of more consequence. The Middle Voice here and in φυλάξασθαι below, limits the advantage of the action indicated, to the subject, *for* or *to himself*. —— εὐορκεῖν ἢ . . . φυλάξασθαι τοὺς ἀπειλοῦντας, to keep his oath than . . . to escape those threatening, i. e., the threats of the people.

19.—Καὶ γὰρ, nam etiam. Γάρ introduces the ground or reason, and καί gives emphasis to what follows: *for* he *supposed* that the gods *even* care for, etc. —— ἐπιμελεῖσθαι . . . ἀνθρώπων, to care for, to take cognizance of the actions of men. For the construction of ἐπιμελεῖσθαι with the Gen., see Kühn. § 274. 1. (b): with Prep. and Gen., see e. g. Xen. Cyrop. I. 6. 12; with Accus. and Infin. *to take care that*, see below IV. 5. 10; with ὅπως and the Indic. Fut., see Kühn. Gr. § 330. 6. —— ὃν τρόπον, the Accus. of the *manner in which* any thing takes place, as an adverbial phrase, Kühn. Gr. § 278. 4. R. 3. —— τὰ μὲν εἰδέναι, τὰ δ' οὐκ εἰδ. Some of the philosophers taught that the gods took cognizance only of more important things, and neglected those of inferior importance. See Cic. Nat. Deor. II. 66. III. 35, 39. —— τά τε λεγόμενα καὶ πραττόμενα καὶ τὰ σιγῇ βουλευόμενα. When several words which would require the article, if standing singly, are connected by καί and τὲ—καί, if they designate but one idea or conception, the article is not repeated, as with πραττόμενα, but when they are considered as independent of, or contrasted with each other, they receive it, as in τὰ σιγῇ βουλευόμενα; see Kühn. § 245. 2. For examples of its omission, see II. 1. 20: αἱ ῥᾳδιουργίαι καὶ ἐκ τοῦ παραχρῆμα ἡδοναί, also τῶν καλῶν τε κἀγαθῶν ἔργων; II. 2. 5; 4. 6; Anab. VIII. 3. 21: οἱ στρατηγοὶ καὶ λοχαγοί; and of its insertion, see III. 10. 5: τὸ μεγαλοπρεπές τε καὶ ἐλευθέριον, καὶ τὸ ταπεινόν τε καὶ ἀνελεύθερον. Hipparchus 1. 19. Even the most secret deliberations of men, according to Socrates, were known to the gods who are every where present. Cf. the sentiment of this passage with I. 4. 18. Sympos. IV. 48.

20.—Θαυμάζω οὖν. This section comprises a repetition of the sentiment in § 1, with reference to one particular in the accusation, as a conclusion, indicated by οὖν, igitur, (see note, § 2 above,) from the preceding arguments, a summary of which (τὸν ἀσεβῆς, κ.τ.λ.) is given as a reason for the conclusion. —— ὅπως ποτὲ. The Latins would express this by a circumlocution: miror igitur, qui tandem factum sit, ut. The particles ὅπως ποτὲ are equivalent to τίσι ποτὲ λόγοις in § 1, but may be rendered *how . . . ever*, or more familiarly: *how in the world.* It should be remarked, that it is frequently difficult, if not impossible, to express in English the shade of idea indicated by ποτέ, as well as by several other of the Greek particles, without too long a circumlocution. It sometimes may be suggested by the collocation of the words of a clause or by the tone of voice in reading, whilst its full force must be felt rather than expressed. See III. 5. 13, for a similar construction, with ὅπως: καὶ θαυμάζω γε . . . ἡ πόλις ὅπως ποτ' ἐπὶ τὸ χεῖρον ἔκλινεν, and cf. note upon § 1. In the following clause, οὐδέν ποτὲ, it has its more usual signif. *ever, at any time.* —— περὶ τοὺς θεοὺς μὴ σωφρονεῖν, was not of sound mind, right judgment, in respect of the gods. The negative μή is used, because this is a mere supposition, opinion of the Athenians, whilst οὔτε is employed below with εἰπόντα and πράξαντα, which express the author's own opinion of the conduct of Socrates. For the distinction in the use of οὐ and μή, see Kühn. Gr. § 318.

Περὶ τοὺς θεοὺς . . . περὶ θεῶν. A change of the construction of the Prep. in this way is not unusual. See Stallb. Plat. Phaedr. p. 231. D.; Aeschin. Timarch. § 52: περὶ τῶν ἀναθημάτων ἀκούω λόγους λεγομένους, and afterwards: περὶ δὲ τὸν τῶν ἀνθρώπων βίον καὶ τὸν λόγον, κ.τ.λ. It is sometimes difficult to point out a distinction in meaning between the construction of περὶ with the Accus. and Gen. as in the cases above referred to. See Fischer, Plat. Phaed. § 11. 276; Plat. Euthyphr. p. 3. B.: καινοτομεῖν περὶ τὰ θεῖα; 5. A.: καινοτομεῖν περὶ τῶν θειῶν. We even find the Accus. where we should expect the Gen. and the reverse. Plat. Menon. p. 90. B; Stallb. Plat. de Repub. VII. p. 538. D. et al. See also Kühn. L. Gr. II. § 624. —— δὲ, answering to μὲν in the preceding phrase, and introducing an affirmation of the reverse of what is there denied. Lat., ac potius. —— εἴη τε καὶ νομίζοιτο, *would be* and *be considered.*

CHAPTER II.

1.—Θαυμαστὸν . . . τὸ πεισθῆναί τινας ὡς, κ.τ.λ. The article τὸ gives the phrase the force of a substantive, (see Kühn. Gr. § 244. 11,) which is the subject of φαίνεται, and θαυμαστόν, is predicate. For the emphatic position of θαυμαστόν at the beginning of the sentence, see Kühn. Gr. § 348. 5, 6, 7. —— τοὺς νέους διέφθειρεν. For a more definite statement of this accusation as answered by Socrates, see Plat. Apol. p. 19 sq. —— δὲ . . . καὶ, *and . . . also;* see note, § 1. 3. —— προς τοῖς εἰρημένοις, in addition to what has already been said.—— πρῶτον μὲν . . . εἶτα. The omission of δέ after εἶτα, and ἔπειτα following πρῶτον μὲν is not infrequent; see Kühn. Gr. § 322. Rem. 4; L. Gr II. § 734; cf. I. 4. 11; I. 7. 2; III. 6. 2, 9, et al.—— ἀφροδισίων καὶ γαστρὸς, res venereas exercendi et edendi potandique. The omission of the article here, giving a kind of verbal force to the nouns, is worthy of notice; so χειμῶνα, θέρος, and πόνους which follow; Kühn. Gr. § 244. R. 3.—— πρὸς χειμῶνα, κ.τ.λ. The change from the genitive used in ἀφροδισίων and γαστρός (Kühn. § 275) to an accusative with the preposition, to express a more objective relation cannot escape the notice of the student. The Latins would continue the genitive: "hyemis, aestatis, laborum omnium tolerantissimus." For the power of Socrates in enduring cold and heat, etc., see Plato, Sympos. 220. B., and cf. I. 6. 2, 3, and Introd.

Ἔτι δὲ, *and besides*, or *nay more*.—— πρὸς τὸ μετρίων δεῖσθαι πεπαιδευμένος οὕτως, he was so trained (or accustomed) to moderation in his desires, ὥστε πάνυ, κ.τ.λ., that having very little he was very easily satisfied with what he had. The use of the participle, κεκτημένος, in the nominative by attraction here, is explained in Kühn. Gr. § 341. 3. 307. 4, compared with § 310. 3; L. Gr. II. § 825; and Viger. Idiot. 163. Cf. § 7; III. 3. 1; 9. 7; 11. 8, 14: τῷ φαίνεσθαι βουλομένῃ, et al. For the construction of the adverbial sentence with ὥστε, to which οὕτως corresponds in the principal sentence, see Kühn. Gr. § 341. 1. For the Infin. ἔχειν, where we might expect the Indic., see also Kühn. Gr. § 341. 3. (a); B. 139. F. 4., and L. Gr. II. § 825. 3. (a). The frugality of Socrates is described in 1. 3. 5 sq.; Oecon. II. 3; cf. also I. 6. 2. The propriety of the strong expression, πάνυ μικρά, in reference to his possessions, is evident from his own declarations found in the Apol. of Plato, p. 38, and Oecon. 2. 3: "If I could find a reasonable purchaser, I should perhaps get five minae for all my property, including my house." Cf. also Cic. Tusc. Disp. 34. 97.

2.—Παρανόμους, *regardless of law*, like our use of the word *lawless*. —— πρὸς τὸ πονεῖν μαλακοὺς, *incapable of enduring hardship*, labores adire. Cf. the meaning of the Infin. with the article with that of the nouns πόνους, κ.τ.λ. above, without it.—— ἂν . . . ἐποίησεν, like our Potential Imperf., Lat. Imperf. Subj., How could he make, or have made, etc. For the use of ἂν with the Histor. tenses in questions, see Kühn. Gr. § 344. 6; L. Gr. § 454. 6. *a*.—— Ἀλλ' ἔπαυσε. Ἀλλ' indicates the contrast with the implied negative answer to the preceding question. He could not, on the contrary he hindered (ἔπαυσε, avocare a,) many, etc. This word is here used as the Latins sometimes used immo vero, *nay rather:* "Si patriam prodere conabitur pater, silebit ne filius? Immo vero obsecrabit patrem."—Cicero. Hartung, Vol. II. 37, says that ἀλλά is often used when one suddenly stops and turns to a thought which gives the whole idea another phase. Comp. § 27; II. 6. 21; Anab. IV. 6. 19. For the construction of verbs of this class with the accusative of the person and genitive of the thing, see Sophocles' Gr. § 180. 2. The verb παύω, in the Act. *to cause to cease*, in the Mid. generally, *to cease* voluntarily, and Pass. involuntarily.—— μέν here has reference to the words, § 3, καίτοι γε οὐδεπώποτε ὑπέσχετο διδάσκ. κ.τ.λ., which restrict the clause with μέν, while that is in contrast with the preceding, as above stated. See note 1. 1.—— ποιήσας, *by making* them to desire virtue, denoting the means. So also παρασχών, see Kühn. Gr. § 312. 4. (e). —— ἂν . . . ἐπιμελῶνται, after a past tense for εἰ ἐπιμελοῖντο; cf. I. 2. 55, 59; III. 2. 4: ὧν ἂν ἡγῆται for ἂν ἡγοῖτο. ἄν for ἐάν, distinguished from the modal adverb ἄν by position at the beginning of a clause or by its connections. We have ἄν with the Subj. here, where we might expect εἰ with the Opt.: εἰ ἐπιμελοῖντο, since the Greeks were fond of recurring from indirect to direct discourse in subordinate clauses; see B. 139. m. 69, and also for the use of the Subj. after Histor. tenses, 139. m. 9.

3.—Καίτοι γε, quanquam or quanquam quidem. The particle γέ like quidem in Latin, gives emphasis to the restriction. See Kühn. Gr. § 317. 2. Cf. IV. 2. 7; Cyrop. III. 1. 38; also Cicero, de Legg. II. 6. 14: de ejus legis laude dicam; quod idem et Zaleucam et Charondam fuisse video; quanquam quidem illi non studii et delectationis, sed reipublicae causa leges civitatibus suis conscripserunt. When γέ is separated from καίτοι by intervening words, it frequently has not respect to the whole clause, but to the word which it follows, as in I. 6. 11; II. 3. 15; III. 12. 7; IV. 7. 5: καίτοι οὐδὲ τούτων γε ἀνήκοος ἦν. See Hartung's Gr. Partik. I. S. 411; Kühn. L. Gr. II. § 704. I. 2. and Tusc. Disp. III. 34, 84.—— ὑπέσχετο διδάσκαλος εἶναι τούτου, he never professed to be a teacher of these things, "se harum rerum doctorem pofiteri." Cf. with ὑπέσχ. here the forms of ἐπαγγέλλεσθαι in § 7, 8.—— τῷ φανερὸς εἶναι, by appearing to be such, etc., or on this account, because he appeared to be such. For the Nom. here by attraction with the Infin., see Kühn. Gr. § 310. 3, also § 1 above, and cf. III. 3. 1.—— συνδιατρίβοντας ἑαυτῷ μιμουμένους ἐκεῖνον. In some Mss. αὐτῷ is found instead of ἑαυτῷ, but the latter pronoun is probably used, as referring to the thoughts of Socrates and not of the author; see note, § 49. In sentiment, Plato Apol. 33 is parallel with this: ἐγὼ δὲ διδάσκαλος μὲν οὐδενὸς πώποτ' ἐγενόμην, κ.τ.λ. Accordingly, (see note 1. 4,) Socrates does not call those to whom he gave instruction μαθητάς, (pupils), but *συνόντας, συνδιατρίβοντας, γνωρίμους*, and *ἐπιτηδείους*, cf. I. 6. 3. In this way he distinguished himself from the Sophists of his time, who boasted that they could effect all things by their teachings.—— *ἐκεῖνον*, *him*, as contrasted with themselves. This Pron. is more emphatic and *distinct* than *αὐτός*, and hence appropriate where another is contrasted emphatically with the person speaking or thinking. Cf. IV. 1. 1; 2. 3; Anab. VII. 3. 4; Plat. Protag. p. 310. D.—— *τοιούσδε*. The pronouns *ὅδε, ὧδε, τοιόσδε*, and *τοσόσδε*, commonly refer to what follows; whilst *οὗτος, οὕτως, τοιοῦτος*, and *τοσοῦτος* have reference to what goes before; as in Cyrop. V. 2. 31: **Καὶ ὁ Κῦρος ἀκούσας τοῦ Γωβρύου τοιαῦτα τοιάδε πρὸς αὐτὸν ἔλεξε.** Yet the latter class somewhat often refer to what follows; as in I. 2. 61; II. 1. 10; IV. 6. 1; see also Krüger. ad Anab. II. 2. 2; and the former more seldom to what goes before, as *τοιούσδε* here. See also *τοιάδε* in I. 7. 5, at the end, with note. Different from this is it, when *τάδε*, etc., refer to an object as present before the eyes, as in Cyrop. III. 3. 35: *ἐγὼ δὲ ὑμῖν μὲν παραινῶν, ποίους τινὰς χρὴ εἶναι ἐν τῷ τοιῷδε*, i. e., in the present state of things. So in Cyrop. III. 3. 38. Anab. VII. 3. 47. In like manner in Latin, for the sake of rendering the narrative of past events more vivid, hic is used for is. See Kühner's note upon Cic. Tusc. Disp. I. 3. 5. p. 53.— Socrates was distinguished from all his predecessors by the correspondence of his life with his teachings. This was one secret of his influence. He lived according to his philosophy; cf. I. 3. 1; IV. 4. 16; 7. 1, etc. See Brandis, Gesch. Gr. and Rom. Phil. II. S. 5.

4.—'Αλλὰ μήν, see Note, I. 1. 6.—— *ὑπερεσθίοντα ὑπερπονεῖν*, that one eating immoderately should labor excessively. Socrates probably alluded to the athletæ whose voracity was proverbial. See Kühner's Note upon Cic. Tusc. II. 17. 40.—— *τὸ δέ*, answering to *τὸ μὲν* above.—— *ψυχή*, the appetite for food and drink; so it is not unfrequently used; Cyrop. I. 3. 18. VIII. 7. 4: *τῷ δὲ ἡ ψυχὴ σῖτον μὲν οὐ προσίετο.* In like manner the Latins use anima and animus. See Kühn. note on Cicero, Tusc. Disp. II. 22. 53. Cf. also, I. 3. 14, upon which Kühner says: de vehementiore amoris appetitione.—— *ταῦτα ἱκανῶς ἐκπονεῖν*, to digest by suitable labor.—— *ταύτην . . . τὴν ἕξιν ὑγιεινήν τε ἱκανῶς εἶναι.* This manner of living (*ἕξιν*) is healthful (for the body), sufficiently so, etc. This position of the adverb is emphatic. See Stallb. Plat. Phaedr. 256. E. for abundant examples, and also Kühn. Gr. § 348. 5, and L. Gr. II. § 863. 1. Cf. Cicero de Oratore, I. 21. 96: jucundum satis fore videbatur. So of other adverbs both in Latin and Greek, e. g. *πάνυ*, admodum, plane, etc.—— *ἐμποδίζειν*, *to hinder;* literally, *to fetter*, from *ἐν* and *πούς*.

5.—Ἀλλ' οὐ μὴν, θρυπτικός γε... οὐ μὴν οὐδ'. The particles οὐ μήν are often used where one phrase is followed by another which might seem to oppose it, but does not. The latter thought is strongly affirmed, whilst the first remains true. The idea here is, that, although Socrates commended the care of the body, yet he was not effeminate, etc. Latin: profecto tamen non or neque tamen; see I. 2. 27: οὐ μὴν τά γε ἄλλα οὕτω κρίνεται, in respect to other things, *surely*, we do not so judge. Thuc. 1. 5; Isocr. Paneg. 54, 68. Where there is no opposition between the antecedent and consequent member, but an agreement in sentiment, the particle μήν, in the phrase οὐ μήν or οὐδὲ μήν, not only connects, but enhances the meaning, like the Latin vero in neque vero. Οὐ μὴν οὐδέ, therefore = neque ... quidem or ac ne ... quidem; see I. 2. 63, and Hartung, Gr. Partik. II. S. 373 sq. Kühn. Gr. § 316. 1. (a). L. Gr. II. § 862. —— ἀλαζονικὸς ἦν οὔτ' ἀμπεχόνῃ, κ.τ.λ. Ἀλαζονικὸς is from ἄλη, a wandering, a roaming: thence ἀλαζών, a wanderer, and impostor, pretender, and the adjective ἀλαζονικὸς, disposed to make false pretensions, and here, desirous of display in dress (ἀμπεχόνῃ, lit. a fine outer garment worn by women and effeminate men), etc. There is undoubtedly a secret thrust, in this passage, at the sophists who were fond of display in dress and equipage; and were hence sometimes called κατ' ἐξοχὴν the ἀλαζόνες.

Ἐρασιχρηματους from ἔρασις (ἔραμαι) love, and χρῆμα, money, = money-loving, avaricious. —— συνόντας, see note, § 3 above. —— τῶν μὲν γὰρ ἄλλων ... ἐπράττετο χρήματα. Γάρ introduces the proof that Socrates did not make his disciples avaricious; and a more condensed argument it would be difficult to find: For he both (μὲν) freed them from other desires, (and of course from a desire of money, as a means of gratifying them), and (δὲ) did not take pay, exact money (ἐπράττετο χρήματα) from those who were desirous of his instructions (ἑαυτοῦ ἐπιθυμοῦντας, lit. those desirous of himself, ii, qui sui cupidi essent; and thus showed himself free from all avaricious desires. His course of conduct was thus strongly contrasted with that of the sophists, who, by their exactions from their disciples, were distinguished in the opinion of the common people for their avarice. See I. 2. 6, 11, 60; I. 5, 6; Stallb. Plato, Hipp. Maj. 282. D. and note; Gorgias p. 519. C; Oecon. 2. 8; Apol. p. 20; and Aristoph. Clouds, 99, 100:

> "These are they,
> Who can show pleaders how to twist a cause,
> So you'll pay them for it, right or wrong."

6.—Τούτου δ' ἀπεχόμενος, abstaining (or, by abstaining) from this; i. e., from taking pay from his pupils. —— ἀνδραποδιστὰς ἑαυτῶν ἐπεκάλει. Ἀνδραποδιστής, a slave-dealer, from ἀνδραποδίζω, to reduce to slavery (prob. from ἀνδρός and πούς), a more emphatic word than δουλόω, to subdue; hence in the plur. with ἑαυτῶν, *sellers of themselves*, of their own liberty. Ἐπεκάλει, to call in reproach, to stigmatize; see I. 5. 6: νομίζων τὸν παρὰ τοῦ τυχόντος χρήματα λαμβάνοντα δεσπότην ἑαυτοῦ καθιστάναι, καὶ δουλεύειν δουλείαν οὐδεμιᾶς ἧττον αἰσχράν. —— διὰ τὸ ἀναγκαῖον αὐτοῖς εἶναι διαλέγεσθαι παρ' ὧν ἂν λάβοιεν, because the necessity was laid upon them of conversing with those, from whom they might receive a reward. In Latin, as in English, the pronoun corresponding to the demonstrative τούτοις, would generally be used before the relative (ὧν): cum iis ... a quibus, with those, from whom. See examples of its omission in Greek in B. 127. 1. d. Kühn. Gr. § 331, Rem. 3, L. Gr. II. § 782. 4; cf. also II. 6. 35. For the use of ἄν here with the optative in *oratio obl.*, see Kühn. Gr. § 333. 6, and Ex.; L. Gr. II. § 798. Cf. a different use, IV. 1. 2.

7.—Εἰ ... πράττοιτο. In the use of this εἰ for ὅτι or ὡς we have an example of the urbanity of the Greeks, who preferred not to express an odious sentiment as actually existing, but as possible; see note I. 1. 13, and notice the different significations of the Indic. and Opt. mode in the two passages. —— τὸ μέγιστον κέρδος ... φίλον ἀγαθόν. A beautiful illustration of this passage is found in the Life of Socrates by Diogenes Laertius, II, 34: Αἰσχίνου δὲ εἰπόντος· Πένης εἰμὶ καὶ ἄλλο μὲν οὐδὲν ἔχω, δίδωμι δέ σοι ἐμαυτόν· Ἆρ' οὖν, εἶπεν (ὁ Σωκράτης), οὐκ αἰσθάνῃ τὰ μέγιστά μοι διδούς; —— μὴ ὁ γενόμενος καλὸς κἀγαθὸς τῷ τὰ μέγιστα εὐεργετήσαντι μὴ τὴν μεγίστην χάριν ἕξοι. After verbs of fearing, etc., instead of μή ... μή we more usually find μὴ οὐ as in II. 3. 10: δέδοικα, μὴ οὐκ ἔχω τοσαύτην σοφίαν. But the double μή is used here to indicate more definitely that the sentiment was Socrates' own. The form of the *oratio obliqua* is retained in minor parts of the sentence as well as in the general enunciation of it. See Kühn. L. Gr. II. § 718. 1. Rem. 2; also cf. Thuc. II. 13. Hartung, Gr. Partik. II. S. 177, compares this construction with that of γέ after γάρ. For an explanation of which Kühner says: subtilior quam verior mihi videtur esse, see Hermann, Adn. Viger. § 265. For the use of the participle with the article here = Latin, is, qui: ὁ γενόμενος ... τῷ ... εὐεργετήσαντι, see Kühn. Gr. § 244. 8. —— χάριν ἔχειν to feel gratitude. Hence the idea of the whole phrase: lest one who had become truly noble and good should not feel the most lively gratitude towards him who had conferred the greatest favors.

8.—Τῶν ξυνόντων ἑαυτῷ = Latin, familiares. See note upon

§ 3 above. —— εἰ μὴ ἄρα, Latin, nisi forte, used ironically. So ἄρα is often used in Attic prose. It must not be supposed, however, that ἄρα loses its inferential force in such cases. The idea in the mind of the writer here was undoubtedly something like this: unless, (which we did not suppose, but might naturally infer from the fact that such a man as Socrates was accused,) virtue is, etc. The employment of particles in this way, as suggestive of trains of thought passing through the mind of the writer or speaker, frequently of so subtle a nature that they could not well be expressed in language, is one of the most decided beauties of the Greek language, and strikingly indicative of the cultivation of the Greek mind. A close attention to such particles as ἀλλά, ἄρα, γάρ, ποῦ, δή, etc., will not only convince the student of this fact, but will repay him by the acquaintance he will thus obtain with the ancient mode of thinking, and the reflex influence of Attic delicacy and refinement upon himself. Εἰ μή without ἄρα is also found in a very similar sense. The exception made is in such cases always an impossible, or at least a highly improbable one. See Kühn. Gr. § 324. 3, L. Gr. II. § 756. 5, and Stallb. Plat. Repub. II. 375, and cf. Kühn. Cic. Tusc. Disp. IV. 23. 51. —— διαφθορὰ, like the Latin, corruptela, that which corrupts, contaminates, is perhaps here well rendered by the Part. adj., *corrupting*, or personifying it, a *corrupter*.

9.—Ἀλλὰ, very often introduces an objection. Hartung, Gr. Partik. II. 37. —— νὴ, followed by the Acc. of the name of the deity invoked, indicates strong affirmation, and is frequently used after ἀλλά in answering objections. See B. 149. m. 23. —— ὁ κατήγορος ἔφη. The common position of the words is the reverse of that found here, as in § 36: ἔφη ὁ Χαρικλῆς. Still this order is not very unfrequent; as in II. 1. 18: ὁ Σωκράτης ἔφη. 2. 7: πρὸς ταῦτα ὁ νεανίσκος ἔφη. Symp. VI. 5: ὁ Καλλίας ἔφη. Cyrop. VIII. 3. 27. Oecon. XIX. 2. We find the same construction in Latin: accusator inquit; see O. M. Müller ad Cic. de Orat. p. 98. —— ὑπερορᾶν, lit., to look over; hence, to overlook, to despise; whilst καταφρονεῖν below means, lit., to think down upon; hence, to consider valueless, to contemn; like the Latin despicere and contemnere. See I. 3. 4: πάντα τἀνθρώπινα ὑπερεώρα. 4. 10: ὑπερορῶ τὸ δαιμόνιον. —— τῶν καθεστώτων νόμων, the established or received laws. —— εἴη, optative in Orat. obliqua. —— τοὺς μὲν τῆς πόλεως ἄρχοντας; for this common construction of the Greek, with the article separated from its noun, by words which are combined with it in expressing a single conception, giving emphasis and *direction* to the qualifying words, see Kühn. Gr. § 245. 3. (a). —— λέγων, *by saying*, or when he said. —— ἀπὸ κυάμου καθίστασθαι. The Athenian magistrates were chosen by putting the names of candidates into an urn with black and white beans (κύαμοι), and those whose names were drawn with the white beans were elected; hence they are called οἱ ἀπὸ κυάμου ἄρχοντες and κυαμευτοί, 'bean Archons;' see Fiske's Man. Class. Lit p. 180. Καθίσταθαι, Mid. Voice, sibi collocare, or creare. —— δὲ after μὲν above, contrasts the conduct of men in respect to their choice of individuals for other occupations and for rulers, and may be rendered *whilst* or *although.*

Θέλειν, for which many read ἐθέλειν. The shorter form, never used by Homer and early Epic writers, and nearly always by the tragedians except in the Impf. ἤθελον, is seldom found in Xenophon and the more ancient Attic prose writers, except in particular phrases; as εἰ θέλεις, ἂν θεὸς θέλῃ; hence the ἐ was probably here erased by the corrector. It is however used in a few passages of the Memorabilia; as in II. 1. 17, and 6. 4. In I. 4. 18, we have the full form after a word ending in a consonant, and the abbreviated form after a vowel. —— κεχρῆσθαι, perfect used as present, indicating possession or continued use, *to have in his service,* v. Kühn. Gr. § 255, Rem. 5; Buttmann, § 113. 7. So this verb is generally used in Attic Greek. It is also used as a present in Epic writers, but frequently with signification, *to be in want,* need of a thing. So in a few cases in Attic writers. Cf. Demosthenes *de Corona,* p. 239, 40; 327, 304, and Homer, Odys. III. 266; XIV. 422 et al. —— κυαμευτῷ, chosen by a bean, i. e., by lot; implied of course with the following nouns, τέκτονι, κ.τ.λ. —— μηδ' ἐπ' ἄλλα τοιαῦτα; Seiffert calls this construction a slight Anacoluthon for μηδ' ἄλλῳ ἐπὶ τοιαῦτα. It is better perhaps with Kühn. to supply κεχρῆσθαι κυαμευτῷ τινί. —— ἃ...ἁμαρτανόμενα...τῶν...ἁμαρτανομένων, which going wrong (or, in which if there is error), do far less injury than when wrong is done to (or, in reference to) the State. —— ἐπαίρειν, *to induce* or *incite.* —— ἔφη, i. e., [κατήγορος] ἔφη. —— τῆς καθεστώσης πολιτείας, the existing government. —— καὶ ποιεῖν βιαίους, and made them violent, turbulent, disobedient; opposed to πραΰς, mild, gentle, obedient. Ποιεῖν is connected by καί to ἐπαίρειν. It will be observed, that Xenophon does not deny the fact that Socrates was not altogether pleased with the democratical government of Athens. Ælian, Var. Hist. III. 17, says: Σωκράτης ἐν τῇ μὲν Ἀθηναίων πολιτείᾳ οὐκ ἠρέσκετο. Τυραννικὴν γὰρ καὶ μοναρχικὴν ἑώρα τὴν δημοκρατίαν οὖσαν.

10.—Φρόνησιν ἀσκοῦντας, may be rendered, *acting prudently,* exercising practical wisdom, prudentiam colere or exercere. So Seiffert; but it seems more in accordance with the spirit of the passage to consider φρόνησις as antithetical to ἀμαθία, and to render the phrase:

those who devote themselves to mental culture. So Kühner: ego vero credo eos, qui animi cultui operam dant. —— *νομίζοντας ἱκανοὺς ἔσεσθαι.* For *ἔσεσθαι* many read *εἶναι*, supposing that after the forms of *νομίζειν*, to be construed with the nominative, Xenophon always uses the present infinitive; but we find both the future and aorist used to indicate different modifications of the same idea. For parallel cases of the Fut. and Aor. after verba putandi, etc., cf. § 8 above; II. 8. 6; III. 1. 1; 7. 8; IV. 1. 5; Cyrop. VII. 2. 28; see Kühn. L. Gr. § 445, note 2, and Gr. § 257. 2. Rem. 2. There seems to be special propriety and beauty in the use of the future here where a contingency is denoted; i. e., those who suppose that (if time and circumstances favor), they shall be suitable, etc.

Πρόσεισιν, *attend, are consequent upon.* —— *οἱ βιασθέντες . . . οἱ . . . πεισθέντες, compelled by force* (*βία*) . . . *induced by persuasion.* It should be observed that in Deponents which have both a middle and passive form in the Aor. (as *βιάζομαι, ἐβιασάμην, ἐβιάσθην*) the passive form *generally,* not always, retains the passive signification. See Rost, Gr. § 113; Kühn. § 252. Rem. Cf. Hellen. VI. 1. 7; VII. 3. 9. —— *ἀφαιρεθέντες . . . κεχαρισμένοι*; these words are here contrasted, as also *βιασθέντες* and *πεισθέντες*, and *μισοῦσιν* and *φιλοῦσιν*, and hence the most forcible rendering of *κεχαρισμένοι* is, *those who have received favors,* beneficio affici, in antithesis with those who are deprived, despoiled; although the common, almost the universal meaning of *χαρίζεσθαι* is to gratify, to bestow favor, beneficio afficere. Cf. however, Herod. VIII. 5: *οὗτοι δὲ ἀναπεπεισμένοι ἦσαν καὶ τοῖσι Εὐβοέεσι ἐκεχάριστο.* —— *τῶν ἰσχὺν ἄνευ γνώμης ἐχόντων,* those who possess force, power, without understanding. In the words of Horace: qui "vim consilii expertem" habent. —— *τὰ τοιαῦτα πράττειν.* This is the reading of all the Mss. and of all the ancient editions of any authority. Some later editors have supplied *τό* before *τὰ τοιαῦτα*, but although strict concinnity of construction would require the article to correspond with that before *βιάζεσθαι*, yet it does not so demand it as to set aside the authority of Mss. and early editions. For the infinitive, *βιάζεσθαι*, standing by itself, seems more to need the support of the *τό* than *πράττειν*, which is attended by its object; and besides, many passages are found in the most accurate Greek writers, where this strict conformity of the parts of the sentence is not observed. Kühn. in h. l.

11.—Ἀλλὰ *μήν*, see note upon I. I. 6. —— *συμμάχων ὁ μὲν βιάζεσθαι τολμῶν δέοιτ' ἂν οὐκ ὀλίγων . . . οὐδενός,* he who ventured to use force, (like vi grassari in Livy,) would indeed (*μὲν*) need allies not a few, etc. This emphatic position of the *οὐκ ὀλίγων, not a few*, at the end of the clause and the corresponding place of the *οὐδενός, not one, none*, should not escape the student's notice.—— καὶ γὰρ. See note I. 1. 19. The *γὰρ* gives a reason for the assertion in the last clause, and *καὶ* strengthens *μόνος, even* by himself, by himself alone; *μόνος* being the Nom. with the Inf., because referring to the same person with the subject of the verb.—— καὶ . . . δὲ. See note I. 1. 3: *κἀκεῖνος δέ*. —— φονεύειν, = Latin, necare, whilst *ἀποκτείνειν* = interficere;—Seiffert. —— ἢ ζῶντι πειθομένῳ χρῆσθαι; the idea is: than to have him, living, as a willing friend.

12.—Ἀλλ' ἔφη γε. The force of the particles *ἀλλ' . . . γε* is nearly that of at enim, in Latin, *but surely*, or *indeed*. The sense is the same as if the objector had said: *καίτοι γε τοῦτο οὕτως ἔχει, ὡς σὺ λέγεις, ἀλλά γε Κριτίας, κ.τ.λ.* The *γέ* not only concedes what precedes, but does it in such a way that the following is more strongly opposed; though what you say is granted in general, yet it certainly cannot be denied that, etc. Cf. note upon *καίτοι γε* in I. 2. 3 above; and also Tusc. Disp. III. 34, 84: verum quidem haec hactenus. The particle *γέ* should seem most naturally to follow Ἀλλὰ, as both refer to the whole phrase, but in Attic Greek they are generally separated by intervening words, and no material difference in its force is discoverable, whether after *ἀλλά* or the predicate that immediately follows, as here. The predicate being the most important part of the enunciation, may properly take after it a word which qualifies the whole phrase. Cf. IV. 3. 3: Ἀλλ' *οἶσθά γ' ἔφη*. But when *γέ* is not subjoined to the predicate, but to some other part of the phrase, it frequently does not qualify the meaning of the whole phrase, but of the particular word with which it is placed. Cf. however, § 49 and 51. For the exceptions with regard to separate positions of these particles, see Ast, Lex. Plat. I. p. 101. In the only instances of their use in N. T. they are written together. See Hackett's Plutarch, De Sera, etc., p. 95.

Κριτίας, the son of Callaeschrus, was one of the Thirty Tyrants who, after the end of the Peloponnesian war, were placed over the Athenians (B. C. 403) by the Lacedemonians, who had obtained the principality of Greece. He possessed much influence and exercised the greatest rigor in his rule until put to death by Thrasybulus. Hellen. II. 3, 15 sq. Thirlwall's Hist. of Greece, Ch. XXIX., XXXI. Mitford, do. Ch. 21. 2.—— Ἀλκιβιάδης, the son of Clinias, the inheritor of one of the largest fortunes in Athens, and possessed of many noble traits of character, excited the interest of Socrates, and led to his untiring exertion to win one possessing such talents and advantages for serving his country, to the side of truth and virtue. They not only lived together for a time at Athens, but served in company at Potidaea, where Socrates saved the life of his pupil, and were afterwards comrades at the battle of Delium. But the subsequent course of Alcibiades is well known. See Thirlwall I. p. 395 sq. Ch. XXIV. sq. The fact that these individuals had been intimate with Socrates, without doubt had great influence upon the minds of the undiscriminating multitude in making up their decision against him. —— μέν . . . δὲ αὖ. The same succession of particles also appears in § 24; II. 2. 14; τοὺς μὲν θεούς . . . τοὺς δὲ ἀνθρώπους αὖ; III. 1. 8. See Kühn. L. Gr. II. § 739. 2. —— ὑβριστότατος, *most insolent*, for which some read ὑβριστικότατος.

13.—Τὴν δὲ πρὸς Σωκράτην συνουσίαν αὐτοῖν ὡς ἐγένετο διηγήσομαι, by a common attraction for ἡ συνουσία αὐτοῖν ὡς ἐγέν., κ.τ.λ. Cf. I. 3. 8; 4. 13, et al. See Kühn. Gr. § 347. 3. A similar construction is found in Latin: "familiaritatem autem eorum cum Socrate qualis fuerit explicabo." With the imperative in Cic. Cn. Pompey XIII.: quae breviter qualia sint in Cn. Pompeio consideremus.

14.—Ἐγενέσθην μὲν γὰρ δή. Γὰρ is used here to begin a promised narration, sometimes called γάρ epexegetic. The δή is added to confirm the declaration, *indeed*. Cf. Sympos. 11. 4; Apolog. § 20. Infra III. 10. 10; 11. 17, et al. See Hartung's Gr. Partik. I. 287, and Kühn. L. Gr. 11. § 692. Sometimes the particle δή following γάρ does not qualify the meaning of that particle, but a preceding word in the sentence from which it is separated by γάρ. Cf. II. 4. 1: τοῦτο μὲν γὰρ δή, i. e., τοῦτο δή, *this indeed;* Cyrop. V. 3. 8: Εὖ μὲν οὖν, ἔφη, δοκῶ εἰδέναι· πολλὰ γὰρ δή ἔγωγε κἀκεῖνος ἐπαῤῥησιασάμεθα πρὸς ἀλλήλους, i. e., πολλὰ δή, prorsus multa. See Hartung and Kühner, as above.—— πάντων ὀνομαστοτάτω γενέσθαι, to become *named*, most celebrated, by all. —— Ἐγενέσθην μὲν . . . ᾔδεσαν δὲ . . . ἐλαχίστων μὲν . . . ἡδονῶν δὲ . . τοῖς δέ. The consecution of the particles is here worthy of notice. The first two parts of the antithetic clause introduced by δὲ, and contrasted by μὲν . . . δέ, belong to one class or one general idea, whilst the last δέ appends something of a different character, and may well enough be rendered by the Latin denique, *and in fine.* —— ἀπ' ἐλαχίστων μὲν χρημάτων, having the least means, or with the least means. Hieron. XI. 1: ἀπὸ τῶν ἰδίων κτημάτων δαπανᾶν εἰς τὸ κοινὸν ἀγαθόν. The same, 6; also Anab. I. 1. 9. The means or instrument with which any thing is accomplished is frequently designated in Greek by the Prep. ἀπό with the Gen. where the simple ablative would be used in Latin. Cf. § 9 above: τοὺς τῆς πόλεως ἄρχοντας ἀπὸ κυάμου καθίστασθαι, to appoint by the *bean*; i. e., by casting lots with it. In like manner the material of which any thing is made, or from which it is derived, is denoted by ἀπό. 3. 3: θυσίας δὲ θύων μικρὰς ἀπὸ μικρῶν. II. 1. 25, 28. See Kühn. Gr. § 288. 1. (e) and (f). L. Gr. II. § 598.—— αὐταρκέστατα ζῶντα, lived most contentedly, or plane contentum vivere. The use of the participle as a complement with εἰδέναι and ἐπιστάσθαι, as seen in ζῶντα, ὄντα, and χρώμενον, where we use the conjunction and finite verb, and the Latins the Accus. with the Inf., is frequent in Greek, and is distinguished from the use of the Infin., inasmuch as the Part. expresses the simple fact, and the Inf. generally indicates the manner; see Kühn. Gr. § 311. 2. —— ἐν τοῖς λόγοις, ὅπως βούλοιτο, cf. Plato, Laches, p. 187. E. For the use of ἐν with the Dat. here, see Kühn. Gr. § 289. 1 (3). (a).

15.—Ταῦτα δὲ ὁρῶντε, perceiving these things, or, when they, etc., Lat. quae quum illi viderent. —— καὶ ὄντε οἵω προειρήσθον, and being such as they have been before represented to be; or, and since they were such, etc., Lat. ac tales essent, etc. The participles ὁρῶντε and ὄντε are doubtless in the Accus. agreeing with αὐτὼ, and yet they may be rendered in Eng. as if Nom. Abs. —— πότερόν τις αὐτὼ φῇ; for the use of the Subj. in *deliberative* questions, or questions implying doubt, see Kühn. Gr. § 259. 1. (b), and L. Gr. II. § 464. Cf. § 45: ὅσα δὲ ὀλίγοι τοὺς πολλοὺς μὴ πείσαντες, ἀλλὰ κρατοῦντες γράφουσι, πότερον βίαν φῶμεν ἢ μὴ φῶμεν εἶναι. —— ἐπιθυμήσαντε, from love or desire, propter cupiditatem. For this use of the participle, denoting the cause, see Kühn. Gr. § 312. 4. (b). —— ὀρέξασθαι, from ὀρέγω, lit. to reach after, to long for, means here, in the Mid. voice, with the preceding Accus. αὐτὼ, *sought*, expetere. Ὀρέξ. τῆς ὁμιλίας corresponds in meaning with Σωκράτους ὠρεχθήτην, in § 16. Cf. Symp. VIII. 35: ἐὰν καὶ ὀρεχθῇ τοῦ σώματος. Ὁμιλίας is the Gen. of the end aimed at; see C. Gr. 373. 1 and 2. —— ἢ νομίσαντε, or because they supposed; see Kühn. Gr. § 312. 4. (b). —— γενέσθαι ἄν; for the use and signification of ἄν with the Infin., see Kühn. Gr. § 260. (5). —— λέγειν τε καὶ πράττειν. The Latin Gerund in the Accus. with ad corresponds to these infinitives: ad dicendum agendumque.

16.—Θεοῦ διδόντος; the Latin would here take the conjunction with the Subj.: si deus iis optionem daret. For the use of the Part. in the Gen. absolute, where in Eng. we use a secondary clause introduced by some particle, see Kühn. Gr. § 312. 3 sq. —— ζῶντα . . . ἑώρων. For the constr. of the Part. as a complement so frequent in Greek, with various classes of verbs, see Kühn. Gr. § 310. 4 sq. With verba sentiendi (espec. of sight), the Part. is generally to be expected, whilst with those verbs which express mere opinion, conjecture, belief, hope, etc., espec. when relating to the future, the Inf. is more frequently used. With verbs of speaking, narrating, both forms are frequently employed In general, from the nature of the two forms, the Inf. is used where the idea is general, indefinite, the Part. where it is limited by time, place, etc.; the Inf. simply *names*, the Part. *describes*. For a more extended discussion, see B. 144. 6 sq., espec. foot note; and for distinctions with particular words, see Kühn. Gr. § 311. —— ἑώρων. Besides ὁράω, the verbs ἀνοίγω and ἁλίσκομαι take both the temporal and syllabic augment. —— ἑλέσθαι ἂν μᾶλλον αὐτῶ τεθνάναι, Latin: "mortem vitae anteponere." —— Δήλω δ' ἐγενέσθην, κ.τ.λ., they became known, etc., i. e., their subsequent conduct revealed their character. —— γὰρ introduces the explanation of what they did, as the ground of the preceding assertion. —— ὡς . . . τάχιστα, ut primum, just as soon as. —— ἀποπηδήσαντε, a stronger word than ἀποφοιτήσαντε. Philostr. Vit. Apoll. IV. 38: εἴ τις διὰ τοῦτο ἀποπηδᾷ φιλοσοφίας, is sometimes compared with this passage. —— ἐπραττέτην τὰ πολιτικά, they immediately broke away from Socrates and *engaged in political life.*

17.—Ἴσως οὖν, *perhaps then*, or perhaps now. The οὖν introduces an inference from what precedes; the conduct of the pupils might suggest this objection to the conduct of Socrates. With ἴσως it denotes possible result or consequence. —— σωφρονεῖν, to be of sound mind, here, to have just views (in relation to government): Socrates ought not to teach his disciples the manner of governing, before he teaches them to do it with moderation, equity. —— οὐκ ἀντιλέγω. Xenophon leaves this reproach unanswered for the present, but resumes it in IV. 3. 1. —— δὲ . . . ὁρῶ, *but this I see*, "hoc certe video," or "tantum video." —— τῷ λόγῳ προσβιβάζοντας, bringing them over to their opinion, persuading them by their arguments. Cf. Aesch. c. Ctesiphon, c. 28: τῷ λόγῳ προσβιβάζων ὑμᾶς; also Aristoph. Avv. 425: προσβιβᾷ λέγων; Eqq. 35: εὖ προσβιβάζεις με, you teach me well, and Xen. Oecon. XIV. 4.

18.—Οἶδα . . . δεικνύντα; for this use of the Part. see note on 14 and 16 above. —— Οἶδα δὲ κἀκείνω, I know too that these men, etc. —— σωφρονοῦντε like δεικν. above. —— ἔστε from ἐς ὅτε, until when = whilst. —— οὐ φοβουμένω . . . ἀλλ' οἰομένω, not because they feared, but because, etc., Lat.: non quod vererentur, etc. The student cannot too carefully notice the frequent and varied constructions of the Greek Participle.

19.—Εἴποιεν ἄν. The Opt. with ἄν is used here to express a possibility, B. Gr. 139. m. 15. —— τῶν φασκόντων φιλοσοφεῖν, those who pretend to be philosophers, the sophists; Seiffert says: qui se volunt esse philosophos. —— σώφρων ὑβριστής, Lat. modestus and insolens, considerate or discreet, and presumptuous or insolent. The same words are used as antithetical in Cyr. 3. 1. 21. —— οὐδὲ ἄλλο οὐδέν; these accusatives depend upon the following verbal adjective ἀνεπιστήμων. See Kühn. Gr. § 279. 7; and cf. Cyr. III. 3. 9: ἐπιστήμονες δὲ ἦσαν τὰ προσήκοντα; Plat. Epinom. R. 979. D.: ὁ ταῦτ' ἐπιστήμων; Aesch. Agam. 1096: πολλὰ κακὰ ξυνίστωρ, and 103, etc. —— οὕτω γιγνώσκω. For more in reference to Socrates' opinion upon the question, so much discussed by the ancient philosophers, Whether virtue can be acquired, and also upon strengthening it by exercise, see III. 9. 1; IV. 1. and Sympos. II. 6. His idea seems to be, that it cannot even be retained without the constant practice of it. —— ὁρῶ γὰρ ὥσπερ . . . οὐ δυναμένους ποιεῖν. We should naturally expect a different constr. here, i. e., ὥσπερ . . . οἱ μὴ τὰ σώματα ἀσκοῦντες οὐ δύνανται ποιεῖν, οὕτω καὶ . . . τοὺς . . . οὐ δυναμένους. This kind of attraction by which the structure in the secondary enunciation, introduced by ὥσπερ, is made to conform to that in the primary, is frequent in comparisons; cf. § 21, and Cyrop. I. 4. 15, and examples collected by Lobeck, in Parerg. c. VI. ad Phryn. p. 755; see Kühn. Gr. § 342. Rem. 3, and L. Gr. II. § 830. 3. For a similar attraction of the Infin. in constr. with the Acc., cf. I. 2. 29. An analogous construction is found also in the Latin. See Cic. de Amicit. I. 1: te suspicor iisdem rebus, quibus me ipsum interdum gravius commoveri; and Tusc. Disp. 1. 17. 39, and Kühner's note in h. l. —— οὔτε γὰρ ἃ δεῖ πράττειν οὔτε ὧν δεῖ ἀπέχεσθαι δύνανται; the Latin language can even excel the beautiful precision of the Greek here: "neque enim facere quae oportet neque abstinere possunt."

20.—Ὡς . . . οὖσαν. When ὡς is connected with a participle, the action expressed by the Part. is indicated as something imagined or conceived of, or a supposed reason, and is the same as a Part. denoting *to think* or *say* followed by an infinitive with or without an Accus. Lat.: Propterea quod putant esse, *because they suppose*, etc. This construction is employed with a simple participle or with the Gen. or Accus. absolute. The construction with the Accus. Abs., as here, is quite frequent; since, as Buttmann says, 145. note 7, "a cause or reason presented as in the mind of another seems to depend on a verb of thinking (sentiendi) implied." See Kühn. Gr. § 312. 6. (a), (b), (d); L. Gr. II. § 673. Cf. I. 3. 2: εὔχετο δὲ πρὸς τοὺς θεοὺς ἁπλῶς τἀγαθὰ διδόναι, ὡς τοὺς θεοὺς κάλλιστα εἰδότας. —— τὴν δὲ τῶν πονηρῶν κατάλυσιν. If the ellipsis were supplied here, it would read: τὴν δὲ τῶν πον. ὁμιλίαν κατάλ. οὖσαι τῆς ἀρετῆς. —— τῶν ποιητῶν ὅ τε λέγων... καὶ ὁ λέγων, one of the poets who says:... and another who says:... The first lines are taken by Xenophon from Hesiod, Theogn. v. 35 and 36. It seems to have been a favorite couplet with Socrates, as it is put into his mouth both in Xen. Symp. II. 4, and in Plat. Menon. p. 95. D. It is not known from what poet the last verse is taken. —— διδάξεαι is here used in the signif. of the Middle voice: to procure instruction for one's self = *to learn*. It is also used in the Mid. with the meaning: *to have one taught.* Cf. IV. 4. 5. —— τὸν ἐόντα νόον, mentis quod fuit ante. This common usage of the Greek Part. is worthy of notice. —— τοτὲ μὲν ... ἄλλοτε δ', *at one time... at another.*

21.—Κἀγὼ δὲ. See note I. 1. 3: κἀκεῖνος δέ. We should naturally expect μέν here, to correspond with the δέ: Ὁρῶ δὲ, at the beginning of § 22. But the μέν is sometimes omitted before the δέ. Here its omission may be accounted for from the distance of the clauses, see note I. 1. 1. —— μαρτυρῶ τούτοις, I give my testimony or assent to them. In the Latin we should, as Seiffert says, have a relative instead of the demonstrative: quibus ego quoque assentior (testis sum). —— ὁρῶ γὰρ, see I. 1. 6. note. —— ὥσπερ; for the form of this comparison, see note, § 19. —— ἐν μέτρῳ πεποιημένων, numeris inclusus. —— τῶν διδασκαλικῶν λόγων, those things communicated by a teacher in his instructions; λόγων is here contrasted with ἐπῶν. —— τοῖς ἀμελοῦσι λήθην ἐγγιγνομένην; lit., *a forgetting occurs to those neglecting*, etc. —— Ὅταν δὲ τῶν νουθετικῶν λόγων επιλάθηταί τις, κ.τ.λ., and when one is unmindful of monitory words (admonitions, exhortations), he also forgets those affections of the mind which led it to desire moderation. —— ὧν ἡ ψυχὴ πάσχ. The antecedent is omitted here, and the relative attracted to its construction; see B. 143. 8, and also a somewhat similar constr., note § 6 above.

22.—Τοὺς εἰς ἔρωτας ἐγκυλ., κ.τ.λ., *those who plunge headlong into love-intrigues.* Concerning the use of the plural here, see I. 1. 11. note: ἀνάγκαις. For ἐγκυλισθέντας some Mss. and editions have ἐκκυλισθέντας. But there is little difference in the use and signif. of the two forms, although, lit. ἐγκυλίω means *to roll in*, and ἐκκυλίω, *to roll out*, in accordance with the prepositions with which they are compounded. Ἐκκυλ. has been compared in respect to signification with ἐκφέρεσθαι, ἐξοκέλλειν, ἐξολισθάνειν, ἐκχεῖσθαι πρὸς ἡδονάς. —— τῶν τε δεόντων, those things necessary to be done; Seiffert: ea quae facienda sunt. —— κερδῶν; concerning the variable use of the contracted and uncontracted forms of this and other similar words, see Kühn. note in h. l. —— καὶ.. δυνάμενοι, *although able*, καί here denoting concession; see Kühn. Gr § 312. R. 8; B. 144. m. 15. The attraction or transposition of the antecedent into the relative clause, and the substitution of a demonstrative Pron. in its place, is somewhat common both in Latin and Greek, see Kühn. Gr. § 332. 4., and cf. Horace, Sat. I. 1. 1, 2, et al.

23.—Πῶς οὖν οὐκ ἐνδέχεται, How then is it not possible—? 'Ενδέχεται is used impersonally as not unfrequently, cf. IV. 7. 9: μανθάνοντας ὅσα ἐνδέχοιτο; III. 9. 4: προαιρουμένους ἐκ τῶν ἐνδεχομένων, choosing from those things which can be chosen from, Stallb. Plat. de Rep. VI. p. 501. C.; and in regard to the sentiment, cf. Plat. Theag. p. 130. A. —— αὖθις, αὖτις in Homer and the Ionic writers, is a lengthened form of αὖ, with which it agrees, for the most part, in signification. Here it is an adverb of time in contrast with πρόσθεν, and = deinde. —— ἀσκητὰ. Weiske supposes that this should be ἀσκητέα, but this conjecture is rejected by Schneider and others. The idea is, that all things good and honorable, are attained unto, established, strengthened, and perfected by practice. —— οὐχ ἥκιστα δὲ, and not *least*, or *and especially*, corresponding substantially with ἀλλὰ μάλιστα, which Herodotus often uses, but more forcible. Cf. § 32: πολλοὺς μὲν τῶν πολιτῶν καὶ οὐ τοὺς χειρίστους ἀπέκτεινον. See Kühn. L. Gr. II. § 590. h. —— σωφροσύνη; we should naturally expect the article, as this is the name of a specific virtue, but see Kühn. Gr. § 244. 2. R. 4; L. Gr. II. § 485. n. 1., and cf. III. 9. 5: δικαιοσύνη . . . σοφία ἐστί; IV. 6. 7: 'Επιστήμη ἄρα σοφία ἐστίν, and other examples cited by Bornemann on Plat. Apol. 1. p. 33. —— ἐν τῷ . . . αὐτῷ σώματι συμπεφυτευμένας τῇ ψυχῇ. The preposition σύν here in composition is best rendered, *together*, and ψυχῇ put in the Dat. after τῷ αὐτῷ; although the meaning is the same if ψυχή is governed by σύν. —— αἱ ἡδοναί. The Greeks as well as the Romans were accustomed to put pleasure for the love of pleasure. For the Plur. number here, see I. 1. 11.

24.—Καὶ . . . δὴ, *now*. Δή here indicates a resuming of the subject of the conduct of Critias and Alcibiades, broken off in § 17 by answering an objection, which led to a disquisition upon the nature of virtue; and also indicates an application of what has been said, a satisfactory conclusion of the whole matter, a confidence that the conclusion about to be stated is established. Cf. § 56 and § 58; and see Hartung, Gr. Partik. I. p. 261 sq.; Kühn. L. Gr. II. § 691. The particles καὶ δή have a somewhat different signification in II. 6, 7, where see note. —— συμμάχῳ, lit. a fellow-fighter, σὺν and μάχη, but here simply, *aid, helper*. ——

ἐκείνου δ' ἀπαλλαγέντε; concerning this Nom. of the participle added by τὸ σχῆμα καθ' ὅλον καὶ μέρος, or partitive apposition, see Kühn. Gr. § 313. 1 Rem. 1: 366. 3., and L. Gr. II. 678. 2. Cf. II. 1. 4. and the passage cited in Krüger Anab. II. 4. 1. p. 112 sq. —— φυγὼν εἰς Θετταλίαν ... ἀνομία; when Critias was banished at a certain time, he fled to Thessaly, where the people were notorious for their extravagance in living, frauds, and other species of immorality. It was even called: nebulonum patriam. Cf. Plat. Crito, p. 53, D., and Stallbaum's note quoted from Fischer; also Hellen. II. 3. 36. —— δ' αὖ, see § 12. above. —— διὰ μὲν κάλλος ... δὲ ... δὲ ... καί. The clauses connected by δέ ... δέ are parts of one general idea, but καί connects something of a different nature. For the position of μέν here, see Hartung, Gr. Partik. II. 415, and cf. I. 1. 12. —— διά ... κάλλος, nearly like διὰ τὸ καλὸν εἶναι; hence, having a verbal force, it is without the article, see note upon I. 1. 9, and cf. III. 3. 11: διὰ λόγου μανθάνειν. The beauty of Alcibiades became proverbial in Greece. —— πολλῶν καὶ σεμνῶν γυναικῶν. A little below we find πολλῶν καὶ δυνατῶν; in II. 9. 6: πολλὰ καὶ πονηρά; III. 11. 4: θεραπαίνας πολλὰς καὶ εὐειδεῖς; cf. also IV. 2. 35, and Anab. IV. 6. 27. In inverse order we find, for example, in Lys. p. 753: πονηροὶ καὶ πολλοί; Aesch. c. Ctesiph. p. 592: ἄφθονα καὶ πολλά. Also in the Comp. and Superl.: πλείω καὶ μείζω, πλεῖστοι καὶ βέλτιστοι; and in inverse order III. 5. 3; Hellen. IV. 2. 5; Cyrop. I. 4. 17; Plat. Phaedr. p. 234. E. et al. From such examples as these we see that the Greeks, as also the Latins, did not consider the notion of multitude or number, as something merely external, but as inherent, a property or quality of things; and were consequently accustomed to connect numerals by καί with other attributive words. Cf. Hermann ad Viger. 323, and Kühn. L. Gr. II. § 726. 3, and 727 Anm. 2; Matth. II. § 444. 4. —— δύναμιν ... τὴν, *the power which* (he exercised or had).

Δυνατῶν κολακεύειν. Many editors, as Weiske, think that κολακεύειν should be omitted here, and that πολλῶν καὶ δυνατῶν ἀνθρώπων should stand in contrast with πολλῶν καὶ σεμνῶν γυναικῶν. But in that case ἄνδρων would have probably been written instead of ἀνθρώπων. And besides, there seems to be no good reason for the change, which is not authorized by the Mss. We are not to understand by τοὺς δυνατοὺς κολακεύειν, simply, men distinguished by the art of flattery (οἱ δεινοί or ικανοὶ κολακεύειν), sycophants, but men able to flatter Alcibiades, i. e., who had great influence upon his mind. Accustomed to flattery from his childhood, he would spurn the common herd of sycophants, and be influenced only by the attentions of men of genius, authority, wealth, and renown. Such men might properly be called δυνατοὶ κολακεύειν. —— διαθρυπτόμενος is well chosen to designate the enervating, corrupting effects of flattery. Cf. Cyrop. VII. 2. 23: ὑπὸ πλούτου διαθρυπτόμενος . . . καὶ ὑπ' ἀνθρώπων, οἵ με κολακεύοντες ἔλεγον, κ.τ.λ. —— οὕτω κἀκεῖνος, for the repetition of the subject here after ὥσπερ, κ.τ.λ., for the sake of emphasis, see Kühn. Gr. II. § 632. Cf. IV. 2. 25, and Hellen. II. 4. 41. It is found even in Homer, Il. II. 474; XVI. 428, 430. This peculiarity is found in Latin as well as in Greek.

25.—Τοιούτων δὲ, κ.τ.λ. Τοιούτων refers to what has been related in the last section. For the Gen. Abs., see Kühn. § 312. —— καὶ . . . δὲ . . δὲ . . . δὲ . . . δὲ . . . καί, *since . . . and . . . and . . . and . . . and . . . and since;* Latin: cum.. et, etc. . . . cum or cum etiam. The clauses more nearly related, it will be noticed, are connected by δέ, and those more distinct by καί. For an explanation of the joining of the Gen. Abs. with nominatives, see I. 1. 18: ὅρκον, κ.τ.λ., cf. also note, § 24. —— ὠγκωμένω, Partic. of ὀγκόω from ὄγκος, bulk, mass, weight; hence *puffed up,* elated. —— ἐπὶ γένει . . . ἐπὶ πλούτῳ, κ.τ.λ. The Latin in such cases frequently varies the construction by interchanging ob and propter.

26.—Εἶτα, *and yet.* Εἶτα and ἔπειτα are used in questions denoting astonishment, indignation, and irony, indicating an unexpected consequence from what precedes. Cf. I. 4. 11; II. 7. 5, 6, 7. Κᾆτα and κἄπειτα are used with still more emphasis; as in Cyrop. II. 2. 31, and Symp. IV. 2. See Kühn. Gr. § 344, 5. (e); B. 149. m. 19. Latin writers might use et tamen, or simply et, as in Cic. Tusc. Quaest. I. 38. 92: et dubitas, etc.? See Kühner's note in h. l. —— ἐπλημμελησάτην, 1st Aor. of πλημμελέω, from πλημμελής (πλήν and μέλος), *out of tune,* means, lit. to make a false note in music; and hence to make a mistake, to do wrong. —— ὅτι δὲ, *on the contrary,* since, etc. Δέ has a strong adversative or contrasting force here. —— ἡνίκα . . . εἰκὸς, *when,* or in the age in which, *it was natural* that they should be imprudent and headstrong, Socrates, etc.

27.—Οὐ μὴν. See note upon § 5 above. —— ποιήσας, after he has, etc. —— φανῶσιν, *show themselves, turn out.* —— αἰτίαν ἔχει τούτου, *is blamed for this,* Lat. crimen habere, or culpam sustinere. —— συνδιατρίβων, passing his time with, being a pupil or disciple of. —— Τῳ . . . ἄλλῳ τῳ, *one, any other one.* Τῳ here is the abridged form of the dative of the indefinite pronoun τίς and is therefore enclitic. —— συγγενόμενος, being with, conversing with, as a disciple with his master. —— ἀλλ' οὐχ, ac non. See note upon I. 2. 2: 'Αλλ' ἔπαυσε μέν. —— ἀλλ' οἵ γε πατέρες. Γέ here is not concessive but emphatic; and it does not qualify the phrase, but the word πατέρες *indeed.* See Hartung, I. S. 414. The whole clause may be rendered: But *even* their fathers themselves, whilst they live with sons (i. e., though even with their sons), are not blamed when their children do wrong, if they themselves conduct properly. How then, the author intends to have implied, can masters be reproached for the faults of their pupils, since they are so much less favorably situated to exert an influence over them than parents.

28.—Δίκαιον ἦν κρίν. The use of the Imperf. Indic. here corresponds with the Latin usage: see Zumpt, Gr. § 518. 2.—— εἰ μὲν αὐτὸς ἐποίει ...ἂν ἐδόκει. By the use of the Indic. mode with εἰ here in the protasis, and the Indic. with ἄν in apodosis, the impossibility both of the thing conditioned and the result is implied, i. e., Socrates did not conduct badly and was not therefore bad. The Imperf. is used of *past time* when we might expect the Aor., because continued action is implied; see B. 139. m. 28 and 29; Kühn. 339. 1. (b).—— εἰ δ' αὐτὸς σωφρονῶν διετέλει, here we have εἰ with the indicative in the protasis, since the condition is a reality or fact, i. e., if he always was of a right mind (which he was), how, etc.; and ἄν with the Opt. in the Apod. to represent the thing conditioned as undetermined, uncertain, Kühn. § 339. II. 3. a. (α); L. Gr. II. § 811. b. Cf. II. 2. 7, and 5. 4: εἴ γε ταῦτα τοιαῦτά ἐστι, καλῶς ἂν ἔχοι, II. 2. 3.

29.—'Αλλ' εἰ, κ.τ.λ., comprises an objection of the opposer of Socrates, in the language of the writer, and grants that if the accusation were well founded, Socrates would be justly reproached: If that be true which is asserted, (but it is not, as is implied in the use of the tenses, see note, § 28 above), that although he did not himself do evil, yet when he saw it in others, he was accustomed to approve, etc.—— Κριτίαν μὲν. The particle μέν is here added, because the author has it in mind to speak afterward of Alcibiades. —— τοίνυν, derived from τοι or τῷ, therefore, and the slightly deductive νύν, introduces the confutation of the preceding objection. It is here μεταβατικήν; i. e., it indicates transition. See Hartung, Gr. Partik. II. 348 sq.; Kühn. Gr. § 324. 3. (c), and Stallb. Plat. Rep. VII. p. 518 D. and VIII. p. 564.—— Εὐθυδήμου. This is the same individual who is called Εὐθύδημος ὁ καλός in IV. 2. 1.—— πειρῶντα χρῆσθαι. The Partic. πειρῶντα may be used here in the middle sense, πειρᾶσθαι (to attempt, conari); but it is perhaps better, supplying αὐτὸν after it, to consider it as active and equivalent to the Latin, tentare aliquem = ad amorem pellicere or pudicitiam tentare; and then χρῆσθαι is the infinitive, denoting design or purpose: *that he might*, etc. Hieron. XI. 11: καὶ τοὺς καλοὺς οὐ πειρᾶν, ἀλλὰ πειρώμενον ὑπ' αὐτῶν ἀνεχέσθαι ἄν σε δέοι, pulchros non tentare, etc. Cyrop. V. 2. 28, and Stallb., Plat. Phaedr. p. 227. C. Χρῆσθαι is elsewhere used of sexual intercourse. Rep. Lac. II. 12: τῇ ὥρᾳ χρῶνται. Symp. VIII. 15: μορφῆς χρῆσις, also 28, and 36 et al.——ἀπέτρεπε φάσκων, *he discouragea him by saying*, or, whilst he thus spoke, Lat. cum ita dictitaret.——ᾧ βούλεται. For the use of the Indicative Present in *oratio obliqua*, see note and references in I. 1. 13.——προσαιτεῖν...ἱκετεύοντα καὶ δεόμενον, to seek with supplications and prayers, supplicando ac precando petere. Προσαιτεῖν is properly used of mendicants or beggars. Oecon. XX. 15: προσαιτῶν διανοεῖται βιοτεύειν. Plato, Phaedr. p. 233. D, and Symp. p. 203. B; VIII. 23.——ὥσπερ τοὺς πτωχούς, by attraction for ὥσπερ οἱ πτωχοί (sc. προσαιτοῦσιν). See note upon § 19 above.——προσδοῦναι, καὶ ταῦτα, κ.τ.λ., that he impart to himself, and that too of what is of no value, is positively bad (φίλημα ἢ ἄλλο τι ψηλάφημα, Symp. VIII. 23). Τὸ μηδὲν ἀγαθόν = vitium. Προσδοῦναι is here followed by the partitive genitive. See Kühn. Gr. § 273. 3. (b), and cf. Eurip. Cycl. 528; Aristoph. Pac. 1111. For the use of καὶ ταῦτα, see B. 150. m. 16.

30.—Τοῦ δὲ Κριτίου...τὸν Σωκράτην...τοῦ Εὐθυδήμου...ὁ Κριτίας. It will be noticed that the article has not been previously used in this narrative with the proper names. It seems to be added here to make the distinction between the individuals more definite. With Critias too: ὁ Κριτίας, it may be considered as denoting contempt, *this* Critias.——λέγεται, Impers. *it is said*, etc.——ὑϊκόν, *like a swine, swinishly*. One Ms. and some editors insert τὶ here with ὑϊκόν, but it might have easily crept in from the ὅτι, and it is not necessary as the neuter adjective is not unfrequently used in this way without τὶ. Cf. II. 7. 13: θαυμαστὸν ποιεῖς; Anab. I. 4. 18: ἐδόκει δὲ θεῖον εἶναι; Cyrop. V. 3. 2; Plat. Legg. II. p. 657. A. θαυμαστὸν λέγεις, Symp. p. 175. A., and Stallb. Plat. Phaedr. p. 274. C. Concerning the word ὑϊκόν, cf. Cyrop. V. 2. 17: τὸ δὲ κεκινῆσθαι ὑπὸ τῶν βρωμάτων καὶ τῆς πόσεως πάνυ αὐτοῖς ὑϊκὸν καὶ θηριῶδες δοκεῖ εἶναι.——προσκνῆσθαι, confricare aliquem.

31.—Ἐξ ὧν δὴ καί. And on account of these things, (the reproofs related in the previous paragraph,) indeed; or, on account of even such things as these. Δή here qualifies the sense of the pronoun ὧν.——τῶν τριάκοντα ὢν νομοθέτης μετὰ Χαρικλέους. Cf. Hellen. II. 3. 2 and 13. Of the thirty tyrants besides Critias the leader, only Charicles is mentioned, because he, conspiring with Critias and aided by a few others, acquired great authority and influence in the republic. Νομο θέτης, *legislator, law-maker.* The νομοθέται were a legislative committee chosen for the final revision of the laws before they were carried into execution; see *nomothetes* in Smith's Dict. of Antiquities. Critias, it seems, was one of this committee. See Thirlwall's Hist. of Gr. Vol. I. p. 460 sq. For the construction of the partitive genitive, τῶν τριάκ. with the Part. ὤν, see Kühn 273. 3. —— ἀπεμνημόνευσεν αὐτῷ. Ἀπομνημονεύειν τινί, to bear something in mind either for or against any one; here of course, *against.* Cf. Il. XXIV. 428; Hesiod. Theog. 503; Thuc. I. 137. —— λόγων τέχνην, not rhetoric merely, but the whole art of discoursing upon public affairs, or upon philosophy and other species of literature. It therefore referred not only to Socrates, but to all who taught any art of this kind. Hence, from its general character, the article is omitted with τέχνην. —— ἐπηρεάζων ἐκείνῳ, lit. threatening, and hence seeking to abuse or calumniate him. The same verb is also used in III. 5. 16. —— ὅπῃ ἐπιλάβ., that on which he might lay hold. —— ἀλλὰ τὸ κοινῇ τοῖς φιλοσόφοις ... ἐπιτιμώμενον ἐπιφέρων αὐτῷ, but applying to him the reproach made by the multitude against the philosophers generally (i. e., that they possessed the art of making the worse appear the better reason, τὸν ἥττω λόγον κρείττω ποιεῖν,) and [thus] calumniating him with them. Cf. Plato, Apol. p. 18. B. and Stallbaum's note; Aristophanes, Nubes, 95–100, et al., in reference to this reproach. —— οὐδὲ γὰρ ἔγωγε οὔτε αὐτὸς ... οὔτε ἄλλου, κ.τ.λ.; I have here followed Schutz, Weiske, and Kühner in reading οὐδὲ γὰρ instead of οὔτε γὰρ. The particles, οὐδὲ γὰρ, in a negative, correspond to καὶ γάρ in a positive declaration; cf. I. 4. 9; and in Mss. οὔτε and οὐδέ as well as μήτε and μήδε are often confounded. The Greek γάρ, like the Latin enim, often refers to a thought to be supplied from the preceding context; here: there was no just cause of complaint against Socrates, but the common reproach of the philosophers was transferred to him; for neither I myself have heard Socrates claiming any such art (as is made a reproach against the philosophers, i. e., τὸν ἥττω, κ.τ.λ., see above), nor have learned that any other one says, etc. Οὔτε is used by Anaphora with ἔγωγε ... αὐτὸς in order to make the contrast of those words with ἄλλου more emphatic.

32.—Ἐδήλωσε δέ. Κριτίας is sometimes considered as the subject of ἐδήλωσε, but it is much better to treat this verb as intransitive and impersonal = δῆλον ἐγένετο, it was evident, or, the thing itself made it plain, viz. that Critias had special reference to Socrates, when he introduced this law. See Kühn. Gr. § 249; Buttm. § 129. 9; Matthiae. II. § 360. 2. and cf. Cyrop. VII. 1. 30: ὡς οὐκ ἔστιν ἰσκυροτέρα φάλαγξ ... ἐδήλωσεν.—δέ, continuative here, *and.* —— ἐπεὶ γὰρ. For the use of the explicative γάρ after such phrases as ἐδήλωσε δέ, see Kühn. L. Gr. 754. B; Hartung's Gr. Partik. § 470. a; cf. III. 4. 12; Symp. IV. 17: τεκμήριον δέ· θαλλοφόρους γὰρ, κ.τ.λ. —— οὐ τοὺς χειρίστους cf. § 23 and *note above*: οὐχ ἥκιστα. Concerning the cruelty and injustice of the thirty tyrants, see Hellen. II. 3. 12 sq.; Thirlwall's Greece, I. 408 sq., Ch. XXXI., and Sallust Catil. LI. 28–31. —— πολλοὺς δὲ προετρέποντο, κ.τ.λ., turned, incited, impelled many; Lat.: impellere ad injuste agendum; see note upon § 64, and cf. Plat. Apol. p. 32. C. Mid. voice used to denote that they did it for their own advantage or gratification. —— που, perhaps, I suppose, or if I am not mistaken; Lat. opinor. It indicates here not that Socrates casually made the remark, but that Xenophon did not know that he made it except from circumstances that afterwards occurred, such as Charicles' allusion to it, as indicated in § 37. —— βοῶν ἀγέλης νομεὺς, κ.τ.λ. Plato uses this same image more fully drawn out in his Gorgias, p. 516. A. B. —— μὴ ὁμολογοίη...μὴ αἰσχύνεται, μηδ' οἴεται, κ.τ.λ. The change from the optative to the indicative mode in these two clauses is worthy of notice, as showing the facility of the Greek in expressing nice shades of thought. The first is a comparison, a supposed case, and hence the optative; but the indicative is used in the last, since a real fact, which was before the eyes of Socrates, is brought to view. See Kühn. L. Gr. II. § 819. Anm. 5.

33.—Καλέσαντες ὅ τε Κριτίας καὶ ὁ Χαρικλῆς... ἐδεικνύτην.. ἀπειπέτην, κ.τ.λ. The interchange of number between the plur. and dual is not unusual, especially with the participle, as here, even in prose, though more frequent in poetry. See Kühn. § 241. R. 8; L. Gr. II. § 426. Anm. 2., and cf. II. 3. 18. —— τόν τε νόμον, the law mentioned in § 31: λόγων τέχνην μὴ διδάσκειν.—ἀπειπέτην μὴ διαλέγεσθαι. For this apparently pleonastic though emphatic use of the negative μή after verbs of forbidding and the like, see Kühn. § 318. 8; Hermann ad Viger. § 271. Cf. IV. 4. 3. De Repub. Lac. IX. 2: ὁ Λυκοῦργος... ἀπεῖπε μηδενὸς ἅπτεσθαι. —— Ὁ δὲ Σωκράτης; δέ may be here rendered by the Latin, tum, *then.* —— Τὼ δ' ἐφάτην. The affirmative answer is frequently made in Greek by some form of φημί, and the negative by the same, with the addition of the negative οὐ.

34.—Τοίνυν; see § 29 above. This particle is not unfrequently used in dialogue where one quickly and promptly answers another, as here: Well then! I am prepared to obey, etc.; cf. § 35, 37 and I. 6. 9. In the last case Socrates answers a question put by himself. —— λάθω τι παρανομήσας. The Partic. here may be rendered as a verb, and the verb as an adverb, *unconsciously;* so frequently with such verbs as λανθάνω, τυγχάνω, etc.; see Kühn. Gr. § 310. 4. (l). —— Πότερον τὴν τῶν λόγων τέχνην σὺν τοῖς ὀρθῶς λεγομένοις; κ.τ.λ., considering the art of speaking as an aid to (adjumento esse) those things which are spoken, etc. Σύν τινι εἶναι or γίγνεσθαι signifies, to be an aid or assistance to any one; the σύν indicating accompaniment, and then, both accompaniment and the consequent aid. See Kühn. Gr. § 289. 2. —— δῆλον ὅτι ἀφεκτέον εἴη. This construction of the optative with ὅτι, after the present, δῆλόν (ἐστιν,) in the primary enunciation, is very rare; and indeed is never used, without there is allusion to what has been spoken by another. Here the reference is to the prohibition which is under discussion. In other cases the present tense is followed by the indicative. See Kühn. L. Gr. § 769. —— πειρατέον ὀρθῶς λέγειν. This whole passage has been thus paraphrased: You prohibit the exercise of the art of speaking. The question therefore arises, whether you mean the art of speaking rightly (ὀρθῶς), or the art of speaking not rightly (μὴ ὀρθῶς). If you prohibit the art of speaking ὀρθῶς, such as I exercise, it is necessary to abstain from speaking ὀρθῶς, which is absurd; but if you forbid the art of speaking μὴ ὀρθῶς such, e. g. as the Sophists exercise, it is necessary to use exertions for speaking ὀρθῶς, and that kind of speaking which I employ must be approved, since it teaches ὀρθῶς λέγειν. For it cannot be supposed that all speech, whether well or ill, is forbidden by you; therefore your prohibition pertains not to me, who commit to my disciples the art of speaking rightly.

35.—Καί = tum, then; the Latin might also employ et and a relative, instead of a personal pronoun where there is a change of persons as interlocutors: cui Charicles. —— τάδε, *something;* referring as τάδε usually does to what immediately follows; see note I. 2. 3. For the use of the plural here, see note upon § 1. 1. 5 ταῦτα. —— σοι εὐμαθέστερα ὄντα προαγορεύομεν, κ.τ.λ., lit. (with τάδε) we announce to you something that is more easily understood. Notice the difference in meaning between the participle, as expressing a fact, and verb in the infin. indicating the result, the thing to be accomplished. —— ὅλως μή, like the Lat. omnino non, Germ. gar nicht, *wholly not*, or *not at all.* —— ἀμφίβολον ᾖ· ὡς, that I may not be in doubt, *so as to do*, or *and so do*, etc. Seiffert compares this construction with that of the Accus. with the Infin. in Latin, after dubito, (see Zumpt's Gr. § 541.), and Kühner renders ὡς, *as*, Germ. wie, but may it not here take the place of ὥστε, and denote result or consequence as above rendered. —— μέχρι πόσων ἐτῶν, *within how many years*, or, *until what age;* cf. III. 5. 27: μέχρι τῆς ἐλαφρᾶς ἡλικίας, as long as active age continues. Hellen. III. 1. 14:

μέχρι τετάρων ἡμερῶν, to the end of four days.—νέους . . τοὺς ἀνθρώπους. Notice the use of the article in designating the subject here. *men are*, etc.—Ὅσου περ, εἶπε, χρόνου, the Gen. of the time within which something happens; see Kühn. § 273. 4. (b). The verb ἔφη is more usually employed in quoting the words of another in this way. Yet εἶπε is somewhat frequently found. Cf. Symp. III. 8: Τί γὰρ σύ, εἶπεν, and Bornemann's note in h. l. where he quotes other instances. In Latin we sometimes find dixit used in the same manner, instead of inquit. Βουλεύειν = βουλευτὴν εἶναι, see I. 1. 18 and note. The age at which one might be chosen to the senate was thirty years. See Smith's Dict. of Ant., Art. βουλή. So in the next clause it is added: you shall not converse with those who are under thirty years of age.—ὡς οὔπω φρονίμοις οὖσι. Ὡς is frequently used with a participle in the same case as the principal subject of the sentence (here a pronoun understood), to give a reason, motive, etc.—μηδὲ σύ, neither indeed shall you. If the preceding clause were positive instead of negative, we should in Attic prose have καὶ μή, although in Ionic and poetic writers μηδέ might even then be used; Kühn. Gr. § 321. 2.

36.—Μηδὲ ἄν . . . ἤν. Great offence has been taken at the change in form, ἄν, ἤν, of this particle and its repetition without a connective; hence some propose καὶ for ἤν. But no change seems to be necessary, for the identity of meaning in the two particles is unquestionable. And when one of two conditional clauses is dependent on another, i. e., used for the sake of explanation, illustration or more accurate definition, they are not connected by a copula. Thus here the action of buying is dependent on that of selling. Cf. the repetition of εἰ in II. 3. 9 and Anab. III. 2. 31 with Bornemann's note. The same construction is found in Latin. Cf. Cic. pro S. Rosc. Amer. I. 2: si quis istorum dixisset . . . si verbum de re publica fecisset; also de Finib. I. 3, and Kühn. Tusc. Quaest. V. 9. 24, and also L. Gr. 823. 9.—ἔρωμαι ὁπόσου πωλεῖ, "ask what he wants for it." In Latin the principle verb would follow the subordinate phrase.—Ναὶ τά γε τοιαῦτα. Ναί followed by ἀλλά makes a qualified assent: *yes*, such things indeed, (sc. it is right for you to ask] but, etc. Γε gives emphasis to τοιαῦτα, and thus strengthens the contrast between *these things* and those introduced by ἀλλά following.—ἀλλά τοι, *but certainly*, (τοι rendering the exception more emphatic); see Kühn. Gr. § 317. 3. These particles are used in the same way in II. 2. 7; III. 6. 10. A verb is frequently interposed between them. Cf. Cyrop. I. 5. 13: Ἀλλὰ πιστεύω τοι.—σύ γε. Γε renders the σύ emphatic. We should give its force by an emphasis on *you*.—Μηδ᾽ ἀποκρίνωμαι . . . ἐὰν εἰδῶ οἷον, κ.τ.λ., shall I not answer . . . if I know, for example, where, etc.

37.—Τῶνδέ. For the use of ὅδε τοιόσδε, etc., as preparatives, see Kühn. Gr. § 304. 2; L. Gr. II. § 631. 2. —— δεήσει = oportet. —— τῶν σκυτέων, κ.τ.λ.; an elliptical phrase for τῶν παραδειγμάτων τῶν ἀπὸ τῶν σκυτέων. Socrates was accustomed in his conversations, to illustrate and confirm his positions by examples or similitudes from common life, from potters, artists in wood and iron, etc. The sophists, on the other hand, far less wisely, drew their illustrations from objects that were splendid and magnificent, and endeavored to captivate their hearers by the elevation of their style. They often even ridiculed the Socratic manner of speaking, as common, low, trite. Cf. IV. 4. 5; Plat. Symp. p. 221. E; 491. A; see also Aristophanes' Clouds, 235. —— κατατετρῖφθαι διαθρυλουμένους, they are worn out by your constant harping upon them, by your constantly having them in your mouth. The verb κατατρίβειν properly refers to the *examples* (which as we say are trite), but is here poetically transferred to the men themselves from whom illustrations were drawn. —— τῶν ἑπομένων τούτοις, those things which are connected with these illustrations, i. e., τοῦ δικαίου, κ.τ.λ., which I am accustomed to connect with these when I make use of them, (sc. must I abstain from, ἀπέχεσθαι δεήσει). The phrase, τά τινι ἑπόμενων, is often so used. See Plato de Rep. III. p. 406. D; p. 412; VI. 486. D. —— τῶν ἄλλων τῶν τοιούτων, such like things, alia id genus. The article before τοιούτων is sometimes omitted. But see examples of its use in Cyrop. I. 22: καὶ τἆλλα τὰ τοιαῦτα; Bornemann, ad Apol. § 33. p. 77. ed. 1824. The Vulg. reading for τοιούτων is δικαίων. —— καί τῶν βουκόλων γε, and at least, from herdsmen. This is adduced as proof that the law was introduced with special reference to Socrates, § 32, above. —— ὅπως μὴ is here followed by the 1st Aor. tense, Subj. mood, ποιήσῃς, in opposition to a canon of criticism which has sometimes been adopted, i. e., that it requires a Fut. indicative. Dawes' canon is now however given up by all scholars. See Kühn. L. Gr. Tom. II. § 777, and cf. II. 1. 19; 10. 1; Woolsey's Gorgias, 480. A. p. 169.

38.—Ἔνθα καὶ, *then indeed.* Καί connects the fact, the *becoming evident,* δῆλον ἐγένετο, with the previous supposition of the fact, § 32 above. —— οὖν. See note on 1. 16 above. —— ὡς εἶχον πρὸς ἀλλήλους, εἴρηται; lit., as they had themselves to each other, it has been related; i. e., their relation and intercourse which each other has been unfolded.

39.—Φαίην δ' ἂν ἔγωγε, *and I would add.* We sometimes give the force of γέ in such cases as this, by emphasis upon *I.* The idea is:

my opinion is, etc. —— οὐκ ἀρέσκοντος αὐτοῖς Σωκρ. ὡμιλησάτην. The negative οὐκ should be joined with ὡμιλησάτην in translating here, and the Gen. Abs. with the Part. indicates the ground or reason: because S. was pleasing, etc. —— ὅν χρόνον, κ.τ.λ., *as long as* they were with, or, in company with, etc. —— οὐκ ἄλλοις τισὶ μᾶλλον . . . ἤ, they did not attempt to converse with others more than with those who, etc.; or, not so much as, etc., like the Latin, non tam . . . quam. Cf. Thuc. II. 40; Demosth. pro Megalop. 10. p. 183. —— τοῖς μάλιστα πράττουσι τὰ πολιτικά, "qui potissimum rempublicam gerunt," most skilled in, etc.

40.—Ἐτῶν, partitive Gen. with εἶναι. See Kühn. Gr. § 273. 3.—— Περικλεῖ, ἐπιτρόπῳ μὲν ὄντι ἑαυτοῦ, κ.τ.λ., with Pericles who was his guardian, and a leading man in the State, he was accustomed to converse; etc. Cf. Plat. Alcib. I. p. 104. B; p. 118. B. —— τοιάδε, as follows. See note § 3 above.

41.—Φάναι. The sudden change here from *oratio obliqua* to *recta* should not escape notice. Such constructions are frequent in Latin, where the words of another are quoted. Cf. e. g. de Orat. I. 56, 239 sq. —— ὦ Περίκλεις. The interjection *O* with the Voc. in Latin, is never a simple form of address, as here, but indicates wonder, displeasure, or some other passion or affection of the mind. —— ἔχοις ἄν, potes ne —— Πάντως δήπου, entirely, *I think*. ——Δίδαξον δή, *now then* teach, etc. Δή sometimes adds urgency to the request, (Cf. II. 3. 11: λέγε δή μοι,) and also, at the same time, indicates a consequence which follows from what has gone before; here an inference from πάντως δήπου, (since you are able), and urgency with the Imper. and the formula of swearing, πρὸς τῶν θεῶν. Cf. III. 6. 5: Λέξον δή, tell me then. See Hartung, Gr. Partik. I. 260 sq.; Kühn. Gr. § 315. 1; L. Gr. II. § 691. B. —— φάναι τὸν Ἀλκιβιάδην. Cf. this with the beginning of the section, where the verb stands by itself with the pronoun implied. —— νόμιμοι, obedient to law, or, observant of law.

42.—Ἀλλ' here denotes opposition to a sentiment implied in the preceding paragraph, i. e., that it is difficult to understand what law is. We need not render it in English, the shade of thought may be given by the manner of uttering the clause following. —— οὐδὲν τι. The indefinite pronoun τί is used here, as elsewhere with adjectives, indefinite numerals, and adverbs, like the Latin quidem, to give emphasis; see Kühn. Gr. § 303. 4; L. Gr. II. § 633. Herbst renders the two words: nihil quicquam; cf. Symp. IV. 21: ἧττόν τί με οἴει μεμνῆσθαι αὐτοῦ. ——

γνῶναι; for the forms of the Aor. of verbs in -ω like verbs in -μι, see Kühn. Gr. § 191 sq. —— πάντες γὰρ οὗτοι νόμοι εἰσίν, by attraction for πάντα ταῦτά ἐστι νόμοι, as in § 43: καὶ ταῦτα νόμος ἐστί. Cf. III. 11. 4: οὗτός μοι βίος ἐστί, he is my life or food to me; IV. 4. 13; Anab. V. 4. 27: ἦσαν δὲ ζειαὶ αἱ πλεῖσται for ἦν δὲ ζειαὶ τὰ πλεῖστα. But this is by no means a universal principle of the language. Attraction does not take place, especially where the relative or demonstrative pronoun precedes. See τί ἐστι νόμος in § 41, and also in the preceding clause; III. 11. 6: ὅ τι ἂν ἐνταῦθα ἐμπέσῃ, τούτῳ τροφῇ χρῶνται, and καὶ ταῦτα νόμος ἐστι in § 43. Cf. other examples collected by Bornemann, Anab. I. 3. 18; see Kühn. Gr. § 240, 1; L. Gr. II. 421. A. 1. This law of attraction is carried much farther in Latin than in Greek; see Zumpt's Gr. § 376; and cf. Cic. Tusc. Disp. I. 10. 20; IV. 10. 23, et al. —— δοκιμάσαν, *approving.* —— ἔγραψε, *propose* or *ordain.* —— φράζον, *indicating* or *explaining,* what, etc. For the Part. as a complement with *verba declarandi,* see Kühn. Gr. § 310. (b). —— ἃ μή. There is a baldness in this form of expression which is seldom allowed in Latin. Either the verb *oportet* with the negative or a verb antithetical to *facere* (ποιεῖν), as, e. g. *omittere,* might be supplied. —— τἀγαθά, things that are good; see Kühn. § 244. 8. In the answer it is unnecessary to repeat the relative form in translating. —— νομίσαν. The common reading is ἐνόμισαν; but the one which we have given, first proposed by Reiske, found in Ms. *F,* and received by Wolf and others, seems to be preferable. The participle is frequently used in this way, with a verb implied from the preceding or succeeding context. Cf. Symp. IV. 53, and also § 2 with Bornemann's note. Also II. 1. 23 below, and note. See Hermann ad Viger. § 215; Kühn. Gr. § 313. R. 1; L. Gr. § 680. —— ὦ μειράκιον. O youth! or in familiar language of address ὦ may be rendered *my:* my son! —— τὰ δὲ κακὰ οὔ. The negative οὔ is rendered emphatic by being placed last. In Latin the same idea would be expressed by minime, but with a reversed position; minimeque mala.

43.—Ἐὰν δὲ, *now if indeed.* —— Πάντα...ὅσα ἄν, *all things whatsoever;* like the Lat.: omnia, quaecunque. —— τὸ κρατοῦν, the ruling power of the city, those who [at the time] rule it. —— κρατῶν τῆς πόλεως, *ruler* of the city; Partic. as a *nomen agentis,* followed by the Genit. —— καὶ ταῦτα νόμος ἐστί;... καλεῖται. In Latin, if there was not an attraction in gender as in the preceding section: πάντες, κ.τ.λ., yet the singular number of the pronoun would be employed: hoc lex est; and, as a general principle, the singular relative, quod, is used where the Greek has the plural; as ὅσα in this same sentence.

44.—*Ἄρ' οὐχ*, nonne. The *οὐχ* indicates that an affirmative answer is expected, cf. note, I. 1. 15, and Kühn. § 344. 5. (b). The deductive force of the interrogative *ἆρα* can scarcely be traced in many cases, although it undoubtedly implies the idea of consequence, result, in the mind of the speaker. —— *ὅταν ὁ κρείττων ... ἀναγκάσῃ*, where the stronger constrains the weaker, not *by persuasion* but *by force.* The participles indicating the means; Kühn. Gr. § 312. 4. (e). —— *ὅσα ἄρα*, whatever things *then.* Ἄρα is here an illative particle, denoting an inference or conclusion from what precedes. Cf. note I. 1. 2, and § 8 above, and see Kühn. Gr. § 324. 3. (a). —— *ἀνατίθεμαι γὰρ τὸ, κ.τ.λ.*, for I retract what I before said, that, etc. This metaphor is drawn from the game of draughts (*πεττῶν*); *ἀναθεῖναι πεττούς*, is to take back the draughts; i. e., to put them in another place, when they are found to be placed wrongly (*θεῖναι πεττούς*, to place the draughts, is antithetical to this). Hence *ἀνατίθεσθαι* receives the meaning: *to correct an error*, or *retract any thing done amiss.* Cf. II. 4. 4. It is often used with this significance in Plato as in Gorg. p. 461. D; Protag. p. 211, etc. Μετατίθεσθαι is used in the same manner in IV. 2. 18. —— For the use of the article *τὸ* with the Infin. *εἶναι*, or with the phrase following, see Kühn. § 308. R. 1; L. Gr. II. § 643.

45.—*Εἴτε μή*, sc. *γράφων*; see note, § 42. —— *κρατοῦν τῶν τὰ χρήματα ἐχόντων*, ruling, prevailing, over those who have wealth.

46.—*Μάλα τοι ... Ἀλκιβιάδη.* The particle *τοί* is used in answers for the purpose of giving emphasis to an assent, or to indicate astonishment or impatience at the question asked. See Kühn. L. Gr. II. § 840; Gr. § 344. 7, and cf. note upon I. 6. 11. In II. 1. 11, 13, it is used in an objection: Ἀλλ' ἐγώ τοι, but I *indeed.* Some editors substitute a comma for the colon after Ἀλκιβιάδη, and connect *μάλα τοι* with *δεινοί.* But these words seem to supply the required answer to Alcibiades' question; and their collocation at so great a distance from *δεινοί* is perhaps a sufficient reason for not connecting them in meaning with that, although such adverbs as *μάλα, μᾶλλον, πάνυ, πολύ*, etc., are often separated by several words from a word which they qualify, for the sake of emphasis. See note upon II. 6. 35. —— *καὶ ἡμεῖς*, *we also.* The use of the plural for the singular, for the sake of modesty, by which the speaker associates others with himself in his views, etc., is unusual in Greek prose, but very common in Latin, and somewhat frequent in the Greek poets. Cf. II. 7. 1 (at the end); Cyrop. (at the beginning), and see Kühn. Gr. § 241. R. 12. —— *τηλικοῦτοι ὄντες*, when we were of such an age [as you], of your age. —— *δεινοὶ ... ἦμεν*, were powerfully much skilled in such inquiries as these. —— *Εἴθε ... ὅτε δεινότατος* σαυτοῦ ταῦτα ἦσθα, O that I had been with you, Pericles, when you excelled yourself [i. e., at other times], in these things, or, when you were in possession of your full vigor and skill in these things. For the use of the Indic. mode, συνεγενόμην with the particle εἴθε, see B. 139. N. 2. For this use of the Superl. with the Genit. of the reflexive pronouns, and its significance, see Kühn. Gr. § 323. 5; B. 132. N. 23, and L. Gr. II. § 750. g. For a similar use of the Comp., (δεινότερος), which some contend, should be read here, see Venat. XII. 20: ἅπας ἑαυτοῦ ἐστι βελτίων, and De Re Equest. 1. 14: ἅπαντα βελτίω ἑαυτοῦ ἔσται.

47.—Ἐπεὶ... τάχιστα, lit., *when they very quickly;* but we may render here, *just as soon as*, see C. 525. R. —— Τοίνυν, Lat. igitur, denotes that the thread of discourse, which has been interrupted, is resumed; see also note upon § 29 above. —— πολιτευομένων ὑπέλαβον κρείττονες εἶναι, supposed themselves superior to those who were employed in governing the State. —— οὔτε γὰρ... ἄλλως... εἴ τε, *for in no other respect... and if,* etc. The particles οὔτε (μήτε)... τε, are often used in Greek like nec (neque)...et (que) in Latin, *not ... and,* indicating denial on the one side and affirmation on the other. Cf. III. 4. 1; Anab. II. 2. 8: ὤμοσαν... μήτε προδώσειν ἀλλήλους σύμμαχοί τε ἔσεσθαι; V. 1. 6, and Krüger, Dionys. Hal. Historiogr. p. 269, where many examples of οὔτε... εἴ τε and οὔτε... ἤν τε are cited. See Rost Gr. p. 695; Kühn. L. Gr. II. § 743. α; and Gr. § 321. 2. (a). For the corresponding Latin idiom, see Cicero, Tusc. Disp. 1. 29. 71: Socrates nec judicibus supplex fuit, adhibuit que liberam contumaciam; and I. 4. 8 with Kühner's note. —— ἐλεγχόμενοι ἤχθοντο. For the use of the participle as a complement with *verba affectuum*, see Kühn. Gr. § 310. 4. (c); L. Gr. II. § 659. III.; and cf. II. 1. 33: ἀπολείποντες, αὐτὸν ἄχθονται; III. 13. 3: ἄχθονται πίνοντες. —— ὧνπερ ἕνεκεν καὶ Σωκράτει προσῆλθον. The καί is omitted in one Ms. but its insertion is according to a common Greek idiom, which employs it after relative pronouns, with the signification *even* or *also*, etiam. Cf. I. 2. 31; III. 8. 2: ἧπερ καὶ ποιεῖν κράτιστον. See Hartung, Gr. Partik. I. S. 136, and Kühn. L. Gr. II. § 728. 2.

48.—Κρίτων, a wealthy Athenian, who having discovered the eminent talents, and being charmed with the manners of Socrates, "is said to have withdrawn him from the shop and to have educated him (καὶ παιδεῦσαι)." He afterward became a faithful and "reverential disciple of the great genius he had discovered." See Introd. Cf. Diog. Laert. 11. 20. —— ὁμιλητής, agrees as predicate with Κρίτων and is understood with the following nouns, see Kühn. § 242. R. 1 with (c). —— Χαιρεφῶν καὶ Χαιρεκράτης; see note, II. 3. 1.—— δημηγορικοί, from δημηγορέω (δῆμος and ἀγορεύω) with the adjective-ending, qualified for public speaking, *orators.* —— οἰκέταις καὶ οἰκείοις, when these words are used together in this way, as they often are, the first, οἰκέται designates servants, and the latter relatives, kindred. See IV. 4. 17, and Bornemann's note. —— καὶ τούτων οὐδείς, Latin: quorum quidem nemo. We can follow either the relative (Latin) or demonstrative (Greek) constr., in English. —— οὔτε νεώτερος οὔτε πρεσβ.... οὔτε ἐποίησε ... οὔτε, κ.τ.λ., neither ... nor ... either ... or, Latin: neque ... neque ... aut ... aut.

49.—Ἀλλά ... γ'; see note, § 12 above. —— προπηλακίζειν, lit., *to bespatter with mud,* or, *to trample in the mud;* hence to treat with contumely, to abuse. For more upon this reproach in reference to the teachings of Socrates, see Apol. § 20, and Aristoph. Nubes, 1407, K., where Phidippides, a pupil of Socrates, is introduced as beating his father and demonstrating its justness. —— τοὺς συνόντας αὐτῷ. Some editions read ἑαυτῷ, as in § 51, where one Ms. has αὐτῷ. See also § 8, § 52, and IV. 5. 1, compared with IV. 7. 1. But there seems to be no good reason for a change where either word is properly used. The difference seems to be that the reflexive ἑαυτοῦ refers the thought to the mind of the person who is spoken of, and αὐτός to the mind of the speaker. Substantially the same principle obtains in the Latin, with this difference, that in Greek αὐτός is oftener used, and in Latin the reflexive pronoun. See Kühn. Gr. § 302. 5; L. Gr. 628. 1; Buttmann, § 127.—— παρανοίας ἑλόντι, *convicting of madness,* folly. The verb αἱρεῖν is used in law as a *term. tech.:* to convict of; cf. Aeschin. contr. Ctesiph. § 156: μηδ' αἱρεῖτε παρανοίας ἐναντίον τῶν Ἑλλήνων τὸν δῆμον τῶν Ἀθηναίων. See, for the causal genitive here, Kühn. Gr. § 274. 2. In respect to the accusation, see Plato, De Legg. XI. 3. p. 928. E, and Meier and Schömann Attic Process III. 1. p. 296. —— τεκμηρίῳ τούτῳ χρώμενος, using this (i. e., the law just specified, κατὰ νόμον ἐξεῖναι, κ.τ.λ.) as an argument, that it is right that the more ignorant should be held in bondage by those who have more knowledge. For the construction of the noun as predicate, with the demonstrative as subject, and the omission of the article, see Kühn. Gr. § 246. 3. R. 1; L. Gr. II. § 488, Anm., and Rost § 98. n. 3. The phrase is equivalent to this: τοῦτό ἐστι τεκμήριον, ᾧ ἐχρῆτο. Cf. § 56 below, and Plat. Gorg. p. 510. D: αὕτη, ὡς ἔοικεν, αὐτῷ ὁδός ἐστι, and Stallbaum's note in h. l. In IV. 6. 15 we find the article used: ταύτην τὴν ἀσφάλειαν εἶναι; see note in h. l.—— δεδέσθαι, Perf. *to keep bound,* and, *to hold in bondage;* see Kühn. Gr. § 255. 2., especially R. 6. for this use of the Perf. tense.

50.—Ἐσκόπει, τί διαφέρει. For the use of the pronoun of direct interrogation instead of the indirect, see I. 1. 1; and for the Indic. in *oratio obliqua* here, see note (and references), I. 1. 13. The difference between μανία and ἀνεπιστημοσύνη is further explained in III. 9. 6.——τῶν τοιούτων ἕνεκα, Latin: adeo, or, "quam ob rem."——τὰ δέοντα, the things that ought to be known.

51.—Ὠφελοῦσιν, are of service to.——τοὺς μὲν...τοὺς δὲ, the former... the latter, or, those... these.——οἱ συνδικεῖν ἐπιστάμενοι, those who were skilled as, or were by profession, advocates. According to the Latin construction, either ὠφελεῖν or some synonymous word would be repeated in the disjunctive clause.

52.—Ἔφη δὲ, [sc. ὁ κατήγορος.——ὄφελος. Supply ἐστίν. For Socrates' sentiments in regard to friendship, see further in II. 4. 5 sq. ——ἑρμηνεῦσαι, lit. to be an interpreter, ἑρμηνεύς; here, to explain in words, to expound. Thus Pericles, in Thucyd. II. 60, says of himself: οὐδενὸς οἴομαι ἥσσων εἶναι γνῶναί τε τὰ δέοντα καὶ ἑρμηνεῦσαι ταῦτα. ——διατιθέναι, *managed* or *influenced.*——ὥστε μηδαμοῦ... εἶναι, *were nowhere, not to be taken into account.* Weiske, whose opinion Kühner adopts, says, that λόγου or τιμήματος and not τοπόυ the more usual ellipsis, is to be supplied with μηδαμοῦ, and hence the idea: *were of no estimation.* Such an ellipsis is found with πολλοῦ, ὀλίγου εἶναι. Plato, Gorg. 456. C: οὐδαμοῦ φανῆναι, and Soph. Antig. 183, but it is unnecessary here.——πρὸς ἑαυτόν; the preposition here indicates *comparison,* with the idea of preference, see Kühn. Gr. § 298. III. (d) and Examples; L. Gr. II. § 616. cf. I. 3. 4; III. 5. 4; Cyrop. III. 3. 20. For a similar construction with the Latin ad, see Cic. Tusc. Disp. I. 17. 40.

53.—Οἶδα μὲν has Ἔλεγε δὲ [= οἶδα δὲ λέγοντα] answering to it, in § 54.——καί; corresponding to this is the καὶ before πρὸς τούτοις, cum... tum, *both... and.*——περὶ πατέρων τε καὶ τῶν ἄλλων συγγενῶν τε καὶ περὶ φίλων. Some editors omit the τε after συγγενῶν, but without Ms. authority, although the τε after πατέρων is omitted by two or three Mss. The true explanation seems to be that συγγενῶν and φίλων are in apposition with ἄλλων, and then the τε is in place: concerning parents and others, both relatives and friends. It is true the περὶ before φίλων seems at first view not to be accordant with this explanation; for we should expect: περὶ πατέρων τε καὶ τῶν ἄλλων, συγγ. τε καὶ φίλ. But φίλων designates a class distinct from πατέρων and συγγενῶν, and may therefore very naturally have the preposition repeated with it. See I. 3. 3. and note, also Symp. V. 3: Ἐγὼ μὲν ναὶ μὰ Δί', ἔφη, (νομίζω τὸ καλὸν εἶναι) καὶ ἐν ἵππῳ καὶ βοῒ καὶ ἐν ἀψύχοις πολλοῖς. Many persons prefer to render here: "Concerning fathers and also the rest of our relatives, and also concerning friends." —— τούτοις γε δή, ὅτι, κ.τ.λ. In regard to the diff. reading γε διότι, see Kühn. in h. l. —— ἐξελθούσης, *going out from*, leaving, sc. the body. —— ἐξενέγκαντες; instead of the form of the 1st Aor. the Attic writers more usually use Aor. 2, ἐνεγκών. Yet there are several cases where the readings vary between the two forms, as in II. 2. 5; III. 6. 18; IV. 8. 1; Anab. VI. 5. 6, et al. —— ἀφανίζουσιν, lit., to make unseen, from ἀφανής (a priv. and φαίνομαι, φανῆναι), and hence, as often, to bury, cf. Soph. Antig. 261, and Aelian. H. An. II. 7.

54.—Ἔλεγε δέ, *and also*. —— ἕκαστος ἑαυτοῦ ὃ πάντων... ἀφαιρεῖ, κ.τ.λ. The construction here is ἕκαστος αὐτός τε ἀφαιρεῖ καὶ ἄλλῳ παρέχει (ἀφαιρεῖν), (τούτου) ὃ πάντων ἑαυτοῦ μάλιστα φιλεῖ, τοῦ σώματος (λέγω), ὅ τι, κ.τ.λ., each one either himself removes, or presents to another to remove, from that which he especially loves, i. e., from his body, whatever, etc. For the construction of ἑαυτοῦ with the relative, see III. 11. 1: ἑαυτῆς ὅσα καλῶς ἔχοι. A relative clause is often added in Greek either with, or, as here, without a demonstrative Pron. for the sake of explanation. So in Latin, see Tusc. Disp. I. 13. 29: qui nondum ea quae multis post annis tractare coepissent, physica didicissent; and also 1. 35, and Kühner's note, p. 53. —— αὐτοί τέ γε. Some editors as Ernesti read γάρ for γε, but the latter is supported by the Mss. The γε is used here like the Latin quidem, and is perhaps one of the most striking examples of the employment of it, much like γοῦν or a mild γάρ, in argumentation. See Hartung's Gr. Partik. I. p. 388 sq., and Kühn. L. Gr. II. 704. 1. —— παρέχουσι... ἀποτέμνειν, κ.τ.λ. The infinitives are used as the object of the verb without the article, and although active in form are taken in a passive sense. See Kühn. Gr. § 306. 1., and Rem. 10; L. Gr. II. § 642. note 2. —— τούτων χάριν; for this use of the Acc. as a preposition, see Kühn. Gr. § 288. 2. R. —— ὠφελεῖ μὲν οὐδὲν αὐτοὺς ἐνόν, κ.τ.λ., being retained, it not only does not . . . but rather, etc.

55.—Οὐ διδάσκων, not that he might teach, etc., non quo doceret. For the use of the participle to indicate purpose, see Kühn. Gr. § 312. 4. (c); B. 144. N. 4. The different construction after the two participles διδάσκων and ἐπιδεικνύων is worthy of notice. We find similar changes in Latin after non quo, e. g. Cic. de Orat. I. 18. 54: non quo aperiret... sed cum maxime tamen hoc significabat. II. 72. 295: non quin imitandum sit, sed tamen est multo turpius. —— τὸ ἄφρον, the neuter adjective with the article used as an abstract noun = ἀφρο σύνη, amentia. —— τοῦ ... εἶναι. For the use of the article in the Genit. with the Infin. denoting purpose, see Kühn. § 308. 2. (b); B. 140. N. 10. —— τῷ οἰκεῖος εἶναι, the being related, *relationship*. —— βούληται. For the ellipsis of the subject, the indefinite pronoun τὶς here, see Kühn. Gr. § 238. 4. (e); L. Gr. II. 414. 5; and Soph. 157. 8. The construction is the same as if: παρεκάλει ἕκαστον ἐπιμελεῖσθαι had preceded. Cf. III. 9. 6: τὸ δὲ ἀγνοεῖν ἑαυτὸν, καὶ μὴ ἃ οἶδε (sc. τὶς) δοξάζειν τε καὶ οἴεσθαι γιγνώσκειν, ἐγγυτάτω μανίας ἐλογίζετο εἶναι, and see the note upon it. The omission of the indefinite subject τὶς is somewhat common in some of Plato's Dialogues. See Woolsey's Gorg. p. 456. D. For the use of the Subj. instead of the Opt. here, see note I. 2. 2; B. 139. m. 50.

56.—Τούτοις μαρτυρίοις; for this constr. see note upon § 49 above. —— Ἡσιόδου μὲν τὸ, *and indeed this* (line or sentiment) *from Hesiod*. The attributive genitive is frequently used without its governing noun when it may be easily supplied. See Kühn. Gr. § 263. β. τό is in the Acc. and is the object of λέγειν, omitted in consequence of its use in the following clause. —— Ἔργον δ' οὐδὲν ὄνειδος, κ.τ.λ. This is from Hesiod's Works and Days (Ἔργ. καὶ Ἡμερ.) I. 309, where the author is speaking of rustic labor, but the opposers of Socrates accused him of quoting it as having reference to every kind of action. They joined the negative οὐδέν with ἔργον, instead of with ὄνειδος, as it appears from what follows: μηδενὸς ἔργου ... ἀπέχεσθαι. —— Τοῦτο δή. For the use of the particle δή in resuming the discourse which has been interrupted (here, by the quotation), see note upon § 24 above, and cf. § 58: ταῦτα δή, κ.τ.λ. —— λέγειν αὐτὸν, ὡς; this he adduced [quoted and explained] *as if* the poet, etc., οὕτως being implied in the preceding clause.

57.—This section, with IV. 6. 3, 4, 13, and 14, has been sometimes adduced as a proof that Socrates was accustomed to enter too much into detail in his conversations. See Wiggers' Life, Ch. IV. —— ὁμολογήσαιτο. For the use of the Optat. to denote repeated action, with such particles as ἐπειδή, see B. Gr. 139. C. note 2; Hermann ad Viger. § 243; Kühn. L. Gr. II. § 809. *b*, and 797. 3. So in I. 3. 4; 4. 19; II. 9. 4 et saepe. —— ἀγαθόν τι ποιοῦντας ἐργάζεσθαι; cf. Plat. Charmid. p. 163. C: τὰ γὰρ καλῶς τε καὶ ὠφελίμως ποιούμενα ἔργα ἐκάλει, καὶ ἐργασίας τε καὶ πράξεις τὰς τοιαύτας ποιήσεις. —— ἐργάτας ἀγαθούς. The word ἀγαθοὺς is omitted by some editors, supposing the idea of goodness to be included in Socrates' mind, in ἐργάζεσθαι and ἐργάτης. But it seems to be added for the sake of emphasis: those who did something good both labored and were good laborers. For the sentiment, cf. III. 9. 9.

58.—Τὸ δὲ Ὁμήρου. This passage is from the Iliad, II. 188 sq. and 198 sq. —— Ὅντινα ... ἄνδρα, *whatever* man, followed by the optative κιχείη, *he might find.* —— βασιλῆα καὶ ἔξοχον, (whether) *king or noble.* —— κακὸν ὥς, like a base man, a coward. —— Δαιμόνι, i. e., δαιμόνιε, used very often, especially by Homer, in salutation, sometimes as a term of regard, but oftener of expostulation and reproach. In the first case, it may be rendered: good sir, or, my friend; in the last: wretch, villain. —— δημότας = δημοτικούς, plebeios, the common people. This word is used by Xenophon alone of Attic writers. Cf. Cyrop. II. 3. 7 and 15; VIII. 3. 5. In Rep. Ath. 1. 4 both δημόται and δημοτικός are used in the same signification. Cf. the use of the latter word in § 60 below.

59.—Ἂν ᾤετο; for the use of this conditional Imperf., see note I. 1. 5. —— ἄλλως τ᾽ ἐὰν πρὸς τούτῳ καὶ θρασεῖς ὦσι, and *besides* or *especially* if in addition to this they are also headstrong. Ἄλλος τ᾽ has here much the same import with which ἄλλως καί is frequently employed. When καί is added it perhaps gives additional emphasis to the clause: see Kühn. L. Gr. for the distinction between the two phrases, and cf. his Gr. § 321. (a), and Examples; Buttm. p. 436; Hermann ad Viger. § 232. Cf. also, II. 6. 30; 8. 1; Plat. Phaed. p. 87. D.

60.—Ἀλλὰ Σωκράτης γε. Ἀλλά here refers to the preceding negative clause: οὐ ταῦτ᾽ ἔλεγε. The force of the γε is not the same as in § 12 above, where see note; but joined with the name Σωκράτης and not with the predicate, qualifies that noun; but S. (however it may be with others), etc. Cf. § 61. —— τἀναντία τούτων, the very reverse of these things. Sometimes also with the Dat. τούτοις instead of τούτων. Cf. II. 6. 5: ὃς τἀναντία τούτων ἐγκρατὴς μέν ἐστι, κ.τ.λ. Also τοὐναντίον in II. 7. 8, and IV. 2. 4. For the use of the Genit. see Kühn. Gr. § 273. R. 9; L. Gr. II. § 522. dd. —— φανερὸς ἦν, presented himself to all, or was evident to all, as, etc. —— ἐπιθυμητάς; a highly descriptive appellation for disciples, those who long for, desire, etc. See I. 2. 5: τοὺς δὲ ἑαυτοῦ ἐπιθυμοῦντας, note upon I. 2. 3., and Apol. § 28. Cf. in Latin, Cic. Brut. XVI. 64: habet (Lysias) certos sui studiosos. —— οὐδένα πώποτε μισθὸν ... ἐπράξατο. See I. 2. 5. above. —— ἀφθόνως, ungrudgingly, liberally. —— ἐπήρκει τῶν ἑαυτοῦ, sc. doctrines, or knowledge. See II. 1. 31: τίς δ᾽ ἄν δεομένῃ (sc. σοί) τινὸς ἐπαρκέσειεν. Kühn. L. Gr. II. § 519. a. In regard to Socrates' liberality to his pupils, see Symp. IV. 43; I. 2. 5. above, and also I. 6. 3. and 11.

Apol. 16. Plat. Hipp. M. p. 300. D. et al. —— ὧν τινες. Perhaps the writer had especially, though not exclusively in view here, Aristippus, who first gave out that he would teach the Socratic philosophy for pay. V. Diog. Laert. 11. 65. —— λαβόντες, *having received*, intrans. —— χρήματα διδόναι, *money to pay*.

61.—Πρὸς τοὺς ἄλλους ἀνθρώπους κόσμον... παρεῖχε. Cf. 1. 3. 3: καὶ πρὸς φίλους, κ.τ.λ. The accusative with the preposition seems to denote the propagation of the renown indicated by κόσμον παρεῖχε, i. e., *among* or *in the estimation of foreigners*. For a similar construction with εἰς, see Plat. Tim. p. 25. B., and Kühn. II. § 603 and 613 with pas sages there quoted. —— Λίχας. Lichas was son of Arcesilaus, and con temporary with Socrates. See Thucyd. V. 50. He is also spoken of in Xen. Hellen. III. 2. 21, but the name is written Λείχας. Cf. also Plu tarch, Cimon, p. 284. C. (c. 10). —— ὀνομαστὸς ἐπὶ τούτῳ. The pronoun οὗτος generally refers to what has gone before, although it may refer to what follows, see note upon I. 2. 3. Kühner seems to refer it to the following account of Lichas, but it is not unreasonable to suppose that its antecedent is implied in the general phrase: κόσμον παρεῖχε. For the use of ἐπί with the dative to indicate design, purpose, etc., see Kühn. Gr. § 296. II. (c) and Examples, and L. Gr. II. § 612. p. 298. Cf. Demosth. Ol. II. (v. 111), p. 35: τὴν ἐπὶ τοῖς ἔργοις δόξαν, and also below II. 1. 27, 28: ἐπ' ἀρετῇ θαυμάζεσθαι; III. 6. 16. —— ταῖς γυμνοπαιδίαις. For an account of the festival of "naked youths," see Smith's Lexicon, Art. *Gymnopaidia*. The time in which any thing takes place is sometimes put in the dative without a preposition. See Rost. Gr. 106. l. d.; Kühn. Gr. § 283. 3, and L. Gr. II. 569. Cf. Plat. Symp. p. 174. A: διέφυγον τοῖς ἐπινικίοις. So also other names of festivals, Παναθηναίοις, Διονυσίοις, Ἐλευσινίοις, etc. In Latin the Ablat. is used in this way: Saturnalibus, etc. See Zumpt § 475, note. —— τὰ ἑαυτοῦ δαπανῶν, expending his own resources, or bearing his own expenses, i. e., living without expense to others. —— τὰ μέγιστα πάντες... ὠφέλει. The verb ὀφείλειν governs two accusatives. The accusative of the thing may be taken adverbially. So in IV. 1. 1: οὐ μικρὰ ὠφέλει τοὺς εἰωθότας αὐτῷ συνεῖναι. In the same manner κακοποιεῖν is constructed in III. 5. 26: πολλὰ τὴν χώραν κακοποιεῖν. In the pass. ὀφείλειν retains the Accus. of the thing effected; as in III. 11. 3: πλείω ὠφελήσεται, et al. See B. 131. 5 and 8; Kühn. L. Gr. II. § 558 b. and Anm. 2. In respect to the article with μέγιστα, cf. Cyrop. 1. 6. 8: ὅτε τὰ ἄριστα πράττοι, and Apolog. § 18, with Bornemann's note in h. l. —— βελτίους... ποιῶν. The Pres. and not the Aor. Part. is used here, because customary and not a single action is indicated.

62.—Μὲν δή. These particles are often used in conclusions. *Now* (since things are as above represented), or *accordingly* Cf. IV. 3. 18. Where after μὲν δή, δέ or δὲ δή follow, they indicate that the discussion of the present subject is concluded, and that something new is entered upon. Indeed the particles μὲν δή not unfrequently begin a new sentiment or argument for which previous preparation has been made. So in IV. 3. 2. Cf. Apol. § 31, § 32, and § 34. See concerning these particles Kühn. II. § 691. B. c; S. 387; Hartung, I. S. 262 sq.; Hoogeveen Doctr. Part. Gr. ed. Schütz, p. 460 sq.—— τιμῆς ἄξιος εἶναι τῇ πόλει, see note upon I. 1. 1.—— Καὶ κατὰ τοὺς νόμους δὲ σκοπῶν, κ.τ.λ. This would in Latin naturally be more closely connected with the preceding sentence: "quod si quis e legibus quoque consideret, idem invenire poterit. See note upon I. 1. 3.—— ἐάν τις φανερὸς γένηται κλέπτων, if any one is clearly caught in the act of theft, or clearly a thief, etc. These same crimes are spoken of as most heinous in Plato, Repub. IX. p. 575. B; Gorg. p. 508. E; Xen. Symp. IV. 36; Apol. 25.—— λωποδυτῶν, a clothes-stealer, lit. a putter on of others' clothes (λῶπος and δύω), especially applied to those who stole clothes from baths, furibus balneatoriis, who were condemned to suffer capital punishment if the value of the theft was more than ten drachms. See Potter's Gr. Antiq. I. 25, or Smith's Dictionary of Mythology; Meier and Schömann, Attisch. Process, III. 1. p. 229 and 359–361.—— τούτοις, Dat. plur. after the singular τὶς *constructio* κατὰ σύνεσιν. See Kühn. L. Gr. II. § 419. 6; Gr. § 241, and cf. II. 3. 2; 8. 6; III. 10. 1.

63.—Ἀλλὰ μὴν denote a passing to another and stronger argument; see note I. 1. 6.—— πώποτε αἴτιος ἐγένετο, was he ever the author.—— Οὐδὲ μὴν ... γε, see note upon I. 1. 6.—— κακοῖς περιέβαλεν. Compounds with περί for the most part govern the Accus., but they are sometimes followed by a Genit., or by a Dat. as here. See Kühn. L. Gr. II. § 610 note. Cf. Isocrat. Paneg. p. 67. B: περιβάλλειν ταῖς μεγίσταις συμφοραῖς. So also in III. 10. 2: ἀνθρώπῳ περιτυκεῖν. 13. 1, and IV. 2. 27: τοῖς κακοῖς περιπίπτουσι.

64.—Πῶς οὖν ἔνοχος ἂν εἴη τῇ γραφῇ, How then could he be subject to indictment? For the use of οὖν conclusive, and the difference between οὖν used to indicate result or consequence, and ἄρα, see I. 1. 2. The force of ἂν with the Opt. in questions, see explained in Kühn. Gr. § 260. 4. (c).—— ὅς. The relative is sometimes emphatically used in Greek after an interrogation, for οὗτος or αὐτὸς γάρ; so in Latin q u i or q u i q u i d e m, as in Cic. Phil. IV. 5: virtus est una altissimis defixa radicibus; q u a e (i. e., haec enim) nunquam ulla vi labefactiri potest, etc.; and in Eng. *who* with the emphasis. Cf. I. 4. 11: Ἔπειτ' οὐκ οἴε (θεοὺς), φροντίζειν οἵ, κ.τ.λ.; III. 5. 15: πότε γὰρ οὕτως Ἀθηναῖον, ... οἵ, κ.τ.λ. Kühn. L. Gr. II. § 800. a. Emphasis is added to the relative by joining γέ with it; ὅς γε as in III. 5. 16; Hellen. II. 4. 41. Ὅς may even be used for οὗτος γάρ when not preceded by an interrogative, as in III. 5. 11. —— ἀντὶ μὲν τοῦ μὴ νομίζειν θεοὺς. This beautiful use of the Infin. as verbal noun, where the Latin would employ a circumlocutory phrase with the Subj.: "pro eo, quod Deos esse non putaret," should not escape notice. —— γέγραπτο, so Bornemann, Kühner, Seiffert, and others give the text instead of ἐγέγραπτο. It should seem that the Augment in the Pluperfect tense is sometimes omitted even in prose for the sake of euphony, when a vowel which cannot be elided precedes and in words compounded with a preposition which ends in a vowel. Cyrop. III. 2. 24, where the authorities are divided between γεγένηντο and ἐγένοντο, also in Cyrop. IV. 1. 9: καταλέλειπτο; VII. 2. 5: καταδεδραμήκεσαν, Hellen. II. 2. 11. ἐπιλελοίπει, et al. —— ᾐτιᾶτο Imperf. tense, referring to the time in which the accusation was made, whilst the Pluperf., γέγραπτο, alludes to the fact of the previous writing of the indictment. —— οἴκου εὖ οἰκοῦσι. Ms. F. and some editions have here: οἶκοι εὖ οἰκοῦσι. It is certain that οἰκεῖν allows this construction, for it is used intransitively, meaning: to be inhabited, to be managed, etc. Cf. Hellen. IV. 8. 5, and examples cited by Stallb. Plato ad Rep. V. p. 463. D, and VIII. p. 543, begin. See Kühn. Gr. § 249. 1, and examples. But all the Mss. except F. without variation have the reading given in the text, and Xenophon uses such forms of expressions elsewhere. See note I. 1. 7. —— προτρέπων ἐπιθυμεῖν. The middle form προτρέπεσθαι is used, § 32 above, and in II. 3. 12; III. 3. 8; 5. 3; IV. 5. 1; 8, 11, and the active in II. 1. 1, et 5. 1; IV. 7. 9; III. 3. 15. From these examples it is evident that the two forms are used with substantially the same signif., the active perhaps denoting the simple notion of exhortation, whilst the middle joins with this a relation to the subject.

CHAPTER III.

1.—Δὲ δή. For this use of these particles = καὶ δή in similar constructions, and introducing a particular under a general principle, see Hartung, Gr. Partik. I. 265, 6, and cf. Arn. Gr. Prose Comp. 257, 8. They may be rendered in Eng. *now* or *now indeed*, Latin *jam* or *jam vero*. —— καὶ refers to a suppressed clause: Socrates not only did not corrupt or injure his disciples as we have seen, but he was even (Lat.: etiam) profitable to them. So in II. 7. 14: καὶ ὑμᾶς αὐτάς. III. 6. 11; 11. 13 Cf. note upon I. 1. 6, and IV. 1. 5; 6. 1. It is used in a similar manner even at the beginning of a treatise, as in Apol. § 1: Σωκράτους δὲ ἄξιόν μοι δοκεῖ εἶναι μεμνῆσθαι καὶ ὡς... ἐβουλεύσατο περί τε τῆς ἀπολογίας καὶ τῆς τελευτῆς τοῦ βίου, i. e., whilst you speak of other things, it seems to me to be important *also*, etc. Cf. also § 3: οὐκ ἐχρῆν μέντοι σκοπεῖν, ὦ Σ., καὶ ὅ τι ἀπολογήσῃ; and Bornemann's note. See Kühn. Gr. § 321. R. 5; L. Gr. § 728, 9. —— τὰ μὲν... τὰ δὲ, *both... and, partim,... partim.* B. 128. n. 5. —— ἔργῳ δεικνύων... καὶ διαλεγόμενος; see I. 2. 59: λόγῳ μετ' ἔργῳ, and note I. 2. 3. —— τούτων, referring to ὡς ὠφελεῖν ἐδόκει, and in the plural, as many kinds of utility are included. —— δή. See note upon I. 2. 24. —— ὁπόσα ἄν. Ἂν is generally supposed to qualify the sense of ὁπόσα in such cases as this, but it is worthy of inquiry whether it does not here qualify the verb which is in the Aor. Sub., giving an air of uncertainty to the declaration: I shall be able, (may chance), to remember; or, answering to Fut. Perf. of the Latin: meminero.

Τὰ μὲν corresponds to διαίτῃ δὲ in § 5 below. —— τοίνυν, see note upon I. 2. 29. —— φανερὸς ἦν, may be rendered as if impersonal, as freq., although strictly personal, *it was apparent.* —— καὶ ποιῶν, κ.τ.λ., that he both did, and *said*, etc. —— ὑποκρίνεται. For this word some modern editors have substituted ἀποκρίνεται, but apparently without necessity; for ὑποκρίνεσθαι is used with the signification: *to answer*, not only in the Ionic writers, as in Herodotus, I. 78, 91, and elsewhere; but also in Thucydides, as in VII. 44. 5. —— περὶ, Latin, de, of, concerning. —— ἥ τε... Σωκράτης τε, see I. 1. 14. —— ἀναιρεῖ, very often used in reference to the responses of oracles. Kühner says: Verbam ἀναιρεῖ de oraculorum responsis proprium est ac legitimum. Cf. Apol. 14; Anab. III. 1. 6; V. 3. 7. —— οὕτως καὶ. This is the reading adopted by Bornemann, Kühner, Seiffert, and others, instead of οὕτω καὶ found in some Mss. and editions. Οὕτως seems to be used by Attic writers even before a consonant, where *so* or *in this manner* is to be expressed with emphasis. Cf. Kühn. in h. l. —— παρῄνει (sc. οὕτω ποιεῖν). Anab. III. 1. 44 with Krüger's note; also IV. 3. 17: καὶ ἀποδὺς ἐλάμβανε τὰ ὅπλα καὶ τοῖς ἄλλοις πᾶσι παρήγγελλε, (sc. ἀποδύντας λαμβάνειν τὰ ὅπλα. —— περιέργους, *busy-bodies*, those who offended against Cicero's injunction, de Offic. 1. 34: Peregrini autem atque incolae officium est nihil praeter suum negotium agere, nihil de alio inquirere minimeque esse in aliena republica curiosum.

2.—Καὶ... δὲ, and further; see note upon I. 1. 3: τἀγαθὰ, and I. 2. 42. —— ὡς, giving a reason, like ὅτι or ἐπεί, and connected with a

Part. in Accus. absolute. See Kühn. Gr. § 312. 6. (d), and note I. 2. 20. —— τοὺς θεούς. We should naturally expect the pronoun αὐτούς instead of the repetition of the noun; but such repetitions are somewhat frequent in Greek. Cf. I. 6. 1, and note. It was a favorite sentiment with Socrates, that we should simply, ἁπλῶς, ask good things of the gods, and not specific blessings. This appears abundantly evident from Plato, as for example, Alcib. II. p. 142 and 143. A, where the following verse from an old poet is quoted:

> Ζεῦ βασιλεῦ, τὰ μὲν ἐσθλά, φησί, καὶ εὐχομένοις καὶ ἀνεύκτοις,
> Ἄμμι δίδου, τὰ δὲ δεινὰ καὶ εὐχομένοις ἀπαλέξειν.

—ἀδήλων ὅπως ἀποβήσοιτο, see note upon I. 1. 6.

3.—Ἀπὸ μικρῶν, from small means; see note I. 2. 14. —— μειοῦσθαι, (from μείων used as a comparative of μικρός and ὀλίγος,) lit. to be less; here, to fall short of, or, to be less worthy, and hence naturally followed by the genitive. —— οὔτε ... καλῶς ἔχειν, κ.τ.λ., lit. the thing has not itself beautifully, i. e., it is not honorable, just. So in *oratio recta* we find καλῶς εἶχε, καλὸν ἦν; and for the opposite idea, αἰσχρὸν ἦν; εἰκὸς ἦν, etc. The Infin. is here without ἄν, see Kühn. Gr. § 260. R. 3; L. Gr. II. § 821. 3. —— οὔτ' ἂν ... ἄξιον εἶναι ζῆν, εἰ, κ.τ.λ. Ἄν is here retained, although it might be omitted for the same reason as above; since in *oratio recta*, the phrase would be: οὔτε τοῖς ἀνθρ. ἄξιον ἦν ζῆν. In reference to the sentiment of this passage, see Plat. Alcib. II. p. 149. E. Voigtlaender as quoted by Kühner explains this passage, thus: "Socrates intended without doubt to indicate by this, that the life of man would be rendered wholly miserable, and all the laws which regulate society be destroyed, if the gods were better pleased with the sacrifices of wicked than of good men. For if the gods prefer the sacrifices of the bad, it necessarily follows that they will also bestow upon them benefits, and in every thing prefer them to the good. Thus the lives of both gods and men would be made miserable. The lives of gods, because they must either love men whom they cannot love, without violating justice and holiness itself, or become themselves bad; of men, because the good must either yield entirely to the bad or probity vanish from the earth. Hence the result would be that the highest things would be confounded with the lowest, and life would not be desirable to any created being." —— Ἐπαινέτης, *laudator, praiser.* —— ἔπους, *verse.* —— Κὰδ δύναμιν, κ.τ.λ. This line is taken from Hesiod, Ἐργ. καὶ Ἡμερ. 366. Κὰδ [= κατά] δύναμιν, *according to (your) ability.* —— ἔρδειν may be considered as depending upon χρή or some such word understood, or it may be rendered as imperative, as the Inf. frequently is, especially among the poets. —— ἀθανάτοισι = ἀθανάτοις.

—— καὶ πρὸς φίλους δὲ. The καὶ here answers to the καί with τοῖς τὴν ἄλλην δίαιταν, and is not connected in import with δὲ, which joins this to the preceding clause. —— πρὸς signifies, *in respect to*, Latin, in with the Abl., and is omitted before ξένους, because that is included in the same idea with φίλους, and they together are contrasted with τὴν ἄλλην δίαιταν; cf. I. 4. 17, where both the preposition and the article: περὶ τῶν, are omitted before ἐν Σικελίᾳ; also II. 1. 6, and III. 10. 13, and I. 2. 53, with the note. —— τὴν Κὰδ δύναμιν, by attraction for τὸ κὰδ δύν. See Kühn. L. Gr. II. § 492. 3.

4.—Εἰ δέ, *but if*, or, *as often as*. —— δόξειεν. This Aor. Opt. denotes not a supposed case, but a frequent occurrence of an actual event. See Kühn. L. Gr. § 819. β.; Gr. § 339. R. 3; Rost § 120. This form of the Opt. in -ειας, -ειε(ν), etc., is more frequently used by Attic writers than the regular form in -αις, -αι, etc. See Kühn. Gr. § 116. 9, and note, I. 1. 5. We find a construction similar to this, but without ἄν in the apodosis, in § 6, and with ἄν and the Impf. in IV. 6. 13: εἰ δέ τις αὐτῷ ... ἀντιλέγοι ... ἐπανῆγεν ἄν. —— παρὰ τῶν θεῶν, *from* (i. e., coming from), etc. Παρά is used with the Genit. of the author, instead of the more usual ὑπό, when a thing is represented as proceeding from the vicinity of one, or caused by his influence. See Kühn. Gr. § 251. R. 4, and § 297. I. (1). —— ἧττον, less, i. e., with more difficulty. —— παρὰ τὰ σεμαινόμενα, sc. παρὰ τῶν θεῶν, as expressed below. With the radical meaning of παρά, *beside*, *near*, *along side*, is connected that of *going by*, *passing beyond*, and, from this, that of *being beyond*, and hence, *contrary to*, *against*. The use of παρά with the three cases, Gen., Dat., and Accus. in this passage, should not escape notice. Cf. B. 147. p. 417, 18. —— ἔπειθεν, *attempted to persuade*, persuadere conatus esset, or, suasisset. —— ὁδοῦ λαβεῖν ἡγεμόνα τυφλὸν ... ὁδόν. It is unnecessary in Lat. or Eng. to repeat ὁδός: to take as guide one who was blind and ignorant of the way, caecum et ignavum viae ducem. —— παρὰ τοῖς ἀνθρώποις. Παρὰ is here used in its causal or figurative signification, denoting *in the judgment* or *opinion of*. —— πρὸς τὴν ... ξυμβουλίαν, *in comparison with* (prae, praeter) divine counsel. No reference is made to the contents of these first four sections in § 15, where there is a recapitulation of the preceding arguments, and there seems to be a rather loose connection between piety towards the gods and temperance in food; but it may not unnaturally be supposed that Xenophon passes from duties owed to the gods, to those which pertain to men.

5.—Διαίτῃ δὲ. This emphatic position at the beginning of the sentence, is given to διαίτῃ, in order to make the contrast stronger with the piety which has been the subject of the preceding sections, and δὲ is antithetical to μὲν (Τὰ μὲν τοίνυν) in § 1. —— εἰ μή τι δαιμόνιον εἴη, = ἢν μή τι δαιμόνιον κωλύῃ or ἢν μή τις θεὸς ἀποκωλύῃ, unless there should be a divine intervention. Cf. Cyrop. I. 6. 18: ἢν μή τις Θεὸς βλάπτῃ, and Bornemann and Herbst, Symp. VIII. 43. —— τοσαύτης δαπάνης, so much money (sc. as would be necessary for the support of Socrates). —— οὐκ οἶδ', εἴ τις οὕτως ἂν ὀλίγα ἐργάζοιτο, whether any one could earn so little. Cf. note I. 1. 6. 8. Concerning the verb ἐργάζ., see II. 8. 2, and in reference to the construction of ἄν with the Opt., see Kühn. L. Gr. II. § 839; and cf. IV. 2. 30; Cyrop. 1. 6. 41, and 10, with Bornemann's note. —— ἡδέως, *with relish.* —— ἐπὶ τούτῳ, *for this*, i. e., that he might eat with a relish, referring to ἡδέως ἤσθιε. —— ἥει, sc. ἐπὶ σῖτον. —— ὄψον, lit., boiled meat, (from ἕψω), as opp. to bread; then, meat in general; and finally, more delicate kinds of food (ἡδύσματα); as here, any thing eaten with food, to give it a relish, a condiment, sauce. Cf. I. 6. 5, and Cyrop. I. 5. 12; III. 14. 2, 3, for different uses of the word, and see Bornemann, Symp. IV. 8. p. 108. Cicero in his Tusc. Disp. V. 34. 97: Socratem ferunt, quum usque ad vesperum contentius ambularet, quaesitumque esset ex eo, quare et faceret, respondisse: se quo melius coenaret, opsonare ambulando famem.

6.—Εἰ... ἐθελήσειεν; see note upon § 4. —— ὥστε φυλάξασθαι. The Infin. is used after such adjectives as ἐργωδέστατον, ὠφελιμόν, etc., with ἔστιν, and some other words and phrases, to define or characterize more particularly; and when ὥστε is added it gives greater force to the Infinitive. See Kühn. L. Gr. II. § 642 *d.* and Rem., and Stallbaum's note upon Plat. Phaed. p. 103. E. We find a similar constr. of the Infin. with the Accus. in Latin, as Cic. de Nat. Deorum III. 1: difficile factu est me id sentire quod tu velis; but the more usual constr. in Latin would be with ut and the subjunctive. —— τὰ πείθοντα, things which persuade, induce. Some read ἀναπείθοντα, but apparently without good reason or sufficient Ms. authority. See Kühn. in h. l. —— γαστέρας καὶ κεφαλὰς καὶ ψυχάς. According to our idiom the Sing. number would be used here, but both the Greek and Roman writers were accustomed to use the Plur. both of abstract and concrete nouns, where there was a direct reference to many objects; see Kühn. L. Gr. § 408. R. 3, and cf. III. 12. 2, and Kühner's Tusc. Disp. IV. 2. 3, where abundant examples are cited from both languages.

7.—Ἔφη ἐπισκώπτων, said sportively. —— τὴν Κίρκην, see Odyss. κ. 239 sq. —— τοιούτοις πολλοῖς, sc. ἃ πείθει μὴ πεινῶντας ἐσθίειν, κ.τ.λ., i. e., by many things which persuade, etc. —— ἀποσχόμενον τὸ... ἅπτεσθαι. Some editors for τὸ read τοῦ, but without good reasons. Verbs generally constr. with the simple Infin. are frequently, for the sake of emphasis, followed by the Accus. of the article with the Infin. Cf. IV. 7. 5 below, and also 4. 11; and see Kühn. Gr. § 308. R. 1.—— διὰ ταῦτα. After a participle introducing the cause or reason, διὰ ταῦτα or διὰ τοῦτο is frequently added for the sake of greater distinctness. Anab. I. 7. 3; VII. 1. 9; Cyrop. III. 1. 39; Kühn. L. Gr. II. § 667. Anm.

8.—'Αφροδισίων. Three explanations are given of the government of this word. Kühner in his L. Gr. § 625, 4, explains it as depending upon περὶ, to be supplied from the preceding clause, and refers to Bernhardy's Gr. Syntax, p. 204. But Herbst governs ἀφροδισίων by the verb ἀπέχεσθαι and τῶν καλῶν by ἀφροδ., and this, which seems to us a more natural explanation than the former, receives some support from such passages as II. 6. 22: τοῖς τῶν ὡραίων ἀφροδισίοις ἡδόμενοι. Even Kühner is inclined to accede to this explanation in his note in h. l. But on the whole it may perhaps be better with Seiffert to consider ἀφροδ. as a partitive genitive (Latin: de rebus autem venereis, etc.) and τῶν καλῶν as governed by ἀπέχεσθαι. The meaning is the same as if τό had been inserted after παρῄνει: In respect to the ἀφροδισίων, he admonished firmly to abstain from that of the τῶν καλῶν.—— ἁπτόμενον; for the omission of the pronoun here, see note upon I. 2. 55, and references there. Cf. also § 11: ἐφ' οἷς οὐδ' ἂν μαινόμενος σπουδάσειεν. II. 1. 17; 6. 26; III. 6. 6; 9. 14; 13. 2; IV. 2. 37. For the same constr. in Latin and abundant examples both from Gr. and Rom. authors, see Kühn. Tusc. Disp. IV. 8. 17.—— σωφρονεῖν, to preserve constancy of mind.—— Κριτόβουλόν; a son of Crito, the friend and disciple of Socrates.

9.—Σωφρονικῶν, modest, as contrasted with θρασέων, impudent, insolent; for the constr., see Kühn. Gr. § 273, 3.—— προνοητικῶν, (from πρό and νοέω), prudent, considerate.—— ἀνοήτων (a priv. and νοέω), silly.—— ῥιψοκινδύνων, (ῥίπτω and κίνδυνος), rash, fool-hardy.—— Πάνυ μὲν οὖν, a frequent formula for an affirmative answer, and hence common in colloquy, as in the dialogues of Plato. See II. 1. 2. sub. fin. Μὲν οὖν = μενοῦν, is also used with other words besides πάνυ, and often with not merely an affirmative significance, but also to extend or correct the preceding idea, like the Lat. immo, or, immo vero, as II. 7. 5: Πάντα μὲν οὖν, ὡς ἔγῳμαι, yea, truly, all things, as I suppose, and in III. 8. 4. Cf. Stallb., Plato, Crito, p. 44. B; Gorg. p. 464. B. See also Hartung, Gr. Partik. II. 399 sq., and Kühn. Gr. § 316. R. (b). It is even used in contradicting and denying, as may appear from the above references.—— Θερμουργότατον, (θερμός and ἔργω,) one who does hot, hasty acts, *most rash.* —— λεωργότατον, probably from adv. λέως = λίαν, and ἔργω, one who will do any thing = πανοῦργος, most audacious. Cf. the use of the word in Aesch. Prometheus 5. —— κυβιστήσειε, to throw headlong upon. On account of the danger attending the casting one's self upon a sword, the expression became proverbial, to indicate any peril however great. —— εἰς πῦρ ἅλοιτο, also proverbial, as is the phrase: διὰ πυρὸς ἰέναι, Sympos. IV. 16. Many editors retain here the Imperf. form, ἅλλοιτο, which is found in almost all the Mss., but the preceding Aor. would seem to indicate that the Aor. should be used here, and the change by the addition of λ might have very easily crept into the Mss.

10.—Καὶ is placed with special force at the beginning of questions where the remark of another is taken up with surprise and its invalidity or absurdity implied. In such cases the Latins sometimes use *vero*, the Germans *aber*, and we *but*. See Kühn. Gr. § 321. R. 1, and L. Gr. II. § 727. 2. It is so used in § 11 and 12; III. 9. 12; IV. 4. 10. —— δή. The δή in such cases as this may indicate more strongly astonishment, impatience, or indignation. So in II. 6. 7; III. 13. 6; IV. 4. 10; Eur. Med. 1001. See Kühn. L. Gr. II. § 833 *d.* —— τί...ἰδὼν ποιοῦντα, the peculiar brevity and beauty of the construction of both the relative and interrogative pronouns, especially with participles, should not escape notice; see C. 539. 2. —— κατέγνωκας αὐτοῦ, have you judged so severely of him. Κατά signifies here in composition, against, opposed to; cf. III. 7. 3. —— Οὐ γὰρ. Kühner calls γάρ in such cases as this, γάρ conclusive in an interrogation, cf. 4. 14; II. 3. 16, 17; III. 4. 1; 7. 7; 11. 17, etc., and L. Gr. II. § 833. i. There is, however, here manifestly an ellipsis to which it refers. Xenophon's question implies the idea of injustice in Socrates' severe reproach of Critobolus, and he replies: I reproach him justly, for has he not, etc. —— Ἀλλ' εἰ μέντοι, but if indeed, at si profecto, as in II. 1. 12. μέντοι very often expresses confirmation, *indeed*, in antithesis with καί, οὐ, ἀλλά, etc. Here it is used to strengthen the objection to Socrates' declaration: if indeed what you say were just, even I, etc. Cf. I. 4. 18, and Kühn. Gr. § 316, R., and L. Gr. II. § 698. a. —— τὸ ῥιψοκίνδυνον ἔργον, this rash deed, i. e., the one just named: τὸν Ἀλκιβ. υἱὸν φιλῆσαι. This phrase seems to be the subject here, and hence the article τό. Kühner however considers it as predicate, and accounts for the article which is not generally used with the predicate noun, from the distinct allusion to a well known fact, and perhaps a direct repetition of the word from Socrates. See Kühn. Gr. § 244. 6; L. Gr. II. § 494. —— κἂν ἐγὼ δοκῶ...ὑπομεῖναι, I seem to be able to come into, to be exposed to this danger.

11.—Ὦ τλῆμον, miserable man.——καὶ τί, see note, § 10.——ἂν...παθεῖν, what do you suppose will happen, you having (i. e., if or when you have,) etc. For the Fut. sense of the Inf. with ἄν, see Kühn. § 260. 5. (a). Cf. Symp. VI. 25: οὗ ἔρωτος (sc. τοῦ φιλεῖν) οὐδέν ἐστι δεινότερον ὑπέκκαυμα, κ.τ.λ.——Ἀρ' οὐκ; these particles in interrogations like the Latin nonne imply an affirmative, whilst ἆρα μή, Lat. numne, imply a negative answer. See Kühn. Gr. § 344. 5. (b), and L. Gr. II. 834. 3. In regard to the former, cf. I. 5. 4; 7. 2 and 3; II. 1. 16; 6. 38; and for the latter, II. 6. 34; IV. 2. 10: ἐφ' οἷς..σπουδάσειεν. The Prep. ἐπί is often put with the dative case after verbs implying motion, to designate the end or design of the motion. Cf. Plat. Phaedr. p. 276. B; p. 278. D. Symp. p. 217. A, where the same verb is used as here. See also many other passages cited by Kühner in h. l.

12.—Ὦ Ἡράκλεις, O Hercules! indicating surprise here. It may also be used as an exclamation of anger or indignation or disgust. So the Latin mehercle and hercle.——δεινήν τινα...δύναμιν. When the Indef. Pron. τὶς is used in this way with adjectives, adverbs, etc., it seems to bring out more distinctly the idea designated by these words; see Kühn. Gr. § 303. 4; L. Gr. II. 633. 4. So quidam is used in Latin, as in Cic. Lael. IX. 2: admirabilis quaedam exardescit benevolentiae magnitudo, cf. also Kühn. Tusc. Dis. II. 4. 11. In regard to the sentiment of the passage, see Symp. IV. 25.——φαλάγγια are small animals similar to the spider. The most poisonous and destructive kinds have been described as belonging to Italy, and are called from the city Tarentum, Tarantula. Cf. Plin. H. N. XXIX. 4.——ἡμιωβολιαῖα, equaling in magnitude half an obolus. The comparison should seem to imply that the φαλάγγια were small in size and round.——τοῦ φρονεῖν ἐξίστησιν, = τὸν νοῦν ἐκπλήττει, expels their reason; cf. IV. 5. 6; II. 1. 4, for similar constructions of the Infin. with the Gen. of the article.——κατὰ τὸ δῆγμα, *on account of*, *by*, or *by means of*, a causal sense. The proper meaning = secundum easily passes into propter.

13.—Τοὺς δὲ καλούς. The adversative δέ is frequently employed in animated interrogations, where the concessive member is to be supplied by the mind as here: τὰ μὲν φαλάγγια ἐνιέναι τι οἴει, τοὺς δὲ καλοὺς οὐκ οἴει. Cf. I. 6. 15; II. 1. 26, 30; II. 6. 10, 14, 37; II. 9. 2; III. 3. 11, et al. Oftentimes too the δέ is copulative, and continues a question interrupted by a preceding answer; cf. III. 5. 2, and see Kühn. Gr. § 322. Rem. 6; L. Gr. II. § 696. 5.——θηρίον, used of man, as in III. 11. 11.——τοσούτῳ δεινότερόν ἐστι...ὅσῳ. The correlatives ὅσον, ὅσῳ, and τόσον, τοσούτῳ, correspond to each other, and indicate an equality in the two things compared, so much ... as much, in what proportion ... in just the same proportion. So: ὅσον τὴν ἀρετὴν ἀσκήσεις, τοσοῦτον εὐδαίμων ἔσῃ, and Xen. Cyrop. VIII. 1. 4. Frequently not only the quantity but the degree of the quantity is indicated: ὅσῳ μᾶλλον ... τοσούτῳ μᾶλλον, or, ὅσῳ μάλιστα ... τοσούτῳ μάλιστα. But sometimes when the quantity of two things is compared, the degree of the quantity of only one of them is indicated; then we have, as in our passage, joined with one of the correlatives an adjective in the comparative degree, and with the other, an adjective in the positive: This animal ... is so much the more dangerous than the tarantula, by as much as this ... infuses poison, etc. Cf. with this, and note the difference in the construction, those passages where with ὅσῳ the comparative μᾶλλον is to be supplied from the other member, as in Xen. Hier. X. 2: οἶδα γὰρ ὅτι ὥσπερ ἐν ἵπποις, οὕτω καὶ ἐν ἀνθρώποις τισὶν ἐγγίνεται, ὅσῳ ἂν ἔκπλεα τὰ δέοντα ἔχωσι, τοσούτῳ ὑβριστοτέροις εἶναι. This constr. is unfrequent in the Latin hist., and yet it occurs, as in Tac. Ann. I. 57: barbaris quanto quis audacia promptus, tanto magis fidus rebusque motis potior habetur. —— ἐκεῖνα ... τοῦτο. The pronoun οὗτος sometimes refers to the more distant noun, (as here to τὸ θηρίον,) where it is the principal subject of the sentence, and ἐκεῖνος not to the more remote, but to the less emphatic noun; as in IV. 3. 10. See Stallb. Plat. Phaedr. p. 232. D. and Kühn. L. Gr. II. § 629. 7. So hic and ille in Latin; see Kühn. Tusc. Disp. 1. 49. 117. —— πρόσωθεν. In some Mss. πόῤῥωθεν. These words are often interchanged and are considered as synonymous in meaning, although Buttmann L. Gr. § 115 note, makes the distinction: in usage πρόσω signifies, *forwards*, and πόῤῥω (Doric πόρσω) *far*. Cf. 1. 4. 6, and Anab. III. 2. 22. —— ἴσως δὲ καὶ οἱ Ἔρωτες ... τιτρώσκουσιν. Bornemann here appropriately compares Achill. Tat. p. 8. 29; Κάλλος γὰρ ὀξύτερον τιτρώσκει βέλους, καὶ διὰ τῶν ὀφθαλμῶν εἰς τὴν ψυχὴν τιτρώσκει. Some have supposed this whole passage, from ἴσως to the end of the Section, to be supposititious, i. e., supplied from the scholiast, but there does not seem to be good reason for this assumption.

14.—Καὶ ἀφροδισιάζειν ... πρὸς τοιαῦτα. Kühner refers καὶ back to § 6, where it is enjoined to abstain from delicate food, here from the indulgence of impure love. —— τοὺς μὴ ἀσφαλῶς ἔχοντας πρὸς ἀφροδισία, those intemperate, not sufficiently guarded, in respect to love. —— οἷα ... οὐκ ἂν προσδέξαιτο ἡ ψυχή, the soul shall not admit i. e., reject with scorn. Cf. the use of ψυχή in regard to the animal appetite in I. 2. 4. —— οὐκ ἂν πράγματα παρέχοι, lit., make business for, i. e., disturb, trouble. The word οἷα is first the object of προσδέξαιτο and then the subject of παρέχοι. Instances of similar construction are not rare.

15.—This section is a kind of summary of the preceding discussion. —— οὐδὲν ἂν ἧττον ἀρκούντως ἥδεσθαι, κ.τ.λ. He supposed that he held the just medium, i. e., had not less delight in the pleasures of sense, and yet had far less trouble. The particle ἂν is to be connected with the Infin. ἥδεσθαι and supplied with the following verb, λυπεῖσθαι. So it is often to be supplied in one of two corresponding clauses, as in II. 1. 27; 1. 18; III. 3. 2, and sometimes where many words intervene. See B. 139. N. 5. Kühn. L. Gr. II. § 458, note 1. —— We should naturally expect μέν here with ἥδεσθαι to correspond with δέ after λυπεῖσθαι, as the words are contrasted. But such omissions are not unknown even in prose authors, as in Anab. III. 4. 7, 41, and in Thucydides and other writers. See Kühn. L. Gr. II. § 735.

CHAPTER IV.

1.—Περὶ αὐτοῦ τεκμαιρόμενοι. The verb τεκμαίρομαι, after the time of Homer, generally signified, to perceive from certain signs, to judge, and was usually followed by the Dat. of the means, but with the Gen. of the thing judged depending on a preposition. There seems to be an evident allusion here to persons who, after receiving the instructions of Socrates, had not continued in the practice of the virtues which he enjoined, and τεκμαιρόμενοι is judging from such examples as these, and therefore from insufficient data, *conjecturing*. —— προτρέψασθαι... προαγαγεῖν. The verb προτρέψασθαι seems to signify, to excite to the consideration of virtue, to praise and commend it, and προαγαγεῖν to lead forward in the practice of it. The objection is, that Socrates' instructions were theoretical and not practical. For the sentiment cf. Cic. de Oratore I. 47, 204: Socratem illum solitum aiunt dicere perfectum sibi opus esse, si quis satis esset concitatus cohortatione sua ad studium cognoscendae percipiendaeque virtutis; quibus enim id persuasum esset, ut nihil mallent se esse, quam bonos viros, iis reliquam facilem esse doctrinam. —— κράτιστον γεγονέναι, that he was most excellent, or had special influence; followed by the Inf. —— οὐκ ἱκανόν, was unable. —— μὴ μόνον, not οὐ on account of the Imper. δοκιμαζόντων. The participle σκεψάμενοι may also be rendered as Imper., connected with δοκιμ.: let them turn their attention to and examine, etc. The propriety of using μή then appears more evident. It may be noticed here that the best Attic writers seldom use the verb σκέπτομαι in the Pres. or Impf. tense, but the forms of σκοπέομαι in its stead. —— ἃ..

ρωτῶν, what things interrogating, i. e., by what questions. —— κολαστηρίου (i. e. κόλασμα) ἕνεκα, for the sake of reproof, castigation. —— τοὺς πάντ' οἰομένους εἰδέναι. The sophists are to be understood as especially referred to here. Socrates strove in every way to restrain and repress their arrogant boastings. —— συνεμέρευε, (σύν and ἡμέρα,) lit., to pass the day with. —— δοκιμαζόντων, the abbreviated Attic form for δοκιμαζέτωσαν.

2.—Τοῦ δαιμονίου; not the divinity of Socrates specifically, but used generically, the divine one = the deity. —— Ἀριστόδημον τὸν Μικρὸν ἐπικαλ. Aristodemus, surnamed the Little, was an austere man, always walking ἀνυπόδητος, but a most devoted and constant attendant of Socrates. —— οὔτ' εὐχόμενον, is omitted in many editions and is probably spurious. See various readings, Kühn. in h. l. —— ἔστιν οὕστινας ἀνθρώπους, *any men.* Ἀνθρώπων is the reading in many editions. For this use of the relative with ἔστιν in either number or any case as a substantive pronoun, see Kühn. Gr. § 331. R. 4; B. 150. m. 21, and L. Gr. II. § 783. Anm. 4; Soph. 150. 5; Rost § 99, note 9. Cf. Plat. Phaed. 111. D. —— τεθαύμακας ἐπὶ σοφίᾳ. Cf. Plat. Sympos. p. 206: σὲ ... ἐθαύμαζον ἐπὶ σοφίᾳ. For the use of the Dat. with the preposition here, see Kühn. Gr. § 296. II. and § 285. R.; L. Gr. II. § 612 and § 584, note. For the Perf. tense denoting rather the result of action in the present time, see Kühn. Gr. § 258. R. 5, and cf. I. 2. 49: δεδέσθαι. —— Ἔγωγε. The affirmative answer is frequently made by the Pron. either with or without the emphatic particle γε. So in Latin, though generally with some strengthening word, as *hercle, profecto,* etc. —— Καὶ ὅς. See note I. 2, 35, καί; and for the use of the ὅς in a demonstrative sense, see Kühn. Gr. § 331. R. 1, and L. Gr. § 781. 3. a. Cf. also III. 1. 5; 3. 3, 4; 4. 1; 12. 1; IV. 3. 3; 6. 2.

3.—Τοίνυν. This particle is often used when one directly and with out opposition answers another's question; see Kühn. L. Gr. II. § 758. 2 —— ἐπὶ δὲ διθυράμβῳ. It has been supposed with some plausibility, that διθυράμβων sc. ποιήσει should be read, since the word is not usually employed in the Sing. like ἔπος and μέλος, but in the plural like ἴαμβοι, ἀνάπαιστοι. —— Μελανιππίδην. This Lyric poet lived about 520 B. C. —— Πολύκλειτον... Ζεῦξιν. Polycletus the celebrated statuary lived about B. C. 430 and Zeuxis, the distinguished painter, near the same time.

4.—Ἄφρονά (a priv. and φρήν) is here contrasted with ἔμφρενά (ἐν and φρήν), the ἐν, as frequently, indicating the possession of the quality denoted by the noun. So in ἐνεργά, which is contrasted with ἀκίνητα, *without motion, motionless.* εἴπερ γε...γίγνεται. The particle γε is here added to give additional force to εἴπερ, *if indeed*, it is true that, etc. Cf. Anab. I. 7. 9; Sympos. V. 6. —— τύχῃ τινί...ὑπὸ γνώμης. The construction here is beautifully varied, the dative being used for the instrumental cause, and the Genit. with the preposition to designate the active, intelligent cause. When persons are designated we more frequently find διά with the Gen., corresponding to *per* in Latin, and sometimes even with words designating things; see B. 133. N. 12, and references to πρός and ἐν, and also Zumpt's L. Gr. 301. —— Τῶν δὲ ἀτεκμάρτως ἐχόντων, κ.τ.λ.; of those things which are in the dark, which furnish no indications, etc. —— τῶν φανερῶς ἐπ' ὠφελ. ὄντων, those which are manifestly for use. —— ἔργα, *the products of*, or rendered as a verb with esse implied, *are caused by*. —— Πρέπει, impersonal, *it is plain*. —— μὲν = μήν from which it is derived, expresses confirmation. So frequently in Ionic writers and sometimes in Attic Greek, especially in answers. See Kühn. Gr. § 316. 1. R.

5.—Οὐκοῦν, *Does not then?* an inductive interrogative particle; sometimes written οὐκ οὖν, and οὔκουν; but for the distinction in the use of these forms, see Kühn. Gr. § 324. R. 7; B. 149. m. 18. In regard to the sentiment, see IV. 3. 3 sq., and cf. Cic. de Nat. Deor. II. 54. —— Ὀσμῶν γε μήν. The particles γε μήν denote transition to a new particular, on which special emphasis is put. Two cases are to be noted: where the γε gives force to a preceding word, as here, to ὀσμῶν; and so in I. 6. 6; III. 6. 12; 8. 10; 9. 6; 11. 10, etc.; and where it is joined to a conjunction, in which case it gives emphasis to the whole sentence or clause. See Apol. § 13: ὥς γε μήν, κ.τ.λ., and § 18; also abundant examples in Hartung, Gr. Partik. I. S. 401 sq., II. S. 383 sq. —— διὰ στόματος. The article is omitted here on account of the verbal force of the noun with the preposition: which are perceived by tasting. Cf. note on I. 1. 9. —— γνώμων, the judge, estimator. —— εἰ μὴ ἐνειργάσθη, had not been made or implanted. The student should notice the use of the Aor. here and in the context, to denote a repetition of *individual* acts. B. 134. 4, and N. 5.

6.—Οὐ δοκεῖ σοι καὶ τόδε προνοίας ἔργον ἐοικέναι, does it not appear to you that this should be, (or is to be,) considered, as the work of foresight? The reading ἔργον is supported by the best Mss. The Dat. ἔργῳ and ἔργοις seem to have arisen from understanding ἐοικέναι to have the signification: *to be like, similar*, instead of *to be supposed* or *considered*, which should evidently be given to it here. It is equivalent to φαίνεσθαι which is often placed in the same way with δοκεῖν.

See II. 1. 22; IV. 2. 20, et al. —— τὸ . . . θυρῶσαι; namely, *the closing it with eye-lids as doors*, etc. For the use of the article here with the Infin. after the preparative demonstrative τόδε, see examples collected by Hase in his note upon Rep. Lac. IX. 1, and Kühn. L. Gr. II. § 631. 2.—— αὐτῇ χρῆσθαί τι, to use it for any purpose; τὶ is the Accus. of the object aimed at. See Kühn. Gr. § 278. 4; L. Gr. II. § 549. b. —— ὡς δ' ἂν . . . βλάπτωσιν; cf. with ὡς . . . κακουργῇ without ἄν. See Kühn. Gr. § 330. 4, and L. Gr. II. § 775. The Subj. is used in the final, because the verb in the principal clause, ἐμφύσαι, is an Aor. with a present signification. See Kühn. Gr. § 330. 2. —— ἠθμὸν βλεφαρίδας, *the eyelashes as a strainer*, or, *sieve*. Ἠθμός was a strainer, originally used for filtering wine; Schneid. —— ὀφρύσι τε; the particle τέ is seldom used as a connective by Xenophon without a καί following; and it is not improbable that δέ was originally written here. See Zeunius, Schneider, et caet. in h. l. —— ἀπογεισῶσαι, *to make jut out like a cornice*, cf. Cic. N. D. II. 57: Primam enim superiora, superciliis obducta, sudorem a capite et a fronte defluentem repellunt. This whole phrase has been very well translated: "that by brows the parts above the eyes are rendered eaveslike," etc. —— τὸ δὲ . . . δέχεσθαι. This and the following infinitives are strictly the subjects of ἐστίν, and are repeated by ταῦτα in the last clause, thus producing a slight anacoluthon. —— οἵους τέμνειν, cf. γομφίους . . . λεαίνειν. So οἷος is used with the Infin. in § 12; II. 1. 15; 6. 37, et al. See Rost's Gr. § 122; Kühn. L. Gr. II. § 788. Anm. 3. Gr. § 306. 1. c. In such cases it has all the properties of an Adj. and nearly = δυνατός; see B. 139. F. 5. Exs. —— τοὺς . . . γομφίους, *the molar teeth*. —— ἐπεὶ δὲ τὰ ἀποχωροῦντα δυσκερῆ, sc. ἐστίν. The ellipsis of εἶναι after conjunctions is rare. See a similar representation in Cic. N. D. II. 57.

7.—Δημιουργοῦ (fr. δῆμος and ἔργω), lit., working for the people, hence workman, worker, maker. In the New Platonic Philosophy it is used as the name of God, the Creator. —— τὸ δὲ ἐμφῦσαι, κ.τ.λ. This is a continuation of Socrates' question from § 6, and the infinitives are in the same construction as there with the clause: ταῦτα οὕτω . . . ἐστίν implied. —— Ἀμέλει, strictly Imper. but here used as an adverb, *truly, without doubt*, Latin: sine dubio. The same word is used in IV. 4. 6. —— τινος . . . βουλευσαμένου, κ.τ.λ., one who has deliberately resolved upon the existence [the making] of living beings.

8.—Σαυτὸν . . . ἔχειν. When the subject of the Inf. is the same as that of the governing verb it is generally omitted, but is retained where any special emphasis is to be put upon it; as here, contrast; notice also the use of σέ below; ὄντα σὲ, κ.τ.λ., see Kühn. Gr. § 307. 4, and R. 4; L. Gr. II. § 646. 1, and cf. II. 6. 35 extr., 38. —— **Ἐρώτα γοῦν καὶ ἀποκρινοῦμαι.** This phrase, although in all the Mss., is omitted by many editors. But it is difficult to see how it could have crept in here, if not written by the author himself. It is true, it somewhat interrupts the continuity of the discourse, but yet it contains nothing so incongruous as to warrant its rejection. Aristodemus does not, it should seem, (perhaps from modesty,) choose to answer Socrates directly, that he believes himself φρονιμόν τι ἔχειν, but in order to avoid the answer says: now continue your questions and I will reply to them (and it is implied, you yourself shall judge by my answers whether I have any reason or intelligence). Socrates understanding this, proceeds to ask further questions. Cf. Symp. V. 2. ἀλλ' ἀποκρίνου. Σὺ δέ γε ἐρώτα. The particle γοῦν is often employed in responses as nearly synon. with οὖν; III. 3. 5, 6, 7; 6. 5; 10. 8, et al. See Hartung's Gr. Partik. II. S. 15. —— **καὶ ταῦτα,** *and that too;* see I. 2. 29, and reference. —— **πολλῆς οὔσης . . . πολλοῦ ὄντος.** The simplicity of the construction of the Greek allows these repetitions which would hardly be admissible in Latin: "te et terrae exiguam partem in corpore et humoris habere, quum ea multa sint." —— **μικρὸν μέρος λαβόντι τὸ σῶμα συνήρμοσταί σοι,** to you taking a small portion *the* body is fitted. The article is used with σῶμα since it is a well known, specific object; we might render either by the indefinite article *a*, or by the possessive, *your*. For the use of the Part. here, see B. 144. 2. —— **νοῦν δὲ μόνον ἄρα οὐδαμοῦ ὄντα, κ.τ.λ.,** *and do you suppose that you alone by some good fortune have obtained possession of mind existing nowhere else.* This seems to be brought in to obviate an objection which might lie in Aristodemus' mind, although he had not expressed it. Cf. Cic. N. D. II. 6: Unde enim hanc (mentem) homo arripuit? ut ait apud Xenophontem Socrates, and III. 11; also Plat. Phileb. § 54. p. 81, and Stallb. note, and IV. 3. 14 below.

9.—**Μὰ Δί',** a formula of swearing, (μά being perhaps connected in origin with μήν, μέν,) which, however, by itself neither affirms nor denies, but is generally connected with an affirmative or negative particle, as **ναὶ μὰ τὸν Δία** and **οὐ μὰ Δία.** When it stands without the affirmative or negative particle, it has generally a negative implied with it either from a preceding or succeeding negative phrase. Here the reference is back to Ἄλλοθι δὲ οὐδαμοῦ οὐδὲν οἴει φρόνιμον εἶναι; for examples of a previous negative phrase, cf. IV. 6. 10; Oecon. XII. 1; for one subsequent, cf. III. 4, 3; Cyrop. VIII. 3. 45. It is however true that the negative οὐ is not found in the immediate context, and yet μὰ

Δία has a negative force. This takes place when it is sufficiently plain without the negative that a negative answer is to be given to a question. Cf. III. 13. 3, and note upon II. 6. 1. See upon this formula of swearing Stallbaum, Plato, Phileb. p. 36, § 72; Gorg. p. 489. E.; B. 149. 23; Kühn. Gr. § 316. 4. —— οὐ γὰρ, κ.τ.λ. It should be distinctly understood here that the reasoning of Aristodemus is not against the existence of the gods, but against their immediate agency in the affairs of life and the consequent appropriateness of worshipping them, which Socrates is inculcating. Hence the appositeness of the following argument: *I do not see*, etc., and the agreement with previous (§ 7 and 8) and subsequent (§ 10) concessions of Aristodemus. —— κυρίους, *authors.* —— ὥσπερ sc. ὁρῶ. —— Οὐδὲ γὰρ. Γάρ here refers to a suppressed clause; as perhaps, ironically: you have spoken excellently, *for*, etc. This kind of ellipsis before γάρ is especially frequent in dialogue in answers to questions. Cf. II. 1. 2, 15; 3. 6; 6. 7, 15; III. 6. 12; 11. 7. Still γάρ is frequently used merely to introduce the answer to a question, like a strengthened γέ which enters into its composition, γὲ ἄρα. See Kühn. Gr. § 324. 2; L. Gr. II. § 840. d., and cf. III. 5. 2. 10, 11, 16, et al. —— ἑαυτοῦ, in many Mss. and editions σεαυτοῦ or σαυτοῦ. But it is easier to account for the introduction of σεαυτοῦ into the Mss. which have it, than ἑαυτοῦ into those where it is found. It seems also to be well established, that the reflexive pronoun of the third person takes the place of that of the first and second person, when the person to whom it refers is clearly denoted by the construction of the sentence, and the attention is not so much directed to a definite individual as to the fact that what is affirmed is restricted to the subject itself. Hence it signifies nearly the same as ἴδιος. Cf. II. 1. 31: τοῦ δὲ πάντων ἡδίστου ἀκούσματος, ἐπαίνου ἑαυτῆς (self-praise), ἀνήκοος εἶ; II. 6. 35; Anab. VI. 6. 15, et al. See Rost's Gr. § 99 note; Kühn. Gr. § 302. 8; B. 127. N. 5; L. Gr. II. § 628. aa. —— κατά γε τοῦτο, according to this (sc. what you affirm).

10.—Οὔτοι, *but not indeed;* the adversative force is not however in the τοί, which is merely restrictive, but in the negative οὐ. See Kühn. L. Gr. II. § 758. Anm. —— ἢ ὡς, for ἢ ὥστε (v. in III. 5. 17), as not unfrequently with the Inf. Cf. a different constr. in Apol. § 16; Hier. X. 1; Cyrop. I. 1. 2. —— ὅσῳ μεγαλοπρεπέστερον (sc. ὄν); κ.τ.λ. In proportion as the divinity is more exalted and yet considers you worthy of regard, the more is he to be honored, or, the more exalted the being who deigns to regard you, the more, etc. For the omission of the participle ὄν, see II. 1. 32: τιμῶμαι δὲ μάλιστα πάντων . . . ἀγαπητὴ μὲν συνεργὸς τεχνίταις, κ.τ.λ. (sc. οὖσα); 3. 15: ἄτοπα λέγεις . . . καὶ οὐδαμῶς πρὸς σοῦ, and in no manner suited to yourself. Cf. also Symp. IV. 25:

καὶ γὰρ ἄπληστον (scil. *ὂν*) *καὶ ἐλπίδας τινὰς γλυκείας παρέχει*; and examples collected in h. l. by Bornemann.

11.—*Ἔπειτ' οὐκ οἴει...?* see note upon I. 2. 26.——*οἳ*. For this use of the relative after an interrogation, see I. 2. 64.——*ὀρθὸν ἀνέστησαν*, *made erect*, Cic. de Nat. Deor. II. 56. 146.——*καὶ ἧττον κακοπαθεῖν*, (*οἷς*) *καὶ ὄψιν καὶ ἀκοὴν καὶ στόμα ἐνεποίησαν*. Nearly all the Mss. have this passage as we have given it above, with the omission of the *οἷς* and a colon instead of a comma: *κακοπαθεῖν· καί, κ.τ.λ.* Still various changes of the text have been proposed, but it seems hardly worth while to enumerate them. Changes of the text, unless it *is manifestly* corrupt, are but an indifferent method of escaping a difficulty. If the *οἷς* is to be admitted from two Mss. which have *κακοπαθεῖνων*, which is very doubtful, the idea seems to be: he made them of erect stature, so... that they may be less liable to injury, *in those parts in which*, *οἷς*, the gods have placed the sight, etc. But it appears not to be altogether clear, how the erectness of man renders the parts of the body enumerated, less liable to injury than the same parts in beasts. It seems far more probable that *οἷς* should be omitted, and that the words from *ἡ δὲ ὀρθότης* to *κακοπαθεῖν* are parenthetical, and that the words *καὶ ὄψιν, κ.τ.λ.*, simply declare that the gods made men with *ὄψιν*, face, in its general sense, and *ἀκοήν*, the power of hearing, and *στόμα*, mouth, not so much as an instrument of tasting as of speaking, by which man is distinguished from beasts.——*ἑρπετοῖς*, lit., *creeping things*, from *ἕρπω*; but as this verb means to walk as well as to creep, its derivative *ἑρπετόν* is put for all things that walk on the earth, and thus is sometimes opposed to *πετεινά*, winged animals.

12.—*Καὶ μὴν γλῶττάν γε.* The particles *καὶ μήν* indicate transition to something new, which is adduced in confirmation (*μήν*) of the general idea, *and indeed, and truly.*——The *γέ* is called *suppletive* by Kühner and Hartung. It seems merely to indicate that the word after which it is placed is emphatic, or the word which is contrasted. This would be denoted by position in Latin and by the tone of voice in English; cf. I. 6. 3, 8; II. 2, 4; III. 4, 4; 5, 3, et al. Sometimes the *μήν* has an adversative force in such a connection: and (*καί*), yet (*μήν*), truly (*γέ*), or, but indeed it is true, but truly. So in II. 3. 4, 14, 19; 8. 4, 5; 10, 3; III. 1. 11, et al. See Kühn. Gr. § 316. 1, and L. Gr. II. § 696. c. and 704. 1. 1; Hartung, Gr. Partik. I. S. 401–404.——*οἵαν... ἀρθροῦν*. See upon the constr. *οἷος* with the Infin. note, § 6. The idea is, that the gods made men with reason and with such organs that they can exhibit it.——*ψαύουσαν*, like the Gerund, or Abl. of means in Latin, by touching, etc.—— καὶ σημαίνειν πάντα ἀλλήλοις ἃ βουλόμεθα, and (such οἵαν,) that we can make known, etc. When two relative clauses succeed each other, the relative is frequently, as here, omitted with the last, or the constr. is entirely changed and a demonstrative takes the place of the relative. See examples in Kühn. Gr. § 334. 1, and L. Gr. II. § 799. The subject of the Infin., ἡμᾶς, is omitted as usual in Greek where there is no special emphasis to be put upon it. —— τὸ δὲ... δοῦναι.., παρέχειν. The Infin. with the article in the Accus. is placed elliptically in exclamations and vivid interrogations, indicating indignation, surprise, etc., the idea on which the Infin. depends being suppressed, as: οὐ θαυμαστόν ἐστιν, or some similar phrase. See Rost's Gr. § 125, note 5; Kühn. Gr. § 308. R. 2, and L. Gr. II. § 652. 1. So in IV. 3. 5 sq.; cf. Bornemann upon Apol. § 17. p. 58. —— τοῦ ἔτους χρόνον. The substantive with an attributive genitive which has the article, is often placed without it, when the idea of both nouns coalesces into one. This usage is represented in Kühner's L. Gr. as confined to poetry, but corrected in his note in h. l. Thus it is omitted in I. 5. 2: ἐπὶ τελευτῇ τοῦ βίου (life's end); Apol. 30: ἐν καταλύσει τοῦ βίου; Anab. I. 1. 1: τελευτὴν τοῦ βίου, Cyrop. V. 1. 13; VII. 2. 20, et al. Sometimes, however, the article is added to both substantives, as in I. 9. 30: ἐν τῇ τελευτῇ τοῦ βίου; De Rep. Lac. X. 1.

13.—Οὐ τοίνυν, see note upon I. 2. 29. Τοίνυν here indicates that care for the soul follows, as a natural consequence, from the great care of the deity for the body, which has just been exhibited. —— τὴν ψυχὴν κρατίστην. The Adj. placed in this way after the noun with the article has the force of a predicate, i. e., κρατίστην οὖσαν, or ἣ κρατίστη ἐστίν. So in II. 1. 30: τὰς στρωμνὰς μαλακὰς παρασκευάζῃ, and in III. 10. 8; IV. 7. 7, et al. Cf. § 12: μόνην τὴν τῶν ἀνθρώπων (γλῶτταν) ἐποίησαν, κ.τ.λ., i. e., ἡ τῶν ἀνθρ. γλῶττα μόνη ἐστὶν, ἣν ἐποίησαν. On the other hand ἡ μόνη γλῶττα, the only tongue. See Rost's Gr. § 98. Anm. 1; Kühn. Gr. § 245. 3. (b); L. Gr. II. § 493. —— θεῶν... ᾔσθηται ὅτι εἰσί. Θεῶν is the Gen. of the person of whom a thing is perceived; Kühn. Gr. § 273. 5. (f). For the attraction, see Kühn. Gr. § 347. 3. In Anab. I. 2. 22, there is a sentence constructed much like this with the Accus. instead of the Genit.: ᾔσθετο τό τε Μένωνος στράτευμα ὅτι ἤδη ἐν Κιλικίᾳ ἦν. For the sentiment, cf. Cic. Nat. Deor. II. 61. —— τῶν τὰ μέγιστα καὶ κάλλιστα συνταξάντων. Compare with this IV. 3. 13: ὁ τὸν ὅλον κόσμον συντάττων τε καὶ συνέχων. —— τί δὲ φῦλον ἄλλο ἢ ἄνθρωποι θεοὺς θεραπεύουσι; and what tribe *other than*, or, *besides*, etc. For the attraction of the verb to the plural here, by ἄνθρωποι, see Kühn. Gr. § 242. R. 4; L. Gr. II. § 429. The same constr. is found also in Latin, as in Sallust, Jug. L. 6: opportunior fugae collis, quam campi fuerant. Cic. Phil. IV. 4: Quis igitur illum Consulem, nisi latrones putant. —— ἢ ψύχη ἢ θάλπη, Accus. plur. contract. of the 3d Decl. For this use of the plur. to denote an abstract idea, see Kühn. Gr. § 243. 3; L. Gr. II. § 408. p. 29, and cf. II. 1. 6. —— ἐκπονῆσαι. The verb ἐκπονεῖν is generally transitive and followed by an Accus.; but here Intrans. and with a Prep. before the Accus.

14.—Οὐ γὰρ, *nonne igitur*, is it not then? Γάρ conclusive; see I. 3. 10. —— παρὰ τὰ ἄλλα ζῷα, *prae*, or, praeter, etc. The Prep. παρά with the Accus. sometimes denotes comparison. So in IV. 4. 1: παρὰ τοὺς ἄλλους εὐτακτῶν. See Kühn. Gr. § 297. III. (b); B. 147. παρά c. Accus. 3· L. Gr. II. § 615. S. 305. —— ἄνθρωποι, without the article; so in the preceding section; III. 12. 5; IV. 1, 2; 3. 7; 4. 6, etc. This is one of the nouns that is sufficiently definite in itself, and consequently does not need the article, but for the sake of emphasis, or to denote some special significance. See Kühn. Gr. § 244. 2. R. 3; L. Gr. II. § 484. Anm. —— φύσει is added to indicate that it is something more than an acquired superiority that man possesses. —— βοὸς ἄν. The particle ἄν is rhetorical, giving emphasis to βοός; so not unfrequently when repeated, whilst at other times it is placed at the beginning of a clause to show at the outset that the predicate is conditional; see Kühn. Gr. § 261. 3. (b) and (a), and L. Gr. II. § 458. 2. See numerous examples of such a use in Bornemann, Apol. § 6, and Krüger Anab. III. 1. 6. —— ἔχων, may agree with ἄνθρωπος to be supplied from ἄνθρωποι or with τὶς, not unusually omitted with a Partic. or adjective. —— ἀμφοτέρων τῶν (i. e. σῶμα and ψύχη) πλείστου ἀξίων τετυχηκὼς, utrumque praestantissimum (animum et corpus) consecutus. —— ὅταν τί ποιήσωσι, κ.τ.λ., *when they do what?* i. e., what must the gods do, so that you shall believe that they care for you? For the change here to a direct interrogation, see Kühn. Gr. § 344. R. 6; L. Gr. II. § 842. 1. —— νομιεῖς, Attic future indicative; for its formation and use, see Kühn. Gr. § 117, and numerous examples in Fritzsch. in Quaest. Luc. p. 134–136.

15.—Σὲ ἐξαιροῦντες ἐν ἀμελείᾳ κατατίθενται, selecting you alone, place you in forgetfulness. The direct discourse is here again assumed, cf. III. 5. 14. Cyrop. 1. 3. 5; II. 3. 8.

16.—Εἰ μὴ δυνατοὶ ἦσαν, sc. εὖ καὶ κακῶς ποιεῖν. —— καὶ, according to our idiom, may be rendered, *or*. —— ἐξαπατωμένους, (sc. τῇ δόξῃ, ὡς οἱ θεοὶ ἱκανοί εἰσιν εὖ, κ.τ.λ.)

17.—Ὠγαθέ. Hermann says: "This is a friendly appellation which is especially employed when it is desired to give one a gentle admonition.

For it designates an almost entirely concealed reproof, like o bone in Latin. The Greeks also make use of ὦ βέλτιστε;" ad Viger. § 64. Cf. III. 7. 9, and II. 3. 16. In this last passage ἔφη is also used, as in h. l., although there is no change of speaker. This repetition is not unfrequent in animated narration, and serves to direct the mind of the hearer more particularly to what is said. So in II. 7. 10, and III. 4. 12. Cf. note upon II. 4. 1. Inquit is repeated in the same way in Latin. —— ἐνών, sc. ἐν τῷ σώματι. The object of the following verb is not unfrequently to be supplied with a participle. Cf. Anab. I. 8. 11: καλέσας παρεκελεύετο τοῖς Ἕλλησι: i. e., καλ. τοὺς Ἕλληνας παρεκ. αὐτοῖς. —— ἐν παντὶ φρόνησιν, intelligence which is in every thing. —— καὶ μή, sc. οἴεσθαι χρή, and you should not suppose, etc. There is also the same ellipsis after μηδὲ just below. The reason of the change from καὶ μή to μηδέ may be seen in Kühn. Gr. § 321. 2. Cf. I. 2. 60, and III. 7. 9. —— περὶ τῶν ἐν Αἰγύπτῳ καὶ ἐν Σικελίᾳ. For the ellipsis of περὶ τῶν, see note upon I. 3. 3.

18.—Ἦν μέντοι, *if truly.* —— ἐθέλοντας . . . θελήσουσι, see note upon I. 2. 9. —— οὕτω, *so,* (inserted for the sake of distinctness after the preceding clause. —— τῶν θεῶν πεῖραν λαμβάνῃς θεραπεύων, to make a trial of the gods by worshipping them. —— εἴ, *whether.* —— γνώσῃ τὸ θεῖον ὅτι, κ.τ.λ. For the constr. cf. § 13 above. —— ἐπιμελεῖσθαι αὐτούς. The different readings, with αὐτούς omitted, and with αὐτό in its place, seem to have arisen from a supposed difficulty in referring the plural pronoun to a singular antecedent (τὸ θεῖον). But such constructions, κατὰ σύνεσιν, are not unusual in both Greek and Latin authors. So in II. 3. 9. Cf. Bornemann Sympos. IV. 63. p. 154. For the repetition of the subject by the pronoun, see Kühn. Gr. § 304. 3; L. Gr. II. § 858. 10.

19.—Ταῦτα λέγων, by saying these things. —— ὁπότε ὑπὸ τῶν ἀνθρώπων ὁρῷντο. See note upon I. 2. 57: ἐπειδὴ ὁμολογήσαιτο. —— ἐπείπερ ἡγήσαιντο. For this use of the Opt., see B. 139. m. 15, and 44. —— μηδὲν ἄν ποτε, . . . διαλαθεῖν, *nothing . . . can ever escape the notice of,* etc.

CHAPTER V.

1.—Εἰ δὲ δή. In Attic Greek a fact or a general thought is frequently introduced by εἴ, and the sentence is ὑποθετικῶς, only in form. The εἴ is nearly the same as ἐπειδή, quoniam, *since;* (Εἴγε is also used in the same manner as ἐπεί γε;) δή then corresponds to the Latin jam, or, vero, and indicates that the thing is established, is beyond doubt. See Hartung, Gr. Partik. I. S. 259 sq.; Kühn. L. Gr. II. § 691, and Gr. § 315. 1. Cf. I. 6. 9; II. 6. 20; Sympos. IV. 18. In Latin the same idea is frequently expressed by inserting ut est, or, ut est certe after si, as: si, ut est certe.——καὶ ἐγκράτεια καλόν τε... ἐστιν, self-government is both an honorable and good possession (acquisition).——προὐβίβαζε; see I. 2. 17.——Ὦ ἄνδρες, in Latin the Voc. viri would not occupy the first place in the sentence.——ἄνδρα, simply, *one*, any one, aliquis. Some suppose that ἄνδρα is used here with some speciality of meaning, *a real man*, but I do not so understand it.——μὲν... δὲ, *both... and.*——ὅντιν' ἂν αἰσθανοίμεθα. The Opt. has the same force here as in a conditional sentence. The particle ἂν refers to a suppressed clause, as εἰ τύχοι, if it might be; see Kühn. Gr. § 260. 3. (4), (a); L. Gr. II. 798; cf. a different use of ἂν with the Opt. in I. 2. 6, and note. The participle ὢν is frequently not expressed with the adjective or substantive, after *verba sentiendi* or *declarandi*. See Kühn. II. § 656. 3.——ἥττω γαστρὸς, κ.τ.λ., *inferior to, subject to*, etc. See Kühn. Gr. § 275. 1. 2; L. Gr. II. § 361; Rost § 108, p. 515, and cf. IV. 5. 11: ἀνδρὶ ἥττονι τῶν διὰ τοῦ σώματος ἡδονῶν. Thus in Latin with the Abl.: inferior voluptatibus.——πόνου. Ἥττων πόνου, = one who is inferior to labor, yields to it, does not bear up under it.——τοὺς πολεμίους κρατῆσαι. Κρατεῖν is more intensive with the Accus. than with the genitive. With the genitive it signifies merely to rule, to have in one's power; with the Accus. to subjugate, to conquer. See Kühn. Gr. § 275. R. 1; L. Gr. II. § 538. Anm. 2 Rost, § 108. Anm. 4.

2.—Ἐπὶ τελευτῇ τοῦ βίου. See note, I. 4. 12: τοῦ ἔτους χρόνον.——θυγατέρας παρθένους; cf. Cyrop. IV. 6. 9: ἔστι δέ μοι ἔφη, καὶ θυγάτηρ παρθένος, κ.τ.λ.——παιδεῦσαι... διαφυλάξαι, κ.τ.λ.; these infinitives denote a purpose, and may be rendered in Eng. passively; see B. 180. 3.——ἀξιόπιστον εἰς ταῦτα, worthy of trust in respect of these things; εἰς = Lat. de.——ἡγησόμεθα. For the use of the Indic. in the Apodosis, after εἰ with the Optat. in the Protasis, see Kühn. Gr. § 339. 3. (b), and L. Gr. II. § 819.——δούλῳ δ', κ.τ.λ. The ἆρα is to be repeated here, by anaphora, from the preceding sentence.——ἔργων ἐπίστασιν. The noun ἔργον is frequently used, as is also the Latin opus (opus facere = agrum colere), for agricultural labor.——τοιοῦτον. Some editors insert the article before this word. And it is so used in § 1, and often elsewhere, when a person well known or previously described is referred to. Cf. § 5; I. 2. 37: τῶν ἄλ. τῶν τοιούτων, also Cyrop. V. 5. 32. Often, too, where the whole class of those who are *such*, is referred to, the article is used, but never where only one individual of the kind is designated

3.—Ἀλλὰ μὴν, simply *but* in the minor proposition, or, *but indeed.* —— εἴ γε μηδὲ δοῦλον ἀκρατῆ δεξαίμεθ' ἄν, if we would not ever receive a servant, who was intemperate; i. e., if he might be intemperate, εἰ οὗτος ἀκρατὴς εἴη, a conditional phrase to which the particle ἄν here refers. Thus it is often used with reference to such a clause, implied in a word, which is to be mentally supplied. The nice shades of meaning, which the Greeks could express by the use of this particle, should not escape the student's notice. Μηδὲ, *not even*, see Kühn. Gr. § 321. 2. For the construction of the Optat. δεξαίμεθ' with ἄν, after εἴ, see Kühn. Gr. § 340. 6; L. Gr. II. 525. Anm. 6; Rost, § 121. Anm. 8. —— αὐτόν γε. Αὐτός in contrast with δοῦλος, in Greek, signifies, one who is free and of good lineage, and here it may be rendered, *we ourselves*, or, one himself, literally, (for the reflexive,) *one's self.* Γέ gives emphasis to the contrast. —— Καὶ γάρ. Καί gives emphasis to οὕτως, not so *also.* —— τῶν, ἄλλων ἀφαιρούμενοι χρήματα. The most common construction of ἀφαιρεῖσθαι, is with two accusatives, yet the construction with the Genit. of the person and Accus. of the thing, as here, is somewhat frequent; so in Cyrop. V. 4. 29; VII. 4. 11; Demosth. De Corona 232. 22, et al. It is very rarely followed by the Accus. of the person and the Genit. of the thing, in which case it signifies to restrain, etc. Ἀποστερεῖν also admits these three modes of construction, but whilst it oftenest has two accusatives, it is very often followed by the Accus. of the person and Genit. of the thing, as in Cyrop. III. 1. 11, and but very rarely with the Genit. of the person and Accus. of the thing, as in D. Venat. XII. 8. —— κακοῦργος ... τῶν ἄλλων. Κακοῦργος has the force and construction of a substantive.

5.—Ἆρά γε οὐ. See note upon I. 5. 11. The particle γέ with the interrogative denotes that having enumerated or passing by all else, the author proceeds to the last particular which is added with confidence in its validity. It may be rendered, *in fine*, denique. See Hartung, Gr. Partik. I. S. 377. Cf. III. 2. 1, and note; also III. 8. 3: Ἆρά γε ... ἐρωτᾷς με, Do you, in fine, ask me. —— κρηπῖδα. The noun κρηπίς signifies, lit., a kind of boot, and then generally a foundation, groundwork. So in Pind. Pyth. IV. 138 (Boeckh.): βάλλετο κρηπῖδα σοφῶν ἐπέων, foundation of a wise discourse. The same, VII. 3, et al. Upon the nature and value of temperance, as held by ancient philosophers, see Cic. Tusc. Disp. IV. 13, 30, and Kühner's note, and also the discussion in II. 1 below.

Διατεθείη καὶ τὸ σῶμα, κ.τ.λ., be constituted both in body and mind. For the constr. of the passive with an Accus., see Kühn. Gr. § 281. 1; L. Gr. II. § 565. 1. —— *Ἐμοὶ μὲν*, *μέν solitaire*, see note upon I. 1. 1. —— *νὴ τὴν Ἥραν*, a common oath among Athenian women, but probably not found in use by other men besides Socrates, although somewhat frequent with him; cf. III. 10. 9; 11. 5; IV. 2. 9, etc. Concerning its use in Plato, see Stallbaum upon Hipp. Maj. p. 291. E. —— *δουλεύοντα δὲ*, opposed to *ἐλευθέρῳ μὲν ἀνδρὶ* in the preceding clause. —— *ἱκετεύειν*. The construction with a verbal adjective, (as here with *εὐκτόν*) often passes into a simple infinitive. Kühn. Gr. § 284. R. 7; L. Gr. II. § 587. Anm. 4. Cf. De Re Equ. III. 7, where *ληπτέον πεῖραν* is changed to *πεῖραν λαμβάνειν*. —— *δεσποτῶν ἀγαθῶν τυχεῖν*. The idea of this passage seems to be that, whilst a free man should pray that he may not have an intemperate servant, he who is already enslaved to his passions and appetites should supplicate that he may have good masters, i. e., those who by good example, precept, and guidance, may exercise just restraint over him. The idea that by *δεσποτῶν ἀγαθ.* virtues are to be understood seems not to be well authorized, for although vices, passions, evil desires, etc., are called *δεσπόται* and *δέσποιναι*, virtues are never so designated; neither are persons spoken of as enslaved to virtue: *δουλεύειν τῇ ἀρετῇ*.

6.—*Ἔργοις ἢ τοῖς λόγοις*, *in deed than in word*. —— *τῶν διὰ τοῦ σώματος ἡδονῶν*, the pleasures of the body, or, which are experienced by the body. The common use of the article, in giving the force of an adjective to the words intervening between it and its noun, is evident here. —— *ἀλλὰ καὶ τῆς διὰ τῶν χρημάτων*, but also of that (*ἡδονῆς*, pleasure) which is obtained by wealth. —— *παρὰ τοῦ τυχόντος*, from any one, quispiam, or, quilibet. —— *δεσπότην ἑαυτοῦ*. Cf. I. 2. 6. —— *οὐδεμιᾶς ἧττον αἰσχράν*. This phrase is in accordance with the Greek usage, although from the analogy of other languages we should expect: *οὐχ ἧττον αἰσχρὰν ἢ ἄλλην τινά*; i. e., the place of the object with which the thing is compared, *τὶς*, is supplied by another pronoun, coalescing with the negative, (*οὐδείς*) in the Genit. with the comparative adjective; see Kühn. L. Gr. II. § 588. Anm. 3 Cf. III. 5. 18; IV. 2. 12; De Vectig. I. 1.

CHAPTER VI.

1.—*Ἄξιον*, sc. *ἐστίν*, *it is worth while*, or, *it is of consequence*. —— *αὐτοῦ καὶ ἃ πρὸς ... μὴ παραλιπεῖν*, is equivalent to *αὐτοῦ πρὸς*

Ἀντιφῶντα λόγους μὴ παραλιπεῖν, not to pass by his conversation with Antiphon; cf. Plat. Rep. IV. p. 439. B. The Genit. αὐτοῦ depends upon the relative clause ἃ ... διελέχθη, which is equivalent to λόγους. —— τῷ Σωκράτει. We should naturally expect αὐτῷ here, as the Pron. αὐτοῦ precedes, but the Greek frequently repeats the substantive after a pronoun or a noun, especially if there will be too great a concurrence of pronouns, as there would have been here, αὐτοῦ, αὐτῷ, αὐτῶν. Cf. II. 5. 4. Proper names, in particular, are often repeated where a pronoun might be expected. Cf. Anab. I. 9. 15; Lycurg. contra Leocrat. 87. p. 220.

2.—Ὦ Σώκρατες; see note upon I. 5. 1. Τἀναντία τῆς φιλοσοφίας ἀπολελαυκέναι, to have been the participant of the very opposite from philosophy. For the construction of the Genit. of the source of enjoyment with the Accus. of the thing enjoyed, see Kühn. Gr. § 273. 5. (c); L. Gr. II. § 526. Anm. 4; Rost, § 108. Anm. 16. See also IV. 5. 10. —— γοῦν, compounded of γέ and οὖν, *surely, at least*, is often used after the general nature of a subject has been explained, and one argument or example, which is especially forcible, is adduced as sufficient proof. Cf. § 11; II. 1. 1; III. 3. 1; 10. 1, etc. It sometimes is simply a particle of affirmation, certainly, surely; see Kühn. Gr. § 324. R. 6. —— οὐδ' ἂν εἷς, emphatic, for οὐδεὶς ἄν. So in II. 6. 4; 7. 14: οὐδ' ὑφ' ἑνὸς ἀδικούμενοι; III. 5. 21, etc. So in Latin, non ullus, is written for nullus for the sake of emphasis. See Kühn. Tusc. Disp. I. 39. 94, Var. Lectt. —— σιτία τε. The explanatory clause is frequently asyndic both in Latin and Greek. The τέ corresponds with the following καί. —— ἱμάτιον ἠμφίεσαι. Verbs which in the Act. voice take two accusatives, retain one in the Mid.; see B. 135. 4. —— οὐ μόνον ... ἀλλά, *not only ... but*. This formula is used where the thought in the first clause is not denied, but the last is added as of more weight or of greater extent than the former, on which it is based. It accordingly differs from οὐκ ... ἀλλά, for the former clause, when these particles are used, is excluded by the latter which takes its place. It is also to be distinguished from οὐ μόνον ... ἀλλὰ καί, where the first idea as it stands alone is denied, but is affirmed as modified by the last clause. There are examples, though rare, where this last formula does not seem to differ from the one in our passage, as Plat. Sympos. p. 219, E: οὐ μόνον ἐμοῦ περιῆν, ἀλλὰ καὶ τῶν ἄλλων ἁπάντων, but Kühner thinks that in such cases the καί may have been carelessly added. Stallb. Plat. Sympos. p. 206. A. in Var. Lectt., and Bremius in Excursus IX. ad Isocr. —— ἀνυπόδητος. This custom of going barefoot adopted by Socrates, was the more conspicuous, since the Athenians especially prided themselves in the beauty of their sandals: and this fact undoubtedly gave rise to his habit, as a reproof of the luxury and effeminacy of the times. See Aristoph Clouds, 103:

> "Those squalid, barefoot, beggarly impostors,
> . . . . of whose sect
> Are Socrates and Chaerephon."

Also cf. Mitchel's note and v. 362; Plat. Phaedr. p. 229. A. —— ἀχίτων, not without the inner garment, ὑπενδύτης, but the outer, ἐπενδύτης which, κατ' ἐξοχὴν, the ancients were accustomed to call tunic; and those who were without it, were ἀχίτωνες. See Ernesti in h. l. —— διατελεῖς. Διατελεῖν used without the participle ὤν. So in Agesil. VI. 8 and 4, et alibi. So also διαγίγνεσθαι, in II. 8. 5, and Cyrop. I. 2. 15; and τυγχάνειν, Hellen. IV. 3. 3; 8. 29; and κυρεῖν. See Kühn. L. Gr. II. § 664. Anm. 1. In reference to Socrates' dress, see Plat. Phaedr. p. 299; Sympos. p. 174, 220.

3.—Καὶ μὴν . . . γέ. See note I. 4. 12. —— ὥσπερ καὶ, for the repetition of καί in comparisons, see note upon I. 1. 6. —— οὕτω καὶ . . διαθήσεις, you also will so dispose your disciples (that they imitate your frugality). Cf. IV. 2. 40.

4.—Εἶπε, . . . Δοκεῖς μοι ἔφη. It is not unusual to interpose ἔφη in the middle of a sentence which is preceded by a verb of like signification. So in Sympos. 1. 15; Plat. Sympos. p. 202. C. et al. Rarely is the same word ἔφη repeated as in Cyrop. II. 2. 13. The same idiom is somewhat frequent in Latin, where inquit follows respondit. See Kühn. Tusc. Disp. V. 36. 105. —— τί χαλεπὸν ᾔσθησαι τοὐμοῦ βίου, i. e., in my manner of life. For the government of the Genit., see Kühn. Gr. § 273. 5. (f.), and L. Gr. II. § 528. Anm. 3. Cf. I. 1. 12; III. 6. 17. Τοὐμοῦ is in many editions written without contraction τοῦ ἐμοῦ.

5.—Πότερον, sc. χαλεπὸν ᾔσθησαι τοῦ ἐμοῦ βίου, ὅτι, *is* the severity which you see in my manner of life this, *that*, etc. —— τοῖς μὲν λαμβάνουσιν . . . ἐμοὶ δὲ μὴ λαμβάνοντι. Two enunciations are frequently introduced by μέν . . . δέ when the first is only intended to give force to the idea in the latter by contrast. So here and in II. 1. 6; II. 1. 8; 7. 11; III. 9. 8, et al. Sometimes two phrases are thus placed in contrast without the μέν, but with far less force. —— φαυλίζεις (from φαῦλος, bad, mean, etc.), do you hold cheap, despise. —— ὡς . . . ἐσθίοντος ἐμοῦ, κ.τ.λ., *that I eat less healthful food than you.* The longer form of the pronoun ἐμοῦ, is here used instead of the shorter μου in the preceding clause on account of the contrast. For the constr. of the participle in the genitive absolute, see note upon I. 1. 4; ὡς τοῦ δαιμονίου προσημαίνοντος. —— ὡς χαλεπώτερα, πορίσασθαι τὰ ἐμὰ διαιτήματα. With χαλεπώτερα, ὄντα is to be supplied from the following clause: ἡδίω ... ὄντα. The Accus. absolute here is to be put in the same construction in translating as the Genit. preceding because that my food, means of living, are more difficult to be procured, etc. See B. 145. N. 7; Kühn. § 312. 6. (c); L. Gr. II. § 673. The first Aor. Infin. πορίσασθαι depends upon the adjective χαλεπώτερα, and may be rendered passively like the supine in –u in Latin. So both the Infin. Act. and Mid. is used after several adjectives, nouns, etc. See Kühn. § 306. 1. R. 10; L. Gr. II. § 640. Anm. 3. Cf. § 9: χαλεπώτατα, εὑρεῖν, κ.τ.λ. II. 1. 22; III. 8. 8. —— διὰ τὸ ... εἶναι, Inf. with διά in giving a reason as often in Greek. —— ὁ μὲν ἥδιστα ἐσθίων, he who eats with an appetite, a relish. —— τοῦ μὴ παρόντος ... ποτοῦ, drink that is not in readiness, obtained with difficulty.

6.—Τά γε μὴν ἱμάτια. The noun is here placed at the beginning of the sentence for the sake of emphasis, and is strictly in what the old Grammarians call a case of synecdoche: *as to* garments, you know, etc. Upon γε μὴν, see note, I. 4. 5: ὀσμῶν γε μήν. —— καὶ ὑποδήματα, sc. οἶσθ' ὅτι. —— ἤδη ... ἐμὲ ... διὰ ψῦχος μᾶλλόν του ἔνδον μένοντα, κ.τ.λ. The idea is: now then have you ever perceived that, I (who do not wear sandals), have either remained at home more than another, του (who wears them), or, on account of the heat, contended with any one, τῳ, for a shade, or, that from suffering, τὸ ἀλγεῖν, in my feet, I have not gone wherever I wished? For the Accus. τοὺς πόδας, see Kühn. § 279. 7. Ἔνδον = Lat. domi, from Prep. ἐν, in. In reference to the idea in this passage, cf. Plat. Symp. p. 220. A. B.

7.—Μελετήσαντες, sc. τὸ σῶμα. Part. denoting the means, as often. —— ἀμελησάντων, *neglecting it.* —— πρὸς ἂν; (many editions have πρὸς ἃ and ἃ ἄν;) in respect to that in regard to, or, for which they exercise. ——Ἐμὲ δὲ ἄρα οὐκ οἴει, κ.τ.λ., do you not suppose that I who always exercise myself to bear with my body whatever happens to it, can do it more easily than you, etc. Τῷ σώματι is to be rendered with καρτερεῖν, as Dat. of means or instrument, and καρτερεῖν depends upon the Part. μελετῶντα; cf. III. 9. 14. Apolog. § 3.

8.—Τοῦ ... μὴ δουλεύειν ... γαστρὶ ... οἴει τι ἄλλο αἰτιώτερον, do you suppose any thing else is more the cause of my not being a slave, etc? The Inf. in the Genit. with the Art. is governed by the Adj. αἰτιώτερον. The negative μή is used, as generally with the Infin., connected with the article, to denote that an idea exists subjectively, in the conceptions of the speaker, Kühn. Gr. § 318. 4. —— εὐφραίνει; this verb belongs to both members of the sentence, and may be translated with the latter only, as if written: ἃ οὐ μόνον ἐν χρείᾳ ὄντα (while we use them), ἀλλά καὶ ἐλπίδας παρέχοντα ἀεί ὠφελήσειν εὐφραίνει. A verb belonging to two members of a sentence is often put in the first only in Greek, as well as in our own language. Cf. I. 7. 3; II. 4. 2, et al. —— Καὶ μὴν...γε, see note upon I. 4. 12. —— οἱ...οἰόμενοι μηδὲν εὖ πράττειν, those supposing that they do not prosper in every thing. The phrase, εὖ πράττειν, is really elliptical for εὖ πράττειν τὰ αὑτοῦ. The phrase εὖ πράττειν has two senses, to do well and to be prosperous; sometimes it passes from one signification to the other in the same sentence. —— ὡς εὖ πράττοντες, as those who are in prosperity. For a similar play upon words, see Stallb. Plat. Charmid. p. 172. A; Alcib. I. p. 116. B. et al. Concerning the sentiment, see III. 9. 14, 15. —— ἢ ἄλλ' ὅ τι ἂν τυγχάνωσιν ἐργαζόμενοι, or *any thing else about which they may be employed.* The verb τυγχάνειν, when used with a Partic. as its complement, need not always be rendered at all. It indicates that the event designated by the Partic. is one which takes place, not by design, but by chance, or in the ordinary course of nature, etc. See Kühn. § 310, 4. (1).

9.—Εἶναι, *is produced, flows from.* —— ὅσην ἀπὸ τοῦ ἑαυτόν τε ἡγεῖσθαι βελτίω, as from the feeling that one's self is becoming better, and is acquiring better friends, καὶ φίλους ἀμείνους κτᾶσθαι, i. e., is so acquiring them that they are better, ὥστε ἀμείνους γίγνεσθαι. This is similar in construction to the phrase: παιδεύειν τινὰ σοφόν, i. e., παιδεύειν τινὰ, ὥστε σοφὸν γίγνεσθαι. This question, as indicating Socrates' two principal sources of enjoyment, and, I might add, incentives to action, (i. e., self-improvement and the improvement of others by friendly intercourse,) is worthy of the prince of heathen moralists and philosophers. —— τοίνυν, see I. 2, 34. —— ταῦτα νομίζων, i. e., that I am becoming better and acquiring better friends. —— ἐὰν δὲ δή; cf. note, and see I. 5. 1. —— πλείων σχολή, κ.τ.λ., more leisure to care for, etc. —— τὸ παρὸν, that which is present or easily procured. —— ἐκπολιορκηθείη; this word seems to be used here in referring to persons, in the sense of ἑλεῖν, *to take captive;* so fought against as to be taken. Hellen. II. 4. 3, and Thucyd. I. 131, have been referred to as examples of this signif. of the word. —— τῶν χαλεπωτάτων εὑρεῖν, of things most difficult to be obtained, with which τοῖς ῥᾴστοις ἐντυγχάνει is contrasted; cf. the use of the latter supine in Latin. —— ἀρκούντως χρώμενος = ἀρκούμενος, *contented.*

10.—Ἔοικας...οἰομένῳ. With the verb ἐοικέναι, the participle may be put either in the Dat. as here, or in the Nominative. See Kühn § 310. R. 2; L. Gr. II. § 656. 2. For the Dat. cf. Sympos. 11. 15, and for the Nom., Hellen. VI. 3. 8, and Anab. III. 5, 13. —— μηδενὸς δέεσθαι θεῖον εἶναι; in regard to this principle of the Socratic philosophy, see Ritter's Hist. Phil. II. p. 66 sq., and Brandis, Gesch. Phil. II. S. 9. For δέεσθαι many editors read, δεῖσθαι. But Xenophon seems to have had a preference for the full form of this word; see Kühn. Gr. § 137. 2; L. Gr. I. 144.

11.—Ἐγώ τοι, *I indeed*, or, *for my part*. See II. 1. 11, 13. The strengthening particle τοί is often used with pronouns, and with other particles esp. in answering questions; cf. note upon I. 2. 46, and also see Kühn. Gr. § 317. 3; L. Gr. II. § 705. 1. —— σὲ μὲν δίκαιον, for which one Ms. and some editors read: σὲ δίκαιον μὲν. It does not seem necessary to deviate from the reading of all the other Mss., since even the best Attic writers do not always maintain perfect regularity in the collocation of the particles μέν and δέ after the word which they qualify. See Kühn. Gr. § 322. R. 2. —— δοκεῖς δέ; in Latin, instead of the Conj. the relative quod would be employed in such a connection as this: "quod etiam ipse mihi videris." —— γοῦν, see note upon § 2. —— πράττῃ, see note I. 2. 5: ἐπράττετο. —— καίτοι ... γε, see note I. 2. 3. —— οὐδενὶ ἂν μὴ ὅτι προῖκα δοίης, ἀλλ' οὐδ', κ.τ.λ., I say not, that you would not give them to any one gratuitously, but not without a full price, i. e., μὴ λέγω ὅτι, κ.τ.λ., like the Latin, ne dicam. Cf. II. 9. 8. Cyrop. I. 3. 10. See Hermann ad Viger. 253; Kühn. Gr. § 321. 3; B. 150. 1. —— ἔλαττον τῆς ἀξίας, i. e., ἔλαττον ἢ ἡ ἀξία τούτων τῶν χρημάτων ἐστί. Cf. II. 5. 5: τὸ πλεῖον τῆς ἀξίας; II. 1. 22; III. 11. 1; 13. 5, et al. See also Kühn. L. Gr. II. § 751. 4. —— ἀξία, sc. τιμή, its price or value.

12.—Εἰ καὶ τὴν συνουσίαν. The particles εἰ καί are not to be taken together, but καί belongs with τὴν συνουσίαν: *also;* and contrasts that word with τὸ ἱμάτιον, κ.τ.λ. Συνουσίαν (from σύνειμι) means literally, a being with; here, the intercourse of teacher and pupil, or, master and disciple. —— Δίκαιος μὲν οὖν ἂν εἴης. The order of the words would here be inverted in Latin: Sis (or eris) ergo sane justus. —— σοφὸς δὲ οὐκ ἄν; sc. εἴης. The particle ἄν is found without a verb where it may be readily supplied from the context: see Kühn. L. Gr. II. § 456. Cf. Anab. III. 2. 24, and passages from Plato, cited in Kühner's Gr. as above referred to. —— μηδενός γε ἄξια, *things worth nothing*, of no value; γέ gives emphasis to μηδενός.

13.—Παρ' ἡμῖν νομίζεται, κ.τ.λ. The order of the thought in this passage is: παρ' ἡμῖν νομίζεται ὁμοίως μὲν καλόν, ὁμοίως δὲ αἰσχρὸν εἶναι τὴν ὥραν καὶ τὴν σοφίαν διατίθεσθαι. It seems to us equally honorable and equally base to set to sale beauty and wisdom; i. e., however base it may be to prostitute physical beauty for gain, it is equally base to make pecuniary gain from wisdom; and as it is honorable to sell (impart) beauty to one who is a lover of the good and true, in order to acquire him as a friend, and for this purpose to impart beauty of mind (i. e., the love of the good and beautiful) to him, so is it to impart wisdom to others who desire it, not from love of gain, but in order to conciliate them as friends. In reference to ὁμοίως μέν ... ὁμοίως δέ, cf. Hier X. 8: ὁμοίως μὲν τοῖς σοῖς ἰδίοις, ὁμοίως δὲ τοῖς ἀνὰ τὴν χώραν. Plat. Sympos. p. 181. B. Διατίθεσθαι, which is used of merchants who expose their goods for sale, is fitly chosen to characterize the conduct of the Sophists, who communicated their wisdom to any one who might desire it, for a pecuniary reward. —— τοῦτον φίλον ἑαυτῷ ποιῆται. The reflexive pronoun is not unfrequently used with the Mid. Voice, especially in antitheses, in order to bring out more distinctly the reflexive sense of the verb. So in Cyrop. III. 2. 22: IV. 2. 22; VIII. 7. 13, etc. Still we have in this same section: φίλον ποιῆται without the pronoun. See Kühn. Gr. § 250. R. 3, and L. Gr. II. § 398. 2. —— τὴν σοφίαν... τοὺς... πωλοῦντας. The noun τὴν σοφίαν is placed at the beginning of the clause for the sake of emphasis. The usual order of the words would be: τοὺς μὲν τὴν σοφίαν πωλοῦντας. Cf. II. 2. 4: τούτου γε τῶν ἀπολυσόντων; IV. 4. 7: περὶ ἀριθμῶν τοῖς ἐρωτῶσιν. —— σοφιστὰς ὥσπερ πόρνους; see note, I. 1. 11. By the addition of ὥσπερ πόρνους here the idea of prostituting wisdom, i. e., giving it for a reward, as the πόρνος did the body, is distinctly expressed. —— εὐφυᾶ. Some few Mss. have the form εὐφυῆ. But there seems to be no reason for changing the text. The form in -ᾶ is found in III. 1. 11: ἐνδεᾶ, and in 3. 13, although in the latter case there are various readings. In Plato both forms are used, but the form in -ᾶ more frequently. Kühn. L. Gr. I. § 15. Anm. 3, says that in such words έα is contracted into ᾶ, although the contraction ῆ is sometimes found. —— ποιῆται. Many editors here adopt the reading ποιεῖται, which is found in two or three Mss. But the subjunctive seems to be required, and although we should expect ἄν with the Subj. in a relative clause, yet it is omitted in the preceding clause: τοῦτον φίλον ἑαυτῷ ποιῆται, to which this seems to be conformed. Still if, as Matthiae supposes, it were necessary, it might easily have been omitted in copying, after ὅστις δέ in consequence of the similar words ὃν ἂν following. See Kühn. L. Gr. II. § 796 1. —— ἔχῃ ἀγαθόν. For the use of ἔχειν with the signification, to be possessed of, to know; cf. § 14: σχῶ; I. 6. 13; II. 2. 6; III. 2. 1. This word is employed in reference to any thing that is in one's power, whether external or internal. Thus we find it followed by κάλλος and σωφροσύνην, as well as δυνάμεις, ἀρκάς, etc.

14.—Ἐγὼ δ' οὖν καὶ, *and I accordingly myself.*—— ἄλλοις συνίστημι, *commend, recommend to others.* So frequently in Xenophon, v. Bornemann in Index to Anab. p. 673, and in note Sympos. IV. 63. p. 154. —— παρ' ὧν . . . ὠφελήσεσθαί . . . ἀρετὴν, from whom I think they will be in any way benefited in respect to virtue. For the future ὠφελήσεσθαι, v. note upon I. 1. 8: ἀνιάσεται . . . στερήσεται, and Kühn. Gr. § 251. 3. R. —— τῶν πάλαι σοφῶν ἀνδρῶν. Some, as C. F. Hermann, have referred these words to the early poets rather than the philosophers. But this rather forced, though by no means impossible interpretation, is not necessary. For Socrates does not affirm that he inculcated the dogmas of the Sophists; but, he says, *if* we find any thing good in them (and he doubtless found much, see Introd.) we cull it and count it a great gain. —— κατέλιπον, the Aor. in the sense of our perfect; see Buttmann Gr. § 137. 3. —— ἐὰν ἀλλήλοις φίλοι, if we (before friends) may become, φίλοι, endeared (by these common pursuits). 'Ωφέλιμοι instead of φίλοι, seems evidently to be a gloss.

15.—Ποτὲ. Notice the use of this particle in introducing each conversation, see § 1, 11. In § 11 connected with πάλιν as here. —— Πῶς . . . ἡγεῖται . . . πράττει . . . ἐπίσταται. These verbs are all found in the Optative, ἡγοῖτο . . . πράττοι . . . ἐπίσταιτο, in a few Mss.; and that reading is adopted by Ernesti and others. But the change probably arose from the feeling, that the indirect question required that Mood. It cannot however be doubted that even the present indicative may be used, when the oblique interrogation takes the form of the direct: see note upon I. 1. 1, and examples there cited. —— δὲ, *whilst.* —— οὐ πράττει τὰ πολιτικὰ, see note I. 1. 18. —— εἴπερ ἐπίσταται, if he really had knowledge of it. This seems to have been added in derision by Antiphon. —— Ποτέρως δ'. The particle δέ here refers to a suppressed clause: Λέγεις μὲν ἐμὲ τὰ πολιτικὰ μὴ πράττειν. You say that I do not engage in political life, *but,* etc.; cf. note upon I. 3. 13. Socrates rightly supposed that the true government of a nation must begin with the education of the youth; and that it is a far higher and better service, to form many to be good citizens, than to be the chief ruler of the State.

CHAPTER VII.

1.—Ἀλαζονείας ἀποτρέπων. The Genitive is here governed by the force of the preposition in composition, or it may be termed, the *separative* Genit. after the Part. ἀποτρέπων. See Kühn. Gr. § 271. 2. For the meaning of ἀλαζ. cf. Cyrop. II. 2. 12; and Aristot. ad Nicomach. IV. 7, and Theophrast. Char. c. 23. —— προέτρεπεν, see note I. 2. 64. —— ἐπ' εὐδοξίᾳ. Schneider, Ernesti, Herbst, and others, have the Accus. εὐδοξίαν. Concerning the sentiment, see II. 6. 39, and Cyrop. I. 6. 22. —— Τοῦτο . . . ὃ, Acc. of limitation. Kühn. Gr. § 279. 7; S. 182.

2.—'Ενθυμώμεθα γάρ. The particle γάρ in exhortations has very much the force of our *now:* Let us now consider. He had before spoken of ἀλαζονείας, boasting, to his disciples, and says: we will now, or let us now illustrate the subject by examples. See Hartung Gr. Partik. I. p. 476 sq.; Kühn. Gr. § 324. 2; L. Gr. II. 754, b. —— μὴ ὢν, *whilst he is not.* —— ἆρ' οὐ, *must he not*, etc.? cf. note upon I. 3. 11. —— τὰ ἔξω τῆς τέχνης, κ.τ.λ. The construction of τὰ ἔξω is the same as that of τἆλλα in Cyrop. I. 3. 10; see Kühn. Gr. § 280. R. 1; L. Gr. II. § 558, Anm. 1. The adverb ἔξω has the force of a noun in consequence of the article. See Kühn. Gr. § 244. 10. For the construction and governing power of verbals, see Kühn. Gr. § 284. 3, 12; B. 134. 9, 10. —— σκεύη. In regard to the expense of the equipage of the ancient chorus of flute-players, see Boeckh, Econ. of Athens, B. III. ch. xxii. —— ἔπειτα, for ἔπειτα δέ, see note upon I. 2. 1. —— ἀλλὰ μὴν . . . γε, see note upon I. 1. 6. —— ἔργον . . . οὐδαμοῦ ληπτέον, he must never make a trial of his skill, give an example of his art. Schneider and Bornemann consider ἔργον . . . ληπτέον as synon. with ἐργολαβεῖν, III. 1. 2. —— καίτοι . . . δαπανῶν, *although at great expense.* For καίτοι with a Partic., see Kühn. Gr. § 312. R. 8; L. Gr. II. § 667. p. 370, and note upon I. 1. 5.

3.—'Ως δ' αὕτως. The δέ is sometimes though seldom written after ὡσαύτως, as in § 4: 'Ωσαύτως δὲ. The adverb ὡσαύτως corresponds in meaning to the adjective ὁ αὐτός, *the same*, from which it is derived. —— ἢ κυβερνήτης. For the position of this word, see I. 6. 8: εὐφραίνει. —— ταύτῃ λυπηρόν, with εἴη understood: it would on this account be a source of misery. Cf. III. 5. 2; IV. 3. 12; Sympos. IV. 17, and Bos' Ellipses Gr. I. p. 333. —— κυβερνᾶν τε κατασταθεὶς. In respect to the construction of the infinitive here, cf. III. 2. 1: στρατηγεῖν ᾑρημένος, and 3. 1: ἱππαρχεῖν ᾑρημένος. The particle τέ here is a great offence to the critics. It is wanting in two Mss., and some editors, following these Mss., have found it to be the easiest way to dispose of it, to exclude it altogether from the text. But Kühner seems to be right in supposing that it cannot be thus summarily got rid of, and gives at least a plausible explanation. The words οὓς ἥκιστα βούλοιτο, are contrasted with αὐτὸς, and the full expression would require τούτους to precede οὕς, κ.τ.λ. But if the demonstrative had been added, the phrase would undoubtedly have been τούτους τε οὕς, κ.τ.λ., and as the demonstrative was omitted the particle τέ very naturally took a place near the beginning of the clause. It is correlative with καί before αὐτὸς αἰσχ. κ.τ.λ. Its influence is to heighten the contrast between evils that are inflicted upon another and upon himself by one who is unskilful in his profession. So τέ is not unfrequently placed at the beginning of a sentence to indicate that one clause and not a single word is contrasted with another. See II. 1. 5, 28, and Bornemann's note; II. 2. 12; III. 12. 4: καὶ διὰ ταῦτα τόν τε λοιπὸν βίον ἥδιον καὶ κάλλιον διαζῶσι, καὶ τοῖς ἑαυτῶν παισὶ καλλίους ἀφορμὰς εἰς τὸν βίον καταλείπουσιν (where we might expect καὶ αὐτοί). It is placed in the same manner where two words blended in one idea are contrasted with another word, IV. 1. 2: ταχύ τε, κ.τ.λ. Some translate τε here: "for instance;" see Knickerbocker for Dec. 1847. —— ἀπαλλάξειεν, *come off*. The verb ἀπαλλάττειν is not unfrequently used in an intransitive or reflexive sense, III. 13. 6; Cyrop. IV. 1. 5; Demosth. de Coron. p. 246. 65.

4.—Μὴ ὄντα δοκεῖν. The Inf. εἶναι is to be supplied from the participle ὄντα after δοκεῖν. —— ἀλυσιτελὲς ἀπέφαινε. With *verba sentiendi* and *declarandi* and especially with φαίνομαι, the participle of εἶναι is frequently omitted; see Kühn. Gr. § 310. R. 5; L. Gr. II. 656. 3; cf. II. 3. 14: μὴ αἰσχρὸς φανῇς; IV. 2. 12; Sympos. III. 8. —— μείζω ἢ κατὰ δύναμιν, greater than (is in accordance with) their ability. For the force of the comparison with ἢ κατά, see Kühn. Gr. § 323. 7; L. Gr. II. § 751. i.; and cf. IV. 4. 24; 7. 10. —— οὐκ ἄν, *not easily*.

5.—Εἴ τις... παρά του... λαβὼν ἀποστεροίη. The participle λαβὼν governs the nouns ἀργύριον and σκεῦος. The full phrase would be, εἴ τις ἀργύριον ἢ σκεῦος παρά του λαβὼν αὐτὸν ταῦτα ἀποστεροίη. —— ἐξηπατήκει, sc. τὴν πόλιν. Some have suspected that this verb should be in the Optative, i. e., ἐξηπατήκοι or ἐξαπατῴη. But Socrates probably wished to represent it as a real fact, and if so, of course would use the indicative. —— μὲν οὖν. The conclusive particle οὖν is omitted in two or three Mss., but it seems to be needed here. Cf. I. 1. 20: θαυμάζω οὖν; I. 2. 62, where δή takes the place of οὖν; I. 3. 15; 4. 9 and 6. 14. —— τοιάδε διαλεγόμενος; we should rather expect τοιαῦτα here, referring to what has gone before; see note I. 2. 3, but τοιάδε is used δεικτικῶς, i. e., in reference to the present conversation, the one now in progress. See Kühn. in h. l., and Gr. § 303. R. 1. Διαλέγεσθαι, originally, perhaps, had reference to discourse between different individuals by way of question and answer; see Socrates' definition of it in IV. 5. 12. So in

I. 6. 1; II. 10. 1. But the idea of dialogue was finally lost in the word, and it was used for discourse carried on by one person, especially in the Socratic method of eliciting truth by questions, etc. Cf. II. 4. 1, and see note, IV. 5. 12, and Woolsey's Gorgias, p. 447. C.

BOOK II.

CHAPTER I.

1.—Καὶ τοιαῦτα λέγων, by saying the following things he also seemed to me, etc. Καί appears to contrast τοιαῦτα λέγων, with what was said in Book I. Chap. V. upon this same subject, and τοιαῦτα, contrary to the general, though not universal principle, refers to what follows; see Kühn. Gr. § 303. 1. R. 1; B. 127. 1. b. The Part. (λέγων), here, as frequently, denotes the means; Kühner, however, in h. l. refers τοιαῦτα to what precedes in the last chapter of the first Book, but it is difficult to see how what is there said, should tend directly to incite men to temperance in eating, drinking, etc., whilst the direct object of what follows is to inculcate that virtue.——πρὸς ἐπιθυμίαν βρωτοῦ... καὶ πόνου. The difficulty in this sentence has caused different editors to propose a variety of changes in the text. But the most natural supposition seems to be, that it is an irregular construction of Xenophon himself, and that the nouns from βρωτοῦ to ὕπνου are governed by ἐπιθυμίαν; and the following, ῥίγους, κ.τ.λ., are governed by ἐγκράτειαν as if ἐπιθυμίαν had not intervened. Ἐγκράτειαν may then be rendered, temperance or moderation with the first nouns and with the last endurance, Latin: tolerantia. So Seiffert; and Kühner assents to the same explanation as proposed by Sauppius.——Γνοὺς δέ. Many editors, as Herbst and Seiffert, substitute γάρ for δέ here. But it seems unnecessary, as δέ is not necessarily adversative but explicative. It not only, however, like γάρ, introduces something for the sake of explanation, but adds with it some new thought which gives force or dignity to the preceding notion; cf. II. 5. 5; Hermann ad Viger. 345, 6; Hartung Gr. Partik. I. S. 167; Bornem. ad Symp. IV. 17. p. 117; and Kühn. L. Gr. II. § 736. 3. So in Latin autem is put for enim. See Kühner's note upon Cic. Tusc. Disp. I. 2. 3, p. 50.——ἀκολαστοτέρως ἔχοντα; ἔχω with Adv. equivalent in signif., as frequently to εἰμί with an Adj.——Ἀρίστιππε, Aristippus, one of the disciples of Socrates, termed "imperfect Socratists." He was a native of Cyrene in Africa, from which the school of philosophy, of which he was the reputed founder, was called the

Cyrenaic school. Born of wealthy parents, he seems to have indulged in all the luxury and pleasure, for which the inhabitants of his native city were notorious. The fame of the discourses of Socrates induced him to go to Athens (Plat. de Curios. 2; Diog. L. 1. 1), where he remained as a disciple of Socrates until his execution, Plat. Phaed. p. 59. He was odious to Xenophon and Plato (Diog. L. II. 65. c. note), termed Sophist by Aristotle (Metaph. III. c. ii.); and his subsequent life shows that Socrates did not wholly cure him of his inclination to sensual pleasure. See Ritter's Hist. Ancient Philosophy, Vol. II. Chap. III. p. 84 sq., and Lewes' Biog. Hist. Phil. Vol. II. Chap. II. p. 10 sq., where several characteristic anecdotes of him are related.——δύο τῶν νέων, two of our youth, young men.——ἀρχῆς; for constr. see Kühn. Gr. § 273. 3. (b) (δ).——Βούλει σκοπῶμεν. For the Subj. after βούλει, see Kühn. Gr. § 259. 1. (b); B. 139. 1. (1); L. Gr. § 464. c; M. II. § 516. 3; cf. § 10. III. 5. 1; IV. 2. 13, 16.——καὶ ὁ Ἀρίσ. The connection here may be made in English as well as Latin by a relative: to whom, cui, Aristippus replied.——γοῦν; see note upon I. 6. 2.

2.—Εἰκὸς γὰρ. For γάρ in response, see I. 4. 9.——Τὸ οὖν προαιρεῖσθαι...μᾶλλον. The comparative μᾶλλον is frequently added to προαιρεῖσθαι when it might be considered as almost redundant; so potius malle in Latin. Cf. III. 5. 16; IV. 2. 9; 4. 4; Isocr. de Pace, p. 153. 37.——ἐθίζοιμεν. This verb governs two accusatives, one however is made by the Infin. with the article τό. See Kühn. L. Gr. II. § 643.——ἄπρακτα γίγνηται, *be left undone or neglected.*——παρὰ τὴν ἐκείνου ἀρχήν, under his government or while he has the control of things.——τὸ δύνασθαι διψῶντα ἀνέχεσθαι, *the being able when thirsty to endure it.*——οὖν; see note upon I. 3. 9.

3.—Τί δέ; this phrase corresponds substantially with the Latin "quid vero," and is used in passing suddenly to another point, to call the attention to it.——τὸ μαθεῖν...ποτέρῳ ἂν προσεῖναι μᾶλλον τρέπει; *to learn...to which would this more properly belong?*——Πολὺ, sc. μᾶλλον ἂν πρέποι.——καὶ γὰρ, *for even;* see Hartung, Gr. Part. I. S. 137 sq. The Vulg. reading is καὶ γὰρ καί, but the last καί is not found in the eight Paris and some other Mss. and should in all probability be omitted. See Kühn. in h. l.

4.—Τούτων...τὰ μὲν, κ.τ.λ., of these (i. e., brute animals), some, to wit, enticed by the appetite, and even some who are very fearful of incurring danger, yet urged on by the desire of gratifying their appetites, are taken, etc. Τὰ μὲν indicates some of animals in general and ἔνια δυσωπούμενα is subjoined by the figure καθ' ὅλον καὶ μέρος. Cf. note upon I. 2. 24; II. 7. 1; III. 10. 11; IV. 2. 31. The same figure is common in Latin. —— ἐξιστάμενοι τοῦ, being withdrawn, allured from thinking of danger. See note upon I. 3. 12: τοῦ φρονεῖν ἐξίστησι.

5.—Ταὐτὰ...τοῖς ἀφρονεστάτοις. Words which contain the idea of likeness, unlikeness, etc., govern the Dat., hence ταὐτά (from ὁ αὐτός) governs ἀφρονεστάτοις. See Kühn. Gr. § 284. 3. (4); L. Gr. II. § 576; Soph. § 195, n. 3. —— ὥσπερ, *just as*, to adduce an example. Cf. III. 3. 12. —— εἱρκτὰς, fr. εἱρκτή, (fr. εἴργω, to shut in,) an inclosed place, and hence here, *the women's apartments*, so called, as secluded from the rest of the house. —— κίνδυνος, sc. ἔστι. —— ὁ νόμος ἀπειλεῖ; see an account of the penalty affixed to this crime in Smith's Dict. *Adulterium*, and Meier and Schöman, Attic Process, B. III. 1. S. 327 sq. —— ὄντων δὲ πολλῶν, κ.τ.λ., since there are many things that can free from the desire of these pleasures. Accord. to Fr. Portus, the study of philosophy, the arts, painting, etc. Thus in II. 2. 4 it is said: τούτου γε τῶν ἀπολυσόντων μεσταὶ μὲν αἱ ὁδοί. The future participle is used in a similar way in II. 8. 3: τῷ δεομένῳ τοῦ συνεπιμελησομένου; IV. 4. 5. —— ἆρ' οὐκ ἤδη...ἐστιν, is not this now the part of one wholly possessed of an evil genius? Upon ἤδη see Hartung, Gr. Partik. I. p. 243, and Kühn. L. Gr. II. § 690. B. The Latins use jam in the same way, and we, *now*, with the emphasis. Cf. II. 1. 14; 9. 7. Plat. Phaedr. p. 260. C: Παγγέλοιόν γ' ἂν ἤδη εἴη, that would *now* be very laughable.

6.—Τὸ δὲ εἶναι μὲν...τοὺς δὲ. The idea is: Is it not a great want of forethought that, although many of the employments of men are in the open air, ἐν ὑπαίθρῳ, where they may be exposed to inclemency of weather, *yet* numbers are entirely unaccustomed to bearing heat and cold; unexercised in, ἀγυμνάστως ἔχειν. For the constr. and the use of μέν and δέ, see I. 6. 5, and cf. § 8 below.

7.—Τοὺς ἐγκρατεῖς. This word is used in a double sense as in § 1. —— τούτων ἑκατέρου τοῦ φύλου τὴν τάξιν, the rank of each kind (genus) of these men.

8.—Τοῦ...παρασκευάζειν; the Infin. as Genit. absol. with ὄντος. —— μὴ ἀρκεῖν τοῦτο, sc. αὐτῷ. The verb ἀρκεῖν is found without the Dat. of the person, as in II. 2. 6; IV. 4. 9. We might naturally expect μὴ ἀρκεῖσθαι τούτῳ, ἀλλὰ προσαναθέσθαι, κ.τ.λ., not to be satisfied with this, but also to take upon one's self to supply, etc. But it is frequently the case in Greek, that the object of one clause is made the subject of the next, even without indicating it by a pronoun. See Kühn. L. Gr. II. § 852. a. Cf. Thucyd. I. 45. 51; II. 65, and Stallb. note upon

Plato, Protag. p. 320. A. B; De Repub. II. p. 360. A.; Gorg. p. 510, B. —— *πολλὰ ὧν βούλεται ἐλλείπειν.* The subject of βούλεται is to be supplied from the preceding words ἄφρονος ἀνθρώπου. Ἐλλείπειν τι ἑαυτῷ, signifies to deny one's self a thing. —— *τούτου δίκην ὑπέχειν*, *to subject one's self to punishment for this.*

9.—*Ἐγώ τε ... αἵ τε πόλεις.* For the use of τε ... τε, see I. 1. 14. —— *ἄφθονα τὰ ἐπιτήδεια παρασκευάζειν.* The Adj. ἄφθονα is a predicate, as the position of the article indicates; see I. 4. 13. The full enunciation of the thought would be: τὰ ἐπιτήδεια παρασκευάζειν, ὥστε αὐτὰ ἄφθονα εἶναι. We, however, may express the word ἄφθονα in English by an Adv. or adverbial phrase, *abundantly, in abundance.* —— *πολλὰ πράγματα ἔχειν αὐτοῖς τε καὶ ἄλλοις παρέχειν.* It is unnecessary to stop to enumerate the various changes of reading and the consequent explanations of this phrase, given by different editors. Those who are curious to see them, may consult Kühner in h. l. The idea seems to be: those who wish to have many cares and labors themselves and to furnish them for others (i. e., make others industrious), I would reckon, etc. The pronouns αὐτοῖς and ἄλλοις are contrasted. Thucyd. 1. 70 has been very justly compared with this passage. The Corinthians there say of the Athenians: ὥστε εἴ τις αὐτοὺς ξυνελὼν (i. e., embracing every thing in few words) φαίη πεφυκέναι ἐπὶ τῷ μήτε αὐτοὺς ἔχειν ἡσυχίαν, μήτε τοὺς ἄλλους ἀνθρώπους ἐᾶν, ὀρθῶς ἂν εἴποι. Cf also Diog. Laert. X. 139, concerning the Epicureans: τὸ μακάριον, κ.τ.λ.; and Cicero's interpretation of it, Nat. Deor. I. 17: Quod aeternum beatumque est, id nec habet ipsam negotii quicquam nec exhibet alteri. Cf. also Cic. de Off. III. 28. 102. In reference to the antithetical use of πράγματα ἔχειν and πράγματα παρέχειν, cf. Hellen. IV. 5. 19, and V. 1. 29. —— *ἐμαυτὸν τοίνυν.* We should expect some adversative particle here as δέ; but the conclusive particle τοίνυν seems to be used by anacoluthon, and the natural completion of the preceding sentence would have been: τοὺς δὲ βουλομένους ἡδέως βιοτεύειν εἰς τοὺς ἀρχῆς ἀπεχομένους; in which case τοίνυν would have been expected. For the use of τοίνυν after μέν in a preceding clause, see Arn. 2 Gr. Comp. p. 196; cf. Cyrop. I. 1. 2.

10.—*Τοῦτο σκεψώμεθα.* This is a plain case of the reference of τοῦτο to what follows; see note upon I. 2. 3. —— *Πάνυ μὲν οὖν*, sc. σκεψώμεθα. —— Ἐν δὲ τῇ Εὐρ. ... ἀρχ. For the extent of the Scythians, see Panegyr. Isoc. p. 22 and note, Felton's Ed. —— *ἡ τῶν Ἑλλήνων.* A strictly regular construction would require εἶτα answering to πρῶτον μὲν. But the preceding question, τούτων οὖν ποτέρους ἥδιον οἴει ζῆν, gives occasion to change to ἡ τῶν, κ.τ.λ.

11.—Ἀλλ' ἐγώ τοι, *but I truly*, or, *indeed*, at ego quidem. For the use of τοί, in answers, see note upon I. 2. 46. —— αὖ, refers back to § 8: καὶ οὐδαμῶς γε τάττω ἐμαυτὸν εἰς τὴν τῶν ἄρχειν βουλομένων τάξιν, I by no means reckon myself among those who wish to rule; so, on the contrary, αὖ, I wish not to be enslaved, εἰς τὴν δουλείαν ἐμαυτὸν τάττω, which is for εἰς τὴν τῶν δούλων τάξιν τάττω. The Latin may imitate the Greek here, and use servitium for δουλείαν; see Zumpt's Gr. § 675. —— τίς . . . ὁδός, so the pronoun τὶς is not unfrequently separated from its noun by several intervening words. —— μέση τούτων ὁδός, *middle way between these.* —— οὔτε δι' ἀρχῆς, οὔτε διὰ δουλείας, sc. ἄγουσα, which is to be supplied, ἀπὸ κοινοῦ, from the following ἄγει; see numerous examples of a similar construction in C. G. Krüger upon Dionys. Histor: p. 17; see also Kühn. L. Gr. II. § 852 sq., and cf. § 12.

12.—Ἀλλ' εἰ μέντοι, *but if indeed.* See note upon I. 3. 10 Although μέντοι has here a confirmatory significance, yet just below it has an adversative meaning, *but.* Cf. Schneider and Bornemann upon Cyrop. V. 2. 12. p. 423. —— δι' ἀνθρώπων, sc. φέροι, which κατὰ σύλληψιν, is to be supplied from the preceding φέρει; see note upon § 11. —— ἴσως ἄν τι λέγοις, you would perhaps say *something*, i. e., something that has meaning, force. So τί is used in Plat. Sympos. p. 173. B: οἴεσθέ τι ποιεῖν οὐδὲν ποιοῦντες. Cf. the use of aliquid in Latin. —— εἰ . . . μήτε ἄρχειν ἀξιώσεις μήτε ἄρχεσθαι, μήτε . . . θεραπεύσεις. The reading of the Mss. here is ἀξιώσῃς . . . θεραπεύσῃς. But Bornemann and most of the other recent editors give the indicative future. The sense seems to require this, and the use of the subjunctive in this way after εἰ by the prose writers of Xenophon's time is not well supported by Mss. See Kühn. L. Gr. II. § 818. Anm. 1, and Matthiae II. 525. b. But still a variation from the Mss. would not be sanctioned, but for the fact that -σεις and -σῃς are often interchanged and confounded in the written Greek. —— κλαίοντας καθιστάντες, *bringing to tears, causing to weep.* Cf. Eurip. Androm. 635: ὃς κλαίοντά σε καὶ τὴν ἐν οἴκοις σὴν καταστήσει κόρην. Schneider writes καθίσαντες in imitation of Cyrop. II. 2. 14 and 15. Cf. also Plato Io. p. 535. E. and Stallbaum's note. —— δούλοις χρῆσθαι. Some Mss. have the Accus. δούλους and some insert ὡς before δούλοις. For the omission of ὡς, cf. I. 2. 49: τεκμηρίῳ τούτῳ χρώμενος; 56; II. 6. 26; III. 11. 6; 14. 4, et al., and examples of the use of ὡς, collected by Sauppius, in note upon I. 2. 56; also Anab. II. 6. 25; III. 1. 30, et al. There seems to be this difference between the two forms of expression: χρῆσθαί τινι πιστῷ φίλῳ is used of one who truly has a faithful friend, whilst χρῆσ. τ. ὡς π. φίλῳ is used of one who supposes he has a faithful friend, though he may not necessarily be faithful. Ὡς then is properly omitted here, as real servitude is designated.

13.—Ἦ λανθάνουσί σε οἱ ... τέμνοντες, *have those escaped your notice; who*, etc. —— Πολιορκοῦντες. The verb πολιορκεῖν, lit., to blockade or besiege a city (from πόλις and εἴργω, ἕρκος), is used metaphorically of other kinds of annoyance. Cf. § 17, and Plat. Alcib. II. p. 142. A. —— καὶ ... αὖ, *and again*. These particles are used together in Anab. I. 1. 7; 9. 19; VI. 1. 18; Plat. Alcib. I. 105. D. —— ξένος πανταχοῦ, *every where* foreigner, citizen of the world.

14.—Μέντοι; a particle of affirmation, *truly*. See Hartung, Gr. Partik. II. p. 393 sq.; Kühn. L. Gr. II. § 698. a. —— ἤδη; see note upon § 5 above. —— πάλαισμα, lit., a trick of the παλαιστής, and then a trick or device in general. The latter, *device* or *counsel*, is evidently the meaning here. —— ἐξ οὗ, sc. χρόνου, *since*. —— Σίννις ... Σκείρων ... Προκρούστης, were infamous robbers, slain by Theseus. See Plut. Theseus, c. 8–11. Apollod. III. 16. 1. The irony of this whole passage cannot escape the notice of the reader; especially in the clause: οὐδεὶς ἔτι ἀδικεῖ. —— τοῖς ἀναγκαίοις καλουμένοις, those called necessary, i. e., relatives or kindred. Cf. Stallb. ad Plat. de Repub. IX. p. 574. C. —— ὅμως, *yet, still*; see Kühn. Gr. § 322. 7, and L. Gr. II. § 667. c, and cf. § 15.

15.—Σὺ δὲ οὐδὲν μὲν τούτων ἔχων, i. e., none of the protection, safeguards, which the citizens have, who are still exposed to injury; and passing much of your time in journeyings, where there is especial danger (ἐν δὲ ταῖς ὁδοῖς ... διατρίβων); and when you come into any city, being the most unprotected of all, etc., (εἰς ὁποίαν δ' ἂν πόλιν ἀφίκῃ, κ.τ.λ.) Both of the last two clauses, ἐν δὲ ταῖς ὁδοῖς ... εἰς ὁποίαν δ' ἂν, κ.τ.λ., are opposed to the first οὐδὲν μὲν ταύτων ἔχων, hence the δέ ... δέ answering to μέν. —— τοιοῦτος, οἵοις, i. e., having no fixed abode, and no friends or companions but wandering from one city to another. For the plural number after the singular, see Kühn. Gr. § 332. R. 1. (a); L. Gr. II. § 784. 2. a. p. 503. —— διὰ τὸ ξένος εἶναι, for the attraction here, see I. 2. 3: τῷ φανερὸς εἶναι. —— ἢ διότι καὶ δοῦλος ἄν; i. e., εἰ δοῦλος εἴης. A conditional enunciation is often implied in a noun; see Kühn. Gr. § 340. 1; L. Gr. II. § 823. 2. Previously it has been shown, that as citizen or guest he could not be protected from injury; and now Socrates reasons on the supposition that he may become a servant. He ironically asks Aristippus, if he places his hope in this, that if he should become a servant, he should evidently be a useless one? —— οἷος ... λυσιτελεῖν; for the relative with the Infin., see note upon I. 4. 6:

οἵους τέμνειν. —— τίς γάρ; before this question a denial of the preceding is implied: by no means, for who, etc.; minime vero, quis enim, etc. See note upon I. 4. 9: οὐδὲ γάρ.

16.—Ἆρα οὐ; see note upon I. 3. 11. —— σωφρονίζουσι, *restore to sanity, correct.* —— ἀποκλείοντες ὅθεν . . . ᾖ, by excluding them from (the places) where it is possible, etc.

17.—Ἀλλὰ γάρ, *but indeed;* the force of the γέ in γάρ here predominates. These two particles often introduce an objection; see Hartung, Gr. Partik. I. S. 470 sq.; Kühn. L. Gr. II. § 754. 5. Cf. upon a similar use of at enim in Latin, Kühner's Tusc. Disp. V. 16. 47. —— ἐξ ἀνάγκης, compelled by necessity. —— εἴ γε, si quidem · for the force of γέ, see Kühn. Gr. § 317. 2, and L. Gr. II. § 704. 1. —— πεινήσουσι κ.τ.λ.; the future here denotes necessity or destination; if they must, or, it is destined to them, to suffer hunger, etc. See Kühn. L. Gr. II. § 704. 1, and Gr. § 256. 3; Rost § 116. Anm. 7. See note upon § 12, and cf. III. 3. 52; 6. 13. —— οὐκ οἶδ', ὅτι διαφέρει τὸ αὐτὸ δέρμα ἑκόντα ἢ ἄκοντα μαστιγοῦσθαι . . . ἄλλο γε, κ.τ.λ., I do not know what other (ὅτι . . . ἄλλο) difference it makes with the same skin, whether one is voluntarily or involuntarily scourged, except, etc.; or we may make the Gr. Accus. of limitation, δέρμα, a nominative; whether the same skin is scourged, etc. Ἄλλο γε are best rendered with ὅτι; they are not strictly necessary to the sense, as the idea is contained in διαφέρει; but they make the distinction introduced more conspicuous, and hence the γέ, and also remove any obscurity that might arise from the separation of διαφέρει from ἢ ἀφροσύνῃ, κ.τ.λ. We should naturally expect the insertion of ὅτι after ἢ: ἄλλογε, ἢ ὅτι ἀφρ. κ.τ.λ., but it is omitted just as it often is after the phrases: οὐδὲν ἄλλο ἤ, ἄλλο τι ἤ, τί ἄλλο ἤ, κ.τ.λ. Cf. II. 3. 17; Stallb. Plat. Lysid. p. 222. D, and see Rost's Gr. § 139; Kühn. Gr. § 346. 2. (d); L. Gr. II. § 852. m. —— πολιορκεῖσθαι, to be harassed; see note, § 13.

18.—Τῶν τοιούτων, i. e., τοῦ πεινῆν, διψῆν, ῥιγοῦν, ἀγρυπνεῖν. The construction is: οὐ δοκεῖ σοι τὰ ἑκούσια τῶν τοιούτων διαφέρειν τῶν ἀκουσίων. —— ᾗ, = ταύτῃ, ὅτι, inasmuch as, just as; see I. 7. 3: ταύτῃ. —— πίοι; the particle ἄν is to be repeated from the preceding clause: φάγοι ἄν. See note I. 3. 15. —— ὁπόταν βούληται. Just before we have ὁπότε βούλοιτο (Optat.) because the preceding clause on which this depends, φάγοι ἄν, denotes an uncertain condition. We naturally have the Subj. here after the present ἔξεστιν. See Kühn. L. Gr. II. § 810. a. —— παύεσθαι; sc. πεινῶντι, διψῶντι, κ.τ.λ. —— ἐπ' ἀγαθῇ ἐλπίδι, resting on good hope, with good hope for his reward. See Kühn.

L. Gr. II. § 612. g; Gr. § 296. II. In reference to the sentiment, cf. I. 6. 8.

19.—*Ἆθλα*, designates the rewards of labor, from ἆθλον, the prize of contest, which is distinct from ἆθλος, the contest itself; although in the plural and perhaps a few times in the singular, ἆθλον may like ἆθλος denote the contest itself. For the distinction, see Liddell and Scott's Lex. h. v.; Pillon's Gr. Synonymes, p. (4). —— *μικροῦ τινος ἄξιά ἐστι*, *are of some small value.* —— *χειρώσωνται*, get the victory over; Schneider in accordance with two or three Mss. reads χειρώσονται. —— *ἢ ὅπως . . . ἢ ἵνα.* The change from ὅπως to ἵνα here seems strange, yet it is not without parallels; cf. IV. 4. 16; Anab. II. 6. 22, et al. —— *δυνατοὶ . . . τοῖς σώμασι*, κ.τ.λ., becoming strong both in body and mind. —— *καλῶς οἰκῶσι*, see note upon I. 1. 7. —— *τούτους*; the noun is not unfrequently followed by a demonstrative pronoun for the sake of perspicuity, or, as here, for emphasis. Cf. III. 7. 4; IV. 6. 5, 11; Cyrop. II. 1. 13, and see Kühn. Gr. § 304. 3; L. Gr. II. § 858. 10. —— *ζῆν εὐφραινομένους*, live happily. —— *ἀγαμένους μὲν ἑαυτούς*, since they admire, are satisfied with themselves, etc.; ἑαυτούς is contrasted with τῶν ἄλλων below. —— *ζηλουμένους*, esteemed happy, emulated.

20.—*Ἐκ τοῦ παραχρῆμα ἡδοναί*, those pleasures which are obtainable immediately (i. e., as soon as sought) and without labor. The explanation: pleasures of the present time, seems to be inadmissible from the use of ἐκ, *post, after*, not *in*; from the usage of the formula τὸ παραχρῆμα = τὸ παραυτίκα, or τὸ αὐτίκα, not that which does not endure beyond the present time (the momentary), but that which immediately follows the present time, and also from the contrast with αἱ διὰ καρτερίας ἐπιμέλειαι, the cares exercised with industry and perseverance. —— *εὐεξίαν*, good state of body, or, good constitution. —— *ψυχῇ ἐπιστήμην ἀξιόλογον οὐδεμίαν ἐμποιοῦσιν.* Kühner says that ἀξιόλογον is justly added here, because it cannot be said that αἱ παραυτίκα ἡδοναὶ impart no knowledge to the mind; for who can deny that the mind obtains knowledge from hearing music, beholding pictures, and other similar pleasures? —— *καλῶν τε κἀγαθῶν ἔργων ἐξικνεῖσθαι.* The verb ἐξικνεῖσθαι, to arrive at, to attain, is construed with the partitive Genit. like τυγχάνειν, λαγχάνειν, and προσήκειν. So also ἐφικνεῖσθαι, Isocrates, Paneg. p. 64. 113, and p. 80. —— Ἡσίοδος; Ἔργ, καὶ Ἡμερ, I. 285. —— *Τὴν . . . κακότητα καὶ ἰλαδὸν*, κ.τ.λ., we can obtain vice easily even in abundance. —— *μάλα δ' ἐγγύθι ναίει*, and dwells, or, has its mansion very near. —— *Τῆς δ' ἀρετῆς*, κ.τ.λ., but the immortal gods have placed before the temple of virtue (or guarded it by) bars of sweat, toil.

—— ὄρθιος, steep. —— καὶ τρηχὺς τὸ πρῶτον, and rough at first —— ἵκηται. Οἶμος seems to be the subject of this verb. Still some, as Goettling, understand τὶς, if any one who chooses this way shall come, etc. —— Ῥηϊδίη. It is perhaps most probable that οἶμος is fem. here, so that ῥηϊδίη agrees directly with it. This noun is used in both genders in later Attic writers, and a few times, though rarely, by the older poets, as in Aesch. Prom. 394, and Eur. Alc. 838. Still the gender of the Adj., ῥηϊδίη, may have been made to correspond with that of ἀρετή. —— Ἐπίχαρμος. This comic poet was a native of Coos, an island in the Egean Sea, and was professor of the Pythagorean philosophy at the Court of Hiero in Syracuse; hence he received the appellation Siculus. He flourished about 470 B. C., and is frequently considered as the first writer of comedy. See Fisk's Manual of Class. Lit. p. 459; and Schöll, Gesch. d. Gr. Lit., *Epicharmus* in Index. —— Τῶν πόνων πωλοῦσιν, κ.τ.λ. The gods sell to us all good things *for labor*. Genitive of the price; Kühn. Gr. § 275. 3, cf. II. 8. 2: μισθοῦ τὰ ἐπιτήδεια ἐργάζεσθαι. —— καὶ ἐν ἄλλῳ... τόπῳ, κ.τ.λ. This quotation is omitted by Bessarius. W. Dindorf supposes that the whole from Μαρτυρεῖ to ἔχῃς is spurious. But the reasons given, do not seem to be sufficient for forcibly excluding it. See Kühn. in h. l. —— μὴ τὰ μαλακὰ μώεο, μή, κ.τ.λ. The idea is: Do not seek an easy life, lest by that means you may procure for yourself a hard and troubled one. Μώεο is the Pres. Imp. of μώομαι = μάομαι.

21.—Πρόδικος, was a Sophist of Ceos. He was, however, often at Athens, and was acknowledged by Plato to be distinguished for his wisdom. He was a disciple of Protagoras. See Plat. Hipp. Maj. p. 282; Theat. p. 151, et al.; and also Brandis' Gesch. Gr. Phil. I. S. 541 and 546 sq. —— ἐν τῷ συγγράμματι τῷ περὶ τοῦ Ἡρακλέους, in the writing relating to Hercules. —— ὅπερ δὴ... ἐπιδείκνυται. The particle δή here indicates the certainty of a thing, *indeed, certainly*. See Kühn. Gr. § 315. 2; L. Gr. II. § 692, and cf. II. 2. 3; III. 5. 11. The present tense, ἐπιδείκνυται, should seem to be used by Xenophon because that Prodicus was accustomed to recite the "choice of Hercules" at the time when this colloquy of Socrates was held. Ἐπιδείκνυσθαι, lit., to exhibit as a specimen of one's art. This word is fitly chosen, to indicate the parade which the Sophists loved so much in the exhibition of their sentiments. —— ὧδέ πως; cf. τοιάδε τις, I. 1. 1. —— Καὶ strengthens the superlative πλείστοις, see Kühn. Gr. § 239. —— ἀποφαίνεται, expressed his sentiments. —— ἐπεὶ ἐκ παίδων εἰς ἥβην ὡρμᾶτο, when having completed his boyhood, he was entering upon the period of youth. —— γιγνόμενοι, becoming (by law). —— εἴτε τὴν δι' ἀρετῆς . . . εἴτε τὴν διὰ κακίας, whether they will proceed on the way through (or the way of) virtue . . . or the way of vice, etc. —— ἐξελθόντα εἰς ἡσυχίαν καθῆσθαι, κ.τ.λ., going out into a solitude, a sequestered spot, he sat down, being in doubt which way he should turn. Thus Cic. de Offic. I. 32. 118: (Herculem) exisse in solitudinem atque ibi sedentem diu secum multumque dubitasse, etc. Schmidt connects εἰς ἡσυκίαν with καθῆσθαι, sat down quietly, or, in quiet. —— ὁποτέραν τῶν ὁδῶν τράπηται. For the use of the Subj. with the Interrog. of doubting, see note, I. 2. 15, and cf. § 23.

22.—Μεγάλας, large in stature. —— εὐπρεπῆ τε ἰδεῖν, καὶ ἐλευθέριον, of a comely and noble appearance; for the constr. of the Infin. see I. 6. 5. Gaisford, according to Cod. Stob. reads ἐλευθέριαν, but the change is unnecessary, as Xenophon uses ἐλευθέριος both as an adjective of two and three terminations. Cf. Sympos. II. 4, and VIII. 16. —— φύσει, the Dat. of the agent with the Perf. Pass., nature being personified. This Dat. of the agent is found with the Perf. and Plup. Tenses, and with verbal adjectives; see C. 417 and Note. The same idiom is found in Latin, though confined mainly in Class. Latin to the Perf. Part. and Tenses formed with it. Zumpt's Gr. 419, note. —— τὸ . . . σῶμα. The Accus. with Pass. Part. to explain it more fully. In English we should use a preposition, *in* or *in respect to;* see Kühn. Gr. § 279. 7. —— καθαρότητι, with purity. The sense may be well expressed in English by joining φύσει as an Adj., to καθαρ., having her body adorned with native purity. Some Mss. and editions have καθαριότητι, but the reading which we have given seems to be most appropriate, as well as to be supported by the best Ms. authority. This phrase is opposed to κεκαλλωπισμένην τὸ μὲν χρῶμα, artificial appliances for ornament; and as καθαριότης includes in it, according to Kühner, the idea of elegance superinduced by art, which καθαρότης does not, the contrast is better preserved by retaining the latter. —— ἐσθῆτι λευκῇ, are in the same construction with the preceding nouns σωφροσύνῃ, etc., depending upon κεκοσμημένην. But such incongruities of expression are not unfrequently found in the best writers. Cf. I. 3. 9. —— τεθραμμένην, κ.τ.λ., pampered into obesity and effeminacy. —— ὥστε λευκοτέραν τε καὶ ἐρυθροτέραν τοῦ ὄντος δοκεῖν φαίν., so that she might seem or be seen to present a fairer and more ruddy appearance than she really had, τοῦ ὄντος. (Upon these last words, see note, I. 6. 11.) Bornemann renders the phrase: that she might seem manifestly (aperte) to be, etc. (sc. κεκαλλωπισμένην). —— τὸ δὲ σχῆμα. The δὲ here answers to μὲν above with χρῶμα. —— τὰ δὲ ὄμματα ἔχειν. The change of construction here should not escape notice. —— ἀναπεπταμένα, wide open, i. e., as indicating boldness (βλέμμα ἰταμόν) in contrast with τὰ ὄμματα αἰδοῖ, or with oculis verecunde demissis. —— ὥρα. Some editors insert the article before this word from Aristaenetus I. ep. 25, where this passage is imitated, but this seems to be one of the nouns that imitate the usage of proper names in omitting the article; see Rost, Gr. § 98. 6; Kühn. § 244. R. 4; L. Gr. II. § 484 note. Cf. IV. 1. 2, where both ὥραν and ἀρετήν are without it. Other similar words also omit the article. Cf. ἥβην § 21 above, and γῆν § 28 below. For its frequent omission with κάλλος, see Bornem. Sympos. I. 8. p. 52. The word ὥρα, lit., *time*, then season, spring, youth and youthful beauty, hence, beauty in general. —— κατασκοπεῖσθαι ... ἑαυτήν; for the use of the Mid. Voice here, see B. 136. 7, note 4.—— ἐπισκοπεῖν δὲ καί, εἴ τις ἄλλος αὐτὴν θεᾶται, and also looks around (to see) if any other one is looking at her. We should rather expect ἑαυτήν here, and it would be necessary if the Opt. were employed instead of the indicative θεᾶται. See note upon I. 2. 49.

23.—Πλησιαίτερον τοῦ Ἡρακλέους. Adjectives denoting approach, are sometimes followed by the Gen. though oftener by the Dat. See Kühn. Gr. § 273. R. 9. —— τὴν ... πρόσθεν ῥηθεῖσαν ἰέναι, Acc. with the Infin. because in indirect discourse. —— τὸν αὐτὸν τρόπον, in the same gait as before, not faster or slower, contrasted with the haste exhibited by her companion (προσδραμεῖν). —— φθάσαι βουλομένην, wishing to anticipate, get before, etc. —— ἀποροῦντα, ποίαν ὁδὸν ... τράπῃ; cf. § 21: ἀποροῦντα ὁποτέραν τῶν ὁδῶν τράπηται, with the note; and for the use of the Pron. of direct interrogation, see note upon I. 1. 1. —— ποιησάμενος; this seems to be the best authorized, although more facile readings are found; as ποιήσῃ, ποιήσει, and ποιήσῃς. After the participle, τὴν ἐπὶ τὸν βίον ὁδὸν τράπῃ must be supplied from the preceding context. A somewhat similar construction is found in I. 2. 42, but for an explanation of this ellipsis, see Hermann ad Vig. § 227. p. 623; Symp. IV. 53. p. 146. —— καὶ ... μὲν ... δέ. These particles may be rendered here: that (and) ... both ... and.

24.—Διέσῃ. This is the best authorized reading, and διεῖναι is construed with the participle in the same manner in which other similar words, διαγίγνεσθαι, διατελεῖν, and διάγειν, often are. See Kühn. Gr. § 310. (1); hence here rendered *always* or *continually*, Lat. semper, and the Part. as a verb. —— ἀπονώτατα, with the least possible labor.

25.—Σπάνεως ἀφ' ὧν ἔσται ταῦτα, i. e., σπάνεως, τούτων, ἀφ' ὧν ἔσται ταῦτα, of want of things from which these (sc. pleasures) are obtained. In reference to the preposition ἀπό, denoting the instrument, see note upon I. 2. 14. —— οὐ φόβος, "metus non est" = "non est quod metuas." —— ἐπὶ τὸ πονοῦντα...πορίζεσθαι, bring you to this, that you must obtain these things (or bring you to obtain) by labor and by various troubles of body and mind, etc. —— οἷς...τούτοις; for the attraction, see Rost, § 99. 9, 10. p. 460 sq.; Kühn. L. Gr. II. 787. 2, and Anm. 3. —— ὠφελεῖσθαι...ἐξουσίαν, the power of receiving benefit from every quarter; for the use of the Infin. without the article as a noun, cf. III. 6. 11: οὐκ οἴει καὶ ἁρπάζειν ἐξουσίαν ἔσεσθαι (i. e., ἐξέσεσθαι) τῷ βουλομένῳ, and see B. 140. N. 8; Kühn. L. Gr. II. § 641. c.

26.—Ὄνομα δέ. The particle δέ need not be expressed in Latin or English: "nomen quodnam tibi est?" The concessive member before δέ is frequently omitted, and thus vivacity is given to the question: (this sounds very well) *but*, etc. See note upon I. 3. 13. —— ὑποκοριζόμενοι. The verb ὑποκορίζέσθαι signifies originally to speak as a child or with fondling terms; then, to smooth or gloss over an odious thing with mild and favorable words, and the reverse here, to detract, to call a good thing by an odious name.

27.—Ἐν τούτῳ...προσελθοῦσα, coming up in the meantime. —— εἰδυῖα τοὺς γεννήσαντας, κ.τ.λ., having known your parents and carefully observed your nature, disposition, in education (i. e., while you have been trained up), etc. —— τὴν πρὸς ἐμὲ ὁδὸν, the way to me, or, which leads to me. —— ἐπ' ἀγαθοῖς διαπρεπεστέραν, κ.τ.λ., more illustrious on account of the good that I confer upon you. See note upon I. 2. 61: ὀνομαστὸς, κ.τ.λ., and cf. § 28. —— προοιμίοις ἡδονῆς, by overtures, promises of pleasure, lit., prefaces; the idea is: I will not begin by alluring with deceptive promises of pleasure. —— φανῆναι; in respect to the omission of ἄν, cf. note, I. 3. 15.—— τὰ ὄντα...μετ' ἀληθείας, I will recount to you things that really are, in truth. See upon the construction here, Kühn. L. Gr. II. § 858. 3, and cf. Stallb. Plat. Phaed. p. 66. C, and Bornemann ad Sympos. VII. 4.

28.—Τῶν γὰρ ὄντων ἀγαθῶν, κ.τ.λ. Schaefer expresses this idea more fully thus: ἃ γάρ ἐστιν ἀγαθὰ καὶ καλά, τούτων οὐδὲν ἄνευ πόνου... θεοὶ διδόασιν. —— ἀπὸ βοσκημάτων; see note upon I. 2. 14. —— τὰς...τέχνας αὐτάς τε. The particle τέ is placed here as if the preceding words, the arts themselves, were contrasted with αὐταῖς ... χρῆσθαι, the practising of them; and the sentence arranged as follows: τὰς πολ. τέχ. αὐτάς τε καὶ ὅπως αὐταῖς δεῖ χρῆσθαι, μαθητέον, not only the arts themselves but the practice of them must be learned. After the ἀσκητέον is added, the natural place of the τέ would be after μαθητέον, contrasting that with ἀσκητέον. But such irregularities of position, arising from the blending of two constructions, are found elsewhere, cf. Cyrop. VIII. 2. 22, and Anab. I. 2. 21. —— ἀσκητέον is considered by some, as Fr. Jacobs, to have a pregnant signif. ἀσκήσει μαθητέον, to be learned by exercise, but it is perhaps better with Bornemann to consider the words ὅπως αὐταῖς δεῖ χρῆσθαι as comprising but one idea = τὴν αὐτῶν χρῆσιν. Cf. De Vectig. IV. 1: ταύτην (τὴν δύναμιν) γνόντες καὶ ὅπως χρῆσθαι δεῖ. For the constr. and governing power of verbals, see note I. 7. 2. —— εἰ δὲ καὶ; after εἴτε... εἴτε several times repeated, the last and most important member of the sentence is more emphatically connected by δὲ καὶ; the adversative δέ contrasting this member with the others as most weighty. Cf. Plat. Apol. p. 40. C, and see Kühn. L. Gr. II. § 746. Anm. So in Latin sive and si vero often answer to one another. See Kühner's Cic. Tusc. Disp. I. 41. 97. —— εἶναι, τῇ γνώμῃ ὑπηρετεῖν ἐθιστέον. Some editors place the comma after ὑπερετεῖν, but erroneously as it seems to us. In respect to the sentiment of the passage, if our pointing is correct, cf. Oecon. XVII. 7: οὐκοῦν... ὅπως δυνήται ὑπηρετεῖν τῇ γνώμῃ; and see also an interpretation of this passage, Cicero de Offic. I. 23: Exercendum corpus et ita afficiendum est, ut obedire concilio et rationi possit. The appropriateness and truth of the idea that the control of the mind over the body conduces to, and is the most certain means of physical health, cannot be doubted. This, too, is evidently implied in the descriptions of the persons and habits of Ἀρετή and Κακία.

29.—Εὐφροσύνας, Lat. hilaritates, *joy*, happiness; for the use of the plural, see note, I. 1. 11: ἀνάγκαις. Notice the choice of the words to characterize the different kinds of happiness, and the contrasting force of the article.

30.—Τί δὲ; for the force of the δέ, see note upon I. 3. 13: τοὺς δὲ καλούς. —— ἥτις; the relative clause does not simply define here but relates to the nature, peculiarities, of the thing itself, sc. ποιότητα. According to our English idiom it would be *since you*, or, *as you*, etc. In Greek as in Latin the relative is used with a verb in the second person. See Kühn. L. Gr. II. § 781. 4, 5. —— πρὶν μὲν πεινῆν ἐσθίουσα; this and the following clause are added as an explanation of the more general phrase: πάντων ἐμπίπλασαι. The finite verb would be used instead of the participle in Latin: "priusquam esurias, comedis," etc. —— μηκανωμένη... παρασκευάζῃ. Strict concinnity of expression would require the finite verb μηχανᾷ instead of the participle μηχανωμένη, in order to correspond with the following παρασκευάζῃ. But Xenophon undoubtedly, as was very natural, carried forward in his mind the construction of the preceding clauses with participles, without noticing the interruption by ἵνα, before he came to the next member, where the importance of the idea caused him to recur to the use of the finite verb. For the interchange of the finite verb and participle, see Kühn. L. Gr. II. § 675. 4; and cf. note, II. 2. 5, and IV. 4. 1. —— οἴνους; for the use of the plural, see Kühn. § 243. 3. (2), and L. Gr. II. 408. b. —— τοῦ θέρους, in summer. For this use of the Gen. of the space of time within which something happens, see Kühn. § 273. 4. (b). —— χιόνα, snow, i. e., for cooling the wine. The Greeks seem to have had subterranean apartments for preserving ice and snow, like our modern ice-cellars, though it was oftener done by covering them with chaff. See Becker's Charicles, p. 256. —— οὐ μόνον τὰς στρωμνὰς μαλακάς, ἀλλὰ καὶ τὰς κλίνας, κ.τ.λ. The climax in the thought is conspicuous here. Men of pleasure are not satisfied with soft matrasses or beds, (στωμνάς from στρώννυμι, *to spread out*,) spread on the ground or floor, but they prepare couches (κλίνας from κλίνω), on which to spread their soft matrasses; and still further, they put under these couches ὑπόβαθρα, as additional appliances of luxury. For the position of μαλακάς, see note upon I. 4. 13. The noun ὑπόβαθρα is generally interpreted foot-carpets, spread under the κλινάς. So in the Lexicons. But Schneider from some passages of Antyllus, a physician, in Fragm. medicor. Oribas, ed. Matthaei, pp. 114, 170, and 172, draws the conclusion that this word designates fulcra diagonalia, supports, put under the feet of a couch, as under cradles for the purpose of procuring motion, rockers. Voigtlaender also, in Observatt. Laud. de ὑπόβαθρον, refers to Stob. I. p. 192, and Theophrast. I. p. 192, Schn. This explanation at least looks reasonable, and gives greater force to the passage than the usual explanation. —— διὰ ... ἀλλὰ διὰ, on account of... but because. —— τὸ μηδὲν ἔχειν, ὅ τι ποιῇς, you have nothing to do, you do not know what to do. For the Subj. deliberative, see Rost, § 119; Kühn. II. § 464. —— δέεσθαι; the Mss. are divided between the full and contracted form of this word; but see note upon I. 6. 10. —— ἀφροδίσια... ἀναγκάζεις, provoke sensual indulgence. —— καὶ γυναιξὶ καὶ ἀνδράσι χρωμένη. Some read καὶ γυναιξὶ τοῖς ἀνδράσι χρ., "et viris tanquam mulieribus uteris," but this reading is not supported by Ms. authority, and the sense requires no change. The vice of licentious indulgence in general, was doubtless aimed at, rather than a specific kind of it. —— ἑαυτῆς; second person, see note upon I. 4. 9. —— ὑβρίζουσα... κατακοιμίζουσα, complements of the verb παιδεύεις. The participle is often so used after a verb with a demonstrative word (οὕτω). See Cyrop. I. 4. 15: οὕτω διῆγεν, κ.τ.λ.; VIII. 4. 5. Cf. Kühn. L. Gr. II. § 663. XI. —— κατακοιμίζουσα. The verb κατακοιμίζειν signifies, lit., to fall to sleep, and metaphorically, to pass time uselessly, i. e., as if falling to sleep. The words in § 33: οὔτε διὰ τοῦτον (τὸν ὕπνον) μεθιᾶσι τὰ δέοντα πράττειν, are strongly antithetical to this word.

31.—Ἐκ θεῶν...ἀπέρριψαι, you have been excluded from the number of the gods.——τοῦ πάντων ἡδίστου ἀκούσματος, κ.τ.λ., "the sweetest strain the ear takes in," your own praise. Cf. upon the sentiment, Hieron. I. 14: τοῦ μὲν ἡδίστου ἀκροάματος ἐπαίνου οὔποτε σπανίζετε, and Cic. pro Archia poet. IX. 32: Themistoclem dixisse aiunt, quum ex eo quaereretur, quod acroama aut cujus vocem libentissime audiret: Ejus, a quo sua virtus optime praedicaretur.——ἀνήκοος εἶ, lit., you are unhearing, but in Engl.: you never hear, so ἀθέατος (sc. εἶ) you never see.——λεγούσῃ τι πιστεύσειε. The Pron. τὶ Accus. is used with πιστεύσειε, but the Gen. τινὸς, with ἐπαρκέσειεν; see note upon I. 2. 60.——εὖ φρονῶν, in his senses, *sane.*——τοῦ σοῦ θιάσου. The word θιάσος seems to signify originally a company of men, assembled for the purpose of sacrificing to the gods. Cf. Herbst, Symp. VIII: τοῦ θεοῦ τούτου θιασῶται, where see many examples. Hence used tauntingly here: Who would in his right mind venture to make one of your band of worshippers.——οἳ (sc. θιασῶται); for the use of the plural, κατὰ σύνεσιν, see Kühn. L. Gr. II. § 418. Cf. II. 2. 3: αἱ πόλεις παύσοντες; III. 5. 20; where ἡ ἐν Ἀρείῳ πάγῳ βουλή is followed by τούτοις.——ἀπόνως μὲν λιπαροὶ διὰ νεότητος τρεφόμενοι, *they* being supported without labor and in affluence, λιπαροὶ, (with an abundance of every thing,) during youth. With this the following clause is contrasted: ἐπιπόνως δὲ αὐχμηροὶ διὰ γήρως περῶντες, passing through age in servile labor and poverty (in want of every thing). The idea is: that whilst in youth they are supported by parents or friends without labor, and enabled to indulge in a most luxurious style of living; but they become old, are deprived of the aid of parents or friends, and in consequence of their effeminacy induced by indulgence and their want of a trade or profession, are compelled to pass the rest of life in toil and penury, doubly severe to them in consequence of early indulgence.——πεπραγμένοις . . . πραττομένοις, by *what they have done,* and . . . *what they are now doing.*——τὰ μὲν ἡδέα... ἀποθέμενοι, exhausting their pleasures in youth, and laying up trouble and hardship for age.

32.—Παρὰ ἀνθρώποις, οἷς προσήκει, (i. e., παρὰ οἷς προσήκει ἐμὲ τιμᾶσθαι. Cf. for similar constructions, III. 7. 3; Sympos. IV. 1, on which see Herbst. and Bornemann. The preposition is more rarely repeated; see III. 3. 6: ἐν τοιούτοις...χωρίοις, ἐν οἵοισπερ. See also

Matthiae Gr. II. § 595; Kühn. L. Gr. II. § 625. 3. The same brevity of expression is also found in the Latin: a hominibus quibus decet. Cic. de Fin. IV. 20: Platonem eadem esse in sententia qua tyrannum Dionysium. Cf. also Cic. Tusc. Disp., Kühn. ed., I. 39. 94, p. 144. In reference to the Infin. *τιμᾶσθαι*, to be supplied from the antecedent finite verb, *τιμῶμαι*, see Kühn. L. Gr. II. § 852, g. This ellipsis is common with such words as *προσήκει, ἔοικε, εἰκός ἐστι, δεῖ, χρή*; cf. II. 6. 22; IV. 5. 7. It is also found with *οἶδα*, III. 8. 3; *καλῶς ἔχει*, in II. 7. 6; III. 11. 1, etc. —— *ἀγαθὴ ... συλλήπτρια, κ.τ.λ.*, a good coadjutor in the labors of peace, and a firm ally in war. —— *ἀρίστη δὲ φιλίας κοινωνός*, in fine, a most excellent participant in friendship.

33.—*Τοῖς μὲν ἐμοῖς φίλοις.* With this *μέν* (solitarium), the contrast is to be supplied in thought; i. e., the friends of *Κακία* in contrast with *ἐμοῖς φίλοις.* —— *ἡδεῖα μὲν ... ἀπόλαυσις*; cf. I. 6. 5, in regard to the sentiment. The *μέν* contrasts *σιτῶν ἀπόλαυσις* with *ὕπνος*, below, with which a corresponding *δέ* is found. —— *ἀπράγμων ... ἀπόλαυσις*, enjoyment at their ease, untroubled enjoyment. —— *οὔτε ἀπολείποντες αὐτὸν* (sc. *ὕπνον*) *ἄχθονται, κ.τ.λ.*, they are neither burthened when deprived of it (sleep), nor do they on account of it omit, etc. The verb is general in signification, including both physical and mental discomfort. The natural position of *εὖ* would be with *πράττοντες*, but it is placed at the beginning of the clause for sake of the antithesis, which is suggested with so much adroitness throughout this whole address of *Ἀρετή*. It also thus corresponds in position with *ἡδέως* in the preceding clause. —— *τίμιοι δὲ πατρίσι*, honored, each one in his own country. —— *τὸ πεπρωμένον τέλος*, end appointed by fate = death. —— *θάλλουσι*, to flourish, i. e., be in honor; so the Latin vigeo; cf. Cic. Tusc. Disp. I. 49, init.; Harmodius in ore et Aristogito, Lacedaemonius Leonidas, Thebanus Epaminondas vigent. —— *Τοιαῦτα ... διαπονησαμένῳ*, having completed such labors. For the omission of the connective here, see note upon I. 1. 9: *τοὺς τὰ τοιαῦτα.* —— *μακαριστοτάτην.* This superlative of *μακαριστός*, from *μακαρίζω*, is peculiar to Xenophon, see Sympos.; and even he sometimes uses *μακαριωτάτος* from *μακάριος*; see Cyrop. VII. 2. 27.

34.—*Τὴν ὑπ' Ἀρετῆς Ἡρακλέους, παίδευσιν*, the instruction of Hercules by *Ἀρετή.* —— *ἐκόσμησε μέντοι τὰς γνώμας ἔτι μεγαλειοτέροις ῥήμασιν, ἢ ἐγὼ νῦν*, although he clothed his thoughts in far more magnificent, splendid words, than I now do. If more magnificent as the genuine modesty of Xenophon would have us believe, certainly not more fitly chosen or gracefully and happily arranged. —— σοὶ . . . ἄξιον, it becomes you, it is worth while for you —— πειρᾶσθαί τι . . . φροντίζειν, to exert yourself, . . . to take some care for those things that pertain to the future time of your life.

CHAPTER II.

1.—Λαμπροκλέα, τὸν πρεσβύτατον υἱὸν ἑαυτοῦ; Socrates had three sons; (perhaps more than three, see Wiggers' Life,) Lamprocles, Sophroniscus, and Menexenus. The eldest is the one who held the following conversation with his father. —— πρὸς . . . χαλαπαίνοντα, treating harshly from anger, ill-tempered to. —— καὶ μάλα, *most certainly* (I do). —— τοὺς τί ποιοῦντας τὸ ὄνομα τοῦτο ἀποκαλοῦσιν. The idea fully expressed would be as follows: καταμεμάθηκας οὖν, τίνας τὸ ὄνομα τοῦτο (sc. ἀχαρίστους) ἀποκαλοῦσιν, καὶ τί ποιοῦσιν οὗτοι, οὓς τὸ ὄνομα τοῦτο ἀποκαλοῦσιν, or less accurately: καταμεμάθηκας, τί ποιοῦσιν οὗτοι, οὓς τὸ ὄνομα τοῦτο ἀποκαλοῦσιν. Thus an interrogation is frequently constructed in Greek with a participle accompanied by the article, from which it is separated by the interrogative pronoun. In this way two interrogations frequently are blended into one. Cf. Plat. de Rep. p. 332. C; Sympos. p. 206, B, and examples cited by Bornemann, Sympos. VIII. 36; and see Matth. Gr. II. § 567; Rost, 123. b. c; Kühn. L. Gr. II. § 843; Gr. § 344, R. 8. In reference to the subject of ἀποκαλοῦσιν, see B. 129. 19, and in reference to two accusatives after it, see Kühn. Gr. § 280. 4; L. Gr. II. § 558. b. The Latin may imitate this simple brevity of the Greek: "quos quid facientes hoc nomine appellent." —— εὖ παθόντας, *those receiving favors.* —— καταλογίζεσθαι; some commentators suppose that δεῖν should be understood with this word, but the idea seems rather to be implied in δοκοῦσι. After verbs of believing, supposing, and the like, such as νομίζειν, οἴεσθαι, ἡγεῖσθαι, δοκεῖν, etc., the idea of intention, wish, approbation, or of thinking to be just or necessary, is implied. See Kühn. L. Gr. II. § 638, p. 337; Bornem. upon Sympos. IV. 42. p. 138 sq., and Cyrop. IV. 5. 16; VIII. 1. 12; Krüger Anab. I. 2. 1.

2.—Ἤδη δέ; see note upon I. 3. 13: τοὺς δὲ καλούς. —— εἰ ἄρα, see note, I. 1. 8. —— τὸ ἀνδραποδίζεσθαι, to reduce to servitude. This clause is the subject of δοκεῖ. —— δίκαιον, καὶ τὸ ἀχαριστεῖν. Before καί, οὕτω, added by Stephanus, probably from the feeling that it was required after ὥσπερ, has crept into most of the editions. But examples are frequent where the other member of a comparison, introduced by ὥσπερ, is without οὕτως. See IV. 4. 7: ὥσπερ σύ, καὶ ἐγώ: III. 1. 4;

Cyrop. I. 6. 3; V. 2. 12; Apol. 33, and Bos' Ellips. p. 778, ed. Schaef. —— ὑφ' οὗ ἄν τις, κ.τ.λ. For the attraction of the relative to the case of the subordinate proposition, see Kühn. § 332. 6; L. Gr. II. § 791. The natural construction would here be: καὶ δοκεῖ μοι, ὅστις ἄν, ὑπό τινος εὖ παθών (or ἐὰν ὑπὸ τινος εὖ πάθῃ), μὴ πειρᾶται χάριν ἀποδιδόναι ἄδικος εἶναι. Cf. § 6. The same manner of construction is common in Latin: videtur que mihi a quo quis beneficiis affectus sive amico sive inimico gratiam referre non studeat, injustus esse. Cf. Kühn. Tusc. Dis. I. 34. 84, and Zumpt's Gr.

3.—Εἴγε οὕτως ἔχει . . . ἂν εἴη, cf. III. 11. 3; Cyrop. II. 1. 8. The optative with ἄν frequently follows εἰ with the indicative, or ἐὰν with the subjunctive, when the thing deduced is contrasted as uncertain, etc. See Kühn. § 339. 3; L. Gr. II. § 817. b, where many examples are cited. —— μείζω ἀγαθά. One Ms. has μείζονα corresponding in form to μείζονα with εὐεργετ. below, but the full and contracted forms are promiscuously used. Cf. Cyrop. III. 3. 20; Agesil. II. 7, and see the Grammars. —— Τίνας . . . ὑπὸ τίνων . . . ἢ παῖδας ὑπὸ γονέων, whom can we find that have received greater favors from whom than, i. e., can we find any persons who have received greater favors from others, than children from parents? For the blending of two interrogative sentences here, see Kühn. Gr. § 344. R. 7; C. 539. 2; L. Gr. II. § 843. 1; Rost, § 123. b, 10. b. —— οὓς οἱ γονεῖς . . . εἶναι. The Latin is far inferior to the Greek in such phrases as this, substituting finite verbs for the Part. and Inf.: quibus cum antea non essent parentes causa exstiterunt, ut essent. —— ἃ δή, which, *as is evident;* for this meaning of δή, see note upon II. 1. 21, and the references there. —— ὥστε . . . φεύγομεν. For the use and significance of the indicative with ὥστε, see Kühn. Gr. § 341. 2; cf. I. 2. 31. —— ἐπὶ τοῖς μεγίστοις ἀδικήμασι; the preposition with the dative here denoting the goal or aim, has the same force as in the phrase: νόμους θέσθαι ἐπί τινι. See Kühn. Gr. § 296. II. (1). (d); L. Gr. II. § 612. —— ζημίαν θάνατον πεποιήκασιν, made death the penalty, punishment. The Greeks were accustomed to say: θάνατος ἡ ζημία ἐστίν but θάνατον ζημίαν τάττειν, ἐπίθεσθαι or ποιεῖν. In the former case the article distinguishes the subject, but in the latter case ζημίαν has not the force of a subject, but is added as an explanation of θανάτον, as penalty, and is consequently without the article. If it were added it might give the ζημίαν the force of fitting, due punishment; see Meatzner ad Antiphon. Or. V. p. 134. 34. Θανάτος, in respect to the article, is used as a proper noun. See Apolog. § 1, where it is, without the article, contrasted with τοῦ βίου. —— ὡς οὐκ ἂν . . . παύσοντες, *supposing that they can deter from crime by the fear of no greater evil.*

For the use of the participle with ὡς as equivalent to a participle of a verb denoting to think or say with the Infin. or Acc. and Inf., see Kühn. Gr. § 312. 6; L. Gr. II. § 671; Rost, § 130. For the use of ἄν with the Part., see Kühn. Gr. § 260. 5. (b); L. Gr. II. § 671; Rost, § 120.

4.—Καὶ μὴν . . . γε. See note upon I. 4. 12. —— ἐπεὶ τούτου γε τῶν ἀπολυσόντων. The pronoun τούτου does not refer directly to ἀφροδισίων, but to the whole idea contained in the preceding words: τὸ τῶν ἀφροδισίων ἐπιθυμεῖν. See Kühn. L. Gr. II. § 421, Anm. 2. For the irregular position of the article, see note upon I. 6. 13: τὴν σοφίαν, κ.τ.λ. —— οἰκήματα = lupanaria. —— φανεροὶ δὲ ἐσμὲν, κ.τ.λ., *moreover it is evident that we even consider*, etc. —— βέλτιστα, most healthy, robust.

5.—Ὑποδεξαμένη τε . . . βαρυνομένη τε; for the τε—τε, see note upon I. 1. 14. It should be further noted, that the καί before σὺν πολλῷ corresponds to the first τε. —— τῆς τροφῆς ἧς καὶ αὐτὴ τρέφ. This is the reading best supported by the Mss. and ancient editions, but the rareness of the attraction of the relative from the dative, has caused several modern editors, as Schneider and Bornemann, to substitute the pronoun in the dative ᾗ. Upon this attraction of the relative pronoun, see Kühn. L. Gr. II. § 787, and Gr. § 332, R. 6. In addition to the references in the grammars, cf. Aeschin. de F. Leg. 43: παρ' ὧν μὲν, κ.τ.λ. —— διενέγκασα; see note upon I. 2. 53. —— οὔτε γιγνώσκον τὸ βρέφος . . . οὐδὲ σημαίνειν δυνάμενον. Most editors govern βρέφος here by τρέφει, but on account of the intervening words, this construction seems to be harsh, and it is more probable that there is a grammatical irregularity in the sentence, which would naturally run thus: τεκοῦσα τρέφει τε καὶ ἐπιμελεῖται, οὔτε προπεπονθυῖα οὐδὲν ἀγαθόν, οὔτε γιγνώσκοντος τοῦ βρέφους, ὑφ' ὅτου εὖ πάσχει, οὐδὲ σημαίνειν δυναμένου, ὅτου δεῖται, ἀλλ' αὐτὴ στοχαζομένη τά τε συμφέροντα καὶ κεχαρισμένα πειρωμένη ἐκπληροῦν· καὶ τρέφει, κ.τ.λ. But Xenophon without regard to grammatical accuracy changed the genitive absolute into the nominative, in order to make it correspond in case with the preceding προπεπονθυῖα and the following αὐτὴ στοχαζομένη, and the participle πειρωμένη, to the finite verb πειρᾶται, on account of the importance of the idea to be expressed by it. Cf. note upon II. 1. 30. —— οὐδὲ . . . δυνάμενον. After οὔτε we not unfrequently find οὐδέ (and not). See Bornem. Anab. III. 2. 27; Rost's Gr. § 134. Anm. 2; Kühn. Gr. § 321. R. 6; L. Gr. II. § 743. Anm. 4.

6.—Ἃ δ' ἂν οἴωνται ἄλλον ἱκανώτερον εἶναι διδάξαι. The Latin sentence takes a very different form here: quibus autem docendis alium magis idoneum putant. —— ἐπιμελοῦνται . . . ὅπως οἱ παῖδες αὐτοῖς γένωνται; this seems to be the preferable reading, although some editors and some Mss. have ὅπως ἂν οἱ... γένωνται (others γένοιντο); see Kühn. in h. l. —— πάντα ποιοῦντες, exerting themselves in every way.

7.—Ὁ νεανίσκος (sc. Λαμπροκλῆς) ἔφη. For the order of the words here, see note upon I. 2. 9. —— ἀλλά τοι, see note upon I. 2. 36. —— εἰ... πεποίηκε... οὐδεὶς ἂν δύναιτο; for the Optat. with ἄν after the Indic., see note upon I. 2. 28: εἰ δ' αὐτὸς σωφρονῶν, κ.τ.λ. There is a peculiar delicacy exhibited in the omission of the words ἡ ἐμὴ μήτηρ before πεποίηκε, as Lamprocles had only his own mother in mind. —— πολλαπλάσια, from πολύς and the termination -ασιος, *many times*, containing the idea of comparison, and hence governing the genitive τούτων; see Kühn. Gr. § 275. 2; L. Gr. II. § 540. β; Rost, § 109. —— τὴν χαλεπότητα, asperitas; cf. Sympos. II. 10. In consequence of the asperity of Xantippe, her name, as is well known, has become synonymous with *shrew*. But it cannot be denied that Socrates was somewhat in fault. In his excessive devotion to philosophy and the State, the duties of domestic life were probably thrown somewhat into the back-ground. See Introd., and Ritter's Hist. Phil. II. p. 33, 34. —— Πότερα δὲ, see I. 3. 13. —— τῆς μητρός. Some editors have here omitted the article, but it can hardly be doubted that it should be retained. Socrates has been speaking of the μητήρ in general, and hence omits the article; but Lamprocles here alludes to his own mother, and hence says τῆς μητρός. —— τῆς γε τοιαύτης, being indeed such a one, since she is of such a character. —— Ἤδη πώποτε, originally only in negative clauses, as in Homer and Hesiod, but in Attic writers, in interrogations that imply a negative, as in IV. 2. 24; 4. 11; 5. 9; Hellen. III. 5. 14. Also after conditional conjunctions; as εἰ, Anab. 5. 4. 6; Cyrop. VI. 4. 5; Aristoph. Acharn. 380; and after relative pronouns; Plat. Apol. p. 19. D; and even with participles in a relative construction, as οἱ ἐμοῦ πώποτε ἀκηκοότες. Cf. Poppo, Thuc. P. III. Vol. 2. p. 647.

8.—Νὴ Δία, a formula of swearing, denoting strong affirmation; often used with ἀλλά in answering questions; see further, 7. 4 below. —— ἐπὶ τῷ βίῳ παντὶ; *for* (at the price of) *my whole life*. For this meaning of ἐπί with the Dat., see Kühn. Gr. § 296. II. (f). —— πόσα ... πόσα δὲ; see note, I. 1. 1: ἀδικεῖ Σωκράτ., κ.τ.λ. The words πόσα δυσάνεκτα... δυσκολαίνων... πράγματα παρασχεῖν in the first clause answer directly to the words of the last clause, πόσα δὲ λυπῆσαι κάμνων, and the rest are explanatory. —— εἶπα; this first person of the Aor. is seldom used in Attic Greek, and hence some editors have substituted for it the more usual 2 Aor. εἶπον. Attic writers employ the second person εἶπας more frequently; the first pers. plŭr. εἴπαμεν, prob. never the second pers. εἴπατε and the imperatives, εἰπάτω (προσειπάτω) and εἴπατε, very often; and the third εἶπαν, very rarely. For the two accusatives after εἶπα and ἐποίησα, see Kühn. Gr. § 280. 4. —— ᾐσχύνθη The Subj. in Lat. erubesceret, or, puderet.

9.—The connection of the thought here is: Stage actors permit the utmost severity of language to be used to them upon the stage, without being enraged, since they know that no insult or injury to themselves is intended; much more ought you to endure the severity of your mother, knowing that she not only does not intend you any injury, but has your highest good most sincerely at heart. —— ὑποκριταῖς. The noun ὑποκριτής, from ὑποκρίνομαι, signif. first, *one who answers*, and then as responding to each other, *stage players;* this is its usual meaning. In later Gr. one who acts a feigned part, a dissembler, and hence our word hypocrite. —— ἀλλήλους τὰ ἔσχατα λέγωσιν, say the *last* things, i. e., the worst, the most severe things. —— 'Αλλ'. Instead of this particle, we may in English use the relative pronoun *which*, etc. So in Latin: quos quidem arbitror, etc. —— ῥᾳδίως φέρουσι, bear calmly, aequo animo. —— τοῦτό γε, lit., this *at least*, but in English we should give the force of the γέ by emphasis on the preceding word.

10.—Ὅπως ὑγιαίνῃς τε καὶ ὅπως . . . ἔσῃ. Two Mss. have the reading ὑγιανῇς, which some editors have changed to ὑγιανεῖς, to avoid a supposed discrepancy in mood between this verb and ἔσῃ which follows. There are also two or three Mss. that have ὑγιαίνεις or ὑγιαίνοις; but the reading given in the text, seems to be the best authorized. There appears not only not to be any objection to the employment of different modes after the conjunction ὅπως here, but a delicacy and beauty peculiar to the Greek in their use. In the first case, the result to be obtained depends more upon agency foreign to the actor, i. e., of the gods, and is hence spoken of with more doubt and contingency, by means of the subjunctive mood. But the future expresses the more certain event which is more in the power of the mother. Cf. II. 4. 2; Bornemann, Sympos. VIII. 25, p. 203, who compares Anab. IV. 6. 10; Agesil. VII. 7. —— πολλὰ τοῖς θεοῖς εὐχομένην ὑπὲρ σοῦ, asking many good things from the gods for you, = αἰτεῖσθαι ἀγαθὰ παρὰ τῶν θεῶν, Cyrop. I. 6. 5. Cf. III. 14. 3, and IV. 2. 36. —— εὐχὰς ἀποδιδοῦσαν. The phrase εὐχὰς ἀποδιδόναι signifies to perform vows to, to pay what is promised to the gods. —— τἀγαθά, the good, things that are good.

11.—Μηδενὶ . . . ἀρέσκειν, μηδ' ἕπεσθαι . . . ἄρχοντι. The words from μηδὲ to ἄρχοντι are explanatory of μηδενὶ ἀρέσκειν, to please no one, neither to follow nor be obedient to one, whether he may be general or other ruler. The first verb ἕπεσθαι which has more direct reference to physical action, is fitly chosen to correspond to στρατηγῷ, and πείθεσθαι, denoting rather mental action, to ἄλλῳ ἄρχοντι.

12.—Ἄν τι σφαλλόμενος τύχῃς, if you shall fall into any calamity, or if any thing evil happen to you. —— οὐδὲν ἄν σοι διαφέροι φίλον ἢ ἐχθρὸν γενέσθαι. Διαφέρειν is constructed with the Accus. of the quantity and Dat. of the person. So in Plat. Ep. 13. p. 362. A; Eurip Troad. 1248. —— τῆς παρὰ τούτων εὐνοίας, good will from these, or, their good will; cf. III. 11. 3, 13; Demosth. de Coron. p. 226, 3, and note upon III. 11. 14: τῶν παρ' ἐμοί.

13.—Εἶτα. See note upon I. 2. 26. —— παρεσκεύασαι, Perf. 2d Pers. in the sense of the present tense as freq.; so in § 11 above. See Kühn. Gr. § 255. R. 5. —— γονέας μὴ θεραπεύῃ; for an account of the law against ingratitude to parents, κάκωσις γονέων, the kind of neglect punished, etc., see Potter's Gr. Ant. B. IV. ch. 15; Meier and Schömann, Attische Process, III. 1. § 2; S. 288, 9. —— ἄρχειν, to become archon, ruler; see I. 1. 18. —— ὡς οὔτε ἂν τὰ ἱερὰ εὐσεβῶς θυόμενα ὑπὲρ τῆς πόλεως, supposing that the sacrifices in behalf of the State will not be reverently performed. —— οὔτε ἄλλο καλῶς καὶ δικαίως οὐδὲν ἂν (sc. πραττόμενον), τούτου πράξαντος. The participle πραττόμ. is to be supplied, ἀπὸ κοινοῦ, from πράξαντος, and τούτου θύοντος and τούτου πράξαντος correspond to each other. For the meaning of the participle with ὡς . . . ἂν, see note, § 3 above: ὡς οὐκ ἂν . . . παύσοντες. —— ἐν ταῖς τῶν ἀρχόντων δοκιμασίαις. The candidates for office at Athens were compelled to pass an examination in regard to their lineage, age, manners, habits, etc., and these examinations were called δοκιμασία; see Fiske's Man. p. 181.

14.—Συγγνώμονάς σοι, indulgent, disposed to pardon you. —— καὶ οὗτοι, even they, they themselves, or, they in turn. —— αὖ. See note upon I. 2. 12. —— εἶτα. Eight Paris Mss. have καὶ εἶτα, from which Zeunius makes κᾆτα, and most of the more recent editors adopt the correction. But Kühner and Seiffert seem justly to retain the common reading which we have given. For εἶτα and ἔπειτα are frequently used after a finite verb, where we might expect καὶ εἶτα (κᾆτα) and καὶ ἔπειτα, signifying: *then afterwards* and sometimes, *and then* = καὶ τότε, as in IV. 5. 3: εἶτα . . . νομίζεις; Plat. Apol. p. 23. C, on which see Stallb., and many other passages. For the reverse καὶ εἶτα or καὶ ἔπειτα for the simple εἶτα and ἔπειτα, see note upon I. 1. 5. The preceding ν ἐφελκυστικόν (ἀτιμάσωσιν) also is in favor of εἶτα, and the change of subject is no valid objection to it. See note, II. 1. 8. —— τοὺς γονεῖς. Several Mss. and editors have γονέας here, but the Accus. in -εῖς from nouns in -εύς is not uncommon in Xenophon. Cf. as examples, III. 5. 19: τοὺς ἱππεῖς, 7. 6. γναφεῖς, σκυτεῖς, χαλκεῖς, et al. saep.

CHAPTER III.

1.—Χαιρεφῶντα. Chaerephon was an intimate friend and disciple of Socrates, but a man of violent passions; see Plat. Charm. p. 153, b; Wiggers' Life of Socrates, Ch. II. He is also called φιλότιμος in § 16. —— ἰδών, when he saw, or, met with. —— οὐ δήπου, not most certainly, or, not I hope; ironically. See Kühn. L. Gr. II. § 835, 3, and cf. IV. 2. 11. —— χρησιμώτερον νομίζουσι χρήματα; so χρήματά ἐστι χρήσιμον, and νομίζω χρήματα χρήσιμον εἶναι, when the idea relates to treasures in general; cf. § 5; 6. 21; 9. 1; III. 8. 5; 6. 9, et al., and Anab. III. 2. 22. Sometimes κτῆμα is added, as in Sympos. IV. 14: εἰδὼς ὅτι χρήματα ἡδὺ κτῆμα. See Kühn. Gr. § 241. 2; Buttmann, § 129. The paronomasia in the words χρήματα and χρησιμώτερον, ἀφρόνων, φρονίμου and βοηθείας, βοηθεῖν, should not escape notice. The choice of words with reference to their similarity of sound, especially in proverbial expressions, was not uncommon in Greek, though much less frequent than in some of the oriental languages; cf. II. 4. 5: ποῖος γὰρ ἵππος ἢ ποῖον ζεῦγος οὕτω χρήσιμον, ὥσπερ ὁ χρηστὸς φίλος. —— ἢ ἀδελφούς; some editors have conjectured that this should be ἀδελφόν in the singular, to correspond with the words in the singular which follow, referring to it. But the plural seems here to be used to make the idea general, and when afterwards the application is made to a specific individual, the brother of Chaerecrates, the singular number is employed. —— καὶ ταῦτα, and that too; see note upon I. 2. 29. —— βοηθείας δεομένων, lit., needing help, i. e., requiring the care of the possessor in order to keep, preserve them. This phrase, obscure in itself, is employed for the sake of the antithesis with τοῦ δὲ βοηθεῖν δυναμένου.

2.—Εἴ; for the significance of this word, see note, I. 1. 13. —— τὰ (sc. χρήματα) τῶν ἀδελφῶν, the wealth, possessions of brothers. —— ἐνταῦθα, there, in respect to these (the citizens). —— λογίζεσθαι, to suppose, to come to the conclusion. —— ἐπὶ δὲ τῶν ἀδελφῶν, in respect to brothers. For this use of ἐπί with the genitive, cf. note upon

III. 9. 3. —— ἀγνοοῦσι, the plural number, κατὰ σύνεσιν, after the singular, εἴ τις, see note upon I. 2. 62.

3.—Ὡς βοηθῶν δεόμενοι, because they need; Lat. quod with the subjunctive, or thinking that they need, etc., according to Kühn. Gr. § 312, 6. —— ὥσπερ...γιγνομένους φίλους; for the accusative absolute with ὥσπερ, see Kühn. Gr. § 312. R. 13; Buttmann, § 145, note 7, and note I. 2. 20.

4.—Καὶ μὴν, *and yet*, = καὶ ἔτι, Lat. atqui. The common use of the particle μήν is to confirm or augment; but it also sometimes indicates a kind of opposition between the clause in which it stands and what precedes. See Hoogeveen, Partic. Gr. p. 271, and Klötz's Devarius, II. S. 651. —— πρὸς φιλίαν μέγα μὲν ὑπάρχει, contributes much to friendship; for this use of πρὸς with the accusative, denoting object or aim, see Kühn. Gr. § 298. III. (3). a. —— τὸ ἐκ τῶν αὐτῶν φῦναι, to be born of the same (parents); the subject of ὑπάρχει. —— μέγα δὲ (sc. ὑπάρχει) τὸ ὁμοῦ τραφῆναι, to be reared, brought up, together. —— πόθος τις ἐγγίγνεται, κ.τ.λ., a kind of love arises among those who, etc.

5.—Ἀλλ' εἰ μὲν. Ἀλλά, ellipt., a particle of assent; see Klötz's Devar. II. S. 8 sq. —— ὁπότε μέντοι παντὸς ἐνδέοι καὶ πᾶν τὸ ἐναντιώτατον εἴη. The most natural explanation of this clause in its connection, is perhaps that of Weiske: but if he is entirely wanting in this (i. e., in respect of being such a brother as it is fitting to be = ὁπότε παντὸς ἐνδέοι τῷ ἀδελφῷ τοιούτῳ εἶναι, οἷον δεῖ), and is entirely the opposite. There is another explanation, which gives a tolerable sense, by supplying αὐτῷ after ἐνδέοι: but if he is in need of every thing, etc. But the former seems more in accordance with the context. —— τί ἂν τις ἐπιχειροίη τοῖς ἀδυνάτοις, why should one attempt impossibilities, i. e., to unite, reconcile things that are wholly opposite?

6.—Πότερα δέ; see note upon I. 3. 13: τοὺς δὲ καλούς. Verbs compounded with prepositions implying approach, junction, etc., are followed by Dat., B. 133. 2. b. —— ἔστιν οἷς, *some*, see note and references, I. 4. 2. —— Διὰ τοῦτο γάρ τοι, on this very account indeed; cf. II. 5. 4: ἐγὼ γάρ τοι... ἀκούω, I hear even that; III. 5. 19; Sympos. II. 3. Τοί gives emphasis to the γάρ; see Hartung, Gr. Partik. II. S. 353 sq.; Klötz, S. 368 sq., and cf. note upon I. 4. 9. —— ἀξιόν ἐστιν ἐμοὶ, it is fitting, just, etc. Cf. II. 1. 34; Sympos. IV. 13, 54, 56 et al. —— καὶ ἔργῳ καὶ λόγῳ; these words are often found in the reverse order: λόγῳ καὶ ἔργῳ. The latter seems the natural order of climax, and when λόγῳ is placed last it appears to be put as a kind of complement to the former, on which special emphasis is placed. For numerous instances of both constructions, see Bornemann in h. l.

7.—Τῷ ἀνεπιστήμονι μέν. The infinitive χρῆσθαι is to be supplied here from the next clause, by the common construction ἀπὸ κοινοῦ.

8.—Ἀλλ' οὐδὲ πειράσομαι, but, so far from it, I will not even attempt it.

9.—Εἰ κύνα μέν, κ.τ.λ., if laying aside anger, you would attempt by kind treatment to conciliate a dog, if you had one which was, etc., i. e., εἰ, ἀμελήσας ἂν τοῦ ὀργίζεσθαι ἐπειρῶ εὖ ποιήσας πραΰνειν κύνα, εἰ σοὶ ἦν, ἐπὶ προβάτοις ἐπιτήδειος ὤν, κ.τ.λ. The noun κύνα is placed at the beginning of the sentence for the sake of emphasis, and then αὐτόν supplies its place with the verb πραΰνειν. For this use of the pronoun, see note I. 4. 18; for εἰ...εἰ, see I. 2. 36. The relation of the members of the sentence indicated by the particles μέν...μὲν—δὲ...δὲ—μὲν...δέ, should not escape notice.——τὸν δὲ ἀδελφὸν φῂς μέν, κ.τ.λ. Strict concinnity of expression would require the Part. φάς, instead of the finite verb φῂς, to correspond with the following participle ὁμολογῶν, but the importance of the thought leads to the use of the verb; see note upon II. 2. 5.——ἐπίστασθαι δὲ ὁμολογῶν, κ.τ.λ., and confessing that you yourself know how to do well, etc.; εὖ ποιεῖν and εὖ λέγειν depend upon ἐπίστασθαι, and have not ἀδελφόν as accusative with them, as they are sometimes rendered; cf. § 8 above.

10.—Δέδοικα...μὴ οὐκ, *I fear that...not*, etc. The Indic. ἔχω is used here to denote the probability that the thing feared does not exist; see Kühn. § 318. R. 6.——καὶ μὴν...γε; see note, I. 4. 12.——οὐδὲν...ποικίλον, lit., nothing various, but here metaphor., skilfully devised, carefully thought out. Cf. Stallb. Plat. Symp. p. 182. B.——οἷς δὲ καὶ σὺ ἐπίστασαι αὐτὸς; by attraction for τούτοις, ἃ καὶ σύ, κ.τ.λ., see note, II. 1. 25.——περὶ πολλοῦ ποιεῖσθαί σε, will make you of much value, esteem you much.

11.—This and the following sections are often cited as a specimen of inductive reasoning of which Socrates was so fond. So II. 10, and III. 7. Οὐκ ἂν φθάνοις...λέγων εἴ, κ.τ.λ., you could not tell me too soon, if, etc., i. e., tell me as soon as possible. For the construction, see Buttmann, Gr. § 150; Kühn. § 310, 4. (1); L. Gr. II. § 664. Cf. III. 11. 1: οὐκ ἂν φθάνοιτ', ἔφη, ἀκολουθοῦντες.——ὃ ἐγὼ εἰδὼς λέληθα ἐμαυτόν, which I have unconsciously known.——λέγε δή μοι, tell me I pray; see note, I. 2. 41.——ὁπότε θύοι, καλεῖν σε ἐπὶ δεῖπνον. It was a common practice after making a sacrifice, to prepare a supper to which relatives and friends, as a special favor, were called. Cf. II. 9. 4. —— κατάρχ... τοῦ καλεῖν ἐκεῖνον, begin by calling him. Verbs signifying to begin, etc., govern the genitive.

12.—Προτρέψασθαι; see note, I. 2. 64.

13.—Εἰς τὴν ἐκείνου, (sc. πόλιν, or, γῆν). ——'Αθήναζε for Ἀθήνας δέ; see Kühn. Gr. § 235. 3, and R. 3. —— αὐτὸν; this pronoun is frequently employed where we use the personal pronoun him, her, it, but it is strictly reflexive = ipsum, *self*, as in the following clause where ἐμέ is to be supplied, and used in all the persons. —— τοῦτο... ἐκείνῳ ποιεῖν; for the construction, see Rost, Gr. § 104. Anm. 9; Kühn. L. Gr. II. § 559. Anm.

14.—'Επιστάμενος...ἀπεκρύπτου, having known for a long time... have you... kept hidden. Cf. § 11: ὃ ἐγὼ εἰδὼς λέληθα ἐμαυτόν; Sympos. I. 6: ἀπεκρυπτόμην ὑμᾶς ἔχων πολλὰ καὶ σοφὰ λέγειν. —— ἢ ὀκνεῖς; ἤ, like the Latin an, is not generally found in the second member of an interrogation, when it is wanting in the first, unless it may be easily supplied from the preceding words, as in h. l: ἢ ἄρα... ἀπεκρύπτου, ἢ ὀκνεῖς. —— μὴ αἰσχρὸς φανῇς. Μή has not, like the Latin ne for ut ne with a finite verb, the force of a final conjunction. We may render it *lest* or *that*, but strictly it is an indirect interrogative, *whether or not;* as in h. l. with ὀκνῶν implied in the preced. verb ὀκνεῖς. So in II. 5. 5: τὰ τοιαῦτα πάντα σκοπῶ μή; i. e., τὰ τ. π. σκοπῶν σκοπῶ μή, and frequently elsewhere. See Kühn. Gr. § 318. R. 6; L. Gr. II. § 779. 1. For the construction of αἰσχ. φανῇς, see I. 7. 4. —— Καὶ μὴν ...γέ, different in signification from the same words in I. 4. 12, but see the explanation there and cf. § 4 above. —— Τοὺς...πολεμίους κακῶς ποιῶν. Cf. a similar sentiment of Socrates in respect to private enemies, in II. 6. 35. —— εἰ μὲν οὖν ἐδόκει μοι X. ἡγεμ. εἶναι σοῦ πρὸς τὴν φύσιν ταύτην. The idea contained in these words seems to be this: If then Chaerephon seemed to me more suitable than you to take the lead toward this state of mind, (i. e., which would cause him first to confer favors upon his friends, φθάνῃ εὐεργετῶν), I would attempt, etc. —— νῦν δέ; the use of these particles after a hypothetical proposition, to indicate the opposite of what is there supposed, has a parallel in the Latin nunc autem, or, nunc vero, Eng. *but now;* see Kühn. Tusc. Disp. III. 1. 2. For the use of the Greek particles, see Kühn L. Gr. II. § 690. 2; Viger. Idiot. p. 360, and Hoogeveen, Gr. Partic. p. 364. —— δοκεῖς...ἐξεργάζεσθαι τοῦτο, you by taking the lead seem rather (i. e., better fitted) to do this. Why does Socrates represent it as more suitable that Chaerecrates should take the precedence in the work of conciliation? Kühner thinks, that it rests upon the age of the brothers. The reasoning is: You Chaerecrates are younger than Chaerephon, and as the younger should serve the elder, it behooves you to begin first to bestow favor upon your brother. But it is not more probable that Socrates means this as commendatory of Chaerecrates? He has before said that whoever does this, πλείστου γε δοκεῖ ἀνὴρ ἐπαίνου ἄξιος εἶναι. And does he not now intend to represent Chaerecrates as better fitted for this work than his brother?

15.—Καὶ οὐδαμῶς πρὸς σοῦ, sc. ὄντα, (see note, I. 4. 10,) and that are by no means in accordance with your character or practice; for this use of πρός with the Gen. to denote what belongs or is appropriate to any thing, see B. 147, πρός c. gen.; Kühn. Gr. § 298. 1; L. Gr. II. § 517. Anm. I. and 616. p. 306. Cf. Sympos. IV. 23: οὐδὲ πρὸς σοῦ ποιῶ, κ.τ.λ. ——Ὅς γε κελεύεις, who indeed (or forsooth) commands. The γέ is not restrictive, but argumentative or explicative. See Kühn. Gr. § 317. 2; L. Gr. II. 704. II. 1. ——ἐμὲ νεώτερον ὄντα, me who am younger. There is no intimation here that Socrates based his recommendation to Chaerecrates on his being younger, but Chaerecrates brings this as an objection, wondering that Socrates should have overlooked it, and thus recommended a thing so adverse to the maxim received by all men, that the elder should take the precedence in all things. —— καίτοι...γέ; see note, I. 2. 3. —— τούτου...τἀναντία νομίζεται; so in § 16, πανταχοῦ νομίζεται, is the custom received, or practised. Thus in IV. 4. 19. Cf. also note, 1. 11: νομίζει θεούς.

16.—Οὐ γάρ; for the use of γάρ in interrogations, see note I. 3. 10. Cf. § 17. ——ὑπαναστῆναι; concerning the construction of this word with the Gen. of place, see Kühn. § 271. 2; L. Gr. II. § 512. 1.—— κοίτῃ μαλακῇ τιμῆσαι. In reference to this mark of respect, see Hom. Il. ι. 617. 659 sq., and Odyss. ω. 254. —— ὠγαθέ; see note, I. 4. 17. ——τὸν ἄνδρα = ἐκεῖνον; perhaps, however, it is used to designate the mature age of Chaerephon, in contrast with the youth of Chaerecrates. —— οὐκ ὁρᾷς; we should naturally expect ἦ as a sign of interrogation here, but it is frequently omitted with this and other phrases like it, as οὐχ ὁρᾶτε, οὐκ οἶσθα. Cf. III. 4. 3; 5. 18, et al. ——φιλότιμος, honor-loving, in a good sense, and ἐλευθέριος, noble-minded, in opposition to δουλοπρεπής. —— μὲν γάρ. Γάρ introduces the ground or reason of the declaration: πάνυ ταχύ σοι ὑπακούσεται. —— ἀνδράπια, diminutive in -ιον indicative of contempt. ——ἢ εἰ διδοίης τι, than by giving him something; for the use of the optative mode here, see Kühn. Gr. § 260. 4. —— κατεργάσαιο, prevail over, conciliate to yourself.

17.—Τί γὰρ ἄλλο...ἢ κινδυνεύσεις; cf. note, II. 1. 17, and Plat. Men. p. 80. A: σὺ οὐδὲν ἄλλο (sc. ποιεῖς), κ.τ.λ. The same ellipsis is also frequent in Latin after nihil aliud quam, and similar phrases; see Zumpt's Gr. § 771. —— ἐπιδεῖξαι...σὺ μὲν...εἶναι. The infinitive is used instead of a participle after δεικνύμι either when it signifies to teach or when the object of this verb is to be represented as a thing merely possible; see Kühn. § 311. 11; L. Gr. II. § 658. Anm. 3. Cf. IV. 4. 18. Σὺ μέν are added after ἐπιδεῖξαι for the sake of the contrast with ἐκεῖνος δὲ, after which κινδυνεύσει ἐπιδεῖξαι... εἶναι are to be supplied. —— προκαλούμενον ἑαυτὸν, challenging him. —— πάνυ φιλονεικήσειν, will be very emulous.

18.—Τὼ χεῖρε, ἃς ὁ θεὸς...ἐποίησεν...ἀφεμένω...ἀλλήλω. For the article and qualifying words in the masculine dual whilst the substantive is in the feminine, see Kühn. Gr. § 241. 5. R. 10. (b); L. Gr. II. § 427. 6, and Anm.; Buttm. § 129. 7, and cf. note, I. 2. 33.

19.—Οὐκ ἂν πολλὴ ἀμαθία εἴη. The harshness of the connection between this and the preceding context, has led some editors to suspect that οὐκοῦν should be substituted for οὐκ ἂν; but paragraphs summing up what has preceded are not unfrequently put ἀσυνδέτως, as was shown in note upon I. 1. 9: τοὺς τὰ τοιαῦτα, κ.τ.λ. —— καὶ μὴν...γε; see note, I. 4. 12. —— χεῖρέ τε καὶ πόδε καὶ ὀφθαλμὼ τἆλλά τε; other readings here are: καὶ τἄλλα; Just. τἄλλα τ' ἕως; Par. C. τἄλλα τέως; Par. G. τἄλλα τε ὡς; L. καὶ ἄλλα τε. But the reading in the text, is not only supported by Ms. authority, but is defensible upon grammatical principles. For, after clauses connected by καί, another is not unfrequently affixed by τέ. The last clause in such cases is not considered as parallel with what precedes, for καί and τέ are not thus used as corresponding particles in Attic Greek, but contains something accessory or additional. See Kühn. Gr. § 321. R. 2. Cf. Thucyd. I. 54 and 108, also III. 52. The same construction is found in Latin; after et...et, a clause with que follows. So in Cic. de Legg. II. 13. 33: Iam vero permultorum exemplorum et nostra est plena respublica, et omnia regna, omnesque populi, cunctaeque gentes, augurum praedictis multa incredibiliter vera cecidisse. —— ἀδελφὰ, *in pairs.* —— ὀργυίας, here = a fathom, six feet and nearly an inch. —— οἱ καὶ δοκοῦντες. The καί here with the participle is concessive: *although;* see Hermann ad Vig. § 322. p. 659: Kühn. Gr. § 312. R. 8; L. Gr. II. § 667, c. It has the same signification just below: καὶ πολὺ διεστῶτε; also in II. 4. 4: καὶ πάνυ πολλῶν ὄντων. Cf. Sympos. IV. 13: ὁ δὲ καλὸς, κ.τ.λ —— τῶν ἔτι ἐγγυτέρω...τὰ ἔμπροσθεν, κ.τ.λ. Ἐγγυτέρω is used as a noun in the Gen. with τῶν, and governed partitively by τὰ ἔμπροσθεν and τὰ ὄπισθεν that follow.——πράττετον ἅμα καὶ ἐπ' ὠφελείᾳ ἀλλήλοιν. Ἅμα καὶ are not to be united in construction here, as just above in the sense of pariter ac, but ἅμα πράττειν signifies to unite in a labor or employment, and καί, *and indeed*, or, *and that too*. See Kühn. Gr § 321, and L. Gr. II. § 727. 1.

CHAPTER IV.

1.—Διαλεγομένου; see note, I. 7. 5.——ἐξ ὧν, from which, sc. reasonings. The relative here is in the plural number, in consequence of an implied plural antecedent in the preceding phrase.——πρὸς φίλων κτῆσίν τε καὶ χρείαν, in respect to the acquisition, etc. For the use of the preposition, see Kühn. § 298. III. (2) (e).——τοῦτο μὲν γὰρ δή. The particle δή here is to be taken with τοῦτο and not with γὰρ, this indeed, hoc ipsum. So it is used after πολλά separated by γάρ in Cyrop. V. 3. 8. See Hartung, Gr. Partik. Vol. I. 287. It is far oftener, when thus placed, to be taken with γάρ, see note and references, I. 2. 14.——κράτιστον ἂν εἴη φίλος σαφὴς καὶ ἀγαθός. The condition which gives rise to the ἄν and Opt. mode seems to be implied in the adjectives, σαφὴς καὶ ἀγαθός; i. e., εἰ σαφὴς κ. ἀγαθ. εἴη. Some however supply εἴ τις εἴη. See Kühn. Gr. § 340, and L. Gr. II. § 823. 2.——ὁρῶν ἔφη. The verb ἔφη is frequently repeated in successive clauses for the sake of distinctness, especially in colloquial, and even familiar style. Cf. § 2; III. 6. 11; 8. 3; 10. 10, et al. and note, I. 6. 4.

2.—Καὶ γὰρ οἰκίας, κ.τ.λ.; Cicero in Lael. XV. 55, has similar language: Quid autem stultius, quam, cum plurimum copiis, facultatibus, opibus possint, cetera parare, quae parantur pecunia, equos, famulos, vestem egregiam, vasa pretiosa; amicos non parare, optimam et pulcherrimam vitae, ut ita dicam, supellectilem?——καὶ τὰ ὄντα, sc. acquired; to be supplied from the correlative participle κτωμένους.——φίλον δέ, ὃ μέγιστον ἀγαθὸν εἶναί φασιν; the relative ὅ, neuter for the masculine ὅν; see Kühn. Gr. § 332. 5. (6) and R; L. Gr. II. 786. 3. Cf. IV. 8. 4, and also note § 7 below, where the relative is not attracted to the predicate. For a similar attraction in Latin, see Zumpt's Gr., and Kühner's Cic. Tusc. Disp. IV. 10. 23.——ὁρᾶν ἔφη before τοὺς πολ. are best omitted in English, as their repetition encumbers the sentence.——ὅπως κτήσονται φροντίζοντας...σώζωνται; after σώζωνται, φροντίζοντας is to be repeated, see note, I. 6. 8. A strict concinnity of expression would require the last clause to read: οὔτε ὅπως, ὃν ἂν ἔχωσι, ἑαυτοῖς σώζωνται, but as φίλον is used generically, it may have a plur. referring to it, κατὰ σύνεσιν; see Kühn. Gr. § 332. 5. (a).

3.—Ἀλλὰ καί, quin etiam, moreover.

4.—Καὶ πάνυ πολλῶν αὐτοῖς ὄντων. Καί is here to be connected with ὄντων and not with πάνυ, and is concessive, *although;* see note, II. 3. 19: οἱ καὶ δοκοῦντες.——τὸ πλῆθος εἰδότας. For a similar expression of the same idea, see Diog. Laert. II. 30; and Cic. Lael. XVII. 62: saepe (Scipio) querebatur quod omnibus in rebus homines diligentiores essent, ut capras et oves quot quisque haberet, dicere posset, amicos quot haberet, non posset dicere.——ἀλλὰ καὶ... πάλιν τούτους ἀνατίθεσθαι, they retract them again, i. e., remove them from the number of their friends. Ἀνατίθεσθαι, literally, to put over again, to change a move in chess; see Woolsey's Gorg. p. 461. D. p. 149. So Cic. in his Hortens. says: tibi concedo... ut calculum reducas si te alicujus dicti poenitet. Πάλιν is frequently used with verbs compounded with ἀνά in the same manner as we often use *again.* So in III. 5. 7; Thuc. I. 109, et al.——τοσοῦτον, only so much, i. e., so little; cf. Cyrop. VI. 3. 22.

5.—Χρήσιμον... χρηστός. For the paronomasia see note, II. 3. 1.——παραμόνιμον, from παραμένω, staying by, steadfast, faithful.

6.—Ἑαυτὸν τάττει, *devotes himself to* (the supplying of) every thing, etc.——Καὶ τῶν κοινῶν πράξεων; with the ellipsis supplied: καὶ τῆς τῶν κοιν. πράξ. κατασκευῆς, as in the preceding member of the sentence. For the omission of the article, see note, I. 1. 19.——εὖ μὲν πράττοντας... σφαλλομένους δέ, those in prosperity... and those cast down by adversity.

7.—Τὰ ὦτα προακούουσι. The plural verb seems here to be used instead of the singular with the neuter plural for the sake of uniformity with the preceding and succeeding plural verbs. Προακούειν, to hear before (another) in a similar manner προορᾶν above.——τούτων φίλος εὐεργετῶν οὐδενὸς λείπεται, a friend fails in no one of these things, (i. e., in whatever the hands supply, etc.) to confer favor. For the construction of the participle with the verb λείπεσθαι, see Kühn. § 310. 4; L. Gr. II. § 661.; Matth. II. § 554. f. Cf. II. 6. 5: μὴ ἐλλείπεσθαι εὖ ποιῶν, κ.τ.λ.——ταῦτα ὁ φίλος... ἐξήρκεσεν, these things a friend... abundantly supplies, etc. The verb ἐξαρκεῖν, to suffice for, etc., seems to be properly rendered in this way, and the necessity of supplying the participle ἐξεργαζόμενος, is avoided.——κτήματος, ὃ καλεῖται φίλος. The relative is not here attracted in gender to the predicate because greater emphasis is laid upon the antecedent κτήματος.

CHAPTER V.

1.—Ὁπόσου τοῖς φίλοις ἄξιος εἴη, how much he is valued by friends. Cf. I. 1. 1, ἄξιος, κ.τ.λ. —— Ἀντισθένη. Antisthenes was a disciple of Socrates and the founder of the school of the Cynics. See Ritter's Hist. Philos. Vol. II. chap. IV. p. 108 sq., and Lewes' Biog. Hist. Phil. Vol. II. chap. III. p. 16 sq. The form of the Acc. found here belongs rather to Plato than Xenophon, although in many passages the Mss. vary, as in III. 8. 1. Sympos. I. 3. —— τοῦ ἀμελοῦντος αὐτοῦ καὶ ἄλλων πολλῶν, before him who was negligent, etc. In respect to the collocation of the words, cf. IV. 6. 14: καὶ τοῖς ἀντιλέγουσιν αὐτοῖς φανερὸν ἐγίγνετο τἀληθές; Anab. VII. 1. 9, et al. Αὐτοῦ and ἄλλων πολλῶν are brought near together for the sake of the contrast. See Kühn. Gr. § 348. 10.

2.—Ἔφη like inquit in Latin is tautologically used after a verb of speaking; see note, I. 6. 4, and also cf. note, II. 4. 1. —— ἀξίαι, prices, estimationes. —— που δύο μναῖν ἄξιός ἐστιν, is estimated at about two minae. The μνᾶ was seventeen dollars sixty-one cents. For the usual prices of slaves, see Boeckh's Econ. of Athens, p. 67. B. I. ch. 13. —— Νικίας, called by Athenaeus (vi. p. 272. e.) the richest of all the Greeks; and according to Xenophon (Vectig. 4. 14) he had 1000 slaves in his mines. See Boeckh, Econ. of Athens, B. IV. ch. 3. p. 480. —— ἐπιστάτην εἰς τἀργύρια, overseer of the silver mines, sometimes called ἀργυρεῖα ἔργα. In the rich silver mines of Laurion many laborers were employed in the time of Socrates by private individuals. See Boeckh's Dissertation on Econ. of Athens, p. 616 sq., where is a full account of this source of the wealth of Attica. Cf. also III. 6. 12, and Vectig. IV. 1 sq. —— ταλάντου, = 60 minae and 600 drachmae, about $1056.60. —— σκοποῦμαι δὴ τοῦτο. The particle δή is here resumptive, i. e., after speaking of the price of slaves, Socrates returns to the original question, this is what I ask, i. e. εἰ ἄρα, etc. in *oratio obliqua*, but *recta* above.

3.—Ναὶ μὰ Δί'; sc. εἰσὶ καὶ τῶν φίλων ἀξίαι. —— ἐγὼ γοῦν; for the force of γοῦν, see note, I. 6. 2. —— τὸν μέν τινα . . . τὸν δ', one, some one, . . . another; so ὁ μέν τις . . . ὁ δέ τις, alius quis . . . alius quis, are often placed; see Kühn. L. Gr. II. § 481. d. —— πρὸ πάντων χρημάτων καὶ πόνων πριαίμην. The idea of preference implied in πρό is most suitable in this passage. Cf. Apol. § 20. Instead of πόνων some editors use πόρων, but without necessity, authority, or, even apparent plausibility, as Antisthenes was doubtless very poor; v. Sympos. III. 8; IV. 34. In II. 1. 20: τῶν πόνων πωλοῦσιν ἡμῖν πάντα τἀγαθ' οἱ θεοί, good things are spoken of as sold for labor. And besides, Antisthenes the founder of the Cynic school of philosophers, might naturally be supposed to set a very high value upon πόνον, labor, trouble; v. Diog. Laert. Antisth. vita, p. 138 and 140. It is, however, more probable that πρὸ πάντων χρημάτων καὶ πόνων had a proverbial significance: before all wealth and labor, i. e., above every thing.—— φίλον μοι εἶναι; in other cases, we find the particle ὥστε added after πρίασθαι. Cf. Cyrop. III. 1. 36: λέξον μοι, πόσου ἂν πρίαιο, ὥστε τὴν γυναῖκα ἀπολαβεῖν; VIII. 4. 23: οὐκ ἂν πρίαιό γε παμπόλλου, ὥστε σοι ταῦτα εἰρῆσθαι.

4.—Εἴ γε ... ἔστι, καλῶς ἂν ἔχοι; for the use of the Opt. mode with ἄν after εἴ, see note, I. 2. 28.—— ὡς πλείστου ἄξιος εἶναι; this ought in strict conformity with the parallel phrase: καλῶς ἂν ἔχοι ἐξετάζειν τινὰ ἑαυτὸν, to read: πειρᾶσθαι ὡς πλείστου ἄξιον εἶναι, but it is attracted to the form of the preceding enunciation: πόσου ἄρα τυγχάνει τοῖς φίλοις ἄξιος ὤν; see Kühn. L. Gr. II. § 646. 2. and 3.—— ἐγὼ γάρ τοι, see note, II. 3. 6.—— τοῦ μὲν ... τοῦ δὲ, from one ... and from another.—— ἀνθ' ἑαυτοῦ μᾶλλον εἵλετο; the preposition ἀντί is often thus placed after a comparative; see Kühn. Gr. § 287. 1. (b); L. Gr. § 588. Anm. 2.

5.—Τὰ τοιαῦτα πάντα σκοπῶ, μή; the participle σκοπῶν is implied in the verb σκοπῶ, see note, II. 3. 14: ἢ ὀκνεῖς, κ.τ.λ., considering all such things, I consider, whether, etc.; or according to Seiffert σκοπῶ may be taken in a pregnant signification: quae quidem omnia considerans, vereor ne, etc.—— ἀποδίδωται τοῦ εὑρόντος, disposes of him for what he is found worth, will bring. So τοῦ εὑρίσκοντος in Aesch. c. Timarch. p. 117. 2. Cf. Oecon. II. 3: πόσον ἂν οἴει εὑρεῖν τὰ σὰ κτήματα πωλούμενα, and De Vectig. IV. 25. 40, where see examples collected by Schneider.—— τὸ πλεῖον τῆς ἀξίας, *more than his worth.* The idea of the passage is: If one has a friend who is bad or of little worth, and he can dispose of him for more than his value, he will easily be induced to sell him; i. e., if a friend of little value can be exchanged for one of more worth, the transfer will be readily made.—— ἐπαγωγὸν ᾖ, *there may be an inducement,* etc.

CHAPTER VI.

1.—'Εδόκει ... φρενοῦν, he seemed to sharpen the mind.—— ἐπιχειροίημεν; the Attic form of the optative of contract verbs in -έω and -όω, is more unusual in the dual and plural than the comm·n form;

although the reverse is true of the singular. See Kühn. Gr. § 137. 4; L. Gr. I. § 144. 5; Buttm. § 105. note 4. 1. 2.—— ἆρα is sometimes equivalent to ἆρ' οὔ, nonne. See Eurip. Alcestis, l. 229, 771. It often indicates doubt, uncertainty, wonder, unbelief, etc., like the Latin num, and is taken negatively and anticipates a negative answer, as in § 16; III. 13. 3; IV. 2. 22. It is also frequently employed as here in accordance with Attic urbanity, where there is no doubt, even in interrogations, when the interrogator knows that the answer of the person addressed will be affirmative. When used for ἆρ' οὐ, there is frequently a shade of irony implied, as in III. 2. 1; 6. 4; 10. 1, 7, et al. So ἆρ' οὖν is sometimes used for ἆρ' οὖν οὔ, as in II. 7. 5; III. 10. 4, et al. See Kühn. L. Gr. II. § 834. 2. For a similar use of ne in Latin for nonne, see Kühn. Tusc. Dis. II. 11. 26.—— πρῶτον μὲν; the construction is changed here, and instead of the εἶτα δέ which would naturally follow πρῶτον μέν, we find τί γάρ (§ 2). Kühner compares in Latin, Cicero, Tusc. Dis. V. 27. 78: primum ii qui sapientes habentur—; mulieres vero; and IV. 35. 74, on which see his note.—— τοῦ μὲν... ἀρχομένου. Upon μέν *solitarium*, see note, I. 1. 1.—— Πάνυ μὲν οὖν, see note, I. 3. 9.

2.—Τί γάρ; these particles are used when one passes with some animation to something new. Γάρ has no reference to the logical connection of the thought, but is merely rhetorical, and gives animation to the question itself. Quid? is used in a similar way in Latin. See Hartung, Gr. Partik. I. S. 480, 1; Kühn. L. Gr. II. § 833. i.; cf. § 3; III. 10. 3.—— *τῶν πλησίων, his neighbors.*—— καὶ λαμβάνων, when he receives, etc. —— Ἀφεκτέον μέντοι; abstinendum vero; μέντοι denotes confirmation. See Kühn. Gr. § 316. R. (a); L. Gr. II. § 840. f. Cf. IV. 2. 12, 14; Sympos. IV. 33.

3.—Δυσξύμβολος, (from συμβάλλω, with the inseparable particle δυς,) hard to agree with, hard at a bargain. See Stallb. Plat. de Rep. VI. p. 486. B.—— Ἐμοὶ μὲν δοκεῖ; cf. I. 2. 62: Ἐμοὶ μὲν ἐδόκει, and see note, I. 1. 1: ἡ μὲν γὰρ γραφή.—— οὗτος... ἐκείνου, this... than that, the other, characterized in § 2. Αὗτος refers to the nearest object and ἐκεῖνος to the more distant; Kühn. L. Gr. § 629. 7; I. 3. 13; see Plat. Apol. 2. So hic and ille in Latin; see Kühn. Tusc. Disp. I. 49. 117.

4.—Τί δέ; (*what then?*) indicates that the writer passes to something different, yet closely connected with what precedes. As τί δέ follows τί γάρ in this passage, so in III. 3. 5, 6 τί γάρ follows τί δέ.—— μηδὲ πρὸς ἓν ἄλλο, see note, I. 6. 2: οὐδ' ἂν εἷς. For the use of πρός, see Kühn. Gr. § 298; III. (3). (a). Cf. III. 6. 6: οὐδὲ πρὸς ταῦτα πω ἐσχόλασε.—σχολὴν ποιεῖται, makes leisure, i. e., allows himself (no) time.—ὁπόθεν αὐτὸς κερδανεῖ; the verb κερδανεῖ in the future is expressed in Latin by a periphrasis with the subjunctive: unde ipse lucrum capturum se sperat.—Εἰ δέ τις... ἔχοι, εὖ δὲ πάσχων ἀνέχεται; some editors change ἔχοι to ἔχει to make it correspond with ἀνέχεται, and others read ἀνέχοιτο in accommodation to ἔχοι, but both badly. For in addition to Ms. authority for the reading given in the text, there is manifestly a change in the shade of thought, that requires a change of tense; the first clause is conditional: if one may have, etc.; the last, declarative of a fact: but he is pleased to receive favor, etc.; see note, I. 2. 32. When after εἰ the indicative occurs first, and then the optative, the action indicated by the latter is conditioned upon the performance of that which is expressed as doubtful by the former. Cf. Cyrop. IV. 6. 7: Εἰ οὖν σύ με δέχῃ καὶ ἐλπίδα τινὰ λάβοιμι. The verb ἀνέχεται, lit., to endure, suffer, is here used ironically; so in Cyrop. V. 1. 26: ὁρῶντές σε ἀνεξόμεθα... ὑπὸ σοῦ εὐεργετούμενοι; upon which see Owen's note.

5.—Οἶμαι μέν; so also ἡγοῦμαι μέν, δοκῶ μέν, οὐκ οἶδα μέν, and similar phrases, are used without a corresponding clause with δέ: *I think* (*but I will not venture to assert it*, or some such phrase implied). There is a modesty and urbanity in such modes of speech, characteristic of the Attic Greek. Kühn. Gr. § 322; L. Gr. II. § 734. 2.—τἀναντία; the Acc. used adverbially. See Kühn. Gr. § 279. R. 10; L. Gr. II. § 557. Anm. 4.—φιλόνεικος πρὸς τὸ μὴ ἐλλείπεσθαι, κ.τ.λ., emulous not to be left behind in doing good (lit., in respect to, etc.) to those, etc. For the constr. of the Part. see 310. 4. (f).

6.—Τοῖς λόγοις... τεκμαιρόμενοι; with verbs of measuring, conjecturing, judging, etc., the dative is used; see Kühn. § 285. (3). (b); L. Gr. II. § 586. e. Cf. I. 4. 1; Sympos. VIII. 11. The verb τεκμαίρεσθαι is also constructed with the prepositions ἀπό and ἐκ in III. 5. 6; IV. 1. 2.—εἰργασμένον *has made*, Act. in signif. here, Pass. III. 10. 9.

7.—Καὶ ἄνδρα δὴ λέγεις; the particles καὶ... δή indicate that the phrase in which they stand, is joined to the preceding enunciation as a consequence or conclusion. They introduce the general truth indicated by previous examples. The phrase would be here expressed in English by: Do you, then, mean or say, etc. See Hartung, Gr. Partik. I. 264. In other cases καὶ... δή merely connect a passage which has greater force than the preceding, *and indeed*, et vero. They are also used to resume an interrupted discourse for the sake of bringing it to a close;

see note, I. 2. 24. See also on the different meanings of these particles, Klotz's Devarius, II. 264. 5, and cf. Stallb. Plat. Phaed. p. 115. C. —— δῆλον εἶναι... εὐεργετήσοντα; for the personal construction corresponding to δῆλον εἶναι, with the participle, see Kühn. Gr. § 310. R. 3; L. Gr. II. § 658. Anm. 2; Buttm. § 151. 7. It seems to be occasioned by the desire to give prominence to the main word, ἄνδρα, which is pushed forward into the leading clause, instead of standing in a secondary clause as in the impersonal construction. See Woolsey's Gorgias, p. 448. D. —— καὶ γὰρ; καί, *even*, is to be joined with ἵπποις, and γάρ gives a reason for the implied answer to the preceding question, (I do) *for*, etc. Cf. II. 1. 3.

8.—Εἶεν, *be it so, well;* formed from the 3d sing. εἴη. For the grammatical form, see Buttm. § 108. p. 193, foot-note. It is sometimes a mere particle of transition, but often used by the Attic writers when they wish to dismiss one topic and pass to another. See Stallb. Plat. Apol. p. 19. A, and Euthyph. p. 88 sq. —— τὰ παρὰ τῶν θεῶν... εἰ συμβουλεύουσιν; for the plural verb, κατὰ σύνεσιν, with a subject expressed by a neuter article with a noun in the genitive plural, see Kühn. Gr. § 241. R. 1; L. Gr. II. § 420. 1. Cf. Apolog. § 4. —— ὃν ἂν ἡμῖν τε δοκῇ, sc. φίλον ποιεῖσθαι.

9.—Κατὰ πόδας, sometimes rendered *by running*, "cursu," or, "velocitate pedum," but perhaps better, "insistendo vestigiis ejus," *following close on his track;* as Livy, xxvii. 2, says: Marcellus... vestigiis institit sequi. Cf. III. 11. 8: ἵνα κατὰ πόδας ἁλίσκωνται; Cyrop. I. 6. 40. —— [οἱ] ἐχθροί, are strictly those who from friends become enemies, Lat. inimici; whilst οἱ πολέμιοι are enemies in war, armed enemies, Lat. hostis. So Ammon: ἐχθρός est ὁ πρότερον φίλος; πολέμιος autem ὁ μεθ' ὅπλων χωρῶν πέλας. But still ἐχθρός is not unfrequently used for an armed or warlike enemy, as ἐχθροί in h. l., and πολέμιος for one who is a bitter enemy and yet not in arms; see IV. 4. 17. Δυσμενής is one who bears an invincible, lasting hatred to another; it is, however, especially in Homer, used with the nouns ἀνήρ, ἄνδρες, for both the former; see Il. κ. 100, and Al. Pillon, Syn. Gr. p. 51. Those who are pursued as prey, and held bound (δήσαντα κατέχειν), are appropriately called enemies, ἐχθροί = πολέμιοι. —— Φίλοι δὲ πῶς. The preceding answer of Socrates was negative, and only informed how enemies could be procured, hence the question: But how, *friends?* See note, I. 3. 13: τοὺς δὲ καλούς.

10.—Ἐπᾴδοντες οἷς ἂν βούλωνται; for ἐπᾴδ. τούτοις, οὓς ἂν βούλ. Ἐπῳδὰς ἐπᾴδειν τινι, incantare aliquem (carmine, or, verbis). —— φίλτρα, from φιλέω, and hence lit., a love-potion, a charm.

11.—Ἃ μὲν; to this μέν, δέ near the end of § 12: Ἄλλας δέ τινας, answers. —— τοιάδε τις; see note, I. 1. 1. Τις is used here because the line is quoted from memory, as heard (ἤκουσας) from those who were accustomed to recite Homer. —— Δεῦρ', κ.τ.λ. This line is from the Odyssey, XII. 184. The sentiment in this and the two following sections, according to Weiske, is that one who wishes another to be his friend must first signify his own love to him by words and then by actions. —— Οὔκ· ἀλλὰ; the general rule is that οὐ should be written before consonants and οὐκ and οὐχ before vowels. But where special emphasis is to be laid upon the particle, it is generally written οὔ even before vowels. This takes place when οὐ stands at the end of a sentence, and there is a break in the discourse, when it corresponds to our *no* in answer to a question, and in antithetical clauses; when, however, closely connected with what follows, οὐκ generally, though here, οὔκ is written. See Kühn. Gr. § 15. 4. —— τοῖς ἐπ' ἀρετῇ φιλοτιμουμένοις, those earnestly striving for virtue.

12.—Σχεδόν τι, *almost;* with λέγεις, these words may be paraphrased in Latin: hoc idem fere est, quasi dicas. —— οἶα μὴ νομιεῖ ...καταγελῶντα λέγειν, as (that) when he hears, he will not suppose the one who praises speaks ironically or in ridicule. For the form of future called Attic, as it appears in νομιεῖ, see Kühn. Gr. § 117. 1 and 2. —— οὕτω, thus, i. e., if he supposed himself ridiculed.

13.—Οὔκ, *no,* see note, § 11. —— ἤκουσα μὲν. The particle μέν is used here much as in οἶμαι μέν in § 5. —— ἐπίσταιτο; the optative is employed on account of its being a mere relation of what had been heard from another. Bornemann thus paraphrases it: ἤκουσα λεγόντων, ὅτι Περικ. ἐπίσταιτο. See Kühn. Gr. § 329 and 345; L. Gr. II. § 769. 3. —— ἐποίει. The sudden transition here from indirect discourse, although somewhat common in Greek, would hardly be admissible in Latin. —— περιάψας τι ἀγαθὸν, by conferring some favor upon it. Socrates supposed that Pericles made himself profitable to the State as an orator and Themistocles as a general.

14.—Μέλλοιμεν; for the optative see note, I. 2. 28. —— κτήσασθαι; for the aorist Infin. after μέλλοιμεν, see II. 7. 10 and note, I. 2. 10. —— λέγειν τε καὶ πράττειν; by λέγειν and πράττειν the two means of becoming useful to the State, illustrated by the two preceding examples, are brought to view. —— Σὺ δ' ᾤου; see note, I. 3. 13: τοὺς δὲ καλούς.

15.—Ἑώρων γάρ; (yes) *for,* etc., see note, I. 4. 9. —— φίλους and ἑταίρους; see note, I. 5. 4.

16.—*Καί, περὶ οὗ διαλεγόμεθα, οἶσθά τινας.* Καί is to be joined with οἶσθά τινας, and περὶ οὗ διαλεγόμεθα, (which is the point in discussion,) is thrown in, to recall Socrates' attention to the question proposed. —— *μέλει μοι, εἰ*, this is my care, this I wish to know, whether, etc. —— *ἐξ ἑτοίμου*, *easily;* see Viger, p. 70, 1.

17.—*Ὃ ταράττει σε, ὦ Κριτόβ. ὅτι.* We may supply after ὃ ταράττει σε, *τοῦτό ἐστιν*, ὅτι. So Stallb. explains Plato Rep. Lib. VI. p. 491. B: ὃ μὲν πάντων θαυμαστότατον ἀκοῦσαι, ὅτι... ἐπηνέσαμεν. Cf. Isocr. Paneg. p. 77. 176, and Stallb. Plat. Lysid. p. 204. C. The relative is here made the principal clause, and that which should be the principal clause is introduced by ὅτι. The natural construction of the sentence would be: ὃ ταράττει σε, πολλάκις ἄνδρας... ὁρᾷς. Cf. Kühn. Gr. § 347; L. Gr. II. § 857. —— *χαλεπώτερον χρωμένους*, sc. ἀλλήλοις.

18.—*Αἰσχρὰ ἥκιστα προσιέμεναι*, which least of all admit, etc. Cyrop. VII. 1. 13: ἐγὼ γὰρ κακόν οὐδὲν... προσήσομαι. —— *πολεμικῶς* = πολεμίως, since it is generally used in a good sense; in a warlike manner, bravely, etc.; while the meaning of πολεμίως is with enmity, hostility, which alone is the appropriate idea here. Cf. § 21.

19.—*Ἀθύμως ἔχω*, *I am disheartened.* The adverb here with ἔχω is used like εἶμι with the adjective as very frequently, see § 18. —— *οὔτε γὰρ τοὺς πονηροὺς ὁρῶ, κ.τ.λ.*; to this, *οὐδὲ ἂν, κ.τ.λ*, in § 20, corresponds. For the anacoluthon, see note, I. 2. 31, and cf. II. 2. 5: οὐδὲ, κ.τ.λ.

20.—*Εἰ δὲ δή*; for the force of δή, see I. 5. 1: but if, as you now say. —— *ἑαυτοῖς... ἀλλήλους*; the reciprocal and reflexive pronouns are often used, where there is no antithesis expressed or implied, without distinction, and even in the same sentence as here, merely for the sake of variety. Cf. II. 7. 12; III. 5. 16. As the reciprocal and reflexive pronouns both express a reflexive idea, and are nearly related to each other, the reflexive may take the place of the reciprocal when it is easily understood that several persons so perform an act in respect to themselves, that it appears as reciprocal. But when the antithesis, ἑαυτὸν ἕκαστος is either expressed or implied, the reciprocal must be used; cf. III. 5. 2, 16. See Kühn. Gr. § 302. R. 7; Soph. 145, n. 2.

21.—*Ἀλλ' ἔχει μέν... ποικίλως πως ταῦτα*, but these things are somewhat diverse. For the use of the Adv. and ἔχω, see note, § 19. The particle μέν is here followed by Ἀλλ' ὅμως, § 22. —— *φύσει γὰρ ..δέονταί τε γάρ*; the second γάρ introduces a parenthetical clause: see note, IV. 2. 38; Bornem. Sympos. IV. 55, and cf. III. 10. 3; IV. 3. 10

—— τὰ . . . πολεμικά, supply: φύσει ἔχουσιν οἱ ἄνθρωποι, have *somethings conducive to hostility*, as opp. to τὰ . . . φιλικά. —— πολεμικὸν . . . ἔρις, κ.τ.λ. The adjective πολεμικὸς here seems to mean: productive of divisions or discord. For the construction, see II. 3. 1: χρησιμώτερον νομίζουσι, κ.τ.λ. —— μισητὸν, worthy of hatred, odious.

22.—Αἱροῦνται μὲν as if followed by δύνανται δέ, but there is a change of construction, in order to indicate an accession of emphasis in the last clause, by means of the καί. —— δύνανται . . . δύνανται δὲ; for the omission of μέν, see note, I. 1. 1: ἀδικεῖ . . ἀδικεῖ δὲ. —— ἐγκαρτερεῖν, *to endure it patiently.* —— οὓς μὴ προσήκει; sc. λυπεῖν; see note, II. 1. 32.

23.—Νομίμως = δικαίως; cf. IV. 4. 1. Τὸ νόμιμον is also defined in IV. 4. 11 and 12 as τὸ δίκαιον. Cf. also 8. 11. —— τὴν ἔριν . . . διατίθεσθαι, to settle a strife "not only without giving pain but also advantageously to one another." Hickie. —— τὸ μεταμελησόμενον, i. e., τὴν μεταμέλειαν γενησομένην προϊέναι, *from proceeding* to what shall cause repentance; for the use of the abstract neuter here, see Kühn. L. Gr. II. § 474, γ; Matth. II. § 570.

24.—Πολιτικῶν τιμῶν, governed in the Gen. by κοινωνοὺς εἶναι, see Kühn. § 273. 3. (b).

25.—Εἰ δέ τις, connected in construction with πειρᾶται. —— τοῖς φίλοις τὰ δίκαια βοηθεῖν; for the construction here, see Kühn. Gr. § 279. 7; L. Gr. II. § 553. Anm. 4, where several similar examples are given. Cf. III. 5. 16; Sympos. VI. 3; Dem. I. c. Aphob, p. 814. 3. —— καὶ ἄρξας. Καί connects ἄρξας to βουλόμενος, if any one wishing to be honored in order that, etc. . . . and having been appointed archon, should attempt, etc.; for the use of the Aor. see note, I. 1. 18.

26.—Ἐξῆν τοῖς κρατίστοις συνθεμένους . . . ἰέναι. The participle is not here put by attraction in the same case as the personal object, but in the accusative. See Kühn. Gr. § 307. R. 2, and note, I. 1. 9. For the use of the Mode and Tense, see note, I. 2. 28. —— συντίθεσθαι, to make a compact, or to unite together. —— πάντας ἂν τοὺς ἀγῶνας οὗτοι ἐνίκων, the Accus. of a kindred signification with the verb, is common to the Greek with other languages. So we find πυγμήν, γνώμην, δίκην νικᾶν (to gain, win, etc.) See Kühn. Gr. § 278. 1. —— Ἐκεῖ μὲν, i. e., ἐν τοῖς γυμνικοῖς ἀγῶσιν. —— πολιτικοῖς, sc. ἀγῶσιν. —— πῶς οὖν; the particle οὖν is here pleonastic, since ἐπεὶ οὖν precedes. It is wanting in some Mss. —— κτησάμενον; see note, I. 3. 8: ἀπτόμενον. —— τούτοις κοινωνοῖς . . . χρώμενον; see II. 1. 12: δούλοις χρῆσθαι.

27.—Ἀλλὰ μὴν; see note, I. 1. 6. —— κἀκεῖνο, *this also.* —— καὶ τούτων. For this use of οὗτος with καί in making an addition to a previous clause, see C. 513. 1, note. —— καὶ μὴν, and indeed; cf. note, II. 3. 4. —— εὖ ποιητέοι; for the signification and use of the verbal in -τέος, see Kühn. Gr. § 234. 1. i; Buttm. § 134. 8. —— τοὺς βελτίστους ἐλάττονας...τοὺς χείρονας πλείονας ὄντας, the best who are fewer than the worse who are more. —— ἐθέλοντες...θέλωσι; see note, I. 2. 9.

28.—Ἔχοιμι, *be able;* see note, I. 6. 13. —— διὰ τὸ ἐρωτικὸς εἶναι, because I am given or inclined to love. Cf. I. 6. 14. The love of true beauty, virtue, and honor, with which Socrates labors to inspire his friends, must be here meant. In reference to the attraction, see note, I. 2. 3: τῷ φανερὸς εἶναι. —— δεινῶς ὅλος ὥρμημαι, *I am strongly all-impelled;* δεινῶς qualifies the phrase ὅλος ὥρμ. —— φιλῶν...αὐτ. ἀντιφιλεῖσθαι, *whilst I love them, to the being loved in turn.* —— ἀντεπιθυμεῖσθαι τῆς ξυνουσίας, to be sought in turn for the sake of intercourse, companionship; ξυνουσίας is the genitive of cause or occasion, see Kühn. Gr. § 274. 1.

29.—Τούτων, *of these* (*qualities* indicated by the preceding clauses). —— δεῆσον; Neut. Part. used impersonally.

30.—Πάλαι ἐπιθυμῶ. The idea is: I have long been and now am desirous, etc. So the Adv. πάλαι is freq. used with a verb in the present tense. —— ἄλλως τε καὶ; see note, I. 2. 59.

31.—Τὸ τὰς χεῖρας προσφέροντα ὑπομένειν ποιεῖν τοὺς καλούς, that he who lays hands upon, will retain those who are beautiful. —— Σκύλλης; see Od. XII. 85 sq. —— τὰς δέ γε Σειρῆνας... ὑπομένειν. The particle δέ here denotes contrast, *on the contrary*, and γέ renders the word on which the strength of the opposition is placed (i. e., Σειρῆνας) emphatic. Cyrop. I. 6. 18, and Bornemann's note in h. l.; Symp. IV. 13; and see Hartung, I. p. 380. Ὑπομένειν, *to await, not to flee from.* In reference to the Syrens, see Hom. Od. XII. 39. 52.

32.—Προσοίσοντος, sc. μοῦ; for the omission of the subject, see Kühn. Gr. § 312. R. 4; L. Gr. II. § 666. Anm. 3. For the use of ὡς with the participle, see note, I. 1. 4, and cf. § 33. —— εὐθύς, κ.τ.λ., you have forthwith, i. e., notwithstanding your assurances (contained in ὡς οὐ προσοίσοντος, κ.τ.λ. and θάῤῥει), etc. —— οἱ μὲν...καλοί. Socrates jestingly gives the word καλός, which is ambiguous, and was applied to physical beauty by Critobulus, an application to mental excellence, whilst αἰσχρός here, designates one who is ugly in appearance, but who trusts to his mental excellence to give him the reputation of being καλός. Critobulus perceiving the irony of Socrates, seeks to avoid the ambiguity of the word by showing that he uses καλός in regard to physical beauty: ὡς τοὺ μεν καλοὺς φιλήσαντός μου, τοὺς δ' ἀγαθοὺς καταφιλήσαντος.

33.—Ἐάσεις με κατειπεῖν σου πρὸς αὐτὸν, you will permit me (lit.) to accuse you to him? The verbs προσκατηγορεῖν and διαβάλλειν are also used in the same playful manner. Cf. Weiske, De Pleon. Gr. p. 29. The idea implied in this question: will you so speak, feel, and act, that I can truly say of you, etc. —— ἄγασαι ... αὐτοῦ; the verb ἄγασθαι is very seldom construed with the genitive of the person without the accusative of the thing on account of which one is admired. But it is sometimes followed by the genitive of the participle, which designates both the person admired, and that on account of which he is admired; as in Oeconom. IV. 21: πολὺ δὲ μᾶλλον ἄγαμαι τοῦ καταμετρήσαντός σοι καὶ διατάξαντος ἕκαστα τούτων. The ascending order of the incentives to friendship should not here escape notice: 1. admiration (ἄγασαι αὐτοῦ); 2. regard, good will (εὐνοϊκῶς ἔχεις πρὸς αὐτόν); 3. real merit as a friend, § 35, (ἐπιμελὴς τῶν φίλων εἶ, κ.τ.λ.). See Weiske in h. l.

34.—Ἆρα μή; see note, I. 3. 11. —— Ἀλλὰ, *on the contrary*, καί, *even;* there is an ellipsis of οὐ μόνον οὐ δόξω διαβάλλεσθαι before ἀλλὰ καί. Cf. the use of the negative phrase: ἀλλ' οὐδὲ, κ.τ.λ., II. 3. 8, and note. —— πρὸς οὓς for πρὸς ἐκείνους οὓς; see note, I. 2. 6.

35.—Καλοῖς ἔργοις ... τοῖς ἀγαθοῖς, the honorable deeds ... prosperity. —— τοῖς ἑαυτοῦ; for σεαυτοῦ, see note, I. 4. 9. —— οὐκ ἀποκάμνεις μηχανώμενος, *you are unwearied in your devices.* —— καὶ ὅτι; the particle ὅτι is somewhat loosely repeated here, as it occurs before ἐπιμελής above. —— ἔγνωκας ... εἶναι; for the use and significance of γιγνώσκειν with the infinitive, as distinguished from the participle, see Kühn. Gr. § 311. 4; L. Gr. II. § 657. Anm. 2. Cf. Apol. § 33, and Hellen. IV. 6. 9; VII. 1. 41. —— πάνυ ... ἐπιτήδειον; this separation (hyperbaton) of πάνυ from its adjective gives it special emphasis; see Kühn. Gr. § 348. 9, and L. Gr. II. § 865. 1. —— οἶμαι ... εἶναί με; see note, I. 4. 8: σαυτὸν, κ.τ.λ.

36.—Ὥσπερ οὐκ ἐπὶ σοὶ ὂν, as if it were not in your power. For the use of ὥσπερ with the participle in the Accus. Abs., marking the objective ground of an action, see note, II. 3. 3: and for the force of ἐπί, see Kühn. Gr. § 296. II. 3; L. Gr. II. § 612. p. 297. —— οὔχ for οὔ, see note upon § 11. —— Ἀσπασίας. This woman, distinguished for the charms of her person, manners, and conversation, acquired an almost unbounded influence over Pericles as well as other literary men of hei age. Precisely how much is meant by Socrates' allusions to her instructions to him is difficult to determine. It has been contended, with considerable plausibility, that he speaks ironically both here, in Plato, Menex. p. 235. E., and in Oecon. III. 14: *συστήσω δέ σοι ἐγὼ καὶ Ἀσπασίαν, ἣ ἐπιστημονέστερον ἐμοῦ σοι ταῦτα πάντα ἐπιδείξει.* Cf. Socrates' Life, by Wiggers, and Thirlwall's Greece, I. p. 320. —— δεινᾶς ... συνάγειν; for the use of the Inf. after Adjj. denoting fitness, ability, etc., see Kühn. Gr. § 306. 1. (c). —— ψευδομένας, is contrasted with ἀληθείας τἀγαθὰ διαγγελλούσας. —— ἐπαινούσας, *when they praise.* —— ἃ δή, *which things*, referring to the preceding instructions of Aspasia.

37.—Οἷος ... συλλαμβάνειν μοι; see note, I. 4. 6: *οἵους τέμνειν.* —— εἰ δὲ μή; we should rather expect ἐὰν δὲ μή to correspond with ἂν (ἐὰν) μέν, κ.τ.λ., above, but εἰ not unfrequently follows ἐὰν when the first of two conditional clauses is more important, and contains a more specific reference to consequences that may result. —— οὐκ ἂν ἐθέλοις; we might perhaps expect the construction with ὥστε instead of the form of a primary enunciation. —— πλάσας, the middle form of the verb πλάττειν, is generally used with the metaphorical signification, deceiving, lying, etc.; see Demosth. pro Coron. p. 288. 10, and Kühn. Gr. § 250. R. 4; L. Gr. II. § 398. 5. But the active form is also sometimes used with the same meaning; see Demosth. de Coron. p. 268, 121: *τί λόγους πλάττεις*; also in 305, 232, although just after, the middle form occurs. Cf. also Plat. Phaedr. p. 246. C.

38.—Ἐκ τῶνδε σκέψαι· εἰ γάρ; see note, I. 1. 6: *τὰ μὲν γὰρ ἀναγκαῖα.* —— τὴν ναῦν; see note, I. 1. 9. —— ὡς ἂν στρατηγικῷ; Weiske conjectures that ἂν should be ὄντι, but that reading is not supported by any of the Mss. For the omission of the participle ὄντι, see note, I. 4. 10 and 5. 1. The particle ἄν is not to be joined with the participle as if the order were: *σοὶ ὡς ἂν εἴης στρατηγικός*, but with πείσειεν, which is to be supplied in thought: *εἰ τὴν πόλιν ψευδόμενός σοι ἑαυτὴν ἐπιτρέψαι πείσαιμι, ὡς ἄν τις αὐτὴν πείσειεν, εἰ σὺ εἴης στρατηγικός*; cf. Kühn. in h. l., and III. 6. 4; 8. 1; Cyrop. I. 3. 8; VII. 4. 3. See Kühn. Gr. § 261. 4; L. Gr. II. § 456. Hence *ὡς ἂν στρατηγικῷ ὄντι*, as or as if, etc., designates a thing by comparison, whilst *ὡς στρατηγικῷ ὄντι* states the thought or supposition of the speaker: that you are, etc.; see note, I. 1. 4. —— τί ἂν οἴει σεαυτὸν ... παθεῖν; see I. 4. 8. —— πεῖραν διδούς, when you made a trial (of your ability).

39.—Συντομωτάτη ... ἀγαθὸν πειρᾶσθαι; concerning the sentiment, see note, I. 7. 1. —— ὅ τι ... τοῦτο, limiting accusatives. ——

μαθήσει γε καὶ μελέτῃ. The idea that virtue is the result of education and practice is a favorite one with Socrates; see I. 2. 19; III. 9. 1; IV. 1. et saep.—— οἶμαι δεῖν ἡμᾶς ταύτῃ θηρᾶσθαι, hunt friends, in the manner in which I have explained, etc.; see note, I. 7. 3: ταύτῃ λυπηρόν.—— σύ πως ἄλλως, *in some other way;* other enclitics as πώς, κ.τ.λ., are placed in the midst of discourse like τὶς. Cf. IV. 6. 9.

CHAPTER VII.

1.—Καὶ μήν, and indeed, or, moreover, jam vero.—— τὰς ἀπορίας... τὰς μὲν... τὰς δὲ; for the demonstrative use of the article, see Kühn. Gr. § 247. 3. (d), and for the partitive apposition, § 266. 3, and cf. note, II. 1. 4.——Ἐρῶ δὲ καὶ ἐν τούτοις ἃ σύνοιδα αὐτῷ, but I will speak even in this matter, what I myself have been witness of; lit., what I know with him, i. e., by being in company with him; συνειδέναι ἑαυτῷ, to be conscious to one's self, conscium sibi esse. Cf. Anab. VII. 6. 18; Oecon. III. 7; Sympos. IV. 62. When συνειδέναι is used of those things which cannot be known from personal observation, it seems to be by a rhetorical figure, the person representing himself as present when he is not; see Isocr. Areop. c. 19; Plat. Phaed. p. 92. D. where λόγους takes the place of persons, in reference to which this word is more properly used. —— σκυθρωπῶς ἔχοντα, "*had a long face on.*"——ἡμεῖς; for the plural here, see I. 2. 46.

2.—Ἀλλὰ μήν... γε; *well,* (if you wish me to tell you my trouble,) I am, *indeed;* see Arn. 2 Gr. Pr. Comp. 34, and cf. note, I. 1. 4, 6, 10. —— ἐστασίασεν ἡ πόλις. For this revolt of the Athenians under Thrasybulus from the dominion of the Thirty Tyrants and its result, see Thirlwall's Hist. Gr. Vol. I. 500 sq. ch. xxxi.; Mitford, ch. 21. 4, and Xen. Hellen. II. 4.——εἰς τὸν Πειραῖα; this is the reading in 4 Mss. for the Vulg. ὡς τὸν Π. The latter preposition probably crept into the Mss. from the ὡς following. It seems at least to be decided that ὡς is used only with words indicating persons, or the names of countries or cities, when they stand for the inhabitants; see Kühn. Gr. § 290. 3; L. Gr. II. § 604; Matth. II. § 578. i. In Hellen. II. 4. 10 we find εἰς τὸν Πειραῖα in reference to the same event.——συνεληλύθασιν ὡς ἐμὲ ...ἀνεψιαὶ τοσαῦται, ὥστ' εἶναι, κ.τ.λ. At first view the indicative ἦσαν with ὥστε should seem to be required here, as the consequence appears to be a reality and not a mere notion; but examination shows that the consequence depends not upon the whole preceding clause but upon one word only: τοσαῦται, upon the idea of number, multitude see Kühn. Gr. § 341. 2. 3; L. Gr. II. § 825. 3; cf. § 3.—— ἐν τῇ οἰκίᾳ, in my house; the article with the force of a possessive pronoun; see note, I. 1. 9. —— τεσσαρεσκαίδεκα; many read τεσσαρακαίδεκα, the undeclined form, which is more common in the writers contemporary with our author, but Xenophon not unfrequently uses forms which are discarded by his contemporaries. —— τοὺς ἐλευθέρους. The article here contrasts the free with slaves: fourteen of the rank of freemen (to say nothing of slaves). For the masculine gender where only personality and not sex is taken into account, see Kühn. § 241. R. 11; L. Gr. II. 430. c. Cf. τοὺς οἰκείους . . . τοσούτους, but in § 8 where female employments are spoken of, the feminine is used. Cf. also Rost's Gr. 100. Anm. 12, and Matth. II. § 436. 2. —— λαμβάνομεν ἐκ τῆς γῆς; see I. 3. 5: ὥστε μὴ λαμβάνειν, κ.τ.λ. Cf. also II. 9. 4 below. —— ὀλιγανθρωπία. Many of the citizens were put to death by the tyrants, others took refuge in Piraeus or removed to Megara, Thebes, etc. Cf. Thirlwall and Mitford, and Xen. Hellen. as above cited under ἐστασίασεν, κ.τ.λ. —— πρότερον, Lat. citius. —— περιορᾶν ἀπολλυμένους; for the construction of the participle here to complete the verbal idea, see Kühn. § 310. 4. (e); L. Gr. II. § 660. V. The use of περιορᾶν (lit., to overlook), with a Part. in the sense of *permit* or *allow*, is frequent in the best writers; see Kühn. Gr. § 311. 14, and cf. Isoc. Panegyr. —— ἐν τοιούτοις πράγμασιν, in the present state of things, his temporibus.

3.—Τί ποτέ ἐστιν, how can it be possible? or, how in the world is this? —— ὁ Κεράμων. The article here is δεικτικῶς Ceramo ille; see Kühn. § 244. 7. The same name is afterwards used, § 4, without the article. —— τρέφων, *whilst he supports*, etc.

4.—Καὶ πότερον, utrum vero, see note, I. 3. 10. —— τοὺς παρὰ σοί, κ.τ.λ.; the strict uniformity of position between the parallel members of the sentence is worthy of notice, and also the force of the words between the Art. and noun. —— ἀπὸ, through, by means of. —— εὐπορεῖν, to have plenty, in contrast with ἐν ἀπορίαις εἶναι. —— Νὴ Δί᾽ ἔφη. The particle νή retains its usual affirmative force here. Aristarchus not perceiving the bearing which Socrates gives to the words οὔκουν αἰσχρὸν, replies: It is indeed base that I am in circumstances of want; for free people are supported by me whilst only slaves by him. This passage is not then parallel with those, where after an interrogation with a negative, Νὴ Δία has the negative implied after it. In such cases the negative phrase has the force of affirmation, and the νή strengthens it. See IV. 6. 10, and cf. Sympos. V. 1: Ὁ δὲ Καλλίας ἔφη· Σὺ δὲ δή, ὦ Κριτόβουλε, εἰς τὸν περὶ τοῦ κάλλους ἀγῶνα πρὸς Σωκράτην οὐκ ἀνθίσταται; Νὴ Δί', ἔφη ὁ Σωκράτης, sc. οὐκ ἀνθίσταται. Notice also the force of the words ναὶ μὰ Δία in § 14, where see note.

5.—Ἆρ' οὖν, see note, II. 6. 1. —— ἄλφιτα, meal for making bread. The grinding was performed by women; see Fiske's Man. p. 158. ἱμάτια...χιτωνίσκοι, κ.τ.λ. The ἱμάτιον was a rectangular (generally square) piece of cloth, worn as an outer garment by both men and women, and nearly corresponding with the Roman toga. The χιτών was an under-garment, substantially like the Roman tunica. The χιτωνίσκος, tunicula, diminutive of χιτών, is attributed to men by Ammonius, χιτώνιον to women; but in Pollux VII. 55, χιτωνίσκους are also dresses of females. The χλαμύς was a coarser and shorter mantle (Pollux X. 124), worn especially by soldiers. The ἐξωμίς (fr. ὦμος), according to Pollux and Fest., a man's vest leaving the shoulders bare. Often worn by the slaves with one sleeve; see Fiske's Man. p. 208, and Smith's Dict.: *Pallium*, p. 717 sq. ——Ἔπειτα, and yet; see note, I. 2. 26. So Εἶτα in § 6, and Ἔπειτ' in § 7 indicate affected astonishment; see Kühn. § 344. 5. (e), and cf. note, I. 2. 26. — Πάντα μὲν οὖν; similar to πάνυ μὲν οὖν, see note, I. 3. 9. Here it is corrective, Those with you know none of these things, etc.? Yes, every one of them, I think, immo omnia. For the use of μὲν οὖν (μενοῦν) to express confirmation, cf. III. 8. 4; 9. 14; IV. 6. 10. See Kühn. Gr. § 316. R.; L. Gr. II. § 698. b, and 840. g, 594. Anm., and 701. e. —— ὡς ἐγᾦμαι, var. Lect.: ὡς ἐγ' ᾦμαι; ὡς ἔγωγε οἶμαι, and ὡς ἐγὼ οἶμαι.

6.—Ἀφ' ἑνός, Genit. of means, with the Prep.; see note, I. 2. 14. —— λειτουργεῖν. For an account of the service called λειτουργία, see the word in Smith's Dict. p. 577. —— τήν τε οἰκίαν πᾶσαν; the article used as possessive pronoun, see note, I. 1. 9. For the more usual position of πᾶς, see Kühn. § 246. 5. (β); for its position here, § 246. 5. (γ), and 245. 3. (b). —— Μεγαρέων. Aristoph. Acharn. 519 says: ἐσυκοφάντει Μεγαρέων τὰ χλανίσκια. —— ὠνούμενοι...ἔχουσιν, *hold* or *have by purchase*. Buttmann calls this a paraphrase for the perfect tense (completion in the present time), see 144, N. 18. —— ὥστε, so that, on condition that. For the constr. of ὥστε here with the infinitive, see Kühn. § 341. 3. (c), and L. Gr. II. § 825. c. —— ἐργάζεσθαι ἃ καλῶς ἔχει, to elaborate, make whatever may be pleasing to them (the masters). For the ellipsis, see note, II. 1. 32.

7.—Μαθεῖν...μνημονεύειν...ὑγιαίνειν τε καὶ ἰσχύειν... κτήσασθαί τε καὶ σώζειν. The beautiful change of tense, so that the Pres. is used where continued action is denoted, and the Aor. where the action is momentary or completed, should not escape notice; see also note, III. 11. 10. —— τοῖς σώμασι, Dat. of the respect in which a thing is taken, Kühn. Gr. § 284. (10). —— ὠφέλιμα ὄντα... χρήσιμα. For the neuter gender after Fem. nouns, see Kühn. Gr. § 242. 1; L. Gr. II. § 431. 2; Buttm. § 129. 5. Cf. III. 1. 7.

8.—Ἔμαθον δέ... πότερον; the verb ἔμαθον is placed before the interrogative πότερον for the sake of emphasis. Cf. III. 5. 2; III. 9. 1; IV. 2. 20, et al. See also note, III. 5. 13: ἡ πόλις ὅπως. —— ὡς οὔτε χρήσιμα ὄντα... οὔτε ποιήσουσαι, supposing that they are neither useful... nor that they themselves will ever, etc.; for ὡς with the participle, see note, II. 2. 3. —— ἐπιμεληθησόμεναι; one Ms. has ἐπιμελησόμεναι, the form of the future of this verb always used elsewhere by Xenophon, as in II. 8. 3. It is not impossible, that the form given in the text crept in from the following ὠφεληθησόμεναι, upon which see note, I. 1. 8, and C. 554. N. —— ἀργοῦντες, *when idle.*

9.—Ἀλλὰ καὶ νῦν μὲν. The idea is: but also, in the present state of things, this additional trouble exists, that, etc. Ἄλλα denotes transition and καί augmentation; together they may be rendered *moreover.* See Hoog. Partic. p. 20. I. and 21. II; for the use of the particle νῦν, to indicate result, see Kühn. L. Gr. II. § 690. 2; Klotz's Dev. II. p. 677. —— κίνδυνος μείζω... ἀπέχθειαν, κ.τ.λ. Κίνδυνος is generally followed by μή and the subjunctive or optative. For examples of the Infin. see Schneid. Anab. VI. 1. 21. —— ὁρῶν, when you see. —— αἰσθόμεναι, κ.τ.λ., when they perceive that you are pleased, etc. —— τὴν ἀπ' ἐκείνων, sc. εὐεργεσιῶν.

10.—Εἰ... τοίνυν, if now. —— θάνατον... προαιρετέον ἦν; the verbal in -τεος indicating necessity, is used without ἄν. See Kühn. Gr. § 354, R. 3; L. Gr. II. § 821. 3. So in Latin the particle in -n d u s is used, with a form of the verb e s s e in the indicative: p r e f e r e n d a e r a t m o r s; see Zumpt, L. Gr. 499, 7, and Kühn. Tusc. Quaes. I. 49, 116. p. 163. For the governing power of the verbal, see note, I. 7. 2. —— πρεπωδέστερα; some editors substitute πρεπωδέστατα, which has very little Ms. authority, and is far inferior to the comparative, given in the text. The idea is: more becoming for women (than any other art or employment). For the connection of adjectives in different degrees of comparison, see Kühn. L. Gr. II. § 591.

11.—Ἀλλὰ is used when one replies quickly and decidedly. See Kühn. Gr. § 322. 6. R. 12. It *need* not always be rendered at all in English, as here. —— ὥστε πρόσθεν μὲν... νῦν δέ, so that *whilst before yet now,* see note, I. 6. 5. —— οὐ προσιέμην, did not dare, or was averse to, unwilling, as in IV. 2. 17. —— εἰς ἔργων ἀφορμὴν, means, necessary for carrying on the work. Ἀφορμή is, in general, that from which one starts, the basis of operations. Cf. III. 5. 11; 12, 4. —— ὑπομένειν αὐτὸ ποιῆσαι, to dare to do this; i. e., δανείσασθαι εἰς ἔργων ἀφορμήν, to borrow money for, etc., whilst in the Act. Voice it means, to *lend on interest.*

12.—Ἐωνήθη. The verb ὠνέομαι is seldom used in the Aor. by good Attic writers; instead of it they use ἐπριάμην. As it forms an Aor. I. middle, the passive form takes the passive signification; (see Stuart's N. T. Gr. § 134, e. g., and Kühn. Gr. § 252. R; and besides, the Act. form of this verb is found, according to Bekker Anecd. I. 95. Cf. Kühn. L. Gr. II. § 403. 3; Rost, § 113. —— ἐργαζόμεναι μὲν ἠρίστων, ἐργασάμεναι δὲ ἐδείπνουν. They took their dinner *while at work*, but their supper *after they had finished their work.* The beauty and definiteness of the use of the tenses in Greek is unsurpassed. The ἄριστον (ἠρίστων), the meal taken near the middle of the day and hence corresponding in time with our dinner, and δεῖπνον (ἐδείπνουν), supper, the principal meal among the Greeks; see Fiske's Man. p. 204. For the force of μὲν . . . δὲ, see I. 1. 1. —— ἀντὶ ὑφορωμένων ἑαυτὰς; the verb ὑφοράω, lit., to look askance at, and hence, to view with suspicion, is contrasted with ἡδέως . . . ἑώρων. When oppressed with want, they looked with suspicion, lest one should receive more food, etc. than another; a very natural effect of want. For the use of ἑαυτάς and ἀλλήλας, see note, II. 6. 20. —— αἱ μὲν . . . ἐφίλουν (sc. αὐτόν), ὁ δὲ . . . ἠγάπα (sc. αὐτάς). Such ellipses in parallel members is frequent. So in Thucyd. I. 73: οὐ γὰρ παρὰ δικασταῖς οὔτε ἡμῶν (sc. πρὸς τούτους), οὔτε τούτων (sc. πρὸς ἡμᾶς) οἱ λόγοι ἂν γίγνοιντο. See Kühn. Gr. § 346. 2. (b), and L. Gr. II. § 852. h. Ἀγαπᾶν as distinguished from φιλεῖν, seems to designate regard and satisfaction rather than love. —— χαίρων διηγεῖτο, he related *with joy*; for the numerous adverbial relations designated by the Partic. in Greek, see Kühn. Gr. § 312. —— διηγεῖτο ταῦτα τε, καὶ ὅτι αἰτιῶνται, he related these things . . . and added, etc.; see Kühn. L. Gr. II. § 762. Anm. For the Indic. αἰτιῶνται, instead of the Opt. after the Praet. followed by ὅτι, see note, I. 1. 13. —— αὐτὸν . . . ἐσθίειν. For the Accus. with the Inf. after αἰτιᾶσθαι, see I. 1. 2.

13.—Εἶτα. See note, I. 2. 26, and § 5 above. —— τὸν τοῦ κυνὸς λόγον, the dog-fable or the fable concerning the dog, as in III. 5. 10: τὴν τῶν θεῶν κρίσιν, judgment in relation to the gods. Cyrop. VI. 3. 10: ἡμῶν λόγος, rumor concerning us; VIII. 5. 28, et al. See Kühn. L. Gr. II. § 528. A. 2; Matt. Gr. II. § 342. 1. The idea here, however.

may be: the word of the dog, i. e., which the dog spake, as in Plat. Alcib. I. p. 44: μῦθος, ὃν ἡ ἀλώπηξ πρὸς τὸν λέοντα εἶπε. —— ὄϊν. Xenophon seems to have preferred the Ionic form of this word, although the readings of the Mss. are various. —— πρὸς τὸν δεσπότην εἰπεῖν, spoke thus *with her* master. —— Θαυμαστὸν ποιεῖς, see note, I. 2. 30: ὅτι ὑϊκὸν, κ.τ.λ. —— ὃς gives a reason and is equivalent to, *in that you*, or, *because you*. See Kühn. Gr. § 334. 2; L. Gr. II. § 802. 3. —— ἡμῖν μὲν ταῖς...παρεχούσαις, who furnish, etc. For this common use of the article with the Partic., resolved as a relative and verb, see Kühn Gr. § 244. 8.

14.—Ναὶ μὰ Δία, he does indeed do this and rightly. Ναὶ μά are frequently used in Attic Greek like ναί simply, with the Accus. Cf. note, § 4. —— εἰμι ὁ...σώζων, *I am he who*, etc. See note, § 13, for the constr. of the Partic. and particle. —— Καὶ ὑμᾶς αὐτὰς, i. e., with the implied clause, ἔρια καὶ ἄρνας καὶ τυρόν, § 13, even you yourselves as well as your lambs, wool, etc.; but others prefer the ellipsis: καὶ αὐτόν, i. e., your master. Cf. upon καί ellipt., note, I. 1. 6, and 1. 3. 1. —— προφυλάττοιμι ὑμᾶς, to guard, keep, whilst προφ. ὑμῶν would be to keep guard over. —— φοβούμεναι μὴ ἀπόλησθε. By the use of the Subj. instead of the Opt. here, the certainty of the fear is indicated. Cf. Anab. I. 3. 17, and Bornem. Sympos. p. 70, and see Kühn. L. Gr. II. § 773; III. p. 486 sq. —— Οὕτω δὴ, *in this manner*, conclusive. —— ἀντὶ κυνὸς, *like a dog*, B. 147. N. 1. —— οὐδ' ὑφ' ἑνὸς. For ὑπ' οὐδενός, but more emphatic, see note, I. 6. 2.

CHAPTER VIII.

1.—Διὰ χρόνου, after a considerable (or long) time, interjecto tempore, i. e., aliquo, or, longo tempore. See Kühn. Gr. § 291. 1; L. Gr. II. § 226. p. 282. Cf. also Stallb. Plato, Hip. Maj. p. 281. A. and IV. 4. 5 below. —— Πόθεν...φαίνῃ; so Plato Protag. at the beginning: Πόθεν, ὦ Σώκρατες, φαίνει; where Stallb. compares Cic. Fragm. apud Prisc. VI. p. 706. ed. Putsch.: Quid tu? unde tandem appares, Socrate? cf. Stallb. in h. l. —— ὑπὸ μὲν τὴν κατάλυσιν τοῦ πολέμου; Latin, sub exitum belli; i. e., without doubt, at the time of the peace between the Spartans and Athenians, made by Theramenes at the end of the Peloponnesian war, in consequence of which the latter lost all of their possessions out of Attica. Plut. Lys. 14; Thirlwall's Greece I. p. 490 sq. ch. 30, and Mitford's Hist. ch. 20. Sec. V. —— ἐκ τῆς ἀποδημίας, sc. ἐφαινόμην. —— αὐτόθεν, here of place = ἐξ αὐτοῦ τοῦ τόπου, i. e., from the city itself. In § 3 below, and III. 6. 12, it has reference to time, illico, on the spot, immediately. Cf. Stallb. Plat. Sympos. 213. A. —— ἀφῃρέθημεν τὰ . . . κτήματα. The verb is here in the plural as the subject includes both himself and fellow-citizens. —— ἐν τῇ ὑπερορίᾳ, i. e., in the country beyond the borders of Attica. Ὑπερόριος from ὑπέρ and ὅρος, beyond, is opposed to ἔγγαιος (ἐν and γῆ), within the borders. See Bornem. Symp. IV. 31. —— ἐπιδημήσας, remaining at home. —— ἄλλως τε καί. See note, I. 2. 59. —— δοκεῖ δέ μοι . . . ἔχοντα. See note, I. 1. 9: ἃ ἔξεστιν, κ.τ.λ. —— ἐφ' ὅτῳ ἂν δανειζοίμην, upon which as surety, I might, etc. See Kühn. L. Gr. II. § 839.

2.—Καί, see note, I. 3. 10. —— ἱκανὸν, (lit., sufficient) *strong enough.* —— μισθοῦ τὰ ἐπιτήδεια ἐργάζεσθαι, to earn daily food. Μισθοῦ . . . ἐργάζεσθαι means, to labor for a reward or pay, but here with the accusative, to earn, or to obtain as the reward of labor. —— καὶ μήν, atqui; see Hoogev. Gr. Partik. p. 271. VIII. and cf. note, II. 6. 27. —— τῶν τοῦ σώματος ἔργων, *for bodily labor.* The contrast denoted by τοῦ σώματος, between the labor that he was now engaged in, and that which Socrates was about to propose, is worthy of notice.

3.—Αὐτόθεν, illico e vestigio, *forthwith;* cf. § 1. —— τῷ . . . τῷ δεομένῳ; after the pronoun τὶς the article is often inserted to designate more particularly that which is indefinitely referred to by τὶς. —— τῷ δεομένῳ τοῦ συνεπιμελησομένου, who wants an assistant in the management of his business; see note, II. 1. 5. —— ἔργων τε ἐπιστατοῦντα; ἐπιστατεῖν is generally followed by the dative. See Kühn. L. Gr. § 538. a. and Anm. 2. ε., and Matth. II. § 359 and 402.

4.—Χαλεπῶς, with difficulty, unwillingly, aegre. —— καὶ μὴν οἵ γε, but surely, atqui certe; cf. note, I. 4. 12; so in § 5.

5.—Ὅλως, *in short,* or, in a word, Lat. denique. —— μήν, adversative here, *but;* see Kühn. Gr. § 316; L. Gr. II. § 696, and Wolf, Demosth. Lept. p. 220. —— τὸ ὑπαίτιον εἶναί τινι οὐ πάνυ προσίεμαι, the being responsible to any one, is not at all pleasing to me, or I am wholly averse to, etc. —— μὴ ἀγνώμονι, *who is not severe*— οἷς, *in respect to those things in which,* etc. For the ellipsis, see C. 523. —— ἀνέγκλητον διαγίνεσθαι; cf. note, I. 6. 2: ἀνυπόδητος, κ.τ.λ.

6.—Ὑπομένειν, *to undertake,* antith. to φυλάττεσθαι, to avoid, to shun. —— ὅ τι δ' ἂν πράττῃς τούτων, κ.τ.λ. For the plural τούτων after ὅ τι in the singular, see note, I. 2. 62. Some Mss. however have τούτου, and some τούτῳ. —— εὑρεῖν; for the use of the aorist here, see note and *references*, I. 2. 10: νομίζοντος, κ.τ.λ. —— ῥᾷστα δὲ καὶ; καί is not connected with ῥᾷστα, but corresponds to καὶ ... διαρκέστατα: both live without exposure to danger and with a most abundant supply for old age.

CHAPTER IX.

1.—Ἀκούσαντα ὡς, *heard from C., how*, etc. Verbs of *hearing*, etc., are frequently followed by the Gen. of the person from whom any thing is heard, and the Acc. of the thing heard, or instead of it an accessory clause, as here. —— Κρίτωνος; see note, I. 2. 48. —— χαλεπὸν ὁ βίος. In respect to the evils to which the wealthy were subject at Athens, see Thirlwall's Hist. I. p. 508 sq. ch. xxxii.; Mitford, ch. xxi. sec. 1; also the word *sycophantes* in Smith's Dictionary. —— ἀργύριον τελέσαι ἢ πράγματα ἔχειν, to pay money than to have business, trouble. Πράγματα, the trouble made by those who brought unjust accusations, συκοφάνται.

2.—Κύνας δὲ τρέφεις ... δέ, is used elliptically, see note, I. 3. 13: τοὺς δὲ καλ. —— ἀπὸ τῶν προβάτων ἀπερύκωσι, with the preposition of which the verb is compounded repeated, but a little after we find σου ἀπερύκειν without a repetition of the preposition. Cf. II. 6. 31: ἐνεῖναι ἔν τινι, III. 5. 21: ἐφ' οἷς ἐφεστᾶσι, etc. Such repetitions are not uncommon both in Greek and Latin. —— φοβοίμην, ὅπως μὴ ... τράποιτο; this is a more unusual construction after verbs denoting fear, for the simple μή. So in Plat. Euthyphr. p. 4. E; Phaed. p. 84. B; Demosth. Phil. III. p. 130. 75. In such cases verbs of fearing seem to imitate those which indicate care, since one who fears lest (μή τι γένηται) a thing may be done, etc., may easily be considered as taking thought, in what manner it may be prevented; see Kühn. L. Gr. II. § 779. note 4.

3.—Οἵῳ σοὶ ἀνδρὶ, i. e., τοιούτῳ ἀνδρὶ, οἷος σὺ εἶ; for this attraction of the relative οἷος, see Kühn. Gr. § 332. 7; L. Gr. II. § 788; Matth. II. 478. n. 2; Rost, § 99. 11. Cf. III. 8. 2. —— χαριζόμενον ... ἢ ἀπεχθόμενον, *gratifying ... than being hated by him.* —— τῶν τοιούτων ἀνδρῶν; we may supply τινές or better consider these genitives as dependent upon the οἵ following. —— φιλοτιμηθεῖεν, consider themselves as honored, or, aspire to.

4.—Ἐκ τούτων, after these conversations. —— οἷος...κερδαίνειν...λαμβάνειν; see note, I. 4. 6: οἵους τέμνειν. —— φιλόχρηστός τε καὶ εὐφυέστερος ὤν; the comparative is placed here after the positive because the one virtue is represented in an absolute, and the other in a comparative manner, referring to a suppressed clause: Archedemus was a man who loved honesty, and of too noble a nature, or of a nature more noble than, to make gain by means of the sycophants; with special reference, doubtless, to taking bribes in order not to prevent them from obtaining the results of their unjust accusations. It is by no means *necessary* that παρά should be used here instead of ἀπό if we adopt this explanation. See examples of the use of ἀπό in Kühn. Gr. and the Lex. —— ὁπότε συγκομίζοι... ὁπότε θύοι; see note, I. 2. 57. —— ἀφελὼν [ἄν] ἔδωκε. The particle ἄν is here added by Kühner. For when the secondary enunciation is introduced by ὁπότε, ὅτι, and similar particles with the optative denoting indefinite frequency of action, in the primary enunciation, the Imperf. (or the Pluperf. used as Imperf.), the iterative Aor. in -σκον, or the Imperf. or Aor. with ἄν is generally found. Cf. I. 2. 57; 4. 9; III. 8. 9, 11; Anab. I. 5. 7; Cyrop. VII. 1. 10 (with ἄν), et saep. It is true that the ἄν might easily be absorbed in the -ών of ἀφελών; but is it not more probable that this is a deviation from strict propriety of speech, such as occurs in every writer in every language? —— ἐκάλει; cf. note, II. 3. 11: ὁπότε θύοι, κ.τ.λ.

5.—Ἀποστροφήν οἱ, a place of refuge for him. —— καὶ εὐθὺς ...ἀνευρήκει, and immediately... he *had found*. The Pluperf. denoting celerity. He had no sooner done this (περιεῖπεν) than he found, etc. Cf. Hellen. VII. 2. 9, and Cyrop. I. 4. 5. —— περιεῖπεν (from περί and ἕπω, *to be busy around*), signif. here with μάλα, diligently served (him, αὐτόν). —— προσεκαλέσατο εἰς δίκην δημοσίαν; for the use of προσκαλεῖσθαι in summoning to court (πρόσκλησις, the summons), see Meier and Schömann, Attische Process, IV. 2. p. 576. —— αὐτὸν ἔδει κριθῆναι, ὅ τι δεῖ παθεῖν ἢ ἀποτίσαι. So in Sympos. V. 8: ἵνα ὡς τάχιστα εἰδῶ, ὅ τι με χρὴ παθεῖν ἢ ἀποτίσαι. The verb παθεῖν means, to suffer, sc. corporal punishment; and ἀποτίσαι, to pay, as a fine. These words are common in reference to the penalty claimed or imposed by the Athenian accusers or judges. Cf. Dem. contr. Mid. 523. 2, et saep., and Meier and Schömann, IV. 13. p. 739 sq.

6.—Ὁ δέ, συνειδὼς αὑτῷ πολλὰ, κ.τ.λ., but he being conscious to himself of many and evil deeds; cf. note, I. 2. 24. —— ἀπαλλαγῆναι, "*to be let off by*," so below, οὐκ ἀπαλλάττετο, he did not "let him off." —— καὶ αὐτῷ, sc. Archedemus.

7.—Ἤδη τότε; for the more usual τότε ἤδη, then indeed, tum vero. So in IV. 8. 1, and Plato, de Legg. VI. 20. p. 326. Bornemann, Sympos. VIII. 40. p. 216, compares ἤδη νῦν, δὴ νῦν; cf. note, II. 5. 14.

8.—Καὶ οὐχ ὅτι μόνος, i. e., καὶ οὐ λέγω, ὅτι μόνος ὁ Κρ., more emphatic than καὶ οὐ μόνον ὁ Κρ. ἀλλὰ καί, κ.τ.λ.; see note, I. 6. 11; Plat. Sympos. p. 179. B., and Stallb. and Ast's notes. The adjective μόνος is here put for the adverb μόνον. So the adjective is somewhat frequently constructed in Greek. See Kühn. Gr. § 264. 3, and R. 7; L. Gr. II. § 685. —— εἰ δέ...ὀνειδίζοι; see note, I. 2. 57.

CHAPTER X.

1.—Ἄν τίς σοι; one Ms. ἄν τίς σε. But σοι should undoubtedly be retained and connected with ἀποδρᾷ. Kühner calls it a Dat. *incommodi.* So just below in § 2: τίς σοι κάμνῃ, and in Oecon. II. 14: προθύμως γε, ὦ Σώκρατες, ἀποφεύγειν μοι πειρᾷ. See Kühn. Gr. § 284. (7). R. 3; L. Gr. II. § 579. 3, and Matth. II. § 412. 9. —— ὅπως ἀνακομίσῃ; see note, I. 2. 37.

2.—Καὶ ἄλλους γε. In answers καί is frequently used, denoting a continuation of the preceding interrogation, taken as an affirmation, i. e., it assents to what has been asked, and adds something else to it, which is here made emphatic by γέ. Cf. III. 8. 6; IV. 2. 12; Hieron. 1. 17; Symp. II. 5. —— παρακαλῶ, κ.τ.λ., I call in aid, offering a reward for his recovery. —— τούτου, sc. τινὸς τῶν οἰκετῶν. —— Τί γάρ; see note, II. 6. 2. —— πολὺ τῶν οἰκετῶν χρησιμώτερος ὤν. For the separation, Hyperbaton, of πολύ from χρησιμώτερος here, see Kühn. Gr. § 348. 9, and L. Gr. II. § 865. 1, and cf. Cyrop. VI. 4. 8: ἥξειν αὐτῷ σὲ πολὺ Ἀράσπου ἄνδρα καὶ πιστότερον καὶ ἀμείνονα. Symp. I. 4; οἶμαι οὖν πολὺ ἂν τὴν κατασκευήν μοι λαμπροτέραν φανῆναι. —— κινδυνεύει...ἀπολέσθαι, see note, I. 2. 10.

3.—Καὶ μὴν οἶσθά γε; see note, I. 4. 12. —— παράμονον, a rare form for παραμόνιμον, (see II. 4. 6; III. 11. 11,) which some editors would read here, but without any Ms. authority. Xenophon, as has been before said, often mingled poetic and dialectic forms and words in his writings: "The Attic bee," says Hemsterhuse, did not refuse to cull poetic and Doric words and phrases which are not found in other Attic Greek, if they would add to the beauty or force of his writings. Cf. note, II. 7. 13: ὄϊν. —— καὶ...τὸ κελευόμενον ἱκανὸν ποιεῖν; these words are repeated so as to make the climax more conspicuous; able to perform the duties enjoined, yea, not only able to perform that which is prescribed, but who of his own will, without any command, is able to be useful. A word or clause is often repeated for the sake of perspicuity · cf. Cyrop. V. 2. 31: ἀσφαλεστέραν οὐδὲ μίαν πορείαν ἡμῖν τῆς πρὸς αὐτὴν Βαβυλῶνα πορείας ἰέναι.

4.—Μέντ. *forsooth*, ironically; see Hartung, Gr. Partik. p. 394; Kühn. L. Gr. II § 698. a. —— διὰ τὰ πράγματα, in the present state of things.

5.—Τοῦ αὐτὸν ἐλθεῖν. We should expect αὐτῷ, but the usual attraction is neglected; see Kühn. Gr. § 307. 2, and R. 2; L. Gr. II. § 648. —— ἐκείνῳ μεῖζον ἀγαθὸν... ἢ σοί, a greater favor to him... than to you. —— τὸ πραχθῆναι ταῦτα, i. e., that he should be received as a friend by you.

6.—Οὕτω δή, see note, II. 7. 14. —— καὶ οὐ πολὺ τελέσας, non magnis sumptibus, at no great expense. —— ὃς ἔργον εἶχε, who made it his work, to see, in what he could, etc.; cf. Cyrop. VIII. 4. 6: ἔργον ἔχειν δεόμενον τούτου κοινωνεῖν τοὺς παρόντας. So ἔργον ποιεῖσθαι as in Plat. Phaedr. p. 232. A. where cf. Stallb. and Heindorf.; also Hieron. IX. 10: πολλοὺς ἂν καὶ τοῦτο ἐξορμήσειεν ἔργον ποιεῖσθαι τὸ σκοπεῖν τι ἀγαθόν.

BOOK III.

CHAPTER I.

1.—Ὅτι; for the ellipsis with ὅτι, sc. ἵνα δῆλον ᾖ, (ὅτι), κ.τ.λ., or something of the kind, see Hoogev. Gr. Partik. p. 391, 2. III. —— τῶν καλῶν, here means public office, or honors. —— ἐπιμελεῖς ὧν ὀρέγοιντο ποιῶν, by making them careful in reference to those things which they desire. The Opt. ὀρέγ. is used to designate indefinite frequency; see Kühn. Gr. § 333. 4; L. Gr. II. § 797. 2. Cf. IV. 4. 1: ἃ οἱ νόμοι προστάττοιεν πειθόμενος; 7. 1: ὅ τι μὲν αὐτὸς εἰδείη, πάντων προθυμότατα ἐδίδασκεν, ὅτου δὲ αὐτὸς ἀπειρότερος εἴη, πρὸς τοὺς ἐπισταμένους ἦγεν αὐτούς. —— Διονυσόδωρον. Dionysodorus first professed to be a teacher of military tactics at Athens, and afterwards joined himself to the Sophists. He was brother of Euthydemus. His vanity and ignorance are made conspicuous here, as well as in the Euthydemus of Plato, which see, with Stallbaum's Prelim. Dissertation. —— ἀκούσας.. ἥκειν; for the construction of ἀκούειν with the Infin. see Kühn. Gr. § 311. 1; L. Gr. II. § 657. A. 2. Cf. also III. 5. 9; IV. 2. 4. —— ἐπαγγελλόμενον... διδάξειν; see note, I. 2. 10: νομίζοντας, κ.τ.λ. —— ᾔσθάνετο; the Lat. would require the Subj. mode.

2.—Μέντοι, confirmatory, Lat. vero, or, profecto; see note, I. 3. 10. —— ἐξὸν. For this Accus. Abs., see Kühn. Gr. § 312. 5; B. 145. R. 10. (2); I. 6. 5. note.

3.—Τά... ἀγαθά, is the subject Accus. before γίγνεσθαι and μηγάλα, the predicate is also to be supplied with τὰ κακὰ. —— κατορθ. αὐτοῦ, Gen. Abs. as also διαμαρτ.

4.—Προσέπαιζεν αὐτῷ λέγων; the imperfect tense is used to denote a repetition of the action, and hence the present participle is appropriately used. The verb προσπαίζειν is sometimes, as here, construed with the dative. See Plat. Euthyd. p. 278. B; Legg. VI. 303, and sometimes with the Acc. as Menex. p. 235. C. —— δοκεῖ... φαίνεσθαι; see note, I. 4. 6. —— Ὅμηρος... ἔφη: i. e., Il. III. 169, 70:

Καλὸν δ' οὕτω ἐγὼν οὔπω ἴδον ὀφθαλμοῖσι,
Οὐδ' οὕτω γεραρόν· βασιλῆϊ γὰρ ἀνδρὶ ἔοικεν.

Cf. these with the preceding verses in h. l. —— στρατηγεῖν μαθὼν; cf. just before μεμαθηκὼς ἧκε. The Aor. Part. denotes simply the fact, that he had learned something, but the Perf. that he not only had learned, but also retained something in mind; see Kühn. Gr. § 255. 2, and 256. 2 sq., and cf. note III. 7. 7. The infinitives are used in a similar way in IV. 2. 5: φυλαττόμενος οὐ μόνον τὸ μαθεῖν τι παρὰ τῶν ἰατρῶν, ἀλλὰ καὶ τὸ δόξαι μεμαθηκέναι τὴν τέχνην ταύτην. —— διατελεῖ στρατηγὸς ὤν, *will always be* or *ceases not to be;* see Kühn. Gr. § 311. 4. (l).

5.—Ἵνα καὶ; sc. ἡμεῖς, supplied from the clause: ἐὰν ἡμῶν τις. —— λοχαγῇ σοι; the dative σοί, here may be rendered: *to you* or *under your command.* See Kühn. Gr. § 284. 3; L. Gr. II. § 581; Matt. II. § 389. —— ἤρξατό σε διδάσκειν; for the distinction between ἄρχεσθαι with the Inf. and Part. see Kühn. Gr. § 311. 16; L. Gr. II. § 660. A. 2. —— Καὶ ὅς; see note, I. 4. 2. —— τὰ... τακτικὰ; every thing relating to the order and arrangement of an army in battle, on marches, etc.

6.—Ἀλλὰ μήν, atqui, but, indeed; these particles are used in the assumption of a conclusion from what has preceded. See Kühn L. Gr. II. § 696, d. and cf. III. 8. 3; Apollon. Alex. de Conj. in Bekker, Anecd. II. p. 518, and 839, where this example is quoted: εἰ ἡμέρα ἐστί, φῶς ἐστιν·

ἀλλὰ μὴν ἡμέρα ἐστί· φῶς ἄρα ἐστίν. —— τοῦτό γε. The particle γέ here gives emphasis to τοῦτο. —— πολλοστὸν μέρος, a very small part. Πολλοστός is literally one of many, one of the common sort; and hence generally: very small, trivial. So in IV. 6. 7. Cf. also Cyrop. I. 6. 14, where μικρόν is used with the same meaning: ὡς δέ μοι καταφανὲς ἐποίησας, ὅτι μικρόν τι μέρος εἴη στρατηγίας τὰ τακτικά. —— καὶ γάρ; see note, II. 1. 3. —— παρασκευαστικὸν τῶν εἰς τὸν πόλεμον...ποριστικὸν τῶν ἐπιτηδείων; for the Gen. with verbal adjectives in -ικος denoting fitness, etc., see note and references, I. 1. 7; Kühn. L. Gr. II. § 530, hh; and cf. I. 1. 7; IV. 1. 4. In IV. 1. 3: ἐπιθετικῶν τοῖς θηρίοις, we find the dative, since the dative follows the verb ἐπιτίθεσθαι. —— μηχανικόν, in inveniendo solers, of a ready invention, skilful in devising expedients. Those who, according to IV. 7. 1, are αὐτάρκεις ἐν ταῖς προσηκούσαις πράξεσιν. —— ἐργαστικόν, quick or ready in execution. —— καὶ φυλακτικόν τε καὶ κλέπτην. So in III. 4. 9: φυλακτικοὺς τῶν ὄντων, i. e., those who are careful to keep what they have. Hence φυλακτικός is contrasted here with κλέπτῃ, a thief. —— προετικὸν καὶ ἅρπαγα, *giving lavishly and rapacious.* —— ἀσφαλῆ καὶ ἐπιθετικόν, himself safe and ready to attack another. Cf. Heindorf's Plat. Soph. p. 231 A, and IV. 6. 15.

7.—Κέραμος, tiles. So κέραμος, λίθος, πλίνθος, etc. are frequently used in the sing. for the plur. (collective). See Kühn. Gr. § 243. 1; L. Gr. II. § 407. 2. —— ἐρριμένα; the neut. plur. is somewhat frequent, after several substantives of different genders, when the substantives denote inanimate things; see S. 157. 2. (a); B. 129. N. 11; Kühn. Gr. § 242. 1 · L. Gr. II. § 304; Matth. II. § 304. Cf. III. 7. 5: αἰδῶ δὲ καὶ φόβον... οὐχ ὁρᾷς ἔμφυτά τε ἀνθρώποις ὄντα καὶ πολλῷ μᾶλλον ἐν τοῖς ὄχλοις ἢ ἐν ταῖς ἰδίαις ὁμιλίαις παριστάμενα; —— κάτω... ἐπιπολῆς, *below... above*, antithetical, and together contrasted with ἐν μέσῳ. —— συντίθεται, in the singular as agreeing with the nearest substantive, the *neuter* plural, τὰ ξύλα; see Kühn. Gr. § 242. R. 1. (b), and § 241. 4; L. Gr. II. 433. 2.

8.—Πάνυ... ὅμοιον... εἴρηκας, *you have made a very good comparison.* —— Τούς τε πρώτους ἀρίστους δεῖ τάττειν. This passage seems, at first, to be in direct opposition to the general principle, that the subject has the article and the predicate not; and we should naturally expect: πρώτους τοὺς ἀρίστους. But when it is compared with Cyrop. VII. 5. 5: ἀνάγκη τοὺς πρώτους ἀρίστους εἶναι καὶ τοὺς τελευταίους ... τετάχθαι, it seems quite certain, that τοὺς πρώτους is subject, and ἀρίστους predicate: *it is necessary to form the front and the rear of the best.* Cf. also Hom. Il. IV. 297 sq., and III. 14. 6 below: παρασκευάζεσθαι, κ.τ.λ.

See Kühn. L. Gr. II. § 494. —— ὑπὸ μὲν τῶν ... ὑπὸ δὲ αὖ τῶν, for ὑπὸ τῶν μὲν ... ὑπὸ τῶν δὲ αὖ. This position of μέν is however very frequent. See Stallb. Plat. Phaedr. p. 263. B. In respect to αὖ, cf. I. 2 12. and note.

8.—Εἰ ἐδίδαξεν; understand καλῶς ἔχει, or something of the kind, as the apodosis. Cf. III. 9. 11, and see Kühn. L. Gr. II. § 823. 3. c.; Matth. II. § 617. a. Ellipsis of the apodosis after εἰ μὲν or εἰ δὲ μή is found in Homer and is quite frequent in Attic prose writers. A corresponding usage can hardly be found in Latin prose. —— ὧν ἔμαθες, i. e., τούτων ἃ ἔμαθες. —— κίβδηλον, prob. from κίβδη, dross; and hence meaning, *spurious, bad.* —— ὥστε ... ἂν ... δέοι. The particle ἂν with the Opt. here indicates that this is a conditional expectation or supposition; see Kühn. Gr. § 341. 4; B. 134. 54; L. Gr. II. § 827. 1. —— αὐτοὺς ... ἡμᾶς, *we ourselves*, emphatic here.

10.—Τί οὖν οὐ σκοποῦμεν, a more forcible and animated expression for σκοπῶμεν οὖν. Cf. Plat. Lysid. p. 211. D: Τί οὖν, ἦ δ' ὅς, οὐκ ἐρωτᾷς; for ἐρώτα οὖν, and Prot. p. 310. E: τί οὐ βαδίζομεν; "come let us go," and Stallbaum's note. The Aor. is used with still more emphasis; see Kühn. Gr. § 256. 4. (e), and L. Gr. II. § 443. 3; cf. note, III. 11. 15: Τί οὖν οὐ σύ μοι ... ἐγένου συνθηρατὴς τῶν φίλων; IV. 6. 14. The Latins use quin with the Indic. Pres. in the same way; quin igitur consideramus, for illud consideremus. —— αὐτῶν; for the constr. see Kühn. Gr. § 271. 2. —— Τί δὲ τοὺς κινδυνεύειν μέλλοντας; sc. εἰ τάττειν δέοι, how shall it be, if we wish to arrange those, etc. —— προτακτέον, the constr. of the verbal Adj. in -τεος, see in Kühn. Gr. 284. 3. (12). —— Οὗτοι γοῦν; see note, I. 6. 2.

11.—Ὅποι καὶ ὅπως, *whither*, and *how*, quo loco quaque ratione, or, with what design and in what manner; for the idea, cf. Cyrop. I. 6. 43. —— καὶ μὴν ... γέ; see note, I. 4. 12. —— οὔτε ἄγειν, the Vulg. reading οὔτε λέγειν. —— αἰσχυνεῖται; upon the constr. of αἰσχύνεσθαι, see Kühn. Gr § 311. 14; L. Gr. II. § 659. Anm. —— σε ἀποπέμψασθαι, *to send you from him.* Cf. Cyrop. I. 3. 18: θάρρει, ὡς ὅ γε σὸς πατὴρ οὔτ' ἄλλον οὐδένα οὔτ' ἐμὲ διδάξας πλεονεκτεῖν ἀποπέμψεται, and see on the use of the Mid. Voice, Kühn. Gr. § 250. (d); L. Gr. II. § 396. γ.

CHAPTER II.

1.—Ἐντυχὼν ... στρατηγεῖν ᾑρημένῳ τῳ. For the Dat. see Kühn. Gr. § 284. 2, and for the Infin. (chosen to command, or, to be commander), c. I. 7. 3, and III. 3. 1. The στρατηγοί, generals, in Attica were ten, chosen from each of the ten tribes, who held the command in regular rotation one day each; see Fiske's Man. p. 196.——Ὅμηρον, Il. II. 243, et al.——ἆρα, is it not? see II. 6. 1.——γέ added to an interrog. qualifies the whole phrase and gives it emphasis; cf. § 2; and III. 8. 8, and see Kühn. L. Gr. II. § 703, 2.

2.—Ἦ, aut.——Ἀμφότερον, κ.τ.λ., Il. III. 179. Alexander the Great is said to have had an especial admiration of this verse of Homer. ——αἰχμητής τε, κ.τ.λ. Τε here corresponds with καί before βασιλεύς, *both ... and.*

3.—Καὶ ... δὲ; see note, I. 1. 3.

4.—Τίς εἴη. The simple for the compound pronoun: ἥτις εἴη. See note, I. 1. 1.——περιῄρει, κατέλειπε, used in contrast: *took away, left.*——ὧν ἂν ἡγῆται, those of whom one may be leader, where we might expect ὧν ἡγοῖτο; see note, I. 2. 2, and B. 139. m. 45 and 67.

CHAPTER III.

1.—Καὶ ... δέ; see note, I. 1. 3.——ἱππαρχεῖν ... ᾑρημένῳ; see I. 7. 3, and III. 2. 1. The ἵππαρχοι, "prefects of the horse," at Athens, were two. They had subordinate officers of the cavalry under them, but were themselves subject to the ten στρατηγοί; see Fiske's Man. p. 196.——Ἔχοις ἄν, can you?——οὐ γὰρ δή, *for surely not;* see Kühn. Gr. § 315. 2; L. Gr. II. § 692, and cf. I. 4. 9, and III. 11. 7.——τοῦ πρῶτος ... ἐλαύνειν, for the sake of riding as first of the horsemen. The preposition ἕνεκα is to be supplied with τοῦ from the preceding clause: ὅτου ἕνεκα. So just below with τοῦ γνωσθῆναί; and very often in responses the preposition is to be supplied from the interrogation. Symp. V. 5: Οἶσθα οὖν, ἔφη, ὀφθαλμῶν τίνος ἕνεκα δεόμεθα; Δῆλον, ἔφη, ὅτι τοῦ ὁρᾶν. See Kühn. Gr. § 300. 5. (c), and L. Gr. II. § 625. 5, where many examples are given. For πρῶτος in the Nom. with the Inf., by attraction, see note, I. 2. 3: τῷ φαν. εἶναι.——γοῦν; see note, I. 6. 2. Ἀλλὰ μὴν ... γε; see note, I. 1. 6.

2.—Ἀλλ' ἆρά; for which perhaps ἀλλ' ἄρα should be read, as in Paris Ms. D: we find ἂν ἄρα, *but perhaps*, or, *perhaps then.* See note, III. 11. 4, and cf. IV. 2. 22. It may however be rendered as it is now pointed: *is it indeed because—?* Seiffert: immone propterea.——οἴει...βέλτιον ἂν ποιήσειας παραδοῦναι. The particle ἂν in fact qualifies the infinitive παραδοῦναι, but is placed after βέλτιον, since that word is emphatic; see Kühn. Gr. § 261. 2; L. Gr. II. § 457. This is more evident, if instead of the infinitive, the finite verb is used: οἴει, ὅτι, εἰ τὸ ἱππικὸν βέλτιον ποιήσειας, τῇ πόλει παραδοίης ἄν.——γενέσθαι; with this Infin. ἄν is to be supplied from the preceding clause; see I. 3. 15.——Ἡ δὲ ἀρχή που, the authority, prefecture is, *if I mistake not,* ni fallor, or, opinor. Cf. I. 2. 32; III. 5. 15, et al.——ἐφ' ἧς ᾕρησαι. We should expect a Dat. or even an Acc. in preference to this Gen. with ἐπί, but see examples of similar construction in Kühn. Gr. § 296. (1), and L. Gr. II. § 611.——ἀμβατῶν, of riders, from ἀναβαίνειν. The form ἀμβάτης is used almost promiscuously with ἀναβάτης, by Xenophon in his work De re Eques. and the Mss. vary much in regard to their use; see III. 12; XII. 8; V. 7; III. 9; VI. 6, and various passages in that Treatise.——γὰρ οὖν; the ellipsis here, for which γάρ introduces a proof, is: ὀρθῶς λέγεις; for, etc.; οὖν expresses confirmation: *surely;* see Kühn. § 324. R. 6, and L. Gr. II. § 706. 2. Cf. IV. 6. 14.

3.—Καὶ ὅς; see note, I. 4. 2.——τοῦτο μὲν...οὐκ ἐμὸν οἶμαι τὸ ἔργον εἶναι. The order here is: τοῦτο τὸ ἔργον οὐκ ἐμὸν εἶναι; and ἐμὸν εἶναι form the predicate. If ἐμόν had belonged to ἔργον it would have been placed thus: τὸ ἐμὸν ἔργον.——ἰδίᾳ ἕκαστον, each one by himself.

4.—Παρέχωνταί σοι, present to you as general, ἱππάρχῳ, *their horses,* i. e., *exhibit them,* Mid. voice.——εἰς τὸ δυνατὸν = in quantum potero.

5.—Ἀναβατικωτέρους ἐπὶ τοὺς ἵππους, more ready, expert in mounting their horses.——γοῦν; cf. with οὖν in § 2 above, and see note, I. 6. 2.

6.—Ἐπαγαγεῖν; sc. τοὺς ἵππους.——ἄμμον, *race course* = ἀμμόδρομος, so called because made upon the sand.——οἱ πολέμιοι γίγνονται, where the enemy make their appearance (adveniunt). Cf. Anab. IV. 3. 29: ὅς ἂν πρῶτος ἐν τῷ πέραν γένηται.——βέλτιον, *better,* sc. is it to do this.

7.—Τοῦ βάλλειν ὡς πλείστους ἀπό, κ.τ.λ., *to throw* as many as possible from their horses. This seems to me the plain meaning of βάλλειν here, followed as it is by ἀπό. —— Θήγειν . . . ἐξοργίζειν . . . ποιεῖν; these infinitives all depend upon διανενόησαι. —— Εἰ δὲ μή, *if I have not* hitherto, etc.

8.—Πῶς . . . μάλιστα, *in what way* could one *best*, etc. —— προτρέψαιτο; for this use of the Mid. Voice, see note, I. 2. 64.

9.—Ἐκεῖνο μὲν. There is no δέ antithetical to this μέν, but the construction changes at the beginning of § 10. —— δήπου, *I suppose;* see note, III. 3. 2: πού.

10.—Βέλτιστος ὢν . . . δῆλος ὦ; see note, II. 6. 7: δῆλον εἶναι . . . εὐεργετήσοντα; here βέλτιστος has the emphatic place in the clause. —— εἰς τὸ πείθεσθαι, κ.τ.λ., for procuring their obedience to me. —— εἴ σοι δέοι διδάσκειν, for the more frequent construction: εἴ σε δέοι διδάσκειν. Cf. Oecon. VII. 20; VIII. 9, and Anab. III. 4. 35, and see Kühn. Gr. § 307. R. 3, and L. Gr. II. § 551. A. 5.

11.—Πρὸς τοῖς ἄλλοις . . . δεῖν καὶ, κ.τ.λ., in addition to other things . . . must take care also, etc. —— Σὺ δ' ᾤου; have you *indeed* supposed; as in II. 6. 14; see note, I. 3. 13: τοὺς δὲ καλούς; —— ὅσα τε νόμῳ, κ.τ.λ. This clause is contrasted with the following καὶ εἴ τι ἄλλο καλὸν μανθάνει τις μάθημα, by the particles τε . . . καί. Νόμῳ, in accordance with the customs and prescriptions of the State, and τι ἄλλο καλὸν . . . μάθημα, i. e., arts which men learn of their own accord. —— ζῆν, here κατ' ἐξοχήν, for life adjusted according to the institutions and laws of the State, in opposition to rustic and uncultivated life. Cf. Isocr. Panegyr. c. 5: εὑρήσομεν γὰρ αὐτὴν (τὴν πόλιν) οὐ μόνων τῶν πρὸς τὸν πόλεμον κινδύνων, ἀλλὰ καὶ τῆς ἄλλης κατασκευῆς, ἐν ᾗ κατοικοῦμεν καὶ μεθ' ἧς πολιτευόμεθα καὶ δι' ἣν ζῆν δυνάμεθα, σχεδὸν ἁπάσης αἰτίαν οὖσαν. —— διὰ λόγου. In accordance with this, is the signification of ἑρμηνείαν in IV. 3. 12: ἑρμηνείαν—, δι' ἧς πάντων τῶν ἀγαθῶν μεταδίδομέν τε ἀλλήλοις διδάσκοντες καὶ κοινωνοῦμεν καὶ νόμους τιθέμεθα καὶ πολιτευόμεθα. For the omission of the article, see note, I. 1. 9: ἐπὶ ζεῦγος, κ.τ.λ.; and cf. I. 2. 24: κάλλος.

12.—Ἢ τόδε οὐκ ἐντεθύμησαι, κ.τ.λ. The general idea contained in this and the following sections is: You perceive that the Athenians, who excel other nations in many things, excel in nothing so much as in the love of honor, which leads them to noble exertions. If then you would make your soldiers better, you must foster this principle by bestowing honor and praise upon them when they do well. —— ὅταν γε χορὸς εἷς ἐκ τῆσδε τῆς πόλεως, when one chorus is made up from this whole State, i. e., the best performers among all the Athenians are chosen. The pronoun ὅδε, ἥδε, τόδε, not only calls the attention to what follows (see note, I. 2. 3), but also designates that which lies before the eyes of the speaker and to which he may be supposed to point, hence called δεικτικῶς. See Kühn. Gr. § 303. R. 1. —— ὁ εἰς Δῆλον πεμπόμενος. In reference to the Delia or expeditions to Delos and festivals held there, to which allusion is here made, see Smith's Dict. of Gr. and Rom. Antiquities, p. 345, and cf. IV. 8. 2. —— εὐανδρία... ὁμοία, *such a store of goodly men.* In reference to the Panathenaea to which allusion is supposed to be made here, and the selection of the handsomest men and boys to take part in the ceremonies of the festival, see the word in Smith's Dict.; Potter's Ant. I. 452, and Kühn. and Hickie in h. l.

13.—Εὐφωνίᾳ, *sweetness of voice,* i. e., in singing. The Dat. indicates that wherein one thing excels or surpasses another, see B. 133. 4. (d). —— φιλοτιμίᾳ... ἥπερ παροξύνει, *in love of honor, which incites,* etc. Cf. III. 5. 3: ἀλλὰ μὴν φιλοτιμότατοί γε καὶ φιλοφρονέστατοι πάντων εἰσίν, ἅπερ οὐχ ἥκιστα παροξύνει κινδυνεύειν ὑπὲρ εὐδοξίας τε καὶ πατρίδος, κ.τ.λ.

14.—Ἱππικοῦ, sc. τέχνης, *horsemanship.* —— τοῦ ἐνθάδε, lit., *which is here,* i. e., with ἱππικοῦ, *our* horsemanship. —— τούτῳ, sc. ἱππικῷ. We should expect ἐν with the dative, and it may have been omitted in copying in consequence of similarity with the preceding ἂν. —— διενέγκοιεν, sc. Ἀθηναῖοι; cf. Kühn. Gr. § 238. R. 3. in reference to the ellipsis. —— παρασκευῇ, κ.τ.λ. These datives give a more definite explanation of the idea contained in τούτῳ. So in Latin we frequently find successive ablatives in a similar relation. —— Εἰκός γε; *so it seems at least.*

15.—Προτρέπειν; see note, I. 2. 64. —— Ἀλλά, *certainly,* a particle of affirmation as freq. in responses, where however there is an ellipsis; see B. 139. m. 16.

CHAPTER IV.

1.—Στρατηγοί, generals, chief commanders, ten in number, one from each of the φυλαί. —— Οὐ γάρ, *are not indeed;* see note, I. 3. 11. —— τοιοῦτοί εἰσιν, *are such* (as they ever exhibit themselves). —— ἐμὲ μέν, contrasted with Ἀντισθένην δέ. —— ὃς ἐκ καταλόγου στρατευόμενος, making war in the regular service. Κατάλογος was the list of persons in Athens who were liable to regular military service.

Hence, those persons who possessed a prescribed amount of property, served in the regular infantry, and were termed: *οἱ ἐκ καταλόγου στρατεύοντες.* Those of inferior rank, *thetes*, were called: *οἱ ἔξω τοῦ καταλόγου.* See *Catalogos* in Smith's Dict., and consult also Wachsmuth Hellen. Alterthumsk. II. sec. 1. S. 376. Cf. Thuc. VIII. 24; Polit. v. 2, and Suidas' explanation, quoted from the Schol. ad Aristoph. Equ. 22. 23: Κατάλογος· ἡ ἀπογραφὴ τῶν ὀφειλόντων στρατεύεσθαι καὶ ἡ ἐξαρίθμησις· ὁ πίναξ, ἐφ' οὗ ἐνέγραφον τῶν ἐκστρατευομένων τὰ ὀνόματα. —— κατατέτριμμαι, *I have worn away my life*, spent my vigor. —— λοχαγῶν, commander of a λόχος, about 100 men. —— ταξιαρχῶν, commander of a τάξις, a division of the army, furnished by one φυλή. —— τραύματα ὑπὸ τῶν πολεμίων... ἔχων. Τραύματα ἔχειν, is passive in signification, to receive wounds, or, to be wounded; hence in construction with the preposition ὑπό. Cf. IV. 8. 10: ἐγὼ ἐπιμελείας τεύξομαι ὑπ' ἀνθρώπων. Venat. I. 11: ἔτυχε τιμωρίας ὑπὸ θεῶν. R. Lac. VI. 2: πληγὰς λαβεῖν ὑπό τινος. Hellen. V. 1. 5: οἱ Ἀθηναῖοι... πράγματα εἶχον ὑπό τε τῶν λῃστῶν καὶ τοῦ Γοργῶπα. —— οὔτε ὁπλίτην πώποτε στρατευσάμενον,... τε. The service of the foot soldiers to whom Nichomachides belonged, and which he considered as giving him a superior claim to the office in question, was more onerous than that of the cavalry, which until the latter ages of the republic, was composed chiefly of the nobility; see Fiske's Man. p. 270 sq. Οὔτε... τε, see note, I. 2. 47.

2.—Εἴγε, if (since) indeed; see Kühn. Gr. § 317. 2; L. Gr. II. 704. II. 1. —— Καὶ γὰρ οἱ ἔμποροι, for even the merchants, etc. Cf. note, II. 6. 7.

3.—Κεχορήγηκε. For an account of the Greek Choregia, see Boeckh's Public. Econ. of Athens, p. 454 sq.; Wachsmuth, Hellen. Alterthumsk. II. § 97. S. 92 sq. —— Μὰ Δί',... ἀλλ' οὐδέν; see note, I. 4. 9. —— ὅμοιον... χοροῦ τε καὶ στρατεύματος προεστάναι; cf. the use of ὅμοιος, IV. 8. 10: ὁρῶ καὶ τὴν δόξαν τῶν προγεγονότων ἀνθρώπων ἐν τοῖς ἐπιγιγνομένοις οὐχ ὁμοίαν καταλειπομένην τῶν τε ἀδικησάντων καὶ τῶν ἀδικηθέντων; and for a parallel use of similem in Latin, see Kühn. Tusc. Disp. V. 3. 9: similem sibi videri vitam hominum et mercatum eum, qui haberetur maximo ludorum apparatu totius Graeciae celebritate.

4.—Καὶ μήν... γε; see note, I. 4. 12. —— ᾠδῆς... χορῶν διδασκαλίας. The first duty of the *Choragus* was to assemble the persons who were to take the several parts in the chorus, and then to provide teachers (διδασκάλοι) for them; hence διδασκαλίας here. The preparation for the musical part of the entertainment was often attended with considerable difficulty; hence ᾠδῆς here. See *Chorus* and *Choragus* in Smith's Dict. of Ant.; Boeckh's Econ. of Athens, p. 456, and Wachsmuth, II. § 97. 2. S. 95. —— τοὺς κρατίστους ταῦτα; i. e., as Schneider says: poetas, citharoedos, tibicines et reliquos artifices, qui scenam Atticam implebant et choros Dionysiacos. —— τοὺς τάξοντας...τοὺς μαχουμένους. For this use of the Art. and Part., cf. III. 8. 2; δεόμεθα τοῦ παύσοντος; IV. 5. 3: τὸ ἔχειν τοὺς κωλύσοντας, and see Kühn. Gr. § 244. 8; L. Gr. II. § 486. 2. 'Ανθ' ἑαυτοῦ is to be supplied in the last clause: others who will fight *instead of him.*

5.—Τούτου νικηφόρος, sc. τῶν πολεμικῶν, or we may supply χρήματος or πράγματος. We should naturally expect the plural number. But cf. Apol. § 7; Cyrop. VIII. 4. 6; Anab. II. 1. 21 sq. —— καὶ... δαπανᾶν δ'; see note, I. 1. 3; κἀκεῖνος, κ.τ.λ. —— ξὺν τῇ φυλῇ, *in conjunction with*, etc. The honor of a victory obtained by a chorus, belonged to the whole tribe, φυλή, from which the chorus was taken. The number of the Attic φυλαί was ten, and they were again subdivided according to the region which they occupied into 174 δῆμοι. See Smith's Dict. of Ant., *Tribus.*

6.—'Εὰν γιγνώσκῃ... ἀγαθὸς ἂν εἴη. For this use of the modes with ἐάν and ἄν, see Kühn. Gr. § 339. 3. (a); L. Gr. II. § 818. 2. b. Cf. III. 6. 18: ἐὰν... ἐπιχειρῇς τὰ τῆς πόλεως πράττειν, οὐκ ἂν θαυμάσαιμι, κ.τ.λ.

7.—'Ακοῦσαι, ὡς; see note, II. 8. 6. —— Πότερον τὰ αὐτά ἐστιν, ἢ διαφέρει τι, whether they are the same, etc.; cf. Oecon. V. 14 sq.

8.—Τὸ προστάττειν... πράττειν, the imposing of each thing (duty) on those competent to perform them.

9.—'Αμφοτέρους εἶναι προσήκει; cf. § 8: τὸ τοὺς κακοὺς κολάζειν... ἀμφοτέροις οἶμαι προσήκειν. The former is perhaps the more usual construction. Cf. note, III. 3. 10.

10.—Οὐκέτι, *no longer*, or better, *not also*, non item. Anab. I. 10. 12, and examples collected by Haase, Rep. Lac. XI. 7. (8). —— ἐχθροί γέ τοι, *certainly at least.* These particles make an emphatic contrast or restriction. See Hartung, Gr. Part. II. S. 365, 6; Kühn. Gr. § 317. 3; L Gr. II. § 705. 4, and cf. Anab. II. 5. 19, and III. 6. 13; IV. 2. 18, 33.

11.—Παριείς. There is an ellipsis of λέξον here. But *passing by this, say, tell me.* By this omission the impetuous, impatient state of mind of Nichomachides is indicated. —— οὐχ ἥκιστα δὲ τούτων, ἐὰν ἀπαράσκευος ᾖ; the idea is: far the most important of these things, if he may be unprepared, is, etc.

12.—Μὴ καταφρόνει; we should naturally expect οὖν after these words, but a paragraph containing the conclusion of a discourse, is frequently asyndic, see Kühn. L. Gr. II. § 760. 2. b; and cf. IV. 2. 39; 8. 7. —— ἔφη; cf. note, I. 4. 17. —— τὸ δὲ μέγιστον, ὅτι; for the construction of this appositional clause, as it is sometimes termed, see Kühn. L. Gr. II. § 500. Anm. 2; and Matt. II. § 432. In Latin it would be changed to a relative enunciation: id quod maximum est. We frequently imitate the Greek construction in English. —— ἄλλοις τισὶν ἀνθρώποις, *different men.*

CHAPTER V.

1.—Περικλεῖ... Περικλέους υἱῷ. This Pericles was the natural son of the great Athenian orator, who was by a formal decree "legitimated" by the Athenians, after the death of the other sons of Pericles, and permitted to take the name of his father. See Thirlwall's Greece, I. p. 345. He was one of the ten generals condemned to death after the battle of Arginusae. Cf. Plut. in Pericle; Hellen. I. 5. 16; 7. 2, and 38. —— τοῦ πάνυ, *the well-known or distinguished;* so πάνυ is sometimes used, where ἐνδόξος, περίβλεπτος, or some similar word might be employed. —— Ἐγώ τοι; see note, I. 6. 11. —— στρατηγήσαντος; for the force of the Aor. see note, I. 1. 18: βουλεύσας. —— ἐνδοξοτέραν... εἰς τὰ πολεμικὰ; for the construction of the Acc. with Prep. see Kühn. L. Gr. II. § 557. b, and Anm. and Gr. § 279. 7. R. 9. —— καὶ ὁ Περικλῆς; the relative construction is usual in Latin and English in such cases: cui Socrates. —— διαλογιζόμενοι περὶ αὐτῶν, in our discussion of this matter. —— ὅπου ἤδη τὸ δυνατόν ἐστιν; this answers to the preceding, ὅπως δὲ ταῦτα, κ.τ.λ. We might expect ὅπως for ὅπου (qua in re), but cf. Apol. § 25: ὥστε θαυμαστὸν ἔμοιγε δοκεῖ εἶναι, ὅπου ποτὲ ἐφάνη ὑμῖν τὸ τοῦ θανάτου εἰργασμένον ἐμοὶ ἄξιον. —— Ἤδη, *now,* i. e., that we may come directly to this point, may omit all circumlocution. Cf. Hartung, Gr. Part. I. 241. 2; Kühn. L. Gr. II. § 690. b.

2.—Οἶδα γάρ; the γάρ here has little more force than an emphatic γέ; cf. I. 4. 9: οὐδὲ γάρ. —— Σώματα δὲ ἀγαθὰ καὶ καλὰ: the position of these words so as to be in contrast with πλήθει μὲν, deserves notice. The Latin can retain the same position by means of the relative circumlocution: quae quidem bona pulchra sint. —— πότερον; see note, II. 7. 8: ἔμαθον δὲ πότερον. —— ταύτῃ; see note, I. 7. 3: ταύτῃ λυπηρόν —— λείπεσθαι to be inferior —— ἑαυτοῖς. The reflexive for tne reciprocai pronoun; see II. 6. 20.

3.—Ἀλλὰ μὴν...γέ (at vero)...Καὶ μὴν...γε (jam vero); cf. note, I. 1. 6, and I. 4. 12. —— προγόνων; cf. Hipparch. VII. 3: καὶ μὴν ἐπί γε τοῖς προγόνοις οὐ μεῖον Ἀθηναῖοι ἢ Βοιωτοὶ φρονοῦσιν. —— ἔστιν οἷς; see note, I. 4. 2. —— μείζω καὶ πλείω; see note, I. 2. 24. —— ᾧ, on account of which, qua re, sc. τῷ προγόνων καλὰ ἔργα εἶναι. —— προτρέπονταί τε; this position of τέ is not elsewhere unknown, when the predicate takes precedence; cf. IV. 2. 40: ἐξηγεῖτο, ἅ τε ἐνόμιζεν εἰδέναι δεῖν καὶ ἐπιτηδεύειν, for: ἃ ἐνομιζεν εἰδέναι τε δ. καὶ ἐπ.

4.—Ἀληθῆ, expressed by an adverb in Latin: vere. —— σὺν Τολμίδῃ...ἐν Λεβαδείᾳ συμφορά. The disaster here alluded to, was the defeat of the Athenians under Tolmides at Lebadea in Boeotia, near Ghaeronea, B. C. 447, Olymp. 83. 2. See Thirlwall's Greece, Ch. XVII. Vol. I. p. 305, and Mitford ch. 12. sec. 5. Cf. Thucyd. I. 113; Plut. Per. c. 18, Ages. c. 19; Diod. XII. 6. —— ἡ μεθ' Ἱπποκράτους ἐπὶ Δηλίῳ. For an account of the defeat of the Athenians at Delium, B. C. 420, here referred to, see Thirlwall, Vol. I. 381. Socrates, then forty-five years old, was himself present at the battle of Delium; and the Athenian general Laches "declared, that if all the Athenians had fought as bravely as he, the Boeotians would have erected no trophies." See Introd. and Wiggers' Life of Socrates, Ch. V. and references there. The use of the preposition ἐπὶ with Δηλίῳ after ἐν with Λεβαδείᾳ, deserves notice. It has been found on examination that wherever this battle at Delium is spoken of, either ἐπί or περί is always used with the name of the place, and never ἐν, as in other cases in accounts of battles. The reason seems to be, that the name Delium was properly given to a temple, and although comprising the city proper, it did not extend to the country around the city, where the battle was fought; hence, ἐπί is appropriate. Cf. the meaning of the prepositions ἐν and ἐπί in Kühn. Gr. § 289, 1. (1), (a), and § 296. (1), (a). —— ἐκ τούτων, after ἀφ' οὗ, as ἐκ τούτου often follows ἐπεί, inde or deinde. Cf. Cyrop. V. 3. 15; VI. 1. 33, et al. —— πρὸς τοὺς Βοιωτούς...πρὸς τοὺς Ἀθηναίους. Πρός here, *in comparison with,* strictly governs δόξαν implied: πρὸς τὴν τῶν Ἀθηναίων δόξαν; cf. III. 6. 8: ἐὰν δὲ (ἡ τῆς πόλεως δύναμις) ἥττων τῶν ἐναντίων (ᾖ); and see Kühn. Gr. § 323. R. 6; L. Gr. II. § 749. d. —— οἱ...τολμῶντες; see note, II. 7. 13.

5.—Ἀλλ', see note, I. 2. 42. It should be noticed that ἀλλά is here after the concessive clause which it introduces: αἰσθάνομαι μέν, followed by the adversative δέ.——ἀνδρὶ... ἄρχοντι... διακεῖσθαι, to be more obediently disposed toward a good leader; cf. Cyrop. VII. 5. 45; ἐγὼ γὰρ ὑμῖν, ὥσπερ εἰκός, διάκειμαι. Διακεῖσθαι is constructed here with the dative, but frequently with the Acc. and the preposition πρός or παρά.——τὸ... θάρσος... ἐμβάλλει, κ.τ.λ., a feeling of security produces in them negligence, etc. Θάρσος is opposed to φόβος.

6.—Τεκμήραιο... ἀπὸ τῶν, κ.τ.λ.; cf. note, II. 6. 6.——ἔστ' ἂν, *as long as, whilst*, quamdiu; cf. I. 2. 18: σωφρονοῦντε ἔστε Σωκράτει συνήστην; Oecon. I. 23: αἰκιζόμεναι... τοὺς οἴκους οὔποτε λήγουσιν, ἔστ' ἂν ἄρχωσιν αὐτῶν.——ὥσπερ χορευταί, as those who dance in the chorus. It was necessary that the dancers should keep their eye on the leader of the chorus; and hence, the force of this comparison.

7.—Ὥρα ἂν εἴη λέγειν, it would be time to consider.——Πάλιν ἀνερεθισθῆναι τῆς ἀρχαίας ἀρετῆς, κ.τ.λ., to be again animated with the desire for the ancient valor, etc. Concerning the verb ἀνερεθ., see Bornem. Anab. VI. 6. 9. For the construction of the Gen. with ὑπό implied, see Schneider in h. l.

8.—Εἰ ἐβουλόμεθα... ἐξορμῷμεν, sc. vellemus, incitemus. In the protasis εἰ with the indicative of a past tense, implies that the negative of the condition is true (i. e., if we wished, *which we do not*), but in the apodosis, on the contrary, the affirmative is true; see Kühn. Gr. § 339. 3. (a); L. Gr. II. § 820. b., and cf. Zumpt's Lat. Gr. § 524.——οὕτως; after the participle, οὕτως and some other adverbs are frequently added, to denote more definitely the result of the action indicated by the participle. Cf. III. 10. 2: ἐκ πολλῶν συνάγοντες τὰ ἐξ ἑκάστου κάλλιστα, οὕτως ὅλα τὰ σώματα καλὰ ποιεῖτε φαίνεσθαι; IV. 8. 11, and see Stallb. Plat. Phaed. p. 260. D, and Kühn. Gr. § 312. R. 7; L. Gr. II. § 666. Anm. 6.——πατρῷα... προσήκοντα, patrimony... estate.——τοῦτ' αὖ, sc. τὸ μετ' ἀρετῆς πρωτεύειν, the being first.——δεικτέον... προσῆκον... καὶ ὡς... ἂν εἶεν κράτιστοι. For the change of construction from the Part. προσῆκον to ὡς with the verb, see Kühn. L. Gr. II. § 771. 4.

9.—Οἶμαι μέν; see note, II. 6. 5.——εἰ τούς γε παλαιοτάτους... ἀρίστους γεγονέναι; the construction is: εἰ ἀναμιμνήσκοιμεν αὐτοὺς ἀκηκοότας τούς γε... προγόνους αὐτῶν ἀρίστους γεγονέναι, if we should remind them that they have heard (or they having heard of it), that their ancestors, the most ancient of whom we have any knowledge, were the bravest of men. In sense αὐτοὺς is connected, ἀπὸ κοινοῦ, with both ἀκηκοότας and ἀναμιμνήσκοιμεν. Cf. Kühn. L. Gr. II § 852. k.

10.—Ἆρα, *an.* —— τὴν τῶν θεῶν κρίσιν, *judgment in respect to the Gods;* the objective genitive. Cf. II. 7. 13: τὸν τοῦ κυνὸς λόγον. —— οἱ περὶ Κέκροπα, not simply Cecrops, as this circumlocution was employed in a later stage of Greek literature, but Cecrops and those with him, the tribunal, with him as presiding over it. See Kühn. Gr. § 263. d; L. Gr. II. § 474. d; Buttmann, 140. m. 25. The allusion here is to the contest between Neptune and Minerva in reference to the guardianship of Attica, of which Cecrops was made umpire. Cf. Apollod. III. 14, and see Grote's History of Greece, Vol. I. 266, 7. —— δι' ἀρετήν; i. e., διὰ τὸ μετ' ἀρετῆς πρωτεύειν, as in § 8. On account of his virtue, Cecrops was counted worthy to be a judge, umpire, among the Gods. —— Λέγω γάρ, *yes, I refer to that;* cf. note, I. 4. 9. —— καὶ ... γε; cf. I. 2. 53; III. 8. 6, and Plat. Menex. p. 235. E: Τίς αὕτη; ἢ δῆλον ὅτι Ἀσπασίαν λέγεις; Λέγω γάρ, καὶ Κόννον γε τὸν Μητροβίου. —— τὴν Ἐρεχθέως γε τροφὴν καὶ γένεσιν; for the figure called ὕστερον πρότερον, cf. the passage of which this is an imitation, in Homer's Iliad, II. 547. Erectheus was a very renowned king of Attica, son of Pandion I. He also appears in the fabulous history of Athens, as a god, Poseidôn Erectheus; and as a hero Erectheus, son of the Earth; Grote's Hist. of Greece, Vol. I. p. 271 sq. —— ἐπ' ἐκείνου, in his age, illius aetate; see Kühn. Gr. § 296. (2), and § 273. R. 12; L. Gr. II. § 611. —— ἐκ τῆς ἐχομένης ἠπείρου, *from the whole adjoining continent,* as opposed to the Peloponnesus; i. e., Thrace, which in most ancient times extended even to the borders of Attica. The war of the Athenians with the Thracians and Eleusinians is here alluded to. Cf. Grote's Hist. Gr. I. p. 275 sq., and references. —— ἐφ' Ἡρακλειδῶν πρὸς τοὺς ἐν Πελοποννήσῳ, the war carried on by the sons Heraclês, the Heraclidae, against Eurystheus and the Peloponnesians; cf. Grote's Hist. II. p. 1 sq. —— ἐπὶ Θησέως. The war under the guidance of Theseus against the Amazons and Thracians. In reference to the character and exploits of Theseus, see Grote's Hist. Gr. I. 282 sq. —— τῶν καθ' ἑαυτοὺς ἀνθρώπων ἀριστεύσαντες, as having excelled the men of their age, their contemporaries. The Gen. is here governed by ἀριστεύσαντες; see C. Gr. Gram. § 362.

11.—Εἰ δὲ βούλει, (sc. ἀναμιμνήσκοιμεν ἄν, (lit., if you please, let us, etc., *moreover,* porro. There is an urbanity in the phraseology which is especially characteristic of the Greek language. —— οἱ ... μὲν ἀπόγονοι, ... δὲ πρὸ ἡμῶν γεγονότες, their descendants, *who* preceded, *though* not long, our age; thus the force of the μὲν ... δὲ is given by our relative *who* and particle *though,* in Latin: qui...tamen. Special allusion is made here perhaps to the Athenians of the age of Miltiades,

Themistocles, and Aristides, who carried on the war with the Persians See Thirlwall, I. p. 233 sq. —— αὐτοὶ καθ' ἑαυτοὺς, *they* by themselves, i. e., *alone.* Nepos however says, Milt. c. 5: Hoc in tempore nulla civitas Atheniensibus fuit auxilio praeter Plataeenses. —— κυριεύοντας, i. e., the Persians. —— πλείστην ... ἀφορμὴν κεκτημένους, *had acquired greater power and resources than any of their predecessors;* cf. note, II. 7. 11. —— οἳ δὴ καὶ λέγονται, *for they,* etc. Ὅς is not unfrequently, as here, used for οὗτος γάρ; cf. note, I. 2. 64. The particle δή, Kühner says, in this place signifies: uti constat inter omnes; cf. note, II. 2. 3, and II. 1. 21. The praise here bestowed upon the Peloponnesians, must have special reference to the Lacedemonians. Λέγονται; the idea of celebrity is contained in this word, as frequently: celebrantur. —— Λέγονται γάρ; see note, I. 4. 9.

12.—Διέμειναν, *remained,* ἐν τῇ [sc. γῇ or χώρᾳ] ἑαυτῶν, *in their own territory.* Hence the Athenians were called αὐτόχθονες and γηγενεῖς; Isocr. Panegyr. p. 65. —— ὑπὲρ δικαίων ἀντιλέγοντες; cf. Aristides, Panathen. p. 109 sq. as cited by Schneider in h. l. —— ἐπέτρεπον ἐκείνοις, committed or referred (the matter in dispute, their difficulties) to them. The subject of ἐπέτρεπον is τὸ ἀντιλεγόμενον, supplied from ἀντιλέγοντες, unless we with Kühner take ἐπέτρεπον as reflexive: *submitted themselves;* so in III. 11. 5: τῇ τύχῃ ἐπιτρέπεις; Demosth. de Cherson. p. 92. 9: δεῖ μὴ ἐπιτρέπειν αὐτῷ (τῷ Φιλίππῳ). See Kühn. Gr. § 249. 1; L. Gr. II. § 392.

13.—Καὶ θαυμάζω γε. The particles καί ... γε here indicate assent to the opinion of Socrates and add an inference: (I know it) and am astonished, etc. —— ἡ πόλις ὅπως; the unusual position of ἡ πόλις before ὅπως gives it emphasis: *this* city [sc. of which such a thing was least of all to be expected]. See Kühn. Gr. § 348. 8; L. Gr. II. § 864. 3, and cf. Stallb. Plat. Phaedr. p. 238. A, also II. 7. 8 below, where an interrogative particle is constructed in a similar manner. For the same idiom in Latin, see Kühn. Tusc. Disp. II. 4. 12. —— ἔφη, οἶμαι, ὁ Σωκράτης. This is the order of the words in most of the best Mss. Cf. in Latin, Cic. Brut. c. 23. § 91: Quid igitur, inquit, est causae, Brutus; and Bornem. Cyrop. I. 6. 3; Plat. de Rep. VI. p. 503. B. —— ὥσπερ καὶ ... οὕτω καί; see note, I. 1. 6: καὶ πράττειν. Cf. for a similar idiom in Latin, Cic. de Nat. Deor. II. 6. 17: ut quod etiam ... hoc idem.

14.—Δοκεῖ μοι, in construction with the Nom. with the Infin. and the Acc. with Inf. (χείρους γενέσθαι). Thus we not unfrequently find the Acc. when the idea of thinking, judging, is contained in δοκεῖ μοι.

Cf. IV. 3. 10; Herod. III. 124: ἐδόκεέ οἱ τὸν πατέρα... λοῦσθαι μὲν ὑπὸ τοῦ Διός, χρίεσθαι δὲ ὑπὸ τοῦ ἡλίου. Both constructions are found in Anab. III. 1. 11: ἔδοξεν αὐτῷ βροντῆς γενομένης σκηπτὸς πεσεῖν εἰς τὴν πατρῴαν οἰκίαν καὶ ἐκ τούτου λάμπεσθαι πᾶσαν. See Kühn. L. Gr. II. § 649. b. So videtur is used in Latin; cf. Kühn. Tusc. Disp. V. 5. 12. —— νῦν πρωτεύοντας, sc. the Lacedaemonians. —— τούτοις τὰ αὐτὰ; for the Dat. after ὁ αὐτός, see Kühn. Gr. § 284. (4); L. Gr. II. § 576. —— ὁμοίως... χρώμενοι; equivalent to a conditional phrase: If they practised the same things in like manner, they would, etc. —— ἂν... εἶεν; the change from the Part. to conditional enunciation should not escape notice here. Cf. I. 4. 15, and I. 1. 18, note. —— εἰ δ' ἐπιμελέστερον, sc. χρῷντο supplied ἀπὸ κοινοῦ from the Part. χρώμενοι, and ἐπιμελεστέρον corresponds to ὁμοίως: *more carefully.*

15.—Πόῤῥω ποῦ εἶναι, *is very far indeed,* procul sane abesse. Πού primarily implies doubt or hesitancy, opposed to δή, and is frequently employed where a thing is certain, to give a more courtly air to an affirmation: *do you not?* or, *if I mistake not.* Cf. Lewis, Contr. Atheos, p. 23. n. 10; and note, III. 3. 2; IV. 2. 31. —— πρεσβυτέρους αἰδέσονται; cf. Cic. Cat. Maj. XVIII. 63: Lysandrum Lacedaemonium dicere aiunt solitum Lacedaemone esse honestissimum domicilium senectutis. Nusquam enim tantum tribuitur aetati, nusquam est senectus honoratior; and Xen. Rep. Lac. X. 2. —— οἳ; cf. note, I. 2. 64: ὅς. —— οἳ ἀπὸ τῶν πατέρων ἄρχονται καταφρονεῖν τῶν γεραιτέρων, who even from their fathers begin, etc. For the use of the Inf. here, to indicate that the thing is done with purpose, instead of the Part. which would merely show that the action was entered upon, see Kühn. Gr. § 311. 16; L. Gr. II. § 551. e. The phrase is much stronger than ἄρχονται καταφρονοῦντες would have been. Cf. III. 1. 5: ἤρξατό σε διδάσκειν; 5. 22: (εἰπεῖν) ὁπότε παλαίειν ἤρξω μανθάνειν; 6. 3: ἐκ τίνος ἄρξῃ τὴν πόλιν εὐεργετεῖν; IV. 2. 3: λέγειν ἀρχόμενος ὧδε προοιμιάσεται.

16.—Οἳ... ἀγάλλονται ἐπὶ, κ.τ.λ., who even exalt, etc. —— συνεργεῖν ἑαυτοῖς τὰ συμφέροντα; for a similar construction with the Acc., see note, II. 6. 25. —— ἀλλήλοις; for the interchange here between ἀλλήλοις and ἑαυτοῖς, see note, II. 6. 20. —— πλείστας δίκας ἀλλήλοις δικάζονται, they bring very many suits, etc.; the Dat. depends upon δικάζονται, from the idea of contending which is included in that verb; see Kühn. § 284. 3. (2); L. Gr. II. § 574. c. —— προαιροῦνταί μᾶλλον; cf. note, II. 1. 2. —— αὖ μάχονται. Αὖ, *again, also,* designates a kind of correspondence between μάχονται and δίκας δικάζονται. See Hartung, Gr. Part. I. S. 155. —— ταῖς εἰς τὰ τοιαῦτα δυνάμεσι, κ.τ.λ. Τὰ τοιαῦτα refers not to τοῖς κοινοῖς, but to μάχονται, κ.τ.λ., i. e., they rejoice especially on account of their ability to contend, etc.

17.—Ἀπειρία καὶ κακία, *ignorance* and *degeneracy*, which arise from neglecting gymnastic exercises and from contempt of the authority of leaders. —— ἔχθρα καὶ μῖσος, *hostility* and *hatred*, arising from spurning the authority of magistrates and intestine dissensions. —— μεῖζον ἢ ὥστε φέρειν δύνασθαι κακὸν; for this construction of the Inf. with ἢ ὥστε after the comparative, see Kühn. § 341. 3. (a); L. Gr. II. § 825. e.

18.—Πονηρίᾳ νοσεῖν. In accordance with an idiom common in other languages, νοσεῖν is metaphorically used in reference to a disturbed condition of the State; cf. Anab. VII. 2. 32: τὰ Ὀδρυσῶν πράγματα ἐνόσησεν; Demosth. Olynth. II. p. 22: Θετταλοῖς νοσοῦσι καὶ στασιάζουσι καὶ τεταραγμένοις. It is also used of the State as visited by famine, Xen. de Vectig. IV. 9. Thus in Latin it is said: aegrota respublica, morbus civitatis, etc. Seiffert renders ἀνηκέστῳ πον. νοσεῖν: insanabili perversitate laborare. —— τοῖς ἐπιστάταις, those who taught gymnastics, παιδοτρίβαις; see Smith's Lex. *Gymnasium*, p. 483. —— οὐδένων δὲ καταδεέστερον ... ὑπηρετοῦσι, i. e., οὐδὲ ἄλλων τινῶν καταδεέστερον ὑπηρετοῦσιν, *inferior to none*, etc., see note, I. 5. 6.

19.—Τοῦτο γάρ τοι; for the force of γάρ in answers, see note, I. 4. 9, and Kühn. Gr. § 317. 3. Τοῦτο is here prospective, i. e., it prepares the way for and makes more emphatic the phrase following: τὸ ... πειθαρχεῖν; see Kühn. Gr. § 304. 2; L. Gr. II. § 631. 2. —— καὶ θαυμαστόν ἐστι, is *even* wonderful (not only true, but also wonderful). Καί is emphatic; see Kühn. Gr. § 321. R. 5. —— τοὺς μὲν τοιούτους, i. e., ναῦται, ἐρέται, ἐπιβάται, etc., the lowest class of the Athenians. —— τοὺς ... ὁπλίτας καὶ τοὺς ἱππεῖς; these nouns are contrasted with τοὺς ... τοιούτους above, as indicating persons belonging to the higher classes of citizens; see Wachsmuth, Hellen. Alterthumsk. P. II. Vol. I. S. 403.

20.—Ἡ δὲ ἐν Ἀρείῳ πάγῳ βουλή; for the force of δέ, see note, I. 3. 13, and for a description of the council called βουλή and the Areopagus (Ἀρείῳ πάγῳ), the most ancient judicial tribunal of the Athenians, v. h. vv. in Smith's Lexicon, and Potter's Gr. Antiquities, I. p. 111 sq. —— ἐκ τῶν δεδοκιμασμένων; see note, II. 2. 13. —— μέμφομαι τούτοις, *I find no fault with these;* τούτοις refers, κατὰ σύνεσιν, to βουλήν; see note, II. 1. 31.

21.—Καὶ μὴν ... γέ; see note, I. 4. 12. —— οὐδενὶ τούτων, i. e., temperance, order, obedience, etc., as implied in the preceding Inff. ——

Ἴσως γάρ, i. e., what you say is true, *for perhaps*, etc. Cf. IV. 4. 13, 14, 21, and see Kühn. L. Gr. II. § 754. 1, and a similar use of the Latin enim in Cic. Tusc. Disp. I. 6. 11. Cf. also note, I. 4. 9. —— οὐδὲ εἷς, emphatic for οὐδείς, see note, I. 6. 2. —— ἐφ' οἷς ἐφεστᾶσι; for the repetition of the preposition, cf. II. 9. 2. —— αὐτοσχεδιάζουσιν, rashly, without the requisite knowledge, take the rule upon themselves.

23.—Δέ, *and also*, itemque. —— πολλὰ μεριμνᾶν, to think much upon, be solicitous; cf. note, I. 1. 11 and 14; Oecon. XX. 25. —— ὅπως μὴ λάθῃς σεαυτὸν ἀγνοῶν, that you may not, without knowing it, be ignorant, etc. See Kühn. Gr. § 310. 4. (1). We find this construction, the Aor. tense λαθεῖν with the present, as well as the Aor. participle; cf. IV. 2. 7; VI. 1. 22, et saep. For the use of the present participle, cf. Cyrop. V. 3. 9: ὅπως λάθῃ φίλος ὢν ἡμῖν. There is no good reason why the present should not be employed with λαθεῖν; indeed the sense seems to demand it as in the passage above cited. —— μὴ εἰδότα. We should rather expect οὐκ εἰδώς. But the attraction appears to be omitted here on account of the contrast with the Acc. τοὺς ἐπισταμένους; and μή (not οὐ) seems to be used on account of the conditional form of the phrase: ἐάν, κ.τ.λ. Cf. Kühn. Gr. § 310. 3. R. 1, and L. Gr. II. § 656. 1.

24.—Λανθάνεις με... ὅτι... λέγεις; personal, for the impersonal construction: λανθάνει με, κ.τ.λ.; see Kühn. Gr. § 329. R. 4; L. Gr. II. § 771. 2, and cf. IV. 2. 21: Δῆλος... ὅτι ἃ ᾤετο εἰδέναι οὐκ οἶδεν, οὐδ' οἰόμενος. Probably the construction ὅτι λέγεις is employed to avoid the ambiguity of the two participles, οἰόμενος and λέγων. —— ὁμολογῶ μέντοι, *still*, I concede, etc. Kühner makes μέντοι merely confirmative here, as in II. 1. 12; but there is perhaps an allusion to the irony in the preceding thought of Socrates, which would naturally lead Pericles to objection instead of assent.

25.—Ὄρη μεγάλα; Citheron, Cerastis, and other mountains guarded the approach to Attica. —— διέζωσται ὄρεσιν ἐρυμνοῖς, is girded around (lit., fenced, secured) by steep hills and mountains; i. e., Parnes, Brilessus, Hymettus, Laurion, etc.

26.—Μυσοὶ καὶ Πισίδαι. The Mysians, inhabitants of Mysia, and the Pisidians, of the country bounded by Phrygia on the west and north, Isauria on the east and Pamphylia on the south. See Owen's Anab. I. 1. 11; III. 2. 23. —— βασιλέως. The king of the Persians was βασιλεύς, κατ' ἐξοχήν, and this noun is accordingly used as a proper name, without the article; see Kühn. Gr. § 244. R. 3, and cf. IV. 2. 33; Symp. IV. 11, et al. —— ἀκούω; for this use of the present as a Perf. after the Perf. ἀκήκοας, see Kühn. Gr. § 255. R. 1, and cf. Woolsey's Gorgias, 4. 470. A, and 503. C.

27.—Μέχρι τῆς ἐλαφρᾶς ἡλικίας ὡπλισμένους; cf. note, I. 2. 35. The youth from 18 to 20, *ephebi*, who were frequently sent into the country under the name of περίπολοι, are here alluded to. In Xen. Vectig. IV. 52 it is said of them: οἱ περιπολεῖν τὴν χώραν ταχθέντες. Cf. Smith's Lex. *Ephebus*, p. 407, and Wachsmuth, Hellen. Alterthumsk. B. III. § 56. S. 476.

CHAPTER VI.

1.—Γλαύκωνα. This Glauco was brother of the philosopher Plato, and a different individual from the one mentioned below and in the next chapter, as father of Charmides. —— οὐδέπω εἴκοσιν ἔτη γεγονώς So in I. 2. 40, it is said: πρὶν εἴκοσιν ἐτῶν εἶναι. Twenty years was the age at which the youth must arrive before taking upon himself all the duties of citizen, and before he was allowed to vote and speak in the public assembly. See Thirlwall, Vol. I. p. 186; Smith's Dictionary, *Ephebus*. —— ὄντων ἄλλων οἰκείων, κ.τ.λ., *although he had* other relatives, etc. —— ἐδύνατο παῦσαι ἑλκόμενόν τε ἀπὸ τοῦ βήματος καὶ καταγέλαστον ὄντα, no one had been able to prevent him from being dragged from the speaker's stand, and from derision, i. e., no one was able to dissuade him from haranguing in public, although hissed from the stand, etc. For the construction of the participles with the Inf. here, see Kühn. Gr. § 310. 4. f; L. Gr. II. § 660. VI. Cf. III. 14. 1: ἐπαύοντο πολλοῦ ὀψωνοῦντες. In illustration of this passage, especially of the means employed to silence a speaker in the public assembly, Schneider quotes Plat. Protag. p. 319. C. —— Χαρμίδην; see III. 7. 1. —— Πλάτωνα. The rare allusion of Xenophon to Plato in his writings, has been attributed by some without very good reason to jealous rivalry. See Gell. N. A. XIV. 13.

2.—Εἰς τὸ ἐθελῆσαι ἀκούειν, in order to excite in him a desire to hear. For εἰς τό with the Inf., see Kühn. Gr. § 308. 2. (d), and cf. Anab. VII. 8. 20. —— τοιάδε λέξας κατέσχεν, having spoken to him, he detained him as follows. For the use and signification of the Aor. Part. here denoting priority in time, see B. 144. 2. N. 3. —— ἡμῖν. The Dat. of the personal pronouns of the first and second persons is used to denote a familiarity or confidence between the speaker and hearer, (Dativus ethicus); see Kühn. Gr. § 284. (10). (d), and cf.

Plat. Alcib. I. c. 56.——καλὸν γάρ; cf. note, I. 4. 9.——εἴπερ τ καὶ ἄλλο τῶν ἐν ἀνθρώποις, if there is any thing else in human affairs, i. e., καλόν, honorable. Cf. Cyrop. II. 2. 17: οὐδὲν ἀνισώτερον νομίζω τῶν ἐν ἀνθρώποις εἶναι. Cf. the use of καί in comparisons, note, I. 1. 6; 6. 3, and also Bornem. Symp. p. 67: εἴπερ τι καὶ ἄλλο, καὶ τοῦτο μαθητόν; Cyrop. III. 3. 42: Συμφέρει δ' ὑμῖν, εἴπερ τῳ καὶ ἄλλῳ, τὸ νικᾶν.

3.—Ἐμεγαλύνετο, from μεγάς, and the termination -ύνω which denotes a transforming into that which the primitive adjective signifies; Kühn. Gr. § 232. 1. (c); hence here, *was elated in mind.*——ἡδέως, *gladly.*——ἀποκρύψῃ; some Mss. and editions have ἀποκρύψῃς, but not well; for ἀποκρύπτειν τι refers to things without ourselves, *to hide a thing;* but ἀποκρύπτεσθαί τι to that within, *to conceal,* plainly the idea here. Cf. II. 3. 14: πάντα τὰ ἐν ἀνθρώποις φίλτρα ἐπιστάμενος πάλαι ἀπεκρύπτου; 6. 29: μὴ σὺ οὖν ἀποκρύπτου με; and IV. 4. 1: περὶ τοῦ δικαίου γε οὐκ ἀπεκρύπτετο ἣν εἶχε γνώμην; and see Kühn. Gr. § 250. R. 4; L. Gr. II. § 398. 5.

4.—Ὡς ἂν τότε σκοπῶν, elliptically for ὡς ἂν διασιωπήσειεν σκοπῶν or εἰ τότε σκοποίη; cf. note, II. 6. 38.

5.—Εἰκὸς γοῦν; cf. note, I. 4. 8, and III. 3. 5: Δεῖ γοῦν.——Λέξον δή; see note, I. 2. 41: Δίδαξον δή.——πόσαι τινές; cf. note and references, I. 1. 1: τοιάδε τις ἦν.——τινὲς αὐτῶν, sc. πρόσοδοι τῇ πόλει.——ἐνδεῶς ἔχουσιν, are deficient or small.

6.—Πρὸς ταῦτά... ἐσχόλασα, lit., had leisure for, hence, *given attention to.* Ταῦτα refers to the whole preceding clause: ὅτι καὶ τούτων τὰς περιττὰς ἀφαιρεῖν διανοῇ; hence the plural number is used; see Kühn. § 241. 3; L. Gr. II. § 423. Cf. at the end of the section: ἐπιμεληθῆναι τούτων, and § 10: διὰ τὸ μέγεθος αὐτῶν.——τὸ... ποιεῖν; the article is used for the sake of emphasis; see Kühn. Gr. § 308. R. 1; L. Gr. II. § 643.——μὴ εἰδότα; the subject is implied in the participle: *one not knowing;* cf. note, I. 3. 8: ἁπτόμενον.

7.—Καὶ τὰ ὄντα προσαποβάλοι ἄν, i. e., he not only would not enrich the city, (οὐ μόνον οὐ πλουτίζοι ἂν τὴν πόλιν,) but *even..* lose, etc.

8.—Ἥττων τῶν ἐναντίων, for τῆς τῶν ἐναντίων, compendious comparison; see note and references, III. 5. 4.

9.—Οὕτως γε ἀπὸ στόματος εἰπεῖν, to speak thus directly from memory, memoriter. Cf. Stallb. Plat. Phaedr. p. 235, C, and

Theat. p. 142. D: οὐ μὰ τὸν Δία, οὐκ οὖν οὕτω (sic statim) γε ἀπὸ στόματος; also III. 11. 7: οὐ γὰρ δὴ οὕτως γε ἀτεχνῶς οἴεσθαι χρή.

10.—Οὐκοῦν; see note, I. 4. 5. ——τὴν . . . πρώτην, sc. ἀρχὴν or ὁδόν, lit., *at first*, primum, but well here: *at present;* cf. Oecon. XI. 1: τὰ μὲν δὴ περὶ τῶν τῆς γυναικὸς ἔργων ἱκανῶς μοι δοκῶ ἀκηκοέναι τὴν πρώτην; and see Kühn. Gr. § 279. R. 8. ——αὐτῶν, not sc. δυνάμεων or πολεμικῶν, but referring to the whole matter in question: rei. ——Ἀλλά τοι; cf. note, I. 2. 36. ——φυλακαὶ . . . φρουροί, praesidia . . . milites praesidearii. —— ἐπίκαιροι . . . ἱκανοί, advantageous . . . sufficient. ——συμβουλεύσειν, i. e., οἶδά σε συμβουλεύσειν, to be repeated from the preceding context, instead of οἶδα, ὅτι σὺ συμβουλεύσεις; but the change from ὅτι with a form of the finite verb to the infinitive is not rare. For the distinction in meaning between these two forms and also between them and the construction with the Part. instead of the Infin., see Kühn. § 329. R. 5, and 311. 2; L. Gr. II. § 771. 5, and § 657. Anm. 2.

11.—Ἔγωγε, sc. ἀφαιρεῖν συμβουλεύσω. ——ἕνεκά γε τοῦ οὕτως . . . φυλάττεσθαι, ὥστε κλέπτεσθαι τὰ ἐκ τῆς χώρας, since the watches are so badly kept (φυλακαὶ φυλάττονται), that, etc. Τὰ ἐκ τῆς χώρας is a constr. praegn. for τὰ ἐν τῇ χώρᾳ (ὄντα) ἐξ αὐτῆς (τῆς χώρας) κλέπτεσθαι, like οἱ ἐκ τῆς ἀγορᾶς ἄνθρωποι ἀπέφυγον for οἱ ἐν τῇ ἀγορᾷ ἄνθρωποι ἐκ τῆς ἀγορᾶς ἀπέφυγον. Cf. III. 11. 13: δωροῖο τὰ παρὰ σεαυτῆς; Sympos. IV. 31: τὰ ἐκ τῆς οἰκίας πέπραται; and see Kühn. L. Gr. II. § 623; Buttm. § 151. 1. 8. The verb κλέπτειν, to take secretly, by stealth, is here contrasted with ἁρπάζειν, to seize openly. Cf. IV. 2. 15: ἐὰν δὲ κλέπτῃ τε καὶ ἁρπάζῃ τὰ τούτων; 17: ἂν . . . κλέψῃ ἢ ἁρπάσῃ . . . ξίφος. ——καὶ ἁρπάζειν ἐξουσίαν, *even* the power of openly plundering, taking by force, i. e., οὐ μόνον κλέπτειν ἀλλὰ καὶ ἁρπάζειν. For the construction of ἁρπάζειν ἐξουσίαν, see note, II. 1. 25. ——τῷ βουλομένῳ, cuilibet, or, cuivis. ——ἀτάρ, ἔφη; for the repetition of ἔφη, see note, II. 4. 1. ——πότερον ἐλθὼν αὐτὸς . . . ἢ πῶς, whether yourself *coming* (being present) . . . or *how*. The particle πῶς answers to the participle ἐλθών. ——ὅταν μηκέτι εἰκάζωμεν . . . εἰδῶμεν, for εἰκάζῃς . . . εἰδῇς, when we no longer conjecture but already know, in accordance with Athenian urbanity.

12.—Γὲ μήν; see note, I. 4. 5. ——τἀργύρια, the silver mines of Laurion; see note and references, II. 5. 2. ——Οὐ γὰρ οὖν ἐλήλυθα. Upon γάρ in responses, see note, I. 4. 9. Οὖν indicates that the reason introduced by γάρ is certain, beyond doubt. Cf. III. 14. 2; Cyrop. II. 1. 7: Οὔκουν ἀκροβολίζεσθαι ἀνάγκη ἐστί, τοιούτων γε τῶν ὅπλων ὄντων.

'Ἀνάγκη γὰρ οὖν, ἔφη; and see Kühn. Gr. § 324. R. 6 L. Gr. II. § 706. 2, and Hartung, Gr. Partik. II. S. 15.——λέγεται βαρὺ τὸ Χωρίον εἶναι, the country is said to be unhealthy, pestilential; Cf. Coraius: 'δυsάερον καὶ νοσῶδες· ἔσωσε δὲ καὶ ἡ συνήθεια τὴν λέξιν, βαρὺν ἀέοα λέγουσα τὸν νοσοποιόν."——σκώπτομαι, I am mocked, or, jeered at; some few Mss. have σκέπτομαι, but they are undoubtedly wrong, since in the present and imperfect, the Attic writers do not use σκέπτομαι, ἐσκεπτόμην, but σκοπῶ, σκοποῦμαι, ἐσκόπουν, ἐσκοπούμην. Woolsey in his Gorgias, p. 166, says, that "there is only one instance of σκέπτομαι in Plato to very many of σκοπῶ." It should be further stated, that, on the other hand, not σκοπῶ but σκέπτομαι is employed in the Fut., Aor., and Perfect.

13.—Γέ τοι; see III. 4. 10.——ἱκανός ἐστιν...διατρέφειν, κ.τ.λ. The provisions of Attica were brought to a considerable extent from foreign countries, hence the peculiar necessity of attention to the supply; see Smith's Dictionary; *sitos*, p. 899.——προσδέεται, sc. ἡ πόλις. So the object of one clause frequently becomes the subject of the following, without even a pronoun to indicate it. See Kühn. L. Gr. II. § 852. a. with examples; Stallb. Plato, Protag. p. 320. A. The same change is also found in Latin.——ἵνα μὴ τοῦτό γε...ἐνδεὴς γενομένη, that the city being in want, in respect to this, may not escape your notice. Τοῦτο seems to be Acc. of more def. limitation; see Kühn. L. Gr. II. § 557. Anm. 4; Gr. § 279. 7. For abundant examples of the same construction in Latin, see Kühn. Tusc. Disp. V. 28. 81.——εἴγε ...δεήσει; see note, II. 1. 17.

14.—Ἀλλὰ μέντοι, *but indeed.* Μέντοι expresses confirmation, Kühn. Gr. § 316. R.; L. Gr. II. § 698. a.——οὐδ' ἂν...οἰκήσειεν εἰ μὴ...εἴσεται. Cf. note, I. 2. 28. The future εἴσεται, seems to be employed on account of the ποτέ preceding, although instances may be found where a similar verb in the Ind. Fut. follows εἰ, after an Opt. with ἄν. V. Bremius, Excurs. VII. ad Lysiae, Orat. p. 444 sq. quoted by Kühner in h. l.——ἐκ πλειόνων ἢ μυρίων οἰκιῶν. According to Boeckh, Oecon. of Athens, B. I. Ch. vii, the mean average of the population of Attica consisted of about 500,000; viz., 365,000 slaves, 135,000 free inhabitants; besides about 45,000 resident aliens.——οἰκιῶν ...οἴκων. The former (from οἰκία) signifies merely the houses, whilst the latter (from οἶκος) every thing pertaining to the houses, the households; hence the appositeness of the words here; as the first is a mere enumeration, and the latter brings to view the objects of care and solicitude. ——ἕνα, τὸν τοῦ θείου, one [οἶκον], that of your uncle.——δέ εται δέ; cf. I. 6. 10. This clause is parenthetical. —— τάλαντον, here of course a weight, and = nearly 57 pounds.

15.—Εἶτα; cf. note, I. 2. 26. —— δυνήσεσθαι ποιῆσαι πείθεσθαί σοι; for a similar accumulation of infinitives, see IV. 6. 6; and Bornemann's Cyrop. I. 3. 13: οἴει τινὰς οἴεσθαι δεῖν μὴ ποιεῖν ταῦτα. For the use of the Infin. to denote purpose or result, see B. 140. 3.

16.—Ἐνθυμοῦ δὲ τῶν ἄλλων ... πότερά, κ.τ.λ. Ἐνθυμοῦ is closely connected with the question πότερά σοι, and not with οἷοι φαίνονται, κ.τ.λ. See also note, I. 1. 17.

17.—Ἐνθυμοῦ ... καὶ ... εὑρήσεις, cogita et invenies. For the construction, cf. II. 3. 16: μὴ ὄκνει, ἔφη, ἀλλ' ἐγχείρει τὸν ἄνδρα καταπραΰνειν, καὶ πάνυ ταχύ σοι ὑπακούσεται. —— εἰδότων ὅ τί τε λέγουσι, κ.τ.λ. Some commentators connect ὅτι, κ.τ.λ., with ἐνθυμοῦ, instead of εἰδότων, but οἱ εἰδότες ὅ τί τε λέγουσι καὶ ὅ τι ποιοῦσι seems to be intended as a contrast with τοιοῦτοι, οἷοι φαίνονται καὶ λέγοντες ἃ μὴ ἴσασι καὶ πράττοντες, and the *objectum rei* is implied in εὑρήσεις ... ἀμαθεστάτων. This will appear more distinctly if the words are thus arranged: ἐνθυμοῦ καὶ τῶν εἰδότων ... ὅτι ἐν πᾶσιν ἔργοις οἱ μὲν εὐδοκιμοῦντες ... ἐκ τῶν μάλιστα ἐπισταμένων εἰσί, κ.τ.λ. Cf. note, I. 1. 17. —— ἐκ τῶν ... ὄντας, Lat. esse ex, or, ex numero, etc.

18.—Ἐὰν ... ἐπιχειρῇς ... οὐκ ἂν θαυμάσαιμι; see note, III. 4. 6. —— τούτῳ διενέγκας τῶν ἄλλων, having excelled others in this; instead of τούτῳ, some Mss. and editions have τοῦτο, and also διενεγκών for διενέγκας. Cf. I. 2. 53.

CHAPTER VII.

1.—Χαρμίδην δὲ τὸν Γλαύκωνος. Charmides the son of Glauco, a youth distinguished for great beauty of person and excellence of character, was placed under the instruction of Socrates, by his guardian Critias. See a further account of him in Stallb. Plat. Prolegom. ad Charmidem. —— δυνατώτερον, sc. τὰ πολιτικὰ πράττειν, to be supplied ἀπὸ κοινοῦ, from what follows. See note, II. 1. 11. —— προσιέναι τῷ δήμῳ, i. e., to harangue, address the people from the forum. The words παρελθεῖν εἰς τὸν δῆμον, have the same meaning. —— στεφανίτας ἀγῶνας νικᾶν. The στεφανίτης ἀγών was a contest in which the prize was a crown or wreath. The στεφάνος does not seem to have been employed as a reward of merit in the heroic ages. Smith's Dict. *Corona*,

p. 309. For the construction of ἀγῶνα νικᾶν, after the analogy of νίκην νικᾶν, see note, II. 6. 26. —— Δῆλον ὅτι, ἔφη; we should naturally expect δῆλον, ἔφη, ὅτι as in IV. 2. 14; the same position of the words is found also in IV. 2. 14; 4. 23; Cyrop. VII. 1. 7, et al.

2.—Ὀκνοίη δή; there are various other readings here, such as ὀκνοῖ ἤδη, ὀκνοίη ἤδη, κ.τ.λ. The δή seems to be used to give force to the idea expressed by the verb which it follows: may (*even yet, in these circumstances*) hesitate, etc. This particle is frequently employed in a similar manner, after the imperative, as σκόπει δή, see note, I. 2. 41; and it is also found after other forms of the verb with similar significance. Cf. Hellen. IV. 3. 2: ἐρομένου δὲ τοῦ Ἀγησιλάου... ἀπεκρίνατο δὴ ὁ Δερκυλλίδας; Anab. IV. 3. 27; 5. 34; Plat. Phaedr. p. 273. D; ἐρεῖ δή. See Hartung, Gr. Partik. I. S. 283; Kühn. Gr. § 315. 2; L. Gr. II. § 692. καὶ ταῦτα, sc. ἐπιμελεῖσθαι τούτων. —— καὶ ταῦτα; see note, I. 2. 29. —— ὧν ἀνάγκη... πολίτῃ γε ὄντι, of those things which it is necessary for you, as a good citizen, etc.

3.—Τὴν δὲ ἐμὴν δύναμιν... For the force of δέ here, see note, I. 3. 13, and cf. § 5 below. —— ταῦτά μου καταγιγνώσκεις; cf. I. 3. 10: τί... ἰδών, κ.τ.λ. —— αἷς, for ἐν αἷς; a similar ellipsis is also found in Latin; cf. note, II. 1. 32. —— ὅταν τι ἀνακοινῶνται, when they *communicate* any thing to you.

4.—Οὐ ταὐτόν ἐστιν... ἰδίᾳ τε διαλέγεσθαι καὶ ἐν τῷ πλήθει ἀγωνίζεσθαι; for a similar construction, cf. IV. 4. 12: ἆρα τὸ αὐτὸ λέγεις... νόμιμόν τε καὶ δίκαιον εἶναι; 7. 7: λέγων μὲν τὸ αὐτὸ εἶναι πῦρ τε καὶ ἥλιον. —— καὶ μήν... γέ; see note, I. 4. 12. κατὰ μόνας; supply χώρας or δυνάμεις. The phrase nearly corresponds to κατ' ἰδίαν; Latin: seorsum, or, privatim. Cf. Thucyd. I. 32: αὐτοὶ κατὰ μόνας ἀπεωσάμεθα Κορινθίους; Plat. Alcib. I. p. 114. B. —— οἱ... καθαρίζοντες, οὗτοι; see note, II. 1. 19. In like manner in Latin is is frequently used after a noun, as e. g. Cic. de Nat. Deor. II. 10. 27: jam vero reliqua quarta pars mundi ea et ipsa tota natura pervida est et, etc.

5.—Αἰδῶ δὲ καὶ φόβον... ἔμφυτα... ὄντα; for the neuter plural in the predicate here, see note and references, III. 1. 7. —— ἐν τοῖς ὄχλοις, i. e., ἐν τοῖς τοῦ δήμου ξυλλόγοις, Lat. in concionibus populi. Cf. Plat. Gorg. p. 454. E: ἐν δικαστηρίοις τε καὶ τοῖς ἄλλοις ὄχλοις, and p. 455. A. —— παριστάμενα, exhibited; the verb παρίστασθαι is used of any affection of the mind. —— καὶ σέ γε διδάξων... ὥρμημαι, ὅτι, κ.τ.λ. Καί here has a kind of adversative force and corresponds nearly with καίτοι or καὶ μήν (and yet). There is a concealed irony in this answer, and we might supply: *you speak well*, and yet I am prepared to show, etc. Cf. Stallb. Plato, Apol. p. 29. B, and see Hartung, I. S. 147, and Kühn. L. Gr. II. § 727. 3. In Latin the particle a t q u e is used in the same way; see Kühner's Cic. Tusc. Disp. III. 2. 4: Qua caecitate homines, quum quaedam etiam praeclara cuperent, eaque nescirent nec ubi, nec qualia essent, funditus alii everterunt suas civitates, alii ipsi occiderunt. A t q u e ii quidem optima petentes non tam voluntate, quam cursus errore falluntur; where see Kühner's note.

6.—Τοὺς γναφεῖς.. σκυτεῖς... χαλκεῖς; this form of the Acc. is somewhat common in Xenophon, but rare in other Attic writers; see Kühn. Gr. § 57. R. 1; and cf. note and references, II. 2. 14. —— ἐμπόρους (ἐν and πόρος, a ford, crossing), ship-masters, those who trade upon ships, hence opposed to οἱ ἐν ἀγορᾷ μεταβαλλόμενοι. After μεταβαλλόμενοι, τὰ ὤνια is to be supplied in thought. —— ὅ τι ἐλάττονος πριάμενοι πλείονος ἀποδῶνται, that they may sell for more [than the value] that which they have purchased for less, or, for a large price what they have purchased for a small. The Gen. is used to express the relation of value after verbs of buying, selling, etc. See Kühn. Gr. § 275. 3; B. 132. 10. c. For the use of the subjunctive mode, see note, I. 2. 15.

7.—Τί δὲ οἴει διαφέρειν ὃ σὺ ποιεῖς ἢ... φοβεῖσθαι. The comparative particle ἤ follows διαφερεῖν on account of the force of a comparative in that word. It is like ἄλλο εἶναι, ἤ, a l i u d e s s e q u a m. Cf. III. 8. 5: οὐδὲν διαφερόντως... ἀποκρίνῃ μοι, ἢ ὅτε σε ἠρώτησα, εἴ τι ἀγαθὸν εἰδείης; 11. 14: τηνικαῦτα γὰρ πολὺ διαφέρει τὰ αὐτὰ δῶρα, ἢ πρὶν ἐπιθυμῆσαι, διδόναι, et al.; Stallb. Plat. Phaed. p. 288. D. See Kühn L. Gr. II. § 540. Anm. 3. —— τῶν ἀσκητῶν... τοὺς ἰδιώτας. Ἀσκηταί = ἀθληταί, those who are exercised, practised (in the palaestra), and hence opposed to οἱ ἰδιῶται, those who are unskilled, unpractised. Cf. Hipparch. VIII. 1; Cyrop. I. 5. 11, where too ἀσκηταὶ and ἰδιῶται are antithetical to each other. —— οὐ γὰρ... ὀκνεῖς λέγειν; for the force of γάρ in interrogations, see I. 3. 10. —— τοῦ τῇ πόλει διαλέγεσθαι, i. e., τοῦ ταῖς πολίταις διαλ. —— περιών, *superior to.* —— μηδὲ πώποτε... μηδὲ σοῦ. The first μηδέ = n e q u i d e m, *not indeed;* the second, n e c, *nor;* cf. note, III. 12. 5: οὐδὲ... οὐδὲ. Μηδέ, and not οὐδέ, is used on account of the concessive thought contained in the participle. —— φροντίσασι... καταπεφρονηκόσιν; the first is in the Aor. tense, as indicating a simple fact, and the last in the Perf., since the action continued until the time in which the declaration was made, i. e., have despised and yet hold you in contempt. Cf. note, III. 1. 4.

8.—Καὶ γὰρ; see note, I. 4. 9: οὐδὲ γάρ. Καί is, however, here to be joined with οἱ ἕτεροι in sense: *others also.* Cf. note, I. 1. 3. The ellipsis is to be supplied thus: οὐ μόνον οἱ ἐν τῇ ἐκκλησίᾳ, ἀλλὰ καὶ οὗτοι, οἷς ἰδίᾳ σύνει ἐν ταῖς συνουσίαις (§ 3), οἱ ἐν τῇ πόλει πρωτεύοντες (§ 7) τῶν ὀρθῶς λεγόντων καταγελῶσιν. —— θαυμάζω ... εἰ; see note, I. 1. 13. —— ἐκείνους, refers to οἱ ἕτεροι. —— τούτοις δὲ. Δέ, after a protasis, or participle which has the force of protasis, may be rendered, *on the other hand* or *whilst;* cf. Kühn. L. Gr. II. § 738, and Hermann ad Viger. 241. —— προσενεχθῆναι. Προσφέρεσθαί τινι, is, to conduct one's self toward, demean, or behave to one. Cf. III. 11. 11, and IV. 2. 1.

9.—Ὠγαθέ; see I. 4. 17. —— μὴ ἀγνόει σεαυτόν. Cf. Cicero, Epist. ad Quintum fratrem, III. 6, where he seems to imitate this passage: Cessator esse noli (μὴ ἀποῤῥᾳθύμει) et illud γνῶθι σεαυτόν noli putare ad arrogantiam minuendam solum esse dictum, verum etiam ut bona nostra norimus; and cf. also a somewhat different explanation in III. 9. 6, and IV. 2. 24. —— μὴ οὖν ἀποῤῥᾳθύμει τούτου, do not then neglect this, from indolence. —— καὶ μή; cf. I. 4. 17. —— εἴ τι δυνατόν ... ἔχειν, *if it may be profited by you in any way.*

CHAPTER VIII.

1.—Ἀριστίππου; see note, II. 1. 1, and I. 2. 60. Instead of the Gen. Abs. Ἀριστίπ. ἐπιχειροῦντος, we might, at first, expect the Dat. after ἀπεκρίνατο, but the construction employed by Xenophon is much more forcible. See Kühn. Gr. § 313. 2; L. Gr. II. § 587. e. —— τὸ πρότερον; the reference here is to II. 1. —— μή πῃ ὁ λόγος ἐπαλλαχθῇ, κ.τ.λ. Lest in some way their discourse be perverted, etc.; i. e., Socrates was not so careful to secure his own reputation for acuteness in reasoning, etc., as he was to inculcate and substantiate the truth. The article is used here with φυλαττόμενοι and not with πεπεισμένοι, because there is an allusion to a distinct class of men, the sophists, in the former, but no definite reference in the latter. —— ὡς ἂν πεπεισμένοι, i. e., ὡς ἂν ἀποκρίναιντο πεπεισμένοι, κ.τ.λ.

2.—Τῶν τοιούτων, οἷον ... τόλμαν. Seiffert says this is not a case of attraction, but that οἷον is to be considered as = for example, viz. Still the concinnity of the construction τοιούτων, οἷον is better preserved by considering it as equivalent by attraction to: τῶν τοιούτ., οἷον ... ἡ ὑγίεια ... τόλμα ἐστίν; cf. note, II. 9. 3. —— δεικνύοι δὴ ... ὄν; see note, III. 7. 2; and for the significance of δεικν. with the Part. see Kühn.

Gr. § 311. 11. —— *τοῦ παύσοντες, of that which will make it to cease.* —— *ἀπεκρίνατο, ᾗπερ καὶ ποιεῖν*; sc. ἀπεκρίνατο ᾗπερ καὶ ἀπ. ἀπεκρίνεσθαι, he answered in the manner in which it was most excellent to answer. Instead of answering as if good were something absolute, he referred it to specific objects, and thus thwarted the captious design of Aristippus, and escaped the snare spread for him. In Latin faciendi is often used in the same manner with ποιεῖν here, instead of repeating another verb. For the use of καί after ᾗπερ, see note, I. 2. 47.

3.—Ἀρά γε; see note, III. 2. 1. —— *πυρετοῦ ἀγαθόν, good for a fever.* The adjective here governs the Gen. from the force of a noun contained in it: *the remedy of;* see B. 132. 13, and note 26. —— Ἀλλὰ μήν, atqui; see note, III. 1. 6. —— εἴ τι ἀγαθὸν οἶδα, ὃ μηδενὸς ἀγαθόν ἐστιν, *if I know* any thing good, that is good for no thing, i. e., in no way useful. Socrates' idea, according to Xenophon, is, that nothing is good or useful in itself, but only in reference to some end or object. —— ἔφη, repeated; see II. 4. 1. —— οὔτε δέομαι, sc. εἰδέναι, to be supplied, ἀπὸ κοινοῦ, from οἶδα; see II. 1. 32. Brandis, Gesch. Philos. II. S. 41, note, supposes that this is the mere fragment of a longer conversation upon *the good*, but imperfectly recorded by Xenophon.

4.—Καὶ πολλά, *even many things* · καί is not strictly intensive, = *very*, but adds something to the simple answer that might have been expected to the question. —— μὲν οὖν, immo, or, immo vero; see note, II. 7. 5. —— Ὡς οἷόν...ἀνομοιότατα ἔνια, *some things are as dissimilar as possible;* cf. just below; for the sentiment, cf. § 5, sq., also IV. 6. 1, where the conclusion is: Τὸ χρήσιμον ἄρα καλόν ἐστι πρὸς ὃ ἂν ᾖ χρήσιμον, § 10, and Sympos. V. 3, from all of which, it is evident that Socrates includes the beautiful, καλόν as well as the good ἀγαθόν, under the useful; cf. Stallb. Plat. Prolog. Hipp. Maj., and Ritter's Hist. Philosophy, II. Ch. ii. —— ἔστι μὲν...ἀνόμοιος, καλὸς, κ.τ.λ., *another, unlike the man* who is *well formed for running*, is, etc. Ἄλλος is contrasted with ἀνθρώπῳ. —— ἔνι for ἔνεστι.

5.—Οὐδὲν διαφερόντως...ἤ; cf. III. 7. 7. —— ἡ ἀρετὴ...ἀγαθόν...καλόν ἐστιν, for the gender of the predicate, see II. 3. 1, and cf. § 6. —— ἔπειτα; see note, I. 2. 1. —— τὸ αὐτὸ...πρὸς τὰ αὐτὰ...λέγονται, are called honorable and good in the same respect, and in relation to the same things. The old grammarians would supply κατά with τὸ αὐτὸ, but according to a common idiom, the accusative is put as a more definite explanation of the word with which it is taken; see Kühn. Gr. § 279. 7. In reference to the sentiment, see Plat. Hipp. Maj. p. 295. D. Cf. Gorg. p. 474. D.

6.—Καὶ χρυσῆ γε ἀσπὶς; the particles καί γε are here employed to introduce something new and unexpected, and are not merely confirmatory.——πρὸς τὰ ἑαυτῶν ἔργα; for their own (respective) uses. ——ὁ μὲν ... ἡ δὲ, *the former* (i. e., κόφινος) ... *the latter* (i. e., ἀσπίς).

7.—Ἀγαθά τε καὶ κακά; sc. τὰ αὐτά, to be supplied as subject from the preceding sentence.——τό τε λιμοῦ ἀγαθὸν, i. e., food. For the constr. of the Gen., see note upon § 3 above.——τὸ πυρετοῦ ἀγαθόν, i. e., fasting.

8.—Οἰκίας; for a full description of the Grecian house, see Becker's Charicles, Excurs. I. to Scene III.——ἡδίστη ... ἐνδιαιτᾶσθαι; for the construction of the Inf. with the Adj. see note, I. 6. 5: ὡς χαλεπώτερα.

9.—Τούτου δὲ ὁμολογουμένου; this being conceded (by those with whom the conversation was held).——Ἐπειδὴ ... συμφαῖεν. The Optat. here indicates that Socrates was accustomed to resort to this illustration of the house, with his pupils, or that he often spoke with them upon its construction. Cf. note, I. 2. 57.——παστάδας. For the situation and object of the παστάς, παραστάς, or προστάς, piazza, see Becker's Charicles, Exc. I. pp. 208, 9, and 11.

10.—Ὡς συνελόντι εἰπεῖν, *to speak briefly;* lit., in order that I may speak comprehensively. For the constr. see B. 140. note 4; for the Dat. of the Part., Kühn. § 284. 10. a.——αὐτός is sometimes used to make a strong antithesis between the one designated by it and others; hence, as here, used for lord or master as antithetical to the rest of the household. In similar manner it is used of a father as opposed to son in Apol. § 31. Cf. Kühn. Gr. § 303. R. 4; L. Gr. II. § 630. Anm. 3.——γραφαὶ δὲ καὶ ποικιλίαι, paintings and stucco-work. See Charicles, as above cited, p. 212. 13. Socrates' objection to painting was undoubtedly, that it required the exclusion of the light, which added to the comfort and healthfulness of a dwelling.——Ναοῖς ... καὶ βωμοῖς χώραν ... ἐμφανεστάτη ... εἴη. Temples and altars in Greece were usually built in a thicket and fenced around with a περίβολος. Socrates did not approve of their being too much concealed, but wished them to be in an open or high spot, where the view would not be obstructed, as aiding in devotion.——ἡδὺ μὲν γὰρ ἰδόντας προσεύξασθαι. Some however contend that ἰδόντας has not reference to the worshippers having an unobstructed view, but to the passers by, who may see the temples and altars and make their salutations; see Vitr. I. 7: aedibus sacris—in celsissimo loco, unde moenium maxima pars conspiciatur, arae distribuantur; and IV. 5, ubi de templis circum vias publicas aedificatis agitur

—— ἡδὺ δὲ ἁγνῶς ἐχόντος προσιέναι, i. e., Socrates would have a retired spot, because the danger of being polluted when entering the sacred inclosure, would be so much less there, than in much frequented places. See Smith's Dict.: *Templum*, p. 958.

CHAPTER IX.

1.—Ἡ ἀνδρία, is opposed to δειλία, and signifies *energy of character*, as opposed to *weakness*. Courage is but a partial representative of it; *manliness* (a word of similar origin), in its best and most extended sense, is perhaps nearest to it of any English word, and virtus nearly corresponds in Latin. Plato defines it as καρτερία τις τῆς ψυχῆς, Laches. p. 192. D; and he elsewhere describes the man who is truly ἀνδρεῖος as one who fears nothing which ought not to be feared, whilst he fears what ought to be feared; see Lewis Contr. Atheos, p. 255 sq. Cf. note, I. 1. 16. In regard to the emphatic position of ἀνδρία, see note, II. 7. 8. The Latin accomplishes the same thing by a circumlocution, with de; interrogatus de fortitudine, utram, etc. —— διδακτὸν ἢ φυσικόν; for the gender, see note, II. 3. 1. —— πρὸς τὰ δεινὰ, in respect to all things difficult or perilous. —— ἐν τοῖς αὐτοῖς νόμοις, *in accordance with* the same laws, etc.

2.—Πᾶσαν φύσιν... αὔξεσθαι; cf. the same idea in II. 6. 39. —— οὔτ' ἄν... ἐθέλοιεν ἄν; for the repetition of ἄν, see note, I. 4. 14. —— ἐν πέλταις καὶ ἀκοντίοις... ἐν τόξοις... διαγωνίζεσθαι. For this use of the Prep. ἐν, see Kühn. Gr. § 289. 1. (1). (a); L. Gr. II. § 600. Cf. III. 11. 4. ὁρῶν—μητέρα παροῦσαν αὐτῇ ἐν ἐσθῆτι καὶ θεραπείᾳ. Demosth. de Coron. p. 279. 155: ἐν τοῖς ὅπλοις παραγενόμενοι. The Latin poets have imitated this construction; see Virg. Aen. V. 37: Acestes horridus in jaculis et pelle Lybistidis ursae. —— πέλταις. The πέλτη was a small light shield, the ἀσπὶς a large one to protect the whole body. —— ἀκοντίοις. The ἀκόντιον, ἄκων, javelin, a weapon for throwing at a distance, whilst δόρατα were perhaps more frequently used for fighting close at hand. Here, however, ἀσπίδας and δόρατα are put for Lacedemonian armor in general, whilst πέλταις and ἀκοντίοις characterize that of the Thracians.

3.—Ὁρῶ... ἐπὶ τῶν ἄλλων πάντων; for ἐπὶ construed with the Gen. after verbs of understanding, seeing, judging, speaking, etc., see Kühn. Gr. § 296, and L. Gr. II. § 611, and cf. II. 3. 2.

4.—*Σοφίαν*, *wisdom*, i. e., in general an accurate knowledge, discernment of our relations as moral beings, and the consequent duties. It is, according to Socrates, the foundation of all virtue; it is virtue. —— *σωφροσύνη* from *σόω* (*σώζω*) and *φρήν*, that which saves the soul, hence, *soundness of mind;* it signifies not merely the power of the will over the passions and appetites, but also includes the voluntary submission of these to the will; and hence is not only a healthy and peaceful state of the mind, but a moderation, medium between too much and too little in action. See Kühn. Tusc. Quaest. IV. 13. 30; Plat. Charmidas and Stallb. Prolog.; Lewis, Contr. Atheos, p. 351 sq. In contrast with *σοφίαν*, *right knowledge* here, it seems to have particular reference to right action, and hence Xenophon says, that Socrates did not separate the two (*διώριζεν*): *ἀλλὰ τὸν τὰ μὲν καλά τε καὶ ἀγαθὰ γιγνώσκοντα χρῆσθαι αὐτοῖς, καὶ τὸν τὰ αἰσχρὰ εἰδότα εὐλαβεῖσθαι, σοφόν τε καὶ σώφρονα ἔκρινεν*, but one who knowing the honorable and good, practises them, and being acquainted with the bad avoids it, he judged to be wise and prudent. Kühner thinks the participles *γιγνώσκοντα* and *εἰδότα* are repeated in sense, and the following Inff. depend upon them, i. e., one who knowing . . . knows how to practise, etc. Cf. II. 3. 14: *ἢ ὀκνεῖς . . . ἄρξαι, μὴ αἰσχρὸς φανῇς*; i. e., *ἢ ὀκνεῖς ἄρξαι, ὀκνῶν, μὴ αἰσχρὸς φανῇς*. A more precise construction would require the omission of *καὶ τὸν* before *τὰ αἰσχρὰ*, thus: *τὸν τὰ μὲν καλὰ . . . τὰ δὲ αἰσχρὰ, κ.τ.λ.* —— *οὐδέν γε μᾶλλον, κ.τ.λ.* The construction here is: *τοὺς ἐπισταμένους μὲν ἃ δεῖ πράττειν, ποιοῦντας δὲ τἀναντία, οὐδὲν μᾶλλον σοφούς τε καὶ ἐγκρατεῖς* (sc. *σώφρονας*) *εἶναι νομίζω, ἢ ἀσόφους τε καὶ ἀκρατεῖς νομίζω εἶναι σοφούς τε καὶ ἐγκρατεῖς* (sc. *σώφρονας*), those who know the right but do the contrary, I suppose to be no more wise than those who are ignorant (*ἀσόφους*) and without self-government (*ἀκρατεῖς*). The words *ἀσόφους* and *ἀκρατεῖς* are without the article, although subject and not predicate, because the subject is intended to be indefinite. Cf. Oecon. XII. 17 sq.: *καὶ τόδε μοι δήλωσον, εἰ οἷόν τέ ἐστιν ἀμελῆ αὐτὸν ὄντα ἄλλους ποιεῖν ἐπιμελεῖς. Οὐ μὰ τὸν Δί', οὐδέν γε μᾶλλον, ἢ ἄμουσον ὄντα αὐτὸν ἄλλους μουσικοὺς ποιεῖν.* —— *πάντας . . . προαιρουμένους ἐκ τῶν ἐνδεχομένων . . . ταῦτα πράττειν, κ.τ.λ.*, *choosing from those they*, etc. The idea of Socrates is, that the man who possesses true wisdom, knows what his own real good is, and acts accordingly. It is impossible for him to act contrary to his own interests and to what is right. Hence he who does not act rightly is not possessed of true wisdom or prudence. In reference to the signification of *ἐνδεχομένων*, see note, I. 2. 23.

5.—*Τὴν δικαιοσύνην καὶ τὴν ἄλλην πᾶσαν ἀρετὴν σοφίαν εἶναι, κ.τ.λ.* The reasoning in this somewhat obscure passage is briefly as follows: Justice and every other virtue is wisdom, for every thing just and virtuous is honorable and good; but he and only he who knows the honorable and the good (i. e., the wise man, the σοφός) prefers and does that which is honorable and good. But that which is just and virtuous is honorable and good; therefore justice and every other virtue is wisdom. It must be acknowledged that we should expect the Greek of the last clause: ἐπεὶ ... πράττεται, to run thus: ἐπεὶ οὖν τά τε δίκαια καὶ τὰ ἄλλα πάντα, ἃ ἀρετῇ πράττεται, καλά τε καὶ ἀγαθά ἐστιν. But it may perhaps be supposed that Xenophon was in fault in this instance, in communicating the precepts of his master. See Kühn. in h. l. —— ἐὰν ἐγχειρῶσιν, for the Opt. εἰ ἐγχειροῖεν; see note, I. 2. 2. —— δῆλον εἶναι, ὅτι ... σοφία ἐστί for the more usual ὅτι σοφία εἴη; see note, I. 1. 13: φανερὸν, κ.τ.λ. —— δικαιοσύνη καὶ ἡ ἄλλη πᾶσα ἀρετή. The article, it is well known, is frequently omitted even with the names of specific virtues and vices; cf. note, I. 2. 23: σωφροσύνη; IV. 6. 7: σοφία. The article is inserted before ἀρετή on account of ἄλλη; cf. Plat. Protag. p. 323. A: δικαιοσύνης τε καὶ τῆς ἄλλης πολιτικῆς ἀρετῆς, and B: ἐν δὲ δικαιοσύνῃ καὶ ἐν τῇ ἄλλῃ πολιτικῇ ἀρετῇ.

6.—Μανίαν γε, *insanity.* Μανία, according to Socrates, is the antithesis of σοφία, and is accordingly an ignorance, want of practical understanding of the virtues, such as temperance, justice, fortitude, etc. Γέ gives emphasis to the contrast between μανία and σοφία. —— οὐ ... τὴν ἀνεπιστημοσύνην μανίαν ἐνόμιζε. The distinction here made between ἀνεπιστημοσύνη and μανία is that the former signifies ignorance in general, such as the world takes cognizance of; the latter, ignorance of virtue, which arises from self-ignorance, τὸ ἀγνοεῖν ἑαυτόν. Ignorance of self, of the metes and bounds of one's own ignorance, is according to Socrates the lowest state of degradation and nearly allied to insanity; Ritter, II. p. 49; cf. also note, IV. 2. 24. —— καὶ μὴ ἃ οἶδε δοξάζειν. The position of μή before the relative is emphatic, and the phrase is equivalent to καὶ μὴ ἃ οἶδεν, ἀλλ' ἃ μὴ οἶδεν; see Kühn L. Gr. II. § 865. Anm. 3. For the omission of the subject with οἶδε, and also with the infinitive δοξάζειν, cf. Stallb. Plat. Apol. p. 29. B: ἡ τοῦ οἴεσθαι εἰδέναι (ἀμαθία) ἃ οὐκ οἶδεν (sc. τὶς). The same idiom is also found in Latin; cf. e. g., De Orat. I. 8. 30: neque vero mihi quidquam praestabilius videtur, quam posse dicendo tenere hominum coetus, mentes allicere, voluntates impellere quo velit, unde autem velit deducere. —— ἃ μὲν οἱ πλεῖστοι ἀγνοοῦσι, τοὺς διημαρτηκότας τούτων, κ.τ.λ., for τοὺς διημαρτηκότας τούτων, ἅ, κ.τ.λ. In the following words: τοὺς διημαρτηκότας, ὧν οἱ πολλοὶ γιγνώσκουσι, there is an attraction of the relative on account of the omission of the demonstrative.

8.—Ἀτυχίαις...εὐτυχίαις...εὐπραξίαις. For the concrete signification of abstract nouns in the plural, see I. 1. 11: ἀνάγκαις. The last two words are here used in their usual signification and not as in § 14. q. v. —— ἀνιωμένους. Cf. with the definition of envy here given, Cic. Tusc. Disp. IV. 8. 17: Invidentiam esse dicunt aegritudinem susceptam propter alterius res secundas, quae nihil noceant invidenti; nam si quis doleat ejus rebus secundis, a quo ipse laedatur, non recte dicatur invidere, ut si Hectori Agamemno; qui autem cui alterius commoda nihil noceant, tamen eum doleat his frui, is invideat profecto. —— ἠλιθίους...πάσχειν αὐτό, envy is a characteristic of little minds (of fools).

9.—Τί εἴη for ὅ τι εἴη; see note, I. 1. 1. —— ἰέναι πράξοντας τὰ βελτίω τούτων, to apply themselves to the doing of something better than these things. The Fut. Part. here denotes purpose, see B. 144. 3. —— ἰέναι...σχολάζειν, no one has leisure to pass from things better to things worse, etc. The latter verb is frequently followed by a simple infinitive; cf. Cyrop. II. 1. 9; VIII. 1. 18. —— τοῦτον ἀσχολίας αὐτῷ οὔσης κακῶς...πράττειν, he, since he had no leisure, did, etc., i. e., one who is engaged in something that is profitable, has no time to turn aside to that which is profitless, and leisure should accordingly be devoted to that which is useful. This sentiment is more distinctly expressed in I. 2. 57: τοὺς μὲν ἀγαθόν τι ποιοῦντας ἐργάζεσθαί τε ἔφη καὶ ἐργάτας ἀγαθοὺς εἶναι· τοὺς δὲ κυβεύοντας ἤ τι ἄλλο πονηρὸν καὶ ἐπιζήμιον ποιοῦντας ἀργοὺς ἀπεκάλει. The inculcation of such sentiments as these, one would think, was a very *indirect* way of "corrupting the youth."

10.—Βασιλεῖς; for this form of the Acc., see note, II. 2. 14. —— ὑπὸ τῶν τυχόντων, by the multitude, or, by any one whoever, quibus libet. —— οὐδὲ τοὺς...ἐξαπατήσαντας, neither those who have obtained it by lot, force, or fraud. —— ἀλλὰ τοὺς ἐπισταμένους ἄρχειν, i. e., they alone are in truth kings who know how to rule. Since knowledge is the only and the true foundation of all right action, and alone secures both individual and general well-being, the conclusion was natural, that it was necessary in order to constitute one a real king.

11.—Ὁπότε...ὁμολογήσειε: Opt. indicating repeated action; see I. 2. 57. —— ἔν τε νηΐ...ἐν τῇ νηΐ; for the omission and use of the article, see note, I. 1. 9. —— τὸν...ἐπιστάμενον, used Abs., Lat. peritus; as in II. 1. 28; III. 5. 21, et al. —— ἂν μὲν αὐτοὶ ἡγῶνται ἐπίστασθαι ἐπιμελεῖσθαι,...εἰ δὲ μή, κ.τ.λ After ἐπιμελεῖσθαι, there seems to be an ellipsis of τοὺς ἐπιμελομένους, (Seiffert says of ἄρχοντα,) depending upon ἐπεδείκνευεν, i. e., if they think they know how to manage these things, they themselves manage them. Plat. Protag. p. 311. D. resembles this passage. When two clauses are introduced by εἰ μὲν...εἰ δὲ μὴ, there is frequently an ellipsis of the apodosis of the first enunciation, but oftenest when the idea is a general one, like καλῶς ἔχει, etc.; cf. III. 1. 9, and see Kühn. Gr. § 340. 1. (c). Ἂν instead of εἰ is found in II. 6. 37. The idea of the whole passage is: In navigation, he who is skilled in the art, is leader, and others obey him; so in all other conditions of life; men who have any business that requires care, if they suppose they have skill in it, manage it themselves, but if not, they yield themselves obediently to those who have.

12.—Εἰ...λέγοι; see note, I. 2. 57.—— ζημιωθήσεται, will suffer loss; we in other cases find the form, ζημιώσεται, as in Demosth. Ol. II. (vulg. I.) p. 17, ad init.: ζημιώσεσθαι.

13.—Τὸν δὲ ἀποκτείνοντα—; Pres. Part. denoting repeated action.—— ὡς ἔτυχε, as it happens, in any manner, i. e., lightly, moderately.—— οὕτω answers to ταῦτα ποιοῦντα in the antecedent clause.

14.—Εὐπραξίαν, a living well, good conduct. The common meaning of the word was prosperity, good fortune, = εὐτυχίαν, but Socrates did not so understand it, as he says: τὸ μαθόντα τε καὶ μελετήσαντά τι εὖ ποιεῖν εὐπραξίαν νομίζω. Εὐτυχία is accidental good fortune, and εὐπραξία, success as the result of science and industry.—— Πᾶν μὲν οὖν τοὐναντίον, κ.τ.λ. I suppose τύχην, (εὐτυχίαν) and πρᾶξιν, (εὐπραξίαν) to be entirely contrary (different). Upon μέν οὖν, see II. 7. 5.—— μὴ ζητοῦντα...μαθόντα; participles involving a subject, see note, I. 3. 8: ἁπτόμενον.—— εὖ πράττειν, to live well, bene vivere.

15.—Καὶ...δέ; see note, I. 1. 3: κἀκεῖνος δέ.—— τοὺς τὰ γεωργικὰ εὖ πράττοντας, those who live well in agriculture; i. e., those who have knowledge of and rightly practise it.—— χρήσιμον οὐδὲν, useful for nothing; cf. II. 7. 7: οὐδὲν χρήσιμα.

CHAPTER X.

1.—Τὰς τέχνας ἐχόντων; cf. upon the signification of ἔχειν, note, I. 6. 13.——καὶ τούτοις. After ἀλλὰ μὴν καί, we frequently find another καί which is nearly redundant, as in comparisons. See I. 1. 6; 6. 3.——διαλέγοιτο; see note, I. 2. 57; and for the sing. τινι after a plural, see note, I. 2. 62.——εἰσελθὼν μὲν. To this particle δέ at the beginning of § 6 corresponds.——Παρράσιον, a distinguished painter, but it should seem from his ignorance, a mere youth when this conversation was held; see Fiske's Man. p. 414.——γραφική ἐστιν ἡ εἰκασία, κ.τ.λ.; is painting the imitation, etc.? Contrary to the general principle, the subject is here without the article, because it is general in its signification; and the predicate has it, because it is intended to be specific, perhaps δεικτικῶς. See Kühn. Gr. § 244. R. 1; L. Gr. II. § 494.

2.—Ὅλα τὰ σώματα καλὰ, *bodies beautiful in all their parts.*——ποιοῦμεν γὰρ. See note, I. 4. 9.

3.—Τί γάρ; see note, II. 6. 2.——τὸ πιθανώτατον... ἀπομιμεῖσθε τῆς ψυχῆς ἦθος, do you imitate the state of mind which is the most winning, etc.? According to Plin. XXXV. 36. 19, the painter Aristides first expressed in his paintings that which the Greeks call ἤθη τῆς ψυχῆς.——ἢ οὐδὲ μιμητόν, or is this not imitable?——πῶς γὰρ. The latter particle refers to a suppressed negation: *certainly not.*——συμμετρίαν. Pliny says, XXXV. 10: (Parrhasius) symmetriam picturae dedit, primus argutias vultus, elegantiam capilli, venustatem oris, confessione artificum in lineis extremis palmam adeptus, etc.——ὧν σὺ εἶπας, sc. τῶν κοίλων, κ.τ.λ., § 1. For the form εἶπας, see note, II. 2. 8.

4.—Ἆρ' οὖν; see note, II. 6. 1.——γίγνεται ἐν ἀνθρώπῳ τό τε φιλοφρόνως... βλέπειν. The verb γίγνεται here signifies: is found in, has place in; hence the use of the preposition ἐν before ἀνθρώπῳ. The article τό with the Inf. might follow it even in the signification: to happen, come to pass. Cf. Demosth. de Coron. p. 287, 177: ἵνα τοῖς ἐν Θήβαις φρονοῦσι τὰ ὑμέτερα ἐξ ἴσου γένηται τὸ παρρησιάζεσθαι περὶ τῶν δικαίων.——ὁμοίως is to be taken with ἔχειν τὰ πρόσωπα: to present the same face, appearance. By the separation from the words which it qualifies, ὁμοίως is made emphatic; see Kühn. Gr. § 348. 9.

5.—Διὰ τῶν σχημάτων... ἀνθρώπων, through the mien, bearing of men both when they are standing, etc.——διαφαίνει, middle signification common in Xenophon: appears, is exhibited. Cf. ἡ ἡμέρα ὑποφαίνει, Anab. III. 2. 1; IV. 2. 7; 3. 9; Cyrop. IV. 5. 14. —— τὰ καλὰ ... ἤθη; there is as much good philosophy as morality in the wish that Socrates insinuates here, that Parrhasius will devote his pencil to the illustration of the honorable, beautiful, and lovely in human character, rather than the reverse.

6.—Ἀλλοίους, *different;* i. e., so that a δρομεύς may be easily distinguished from a παλαιστής, etc.; cf. IV. 8. 2: οὐδὲν ἀλλοιότερον διαβιοὺς ἢ τὸν ἔμπροσθεν χρόνον. The idea may be: in different attitudes or circumstances, as contending, running, etc. The former seems preferable. —— τὸ ζωτικὸν φαίνεσθαι, *a life-like appearance.*

7.—Τά τε ὑπὸ τῶν σχημάτων κατασπώμενα, κ.τ.λ., those parts drawn down, etc., by the positions of the body (in wrestling), etc. —— πιθανώτερα, *more fitting*, or, *more pleasing* (as more in accordance with nature).

8.—Εἰκὸς γοῦν; see note, I. 4. 8; III. 3. 5, and 2. —— ἀπειλητικὰ τὰ ὄμματα ἀπεικαστέον ... ἡ ὄψις μιμητέα. The change from the impersonal to the personal construction will not escape the student's notice. Ἀπειλητικὰ (as menacing), predicate as the position of the article shows; so εὐφραινομένων; cf. note, I. 4. 13.

9.—Εἰργασμένους; see note, I. 2. 10. —— Νὴ τὴν Ἥραν; see note, I. 5. 5. —— καλόν γε ... τὸ εὕρημα, beautiful indeed is your invention. Καλόν is emphatic both by position and by the addition of γέ. —— τῷ τὰ μὲν δεόμενα σκέπης ... σκεπάζειν, κ.τ.λ., on this account, that the breast-plate protects those parts ... that need protection, etc. In respect to this unusual construction, τῷ ... σκεπάζειν, cf. Plat. Gorg. p. 490. C: τῷ μὲν ἄρχειν.

10.—Πολυτελεστέρους, of more expensive materials. —— Τὸν δὲ ῥυθμόν. In respect to δέ, cf. note, I. 3. 13. Ῥυθμός, when applied to a breast-plate, must denote relative adjustment of parts, due proportion. —— πότερα μέτρῳ ἢ σταθμῷ ἐπιδεικνύων, whether showing (to the purchaser) the proportion by measure or weight, etc. —— ἴσους ... ὁμοίους, equal in all their parts ... similar. Cf. Hellen. VII. 1. 33: ὡς τῆς πολιτείας ἐσομένης ἐν τοῖς ἴσοις καὶ ὁμοίοις; 1. 1: ὡς δέοι ἐπὶ τοῖς ἴσοις καὶ ὁμοίοις τὴν συμμαχίαν εἶναι; Ibid. § 13 and 45; Thuc. IV. 105; V. 27. —— Ἀλλὰ νὴ ... ποιῶ; sc. ἁρμόττοντας. The insinuation, that he might not make his breast-plates fitting (εἴγε ἁρμόττοντας ποιεῖς) immediately calls forth this strong asseveration.

11.—Σώματα...τὰ μὲν...τὰ δὲ; see note and references, II. 1. 4. ——ὥσπερ καὶ ἁρμόττοντα, i. e., ὥσπερ καὶ ἁρμόττοντα ποιῶ τὸν θώρακα, οὕτω καὶ εὔρυθμον ποιῶ αὐτόν; for καί in comparisons, see note, I. 16.

12.—Ὥσπερ ἂν εἰ φαίης; i. e., ὥσπερ ἂν φαίης, εἰ φαίης. Such an ellipsis is not uncommon with ὥσπερ ἄν; see Kühn. L. Gr. II. § 456. ——τῷ σῷ λόγῳ, "according to what you say."

13.—Εἴ τι ἔχεις; see note, I. 6. 13. ——τὸν αὐτὸν σταθμὸν ἔχοντες, although they have the same weight. ——διειλημμένοι τὸ βάρος...τὸ μὲν...τὸ δὲ, κ.τ.λ., having their weight divided, a part being borne by the shoulders, a part, etc. The participle φερόμενον is to be mentally supplied, and hence the use of the preposition ὑπό. ——ὀλίγου δεῖν, *almost;* used adverbially for ὡς ὀλίγ., κ.τ.λ., so ὀλίγου, πολλοῦ, etc., are sometimes used without δεῖν. Cf. Aristoph. Clouds, l. 722, and see B. 140. n. 4, 150. m. 18; Kühn. Gr. § 341. R. 3. ——προσθήματι, *an appendage.* The weight is so distributed upon the different parts of the body, that it seems like an appendage, a part of the body itself rather than a burden.

14.—Αὐτό δι' ὅπερ, κ.τ.λ., the very thing, on account of which, etc. Αὐτός stands for that which is especially the subject of discourse, = αὐτὸ τοῦτο, hoc ipsum; see Kühn. L. Gr. II. § 630. Anm. 5; Gr. § 303. 3. ——διὰ ταῦτα; i. e., διὰ τὸ ποικίλους καὶ ἐπιχρύσους εἶναι.

15.—Ἀκριβεῖς θώρακες, breast-plates, accurately adjusted to the body. ——Αὐτὸς...τοῦτο λέγεις, you yourself say the very thing I mean. ——καὶ πάνυ ὀρθῶς ἀποδέχῃ, and you fully understand me.

CHAPTER XI.

1.—Θεοδότῃ. In regard to the Heterae of Athens, with whom Theodote may be classed, see Becker's Charicles, Exc. to Scene, II. p. 194 sq. For the Nom. after ὄνομα εἶναι, see Kühn. Gr. § 266. R. 1; L. Gr. II. § 506. Anm. 1. ——οἵας συνεῖναι τῷ πείθοντι; i. e., τοιαύτης οὔσης, ὥστε συνεῖναι τῷ πείθοντι; for the construction of the infinitive, see note, I. 4. 6. This phrase characterizes the profession of Theodote. ——κρεῖττον...λόγου, beyond description in words; cf. I. 6. 11: ἔλαττον τῆς ἀξίας. So below: οὐ γὰρ δὴ ἀκούσασί γε τὸ λόγου κρεῖττον ἔστι καταμαθεῖν, for not indeed to those merely hearing, is it permitted to know that which is beyond the power of description. —— ἀπεικασομένους; the Mid. voice: representing *for themselves*, hints at the object of the artists in making copies of her, i. e., for use as models of human beauty. —— οἷς, for the more usual καὶ τούτοις. —— ἑαυτῆς ὅσα καλῶς ἔχοι. The genitive ἑαυτῆς depends upon ὅσα, partitively. With καλῶς ἔχοι, ἐπιδεικνύειν is to be supplied: it might be decorous to exhibit. Cf. II. 1. 21 and 32. Others, however, render: Quaecunque haberent pulchritudinis commendationem. —— Ἰτέον ἂν εἴη θεασομένους, = ἰέναι ἂν δέοι (ἡμᾶς) θεασομένους. The idea expressed by δεῖ is implied in the verbal in -τέον, and hence the following Acc. This construction is somewhat frequent in Attic writers. See § 2: ταύτην ἡμῖν χάριν ἑκτέον, it is meet that she should give us thanks; cf. with the preceding clause: ἡμᾶς δεῖ μᾶλλον Θεοδότῃ χάριν ἔχειν ... ἢ ταύτην ἡμῖν. See also Kühn. L. Gr. II. § 587. Anm. 4. —— Οὐ γὰρ δή; see note, I. 2. 14, and II. 4. 1. —— οὐκ ἂν φθάνοιτ' ... ἀκολουθοῦντες, Follow me at once, "Quin statim sequimini;" for the construction, see Kühn. Gr. § 279. 4; cf. note, II. 3. 11.

2.—Παυσαμένου δὲ τοῦ ζωγράφου; sc. γράψαντος, to be supplied from ζωγράφου, = ἐπεὶ δὲ ὁ ζωγράφος ἐπαύσατο γράψας. —— ἆρ'; cf. note, II. 6. 1.

3.—Πλείω ὠφελήσεται, she will receive greater advantage; cf. note, I. 1. 8; I. 2. 61. —— ἐκ δὲ τούτων ... θεραπεύεσθαι, the natural consequence is, that we shall pay court to, honor her and she be honored. —— εἰ ... ἔχει, ... ἂν δέοι; for the use of modes here, see note, II. 2. 3.

4.—Πολυτελῶς κεκοσμημένην, κ.τ.λ. The decency and comfort, and even splendor, which Socrates found in the house of Theodote, does not prove that this was the general condition of the women of her class. Indeed the astonishment, indicated by him, shows that he expected to find a very different state of things. Cf. Charicles, p. 198, 9. —— θεραπείᾳ, cultu, ornaments; others render it: attendance or train of servants, like θεραπαίνας. —— οὐ τῇ τυχούσῃ, *which is not vulgar*, or *poor;* connected in sense with ἐσθῆτι as well as θεραπείᾳ. Cf. I. 1. 14. —— Ἀλλ' ἄρα, *but then*, or, *but perhaps*. The ἄρα retains in a degree its conclusive force and also indicates wonder. The idea is: if you have not land, which surprises me, I conclude you have a house, etc. These particles are often used in dialogue where one brings an objection which has somewhat the nature of an inference from what precedes; cf. Kühn. L. Gr. II. § 757. b. —— οἰκία προσόδους ἔχουσα, a house furnishing a revenue, rent. —— Ἀλλὰ μή, *but yet ... not.* ——

χειροτέχναι, servants who engage in mechanical employments, many of whom were owned by the wealthy Athenians.——οὗτος μοι βίος ἐστί; for τοῦτο, κ.τ.λ., by attraction; see Kühn. Gr. § 240. 3, and note, I. 2. 42.

5.—Κρεῖττον οἰῶν...φίλων ἀγέλην κεκτῆσθαι; i. e.: κρεῖττόν ἐστι φίλων ἀγέλην κεκτῆσθαι ἢ οἰῶν ἀγέλην; for the use of the Perf. Tense, see note and references, I. 2. 49.——ἐπιτρέπεις; for the meaning of this word, see note, III. 5. 12.

6.—Ἐνταῦθα ἐμπέσῃ; cf. § 8: εἰς ταῦτα ἐμπίπτοντες. The adverbs ἔνθα, ἐνθάδε, ἐνταῦθα are used both with verbs of rest and motion; see Kühn. L. Gr. II. § 571. Anm. 3, and cf. Anab. II. 3. 19: ἔνθα βασιλεὺς ἀφίκετο; Isocr. Panegyr. p. 46. 30: ἐνταῦθα καταφυγεῖν ἔχομεν.

7.—Οὐ γὰρ δή; see note, I. 4. 9, and II. 4. 1.——θηράσειν; the future of the verb θηρᾶν is in Attic writers for the most part of the Mid. form θηράσομαι, but the active form of the Part. θεράσων occurs in Anab. IV. 5. 24; Cyrop. I. 4. 16.——θηρῶντες...τεχνάζουσιν. We may either consider the subject as implied in the verb here, or infer the noun οἱ θηρευταί from the participle.

8.—Ὅτι μὲν γὰρ, κ.τ.λ. Cf. a similar passage, Cyrop. I. 6. 40.——ἐκ τοῦ φανεροῦ τρέχοντες ἀποφεύγειν, that they flee hastily (running) from, etc. Cf. for the construction of τρέχοντες, the participle in the Nom., note, I. 2. 1.——κατὰ πόδας; see note, II. 6. 9.

10.—Ἓν μὲν...περιπλεκόμενον. This reply by the collocation of the words, answers the implied doubt, (i. e., whether she had any net at all,) in the previous question: you have one I think, and one that clings around (embraces) very well.——τὸν δὲ τρυφῶντα, a wanton lover. Τρυφάω, originally: to live delicately, and, to be licentious, wanton. It is worthy of notice, that Socrates, by attributing to Theodote many of the offices of an honorable love, places before her the contrast between her present mode of life and that which she might follow.——ἐπισκέψασθαι, Aor. tense, to designate an action done for once; that is, to visit a friend, if a friend ever happens to be sick. The variation from the present tense, which designates continued action, to the Aor. when temporary action is brought to view, is worthy of notice here both in the infinitives and participles: ὑποδέχεσθαι, ἀποκλείειν, ἐπισκέψασθαι, συνησθῆναι, ἐπιμελόμενον, τρυφῶντα, ἀῤῥωστήσαντος, πράξαντος; and cf. II. 7. 7; IV. 4. 4: προείλετο μᾶλλον τοῖς νόμοις ἐμμένων ἀποθανεῖν, ἢ παρανομῶν ζῆν.——κεχαρίσθαι, κ.τ.λ. For the Perf. here, see Kühn. Gr. § 255. R. 5, and note, I. 2. 49: δεδέσθαι.——φιλεῖν γε μήν; cf. note, I. 4. 5: ὀσμῶν γε μήν.——ὅτι ἀρεστοί...ἀναπείθεις, because friends are pleasing to you, I know that you conciliate them, not only by word but by deed. Λόγῳ and ἔργῳ correspond respectively to μαλακῶς and εὐνοϊκῶς, indicating not merely the blandishments but the advantages of friendship.

11.—Πολὺ διαφέρει τὸ κατὰ φύσιν τε καὶ ὀρθῶς ἀνθρώπῳ προσφέρεσθαι, it makes much difference, (is of much importance,) to demean ourselves towards men according to nature and rightly. In reference to διαφέρει, cf. III. 12. 5: πολὺ διαφέρει ὡς βέλτιστα τὸ σῶμα ἔχειν; and, for the meaning of προσφέρεσθαι, cf. III. 7. 8. —— τὸ θηρίον, used in reference to man, as in I. 3. 18. The change from the Opt. with ἄν: ἕλοις ἄν to the indicative ἐστίν is worthy of notice.

12.—Τοὺς φροντίζοντάς σου τοιαῦτα ἀξιοῦν. The verb ἀξιοῦν, which when it signifies *to ask, demand,* is followed by an Accus. with the Inf. as in Anab. I. 1. 8; Hellen. II. 4. 42. et al., like other verbs of similar meaning, takes here two accusatives. —— οἷα ποιοῦσιν αὐτοῖς... μελήσει as will be least trouble to those doing them.

13.—Τὰ παρὰ σεαυτῆς; cf. § 14: τῶν παρ' ἐμοί. The latter is the natural construction, and explains the former which is a mingling of two constructions, i. e., δωροῖο παρὰ σεαυτῆς τὰ παρὰ σεαυτῇ, as in the phrase: οἱ ἐκ τῆς ἀγορᾶς ἄνθρωποι ἀποφεύγουσιν. Cf. III. 6. 11.

14.—Προσφέροις, sc. τὰ παρὰ σεαυτῇ. —— ὑπομιμνήσκοις, sc. τῶν παρὰ σεαυτῇ, cf. § 13. —— ὡς κοσμιωτάτῃ ὁμιλίᾳ καὶ τῷ φαίνεσθαι, κ.τ.λ., by the most decorous intercourse and by appearing as wishing, etc. Τῷ φαίνεσθαι Dat. of means together with ὁμιλία. —— ὑπομιμνήσκοις... δεηθῶσι. The wisdom of this advice in respect to accomplishing the end proposed, is unquestionable, and the spirit of it might well be applied to other and worthier objects. Ruhnken compares Alciphron. Epist. II. 1, 40: μέγα τῶν ἑταιρουσῶν ἐστι σόφισμα ἀεὶ τὸ παρὸν τῆς ἀπολαύσεως ὑπερτιθεμένας ταῖς ἐλπίσι διακρατεῖν τοὺς ἐραστὰς, κ.τ.λ. Terent. Heaut. II. 3, 126. hac arte tractabat virum, ut illius animum cupidum inopia incenderet. In respect to the Nom. βουλομένη, see note, I. 2. 1.

15.—Τί οὖν οὐ... ἐγένου συνθηρατὴς τῶν φίλων; why will you not *forthwith* become, etc. This use of the Aor. in urgent requests, indicating the wish that the desired object were already accomplished, is somewhat frequent with τί οὐ and τί οὖν οὐ; see Kühn. Gr. § 256. 4. (e), and cf. III. 1. 11.

16.—Ἴδια πράγματα πολλὰ καὶ δημόσια. By δημόσια as contrasted with ἴδια πράγματα, Socrates designates political employments specifically, but as he did not engage in political life (*τὰ πολιτικὰ οὐκ ἔπρατ τε*), but *ἄλλους πολιτικοὺς ἐποίει*, I. 6. 15; he probably intends to use the phrase in a general way to designate the busy life which he led.—— *φίλαι*, lit., *female friends*, playfully used for his disciples who learned *φίλτρα τε καὶ ἐπῳδὰς* from him. Cf. with II. 6. 11 sq.—— *ἐάσουσι*; the future is sometimes used for the present when there is an implied condition, as here; who would not permit me to be away, if I were disposed to enter your service. See Kühn. Gr. § 255. 3; L. Gr. II. § 446. 4.

17.—*Ἐπίστασαι γάρ*; do you *then?* *Γάρ*, conclusive, cf. with I. 3. 10: *οὐ γάρ;*——*Ἀπολλόδωρον*. This man was entirely devoted to Socrates, and was one of those of his friends, present at his last trial. Cf. Apol. § 28: *Ἀπολλόδωρος ἐπιθυμητὴς μὲν ἰσχυρῶς αὐτοῦ (τοῦ Σωκράτους), ἄλλως δ' εὐήθης.*—— *τόνδε*; when the demonstrative pronoun is used with a proper name, the latter does not take the article; see Kühn. Gr. § 246. R. 1. (b) and references; L. Gr. II. § 488. Anm. ——*Ἀντισθένην*; see note, II. 5. 1; Symp. I. 3; IV. 44: *Σωκράτει σχολάζων συνδιαμέρευεν.*——*Θήβηθεν*; for the termination *-θεν*, see Kühn. Gr. § 235. 3, and R. 1. 2.

18.—*Χρῆσον*, *lend.*—— *ἐπὶ σοί*, *against you*, i. e., for taking or charming you; cf. note, I. 3. 11: *ἐφ' οἷς, κ.τ.λ.*—— *ἐὰν μή τις φιλωτέρα σου ἔνδον ᾖ*; Socrates here as in § 16: *φίλαι*, humorously applies to his disciples the language used of harlots. Thus *ἔνδον ἕτερος* was the common formula for excluding one lover when another was present; cf. Lucian Dial. Meretr. XII. p. 310: *ἀπέκλεισα ἐλθόντα, Ἔνδον ἕτερος, εἰποῦσα*; VIII. p. 300: *ἐπειδὴ δὲ ἐλθόντα ποτὲ ἀπέκλεισα· Καλλιάδης γὰρ ἔνδον ἦν.*

CHAPTER XII.

1.—*Τῶν ξυνόντων τινά*, one of his disciples.—— *νέον τε. καί, κ.τ.λ.*, lit., both young and having, etc., i. e., *although* young, etc., so et...et are sometimes employed in Latin.—— *ἰδιωτικῶς... τὸ σῶμα ἔχεις... Ἰδιώτης.* The noun *ἰδιώτης*, designates a private person, one who has no professional knowledge, and hence unskilled, unpractised, and here, one who does not practise gymnastics, neglects bodily exercise. So in III. 7. 7: *οἱ ἰδιῶται* is antithetical to *τοῖς ἀσκηταῖς*, where see note. Cf. Plato as quoted by Weiske, Vol. VIII. p. 420: *εὖ τὸ σῶμα ἔχων καὶ μὴ ἰδιωτικῶς ἢ φαύλως. Ἰδιωτικῶς τὸ σῶμα ἔχειν*, to have a body unpractised in athletic exercises, and hence *feeble*, sickly. In respect to the construction of τὸ σῶμα κακῶς, ἰδιωτικῶς ἔχειν, cf. III. 13. 1: τὸ σῶμα κάκιον ἔχοντι; Oecon. I. 13: ὥστε ... κάκιον μὲν τὸ σῶμα ἔχοι, κάκιον δὲ τὴν ψυχήν, κάκιον δὲ τὸν οἶκον. —— Ἰδιώτης μέν; the contrast implied in the μέν *solitarium* is τοῦ δὲ διανοεῖσθαι ἐπιμέλομαι, or it may be expressed in English by a paraphrase: I am indeed unpractised in gymnastic exercises; this does not pertain to my course of life; I give my attention to intellectual pursuits; cf. I. 1. 1 ἡ μὲν ... γραφή. —— Οὐδέν γε μᾶλλον, sc. ἰδιώτης εἶ. You are not more an ἰδιώτης, i. e., not less an ἀθλητής than those who are about to contend in the Olympic games, τῶν ἐν Ὀλυμπίᾳ μελ., κ.τ.λ. The idea here is: You have as much need to accustom yourself to ἄσκησις τοῦ σώματος as the literal ἀσκηταὶ τῶν Ὀλυμπίων. For when your country calls you to her defence in war you must be there. And you will as much need strength and activity of body as the combatant in the Olympic games. —— ὃν Ἀθηναῖοι θήσουσιν, lit., which the Athenians place, i. e., institute. The language is derived from the Games. So in Virg. Aen. V. 66: Prima citae Teucris ponam certamina classis. —— τύχωσιν; sc. ἀγῶνα θέντες: quam fors tulerit, as in § 2: ἐὰν οὕτω τύχωσι; q. v.

2.—Δι' αὐτὸ τοῦτο, on account of this very thing: sc. τὴν τοῦ σώματος καχεξίαν. —— ἐὰν οὕτω τύχωσι, *if they shall so chance*, sc. δουλεύοντες τὸν λοιπὸν βίον; i. e., if it shall so happen. Cf. Hellen. VII. 2. 34; IV. 1. 34; Anab. II. 2. 17; III. 1. 3. —— ἐκτίσαντες ἐνιότε πλείω τῶν ὑπαρχόντων αὐτοῖς, sometimes paying more for their redemption than they really possess, they, etc.

3.—Τῶν ἐπιτιμίων τῆς καχεξίας τούτων, i. e., these miseries which follow the neglect of physical exercise; i. e., poverty, disgrace, captivity, slavery, ignominy, death, etc. The word ἐπιτιμίων is well chosen to indicate that these evil are of the nature of punishment for neglect of the physical powers. Καὶ μὴν ... γε, atqui certe. —— πολλῷ ῥᾴω καὶ ἡδίω; these adjectives are in the predicate, agreeing with the implied antecedent of ἅ, and τὸν ἐπιμελόμενον is the Accus. subject of ὑπομένειν. —— τούτων; sc. τῶν τῆς καχεξίας ἐπιτιμίων. —— ὑγιεινότερον; sc. τί, a change of gender which has frequently been noted.

4.—Τἀναντία ... ἤ. So ἤ, *than*, is used after ἐναντίων in IV. 5. 8: τὴν ἐγκράτειαν τῶν ἐναντίων ἢ τὴν ἀκρασίαν — αἰτίαν εἶναι. See Kühn. Gr. § 323. 2; L. Gr. II. § 540. Anm. 3, and cf. note, III. 7. 7: διαφέρει ... ἤ. —— τόν τε λοιπὸν βίον ... καὶ τοῖς ἑαυτῶν παισί. The contrast here strictly requires the pronoun in the first clause: αὐτοί τε ...

καὶ τοῖς ἑαυτῶν παισί. The contrast of the τόν τε λοιπὸν βίον with the time after death, probably gave rise to the present construction. —— ἀφορμὰς, here, *wealth, means of living;* cf. note, II. 7. 11.

5.—Ἡ πόλις . . . ἀσκεῖ δημοσίᾳ τὰ πρὸς τὸν πόλεμον, our State does not publicly institute the practice of those things that pertain to war. A difference is here suggested between Athens and Sparta. In the former place, education, and hence gymnastic exercises, were not demanded by law, as in the latter, but only by custom. —— ἐπιμελεῖσθαι, to be cared for. —— οὐδὲ ἐν ἄλλῳ . . . οὐδὲ ἐν πράξει, κ.τ.λ. The first οὐδέ = n e q u i d e m, *not even,* the last = *nor.* Ἄλλῳ οὐδ. ἀγῶνι, is contrasted with πολεμικὸς ἀγὼν, the subject of the preceding paragraph. It should be noticed that οὐδέ . . . οὐδέ are never properly used as parallel with οὔτε . . . οὔτε: *neither . . . nor.* See Kühn. Gr. § 321. R. 7; L. Gr. II. § 744. 2. —— πολὺ διαφέρει, it is far better. There is however an ellipsis of the contrasted clause with this word, as well as with i n t e r e s t in Latin: πολὺ διαφέρει ὡς βέλτιστα τὸ σῶμα ἔχειν καὶ ὡς κάκιστα. Cf. note, III. 11. 11, and Bornem. Cyrop. II. 3. 4.

6.—Ἐπεὶ . . . τίς οὐκ οἶδεν. The sentence begins as if it were to proceed with πάντες ἴσασιν; such changes are not unfrequent especially with enunciations introduced by ὥστε; cf. Kühn. L. Gr. II. § 828. 1. —— καὶ λήθη, κ.τ.λ. The effects of the neglect of physical culture upon the mind, here enumerated by Socrates, are but too well and too often verified in the fate of those of studious habits. —— πολλάκις πολλοῖς; for similar instances of paronomasia in Greek, cf. Kühn. L. Gr. II. § 865. 2.

7.—Καὶ τὴν εὐεξίαν. There is generally supposed to be a trajection of the καί, which is to be rendered with πρὸς τὰ ἐναντία, κ.τ.λ. This position may have been chosen to bring out more clearly the contrast expressed in the πρὸς . . . γιγνομένων; cf. a trajection of καί in IV. 7. 7. A more natural explanation of this passage is perhaps, to consider the καί as in its proper place with the meaning of also or *even,* and καὶ τὴν εὐεξίαν χρήσιμον εἶναι, κ.τ.λ. = soundness of body should *even* be useful, etc. —— καίτοι, a t q u i, or, a t v e r e, not q u a n q u a m.

8.—Τὸ . . . γηρᾶσαι; sc. τινά. Kühn. Gr. § 238. R. 3; L. Gr. II. § 414. 5. There is also an old form of the Aor. of this verb γηρᾶναι; cf. Kühn. Gr. § 161. 8; L. Gr. I. § 186. p. 190. Thus Thomas Mag. p. 78. ed. Ritsch., says: Γηρᾶναι καὶ καταγηρᾶναι. ἀρχαιότερον· οἱ δ' ὕστερον γηρᾶσαι καὶ καταγηρᾶσαι. —— ἐθέλει αὐτόματα γίγνεσθαι, come not of their own accord, i. e., without practice.

CHAPTER XIII.

1.—Προσειπών τινα χαίρειν; with the formula of greeting: προσεῖπ. χαίρειν, we find the Dat. instead of the Acc. in Hellen. IV. 1. 31: ἀλλήλοις χαίρειν προσεῖπον. Cf. Kühn. Gr. § 285. 1. (1). ——γελοῖον, *absurd.* ——ἀγροικοτέρως. This adverbial ending, properly belonging to the positive, is however somewhat frequently found in comparatives; see Kühn. Gr. § 85. R.; L. Gr. I. § 327. 3, and cf. Venat. XIII. 3. μειζόνως; de Rep. Lac. I. 5. ποθεινοτέρως. II. 7. (5). ὑγιεινοτέρως; Symp. IV. 3. ἐχθιόνως; de Re equ. I. 6. ὑγροτέρως, et al. ——διακειμένῳ περιέτυχες, "*rather churlishly disposed.*" Hickie. ——λυπεῖ; an anacoluthon for λυπεῖν, to answer to ὀργίζεσθαι.

2.—Ἀκουμενός, a physician of the age of Socrates, and his friend. See Plat. Phaedr. p. 227. A.; p. 268. A. B.; Symp. p. 176. B. ——παύσασθαι ἐσθίοντα, *that he should cease eating;* i. e., before satiety. The subject is here implied in the participle; see note, I. 3. 8. So in: ὑγιεινότερόν φησι διάξειν παυσάμενον.

3.—Παρ' ἑαυτῷ, *with him,* i. e., at his house. ——ψυχρὸν... ὥστε λούσασθαι, cold for bathing; so the Latin: frigida ad lavandum. The adjective in the positive with ὥστε is used for the comparative with ἢ ὥστε. See B. 139. m. 56. ——ἄχθονται πίνοντες; see I. 2. 47. ——Μὰ τὸν Δί'; sc. οὐκ ἄχθονται, the negative being implied in the preceding interrogation; see note, I. 4. 9. ——τεθαύμακα, ὡς ἡδέως, i. e., τεθαύμακα, ὅτι οὕτως ἡδέως χρῶνται. So ὡς is used for ὅτι οὕτως in Plat. Crito, p. 43. B; θαυμάζω αἰσθανόμενος, ὡς ἡδέως καθεύδεις; see Kühn. Gr. § 329. R. 8; L. Gr. II. § 771. 8. ——ἐν Ἀσκληπιοῦ; sc. νεῷ; so with Ἀμφιαράου; see Kühn. Gr. § 363. b; L. Gr. II. § 474. b., p. 118.

4.—Ἀκόλουθον, his footman, an attendant who followed his master in public; as really a part of the family, as the master himself, and hence, like a proper name, without the article.

5.—Οἴκοι, at home, i. e., in Athens. ——πορευόμενος, περιπατήσας; for the anaphora here, see I. 1. 18. ——ἐκτείναις; the idea is: if you would just extend these walks that you make about the city in a direction toward Olympia, and continue them five or six days, you would arrive there without having walked more than if you had been at home. ——χαριέστερον... μᾶλλον. The adverb μᾶλλον may be, though it is not often, joined to a comparative to give it force as in Il. ω. 243: ῥηΐτεροι γὰρ μᾶλλον, much more easily; cf. Kühn. Gr.

§ 239. R. 1. A much more frequent use of it is, after several words, to call to mind the comparative, and, as it were, repeat its significance; so in Sympos. I. 4: οἶμαι οὖν πολὺ ἂν τὴν κατασκευήν μοι λαμπροτέραν φανῆναι, εἰ ἀνδράσιν ἐκκεκαθαρμένοις τὰς ψυχὰς . . . ὁ ἀνδρῶν κεκοσμημένος εἴη μᾶλλον, ἢ εἰ στρατηγοῖς καὶ ἱππάρχοις. In such cases as this μᾶλλον ἢ introduces a clause that is to be considered as supplementary to the main thought. —— προεξορμᾶν ἡμέρᾳ μιᾷ, *to set out one day sooner;* for the Dat. of measure or excess, see Kühn. Gr. § 285. 1. (3). (c); L. Gr. II. § 400. 8. So just below; τὸ δὲ μιᾷ ἡμέρᾳ πλείονας, more by one day; sc. than is commonly consumed in the journey. —— περαιτέρω τοῦ μετρίου; cf. note, I. 6. 11: ἔλαττον τῆς ἀξίας.

6.—Παρετάθη, lit., was stretched out, but here, weary, fatigued, cf. Cyrop. I. 3. 11: ἕως παρατείναιμι τοῦτον, ὥσπερ οὗτος ἐμὲ παρατείνει. Plat. Symp. p. 207. B: (τὰ θηρία) τῷ λιμῷ παρατεινόμενα. Lysid. p. 204. C: ἐὰν δ' οὗτος καὶ σμικρὸν χρόνον συνδιατρίψῃ σοι, παραταθήσεται ὑπὸ σοῦ ἀκούων θαμὰ λέγοντος; where see Stallbaum's note. —— τὸ ἱμάτιον; before these words μόνον is to be supplied. Herbst compares Anab. I. 4. 18: ἔλεγον, ὅτι οὐ πώποθ' οὗτος ὁ ποταμὸς διαβατὸς γένοιτο πεζῇ, εἰ μὴ τότε, ἀλλὰ πλοίοισιν, and Sauppius adds III. 2. 13; VI. 22. See Bos' Ellipses Gr. p. 307, where many examples are given. —— ἀκόλουθός; see note, § 5. —— μᾶλλον δέ, *even more*, or, *rather.* Cf. Cyrop. V. 4. 49; Plat. Lach. p. 196, C; Stallb. ad Phileb. p. 58, et al. —— ἠσκημένου . . . ἀνδρὸς; Gen. after a general word understood in the predicate with εἶναι, *running;* lit. a man exercised in the Palaestra, ἀσκητής; and then, one who is liberally educated. It is thus antithetical to παῖς; since slaves were not allowed to take part in the exercises of the Palaestra at Athens.

CHAPTER XIV.

1.—Δεῖπνον. This word here designates an entertainment where each one brought his own provisions; hence sometimes called δεῖπνον ἀπὸ σπυρίδος, because the provisions were brought in baskets. Where each guest contributed to the *expense* of the feast it was called ἔρανος. See Smith's Dictionary *Deipnon*, p. 343. —— φέροιεν; Opt. to denote repeated or customary action; see note, I. 2. 57; φέροντες first follows and then φερομένων. So we not unfrequently find φέρειν where we might expect φέρεσθαι, as μισθὸν φέρειν for μισθὸν φέρεσθαι; cf. Stallb. Plat. Lysid. p. 208. A., and Kühn. Gr. II. § 398. 3. —— ᾐσχύνοντο τό; it is quite doubtful whether this τό should be added. It is not found in the Mss. but might have easily been omitted in consequence of the preceding -το. —— ἐπαύοντο... ὀψωνοῦντες; see Kühn. Gr. § 310. 4. (f).

2.—Σίτου; here, *bread*, though lit., wheat-flour, as ἄλφιτα was the flour from barley; Smith's Dict. *Sitos.* —— ὄψον, antithetical to σίτου; see note, I. 3. 5, and Boeckh's Econ. B. I. ch. 17. p. 101, 2. —— λόγου ὄντος περὶ ὀνομάτων, i. e., λόγου ὄντος, ἐφ' οἵῳ ἔργῳ ἕκαστον ὄνομα εἴη. This clause is parenthetical, λόγου ὄντος being in the Gen. Abs. For the use of the Prep. ἐπί with the Dat. see Kühn. Gr. § 296. II. (d); L. Gr. II. § 612. In like manner we find: ὀνομάζειν, καλεῖν τι ἐπί τινι. Plat. Sophist. p. 218. C: Νῦν γὰρ δὴ σὺ κἀγὼ · οὔτου πέρι τοὔνομα μόνον ἔχομεν κοινῇ· τὸ δὲ ἔργον, ἐφ' ᾧ καλοῦμεν, ἑκάτερος τάχ' ἂν ἰδίᾳ παρ' ἡμῖν αὐτοῖς ἔχοιμεν. Parmenid. p. 147. D: ἕκαστον τῶν ὀνομάτων οὐκ ἐπί τινι καλεῖς. —— ἐπὶ ποίῳ ποτέ; see note, I. 1. 1. —— γὰρ δή; cf. note, II. 4. 1. —— Οὐ γὰρ οὖν; see note, III. 6. 12.

3.—Τὸ ὄψον αὐτὸ, lit., meat itself, i. e., alone, solum, as in § 2: τὸ δὲ ὄψον αὐτὸ καθ' αὑτό. See Kühn. Gr. § 303. R. 4; L. Gr. II. § 630. Anm. 3. —— ἀσκήσεως; the life and habits of an *athlete.* This passage is well paraphrased by Ernesti: Si quis opsonium edit sine pane, non quod athleta est, nec ex athleticae vitae consuetudine et lege, sed voluptatis causa, poteritne is ὀψοφάγος dici? —— σχολῇ γ' ἂν (scarcely), i. e., according to Suidas = οὐδ' ὅλως, οὐδαμῶς, or, βραδέως. Cf. IV. 2. 24; 4. 25. —— ἐπεσθίων, sc. τί δοκεῖ εἶναι; what do you think of him who with little bread eats much meat? —— τοῖς θεοῖς... πολυκαρπίαν; cf. note, II. 2. 10.

4.—Παρατηρεῖτ', ἔφη τοῦτον οἱ πλησίον. Οἱ πλησίον is in apposition with ὑμεῖς implied in παρατηρεῖτε. We should use a vocative in English; cf. Kühn. Gr. § 269. 2. (b). Cf. as quoted by Kühn. Hellen. II. 3, 54: ὑμεῖς δὲ λαβόντες καὶ ἀπαγαγόντες οἱ ἕνδεκα οὗ δεῖ τὰ ἐκ τούτων πράσσετε. Cyrop. VI. 2. 41: ὑμεῖς δὲ οἱ ἡγεμόνες πρὸς ἐμὲ πάντες συμβάλλετε. Also Krüger, Anab. III. 1. 46, and Stallb. Plat. Hip. Maj. p. 281. A. —— τῷ σίτῳ ὄψῳ, ἢ τῷ ὄψῳ σίτῳ χρήσεται. Ὡς is implied here; cf. note, II. 1. 12. Athenaeus thus paraphrases this clause: ὦ παρόντες, τίς ὑμῶν τῷ μὲν ἄρτῳ ὡς ὄψῳ χρῆται, τῷ δ' ὄψῳ ὡς ἄρτῳ.

5.—Ἆρα γένοιτ' ἂν... ὀψοποιία, κ.τ.λ., could there be a preparation of food, more expensive or more contrary to the art of making viands, than that which, etc. —— ἣν ὀψοποιεῖται; for the verb with an Acc. of kindred meaning, see Kühn. Gr. § 278. 1. 2. —— μέν γε the particle γέ here refers to the whole clause, and indicates that it is introduced as an argument for the preceding declaration; much like γάρ. For this signification, see Hartung, Gr. Partik. I. S. 390, 1, and references there: Cyrop. II. 2. 2; Plat. Symp. p. 215. C., et al.

6.—*Τοὺς ἄριστα ἐπισταμένους*; we may supply τὴν ὀψοποιίαν or consider ἐπιστ. as used Abs., as in III. 9. 11. For the use of the Art. with the subject here, see III. 1. 8. —— *τὸν ἕνα ψωμὸν ἑνὶ ὄψῳ προπέμπειν.* The article gives a distributive character to the phrase: to accompany each piece of bread by a single, etc. Cf. Kühn. Gr. § 244. 5; L. Gr. II. § 484. —— *ὅτε μὴ παρείη πολλά.* The Opt. is perhaps here employed to correspond with the following Opt. δύναιτ' ἄν; cf. IV. 2. 20: *δύναιτο γὰρ ἄν, ὁπότε βούλοιτο, καὶ ὀρθῶς ταῦτα ποιεῖν*; μή is employed, because ὅτε has a conditional as well as a temporal signification, and is in that respect nearly equivalent to εἰ.

7.—*Τὸ εὐωχεῖσθαι*, κ.τ.λ., in the dialect of the Athenians, synon. with ἐσθίειν: τὸ εὐωχεῖσθαι ἐσθίειν ἐστίν. —— *τὸ δὲ εὖ προσκεῖσθαι... ἐπὶ τῷ ταῦτα ἐσθίειν*, κ.τ.λ.; the εὖ is added, that we may eat, etc.; i. e., the εὖ is added to give the word the signification of eating those things that injure not, etc. The Prep. ἐπί indicates *end* or *design.* —— *ὥστε... τὸ εὐωχεῖσθαι... ἀνετίθει* so that he applied the word εὐωχ. to those who made a proper use of food.

BOOK IV.

CHAPTER I.

1.—*Καὶ εἰ μετρίως αἰσθανομένῳ*, *even if*, or, *although*, καίπερ. For this use of καὶ εἰ and the distinction between it and εἰ καί, *if also*, see Kühn. Gr. § 340. 7; L. Gr. II. § 824. Cf. Stallb. Plat. Apol. p. 52. A. Bornem. Cyrop. III. 3. 69: Μετρίως αἰσθανόμενος, of moderate capacity = μετρίαν αἴσθησιν ἔχων. Cf. Thucyd. 1. 71: δρῷμεν δ' ἂν ἄδικον οὐδὲν οὔτε πρὸς θεῶν τῶν ὁρκίων, οὔτε πρὸς ἀνθρώπων τῶν αἰσθανομένων, which the scholiast interprets by φρονίμων. Cf. also the absolute use of intelligere in Latin; Cic. Brut. XLIX. 183: an alii probantur a multitudine, alii autem ab iis, qui intelligunt. —— *ὁπουοῦν καὶ ἐν ὁτῳοῦν*, wheresoever and in whatever business (they may be). In like manner absolutely or with a verb implied, the Latin compounds, ubicunque, quicunque, etc., are used; cf. Ovid. Am. III. 10. 5: Te,

Dea, munificam gentes ubicunque loquuntur h. e. ubicunque sunt. —— ἀποδεχομένους ἐκεῖνον, lit., approving of him, and then following his instructions; cf. I. 2. 8. For the use of ἐκεῖνον, see note, I. 2. 3. —— παίζων . . . σπουδάζων, *sportive . . . serious.*

2.—Ἔφη . . . ἄν, *he would say;* for the signification of ἄν, cf. note upon I. 1. 16. —— τινος ἐρᾶν, verbs denoting an affection of the mind govern the genitive. Kühn. § 274. 1. a. For the idea, cf. note, II. 6. 28: διὰ τὸ ἐρωτικὸς εἶναι. —— φανερὸς δ' ἦν . . . ἐφιέμενος; *not desirous of those well endowed in person with beauty,* etc.; see note, II. 6. 7: δῆλον εἶναι. —— ὥραν; see note, II. 1. 22. —— οἷς προσέχοιεν . . . ἃ ἂν μάθοιεν. In indirect discourse, the Optative is often used after a preceding preterite or historical present tense, where the subjunctive or indicative would stand in direct discourse; and in such cases ἄν may be compounded or associated with any of the relatives or relative conjunctions, if, in the direct discourse, the subjunctive would have been employed. In direct discourse the form here would have been αἱ ἀγαθαὶ φύσεις μνημονεύουσιν ἃ ἂν μάθωσιν, κ.τ.λ.; i. e., quickly learn what they attend to and retain in mind what they may have learned. See Kühn. Gr. § 345. 4, and R. 4; L. Gr. II. § 845. 3, and cf. II. 7. 7; Anab. I. 5. 9: νομίζων, ὅσῳ μὲν ἂν θᾶττον ἔλθοι τοσούτῳ ἀπαρασκευαστοτέρῳ βασιλεῖ μαχεῖσθαι; VII. 2. 6: ὁ Ἀναξίβιος τῷ μὲν Ἀριστάρχῳ ἐπιστέλλει (Pres. hist.) ὁπόσους ἂν εὕροι ἐν Βυζαντίῳ τῶν Κύρου στρατιωτῶν ὑπολελειμμένους, ἀποδόσθαι. —— μνημονεύειν . . . ἐπιθυμεῖν; the article is to be supplied here from the preceding Infin. τοῦ . . . μανθάνειν, etc. —— ἔστιν, *it is permitted,* or, *one can.*

3.—Οὐ τὸν αὐτὸν δὲ. This position of δὲ in the fourth instead of the second place in the enunciation, is not without example; cf. Anab. V. 2. 2: εἰς τοὺς Δρίλας δὲ προθύμως ἦγον; Hellen. VI. 4. 17: καὶ τοὺς ἐπ' ἀρχαῖς δὲ τότε καταλειφθέντας ἀκολουθεῖν ἐκέλευον; De Re Equ. V. 9: καὶ τὴν ὑπὸ γαστέρα δὲ ἄγαν κάθαρσιν. This position seems to be owing to the close relation of the preceding words, which make, as it were, but one. At least this accounts for it in most cases. —— ἐπὶ πάντας ᾔει, *he was not accustomed to approach all,* etc. The imperfect denotes customary action; and the phrase is nearly equivalent to: προσφέρεσθαί τινι (III. 7. 8. note), yet with the accessory idea of approaching. —— φύσει ἀγαθοὺς, good in respect to nature, or endowed with a good nature. So ἐρρωμενεστάτους ταῖς ψυχαῖς in § 4. The dative here denotes that *in respect to* which, etc.; see Kühn. Gr. § 284. 3. 10, and cf. Anab. III. 1. 42: ταῖς ψυχαῖς ἐρρωμενέστεροι—τῶν τε ἵππων, κ.τ.λ.; the particle τέ corresponds to καί before τῶν κυνῶν.

With δυσκαθεκτοτάτους and φαυλ., γιγνομένους is to be supplied and rendered like the Inf. after ἐπιδεικνύων. —— τὰς μὲν ἀχθείσας, *some being trained.* The τὰς which according to the usual construction would answer to the one here, with the δέ below (ἀναγώγους δὲ), is omitted and implied in the participle γενομένας; cf. Kühn. L. Gr. II. § 732. Anm. 1. —— ἀναγώγους, antith. to ἀχθείσας, signif. as its composition shows: *untrained.* The same word is applied to horses in III. 3. 4. —— ἀρίστας γίγνεσθαι; the change to the Inf. from the Part. γιγνομένους is less strange here, after ἐπιδεικνύων, since the verb from which that participle is derived, in the sense of *teach,* is more frequently followed by the infinitive; see note, II. 3. 17.

4.—Ἐξεργαστικωτάτους ὧν ἂν ἐγχειρῶσι; for the Gen., see note, III. 1. 6. With ἐγχειρῶσι the verb ἐξεργάζεσθαι is to be supplied from the preceding adjective ἐξεργαστικωτάτους. Sauppius compares III. 9. 5: οὔτε τοὺς μὴ ἐπισταμένους δύνασθαι πράττειν, ἀλλὰ καὶ ἐὰν ἐγχειρῶσιν (sc. πράττειν), ἁμαρτάνειν. —— διὸ ... κακὰ ἐργάζονται. In respect to the change from *oratio obliqua* to *recta;* see Kühn. L. Gr. II. § 850.

5.—Ἐφρένου λέγων, *he instructed them by saying.* —— Εἴ τις οἴεται; the indicative in *oratio obliqua* is not unfrequent when a thing is intended to be represented as a fact, or as passing before the eyes; cf. Kühn. Gr. § 345. R. 5, and note, I. 1. 13.

CHAPTER II.

1.—This conversation with Euthydemus, and chap. IV. of this same book, are frequently referred to, as a specimen of the manner in which Socrates was accustomed to reason with the arrogant and self-conceited persons whom he met; see especially IV. 4. —— μέγα φρονοῦσιν ἐπὶ σοφίᾳ, who pride themselves on account of their wisdom. —— ὡς προσεφέρετο; for the signification of this word, cf. note, III. 7. 8; the imperfect tense, denoting customary action, as frequently. —— Εὐθύδημον; see I. 2. 29, and Plat. Hipp. Minor, with Stallbaum's Prolegomena. —— τὸν καλόν, an appellation frequently given to the learned men of Athens; cf. Plat. Phaedr. p. 278. E: Ἰσοκράτην τὸν καλόν; Phileb. p. 11. C: Φίληβος ὁ καλός; Protag. extr.: Καλλίᾳ τῷ καλῷ; Xen. Hellen. II. p. 470. C: Κριτίᾳ τῷ καλῷ; and in Latin, Cic. Tusc. Disp. I. 40. 96: Propino hoc pulchro Critiae. —— γράμματα, = συγγράμματα, συγγεγραμμένα, books of extracts, precepts, and examples, selected from other authors. —— σοφιστῶν των εὐδοκιμωτάτων here refers to former prose writers as contrasted with ποιητῶν, and not to "the Sophists" specifically; see Grote's Greece, Vol. VIII. p. 480. —— ἐκ τούτων, *hence*, or, on this account. —— διαφέρειν τῶν ἡλικιωτῶν ἐπὶ σοφίᾳ; the more usual construction would be without the preposition ἐπί. The idea here is similar to that in: μέγα φρονεῖν ἐπὶ σοφίᾳ. —— ἐλπίδας; see note, I. 1. 11: ἀνάγκαις. —— πρῶτον μὲν; the idea in these words is resumed by κατ' ἀρχὰς μὲν in the beginning of § 8, and the going with his disciples (τῶν μεθ' ἑαυτοῦ τινας ἔχων) is contrasted with the going alone (μόνος ἦλθεν) in § 8. —— διὰ νεότητα οὔπω εἰς τὴν ἀγορὰν εἰσιόντα; i. e., he was not yet twenty years old; see note, III. 6. 1. —— καθίζοντα εἰς; sometimes verbs of rest involve the idea of the motion that preceded, and may hence be followed by εἰς. —— ᾔει, *was accustomed to go*, Impf. —— τῶν μεθ' ἑαυτοῦ τινας, certain of those with him, his disciples.

2.—Καὶ πρῶτον μὲν; to which πάλιν δὲ in § 3 and ἐπεὶ δὲ in § 6 correspond. —— πρὸς ἐκεῖνον ἀποβλέπειν; in like manner we say that children *look to* parents (for support), and people *direct their eyes to* rulers (for counsel, succor, etc.). Cf. in Greek § 30: τοῦτο πρὸς σὲ ἀποβλέπω εἴ μοι ἐθελήσαις ἂν ἐξηγήσασθαι. 'Αποβλέπειν is also followed by εἰς; as in Hellen. VI. 1. 8: ἡ σὴ πατρὶς εἰς σὲ ἀποβλέπει; Anab. VII. 2. 33: εἰς ἀλλοτρίαν τράπεζαν ἀποβλέπων. —— κινεῖν, move or draw into conversation. Cf. Stallb. Plat. Lysid. p. 223. A. —— τὰς... τέχνας... σπουδαίους. Σπουδαῖος τὴν τέχνην = δεινὸς τὴν τέχνην; cf. § 6. The subject of γίγνεσθαι (τινάς) is implied in σπουδαίους. The words τὰς μὲν ὀλίγου ἀξίας τέχνας form a strong contrast with τὸ δὲ προεστάναι πόλεως. —— ἀπὸ ταυτομάτου, by one's own natural endowments, *by nature;* like φύσει in IV. 1. 3. Cf. § 4 and 6; Plat. Alcib. I. p. 118. C: Λέγεται (ὁ Περικλῆς)... οὐκ ἀπὸ ταὐτομάτου σοφὸς γεγονέναι ἀλλὰ πολλοῖς καὶ σοφοῖς συγγεγονέναι. So in Demosthenes, Coron. p. 296. 205: τὸν αὐτόματον θάνατον = natural death.

3.—Τῆς συνεδρίας, the session, assembly, i. e., at the ἡνιοποιεῖον. —— Εὐθύδημος οὑτοσί; proper names with the demonstratives οὗτος, ἐκεῖνος, ὅδε and αὐτός do not take the article; see Kühn. Gr. § 246. 3. (6); L. Gr. II. § 488. Anm. For the use of the demonstrative ί with οὗτος = this *here*, see Kühn. Gr. § 95. (ε). —— ἐν ἡλικίᾳ γενόμενος, when he shall arrive at the age of manhood. 'Ηλικία is used, κατ' ἐξοχήν, for manly age, i. e., from eighteen to fifty. —— τῆς πόλεως λόγον περί τινος προτιθείσης, the State giving the opportunity of speaking, i. e., proposing a consultation. Λόγον, or, γνώμας προτιθέναι was the office of the πρόεδροι, who, when the people were assembled called out: τίς ἀγορεύειν βούλεται;

4.—Ἐπισταμένων, used absolutely without an object; cf. note, III. 9. 11 and references. —— τἀναντία, sc. ἐποίησα, (*contra feci,*) to be supplied from the preceding context. —— τὸ δόξαι, sc. μεμαθηκέναι. Cf. § 8: φυλαττόμενος οὐ μόνον τὸ μαθεῖν τι παρὰ τῶν ἰατρῶν, ἀλλὰ καὶ τὸ δόξαι μεμαθηκέναι τὴν τέχνην ταύτην.

5.—Ἁρμόσειε... ἄν, *it would be fitting;* nearly synonymous with a form of πρέπειν. —— καὶ τοῖς βουλομένοις παρὰ τῆς πόλεως ἰατρικὸν ἔργον λαβεῖν, those also who wish to receive, etc. Physicians were appointed by the State and received a salary from the public treasury; cf. Boeckh's Oecon. I. 21, and Weiske in h. l. Cf. Schol. to Aristoph. Acharn. 1029: Δημοσίᾳ χειροτονούμενοι ἰατροὶ καὶ δημόσιοι προῖκα ἐθεράπευον. —— ἐπιτήδειον γ', useful *indeed,* γέ = γοῦν; cf. note, I. 2. 54. —— μαθεῖν... μεμαθηκέναι; for the difference of signification in the Pres. and Perf., see note, III. 1. 4. —— ἐν ὑμῖν ἀποκινδυνεύων, "hazarding experiments upon you,"—Packard in h. l. Cf. Plin. H. N.; cited by Schneid. XXIX. 1: Discunt (medici) periculis nostris et experimenta per mortes agunt.

6.—Ἤδη μὲν, κ.τ.λ. There is little doubt that this refers to a time subsequent to the interview above alluded to, and indicates the result of Socrates' previous efforts. He had now gained his ear. —— περιβάλλεσθαι, lit., to throw around, here, *acquire* (for himself, Mid. voice). —— Θαυμαστὸν γάρ. There is an ellipsis here: οὐκ ὀρθῶς ποιεῖς φυλαττόμενος αὐτός τι φθέγγεσθαι. Still we may give the idea substantially in English or Latin by an affirmative particle: *surely,* sane or, profecto. —— ὡς συνεχέστατα, most assiduously. —— παρὰ τοῖς ἀρίστοις... εἶναι. Ἀρίστοις is in the predicate and attracted into the Dat. by the antecedent τοῖς, and the whole phrase is contrasted with καθ' ἑαυτούς, *alone.* —— ὡς οὐκ ἂν... γενόμενοι; i. e., νομίζοντες, ὅτι οὐκ ἂν ἄλλως ἀξιόλογοι γένοιντο, or, οὐκ ἂν ἄλλως... γενέσθαι; cf. II. 2. 13

7.—Καίτοι γε; see note, I. 2. 3. —— ταῦτα ἐκείνων. Ταῦτα according to general usage refers to the nearer thing (δυνατῶν..., λέγειν, κ.τ.λ.), and ἐκείνων to the more remote (οἱ βουλόμενοι κιθαρίζειν, κ.τ.λ.). —— περ πλειόνων... ἐλάττους, κ.τ.λ., lit., *fewer* succeed although *more* devote themselves to them, i. e., fewer in proportion to the number, etc.

8.—Οὖν is here conclusive, and forms a transition to something new —— ἀκούοντος Εὐθυδήμου; this is contrasted with the προθυμότεροι ἀκούοντα that follows. Upon the perfect signification of ἀκούω, just below, see note, III. 5. 26. —— τῷ ὄντι, *really, in truth.* —— γράμματα; see § 1. —— συνῆχας; cf. § 1: συνειλεγμένον; § 10: συλλέγεις.

9.—Νὴ τὴν Ἥραν; see I. 5. 5. —— προείλου . . . μᾶλλον; cf. note, II. 1. 2. —— μετιέναι τὴν σοφίαν, to pursue, engage in the pursuit of, wisdom.

10.—Διεσιώπησεν ὁ, κ.τ.λ.; cf. III. 6. 4. ——Ἆρα μή; these particles presuppose a negative answer; cf. I. 3. 11. —— Ἀλλὰ μή; cf. III. 11. 4. —— τοῦτο δεῖ. Τοῦτο is accusative here. See B. 131. N. 4. The more usual constr. is the Dat. of the person and Gen. of the thing. Woolsey, Gorg. p. 491. D. says: δεῖ sometimes takes the Acc. of the thing when that is a pronoun. —— Οὔκουν, certainly, . . . not. —— ἀστρολόγος = astronomus as ἀστρολογία = astronomia. Still ἀστρονομία was in use; see IV. 7. 5. In like manner Latin writers even in the golden age of the language, use astrologus and astrologia for astronomus and astronomia, which were employed in a later age. See Andrews' L. Lex. h. v. —— ῥαψῳδοὺς . . . πάνυ ἠλιθίους ὄντας. This judgment of the *rhapsodes* applies only to the age of Socrates and to the philosophers; their offices were highly valued in an earlier age. For an account of them, and their services, and the depreciation of them by Socrates and others, see Grote's Hist. of Greece, Vol. II. Part I. ch. 21. p. 184 sq.

11.—Οὐ δή που—; these particles strictly presuppose a negative answer to the interrogation, but are of course used ironically here, as in II. 3. 1. —— βασιλική, sc. τέχνη: "the *kingly art*," i. e. the science of government. —— ταῦτα; for this Acc. see Kühn. Gr. § 279. 7. Example. —— καὶ μάλα . . . καὶ οὐκ οἷόν τέ γε, most certainly (I have thought upon it), and it is not indeed possible, etc.; καὶ . . . γε extend the answer to the question, or, introduce something in addition to the simple answer, and hence, are in place here. Cf. IV. 5. 2: ἆρα καλὸν . . . νομίζεις εἶναι . . ἐλευθερίαν; Ὡς οἷόν τέ γε μάλιστα, ἔφη.

12.—Τοῦτο κατείργασαι; τοῦτο. sc. δίκαιον εἶναι, have yo attained to this, i. e., to be just? —— οὐδενὸς . . . δίκαιος; cf. note, 1 5. 6, and I. 7. 4: ἀλυσιτελὲς ἀπέφαινε. ——Ἆρ' οὖν; see note, II. 6. 1 ——Ἔστι μέντοι; see note, II. 6. 2. —— Μὴ οὖν . . . οὐ δύναμαι Μή ουν . . . οὐ δυνάμαι, am I then not able, &c. In reference to the construction, see Kühn. Gr. § 344. 5. (d); L. Gr. II. § 779. Some Mss. and

Edd. have the Subj. δύνωμαι instead of the indicative. But the latter seems preferable, as Euthydemus speaks with strong confidence. —— Καὶ... τὰ τῆς ἀδικίας; i. e., οὐ μόνον τὰ τῆς δικαιοσύνης ἔργα δύναμαι ἐξηγήσασθαι, ἀλλὰ καὶ τὰ τῆς ἀδικίας.

13.—Ἐνταυθοῖ. Some editors read ἐνταυθί, supposing the former to belong to the Ionic Dialect, but Stallbaum, Plato Phileb. p. 23, cites several examples of the use of ἐνταυθοῖ in Attic Greek, as Plat. Apol. p. 33; Aristoph. Nubes 814, et al. —— Εἴ τι... προσδεῖν, if it seem to you *there is need of these things also*, i. e., in addition to other facilities, as indicated by προς in προσδεῖν.

14.—Δῆλον ὅτι, ἔφη; see note, III. 7. 1. —— οὐδὲν ἡμῖν τούτων κείσεται. The Dat here denotes *in the opinion or judgment of*; see Kühn. § 284. 3. (10), (a); L. Gr. II. § 581, d. Cf. IV. 6. 4: ὁ ἄρα τὰ περὶ τοὺς θεοὺς νόμιμα εἰδὼς ὀρθῶς ἂν ἡμῖν εὐσεβὴς ὡρισμένος εἴη; Cf. in Lat., Tacitus' Annal. I. 42: cives, quibus tam proiecta senatus auctoritas, i. e., quorum iudicio. Δεινὸν γάρ, (no), *for that would be terrible*, a common ellipsis before γάρ.

15.—Καὶ μάλα, sc. φήσομεν. —— κλέπτῃ τε καὶ ἁρπάζῃ; for the distinction in meaning between these words, see note, III. 6. 11. —— πρὸς τῇ ἀδικίᾳ ἐθήκαμεν. This is a *constructio praegnans* for: πρὸς τὴν ἀδικίαν ἐθήκαμεν, ὥστε κεῖσθαι πρὸς αὐτῇ. See Kühn. Gr. § 300. 3; L. Gr. II. § 621. cf. 17: ποτέρωθι τὴν ἀπάτην ταύτην θήσομεν; but a little after, πρὸς τὴν δικαιοσύνην et ταύτην αὖ τὴν ἀπάτην ποῖ θετέον; εἰς τὸ αὐτό, τοῦτο αὖ ποτέρωσε θετέον; Ἐθήκαμεν is a more rare form in Attic Gr., for ἔθεμεν, see Kühn. L. Gr. I. § 203.

16.—Πρὸς μὲν τοὺς πολεμίους... τοιαῦτα ποιεῖν; cf. Cyrop. I. 6. 31: διώριζε δὲ τούτων ἅ τε πρὸς τοὺς φίλους ποιητέον, καὶ ἃ πρὸς τοὺς ἐχθρούς. Plat. Phaed. p. 113. E.: πρὸς πατέρα ἢ μητέρα ὑπ' ὀργῆς βίαιόν τι πράξαντες, and Stallb. Plat. Repub. VIII. p. 559. A. —— ἁπλούστατον εἶναι, *wholly free from guile*; the subject here may be τινά, although Kühner says: στρατηγόν.

17.—Διαχρήσηται ἑαυτόν, commit suicide; the verbs διαχρῆσθαι and καταχρῆσθαι with the meaning to kill, are construed with the Accusative. See Kühn. Gr. § 285. (2), and examples; L. Gr. II. § 585. Anm. 3. Cf. Thucyd. I. 126: καθεζομένους δέ τινας... διεχρήσαντο. —— κλέψῃ ἢ ἁρπάσῃ; see note, III. 6. 11.

18.—Ἅπαντα, *in all things*. —— ἀνατίθεμαι τὰ εἰρημένα; cf. note, I. 2. 44; ἀνατίθεμαι — Δεῖ γέ τοι, certe quidem; see note, III. 4. 10.

19.—Socrates here argues for the sake of curing the vanity of Euthydemus; and in apparent contradiction of his principles, as elsewhere laid down (cf. III. 9. 4 sq.; IV. 6. 6), since he separates knowledge and action, and makes virtue consist in mere theoretic knowledge, instead of action founded on knowledge, i. e. voluntary and intelligent action. He however probably intends to speak only in a comparative manner, and to say, that the man who is ἑκόντα ψευδόμενον is δικαιότερον than one who is ἄκοντα, but yet is not δίκαιον. According to his notion, virtue is knowledge, but he who knows, both approves and practises the right. See a more full explanation in Ritter's Hist. Philos. Vol. II. p. 71 sq. —— εἰρήσθω μοι, *let it be said by me*, i. e., *I venture to say.*

20.—Ὁπότε βούλοιτο; cf. note, III. 14. 6: ὅτη μὴ παρείη. —— αὐτὰ, i. e., γράφειν καὶ ἀναγιγνώσκειν. —— τὰ δίκαια; emphatic by position; see note, II. 7. 8. —— Φαίνομαι; sc. τοῦτο λέγων. *I seem* to say that, etc. This verb is contrasted with the following δοκῶ, *I think*; cf. note, I. 4. 6: οὐ δοκεῖ . . . ἐοικέναι.

21.—Φράζων . . . φράζῃ; for this pleonasm of the Part. with a finite tense of the same verb, defining more accurately the action, see Kühn. L. Gr. II. § 675. 3. So it is employed in IV. 6. 3: ὁ τοὺς νόμους τούτους εἰδὼς εἰδείη ἄν; 6: ὀρθῶς ἄν ποτε ἄρα ὁριζοίμεθα ὁριζόμενοι, κ.τ.λ. For other examples, see Stallbaum's Plat. Hipp. Maj. p. 292. A. —— λογισμὸν, reckoning, computation. —— τοτὲ μὲν . . . τοτὲ δὲ, like ποτὲ μὲν . . . ποτὲ δὲ. The same formula is also used in III. 10, 14, and in the poet as quoted in I. 2. 20, et al.

22.—Ἆρ' οὖν; see note, II. 6. 1. —— Ἀλλ' ἄρα, *but perhaps*; see note, III. 11. 4. Stobaeus has Ἀλλ' ἆρα; cf. the reading in III. 3. 2. —— Οὐδὲ δι' ἓν τούτων, *by none of these things.* Euthydemus, evidently somewhat impatient at Socrates' captious questions, answers him a little tartly. Cf. note, I. 6. 2. —— ἀλλὰ καὶ τοὐναντίον; sc. διὰ τὴν τῶν τοιούτων σοφίαν τοῦ ὀνόματος τούτου τυγχάνειν. For the construction of τοὐναντίον, see II. 6. 4.

23.—Φιλοσοφεῖν φιλοσοφίαν, to investigate the reasons of things; φιλοσοφεῖν signifies frequently: to discover by careful investigation; here with ᾤμην: *I supposed I was pursuing a course of investigation.* —— παιδευθῆναι τὰ προσήκοντα; Pass. verbs, which in the Act. govern two accusatives, frequently retain the Acc. of the thing or effect; cf. Kühn. Gr. § 281. 2; L. Gr. II. § 562. Anm. 5. —— διὰ μὲν τὰ προπεπονημένα, *by the aid of previous labor.* The Accus. is probably used here where we might expect a Gen. to indicate a defect in his previous studies. Lit. *on account of*, etc. —— οὐδὲ τὸ ἐρωτώμενοι ἀποκρίνεσθαι, κ.τ.λ., not able to answer when interrogated concerning that which it is necessary to know, etc. For the constr. of τὸ ἐρωτώμ. ἀποκρίνεσθαι, see Kühn. L. Gr. II. § 547. 2. fin. Ὑπέρ here for the more usual περί; see Kühn. Gr. § 293. E.; L. Gr. II. § 608; and cf. Apol. § 14: ἐπερώτωντος ... περὶ ἐμοῦ; below, IV. 3. 12: προνοεῖσθαι ὑπὲρ τῶν μελλόντων, and so very frequently in the orators.

24.—Εἰς Δελφοὺς δὲ ἤδη πώποτε ἀφίκου; the δέ here refers this question to the words of Euthydemus: ἄλλην ὁδὸν οὐδεμίαν ἔχοντα, κ.τ.λ., *but* have you, etc. In respect to πώποτε, see note, II. 2. 7. —— τὸ Γνῶθι σαυτόν. The idea contained in this inscription upon the temple at Delphos, ascribed to the Delphic God, was adopted by Socrates as the basis of all philosophical investigation. The original author of it was either Thales or Chilo. Socrates' view of its import is thus given by Ritter, Hist. Philos. II. p. 57: "This self-knowledge was regarded by Socrates not merely as a knowledge of one's own ability or inability to know certainly, but he also referred it to the cognition of man's moral value, and thus it appears to come back again to the well known saying, that Socrates had called down philosophy from heaven, and forced her to inquire into the good or evil of humanity." Cf. § 25, 26; Plat. Phaedr. p. 229, 30; where Socrates is made to say: Οὐ δύναμαί πω κατὰ τὸ Δελφικὸν γράμμα γνῶναι ἐμαυτόν; Charmid. p. 164. D.; Protag. p. 343. B, and Stallbaum's note; Cic. Legg. I. 22; Tusc. Disp. I. 22. 52, and Kühner's note. —— οὐδέν σοι τοῦ γράμματος ἐμέλησεν. Cf. Plat. Apol. p. 24. C: οὐδέν τούτῳ πώποτε ἐμέλησεν; p. 25. C: οὐδέν σοι μεμέληκε, and see Kühn. Gr. § 274. R. 1. Γράμμα, here = inscriptio. —— σαυτὸν ἐπισκόπειν, ὅστις εἴης; also in § 25: ὁ ἑαυτὸν ἐπισκεψάμενος, ὁποῖός ἐστι πρὸς τὴν ἀνθρωπίνην χρείαν. For this construction, see Kühn. Gr. § 347. 3, and cf. note, I. 2. 13. The same idiom is not uncommon in Latin and English. γὰρ δή; cf. note, II. 4. 1 —— σχολῇ; cf. note, III. 14. 3.

25.—Ἢ ὅστις, ... ὁ ἑαυτὸν ἐπισκεψάμενος; the subject is resumed by the article after the long intervening relative clause introduced by ὥσπερ; cf. note, I. 2. 24, ad fin.

26.—Ἐψεῦσθαι ἑαυτῶν, lit. *to deceive*, but here = μὴ εἰδέναι ἑαυτούς; so διεψευσμένοι is followed by the genitive in § 27. The genitive here comes under the general relation of *separative genitive*; cf. Kühn. § 271. 2; L. Gr. II. § 513. 3. εὖ πράττουσιν ... κακῶς πράττειν. The verb is here as very frequently taken in an intrans. sense: *are in prosperity ... adversity.* —— καὶ ... δυνάμενοι ... καὶ διά, κ.τ.λ.

The repetition of *καί* denotes a kind of comparison, *both... and also*, Kühner explains them by ut... ita. So a participle is sometimes joined to a preceding finite verb, as in Anab. III. 3. 2: *ἔλθοιμι ἂν πρὸς ὑμᾶς καὶ τοὺς θεράποντας πάντας ἔχων*, which Krüger explains as equivalent to: *ἔλθοιμι αὐτός (τε) καὶ οἱ θεράποντες πάντες.*

27.—Οἱ δὲ μὴ εἰδότες; sc. *ἑαυτούς* or *τὴν ἑαυτῶν δύναμιν.* —— διεψευσμένοι τῆς ἑαυτῶν δυνάμεως; see note, § 26 —— πρός τε τοὺς ἄλλ. ἀνθρώπους καὶ τἆλλα. The idea is: as they are ignorant of themselves, in like manner are they of other men, and of human affairs. In respect to the omission of *πρός* with the last clause, cf. Apol. § 1. —— τοῖς κακοῖς περιπίπτουσι; for the Dat. here, cf. note, I. 2. 63.

28.—Ἐπιτυγχάνοντες ὧν, *κ.τ.λ.*, succeeding in what, etc. Οἵ τε ὅμοιοι τούτοις... κρῶνται, those who are like them in character; or as others suppose, are equally prosperous. *Τούτοις* is to be joined with *χρῶνται*, and not, as some have done, with *ὅμοιοι*. In reference to τέ... τέ, see note, I. 1. 14. —— καὶ προΐστασθαί τε. Some for *τέ* write *γέ* here; others mark *τέ* as suspicious, and still others give to *καὶ ...τέ* the questionable explanation: etiamque or praetereaque; but all these methods of interpretation seem objectionable. There is undoubtedly an anacoluthon, and the sentence would naturally be arranged thus: *καὶ προΐστασθαί τε βούλονται ἑαυτῶν τούτους, καὶ τὰς ἐλπίδας... ἔχουσι.*

29.—Κακῶς δὲ αἱρούμενοι, choosing badly, i. e., what shall be done, rem agendam. —— οἷς ἂν ἐπιχειρήσωσιν ἀποτυγχάνοντες, failing in whatever they undertake. —— ἐν αὐτοῖς τούτοις, in respect to these very things, sc. *οἷς ἂν ἐπιχειρήσωσιν ἀποτυγχάνοντες.* —— ζημιοῦνταί τε καὶ κολάζονται, i. e., they are fined and punished. The two words, *ζημιοῦν* and *κολάζειν*, are frequently found together; the former designates a punishing by loss or detriment, as in money or possessions, for something done contrary to law; the latter, a punishing by words, blows, etc. for the purpose of producing amendment. —— τῶν πόλεων ὅτι. *Πόλεων* here precedes the conjunction *ὅτι* for the sake of emphasis, i. e., the contrast of *the many* occupying States (*πόλεων*) with single individuals. See Kühn. Gr. § 348. 8; L. Gr. II. § 864. 3, and cf. Thucyd. I. 144: *τούτοις ἀποκρινάμενοι ἀποπέμψωμεν,* Μεγαρέας *μὲν* ὅτι *ἐάσομεν ἀγορᾷ καὶ λιμέσι χρῆσθαι*; Ibid.: *εἰδέναι δὲ χρὴ... ἐκ* τε τῶν μεγίστων κινδύνων ὅτι *καὶ... μέγισται τιμαὶ περιγίγνονται.* A similar construction in interrogative sentences has also been noticed in II. 7. 8.

30.—Ὡς . . . δοκοῦν; the participle is not Acc. abs. here as in I. 2 20; 3. 2; but the object of the verb ἴσθι: know thou that it seems en tirely to me, etc. The phrase is nearly equivalent to ἴσθι δοκεῖν μοι Cf. Kühn. L. Gr. II. § 673. Anm. But this construction is not frequent. Such verbs as εἰδέναι, ἐπίστασθαι, νοεῖν, ἔχειν γνώμην, etc. are oftener followed by a Gen abs. with ὡς; cf. Kühn. Gr. § 312. R. 13; L. Gr. II. § 672. —— τοῦτο πρὸς σὲ ἀποβλέπω, this I expect from you, look to you for; cf. § 2. —— εἰ . . . ἐθελήσαις ἄν; cf. I. 3. 4, 5. This form of the Opt. is not unfrequently found in Xenophon; Hellen. I. 3. 21: ποιήσαιεν; 19: σῶσαι; 4. 12: τολμήσαι; 17: κινδυνεύσαι; IV. 3. 2: ἀπαγγείλαις; V. 4. 34: ἐπαινέσαιεν; VI. 1. 9: ἀξιώσαιεν; 10: ποιήσαιεν; 3. 9: ἐάσαιεν; 14: βλάψαι; 4. 36: πράξαιεν; VII. 1. 34: first πολεμήσειαν, and then ἐθελήσαιεν and ἐάσαιεν; 5. 24: βοηθήσαιεν; Cyrop. I. 3. 11: ἄρξαις; II. 4. 21, et al.

31.—Πάντως που γιγνώσκεις, are you *perhaps* entirely acquainted with, etc.; cf. note, III. 5. 15. —— εἰ . . . οἶδα, . . . ἂν εἴην; see note, I. 2. 28. —— τὰ αἴτια . . . τὰ μὲν . . . τὰ δὲ; see note, II. 1. 4. —— τὸ ὑγιαίνειν φέροντα, ἀγαθὰ . . . κακά, those which contribute to health, to be good, etc. Ἀγαθά and κακά are in the predicate.

32.—Οὐδὲν; sc. μᾶλλον ἀγαθὰ εἶναι. —— Στρατείας and the following genitives are governed partitively by μετασχόντες, which is contrasted with ἀπολειφθέντες in the next clause, *taking part in . . . left behind.*

33.—Ἀλλ' ἥ γέ τοι σοφία . . . ἀναμφισβητήτως ἀγαθόν ἐστιν, but wisdom *at least* is certainly, etc. Cf. note, III. 4. 10. Hartung, Gr. Partik. III. S. 366 and examples. Euthydemus might well adduce σοφία as an example which Socrates could not deny to be unquestionably good, for in IV. 5. 6 he calls σοφίαν, the summum bonum, and in III. 9. 5, he says that every virtue is σοφία. The only way of reconciling his reasoning in these different passages is, by supposing that he did not profess to find this σοφία in its unalloyed state, as the supreme, absolute good, in man, but only as it ministers to good. Cf. I. 6. 13. Plat. Meno. p. 8, and see Ritter's Hist. Philos. II. p. 73. Thus in order to carry his point with Euthydemus he uses σοφία with a different signification from what he gives to it in the other passages referred to, and reasons from its consequences. —— Τί δαί; = τί δή; it here indicates transition to something new, with astonishment, surprise: what is it you are saying? or, *how so?* Lat. ain' tu? itane? or, itane vero? See Kühn. Tusc. Quaest. I. 17. 40. —— τὸν Δαίδαλον . . . οὐκ ἀκήκοας. In reference to construction see note, I. 2. 13. The article is used to indi cate notoriety: the celebrated Daedalus. For the legend concerning Daedalus, see Ovid. Metam. VIII. 159 sq.; Hygin. c. 39, 40, and Grote's Greece, Vol. I. p. 307 sq. —— ἐκείνῳ; cf. note, I. 2. 3. —— Παλαμήδους. For an account of the legend of Palamedes, his treacherous death by Ulysses and Diomede, etc., see Grote's Greece, I. p. 400 sq. Cf. also Apol. § 26; Plat. Apol. p. 32. —— φθονηθεὶς... ἀπόλλυται, having been envied is slain. The present is used on account of the representations of the fact in existing well-known poems; see Grote as cited above. —— διὰ σοφίαν, so just above; but near the beginning of the section, διὰ τὴν σοφίαν. Where the article is used, it has more particular reference to wisdom of an individual, and where it is omitted, wisdom as a general term. —— Πρὸς βασιλέα; cf. note, III. 5. 26.

34.—Κινδυνεύει; used impersonally: *it seems.* We should expect οὖν or ἄρα here; but a conclusion is sometimes placed emphatically without a copula; cf. note, III. 4. 12; Hieron. I. 26; Oecon. XVI. 12. The idea here is: since you have called in question all of the instances of absolute good that I have hitherto adduced, it must be that *happiness*, τὸ εὐδαιμονεῖν, is a good by no means questionable. εἴγε μὴ προσθήσομεν if we shall not add to it, i. e., reckon as an element of it.

35.—Ὑπὸ τῶν ἐπὶ... ὡραίοις παρακεκινηκότων, by those who are greatly excited from love to the beautiful. See Stallbaum's note, Plat. Phaedr. p. 249. D. In reference to the signification of ἐπί, see Kühn. Gr. § 296. II. (3); L. Gr. II. § 612. p. 298. In like manner we find it used in the phrase: μαίνεσθαι ἐπί τινι. —— κακοῖς περιπίπτουσι; cf. note, I. 2. 63; IV. 2. 27.

37.—Τούς... μὴ ἱκανὰ ἔχοντας εἰς ἃ δεῖ τελεῖν πένητας, I suppose those to be poor, who have not enough to purchase the necessaries of life. Τελεῖν εἰς, to expend upon, here, to procure, provide, as in II. 9. 1: ἀργύριον τελέσαι; 10. 6: οὐ πολὺ τελέσας ἐκτήσατο φίλον, and εἰς ἃ δεῖ.

38.—Ὀρθῶς γάρ με ἀναμιμνήσκεις; the clause is parenthetical, and disturbs the regular sequence of the words in the sentence, which would naturally be arranged thus: Καὶ νὴ Δί', ἔφη ὁ Εὐθ., οἶδα (ὀρθῶς γάρ με ἀναμιμνήσκεις) καὶ τυράν. Cf. II. 6. 21; III. 10. 3; Anab. II. 5. 12 sq.: Ἀλλὰ μὴν ἐρῶ γὰρ καὶ ταῦτα, ἐξ ὧν ἔχω ἐλπίδας καὶ σὲ βουλήσεσθαι φίλον ἡμῖν εἶναι· οἶδα μὲν γὰρ ὑμῖν Μυσοὺς λυπηροὺς ὄντας; III. 2. 11: Ἔπειτα δέ, ἀναμνήσω γὰρ ὑμᾶς καὶ τοὺς τῶν προγόνων τῶν ἡμετέρων κινδύνους, κ.τ.λ. Cf. note, II. 6. 21.

39.—Ἁπλῶς οὐδέν, omnino nihil, nothing at all. —— τῷ ὄντι, *really, in fact.*

39.—Οὕτω διατεθέντων; cf. note, I. 6. 3. —— ἅ τε ἐνόμιζεν. The natural collocation of the words in the sentence would be: ἃ ἐνόμιζεν εἰδέναι τε δεῖν καὶ ἐπιτηδεύειν; but see note, III. 5. 3.

CHAPTER III.

1.—Λεκτικοὺς καὶ πρακτικοὺς καὶ μηχανικούς. The manner in which Socrates made his disciples λεκτικούς (διαλεκτικούς) is explained in chap. VI.; πρακτικούς, in ch. V.; μηχανικούς, ch. VII. In reference to the meaning of this last word, see I. 3. 7. —— ταῦτα, in these things (Acc. of limitation), i. e., τὸ . . . λεκτικοὺς . . . γίγνεσθαι.

2.—Ἄλλοι . . . διηγοῦντο. Whether Xenophon intends to say that others related other such conversations of Socrates to him, which he passes by, and merely gives one which he himself heard, or that they related them to others, is uncertain. Bornemann in h. l. says: narrabant vel aliis, vel quod malim, mihi. This passage is, however, conclusive in reference to the historical fact, that Socrates held other conversations upon his notions of God.

3.—Σοι ἐπῆλθεν, has it ever yet occurred to you; cf. ἐπίῃ μοι, IV. 2. 4. —— Ἀλλ' . . . γε; see note, I. 2. 12. —— Νὴ Δί' . . . ὃ δ'; for the use of γέ to give emphasis in formulas of swearing, cf. III. 11. 5, and Kühn. Gr. § 317. 2. —— ἕνεκά γε τῶν ἡμετέρων ὀφθαλμῶν, "for all the good our eyes would do us;" Crosby's Gr. Gram. § 395. γ. ἀναπαυτήριον, lit., resting-place, i. e., time of repose. For the form of the word, cf. Kühn. Gr. § 233. 2. (d).

4.—Ὥρας τῆς ἡμέρας, the times of the day, i. e.: ὄρθρον, μεσημβρίαν, δείλην, ἑσπέραν. In the signification of *hour* this word was not used in Xenophon's time, probably not until the time of the Astronomer Hipparchus (B. C. 140). It is used in reference to the watches of the night in IV. 7. 4. In the same passage ὧραι μηνός = τοῦ μηνὸς τὰ μέρη, sc. ἱσταμένου, μεσοῦντος, and φθίνοντος. It is, however, far most frequently employed to designate the seasons of the year, as in § 5 below. —— διὰ τὸ σκοτεινὴ εἶναι; cf. note, I. 2. 3. —— ἀσαφεστέρα, more obscure, sc. than to allow its single parts to be distinguished. Others however interpret this word actively: too obscure to allow any thing to be discerned with the eyes. —— ἀνέφηναν; the Aor. tense indef. as to time and hence denoting what has been and is. —— διὰ τοῦτο πολλὰ...πράττομεν; sc. such things as are enumerated in IV. 7. 4. —— μηνὸς τὰ μέρη; see above.

5.—Τὸ...ἀναδιδόναι; sc. τί δοκεῖ σοι; and τοὺς θεούς. Cf. note, I. 4. 12. —— ταῦτα, refers to πολλὰ...εὐφραινόμεθα, and hence is in the plural. —— φιλάνθρωπα; magnae erga homines benevolentiae est; Seiffert.

6.—Ὥστε καὶ; the latter particle corresponding to καί with μιγνύμενον. —— φυτεύειν; with this verb the preposition, σύν (with, in connection) seems to be implied from the following συναύξειν. The reverse, i. e., a simple following a compound verb, is not unfrequent.

7.—Ἐπίκουρον μὲν ψύχους, ἐπίκουρον δὲ σκότους, both defending against cold and helping in darkness. For μέν...δέ, see note, I. 1. 1, and for the government of the Gen. Kühn. L. Gr. II. § 513. 4. —— ὡς συνελόντι εἰπεῖν, in few words, in short; for the constr. see Kühn. Gr. § 284. (10), and III. 8. 10. —— Ὑπερβάλλει...φιλανθρωπίᾳ, lit., excels other things in kindness to man, i. e., this is a conspicuous example of the love of the gods to man.

8.—Τὸ δὲ...Ἀνέκφραστον. This whole passage seems most probably to have crept into the text from the hand of the glossator; see Kühn. in h. l. —— πελάγη περᾶν, κ.τ.λ., so that we cross the seas by means of it. —— τὰ μὲν ἁδρύνοντα τὰ δὲ ξηραίνοντα. These participles agree with ἥλιον and govern τὰ μὲν and τὰ δὲ. Herbst well compares this passage with Odyss. VII. 119 sq. —— ὧν καιρὸς διελήλυθεν, the time of which has passed, i. e., which are past maturity. —— μᾶλλον τοῦ δέοντος, plus aequo; cf. note, I. 6. 11. —— αὖ πάλιν; the reverse order πάλιν αὖ is much more frequent, see just below. —— ἔοικεν = *apparet*.

9.—Κατὰ μικρὸν προσιέναι...κατὰ μικρὸν ἀπιέναι. A similar anaphora is found in Latin: digitorum enim contractio facilis facilisque porrectio propter molles commissuras et artus nullo in motu laborat; Cic. de Nat. Deor., II. 60. 150. —— ὥστε λανθάνειν...καθισταμένους, so that we insensibly (i. e., without noticing it) come into either extreme. —— εἰ ἄρα τί...ἔργον ᾖ, κ.τ.λ., whether forsooth the gods have any other employment than, etc. See Kühn. Gr. § 324. 3. (a); L. Gr. II. § 833. c, and also § 747. Anm. 1. —— τούτων, the favors before enumerated.

10.—Οὐ γὰρ; see note, I. 3. 10. —— καὶ ταῦτα, sc. ταῦτα ζῷα. —— ἀνθρώπων ἕνεκα; a similar idea is found in Cic. Nat. Deor. II. 62

——τί...ἄλλο ζῷον, the subject of ἀπολαύει.——ἐμοὶ μὲν...δοκεῖ ...φυτῶν; sc. ἀπολαύειν τοὺς ἀνθρώπους. There is also an ellipsis of ἤ after πλείω. Cf. III. 11. 5.——γοῦν; cf. note, I. 6. 2.——ἀπὸ τούτων ἢ ἀπ' ἐκείνων, i. e., from animals than from plants, cf. note, I. 3. 13. —— πολὺ...γένος ἀνθ....χρῶνται...ζῶσι, a great part (race) of men (i. e., the nomadic tribes, the Scythians). For the number here, see Kühn. Gr. § 243. 1; L. Gr. II. § 420. 2.——ὅτι ἂν βούλωνται, sc. χρῆσθαι.

11.—Τοῖς ἀνθρώποις...ἀπολαύομεν. The change from the third person to the first in such cases, is not uncommon in Greek or English; cf. Plat. Gorg. p. 514. E: εἰ μὴ ηὑρίσκομεν δι' ἡμᾶς μηδένα βελτίω γεγονότα τὸ σῶμα, οὐ καταγέλαστον ἂν ἦν τῇ ἀληθείᾳ εἰς τοσοῦτον ἀνοίας ἐλθεῖν ἀνθρώπους; and Woolsey's note.

12.—Τὸ δὲ καί, εἰ, κ.τ.λ. Τὸ is here in construction with the Inf. (συνεργεῖν), as with the preceding infinitives. ——ὑπὲρ τῶν μελλόντων; for the use of ὑπέρ here see note, IV. 2. 23.——ἄριστα γίγνοιντο; for the use of the plural verb with the neuter plural subject, see Kühn. Gr. § 241. 4. (b); L. Gr. II. § 424. ——εἴ γε, since indeed. ——μηδέ, cf. I. 2. 36.

13.—Ὅτι δέ γε ἀληθῆ λέγω...ἂν μὴ ἀναμένῃς, κ.τ.λ This passage has caused much perplexity among the commentators, and although somewhat obscure, yet when carefully considered in its connection, it does not seem to be so desperate as some suppose. After, in the preceding sections, illustrating the special care of the gods for men, Socrates, in section 12, alludes to their special kindness in imparting a knowledge of the future by means of divination. But Euthydemus, alluding to the δαιμόνιον which Socrates said: ἑαυτῷ σημαίνειν ἅ τε χρὴ ποιεῖν καὶ ἃ μή, I. 1. 2 sq., replies in the way of objection: Σοὶ δ'... ἔτι φιλικώτερον, κ.τ.λ., the gods seem to be more benignant to you than to other men, since without your asking they make known to you what it is necessary to do and what not to do. Socrates proceeds in the present section to confute this idea of Euthydemus, and thus substantiate the general truth of his argument: This δαιμόνιον, of which he was accustomed to speak, was not given by the gods as a special favor to him alone, but to him in common with Euthydemus and others. And if others do not experience its guidance it is because they do not yield the fitting obedience and reverence to the gods as unseen and spiritual, but distrusting them, seek a physical form which can be seen by the eyes. Thus Ritter. Hist. Philos. II. p. 39, says· "He [Socrates] gives the exhortation to Euthydemus to renounce all desire to become acquainted with the forms of the gods, and to rest satisfied with knowing and adoring their works, for then he would acknowledge that it was not idly and without cause that he himself spoke of demonical intimations. By this, Socrates evidently gave him to understand, that this demonical sign would be manifest to every pious soul, who would renounce all idle longing for a visible appearance of the deity." Ἀληθῆ refers to the words immediately preceding, sc.: τὸ δαιμόνιον σημαίνειν ἐμοὶ ἃ χρὴ ποιεῖν καὶ ἃ μή, and σὺ is contrasted with the subject of λέγω. —— σὺ γνώσῃ, you shall know, sc. by your own experience, by like intimations to yourself. —— οὕτως ὑποδεικνύουσιν, sc. that their physical appearance in divination is not to be expected: μὴ ἀναμένειν ἕως ἂν τὰς μορφὰς θεῶν ἴδῃς.

14.—Οἵ τε γὰρ ἄλλοι; sc. θεοί, omitted because αὐτοὶ οἱ θεοὶ precede. Socrates and his followers, Plato, the Stoics, Cicero and others, believed in the existence of deities subordinate to the supreme deity, who were employed as ministering spirits in the government of the world. To these allusion is here made. See Kühn. Libr. de M. T. Ciceronis in Philosophiam Meritis. Hamburg, 1825, p. 185–88, and cf. Plat. Cratyl. p. 255; Cic. de Nat. Deor. 1. 12; et al. The argument here to the end of § 14, in three particulars, is designed to show the unreasonableness of skepticism with regard to the gods, because they are unseen: "The best," he would say, "in every species, is unvariably unseen, and only noticeable in its effects, and that in like manner the soul, which participates in the divine nature, and is clearly the ruling principle within us, nevertheless cannot by any means be discerned. He therefore who has emancipated himself from all foolish desire to behold some palpable and substantial shapes of the gods, may soon recognize the operations of the Deity within him, for the gods have implanted in man's mind a knowledge of their power." Cf. I. 4. 16; Ritter, Hist. Philos. II. p. 58, 9, and references there. —— ἀτριβῆ ... ἀγήρατα; these adjectives qualify πάντα (καλὰ καὶ ἀγαθά ἐστιν). Some editions read ἀγήρατον, and make all these Adjj. agree with κόσμον. —— θᾶττον ... νοήματος; cf. note, I. 6. 13. —— οὗτος τὰ μέγιστα μὲν πράττων ὁρᾶται, κ.τ.λ., he is indeed seen to be the doer, artificer of the greatest things, but is unseen in the doing, management of them. Τάδε seems to be used with reference to these things as exhibited before our eyes.

15.—Τοὺς ὑπηρέτας ... τῶν θεῶν ... κεραυνός ... ἄνεμοι. These latter nouns are frequently without the article where we might expect it, as being the names of objects well known. The student scarcely needs to be reminded how often the Old Testament speaks of the lightning and winds as ministers of God.

16.—Ἐκεῖνο δὲ ἀθυμῶ; so in § 16: μὴ τοῦτο ἀθύμει; we also find, ἀπορεῖν τι. Thuc. V. 40: ἀποροῦντες... ταῦτα. For this constr. of the Acc. see Kühn. Gr. § 279. 7; L. Gr. II. § 557. —— οὐδ᾽ ἂν εἷς; see note, I. 6. 2.

17.—Νόμῳ πόλεως, in accordance with the law of the State; cf. I. 3. 1. —— κατὰ δύναμιν, each one according to his ability; cf. I. 3. 3. —— ἱεροῖς θεοὺς ἀρέσκεσθαι. This is a Homeric construction, but we frequently find the Dat. instead of the Acc.; see Oecon. V. 3: ὥστε ἔχειν καὶ θεοῖς ἐξαρέσκεσθαι θύοντας. So ἐξαρεσκεύεσθαι in 19: τοὺς μὲν ἐν τῷ πολέμῳ ὁρᾷς... πρὸ τῶν πολεμικῶν πράξεων ἐξαρεσκευομένους τοῖς θεοῖς. —— οὕτω ποιῶν, *by so doing*, Part. denoting the means.

18.—Ἐλλείποντα is to be joined in construction with τιμᾶν, κ.τ.λ. The verb ἐλλείπειν is usually followed by a participle, but the Inf. is probably here substituted to avoid the concurrence of too many participles. —— οὐ γὰρ παρ᾽ ἄλλων γ᾽ ἄν τις μείζω ἐλπίζων σωφρονοίη; i. e., οὐ γὰρ ἄν τις σωφρονοίη, εἰ παρ᾽ ἄλλων μείζω ἐλπίζοι. —— ἄλλως μᾶλλον, sc. σωφρονοίη.

CHAPTER IV.

1.—Καὶ ἔργῳ; when these words were written, the author undoubtedly intended to continue the discourse by καὶ λόγῳ, but after the several intervening clauses explanatory of ἔργῳ, we find in § 5: καὶ ἔλεγε δέ. —— ἰδίᾳ... χρώμενος, κ.τ.λ.; cf. 8. 11: δίκαιος δὲ (ἦν Σωκράτης), ὥστε βλάπτειν μὲν μηδὲ μικρὸν μηδένα, ὠφελεῖν δὲ τὰ μέγιστα τοὺς χρωμένους αὐτῷ. —— τε ἃ. The particle τέ here answers to καί before ὅτε ἐν ταῖς ἐκκλησίαις, κ.τ.λ., in § 2, and there is a slight anacoluthon, for strict grammatical accuracy would require the following construction: ἰδίᾳ τε... χρώμενος, καὶ κοινῇ ἄρχουσί τε... πειθόμενος... καὶ ἐν ταῖς ἐκκλησίαις ἐπιστάτης γενόμενος οὐκ ἐπιτρέψας τῷ δήμῳ παρὰ τοὺς νόμους ψηφίσασθαι; but cf. note, II. 1. 30 for changes from Partic. to verb. After τέ with a Part. to express a more general idea, καί with a verb may naturally enough follow, to add a more particular and emphatic circumstance; or after μέν and Part., δέ and verb, may contrast an idea of more importance. —— κατὰ πόλιν... ἐν ταῖς στρατείαις, domi milit aeque. —— παρὰ τοὺς ἄλλους, in comparison with others, i. e., beyond, or, *more than others*, praeter ceteros.

2.—Παρὰ τοὺς νόμους ψηφίσασθαι; for a more particular account of the transaction here alluded to, see I. 1. 18, note and references. —— σὺν τοῖς νόμοις contrasted with παρὰ τοὺς νόμους, and signif. *in adhering to the laws.*

3.—Τοῖς τε γὰρ νέοις...διαλέγεσθαι; cf. I. 2. 35, and for the use of μή, cf. note, I. 2. 33. —— ἀπαγορευόντων...προσταξάντων. The former Part. the present, because this prohibition was of the nature of a law that is to be in force at all times, the latter Aor., as done in a specific instance. —— ἐκείνῳ τε καὶ ἄλλοις τισὶ. The circumstance here referred to, is the command of the thirty tyrants to Socrates and four others, to bring Leon of Salamis to Athens, where he had been naturalized and had exiled himself to his fraternal city, fearing that the tyrants might put him to death, as he was wealthy and distinguished. Socrates himself says in Plato's Apol. chap. XX: "Then indeed I showed by my actions and not merely by my words, that I did not care (if it be not too coarse an expression) one jot for death; but it was an object of the greatest care to me to do nothing unjust or unholy. For that government, though it was so powerful, did not frighten me into doing any thing unjust; but when we came out of the Tholos, the four went to Salamis and took Leon, but I went away home. And perhaps I should have suffered death on account of this, if the government had not soon been broken up." Wiggers' Life, p. 59. Cf. Xenoph. Hellen. II. 3. 39; Diog. Laert. II. 24. —— ἐπὶ θανάτῳ; for the signif. of the Prep. ἐπί here, see note, I. 3. 11. —— διὰ τὸ παρὰ τοὺς νόμους προστάττεσθαι, *because it had been enjoined upon him* to act, etc.

4.—Τὴν ὑπὸ Μελήτου γραφὴν ἔφευγε. Ὁ φεύγων signifies *an accused person*, and is opp. ὁ διώκων, *an accuser;* accordingly γραφὴν φεύγειν, to be accused, is antithetical to γραφὴν (δίκην) διώκειν, to prosecute a suit. Cf. Plat. Apol. p. 19. C: μή πως ἐγὼ ὑπὸ Μελήτου τοσαύτας δίκας φύγοιμι. The use of the preposition ὑπό is generally explained as arising from the combining and assimilating of two constructions: ὑπό τινος φύγειν and τὴν γραφήν τινος φεύγειν, as in III. 6. 11: κλέπτ. τὰ ἐκ χώρας. But it perhaps arose from the passive signification of the verbal noun γραφήν, *accusation made by;* cf. Cyrop. III. 3. 2: ἥδεσθαι τῇ ὑπὸ πάντων τιμῇ; Thuc. II. 65: ἐγίγνετό τε λόγῳ μὲν δημοκρατία, ἔργῳ δὲ ὑπὸ τοῦ πρώτου ἀνδρὸς ἀρχή; Plat. Symp. p. 216. B: ἡττημένῳ τῆς τιμῆς τῆς ὑπὸ τῶν πολλῶν; Protag. p. 354. A: τὰς ὑπὸ τῶν ἰατρῶν θεραπείας; Politic. p. 291. D: τὴν ὑπὸ τῶν πολλῶν δυναστείαν. In respect to Meletus, cf. note and references, I. 1. 1. —— πρὸς χάριν τε τοῖς δικασταῖς διαλέγεσθαι, κ.τ.λ., to implore the compassion of the judges and to flatter and entreat them. Cf. Apol. § 4, and Plat. Apol. p. 38. D. E. —— *παρὰ τοὺς νόμους*; this clause is added because laws had been passed against attempting to excite the compassion of judges, etc. Cf. Pollux, VIII. 117. de Areopagitis: *προοιμιάζεσθαι δὲ οὐκ ἐξῆν οὐδὲ οἰκτίζεσθαι.* Quintil. VI. 1. 7: Athenis affectus movere etiam per praeconem prohibebatur orator. —— *τῶν εἰωθότων*, sc. *ποιεῖσθαι*, or we may consider these words as used absol.: things that are customary. —— *ῥᾳδίως ἂν ἀφεθεὶς*, i. e., *ὃς ῥᾳδίως ἂν ἀφείθη, εἰ, κ.τ.λ.* Cf. note, II. 2. 3 and 13. —— *προείλετο μᾶλλον*; cf. note, II. 1. 2.

5.—*Καὶ ἔλεγε δὲ οὕτως*; and he also spoke in the same manner, cf. note § 1. —— *Ἱππίαν τὸν Ἠλεῖον.* For an account of this distinguished Sophist, his vanity, arrogance, etc., see Plato's Dialogues, which received his name, with Stallbaum's Prolegomena, and especially his note, Hipp. Maj. p. 148. —— *διὰ χρόνου.* It appears from what follows that this was not his first visit to Athens. —— *διδάξασθαί τινα*, to have one taught. The Act. form is sometimes used in the same way, just as in other languages, persons are represented as doing that which they cause to be done by others. See Liddell and Scott's Lexicon upon this word. —— *μὴ ἀπορεῖν*, in construction with *τὸ*, as the subject of *εἴη*. —— *δικαίους.* *Δίκαιος*, that is as it should be, suitable for the offices incumbent upon it; = Lat. justus, which signifies, according to Krüger: e u m q u i e s t t a l i s, u t r e c t e m u n e r e s u o f u n g a t u r, v i c e s s u a s e x p l e a t. Cf. Cyrop. II. 2. 26: *οὔτε γὰρ ἅρμα δήπου ταχὺ γένοιτ' ἄν, βραδέων ἵππων ἐνόντων, οὔτε δίκαιον, ἀδίκων συνεζευγμένων.* The word is probably here chosen, in order to place this kind of *justitia* in contrast with real justice, which is the general subject of the conversation. —— *μεστὰ ... τῶν διδαξόντων*, briefly and familiarly, in Lat., d o c t o r u m. For this use of the participle, cf. II. 1. 5: *ἀπολυσάντων, κ.τ.λ.*; II. 2. 4: *τούτου γε τῶν ἀπολυσόντων μεσταὶ μὲν αἱ ὁδοί*; II. 8. 3: *τῷ δεομένῳ τοῦ συνεπιμελησομένου*, indigenti adiutore; III. 8. 2: *δεόμεθα τοῦ παύσοντος*; IV. 4. 5: *πάντα μεστὰ εἶναι τῶν διδαξόντων.* —— *ἐὰν δέ τις βούληται*, as preceded by a verb in the present tense, *φασί*, but above *εἰ μέν τις βούλοιτο*, on account of the antecedent preterite.

6.—*Ἐπισκώπτων*, deriding him. —— *Ἔτι γὰρ σύ ... λέγεις*, are you then, yet talking about, etc. *Γάρ* is conclusive = i g i t u r. —— *οὐ μόνον ἀεὶ τὰ αὐτὰ λέγω, ἀλλὰ καὶ περὶ τῶν αὐτων.* Cf. with this Plat. Gorg. p. 490. E: *Ὡς ἀεὶ ταὐτὰ λέγεις, ὦ Σώκρατες. ΣΩ. Οὐ μόνον γε, ὦ Καλλίκλεις, ἀλλὰ καὶ περὶ τῶν αὐτῶν*; p. 491. B. —— *διὰ τὸ πολυμαθὴς εἶναι*; see note, I. 2. 3. —— *Ἀμέλει*; see note, I. 4. 7.

7.—Πότερον is seldom used in a simple interrogation, and when it is, the contrasted phrase may be easily supplied. According to some commentators the phrase: ἢ περὶ ἀριθμῶν . . . οὐ τὰ αὐτὰ νῦν ἃ καὶ πρότερον ἀποκρίνῃ answers to this. But it seems hardly to be possible. For examples of similar constructions of πότερον, see Thucyd. I. 80; Plat. Phaed. p. 78. B; Lysid. p. 205. A, and other passages cited by Bornemann. —— πόσα καὶ ποῖα Σωκράτους ἐστίν, how many and what are the letters in the word Socrates? The same example is employed in Plat. Alcib. I. p. 113: Τί δ', ἂν ἐγὼ μὲν ἔρωμαι, ποῖα γράμματα Σωκράτους—; and Xenoph. Oecon. VIII. 14: εἴποι ἄν, Σωκράτους καὶ ὁπόσα γράμματα καὶ ὅπου ἕκαστον τέτακται. —— ὥσπερ σύ, καὶ ἐγώ; cf. note, II. 2. 2. —— ἃ οὔτε σύ, οὔτ' ἂν ἄλλος οὐδεὶς δύναιτ' ἀντειπεῖν. The verb agrees with the nearest subject since the two subjects are regarded as independent of each other. Cf. Kühn. Gr. § 242. R. 4; L. Gr. II. § 432. Anm. 2.

8.—Νὴ τὴν Ἥραν; see note, I. 5. 5. —— οὐκ οἶδ', ὅπως ἂν ἀπολειφθείην σου, I do not know how I can leave you, before, etc.; a more courtly phrase for I cannot possibly leave you, etc.

9.—Οὐκ . . . πρίν γ', *not before certainly.* Kühner and Hartung call the γέ here suppletive. Cf. numerous examples of a similar use of it with πρίν, in Hartung, Gr. Partik. I. S. 409, 10, and cf. Kühn. Gr. § 317. 2; L. Gr. II. § 704. —— ἀρκεῖ γὰρ ὅτι τῶν ἄλλων καταγελᾷς, κ.τ.λ., for it is enough that you laugh at others (sc. ἐμοῦ δ' οὐ καταγελάσεις, you shall not ridicule me), proposing questions, etc. —— ὑπέχειν λόγον, to make a statement. —— γνώμην ἀποφαίνεσθαι, give your opinion. Γνώμη is very often without the article in such cases as this; cf. Anab. I. 6. 9; V. 5. 3; 6. 37; § 11 below, et al. We, in English, should use the indefinite *an* or a possessive pronoun.

10.—Οὐδὲν παύομαι. Οὐδέν, *by no means,* nullo modo, a more emphatic negative than οὔ; cf. Kühn. Gr. § 279, R. 10; L. Gr. II. § 557. Anm. 4. Cf. Cyrop. I. 6. 16: καὶ γὰρ λέγοντες οὐδὲν παύονται οἱ ἄνθρωποι; Oecon. XI. 23: οὐδὲν μὲν οὖν παύομαι λέγειν μελετῶν. In like manner nihil is employed in Latin for non, especially in such phrases as nihil me fallis, nihil te moror, et al.; see Zumpt, Gr. § 677. 6. —— ποῖος δή σοι . . . ὁ λόγος ἐστίν; what is . . . *your* explanation of it? —— ἀξιοτεκμαρτότερον, more convincing.

12.—Σκέψαι, ἐάν, . . . ἀρέσκῃ. Ἐὰν with the subjunctive frequently corresponds nearly with εἰ followed by the future indicative; the latter, however, implies that the condition will take place, whilst the subjunctive merely indicates, that it is supposed or expected by the speaker, to take place; see Kühn. Gr. § 339. II. R. 2; L. Gr. § 837. b. —— τὸ νόμιμον δίκαιον εἶναι; cf. II. 6. 23.

13.—Οὐ γὰρ αἰσθάνομαί σου. Γάρ refers to a suppressed clause: how so? for, etc.; or we may with Bornemann supply κακῶς λέγεις; cf. note, III. 5. 21. —— ὁποῖον... ἢ ποῖον, κ.τ.λ.; for the rather unusual change from the particle of indirect interrogation to the direct, see note, I. 1. 11, and cf. Plat. de Rep. III. p. 414. D: οὐκ οἶδα, ὁποίᾳ τόλμῃ ἢ ποίοις λόγοις χρώμενος ἐρῶ, where however some Mss. have ποίᾳ τόλμῃ; Demosth. de Coron. p. 275. 144: ἥτις δ' ἡ φύσις... γέγονε τούτων τῶν πραγμάτων, καὶ τίνος ἕνεκα ταῦτα συνεσκευάσθη, καὶ πῶς ἐπράχθη, νῦν ἀκούσατε. —— νόμους... γιγνώσκεις, have you known, etc.; not merely the Lat. cognoscere but nosse; cf. note, III. 5. 26: ἀκούω.

14.—Οὕς γε; cf. note, II. 3. 15. —— καὶ γὰρ; the ellipsis here to which γάρ refers, is: what you say, i. e., that laws are changed, is no ground for disobedience to them; (*for* States also undertake wars and make peace again). —— Διάφορον... ἤ; cf. note, III. 7. 7.

15.—Λυκοῦργον; emphatic by position. —— οὐδὲν ἂν διάφορον, κ.τ.λ., nulla in re praestantem reliquis civitatibus; Weiske. For the idea, cf. III. 5. 16; Hellen. VII. 1. 8; de Republ. Lac. VIII. 1. —— καὶ πόλις. The noun πόλις depends upon the phrase: οὐκ οἶσθα ὅτι.

16.—Ὁμόνοιά γε, κ.τ.λ.; the idea is: but concord also which seems to be the greatest good of a State, is nothing else than unanimity of the citizens in obeying the laws. —— νόμος... κεῖται, the law is established; cf. Lycurg. adv. Leocrat. p. 189. —— κρίνωσι. In κρίνειν the idea of approving, assenting to, is conjoined with that of judging, deciding. Thus in Hellen. I. 7, 34, the notion of giving judgment is prominent: μιᾷ ψήφῳ ἅπαντας κρίνειν, and afterwards, that of approving: τὸ μὲν πρῶτον ἔκριναν τὴν Εὐρυπτολέμου (γνώμην), κ.τ.λ. —— αἱρῶνται, choose, in order to bestow the prize upon them, in the scenic representations at the festivals of Bacchus. Concerning the change from ὅπως to ἵνα, see note, II. 1. 19. —— ἄνευ δὲ ὁμονοίας; these words form a strong contrast to τούτοις... ἐμμενόντων, above. —— οὔτ' ἂν πόλις... πολιτευθείη, οὔτ' οἶκος... οἰκηθείη. Ἄν is to be supplied in the last clause from the first; see note, I. 3. 15.

17.—Ἰδίᾳ... τις, any one by himself, in private life. —— ἡττῷτο .. νικῴη, lose his cause... obtain it, or more lit. be defeated.. conquer. Not unfrequently the language of military affairs is transferred to the forum. —— τίνι . . . παρακαταθέσθαι. Τίνι depends not upon πιστεύσειε but upon παρακαταθέσθαι: to whom would any one prefer to commit, etc. —— οἰκεῖοι . . . οἰκέται; cf. note, I. 2. 48. —— τίνι . . . πιστεύσειαν . . . ἀνοχάς, κ.τ.λ.; the idea is: in whom can the enemy have more confidence in making treaties, etc.? The construction of the nouns ἀνοχάς, etc., is after the analogy of πιστεύειν πίστιν.

19.—Ἀγράφους . . . νόμους. Socrates meant by these "unwritten laws," those precepts and principles of action, which, given by the gods, are every where recognized both by States and individuals; and consequently, as universally valid, not needing to be written. They also do not require arbitrary enactments for their enforcement, since their infringement invariably brings its own penalty along with it. These laws are the voice of the deity speaking to the inner sense of every man; some of them are enumerated in § 20 sq. See a more extended explanation, in Ritter's Hist. Philos. II. p. 74, 5, and cf. references there. —— κατὰ ταὐτὰ νομιζομένους, received in the same manner. Νομίζεται below is employed with a similar signification; cf. also note, II. 3. 15. —— οἱ ἄνθρωποι αὐτοὺς ἔθεντο. The active voice is also used below: τεθεικέναι τοὺς νόμους, and just after: θεοὺς . . . τοὺς νόμους τούτους τοῖς ἀνθρώποις θεῖναι. In the first instance, men who are themselves subject to the laws make them, and hence the propriety and beauty of the use of the middle voice. So in § 13: ἃ οἱ πολῖται . . . συνθέμενοι ἅ τε δεῖ ποιεῖν καὶ ὧν ἀπέχεσθαι, ἐγράψαντο; IV. 3. 12: καὶ νόμους τιθέμεθα καὶ πολιτευόμεθα; II. 1. 14: οἱ μὲν πολιτευόμενοι . . . νόμους τίθενται. But when the gods or those who are not themselves the subjects or not conceived of as the subjects of them, are spoken of as making laws, the active form is used. So in I. 2. 45: ὅσα δὲ ὀλίγοι τοὺς πολλοὺς μὴ πείσαντες, ἀλλὰ κρατοῦντες γράφουσι, πότερον βίαν φῶμεν ἢ μὴ φῶμεν εἶναι; Rep. Lac. I. 1: Λυκοῦργον . . . τὸν θέντα αὐτοῖς τοὺς νόμους. In Plato, Hipp. Maj. p. 284. D, both forms are appropriately used, as, in the last clause, the persons indicated are considered as having discarded the authority of law. See Kühn. Gr. § 250. 1. (a); L. Gr. II. § 395. —— οἵ γε; cf. note, II. 3. 15. —— θεοὺς σέβειν; the active form of this verb is seldom used in prose writers. See Liddell and Scott's Lex. h. v.

20.—Οὐκέτι; what you have before said I approved, but now I am *no longer* able to yield assent. —— Τί δή; these particles here indicate astonishment; cf. Hartung, Gr. Partik. I. S. 268; Kühn. L. Gr. II. § 691.

21.—Καὶ γὰρ, sc. that is not strange, nil mirum, *for*, etc. —— Ἀλλ' οὖν, but yet, but, however. Cf. Hartung, II. S. 12. —— γέ τοι, give emphasis to δίκην; see Hartung, Gr. Partik. II. S. 366, and cf. IV 2. 33. —— ὑπὸ τῶν θεῶν κειμένους, a diis latos, established by the gods; many intransitive verbs are sometimes employed as passives; cf. Kühn. L. Gr. II. § 392. b.

23.—Οὐ γὰρ οὖν; sc. you have well said; *for* by no means, etc. Οὖν is joined in sense with οὐ from which, as not unfrequently, it is separated by γάρ; see Hartung, Gr. Partik. II. p. 17. It is used in a similar manner in IV. 6. 3; Soph. Oed. C. 984: οὐ γὰρ οὖν σιγήσομαι. Cf. also, IV. 2. 10.

24.—Διώκειν, sequi, or, sectari. —— θεοῖς ταῦτα πάντα ἔοικε, all these things are similar to the gods [sc. not to men]. Some editors have θείοις, and the meaning is then supposed to be: all these things are similar to divine institutions, but aside from the absence of almost all Ms. authority, the sentiment in its connection is jejune. Others render ἔοικε, decet, convenit, but this meaning, although found in Homer, does not seem to belong to Attic writers except when followed by an Inf. as in Plat. Legg. IX. 16, p. 879. C. Besides, the idea which we have given, aside from being the natural version of the authorized text, is more congruous with the words in § 19: θεοὺς οἶμαι τοὺς νόμους τούτους τοῖς ἀνθρώποις θεῖναι, and in § 20: θεοῦ νόμος εἶναι. The reasoning which follows is also appropriate: For that in the laws themselves the punishment of transgressors is contained, (so that it is not necessary to look for it from without,) seems, etc. —— βελτίονος ἢ κατ' ἄνθρωπον νομοθέτου...εἶναι, *to belong to legislation superior to that of man.* ἢ κατά frequently follow a comparative when a relation or proportion is to be indicated. See B. 149. m. 7; cf. note, I. 7. 4. The same idiom is found in Latin. Cf. Livy, XXI. 29. 2: atrocius proelium quam pro numero pugnantium editur; Cic. de Fin. V. 16. 44: quod praeceptum majus erat quam ut ab homine videretur.

25.—Ἄλλα τῶν δικαίων. Ἄλλα, other than, different from. For the construction here, see Kühn. L. Gr. II. § 512. 4. —— θεοῖς ἄρα...τὸ αὐτὸ δίκαιόν τε καὶ νόμιμον. The reasoning of Socrates is: That which pertains to the laws of God, which are right, is lawful (νόμιμον) and just (δίκαιον); in divine and human laws the same thing is true, (for Socrates had maintained, § 12 et al., that in human laws νόμιμον δίκαιον εἶναι,) that the νόμιμον is δίκαιον. Socrates accordingly demanded implicit obedience to the laws of the State, not considering here that the human law might conflict with the divine. In Plato's Crito he is made to go even further and argue that the human law must not be violated even when it comes intc conflict with the law of right. Cf. that dialogue and Stallb. Pro legomena.

CHAPTER V.

1.—Πρακτικωτέρους, ad agendum idoneum; cf. note, IV. 3. 1. —— ὑπάρκειν, is rejected by some few Mss. and Stephanus; but there does not seem to be sufficient reason for its omission. There are several instances of the use of this verb with εἶναι joined with an adjective as here with ἀγαθὸν, (the construction is νομίζων ἀγαθὸν εἶναι ὑπάρχειν ἐγκράτειαν,) having the meaning: adesse, suppetere; cf. Schneid. de Venat. XIII. 17; Oecon. XXI. 11, and Bornem. Cyrop. VIII. 8. 20. Entirely different from this are the passages where εἶναι depends upon ὑπάρχειν, which then has the signification of licere; as in Venat. XIII. 17: ὥστε ὑπάρχειν . . . θεοφιλεῖς τ' εἶναι καὶ εὐσεβεῖς; de Rep. Ath. III. 9: ὥστε μέντοι ὑπάρχειν δημοκρατίαν μὲν εἶναι. —— πάντων μάλιστα . . . πρὸς ἐγκράτειαν, most of all things to temperance. Πάντων is neuter and has regard not to the subject but to the object ἐγκράτειαν.

2.—Περὶ τῶν . . . χρησίμων . . . μεμνημένος. The preposition περί instead of the simple genitive is employed after μεμνημένος for the sake of distinctness; it is especially so used when the verb signifies: to make mention of. See Kühn. L. Gr. II. § 529. Anm. 1, and cf. Hellen. IV. 5. 9: περὶ μὲν τῆς εἰρήνης οὐκέτι ἐμέμνηντο. —— ἄρα; cf. II. 6. 1. —— ὡς οἷόν τέ γε μάλιστα; see IV. 2. 11.

3.—Τῶν διὰ τοῦ σώματος ἡδονῶν. Διὰ τοῦ σώματος has the force of an adjective, as is indicated by the position between the Art. and noun: *physical*, or a noun in the genitive *of the body*. So we find the simple genitive in Hellen. IV. 8. 22: αἱ τοῦ σώματος ἡδοναί; Apolog. 16: ταῖς τοῦ σώματος ἐπιθυμίαις. But such constructions as the present with a preposition are also not unfrequent; cf. I. 4. 5: τὰ διὰ στόματος ἡδέα; I. 5. 6; II. 6. 5; IV. 5. 11. —— Ἴσως γάρ, perhaps then. Γάρ is conclusive; cf. note, I. 3. 10. —— ἐλεύθερον νομίζεις. Ἐλεύθερον here = ἐλευθέριος, suitable, fitting for a free man, liberale; different from the meaning in the preceding sentence, and antithetical to the following ἀνελεύθερον, illiberale, which in turn differs from the same word in the next section. —— τοὺς κωλύσοντας; cf. note, III. 4. 4.

4.—Ταῦτα ἀναγκάζεσθαι ἢ ἐκεῖνα κωλύεσθαι, sc. ποιεῖν or πράττειν; so in § 5: τοὺς τὰ μὲν ἄριστα κωλύοντας, τὰ δὲ κάκιστα ἀναγκάζοντας. The Latin employs a preposition after such verbs: ad haec compelli...ab illis retardari.

5.—Ποίους δέ τινας; what sort of? Ποῖος and τίς conjoined give an air of indefiniteness to the question. —— δεσπότας...δουλείαν...δουλεύουσιν; cf. note, I. 5. 5.

6.—Ἦ οὐ δοκεῖ σοι; sc. ἢ οὐ δοκεῖ σοι (ἡ ἀκρασία) κωλύειν προσέχειν, κ.τ.λ. —— ἐκπλήξασα. The verb ἐκπλήττειν, originally and lit., *to strike out of*, then, to drive out one's senses by a sudden shock, is often used in reference to the effect of any *overpowering* as well as sudden passion upon the mind. Cf. the signif. of ἐξιστάναι in I. 3. 13. —— ποιεῖν depends upon δοκεῖ.

7.—Σωφροσύνης...τίνι...προσήκειν, to whom can we say that temperance less belongs... than to the ἀκρατεῖ? For the construction and signif. of προσήκειν with the Gen. and Dat. see Kühn. Gr. § 273. 3. (b); L. Gr. II. § 521. —— αὐτὰ τὰ ἐναντία...ἔργα ἐστίν. The construction is: σωφροσύνης καὶ ἀκρασίας ἔργα (subject) ἐστὶν αὐτὰ τὰ ἐναντία (predicate). For the use and omission of the article see note, III. 10. 1. —— τοῦ...ποιοῦντος...οἴει τι ἀνθρώπῳ κάκιον εἶναι, do you suppose that any thing is worse for a man than that... which makes him do the very contrary to those who are under self-control. —— Αὐτὰ...τὰ ἐναντία, *directly* the opposite.

8.—Τὴν ἐγκράτειαν τῶν ἐναντίων ἤ, κ.τ.λ., is it not reasonable that temperance is the cause of directly the opposite things to men, of intemperance. For the constr. see note, III. 12. 4. Weiske: Non igitur consentaneum est, continentiam efficere contraria iis, quae incontinentia effecit?

9.—Ἐφ' ἅπερ μόνα, to which alone, i. e., to nothing else except. Ὥσπερ answers to πῶς: *how so*, quid ita? *inasmuch as*, or, *because*, etc. —— περιμείναντας, κ.τ.λ. Cf. this with the sentiment expressed by Arete in II. 1. 30, 33. —— ἀναγκαιοτάτοις...συνεχεστάτοις, those pleasures most necessary (i. e., natural)... continuous (i. e., constantly recurring), such as eating, drinking, sleeping, etc. —— ἀξιολόγως, recte, or, honeste = ἀξίως μνήμης, just below. So in I. 5. 5, where it is antithetical to αἰσχρῶς. Cf. also II. 1. 20 and III. 7. 1. ἀξιόλογον.

10.—Τοῦ μαθεῖν...τοῦ ἐπιμεληθῆναι. These genitives depend upon ἀπολαύουσι. The phrase might be arranged thus: οἱ ἐγκρατεῖς τοῦ μαθεῖν ... καὶ τοῦ ἐπιμεληθῆναι ... ἀπολαύουσι. —— ἀφ' ὧν, sc. ἀπὸ τοῦ καλῶς διοικῆσαι τὸ ἑαυτοῦ σῶμα, κ.τ.λ. —— πράττοντες αὐτά, in the exercise of these things, sc. τὸ μαθεῖν τι καλὸν, κ.τ.λ. —— προσήκειν; see note, IV. 5. 7. —— κατεχομένῳ ἐπὶ τῷ σπουδάζειν. Sauppius says, the proposition here seems to denote the place about which (locus, circa quem, etc.) the desire is exercised and at the same time the end or design. Cf. Kühn L. Gr. II. § 612; Gr. § 296. II. —— τὰς ἐγγυτάτω ἡδονάς, pleasures that are at hand, come within one's way, in promptu positas, cf. note, II. 1. 20. The Adv. here with the Art. is used as an adjective, as elsewhere. Cf. Socrates' reasoning here with that in I. 5, and II. 1.

11.—Ἥττονι ... ἡδονῶν; see note, I. 5. 1. —— Τί γὰρ διαφέρει. Some Mss. read τίνι for τί; either is good Greek, and both are employed by our author, as well as other Attic writers. Cf. for the Acc. I. 2. 50: ἐσκόπει, τί διαφέρει μανίας ἀμαθία; II. 1. 17; III. 7. 7; dative, III. 3. 14: πολὺ ἂν καὶ τούτῳ διενέγκοιεν τῶν ἄλλων. —— διαλέγοντας κατὰ γένη, discriminating according to their kinds; cf. § 12, and Chap. VI. ad init. For the use of the Acc., see note, I. 1. 9: ἃ ἔξεστιν ἀριθμήσαντας ... εἰδέναι.

12.—Καὶ οὕτως ... δυνατωτάτους. This clause is supposed by many to have crept into the text from the margin; see Kühn. in h. l. —— τὸ διαλέγεσθαι. The distinction in meaning between διαλέγειν and διαλέγεσθαι is strongly marked in this and the preceding section. Cf. note, I. 7. 5. —— ἐκ τοῦ συνιόντας βουλεύεσθαι διαλέγοντας, from the circumstance that those who come together for consultation, discourse, etc. —— διαλεκτικωτάτους, *especially qualified to speak*, is derived from the verb διαλέγεσθαι, by which and διαλέγειν, the way is prepared for its use here. By speaking is here meant the ability to arrive at the truth of things by discussion, which according to Socrates only the ἐγκρατεῖς could do.

CHAPTER VI.

1.—Διαλεκτικωτέρους; see note at the end of the preceding section. —— ᾗ, *as.* —— καὶ τὸν τρόπον, also the manner, i. e., οὐ μόνον αὐτὴν τὴν ἐπίσκεψιν, ἀλλὰ καὶ τὸν τρόπον αὐτῆς. Cf. note, I. 3. 1.

2.—Ὧδέ πως, somewhat thus. Πώς is here used much as the pronoun τὶς frequently is = Latin fere. So just below and in IV. 5. 5 —— ποῖόν τι . . . ὁποῖός τι; see note, I. 1. 1, and IV. 5. 5.

3.—Εἰδὼς εἰδείη; see note, IV. 2. 21. —— οὐ γὰρ οὖν; see note, IV. 4. 23.

4.—Νόμιμα, established by law. —— ἡμῖν, in our judgment; for this meaning of the Dat., see note, IV. 2. 14.

5.—Ἀνθρώποις . . . ἆρα. For the position of the noun before the interrogative particle, see note, II. 7. 8. Men here are contrasted with gods. —— καθ' ἃ δεῖ πως ἀλλήλοις χρῆσθαι, in accordance with which it is in some manner (πώς) necessary for men to have intercourse with one another. —— οὗτοι; for the pleonastic use of the pronoun here, see note, II. 1. 19.

6.—Οἴεσθαι δεῖν μὴ ποιεῖν; see a similar accumulation of infinitives in III. 6. 15, and cf. note. —— οἶδας; an Ionic form for οἶσθα. Xenophon perhaps uses two other Ionic forms of this same verb: οἴδασιν, Oecon. XX. 14, and οἴδαμεν (al. ἴσμεν), Anab. II. 4. 6. The writers of the age of Xenophon, and especially Xenophon himself, did not rigidly discard every Ionic form. Some of the Lexicons erroneously say that this form is "never used in the classic prose writers." See Veitch's Irreg. Gr. Verbs, εἰδέω. —— ὀρθῶς ἄν ποτε. Ποτέ is not here a simple particle of emphasis as often with the interrogative pronouns, but = the Latin aliquando, *at length;* i. e., after so many turnings, do we come to this definition? —— ὁριζοίμεθα ὁριζόμενοι; cf. note, IV. 2. 21. The similarity of this idiom, which has been several times noticed, to a very common construction in Hebrew, cannot fail to occur to any one at all familiar with that language.

7.—Ἄλλο . . . ἢ ᾧ σοφοί εἰσιν; do you suppose that wisdom is any thing else but that by which men are wise? For the change from the singular τὶς in the preceding clause to the plural, see note, I. 2. 62. —— Ἐπιστήμη ἄρα σοφία ἐστίν; Socrates reasons in a similar manner in Plat. Theaet. p. 141. D. The article is omitted with the subject; cf. note, I. 2. 23. —— Οὐδὲ μὰ Δί' . . . πολλοστόν. Οὐδὲ belongs with πολλοστόν, and the logical order of the words would be: Μὰ Δί', ἔμοιγε οὐδὲ πολλοστὸν μέρος αὐτῶν. For the meaning of the word πολλοστόν, see note, III. 1. 6, and for the idea, III. 8. 2–8.

8.—Τὸ ἄρα ὠφέλιμον, κ.τ.λ. It should be distinctly borne in mind, that Socrates in all his arguments for *the profitable*, does not treat it as the motive or end of action, but the rule. True happiness, he contends, is the measure of the good will of the gods to men, the interpreter of their designs; but it is not merely our interest, but our *duty*, to comply with the rule of action thus discovered. "In a word," it has been well said, "the great principles of conduct as set forth by his [Socrates'] philosophy, are: piety as the motive, usefulness as the measure, and self-command [ἐγκράτεια] as the means." The Greek Philosophers, Socrates and Plato, by Potter, p. 53.

9.—Τὸ δὲ καλὸν...πάντα καλὸν ὄν. The difficulty of this passage has given occasion to various changes of the text by different editors; but as almost all the Ms. authority is in favor of the reading which is here given, it is perhaps better to attempt an interpretation, even if it shall be only a probable one, than to take time in making a new text. The most natural explanation seems to be: can we *otherwise* (πως ἄλλως), sc. ἢ τὸ ἀγαθόν, § 8, (cf. III. 8, where it is demonstrated that καλόν, ἀγαθόν, and χρήσιμον are the same), define the beautiful, or do you name that beautiful, if there be any thing beautiful (εἰ ἔστιν), whether body or vessel, or any thing else, which you know to be in every respect (πρὸς πάντα) beautiful? The explanation of Seiffert accords substantially with this: jam vero pulchrum num aliter definire possumus (sc. ἢ τὸ ἀγαθόν)? an si quid est, quod scias ad omnia pulchrum esse vel corpus...hoc pulchrum appellas? Another interpretation is however possible, i. e., How else can we define the beautiful than, if it is admissible (εἰ ἔστιν), or (according to others) exempli causa, you call that beautiful, whether, etc. This is rather favored by a marginal reading in Stephanus, ἢ ἔνεστιν ὀνομάζειν, but on the whole, seems to do greater violence to the Greek, than the former explanation.

10.—Ἀνδρίαν. This virtue is more fully discussed in Plato's Laches where we find that Socrates' idea, with which what follows here substantially accords, is: that valor comprises two principal ideas, knowledge and a conscientious regard to what is right and good, which enables one to conduct himself properly, especially in all dangerous emergencies, avoiding the evil and pursuing the good. Thus when Nicias, p. 195. A, defines ἀνδρία to be τὴν τῶν δεινῶν καὶ θαῤῥαλέων ἐπιστήμην καὶ ἐν πολέμῳ καὶ ἐν τοῖς ἄλλοις ἅπασιν, Socrates is not satisfied, but contends that the valiant are only those, οἱ ἐπιστάμενοι τοῖς δεινοῖς τε καὶ ἐπικινδύνοις καλῶς χρῆσθαι. Cf. Stallbaum's Prolegomena ad Lachetem.——τῶν καλῶν...εἶναι; partitive Gen., see Kühn. Gr. § 273. 3. (a).——Κάλλιστον μὲν οὖν, and just after: μέγιστα μὲν οὖν; see note, II. 7. 5.——Μὰ Δί' ἔφη; cf. note, I. 4. 9.——Νὴ Δί' ἔφη; sc. οὐκ ἀνδρεῖοί εἰσι, to be supplied from the preceding interrogation; cf. note, II. 7. 4.——Τί δὲ οἱ...δεδοικότες; sc. δοκοῦσί σοι. Ellipses of this kind, which may be easily comprehended without being expressed, are common in interrogations in Greek as well as other languages.

11.—Οὔκ ἀλλά; cf. note, II. 6. 11. —— τοὺς οἵους . . . χρῆσθαι, who are such as to, etc. The construction of the infinitive as in I. 4. 6. The article is not unfrequently used with οἷος, see Kühn. Gr. § 332. R. 9; L. Gr. II. § 788. Anm. 4.

12.—Κατὰ νόμους τῶν πόλεων, κ.τ.λ. According to Socrates' idea, the government of Athens in the time of Aristides and Themistocles was a βασιλεία, a monarchy, because these men possessed supreme authority, but governed willing subjects according to the laws; on the other hand, the government in the time of Pericles and Alcibiades, was a τυραννίς, a tyranny, because they governed unwilling subjects according to their own will. —— ἐκ τῶν τὰ νόμιμα ἐπιτελούντων, from those who are obedient to the laws. Socrates' preference for an aristocratical form of government here appears: cf. Plat. Menex. p. 238. C, and Wiggers' Life, chap. VII. 4. —— ἐκ τιμημάτων, chosen according to their property.

13.—Εἰ . . . ἀντιλέγοι; see note, I. 3. 4. —— περί του; the pronoun is masculine, as appears from what follows. —— ἤτοι . . . ἤ; by the addition of τοί to the first ἤ, the disjunctive relation is more marked; see Kühn. L. Gr. II. § 745. 4, and cf. III. 12. 2; Cyrop. IV. 5. 22. —— σοφώτερον . . . ὃν αὐτὸς λέγοι; i. e., σοφώτερόν τινα εἶναι, ὃν αὐτὸς λέγοι, ἢ ὃν ὁ Σωκράτης λέγοι. —— ἐπὶ τὴν ὑπόθεσιν, to the subject matter of the discussion.

14.—Τί οὖν οὐκ . . . ἐπισκεψάμεθα; cf. note, III. 1. 10. —— καθυπερτέραν τῶν ἀντιπάλων; compendious comparison for τῆς τῶν ἀντιπάλων; see note, III. 5. 4: πρὸς τοὺς Ἀθηναίους. —— ἐπαναγομένων; sc. ἐπὶ τὴν ὑπόθεσιν.

15.—Ὁπότε . . . διεξίοι. The Opt. denoting repeated or customary action; see note, I. 2. 57. —— διὰ τῶν μάλιστα ὁμολογουμένων ἐπορεύετο, he carried on his argument by means of the most evident propositions. So at the end of the section: διὰ τῶν δοκούντων τοῖς ἀνθρώποις ἄγειν τοὺς λόγους, and in Oecon. XIX. 15: ἄγων γάρ με δι' ὧν ἐγὼ ἐπίσταμαι. For the use of διά here, see Kühn. L. Gr. II. § 605. p. 281; Gr. § 291. 1. (b). Socrates' habit of beginning and carrying on an argumentation by successive propositions most generally received as true, is well known; cf. Ritter, II. p. 52. —— ταύτην τὴν ἀσφάλειαν εἶναι λόγου. Ταύτην is predicate, and hence the article with ἀσφάλειαι The phrase τὴν ἀσφάλειαν λόγου, is equivalent to: an argument that produces conviction. ——῞Ομηρον...ἀναθεῖναι, κ.τ.λ. The reference here is to Odyss. VIII. 171: ὁ δὲ ἀσφαλέως ἀγορεύει. —— τὸ ἀσφαλῆ ῥήτορα εἶναι, that he should be a persuasive orator. —— διὰ τῶν δοκούντων τοῖς ἀνθρώποις, through those things that are readily acknowledged by men. See above: διὰ τῶν ὁμολογουμένων

CHAPTER VII.

1.—Τὴν ἑαυτοῦ γνώμην ἀπεφαίνετο. For the reflexive pronoun with the verbs in the middle voice, see note, I. 6. 13. —— αὐτάρκεις ἐν ταῖς προσηκούσαις πράξεσιν, κ.τ.λ., competent of themselves (without foreign aid), in whatever labors devolve upon them; i. e., according to the promise made in IV. 3. 1, μηχανικούς. Ἐπιμελεῖσθαι is very seldom followed by an infinitive either with or without an accusative, unless the Inf. be accompanied by the article in the Gen., or Acc. (rare), as in passages like I. 2. 55; III. 3. 11; IV. 8. 6, et al. It however frequently happens that with verbs, which take noun in the Gen. or Dat. after them when by themselves, if an Inf. is added, this noun in the Gen. or Dat. is changed to the Acc. so as to avoid the repetition of the object of the verb; cf. Kühn. L. Gr. II. § 647. Seiffert compares the construction here with the Lat. non dubito fore plerosque, and similar phrases. —— εἰδείη; Opt. because indicating indefinite frequency, and preceded in construction by a verb in a past tense.

2.—Μέχρι ὅτου, how far, quatenus. —— πράγματος, negotii ex doctrina et scientia pendentis; Schneid. —— αὐτίκα, *for example*, a meaning confined to Attic Greek. It seems to be an elliptical form of expression, signifying strictly: I forthwith (without delaying to select), take as an example, etc. —— ἔργον ἀποδείξασθαι, to designate, lay out work, i. e., building spots, or any thing where geometrical figures are employed. This seems to be much the most facile and natural interpretation of this phrase, although various others have been given. Kühner, following the interpretation of Coray, makes the words equivalent to γῆν ἔργον ἀποδείξασθαι ἀγρὸν ἑαυτῷ ποιῆσαι σπείραντα, or more briefly: γῆν ἀγρὸν ἑαυτῷ ἐργάσασθαι, but it is difficult to see what the process here indicated, has to do directly with γεωμετρία. He indeed says that it denotes that which *follows* the acceptance, transmission, or division of land, according to correct measurement, and in explanation of ἐργόν adduces from Coray: ἔργον γὰρ κατ' ἐξοχὴν λέγεται ἡ γεωργία καὶ αὐτὴ προςέτι ἡ γεγεωργημένη γῆ; cf. Il. β, 751. μ. 283. But it does not seem to us probable, that such an idea should be introduced here. —— τήν...γῆν; the use and omission of the article here with γήν and the obvious reason for it cannot escape notice. —— καὶ ὡς μετρεῖται ἐπιστάμενον ἀπιέναι, and go away knowing (i. e., would retain in memory), etc. 'Απιέναι has here very much the signification of the verb in such Latin phrases as: victorem discedere.

3.—Οὐκ ἄπειρος...ἦν. It is evident from such passages as this that Socrates was not unskilled in science, and that the instructions of his master in geometry, Theodorus, were not lost upon him. The same thing is evident from the ridicule of Aristophanes, some of the most pointed and amusing passages of which (as in the Clouds, 182 sq.) have reference to the geometrical and astronomical pursuits of Socrates and his pupils. It is also plain, that Socrates' dissuasions from scientific pursuits, only (or at least mainly) had regard to those speculations in science, which had no practical utility, and only took the attention and time from more important objects. It cannot be doubted that Xenophon had in mind in writing this chapter, not only the actual confusion of many of the scientific investigations of his day, and their exaltation of irrational above rational nature; but also the fact that the engaging in such speculations had been brought into the accusation of his master. It is not strange, that in these circumstances, the devoted disciple and friend should withhold and conceal the acquisitions of Socrates, that in a later age would have been considered rather an ornament to than a blemish upon his character. Cf. note, I. 1. 11; IV. 2. 10; Plat. Meno. p. 82 sq.; Brandis' Hist. Philos. II. S. 10; and see Introd.

4.—'Αστρολογίας; cf. note, IV. 2. 10. —— ὥραν; cf. note, IV. 3. 4.

5.—Τὸ... μανθάνειν... ἰσχυρῶς ἀπέτρεπεν, as it respects learning...he urgently dissuaded, etc. Cf. note, I. 3. 7. —— μέχρι τούτου, is preparatory to μέχρι τοῦ. Cf. Plat. Legg. p. 670. D: μέχρι γε τοσούτου πεπαιδεῦσθαι σχεδὸν ἀναγκαῖον, μέχρι τοῦ δυνατὸν εἶναι; de Rep. I. p. 341. D: ἐπὶ τούτῳ πέφυκεν, ἐπὶ τῷ τὸ ξυμφέρον ἑκάστῳ ζητεῖν; Lach. p. 183. C; 191. B; Protag. p. 356. D, et al. See Kühn. L. Gr. II. § 631. 2. —— τὰ μὴ ἐν τῇ αὐτῇ περιφορᾷ ὄντα. Edwards, as quoted by Kühner, in accordance with Diog. Laert. VII. 144: τῶν δὲ ἄστρων τὰ μὲν ἀπλανῆ συμπεριφέρεσθαι τῷ ὅλῳ οὐρανῷ, τὰ δὲ πλανώμενα κατ' ἰδίας κινεῖσθαι κινήσεις, explains these words: quae non communi eodemque coeli motu circumacta proprio sibi motu feruntur. —— ἀσταθμήτους ἀστέρας, lit., unsteady, unstable stars, i. e., comets. —— τὰς περιόδους, the time of their return to the same point. —— τὰς αἰτίας αὐτῶν; these words probably have reference to περιόδους and not to ἀσταθ. ἀστέρας. Still some, as Weiske and Bornemann, refer them, with some plausibility, to the latter words, and in illustration quote Seneca, Quaest. Nat. VII. 11. —— οὐδὲ τούτων γε ἀνήκοος, skilled in these things. He is said to have been instructed in astronomy by Archaelaus, a disciple of Anaxagoras; see Cic. Tusc. Disp. V. 4. 10.

6.—Τῶν οὐρανίων, κ.τ.λ.; cf. in respect to the idea here, Cic. Acad. I. 4. 15, and note, I. 1. 11. —— φροντίστης, *a thinker*, κατ' ἐξωχήν; applied in derision to Socrates by Aristoph. Clouds, 267, and hence its introduction here to wipe off this reproach. —— κινδυνεῦσαι δ' ἂν ἔφη καὶ παραφρονῆσαι, κ.τ.λ., he said that there would be danger that one anxiously inquiring into these things would even become insane. In reference to ταῦτα μεριμνῶντα, see note, I. 1. 14. —— Ἀναξαγόρας, a native of Clazomenae in Lydia. He flourished in the age of Pericles, and was banished, on the decline of the power of the latter at Athens, to Lampsacus, where he died. See Ritter's Hist. Philos. II. Chap. VIII.; Lewes' Biog. Hist. Philos. I. p. 114 sq., and cf. Diog. Laert. II. 6 sq.; Cic. Tusc. Quaest. V. 4. 10.

7.—Τὸ αὐτὸ εἶναι πῦρ τε καὶ ἥλιον, κ.τ.λ.; for the speculations of Anaxagoras here referred to, see references in the preceding section. —— τὰ χρώματα μελάντερα ἔκουσιν; cf. note, I. 4. 13: τὴν ψυχὴν κρατίστην.

8.—Λογισμοὺς. Ernesti and Weiske consider this word as equivalent to τὴν ἀριθμητικήν, the theory of numbers, but those rather seem to be in the right who make it = τὴν λογιστικήν, practical arithmetic, as opposed to theoretical, i. e., keeping and computing of accounts, etc. Plat. Gorg. p. 451. C. explains the difference between λογιστική and ἀριθμητική. Cf. Woolsey's note in h. l.

9.—Προέτρεπε; cf. note, I. 2. 64. —— ἐνδέχοιτο; cf. note, I. 2. 23. —— πόμα, for the usual πῶμα. —— τοῦ γὰρ οὕτω προσέχοντος ἑαυτῷ, κ.τ.λ. We should naturally expect an Acc. here, instead of the Gen., but that reading is found in only one Ms. (Voss. I.), and that of little value. We must therefore take the text substantially as we find it. It is not improbable, however, that ἑαυτοῦ at the end of the sentence is for αὐτοῦ, found in the marg. Villois; as ἑαυτοῦ is easily changed to αὑτοῦ, and that into αὐτοῦ. Then the words, τοῦ ... προσέχοντος ἑαυτῷ, in which the principal idea of the sentence is contained, may be supposed to be placed absolutely at the beginning of the clause for the sake of emphasis, and the idea is this: if any one thus gave heed to himself, he said, it would be difficult (ἔργον... εἶναι) for him to find a physician, who could designate things that would be more conducive to health; i. e., than himself doing what was before enumerated. Αὐτός is frequently used for the sake of perspicuity or emphasis to recall to mind a preceding word; see note and references, I. 4. 18. Schneider refers to similar sentiments in Tacit. Annal. VI. 46, and Plutarch de tuenda Sanit. p. 407, ed. Hutter; Kühner also adds Cic. de Offic. II. 24. 86.

10.—Μᾶλλον ἢ κατὰ τὴν ἀνθρωπίνην σοφίαν ὠφελεῖσθαι, greater than that which is the result of human wisdom. For the construction, see note, I. 7. 4. —— μαντικῆς... συμβουλῆς θεῶν; cf. I. 1. 9.

CHAPTER VIII.

1.—Ὅτι φάσκοντος αὐτοῦ... θάνατος, because, whilst he said, etc., the sentence of death was, etc. —— ἐλέγχεσθαι... ψευδόμενον, convicted of falsehood, i. e., inasmuch as his δαιμόνιον had not made known what he should do to escape death. —— πόῤῥω, later Attic = πρόσω, *so far on* in life; according to Diog. Laert. II. 44; Max. Tyr. Dissert. IX. 8, he was seventy years of age. —— οὐκ qualifies the sense of πολλῷ ὕστερον, and not of the whole clause. —— εἶτα; cf. note, I. 2. 1. —— ἀπέλειπεν; Imperf. tense, left, i. e., when he died. —— τήν... δίκην... εἰπών, having pleaded his cause, etc.

2.—Δήλια. In regard to this festival of Apollo and the reasons for the delay of the execution until after its celebration, see note and references, III. 3. 12; and also Plat. Phaed. p. 58, and Wiggers' Life of Socrates, Ch. VIII. p. 112. —— τὸν δὲ νόμον, sc. διὰ τό: διά τε τὸ τὸν νόμον ἐᾶν.

3.—Some editors, in consequence of obscurities and difficulties in this chapter, especially from this section to § 11, reject it; or at least, suppose that it is corrupt, or the work of some other author than Xenophon. See Bornemann, Schneider, and others in h. l. For its appositeness here as a conclusion of the whole work, cf. the Argument at the beginning of the chapter. The prominent object of the first three sections, which Dindorf rejects, is to show that Socrates' condemnation and death was no argument for the falseness of his claims in respect to the guidance of his monitor. And § 3 in connection with what goes before, constitutes a cumulative argument: By such a death as Socrates died he not only escaped evils, but was a participant of the greatest good, and hence the regard and truthfulness of his guiding spirit in not warning him to avoid it. —— ἢ οὕτως ἀποθάνοι; i. e., as just said: πρᾳότατα καὶ ἀνδρωδέστατα.

4.—Ἑρμογένης, was the son of a rich man, Hipponicus; but as his brother Callias inherited his father's wealth, he was himself poor, but a fond and faithful friend of Socrates; cf. II. 10. 3. —— ἤκουσα. Xenophon was himself absent on a military expedition with Cyrus at the time of Socrates' death. The same account substantially, though much more full, is found in Apolog. 2 sq.; which the student will do well to compare throughout in reading this chapter. —— Μελήτου; cf. note, I. 1. 1. —— γεγραμμένου αὐτὸν τὴν γραφήν; the verb and noun are blended together and take a personal object, αὐτόν; see Kühn. Gr. § 280. 1; L. Gr. II. § 558, and cf. Demosth. de Coron. p. 311. 251: οὐδεμίαν γὰρ πώποτ' ἐγράψατό με οὐδ' ἐδίωξε γραφήν. —— τοῦτο μελητῶν; sc. τῷ ἀπολογεῖσθαι, my defence.

5.—Αὐτὸς (Hermogenes), sc. ἔφη. —— ἤδη μοῦ ἐπιχειροῦντος ... ἠναντιώθη. The opposition of his guiding deity is more particularly stated in Apol. § 4: καὶ δὶς ἤδη ἐπιχειρήσαντός μου σκοπεῖν περὶ τῆς ἀπολογίας, ἐναντιοῦταί μοι τὸ δαιμόνιον.

6.—Οὐδενὶ ... ὑφείμην ἂν ... βεβιωκέναι, I would not concede to any man, that he has lived either better or more pleasantly than I, up to the present time.

7.—Ἃ ἐγώ. Ἃ refers to what immediately precedes. For the omission of the connective particle here, see III. 4. 12. —— ᾐσθανόμην, Imperf. sentiebam (sc. dum vivebam). The experience of his whole past life, continued until that time, as opposed to the impending events of the nearest future, is designated by this verb; whilst the perfect διατετέλεκα only affirms without regard to this contrast. —— οὕτω διατετέλεκα περὶ ἐμαυτοῦ, γιγνώσκων, I have so concluded concerning myself; (i. e., that I live better and more pleasantly than other men). —— οὕτως ἔχοντες περὶ ἐμοῦ, thinking thus of me. —— καὶ γὰρ οἱ ... φιλοῦντες ... φίλους. This whole clause is parenthetical, and the idea of the passage seems to be: not on account of their love to me, (for even those who love others are thus disposed toward their friends,) but because they suppose that, if they associate with me they shall become very good. The last clause has been so paraphrased as to show plainly the force of the words: διόπερ οἴονται, ὅτι, εἰ ἐμοὶ συνεῖεν, καί αὐτοὶ ἂν βέλτιστοι γίγνοιντο, ὥσπερ ἐγώ εἰμι.

8.—Τὰ τοῦ γήρως ἐπιτελεῖσθαι, to pay a tribute to, be subject to the burdens of old age. —— ἀβίωτος ... βίος, a life not to be lived, i. e., not worthy the name of life, or it may be rendered *insupportable.* The Latins say: vita vitalis (cf. Cic. de Amicit. VI. 22), and similar phrases are common in Greek, as ζωὴ ἄβιος, θάνατος ἀθάνατος, γάμος ἄγαμος, γένος ἄγονον, σοφία ἄσοφος. —— χεῖρόν τε καὶ ἀηδέστερον; i. e., worse, etc., than other men; antithetical to βέλτιον ... ἥδιον in § 6.

9.—Εἰ γὰρ ... ποιεῖν, κ.τ.λ., for if it is base to do injustice, why is it not base to do any thing whatever unjustly; but what fault of mine is it, that others are not able to know or do that which is just in respect to me?

10.—Τῶν τε ἀδικησάντων ... ἀδικηθέντων, of those who have done and those who have suffered injustice. —— ἐγὼ ἐπιμελείας τεύξομαι, I shall be cared for, had in reverence; passive in sense, and hence followed by ὑπό, cf. note, III. 4. 1. —— μαρτυρήσεσθαί μοι; the Fut. Mid. for the Pass.; cf. note, I. 1. 8, and Apol. § 26: ἐμοὶ μαρτυρήσεται ὑπό τε τοῦ ἐπιόντος καὶ ὑπὸ τοῦ παρεληλυθότος χρόνου, ὅτι ἠδίκησα μὲν οὐδένα, κ.τ.λ.

11.—Σωκράτην, κ.τ.λ.; by attraction for γιγν., οἷος ἦν Σωκράτης; see note, I. 2. 13. —— ὠφελιμώτατον; thus paraphrased in Apolog.: εἰ δέ τις τῶν ἀρετῆς ἐφιεμένων ὠφελιμωτέρῳ τινὶ Σωκράτους συνεγένετο, ἐκεῖνον ἐγὼ τὸν ἄνδρα ἀξιομακαριστότατον νομίζω. —— εὐσεβὴς μὲν οὕτως, κ.τ.λ., these words down to καλοκἀγαθίαν are thrown in parenthetically, as a sort of summary of the points of Socrates' character that had been brought to view in the preceding work. —— τὸ ἥδιον ἀντὶ τοῦ βελτίονος; see note, IV. 5. 6: τὸ χεῖρον ἀντὶ τοῦ βελτίονος. —— προτρέψασθαι; cf. note, I. 2. 64. —— εἰ δέ τῳ μὴ ἀρέσκει, κ.τ.λ., if these things (i. e., the summary and conclusions which precede) do not meet the approbation of any one, let him, comparing the character of others with these things, thus judge. This simple declaration of the confidence of Xenophon, is a genuine and truthful expression of his deep reverence for one of the most illustrious heathen philosophers, and is a fitting close, as it is a just exhibition of the confident and trustful spirit, of his whole defence of his master and friend.

ENGLISH INDEX.

P.

W.

X.

Y.

Z.

GREEK INDEX.

A.

B.

Γ.

E.

Z.

H.

Λ.

P.

Υ.

Φ.

X.

Ψ.

Ω.

CPSIA information can be obtained
at www.ICGtesting.com
Printed in the USA
LVHW100510130422
716029LV00002B/52

9 783752 591798